JAIME
CASTLE   PELOQUIN

RED CLAW

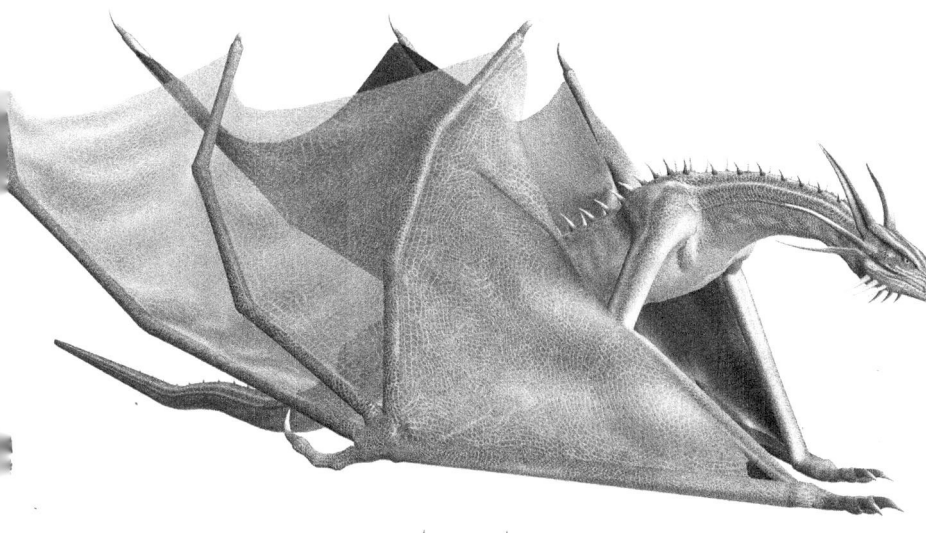

aethonbooks.com

RED CLAW
©2023 CASTLE/PELOQUIN

This book is protected under the copyright laws of the United States of America. No part of this publication may be reproduced, stored in a retrieval system, or transmitted, in any form or by any means, without the prior permission in writing of the publisher, nor be otherwise circulated in any form of binding or cover other than that in which it is published and without a similar condition including this condition being imposed on the subsequent purchaser. Any reproduction or unauthorized use of the material or artwork contained herein is prohibited without the express written permission of the authors.

Aethon Books supports the right to free expression and the value of copyright. The purpose of copyright is to encourage writers and artists to produce the creative works that enrich our culture.

The scanning, uploading, and distribution of this book without permission is a theft of the author's intellectual property. If you would like to use material from the book (other than for review purposes), please contact editor@aethonbooks.com. Thank you for your support of the author's rights.

Aethon Books
www.aethonbooks.com

Print and eBook formatting, and cover design by Steve Beaulieu. Artwork provided by Antti Hakosaari.

Published by Aethon Books LLC.

Aethon Books is not responsible for websites (or their content) that are not owned by the publisher.

This book is a work of fiction. Names, characters, places, and incidents are the product of the author's imagination or are used fictitiously. Any resemblance to actual events, locales, or persons, living or dead is coincidental.

All rights reserved.

The Northern Gate

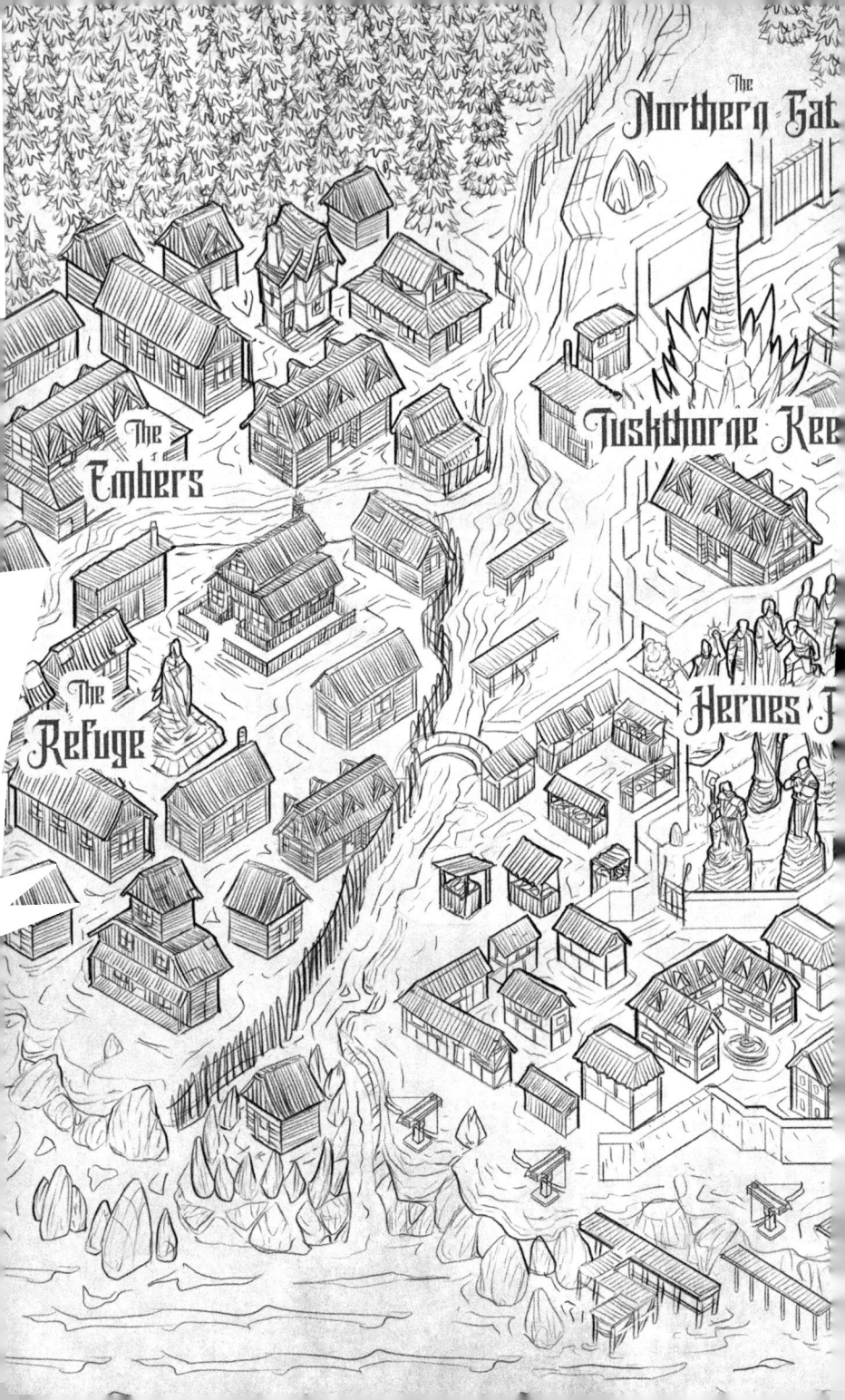

The Embers

Tuskthorne Keep

The Refuge

Heroes

The Wildgrove Forest

The Stacks

Court of Justice

The Palace

Blackwater Bay

To my beautiful wife.

You were sick during most of the writing of this book, and as far behind as you are in reading, I figure this'll be a nice surprise when we are old and gray.

You are the light in my eyes
The joy in every tear I've cried
You are the breath in my lungs
The heart in every song I've sung
—JC

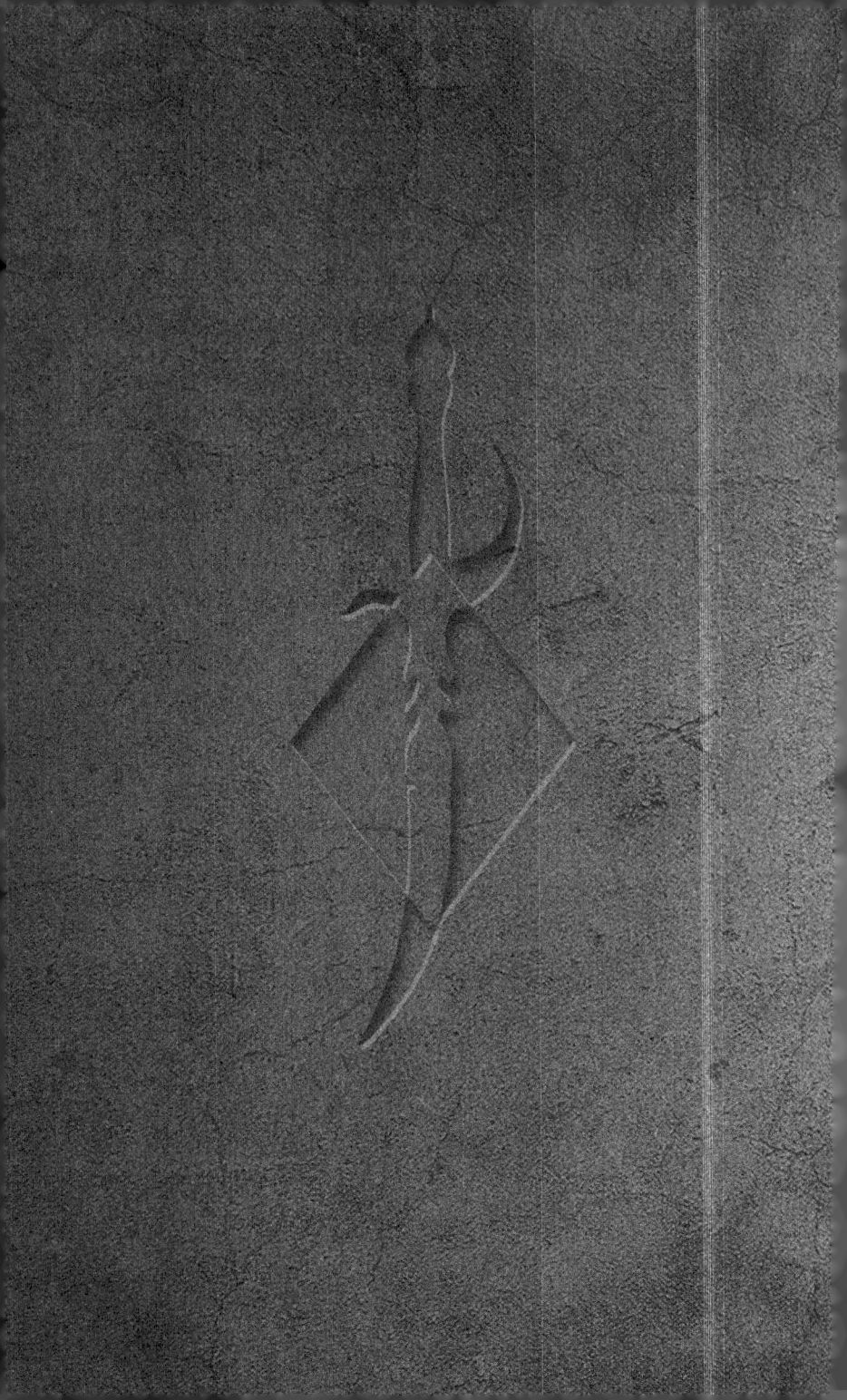

ALSO IN SERIES

BLACK TALON
RED CLAW
SILVER SPINES
GOLDEN FLAMES

I
Natisse

Natisse burned.

Searing fire raged across her flesh, seethed in her veins, blazed in the core of her being—a raw, savage energy she could neither control nor extinguish. The flames lit up the darkness of the old theater, their orange light illuminating Jad's broad face and bulky frame. The mammoth man stared wide-eyed at the tongues of fire rolling across her in a macabre dance.

"Ezrasil's bones!" Jad's rumbling voice pierced Natisse's mind, putting an end to her momentary stupor. Tearing at his black coat, still soaked with the blood of the guards he'd killed, he shouted, "Hold on, Nat! I'll put out the—"

"Wait!" The word spilled from Natisse's lips unbidden. Then, gathering herself, she added, "Just... wait."

Lifting her arms, studying the inferno, the sizzling heat swallowing up the air in a brilliant corona around her, she marveled. Despite it all, she felt nothing. No pain. No howling anguish like she'd experienced the day an Ember Dragon's breath turned her family to wisping ash. But that wasn't true. She did feel something. Power—so much power, rushing through every muscle and nerve with the force of erupting lava.

"It doesn't hurt," she breathed, her mind scarcely able to reconcile her words to the evidence before her very eyes. She turned over her hands, letting the flames leap from fingertip to fingertip. Then she lifted her gaze to Jad, who stood frozen, halfway out of his huge coat.

"Nat," he started, words coming out strangled, confused. "What...?" The rest of his question was choked off before it could form.

As quickly as the fire had sprung to life, it died. One moment, Natisse was wreathed in brilliant red-gold flames; the next, all that remained was a halo of smoke billowing around her like death's cloud. Had it not been for the memory of what had just transpired and the stunned look on Jad's face, she might've imagined it a dream.

Yet she knew the truth. It *had* happened. She *had* been transported to the Fire Realm—some alternate plane of magic or energy, she did not truly know—and stood face-to-face with Golgoth, the mighty red Ember Dragon. And Golgoth had chosen her, had called her *bloodsworn,* had somehow given her access to the firestorm burning within the dragon's own eyes.

"Hey!" Haston hurried up the aisle toward them, having just missed the spectacle. His face was pale, pinched with his own pain from the still-healing wound he'd sustained days earlier, but he refused to let his injuries slow him. He'd arrived in Magister Onathus's caravan yard just in time to help Natisse and Jad escape the confusion sown by their attack on Magister Branthe's slave fighting pits.

"Uncle Ronan says we need to move *now,*" he continued. "We should be outside the Imperial Scales' search radius, but he doesn't want to take chances. He's getting those Orken... er... things ready to move. Athelas, too. Just you two and your new friend." His eyes dropped to the unmoving figure of the young man lying at Jad's feet.

Natisse blinked. "Yes," she said, her voice strangely hoarse, throat parched—by the fire, perhaps? "We'll..." She swallowed, tried again. "We'll be ready to move."

With a nod, Haston turned and headed back down the stairs to the crumbling stage where Uncle Ronan and Athelas—back on his feet after a half dose of the Gryphic Elixir Natisse had found lying on the sands of the fighting pit—were gathering the strange Orken-like creatures into a tight cluster.

"Nat..." Jad's hand gripped her arm in an iron vise.

Her head snapped around and up to meet his gaze.

"What in Shekoth's fiery pits just happened?" the big man demanded. His normally kind face was hard, eyes narrowed in suspicion—or fear. "You just caught on bloody *fire,* and—"

"I don't know," she whispered. It wasn't a lie. Natisse honestly had no explanation for what she'd done or how she'd done it—if she'd indeed been responsible for any of it at all. Her head still spun like she'd sunk to the depths of a deep, dark sea. Her breathing had steadied, but her heart pounded in her chest. The sudden shift between this dank abandoned theater and the Fire Realm, then back again, left her reeling, disoriented. And her conversation with the dragon or why she'd accepted whatever bond had been formed between them—none of it made any kind of sense to her.

"You... don't know?" Jad asked, his colossal jaw muscles clenching. "Nat—"

"Listen to me," Natisse hissed. "A lot of things happened all at once; things I'm still struggling to make sense of. Right now, we have not the time to dissect it. *Any* of it. We've got to get out of here, past the Imperial Scales, and get to the Burrows."

She saw the look in Jad's eyes, the protest forming on his lips.

"I swear, once safe, I'll tell you everything," she said before he could speak. "Just give me time to figure it all out. When we get back to the Burrows, I promise."

Reluctance and uncertainty filled Jad's expression, but he slowly nodded. "Okay," he growled. "You'd damned well better."

Squeezing Jad's arm, offering a reassuring gesture, she nodded back. "You take care of the…" She stopped herself. "Of him."

Jad followed the line of her eyes, staring down at the unconscious young man they'd just saved. "By Ezrasil." He whistled through his teeth and glanced back at Natisse. "What have we gotten ourselves into?"

"I don't know," she said, shaking her head. "Just get him safely back to the Burrow." Her voice hardened as a measure of her usual confidence returned. "We can deal with all this once we know he's not going to die on us."

"I'll do what I can," Jad said. "But wouldn't it be best to drop him off somewhere? An infirmary? Anywhere."

"Kind of hard to explain how we found him."

Jad didn't argue that. He let out a long, loud breath through his nose, then nodded. "So be it." Turning away, he knelt and set about, lifting the unconscious form of Jaylen, Crown Prince of the Karmian Empire, grandson of Emperor Wymarc himself.

Natisse couldn't quite remember what had happened. She only vaguely recalled finding the young man lying mostly unconscious in the dirt of Magister Onathus's shipyards. She'd insisted Jad tend to him. Why had she not left well enough alone? Had she realized then what she knew now… Who he was—heir to the Empire, grandson of the Emperor she'd spent so many years hating, the very embodiment of the power and privilege the Crimson Fang had dedicated their efforts to destroy.

Looking at the pale-faced young man, she couldn't feel much loathing. Only pity. Prince or no, he would've died if not for their intervention.

But they hadn't saved him alone. Her regard shifted from Prince Jaylen, now cradled in Jad's arms, to where Uncle Ronan stood directing the rest of the Crimson Fang and the Orken-like creatures.

Uncle Ronan. Proud, tall, and commanding, with a soldier's stern nature and a military precision that made him ideally suited to leading the Crimson Fang. But he was so much more than just the grizzled man she had answered to for the last decade-and-a-half.

He was General Andros, hero of Blackwater Bay, savior of Kollick, conqueror of Hudar, and defender of Dimvein. Magister Branthe had called him "a man unlike any other. One of the greatest military commanders the Karmian Empire has ever seen."

Natisse's mind still struggled with that. The Uncle Ronan she'd known contrasted so sharply with the General Andros of whom Baruch had spoken with such admiration. One was quiet and paternal, the other a roaring figure of legend, champion of the greatest Empire their world had ever seen. One was the man who had raised her, the other, a mythical hero, impossibly distant.

She watched Uncle Ronan—she couldn't yet think of him as General *anything*—issuing quiet orders to Haston while helping Athelas corral a frail-looking Orken child who had escaped his mother's weak grasp. Gone was the coat he had so dearly loved, given to a beggar the day he tricked his way into the fighting pit. He wore no shirt, displaying a mess of fresh wounds sustained from his combat with Magister Branthe's fighters atop decades-old scars. Knotted and tangled, they striped his back and sides, the mark of torments suffered at the hands of enemies untold.

Who *was* this man? How had the Empire's greatest general wound up leading a rebellion against the very nation he'd served?

And that was only half of it. The other half, discovered days earlier, was the fact that Uncle Ronan also wielded the magic of the Lumenators. He'd summoned a globe of unnatural light to illuminate the tunnels—yet *another* secret she hadn't known about—and driven back vicious gnashers. That same power had just saved Prince Jaylen's life by cauterizing his wounds.

"Natisse!" The man himself marched up the aisle toward her. How had she missed it all these years? She could see the "General" now, in every precise step, in his imperious bearing, the expectant look on his statuesque face, as if he *knew* she would obey his orders without question. "Everyone's ready to move out. Athelas and Jad will help me keep the *Ghuklek* together, and Haston will bring up the rear. I need you to take the lead. You know the ways around Dimvein best of any of them, so—"

"That's *it?*" Natisse snapped. "Just like that? No explanation, nothing?" Anger blazed bright within her, the flames amplified by the strange new reservoir of what had to be magic—*dragon's* magic—burning in her belly. "Like everything just goes back to the way it was?"

"Right now, yes." Uncle Ronan's face hardened, his expression growing unreadable. "Until we're safely in the Burrow, everything else takes second place. Survival first, then we can deal with this."

Natisse wanted to hurl the words back in his face, but he was right. She'd told Jad exactly the same thing. Only she hadn't been lying to Jad for decades.

"Fine." She snarled the word; bit it off like a curse. "I'll lead the way." Only then did it register in her mind what he'd said. "Wait, you want to bring them back to the *Burrow?* To our stronghold that no one but we know about? All of *them*"—she flicked a hand toward the huddled, gold-skinned creatures—"whatever in Shekoth they are?"

"Yes." Uncle Ronan remained impassive, fully in control despite her anger. "You don't know the *Ghuklek* as I do. We can trust them. They're no threat to us. On the contrary, they—"

"Trust?" Natisse bared her teeth. "Don't you dare speak to me about trust!"

Uncle Ronan growled low in his throat. "Damn it, Natisse, we don't have the time for this now. Just. Do. As. I. *Say!*" His voice thundered into her like hurricane gales, and something sparked behind his eyes.

Natisse took a reflexive step back, hand dropping to the hilt of her lashblade. That was no Uncle Ronan. Not the man she'd known. Once again, she'd seen a hint of General Andros peeking through.

Uncle Ronan's face hardened, and his scarred fists clenched and relaxed. "Get us back to the Burrow, Natisse. Now." With that, he turned on his heel and stalked away.

Natisse's eyes stabbed daggers in his back, anger boiling within her—and a hint of fear accompanying it. She was keenly aware of her comrades' eyes upon her. The rest of the Crimson Fang hadn't seen what she had, hadn't heard what she had. None but she and Jad knew the truth—or what little truth had been unmasked in the last few hours. But so much more remained to be discovered.

That thought gurgled like vomit in her throat. What more? What more could she possibly learn after all this?

Yet Uncle Ronan was right. Everything else *had* to come secondary. Survival first. The mission above all. Those were the words that had driven Ammon and Baruch—had gotten them killed, perhaps—but they held true at this moment.

Closing her eyes, Natisse let out a long breath, expelling the fire of rage surging within her. The flames did not fully die, though, feeding on or fed by the wellspring of Golgoth's magic. But she managed to cast them away enough for the icy veil to envelope her heart. With the cold came calm composure. Stuffing the emotions down deep, locking them away until later, her breathing steadied again; her heart slowed its furious racing, and Natisse was once more in control of herself.

When her eyes opened, she found herself once more in the darkened theater, but it felt somehow… different. Colder. Frigid even. It was just her, she knew. But it brought a sense of comfort. That, at least, remained the same though everything else in her world had changed.

"Let's go," she said, marching down the stairs toward the stage, and the people—human and Orken both—huddled there. "Stay close, and keep quiet. All of our lives depend on getting out of here unseen."

2
KULLEN

"Nobody move! Every Ezrasil-damned one of you bastards is under arrest by order of the Emperor himself!"

Captain Angban's shout, accompanied by the dazzling light of two dozen Lumenators, resounded throughout the shipyards with the force of command enough to paralyze the already terrified aristocrats cowering in the aftermath of the chaos.

Kullen, however, had no time for surprise. Not with two companies of Imperial Scales bearing down on him and Ulnu-knew-how-many Orkenwatch on their heels. He couldn't risk his scent being picked up by the Sniffers—*especially* not the one he'd given the slip just two nights earlier. That would lead to far too many questions he had no desire to answer.

He deftly spun away from the gate and sprang into the long shadows of a towering stack of crates nearby. With his dagger still tightly clutched in his right hand, he brought his left to the chain at his neck, and the vial hanging from it. Jamming his thumb against the golden cap, a needle-prick pain pierced his skin. A multitude of things happened at once. First, icy air seeped into his lungs. Power burst to life from within the reservoir deep within his soul, and the world ground to a halt around him. Umbris's energy flooded his veins and set every nerve into spasming vibrations. And the dragon's voice echoed in his mind like a swirling dream.

"*What would you have of me, Kullen Bloodsworn?*"

Lend me your powers, Kullen answered mentally, *so I can get bloody well gone from here!*

"*As you will,*" came the Twilight Dragon's fathomless resonance.

Kullen's flesh tingled, lightning crackling in his veins, and the world filled with shadow and shades of gray and black. He took a step—not with his physical form, but merely allowing the magic to propel him forward—and gave in to the power of the bloodsurge. An invisible hand dragged him into the darkness with inexorable force. He was the shadow itself, intangible and invisible to all around him.

He fixed his focus on a patch of night on the riverbank opposite the shipyards, some three hundred paces distant. His destination, the sloping roof of a three-story mansion overlooking the Talos River, doubtless belonging to some merchant wealthy enough to afford the property but not an aristocrat's title. It was there, to the cover of shadow where no torches shone, where the tiled pergola blocked out the light of the sky, that Kullen directed his form.

The world shuddered around him, reality rippling and giving way with an almost tangible tearing sensation. Kullen hurtled through the night, weightless and formless. Shrieks greeted his transition to the Shadow Realm as the air itself closed around him like quicksand. Only the combined might of his and Umbris's wills enabled him to fend off the relentless grip seeking to drag him into the eternal void. His mind and soul quivered with the effort, but he returned to his flesh and bone with an audible *snap*.

His legs gave out beneath him, and he collapsed to the sloping roof. Tiles cracked and clattered beneath his weight, but the roof held. For long seconds, Kullen lay there, gasping for breath, focusing on the pounding of his pulse as warm blood shoved back the chill that had flooded his veins.

What was wrong? Confusion thrummed at the back of his mind. The bloodsurge should not have taken so much effort. He hadn't overexerted himself or overused the power, not since his near-capture by the Orkenwatch days earlier. That night, he'd come closer than ever before to being ensnared by the creatures lurking within the Shadow Realm. Perhaps he merely hadn't rested enough for his body to be fully recovered, or the void magic of the Shadow Realm had somehow sunk its claws into him.

Whatever the case, it left him weak, drained. Luckily for him, he had a nice, quiet rooftop across the Talos River from the commotion in the shipyards—more than a safe distance away. Even the Lumenators' light wouldn't reach this far, not unless they waded into the middle of the icy river.

Slowly, Kullen dragged himself up the sloping tiled roof until he reached the crest. There, he managed to sit upright, confident the roof beam would support his weight. Hood drawn, within the shadows of his cloak, he had no fear of discovery as he watched the goings-on in the shipyard with interest.

Kullen could see why Emperor Wymarc had set the punctilious Captain Angban as one of the highest-ranking officers in the Elite Scales. The man—pile of hog's shite that he was—had taken over the scene with impressive speed, setting the Imperial Scales to block the shipyards' lone gate and herding all of the pampered aristocrats into the southeast corner of the stockade.

Not that the pompous lordlings and lace-festooned ladies had put up much resistance—between the fire that had broken out in the underground fighting pit and the sudden collapse of the tunnel through which they'd escaped, they were far beyond overwhelmed. A few tried to protest. Kullen could hear their whining even from this distance, but the Imperial Scales had none of it. A few well-placed cuffs and one kick to the fork of a particularly obese gentleman's legs set the tone for the night clearly enough.

A pillar of smoke rising to the north caught Kullen's attention. Nothing burned there that he knew of—that section of the

Western Docks had chiefly been one large caravan yard—but whatever had been set to torch, it would not survive the night. Already, ash began to fall like snow in light flakes on both sides of the Talos, dissolving into nothing as they touched the waters.

Kullen returned his focus to the shipyards. Captain Angban's booming voice alternated between barked commands to his men and sharp rebukes to any aristocrat foolish enough to get out of line. Kullen had no doubt these fops would feel the sting of the Emperor's justice in full force—likely for the first time in their pitiful lives. He'd make damned well certain of it, make sure Emperor Wymarc knew the identities of every one of these bastards who had made sport out of the suffering and violent deaths of slaves.

But at the moment, Kullen had greater concerns than the cruelty of the now-deceased Magister Branthe to occupy his mind.

Prince Jaylen was missing.

He'd last seen the young man stumbling through the tunnel amidst a stampede of nobles trying to escape the flames consuming the underground fighting pit. Kullen had been forced to leave the Prince—both to hunt down Magister Branthe and recover the vial Branthe had stolen from Jaylen—the vial that bonded the boy to Tempest, a silver wind dragon he'd inherited from his father, Prince Jarius.

Kullen had succeeded on both counts. Magister Branthe and his guards lay dead, soon to be forgotten. Tempest's vial rested safely in one of his many pouches, along with the vial through which Magister Branthe had commanded his bronze dragon, Isaax.

And yet, success had come at a fine cost. When Kullen emerged into the night, he found Prince Jaylen gone. Not crushed in the stampede or killed in the chaos, but *missing*. He was somewhere in Dimvein, wounded, beaten, and alone, and it was Kullen's job to locate him.

Kullen, the Black Talon, the Dragonblood Assassin, now Royal

Babysitter. And worse, if the boy turned up dead, Kullen had no doubt he would soon follow him to Shekoth. Unfortunately, Kullen was short on ideas of how to find the Prince and even shorter on time. He could already hear the Orkenwatch, boots pounding the streets around him, closing in on his location.

The Prince had come close to death *once* tonight. Magister Branthe had set him to fight some grizzled old former soldier—General Andros, he'd called him, a thought that brought up a host of questions in Kullen's mind for later—and only Kullen's intervention had kept Jaylen's blood from staining the sands. He'd be damned if he let the Prince die somewhere in the darkness of the Western Docks at the hand of a cutthroat or mugger seeing him as an easy mark.

He'd clearly managed to escape through the shipyards' lone gate before Captain Angban and the Imperial Scales showed up. But not *long* before. It couldn't have been more than a few minutes. Kullen considered that carefully. Perhaps Jaylen *hadn't* gotten himself lost, then. If the young man had managed to keep his head—Kullen gave it roughly even odds—he might have seen the Imperial Scales and Lumenators marching toward the gate and gone to them for assistance. There was a decent chance that Prince Jaylen was even now being hustled away in the safety of a company of soldiers and back to the Palace.

That could be both good news and bad. Captain Angban was Emperor Wymarc's hand-picked guard; he'd have chosen trustworthy men—at least, trustworthy to Angban—to escort the Prince. But there were more knives waiting in the dark than even Angban might be aware of.

Kullen's assassinations of Dimvein's wealthy and powerful Magisters had turned up a number of interesting discoveries: someone calling themself "Red Claw" was calling the shots, using the Blood Clan pirates to weaken the Emperor's power, and apparently had the support of both former Imperial soldiers and at least *one* high-ranking member of the Orkenwatch.

In truth, Kullen envied Angban. At least he knew who he could trust. Kullen couldn't place his faith in a single soul save the Emperor himself. Not even Captain Angban could be above suspicion.

Sighing, Kullen pulled himself to his feet. Much as he wanted to sit and watch the overweening aristocrats suffering through some much-deserved comeuppance, he had a mission to be about tonight. And that mission led him right back into the waiting arms of the Imperial Scales occupying the shipyards.

He scanned the entire walled property, searching for a patch of shadow to shadow walk into. He could push through one last use of Umbris's power tonight. He *had* to get back across the river and quickly if he wanted to pick up Prince Jaylen's trail—either on horseback to the Palace or stumbling on foot into the darkness of the Western Docks.

The Lumenators' presence complicated the task. Captain Angban had distributed the light magic-wielders throughout the shipyard, and their cool blue globes illuminated virtually *every* nook and cranny. Indeed, it was so bright Kullen didn't need his dragon-eyes—a gift granted to him by Umbris to see clearly in the darkness.

Finally, he spotted a suitable destination for his shadow-slide. A set of wooden stairs descended from the shipyards to a floating jetty built at river level. The light from the nearest Lumenator's globe emblazoned the topmost steps, but there was a patch of darkness at the staircase's base. Large enough, Kullen surmised, to envelop him and provide him a place to emerge from the Shadow Realm back into reality.

He couldn't help hesitating a moment as he reached for Umbris's vial. That last shadow-slide had felt strange, and it had taken a supreme effort of will to regain corporeal form. Whether it was the shadow magic seeping into his soul or mere fatigue, he didn't know.

Whatever the cause, this time, he was prepared to face it. Clutching the hilt of his dagger tighter, he steeled his resolve and summoned the bloodsurge once more.

Umbris, he directed his thoughts through his link with the dragon, *lend me your will.*

Umbris did not answer but responded with a deluge of power. Kullen felt it first in his toes, then like lightning, magical energy shot like bolts through his legs, spine, and down his arms. Drawing in a deep, shaky breath, Kullen gave in to the *bloodsurge.*

His solid form dissipated, and he hurtled through the night, sliding between shadows like a breath of smoke on the wind. The chill stabbed into his flesh like a thousand rimy needles, burrowing to the core of him, to his very soul. He could feel claws sinking into him—those lost to the Realm, desperate for companionship. Felt them dragging at him, tearing at his form, seeking to suck him into its depths. It wanted him. Wanted to consume him and make him as empty as the void itself.

With effort, Kullen tapped into his resolve, felt the steel of his willpower joined by Umbris's, strengthening him. His gaze fixed on the jetty's shadow. He was nearly there, almost back in his body. Just a few more moments until—

He *felt* it, then. A queer, rippling distortion of reality. One moment he was drifting through the darkness; the next, it was as if a *second* force pried at him. Not the void, but something equally ravenous and powerful.

And in that instant, trapped between worlds, the tether binding Kullen to Umbris suddenly *snapped,* and the icy void devoured him whole.

3
Natisse

Haston stood waiting just outside at the theater's back doors, keeping watch on the narrow muddy alley as Uncle Ronan had instructed him.

"Anything?" Natisse whispered.

"Quiet here," Haston said. "But things have gotten noisy back at the shipyards."

Indeed, Natisse could hear shouts coming from the walled enclosure she and the Crimson Fang had just escaped. No doubt the Imperial Scales would be there en masse, perhaps a detachment of the Orkenwatch for good measure.

That thought worried her. Her encounter with the Orkenwatch patrol had taken place just a few nights past and less than a quarter mile away. If the same company of Orken was out in this part of Western Docks tonight, that damned Sniffer could very well pick up her scent.

"Go, take a look at the situation," Natisse told Haston. "I'll watch. Any sign the Imperial Scales catch so much as a whiff of us, you shout a warning and leg it hard."

"What's your plan?" Haston asked. "Sewer system?"

Natisse nodded. "Tanneries first, just to make sure there's no trace of our scent. Then we head underground and back to the Burrow."

"Right." Haston peeled himself away from the wall and set off north up the alley. "Be safe," he hissed over his shoulder.

"Be lucky," Natisse called after him. He quickly vanished into the shadows. Haston had a knack for sneaking and becoming nigh on invisible, which was what made him such a valuable addition to the Crimson Fang. Half of her lessons on stealth had been learned from him. The years he'd spent as a thief in the One Hand District had taught him well.

She listened, and sure enough, the noise emanating from Magister Onathus's shipyards grew louder. The Imperial Scales would likely have their hands full putting out the blaze Leroshavé, Nalkin, L'yo, and Tobin had set in Magister Perech's caravan yards, not to mention sorting out all the nobles unlucky enough to be caught in connection with Magister Branthe's underground fighting ring—a highly illegal endeavor long ago outlawed by the Emperor. Natisse felt a grim satisfaction at that notion that every one of those dandy men and lace-festooned women would soon get a taste of Imperial justice.

The door creaked open behind her, and Athelas peeked out. "Ready?"

"Ready," she whispered back. "South, then east to the tanneries."

The young man's handsome face screwed up in a wince, but he nodded. "We're right behind you."

Natisse set off in the opposite direction Haston had gone. The caravan yards along the Talos River lay directly west of the theater, far enough away that the Imperial Scales wouldn't have reached them yet. Soon enough, however, the city guards might think to cast a wider net, and Uncle Ronan had been right to hurry them to safety before the Crimson Fang—and the freed Orken captives under their protection—got caught up in the sweep.

She paused at the intersection, peering out of the alley. The streets in her immediate vicinity remained dark, despite the brilliant blue glow of the Lumenators' magical light washing a half-dozen city blocks around the shipyard. A moment spent listening satisfied her concerns. No bootsteps, clattering weapons, or horse hoofs echoed in the night, nothing to indicate the Imperial Scales were headed this way.

Drawing in a deep breath, she slipped out from the alley and darted across the street into the shadows beyond. Luck was with them; tonight, a wispy veil of clouds concealed the stars and the moon, casting Dimvein into darkness. Not the eerie, almost unnatural gloom that filled the Embers—the part of the city located outside of Thanagar's protective dome—after nightfall, but a welcoming obscurity that secreted her and her companions from any watching eyes.

That didn't stop her heart from hammering a furious beat against her sternum. After literally bumping into an Orkenwatch patrol she hadn't seen coming, there was reason enough to be worried—and cautious. That in mind, she chose a route leading directly southward using only back alleys where beggars, lepers, mangy hounds, and feral cats made crude homes crafted with dirt and refuse.

Thoughts of the Orkenwatch brought back a memory: a giant stood at Magister Branthe's side, his face hidden beneath the hood of his cloak but gold bands gleaming from the long, thick, bristling black beard that hung down to his chest. That wasn't just *any* Orken conspiring with the now-deceased Magister. A high-ranked member of the Orkenwatch had played a hand in everything that transpired in the slave fighting pits.

Including the capture and imprisonment of their own people?

She couldn't help casting a glance over her shoulder. Fifty yards behind her, the group of strange-looking creatures shuffled along between Uncle Ronan, Athelas, and Jad. They were Orken, Uncle Ronan had said, and yet… not. Ezrasil alone knew what that meant. They looked like no Orken Natisse had encountered—they were far too petite and frail, their complexion a rich golden hue, a stark contrast with the sallow yellows, greens, and browns more common among the Orken of Dimvein. Where had they come from? More importantly, why had they been trapped in cages behind the fighting pits? What purpose did they serve? More blood for Magister Branthe to spill into his sands, or was it more?

Movement in the shadows ahead snapped Natisse out of her thoughts. Throwing herself to one side, she pressed her back flat against a stone wall. Heart hammering, breath frozen in her lungs, she waited for the inevitable howl signaling an Imperial Scales or Orkenwatch patrol had fingered her.

Instead, she heard only a low voice—which, as it grew louder, Natisse recognized as off-key singing. She peered around the corner and spotted a filthy, rag-clad drunkard tottering through the alley toward her. No doubt he'd come from the Spotless Trousers, a tavern of ill repute that hadn't lived up to its name a single day since it was first built three years ago. Just one of the many establishments constructed by desperate people attempting to scrape a meager living in the wake of the Embers' destruction.

Natisse frowned. Her mind worked at that thought as she turned back to signal for Uncle Ronan and the others to wait for the dipsomaniac to wander past. A ball of unease festered in her belly. Her hand fell to her pocket where the strange vial of liquid resided. The Embers had been destroyed by Golgoth—the very same dragon now somehow bonded to her.

She hadn't understood everything the dragon had said about "mixing their blood" or "offering a bond," but there was no mistaking the power that now hummed within her. Like fire, it was restless, ever shifting, ever hungry, aching to be set free of its restraints and allowed to burn free.

How odd, then, that Golgoth had seemed hesitant to wield her power as she once had the day she destroyed the Embers. No, Natisse thought, that wasn't right. In that moment, she had glimpsed the truth even as the dragon spoke the words. Golgoth *hadn't wanted* to unleash her fire. That had been the fault of the one who sought to use her, to claim her power for himself.

"*I wrestled with him,*" the dragon had said, "*but I could not stop him from using my power.*"

Had she been wrong about the dragons? She had spent so many years hating them for what had happened to her family, but Golgoth's remorse had been genuine—as real as her disgust for what her former mate, Shahitz'ai, had done that day.

Natisse shoved the thought aside. Now wasn't the time for such thinking. Just as she'd buried her anger over Uncle Ronan's lies, she could lock away these concerns until a time better suited for dealing with them.

To her relief, the swaying drunkard soon staggered off down another east-bound alley—though not far, judging by the heavy *thump* and resulting *crash* indicating he'd collapsed atop one of the many piles of detritus littering this part of the Western Docks.

"Hey!" came a half-hearted shout from one of the alley's many residents. "Watch it!"

After a few breathless moments waiting for any further sound, Natisse gestured for Uncle Ronan to resume their advance, then slipped out into the now-vacant alleyway.

She paused as she approached the street where the drunkard had collapsed. Sure enough, loud snores drifted up from a dark, lumpy form lying amidst a tangle of discarded cloth scraps, sawdust from the nearby carpentry shops, and what smelled like week-old poultry gizzards. The stink curdled Natisse's nostrils, and she hurried on past, stepping over another passed-out vagabond. She could always cut east, one—hopefully less foul-smelling—street south.

Natisse finally felt herself relaxing fractionally when she began her trek eastward. They'd traveled over a mile from the theater, which put them closer to two miles away from the scene at Magister Onathus's shipyards. Even if *every* Imperial Scale in Dimvein had been summoned and set to search the city, there was no way they could've made it this far in such a short time. Not that they would've wasted the effort. They had scores of Dimvein's richest aristocrats cornered within the shipyards' walls. The capital city's finest would have their hands full dealing with the inevitable judicial morass resulting from the night's events.

A deep rumble in the distance made Natisse stop in her tracks. She knew that sound all too well. Her hand shot up, a warning to Uncle Ronan and the others. The sound grew louder. The Orkenwatch had arrived. Their heavy boots pounded the cobbled streets. By her ears, she placed them no more than two streets over. If they even had one Sniffer with them, it was over.

She dared to stick her head around the corner. A long line of Orken marched down Ferrin Way. She watched them, hoping they'd keep to their route. Then, one head snapped toward her, nose twitching in the air.

"Shit, shit, shit," she swore under her breath. She waved back at Uncle Ronan, and he quickly got the hint, dragging their rescued survivors back out of the alley with the hobos and downtrodden. There, behind stone walls, they would be obscured from sight but not from smell. She just had to hope the Sniffer would give up its search before it came to that.

She rushed back to the alley, taking less care with the sleeping men. She found what she was looking for and nearly retched. Bending down, she scooped up the fetid remains of a galler bird and smeared the sludgy innards all over her exposed flesh and clothing. Then, she did her best to look as if she belonged there amongst Dimvein's lowliest.

It wasn't long before the Orken Sniffer entered the alley. She couldn't bear to look at him for fear of being noticed. Lying with her back to the creature, she buried her face in the back of the drunk, eliciting a soft moan. Then she felt it—hot, humid breath on her neck. Her heart pounded. She felt blood pumping in her ears, her face growing hot. The Orken grunted, nudged her with his boot. A moment later, the sound of a glass bottle tinkling against the wall. Then, silence.

She waited long moments before rolling over to find the way clear. She sat up, pressed her back against the wall, and breathed deeply. She regretted it immediately. Scrambling to her feet, she rushed back to Uncle Ronan.

His face crinkled at the sight and smell.

"Better than the alternative," Natisse said. "C'mon. We're almost there."

She rushed ahead, scouting for any more unexpected visitors, and the stink of the tanneries soon greeted her, and nothing had ever smelled so good. She quickened her pace, eager to get off the streets. Not that the sewers beneath Dimvein were particularly pleasant, but they would be safe from Imperial patrols, and they smelled loads better than she did at the moment. Anyone traveling the underground maze of tunnels would be doing so to *avoid* the law. Natisse's lashblade could handle trouble of that nature.

Relief flooded her as she finally turned down the narrow side street that cut behind a skinner's shop, just west of the nearest tannery. There, she found the metal grille barring to the circular opening that descended into the sewers.

She set about wrestling with the grille and had it off by the time Uncle Ronan and the foremost of the Orken creatures caught up.

"In," she hissed to the gold-skinned Orken at the front of the pack. A male by the look of him, though their features were so distorted by lack of care and nutrition, it was difficult to tell.

The creatures scrabbled down the ladder without hesitation—either too afraid for their lives to protest, or their time in Magister Branthe's cages had inured them to such trivialities as human ordure.

"Well done," Uncle Ronan said, clapping Natisse on the shoulder. Though it was an entirely ordinary gesture—he'd done it a thousand times before—tonight, it bothered Natisse. She shifted away, sliding her shoulder out from beneath his hand.

Uncle Ronan's face was cast in shadows, so she couldn't see his expression, but she felt the tension radiating off him. Without a word, he turned away, wiped the galler guts from his hand, and climbed down the ladder into the sewer system.

A hulking figure loomed large in the shadows in front of her.

"All here and in one piece," Jad said.

"How's our new friend?" Natisse asked.

Jad looked down at Prince Jaylen—who appeared almost childlike—cradled in the big man's muscular arms.

"Still unconscious," he said. "He'll be out cold for a while. Blood loss nearly did him in. But if I can get him on my table, I'll be able to stop any further hemorrhaging, maybe give him one of Serrod's potions to help him back onto his feet. Won't sort out the mess completely—"

"But it's better than trying to explain how we let him die," Natisse finished.

Jad grunted and nodded. "Help me get him up on my shoulders. Can't climb down without hands."

Natisse helped shift Prince Jaylen's weight. Jad should've managed with ease, but he grimaced with the effort of hefting the dead weight. He'd taken a nasty dagger wound to the shoulder—nowhere near fatal but painful enough to make every rung misery. But Jad was the sort to suffer in silence, so Natisse said nothing either. That wound was *her* fault. He'd wanted nothing to do with tonight's events, but she'd coerced him into it. They'd have to talk about that later. After what he'd done...

"Hurry!" Haston's harsh whisper echoed through the alley.

Natisse spun toward the sound and spotted the dark shadow racing toward them.

"Orkenwatch patrol!" Haston hissed.

"They must've circled back around," Natisse said through her teeth. "Hurry up. Everyone in."

Haston came to a skidding stop in front of her. "Sniffer's with 'em." Then, he spotted the state of her and added, "Looks like you already knew."

"Yeah," she said. "Close call already."

She turned back to the opening where Jad's bulk still blocked the ladder descending into the sewers. Thankfully, most of the Orken had already descended, as had Uncle Ronan and Athelas.

Only she, Haston, and a half dozen of the gold-skinned creatures remained.

The rumble of the Orkenwatch bootsteps... they were close.

"C'mon, c'mon, c'mon," Natisse said.

Finally, the last of the Orken vanished into the darkness, and Natisse turned to tell Haston to follow.

"Go!" he said before she could.

She didn't argue. Slipping through the hole, she slid down the ladder, barely catching herself before she collided with the hairless top of an Orken's head.

"Haston!" she hissed as she leaped off the ladder, landing in the muck with a splash.

The opening above was suddenly blocked by a solid shadow, and the metal grille slid shut with the faint rasp of metal on stone. Then Haston clamored down the ladder, stopping with his feet planted on the last rung, just above the scummy surface of the sluggishly flowing sewage.

Tense silence thundered in the sewers. Humans and Orken alike waited with bated breath, listening for the approaching patrol. The *tromp, tromp* grew louder, echoed through the tunnels, the sound of hobnailed boots striking stone.

Natisse's heart hammered in her throat. Her hand dropped to the hilt of her lashblade. She'd been lucky enough to survive *one* Orkenwatch patrol—would her luck hold out? With just her, Jad, and Uncle Ronan in anything approaching fighting shape, they'd be hard-pressed should it come to a clash with the brutish Orken.

Shadows fell over them through the grate. One after another, the Orken stomped past, not even slowing as they passed above. The bootsteps faded into the distance. Natisse let out a long breath and heard dozens of others around her doing likewise. Her heart settled once more into her chest, her pulse slowing, the roar of blood in her ears quietening. When she removed her hand from the lashblade, her palms were clammy with sweat. A trickle ran down her forehead and stung her eye. Wiping it away, Natisse gathered herself.

"C'mon," she told the figures she knew filled the darkness around her. "We got lucky here. But we've still a long way to go before we're truly safe."

She eyed Uncle Ronan as she passed him to take the lead.

"Good job," he said.

"Thanks, *General*," Natisse said as she pushed forward.

4
KULLEN

Kullen screamed into the abyss. He roared with all the force his incorporeal form could muster. But it was like grasping for breath in the ocean. Silence, thick and all-consuming, was his only answer.

The ever-present chill of the Shadow Realm collided with him, no longer a creeping trickle but a tidal wave that crashed atop him and buffeted him with soul-crushing force.

He tried to fight, desperately tried to claw his way back to the Mortal Realm, but he couldn't find it. He sensed nothing beyond the gaping darkness enveloping him. Nothing behind, before, or in all directions. Only the void. An empty absence of life.

Umbris! He tried to call for help—the Twilight Dragon *had* to be somewhere in the lightless void—but the bond that had tethered them had been severed. How, he didn't know. In that moment, he knew only bone-deep terror as razor-sharp talons gouged into him.

He had no flesh to pierce, no bone to break, but the claws found purchase on his soul. Dragging, rending, pulling him backward with the inexorability of quicksand.

Kullen couldn't truly see the creatures, but he sensed them—the swirls of power encircling them like wispy strands of frayed fabric. The hollow, sunken features that might once have been human—or Ezrasil knew what else—yet had deteriorated over the passage of time to little more than hideous, snarling visages. Monsters. Bared teeth and sharp talons, eyes of pure nothingness that locked on him, black maws that unhinged in wordless shrieks of delight.

They *wanted* him. Wanted to tear apart the last lingering remnants of Mortal Realm permanence, to shred his very essence until he was as much *nothing* as they were. Eternally hungry creatures of the Shadow Realm that existed only to consume. To devour until the world was naught but shadow, where all traces of reality and life were gone, and only the void existed.

He had heard the tales of horror enough times to know the fate awaiting him. Umbris had warned him of the danger of overusing the bloodsurge. Though the Twilight Dragon had refused to speak on the matter of Heshe, Emperor Wymarc had told him of the former Black Talon who had been consumed by the Shadow Realm. Kullen knew to fear the creatures and fear he did.

But fear had never stopped him from fighting. Not since the first day he'd stood up to bigger, stronger toughs on the streets outside of Mammy Tess's Refuge for the Wayward. They'd left him bloody and beaten, yet every time they'd knocked him down, he'd gotten right back up. He'd fought until they had grown tired of beating him, until blood soaked his clothing, until the bones of their knuckles cracked against his ribs and skull. He would not yield, would not quit. Not to those nameless cunts, and certainly not to the creatures tearing apart his soul.

He had no weapons with which to do battle, but fought anyway. Wielding his determination and willpower like a shield, his rage like a sword, he wrestled with the nightmares trawling him deeper into the endless void. He didn't know what good it did—there was neither time nor place in this chasm of despair, no way to know if he gained or lost ground—for there was no ground to speak of. But he *had* to fight. Had to resist the stinging chill rushing through his veins, turning his limbs to lead.

The moment he stopped fighting, he was done. The moment he gave in, the creatures of the Shadow Realm would take him, make them one of their own.

They clawed, and Kullen clawed right back at them. His hands were no more real than theirs, yet he envisioned himself striking out, raking at hideous, deformed faces, digging into empty eye sockets. Though the swirling nightmarish forms closed about him, overwhelming him, suffocating him, he continued struggling, battling their hunger and cold for as long as his strength would sustain him.

Which was not very long. He was weakening, the numbness of the void seeping deeper into his veins, sapping his life force. He had nothing to tether him to his corporeal form beyond conscious thought and the will to stay alive, but he clung to those with every shred of his iron will. Despite it all, he was slipping, slipping, slipping ever farther into the barren desolation.

It was absorbing him. One iota at a time, slowly but inexorably. Creeping in increments like sin upon the hearts of man. He fought a losing battle. Despair threatened to steal the last of his vitality, and dread of the inevitable, permanent nonexistence that awaited him, tested even his mettle. He was breaking; he could feel it. His will alone could only sustain him for so long, and he had already spent what felt like an eternity trapped in the Shadow Realm. There would be no end to this fight. No end unless he gave in.

And then, suddenly, he was not alone.

A mighty wind roared through the void around him, a surge of power so tangible it felt like the heat of the brightest summer sun on the coldest winter's day. Empty darkness coalesced into a solid form that gleamed with a brilliance not seen by his eyes but sensed by his spirit.

"Kullen Bloodsworn!" roared Umbris's voice in Kullen's mind. *"What have you done?"*

Kullen heaved against the icy, phantasmal hands dragging at

him, tearing free just in time to feel himself scooped up by Umbris's enormous dragon body. He experienced the same rush of relief that had come over him when Umbris rescued him from the onyx sharks. Only this darkness was far colder, the enemies far more deadly, and he had *no* chance of escaping without the dragon's aid.

But Umbris *was* there. As real and corporeal as Kullen himself in the Mortal Realm. The Twilight Dragon's power here was immense—a mountain towering over ants in comparison to the nightmarish creatures encroaching upon him from all angles. When Umbris opened his mouth, a roar thundered through the void, drowning out the shrieks and screams. A pillar of black fire, somehow *darker* than the void itself, reduced the phantasms to motes of shadow no larger than the finest grain of dust.

"*Hold on!*" Umbris rumbled in his mind. "*I've got to get you out of here.*"

Kullen had no hands, but he envisioned himself clinging to Umbris's back, the same way he had the night the dragon saved him from the depths of Blackwater Bay. The void rushed past him, and the screams of the hideous shadow creatures were left far behind as Umbris hurtled through the darkness. Kullen didn't know where they were going, but he was all too glad to be away from those…things.

Then he saw it: a pinprick of light shining in the endless void. His incorporeal form raced toward it at incomprehensible speeds. The Mortal Realm, he knew somehow. And there, life.

He returned to his body with a jerk. The transition was so abrupt, from shadow to flesh in the space between heartbeats, his mind could not make full sense of it. He collapsed on rubbery legs and fell face-first to the jetty's hard, wooden planks. The impact jarred him, sent pain shivering through his face and chest. Yet even those twinges of discomfort felt distant, almost dissociated from him, as if someone *else* felt that pain. Someone made of bone and muscle, not the intangible being he had been for that terrifying eternity.

The chill of the Shadow Realm did not easily release its hold on him. For long moments, he lay in the shadows at the base of the stairs, struggling to make sense of what had just transpired. To regain the sensation in limbs that felt heavy, unwieldy, *wrong*.

What... happened? Even his thoughts felt sluggish, his brain reeling from the transformation.

"*I do not know,*" Umbris said, real anger—and was that a hint of fear?—in his voice. "*Our bond was lost. Severed, as if you had died. Yet I could feel your presence within the Shadow. I have never before experienced that.*"

Any idea... what could have... caused it? Kullen struggled to marshal his thoughts, to clear the fog from his mind. With an effort of will, he pushed himself up onto one elbow. The pins-and-needles sensation had just begun to fade from his arms, but his legs still felt frozen, as if he'd been buried alive in snow for a month. His dagger had fallen from his right hand and lay on the wooden jetty. He made no move for it yet.

"*None whatsoever,*" Umbris said. "*Which is all the more concerning. Nothing should be able to sever the bond between bloodsworn, and yet, there is no denying the truth of what happened.*"

Kullen didn't know exactly what had happened, but he knew one thing for certain: he'd get nothing accomplished by lying around. He forced his other arm—still half-numb—to respond and pushed himself up to both knees. His legs were finally regaining some feeling, enough that he could rise unsteadily to his feet after just a few more labored heartbeats. He clung to the stone wall and took deep, steadying breaths.

Eventually, the blood rushing in his ears slowed, and he could hear the sounds coming from the shipyards above. He wasn't certain how much time had passed—it had felt like forever in that void, but judging by the shouts of the Imperial Scales, it had been mere seconds, minutes at most.

Kullen looked toward the top of the steps, and what he saw nearly sent him back down to his knees. Above him, a corona of... he hesitated to call it light. The red-black blaze brightened the darkness, but with it came an uneasy feeling, like flames seeking to immolate him, like Ulnu's raking claws or Binteth's snapping jaws.

The heat of it made its way down to where he stood, drawing sweat from his pores and a tingling sensation on the top of his skull.

It was the Lumenator's light and yet like nothing he'd seen before. Nothing like the cool blue glow given off by the floating globes generated by the Emperor's light magic-wielders.

Realization sank home a moment later. It had always appeared cool and blue to *his* eyes. Yet he saw not through his human eyes now. Umbris's dragon-eyes had triggered to brighten the darkness, and they perceived the Lumenators' light far differently than he. Where Kullen's eyes saw refuge and strength, Umbris saw this... something Kullen could only describe as hateful and ugly.

His mind reeled, yet something clicked into place. *That* was the only thing different from every other time he'd used the bloodsurge. It seemed impossible to believe it, yet he couldn't remember a time he'd tapped into Umbris's power anywhere near a Lumenator. How could he, given that their light kept all shadows at bay?

Could *they* be responsible for what'd happened? He'd been speeding his way across the Talos River just as he had when fleeing the Imperial Scales, but had that light—or the magic used to generate it—somehow severed his connection to Umbris and the Mortal Realm? Was there something about the Lumenators' gift that adversely affected Umbris's Shadow Realm powers? It *could* be. After all, light and shadow were opposites, in a way.

What do you think? he asked Umbris, knowing the dragon could read his thoughts.

"*It could be,*" Umbris rumbled back, voice pensive. "*It appears we must learn more about this Lumenator magic in order to understand what occurred. I will not risk you again. You must not use the bloodsurge anywhere near the Lumenators until we are certain of its effects.*"

No argument from me on that one, Kullen said, grimacing. *That was one experience I'd rather never repeat.*

"And you must rest before calling on my power again." Umbris's tone had a chiding edge that reminded Kullen of Mammy Tess.

I will. Kullen nodded. He'd get about as far arguing with Umbris as he ever had with the Refuge's head ministrant. *But we've got more important things to deal with before I can loaf about. Jaylen first, then sleep.*

Umbris's growl echoed in Kullen's mind, but the dragon didn't protest. He could sense Kullen's thoughts, knew how he felt about his vow to the Emperor—and, by extension, his grandson.

Kullen found his legs *mostly* heeded his commands, and he could feel all the way down to his feet. Taking that as a good sign, he retrieved and sheathed his fallen dagger and ascended the stairs from the jetty to the shipyards. Far too slowly for his liking, it turned out. Every step proved a laborious effort, as if his soul was terrified of the prospect of drawing nearer to that dark illumination.

Though when he reached the top step, the heat of the light washing over him, he felt no different other than the immediate return of the cool blue light when Umbris's dragon eyes shifted back to the steel gray Kullen had known his whole life.

Kullen half expected the Lumenator to react to his presence, but the woman—short, well-built, with smooth features despite her white hair—didn't even glance his way. Her face remained impassive, registering no surprise to find him emerging from the darkness beside her.

The stoic Lumenators had always unnerved Kullen slightly, but after seeing how Umbris viewed them, he was fully unnerved.

But he had no choice but to press forward, unable to spare a moment's attention for the emotionless, statue-still Lumenator.

"Hey, there!" Kullen shouted to the Imperial Scales guarding the aristocrats. "Who's gonna point me in the direction of Captain Angban?"

5
NATISSE

Darkness reigned like a god in the sewer tunnels, the gloom broken only by the faintest glimmers of night leaking through the grille at the top of the ladder. Natisse cursed herself for not thinking to bring a light source—a lamp, lantern, even an alchemical scratch-stick, anything to generate a few minutes worth of illumination.

She couldn't bring herself to even consider calling upon the fire that had wreathed her flesh back in the theater. Not in front of the rest of the Crimson Fang. She hadn't yet fully come to terms with her actions—why in Ezrasil's name *had* she accepted the dragon's bond?—and had no desire to answer the inevitable bombardment of inquiries it would elicit.

She *almost* asked Uncle Ronan for a light. Not that she expected him to use his Lumenator magic in front of the rest of the Crimson Fang, either. He'd kept it a secret for decades not only from her but *all* of them and wasn't about to take the lid off now. But the anger welling within her wanted to lash out at him, even in this small way.

Before long, Haston solved the problem for her. Light sprang up from a small alchemical lantern in his hand.

"Serrod?" she asked.

"Indeed," Haston replied. "I just had an inkling we'd need them."

He handed a second one to Athelas, who quickly pulled the tab on the side of the glass flask. A sliver of metal slid out from one side, allowing the small hole in the flask's center to open. The silvery liquid in the top compartment dripped slowly into a second reservoir. When it connected with the water within, it bubbled and burst to life in a blinding eruption of light.

"That should do," Haston said.

Natisse nodded her approval. "Good thinking. Lead the way?"

"Will do," Haston said, a grin on his face. He strode past her and headed eastward along the sewer tunnel. Down that way, Natisse knew, they could find an exit that spilled out into the Talos River near the One Hand District. From there, it would be a short trek at street level to—

"No." The word came from the old Orken who had spoken to Natisse in the cages beneath Magister Branthe's fighting pits. He looked to Uncle Ronan and barked something in a harsh, discordant language Natisse didn't understand.

Uncle Ronan nodded. "Yes," he said in the common tongue, "I am taking you to the *Kha'zatyn*."

"We go this way." The old Orken pointed in the *opposite* direction Haston had gone, farther west.

"What?" Natisse slipped through the crowd of huddled, fearful Orken creatures—none taller than her shoulder, a stark contrast with the towering brutes who made up the Orkenwatch—until she stood before the white-haired speaker. "What is he talking about?"

Uncle Ronan ignored the question. His eyes remained fixed on the old Orken. "You are certain?"

"Certain, yes." The Orken nodded, his leathery features etched with confidence. "Urktukk show you."

"Show us what?" Natisse demanded. Her anger flared again, furious at Uncle Ronan's disregard. "Uncle Ronan—"

"Follow, Ketsneer," the old Orken said to Natisse, using the

Orken word for second-in-command. It was interesting that he'd made that assumption, but Natisse let him continue. "Urktukk show you to *Kha'zatyn*."

He turned and spoke in his throaty language to the rest of his people, and as one, the Orken set off at a brisk pace behind their leader.

Caught between aggravation and surprise, Natisse could only stare wordlessly at the fast-moving pack of Orken. Something in the old Orken's words had banished their fear and excited them.

Natisse rounded on Uncle Ronan. "What the—"

But Uncle Ronan was no longer there. He moved along at Urktukk's side, Athelas's alchemical lantern held high to illuminate the tunnels ahead.

A grunt from Jad drew Natisse's attention. The big man stood watching the procession of Orken, a dark scowl on his face. He, too, appeared less than elated by yet another display of Uncle Ronan's secretive nature.

"You got *any* idea what's going on?" she asked quietly. "Where they're taking us?"

"Not a one," Jad rumbled, shifting Prince Jaylen on his shoulder. "But if Uncle Ronan's going with them, might be we should, too."

"Depends entirely on where they're taking us." Natisse's fist tightened around the hilt of her lashblade. "Tuskthorne Keep's not exactly the sort of place I'd want to end up."

"You don't trust him?" Jad asked, voice quiet, his expression pensive.

Natisse considered the question. "I don't know."

"Secrets or no," Jad said, placing his free hand on Natisse's shoulder, "he's the same man we've all followed for so long."

"Yeah." Natisse nodded. "I suppose. Watch my back." She strode ahead of Jad and joined the procession.

"Always," came the big man's quiet response.

She watched Uncle Ronan and Urktukk lead the way through the tunnels, mind racing. Where was the creature taking them?

What was the *Kha'zatyn?* She'd thought Uncle Ronan wanted to escort the Orken back to the Burrow, but it seemed plans had changed, and he hadn't bothered telling them. Sounded about right to fit in with the events of the past couple of days. Secrets, secrets, and more secrets. She was growing tired of this pattern. First chance she got, she was going to have a long, pointed talk with Uncle Ronan. Very likely involving fists as well as words.

Despite her anger, she refused to allow herself to lose sight of the task at hand. Everything they'd done tonight had been to free the slaves from Magister Branthe's fighting pit. It didn't matter that the "slaves" were Orken—distant as they appeared—instead of human, the mission remained the same.

She helped an old, frail-looking female Orken—they were all so frail—through the tunnels. She shuffled her feet, dragging them through the slushy waters. Sympathy swelled within Natisse. With her other hand, she accepted one of the children, the sickly mother nursing a sicklier infant, too tired to carry her on her back. The little Orken mewled and gurgled up at her, baring teeth to reveal too-few and too-small fangs. It took Natisse a moment to realize the baby was *smiling.* She'd never known Orken could do such a thing outside of combat—those sickly grins. The Orkenwatch weren't exactly renowned for their friendly disposition.

Though Urktukk's words had initially buoyed the spirits of his people, not even the promise of the *Kha'zatyn* could fully alleviate the effects of the hunger, thirst, and privation they'd clearly suffered in the cages. Their pace soon slowed, and Natisse found herself near the head of the column—just a few yards behind Uncle Ronan and Urktukk. In fact, she was so close, she nearly bumped into the Orken leader's back when he stopped abruptly.

"Here," the old Orken growled in the common tongue.

Natisse spun a slow circle, confused. The tunnel in which they stood appeared just like every other in the sewers. No ladder led up to street level, and the nearest intersection was well beyond the globe of the little alchemical light in Haston's hand. There wasn't so much as a crumbling brick, a grate in the tunnel ceiling, or a pipe delivering fresh sewage. Just plain stone surrounded them, foul-smelling muck underfoot.

Yet Urktukk moved with confidence, striding toward the left-hand tunnel wall and placing a claw-tipped finger against the stone. He did something Natisse could not see, and suddenly a seam split the wall directly in front of him. Light spilled out of the aperture, which opened to reveal some manner of doorway.

Natisse sucked in a breath of stale air. Another hidden passage? It appeared much like the one through which she'd followed Uncle Ronan for his secret meeting with his mysterious "contact." Only, this one shone with its own internal light. It was a strange light, oddly subdued, like a lantern with its shutters drawn. And it was from no fire Natisse had ever seen—not even the cool blue fire of Lumenator magic. The glow, a deep, rich gold the same hue of Orken skin, came from spidery veins slithering through what was otherwise solid rock.

No, not *through* the stone. Whatever was giving off the light had grown atop the stone, like lichen on tree branches or barnacles clinging to a ship's hull.

Urktukk turned back to Uncle Ronan and gestured toward the opening. "To *Kha'zatyn*," he said, a proud smile on his face.

"Lead the way, Tuskigo Urktukk," Uncle Ronan replied. "Kill the lights," he said to Haston and Athelas, who were at the back of the line. Their alchemical lanterns went dim the moment they slid the metal back through the slot.

Urktukk rattled off a few words in his own language to his people, then shambled into the secret threshold. Uncle Ronan followed on his heels, and Natisse was pushed forward by the once-again animated Orken behind her. She had no time for curiosity or amazement. Indeed, she could barely keep her feet in the excited press of the Orken hurrying to enter the narrow passage with its gleaming veins of gold.

Natisse's head spun, and it wasn't merely from the stink of galler guts and the sewer layered atop the distinctly potent livestock smell of the filthy, rag-clad Orken around her. Too much had happened in quick succession—Uncle Ronan as General Andros, the fire, battling Magister Branthe's guards, the reappearance of the mysterious assassin who'd killed Baruch and just saved her life, Golgoth, and now this. All one after another. Her mind, exhausted after the day's events, reeled.

She moved as if in a trance, one foot in front of the other, guided—or, in truth, propelled—along by the crowd of diminutive Orken creatures flooding down the tunnel. How long they traveled through that gold-glowing corridor, she didn't know. One moment she was in that passage, marveling at the beauty of the strange illumination; the next, she was stumbling out into the oil lantern-lit stone cavern she recognized so well.

"What the..." They were at the Burrow. She glanced back at Jad, who wore a similarly stunned expression. How was it possible Urktukk had known of this place?

Urktukk stopped twenty yards away from the enormous steel door that barred the entrance to the Burrow. "Long I hear of *Kha'zatyn*," he said in a voice sonorous, reverent. "Stories told father to son to son. But only dream of seeing it. Until today."

"I welcome you to *Kha'zatyn*," Uncle Ronan said. To Natisse's ears, the words sounded strangely ceremonial, like a priest's liturgy or the formal greeting of a diplomat. "May you find shelter within its walls, and may your children know peace."

Urktukk placed one dirty, shaking hand on his forehead, the other on his throat, and bowed to Uncle Ronan. He spoke in his own language, and though Natisse didn't understand its meaning, she felt the solemnity to the core of her being. Something momentous was happening here, but what?

Her chance to ask was quickly swept away with Uncle Ronan's turn from Urktukk. He appraised the crowd for someone. "Haston, the key?"

"Of course," Haston said, producing a heavy brass key and handing it to Uncle Ronan.

The Crimson Fang's leader inserted the key and twisted it to precisely the right angle to disarm the hidden traps and mechanisms, then turned it the other way until the lock *click-clicked* again and again. With Haston's help, he set to work pushing open the heavy door, then gestured for Urktukk to follow him inside.

Natisse handed the Orken child back to its mother, then stepped back to admit the flood of gold-skinned creatures into the Burrow. She retreated until she stood along the edge of the steep cliff. Behind and far below her, the Talos River rushed past—an oddly apropos resemblance to the precipitous pace of tonight's events.

"How did they know?" Athelas's whispered question to Jad reached her ears. The two stood a few paces away, waiting their turn to enter. "How did they know about this place or how to get here?"

"Don't rightly know," Jad rumbled back. "But Uncle Ronan seems to have those answers."

"And more," Natisse said under her breath, teeth grinding, jaw clenched. Just as soon as the Orken were sorted, she fully intended to get them from him. He'd kept secrets and lied to her—lied to them *all*—long enough.

6
KULLEN

Though Kullen's presence might've elicited no reaction from the Lumenator, the Imperial Scales responded with violent alacrity. A half-dozen heavily armed city guards swung around to face him, drawing swords or raising crossbows at his head.

"Stay where you are!" roared one in a strident voice.

Kullen made no move. He stood perfectly still, hands held high to show they were empty, a calm smile on his face.

"Captain Angban," he repeated slowly, as if the Imperial Scales hadn't heard it. "Where is he?" There was no time to search the entire shipyard for the Elite Scales' officer.

"Get him!" shouted the one who'd spoken, addressing the sword-wielding guard at his side. "Gather him with the others."

"Get over here, you bastard," demanded the guard rushing toward him, sword drawn.

"I'd rather not, if it's all the same to you," Kullen said in a calm tone. "Just point me in the good captain's direction, and I'll be on my way."

"On your way?" The guard barked a harsh laugh. He stopped three feet from Kullen, brandishing his sword as if to spark fear.

"Boyo, you're not going anywhere. You're under arrest like everyone else!"

"That won't be necessary." Kullen's voice was almost flippant, far too scornful considering the crossbow bolts pointed squarely at him and the oversized Imperial Scale standing before him with bared steel and a serious expression. "I'm sure it's just part of you doing your job and all, but I'd rather not waste either of our time here."

"Waste our...?" The man spluttered in surprise. "Listen here—"

"No, *you* listen." Kullen darted forward to close the remaining space. He was so quick the guard had no time to respond before he was disarmed, his wrist wrenched around behind his back, and his body between Kullen and the crossbow bolts. "I've asked quite politely a few times now. But I'm starting to lose my patience, and when I do, things are going to get... messy." He sucked in a breath and bared his teeth in a snarl. "Now, one last time, kindly do us both a pissing favor and point. Me. To. Angban!" He emphasized each word as if speaking to someone both deaf and dim-witted.

The first guard's face flushed, his eyes narrowing, but he was smart enough to recognize the danger his companion faced. Kullen held the man's own sword against the soft of his neck, in perfect position to slice his jugular vein with a flick of his wrist. And the three crossbow-wielding guards were getting awfully twitchy.

"I heard my name!" came a familiar voice, followed a moment later by a blond-haired and bearded figure. "Who has the audacity to summon me like a hound to—" He cut off as he recognized Kullen's hood and cloak. "Oh, *you*." His upper lip curled into a sneer.

Kullen half expected the man to issue the order for the Imperial Scales to loose their bolts and rush into the attack. The two of them hadn't exactly parted on the friendliest of terms. Only Emperor Wymarc's intervention had stopped Captain Angban from summarily executing Kullen after he'd used an alchemical smoke sphere to sneak past the Elite Scales guarding the Emperor's private study. That was mere hours earlier. Kullen had no doubt the man could harbor a grudge far longer than that and would love nothing more than to enjoin the soldiers to ensure Kullen's death.

But Captain Angban just gave a disgusted grunt. "Release him," he said, gesturing toward the guard Kullen held with a contemptuous flick of his wrist.

Kullen smiled. "But of course, my good captain." He feigned releasing his captive, then stopped. "But what will certify my safety from your men?"

Angban took a step forward.

"Uh-uh," Kullen said, tugging the guard back a hair.

Captain Angban turned toward the nearest of the crossbowmen. Kullen saw the faintest twitch of the man's lip as if he was *dying* to speak the words that would end Kullen's life but only held himself in restraint by sheer willpower. After a long moment, the Captain shook his head.

"Lower your bows," Angban ordered. "He is the Emperor's loyal man." He spoke with audible effort through half-clenched teeth, every word painful.

The Imperial Scales obeyed in an instant, but they shot angry, wary, and suspicious looks at Kullen. For his part, Kullen just met their gazes with a smile that stopped just short of mocking.

"Does that satisfy you?" Angban asked.

"I'd feel better if they placed them on the ground," Kullen said.

"You go too far, and we've reached the end of my grace."

"Very well," Kullen said, releasing his captive with a gentle shove that sent the man stumbling forward a few steps. When the Imperial Scale turned with a glower, Kullen tossed the guard his sword hilt first. The Imperial Scale managed to catch it... barely.

He knew he shouldn't have baited the Imperial Scales—as he'd said, they were merely doing their job. But fatigue, lingering fear of what had nearly transpired in the Shadow Realm, and concern for Prince Jaylen conspired to sour his mood, leaving him irritable and short on temper. And finding Captain Angban had proven far easier than if he'd tried to slip through the shipyards unseen. This way, the only thing wounded or injured tonight was one Imperial Scale's pride.

"Follow," Captain Angban snapped, then turned on his heel to stalk away.

Kullen obeyed—if the Captain needed to feel *he* was in command of the situation, so be it—and marched along behind the stiff-backed Angban. The Imperial Scales' glares followed him, but they were no longer of concern to him. His focus was entirely on finding the information he'd come for.

Captain Angban led him only a short distance away, just beyond the shipyards' front gates, then stopped and whirled on Kullen.

"What?" he demanded in a curt tone.

"The Prince," Kullen answered calmly. "Have you or any of your men seen him tonight?"

"No." Captain Angban's jaw muscles twitched. "And here I thought *you* had gone to retrieve him."

Kullen cursed inwardly. The captain must have read the dismay in his expression, for he frowned, his pale-blond eyebrows knitting together.

"Did you fail at this one task—the *only* task to which the Emperor set you to?" Captain Angban couldn't hide the smugness from his tone. "The Emperor may not doubt your loyalty, but clearly your competence is at que—"

"You're certain?" Kullen cut the man off. He hadn't the time for insults, not now. "None of your men encountered him on your way here? He's not riding back to the Palace with a company of guards?"

"He is not." Captain Angban's words were clipped.

Kullen doubted the man would piss on him to put out a fire, but he could see no hint of deception in the captain's face or posture.

"How badly did you cock this up?" Captain Angban demanded.

"Do I need to set the Imperial Scales to tear apart the city in search of our Prince?"

"No." Kullen shook his head. That would only make the situation worse. The Imperial Scales would approach the task with all the delicacy of an enraged dragon and likely cause about as much damage. "I'll handle it. You focus on dealing with these pissants."

Captain Angban turned a baleful glare on the shivering, sooty, nervous aristocrats huddled under the watchful eye of the Imperial Scales. The cool blue light emanating from the Lumenators' magical globes cast the faces of the noble lords and ladies in a truly unhealthy pallor.

"A fine shame we can't just lock them up," Angban growled. "Better for all of us—all of Dimvein—they sat rotting in the Emperor's dungeons."

"On that, at least, we can agree," Kullen said, giving the man a wry grin.

"Unfortunately, most of them will walk away from this a good deal poorer but no less likely to break the Emperor's laws once again when it suits their greedy desires." Captain Angban spat a wad of phlegm onto the muddy street. "A slap on the wrist when they deserve far worse."

Kullen's grin grew wider and turned ugly, cold. "If it's any consolation, Captain, those orchestrating this travesty have already received all the justice this world has to offer. The rest, we will leave in the claws of Binteth and Ulnu. I suspect the twin gods of death will find Magister Branthe, Baronet Ochrin, and the rest of his little conspiracy sorely lacking in goodness, and they'll enjoy the luxuriousness of Shekoth's deepest pits for an eternity or two."

Captain Angban gave Kullen a nod. "That is some small comfort, indeed."

Kullen knew Angban had no place in his heart for the poetic nature of most gods and goddesses. The kind, pretty, wistful ideals of the Brendoni deity, Yildemé, or any of the thousands found in the southern provinces paled in comparison to the just and swift actions of one such as Ezrasil—stern, unyielding, the balancer of justice's heavy scales.

Many soldiers wore the mark of Dumast, the leader of the Ophahir, an army of righteous soldiers who had fallen in the eternal battle against the ravages of the Nitzlotl—the ever-hungry embodiment of evil. It was believed in many circles that Dumast went on to godhood based on that deed alone. Kullen found it hard to believe that any man could ascend to such a position. He surely had no hopes of it himself.

However, no one with breath in their lungs and eyes in their skulls could deny the fury of Binteth or Ulnu. Their stain was evident upon the hearts of all mankind. The twin bone dragons, the bearers of Ezrasil's judgment, meted out punishments in accordance with his will and their own devices. And they delighted in it.

Kullen turned to march away but stopped as he nearly collided with a Lumenator. Though his human eyes could not see the vile nature of their light as seen by Umbris, he couldn't shake the truth from his mind any more than he could fully banish the chill of the Shadow Realm from his soul.

Why do you see it so differently, my friend? Kullen asked Umbris in his mind.

The only response he received was the feeling of a thousand icy spiders crawling down his spine.

"And what do I tell the Emperor?" Angban called out, causing Kullen to stop and turn.

He regarded the Elite Scale in the manner one would a child who'd asked one too many questions.

"He'll ask about his grandson; you know he will." Captain Angban's expression was hard, worry furrowing his brow. "I'll have to tell him I saw you here, and when I do—"

"I know." Kullen nodded. "Tell him that the Prince is alive and that I'm going after him. Even if I have to search every corner of the Karmian Empire, I'll find him. He has my word on that."

"For your sake—and mine—I hope that is true." Captain

Angban inclined his head. "Good hunting. May Dumast and his Ophahir guide you true."

Kullen had no response for that—the words surprised him almost as much as the tiniest flicker of respect he saw in the Elite Scale's eyes—but Captain Angban turned and marched back into the shipyards, gone before Kullen could speak.

Kullen, too, hoped his word would not be returned void. If he was ever to return to the Palace, it would need to be with a living, breathing Prince Jaylen by his side.

7
Natisse

When the last of the Orken finally entered the Burrow—or the *Kha'zatyn,* as they'd been calling it—Natisse and Jad followed. Athelas remained behind to close the heavy door; apparently, the half-dose of Gryphic Elixir had done wonders to heal the wounds he'd sustained in the clash with Magister Onathus's guards. All that remained of what should've been a mortal wound was a faint scar along the left side of his neck. He'd gotten lucky, indeed.

Unfortunately, the same couldn't be said about Prince Jaylen. In the light of the oil lanterns burning on the Burrow's walls, the young man's face appeared paler than before, and fresh blood glistened wetly on his bare abdomen. Jad's coat, too, was stained with new streaks of crimson. The wounds left by Magister Branthe's lash on the Prince's back had reopened.

"Ezrasil's bones!" Jad cursed and pushed through the crowded Burrow. "Move aside!"

Even if the Orken didn't understand his words, they parted to let him pass. How could they know a man of his size wouldn't simply bull through them or crush them? They were surely used to harsh treatment from Magister Branthe and Onathus's guards. They had no idea how tenderhearted he truly was.

"Sparrow! Sparrow!" he roared at full volume, his deep voice echoing through the earthen-walled passages. "Sparrow, get the table ready."

Jad disappeared down the corridor that led to the Crimson Fang's living quarters. Natisse couldn't help worrying—Prince Jaylen dying down here wouldn't be good for anyone—but if anyone could handle the task of caring for the young man, it was Jad.

The press of Orken soon thinned. Haston and a surprised-looking Nalkin, L'yo, Leroshavé, and Tobin stood at the entrance to the high-ceilinged training room, herding the Orken inside.

"Tobin, bring blankets, sheets, clothing, anything you can find!" Uncle Ronan ordered.

The sandy-haired, freckled Tobin stumbled off to obey.

Uncle Ronan rounded on L'yo. "See what supplies we have. Food, wine, ale, anything we can offer them. They've been caged for days and given little to eat or drink."

"Aye, sir," L'yo said. His eternal smile was gone, replaced by a look midway between confusion and surprise. But he obeyed, as everyone always did when Uncle Ronan started barking commands.

"Nalkin, Haston, Leroshavé, see to it they're settled."

"Yes, sir," Nalkin said, giving him a nod of her head. Haston did likewise. His face was pale, pinched by the pain of his head wound not yet fully healed. He looked half-dizzy, clinging to the wall for support. Clearly, he wasn't quite as recovered as he'd claimed to be earlier. The night's events had drained him. Had drained them all.

Uncle Ronan seemed not to notice. He spoke a few words in the Orken tongue to the aging female Natisse had helped through the tunnels, and she responded in kind. Whatever was spoken seemed to satisfy him. He placed his hand on his forehead as Urktukk had but didn't place his other hand on his rope-burned throat or bow. Another gesture that Natisse couldn't possibly begin to comprehend, just as she couldn't comprehend the enormity of everything Uncle Ronan had kept from her and the rest of them.

Even that discoloration on Uncle Ronan's throat now had a deeper and more significant meaning in her mind.

When he turned away and marched in the direction of his room, Natisse could contain herself no longer. The mission was *done.* The danger was behind them; their freed captives brought to safety. The anger churning within her belly boiled over. So, she stalked after Uncle Ronan and barged through the door to his room before he could slam it shut.

"Talk!" she shouted, unable to restrain her fury.

Uncle Ronan's face hardened, his gray eyes going as cold as the bitterest winter.

"Natisse—" he began.

She cut him off. "Now!" The word rang through the small, roughhewn stone room with force far greater than mere sound. The magic burning in the core of her being amplified it a thousandfold until it set the ground beneath her feet trembling.

Uncle Ronan actually took a step back, hands clenching into fists as if in expectation of attack.

At the moment, Natisse *wanted* to attack, to lash out with all the force of the emotions built-up inside of her. Perhaps then, he would truly understand the full truth of what he'd done by lying to her all these years.

"*General Andros?*" Again, the words came out in a thunderous bellow, as if issuing from a dragon's throat. Natisse could feel the heat burning through her veins, begging to be unleashed, to burn.

Uncle Ronan struck out with a hand, driving his palm into the still-open door and slamming it shut hard enough to shake its wooden frame. Jaw muscles tightening, every muscle in his exposed torso stiffening, he opened his mouth to speak, but Natisse gave him no such opportunity.

"First a Lumenator, and now this?" She stomped forward, dangerously close, glaring up at him with such fury her eyes felt ready to burst aflame. "What else are you lying about? What else have you kept from us while you trained us to be your little army?" The truth of that struck her like a blow to the gut. "Is that what this is? Eh, *General?*" She spat the word like a curse. "You lost your actual army, so you had to mold us as a replacement? You need someone to command, anyone?"

"Natisse—" Again, Uncle Ronan tried.

Again, Natisse's fury overrode him. "Tell me the truth!" She slammed a palm into his chest, surprising herself by how much force she packed into the blow—enough to send him staggering back into the hard earth wall—and how good it felt to do it. "Who are you? And what in Shekoth's pits do you *really* want with us?"

She stood, breaths heaving, fire coursing through her, gaze pinning Uncle Ronan—*General bloody Andros!*—in place. He stared back with that stony-faced look he always got when in command mode, jaw tight, eyes hard.

"Talk!" she roared up at him.

"Just wanted to make sure you were done," Uncle Ronan said sharply.

Natisse nearly punched him in the mouth. She actually began curling her fist. She subconsciously began to reach for the fire burning within her, fully intending to knock him senseless. But something in the back of her mind stopped her. A feeling—not her own, but Golgoth's. The dragon's words rang through her thoughts. *"A careful mind will not lightly unleash my power—nor seek to abuse it as others have in the past."*

With a supreme effort of will, Natisse forced her fingers to unclench. She took a step back, opening space between her and Uncle Ronan.

"I'm done," she growled, her voice fractionally quieter as she fought to remain in control of her anger.

"What, exactly, do you hope for me to say?" Storm clouds brewed in Uncle Ronan's eyes as they bored into hers. He pushed off the wall, brushed off his bare, blood-soaked chest with a scarred hand. "Nothing I say right now is going to matter."

"Dragon-piss!" Natisse snapped.

"I know you, Natisse," Uncle Ronan said in a tone infuriatingly calm. "Right now, you want something to hit. A target for your anger. You have no interest in the truth."

"And what truth is that? Please, tell," Natisse bit off each syllable. "You've been lying to us for so long that I can't believe a word you say."

"I've been lying to you." Uncle Ronan repeated the words back to her. There was no malice or sarcasm in his voice, merely a dry statement of fact. "I've been lying to you because I didn't tell you I was a Lumenator. Or General Andros."

"Or about mysterious passages. Or that you speak pissing Orken. Or about your little meeting in those tunnels. Or about any other countless secrets you've been hiding from us!" Natisse threw up her hands.

"And what would have changed, telling you all that?" Uncle Ronan cocked his head. "Would that have changed the nature of our mission? The nature of what we do and how we do it?"

Natisse opened her mouth to snarl a retort, but the questions caught her wrong-footed.

"Yes, I *am* General Andros," Uncle Ronan said. "Or I was. Long ago. But that's not who I am now. Who I have been since the day we first met."

"Well, you're certainly not Uncle bloody *Ronan!*" Natisse retorted.

"Then who am I?" Again, that infuriating calm, the stony look in his gray eyes. "Did learning my true name—a name I haven't cared to use for decades—alter anything tonight? Did we free fewer slaves because I was once a general in the Imperial Army? Did the nature of our mission to make Dimvein a better place change?"

"I don't know!" Natisse shouted. "Don't you see? That's the problem!" She re-balled her fists, took a step closer—not within striking range, but near enough to drive home her point. "Uncle Ronan was a man I could trust. A man who I thought I knew—perhaps not completely, but enough that I could trust his word.

But General Andros is a different man. A man who might very well have some hidden agenda that only *he* knows about but has conveniently failed to share with us."

She shook her head wildly, setting her carmine hair flying. "As you said, *nothing* changed in our actions. My actions, and those of Jad, Haston, Athelas, and all the rest. But what changed tonight is *you*." She took another step closer and jabbed a sharp fingernail into his chest. "The man we've followed for years now has just been proven to be a liar, and there's no way we can trust a word he says. Everything we are just came crumbling down because the foundation it was built upon—*you*, Uncle Ronan—turned out to be no better than a mud pit."

"Is that really how you see this?" Uncle Ronan asked, raising one steely eyebrow. "Because I can tell you right now, nothing is different for us. The Crimson Fang continues to be who we are, to operate the way we have, and to do what we do for the same reasons we always have."

"So says you," Natisse said, nostrils flaring. "But those are more meaningless words. As meaningless as the Emperor's promises to rebuild the Embers."

Uncle Ronan winced as if she'd slapped him. They had all heard the grand proclamations made by Emperor Wymarc in the weeks and months following Golgoth's destruction of the Embers. Yet one had only to look at the poorest part of Dimvein to know precisely how much effort had actually been made on behalf of those affected.

"Don't you see, Uncle Ronan?" Natisse's anger finally gave out, her fury expended, and in its place took root a deep sorrow. "All these years, we've been seeking to take Dimvein's rich and powerful to their knees because they use their wealth to build greater storehouses, use deceit to get what they want, and cover it all up beneath a veneer of respectability. And that's exactly what you've done here."

"What I've done?" Uncle Ronan's eyebrows shot up. "Nat, this is not the same as—"

"It's exactly the same." Natisse stepped back, her shoulders slumping. "Every one of those people you call your brothers and sisters of the Crimson Fang joined because you promised a better life, the hope of a better future for Dimvein and the Karmian Empire. You said what they wanted to hear—truth or not—and you gave them the closest thing many of them had to a home, a family. That's a sort of power in itself. Power that you have over all of us. And what did you do with it?"

"Helped people," Uncle Ronan said, his voice cold. "The people of the Embers and all of Dimvein."

"Yes, you did." Natisse nodded. "But for all we know, that's just the veneer. What lies beneath—what *real* truth that you keep in your heart—that's what really matters. Isn't that what you always told me? That no amount of wealth could make an evil man truly good, just as poverty cannot truly soil a good man's spirit."

She let out a long breath, all but the faintest glimmer of her anger extinguished. She felt only cold, hollow. The same way she'd felt after watching Ammon being tortured to death in the Court of Justice and again after Baruch's death—the chill, numbing ache of loss. Because, tonight, she *had* lost something. She'd lost Uncle Ronan, the closest thing to a father she could remember.

For the first time, she looked around the room. She'd never been inside Uncle Ronan's chambers before. No one was allowed to enter his room, ever. She, Baruch, and Ammon had spent countless hours debating what treasures it might conceal, what secrets Uncle Ronan kept locked behind his door. But none of them thought *secrets* in a malicious manner. None thought the man capable of this level of manipulation and deceit.

What she saw disappointed her. Aside from the simple cot with its straw ticking mattress, blankets, and pillow, the room had only a three-legged wooden camp stool, a leather-bound chest, and a small shelf upon which sat Uncle Ronan's sparse clothing. The only adornments in the room were a brass hook behind the door—doubtless where he'd hung his treasured coat, now as lost to him as he was to her—and a sheathed sword. Not an ornate ceremonial sword like those the foppish nobility carried, but a well-worn military blade in a battered scabbard.

The sword of General Andros. The last vestige of who he'd been in his former life.

It felt fitting. The fancies she, Baruch, and Ammon had conjured about Uncle Ronan were as fake a façade as the man he pretended to be. Now that she had seen beneath, she felt only disappointment.

She looked back to Uncle Ronan, expecting him to argue her words. But she found only an old man staring wide-eyed at her. A man weathered by years, scarred by a hard life of fighting—and Ezrasil alone knew what other torments—and sagging beneath some nameless weight. A man who might once have been the Imperial champion and hero, but who had been battered by decades of solitude.

Natisse knew the truth at that moment. "Whatever has been driving you all these years," she said in a quiet voice, "you've chosen to bear that burden alone. Alone, rather than bringing in the people you've claimed to trust the most." Her lip curled up into a half-snarl, half-sneer. "I pity you, General Andros, Uncle Ronan, whoever you are. But that doesn't mean I'm going to let you get me killed like you got Baruch and Ammon killed."

"Natisse—" Uncle Ronan began, his voice now hoarse, strangled.

"You're right." She cut him off with a slashing gesture of her hand. "Nothing you say right now is going to matter. So don't say anything. Because I won't be here to listen."

With that, she stalked toward the door, pulled it open, and marched away, leaving the man she'd called Uncle Ronan alone in the silent emptiness of his room.

8
KULLEN

Finding Prince Jaylen was going to prove even more difficult than Kullen had first anticipated—largely thanks to Captain Angban. The Imperial Scales had stamped through apparently *every* street and alleyway around the shipyards. Now, only a mess of hobnailed boot prints remained visible in the churned-up mud, effectively killing the already-infinitesimal chance Kullen might have had of locating the Prince's trail and tracking him through Dimvein.

That left him with an entire city to search and no way to narrow down Prince Jaylen's possible whereabouts.

Any halfwit would doubtless head in a direction that led to safety. In the Prince's case, the Palace. The enormous walls and looming towers were visible even from the Western Docks, and no one in Dimvein could miss Thanagar's colossal bulk squatting on his perch overlooking the city.

But there was a great deal of city between the Western Docks and the Palace. The fastest route led south to Heroes Row, then directly eastward through the Court of Justice to the Palace's front gates. But traveling as the crow flew would send him directly past Tuskthorne Keep and into the Stacks, there to wander through the maze of lumber mills, forges, brickworks, and stone yards. He'd eventually find himself in the Upper Crest, where the Imperial Scales paid by the aristocrats to keep out the "riffraff and undesirables" would turn him away long before he reached the Palace walls.

Therein lay the problem. Since his parents' deaths, Jaylen had spent the last years of his life cloistered behind those protective walls. Kullen suspected the Prince had only the merest inkling of how to traverse the city. Though Jaylen had seen most of the Imperial capital from atop the Palace's tallest towers, he couldn't begin to comprehend just how complex navigating the lower reaches of Dimvein could truly be.

Which meant he was likely lost and wandering somewhere in a sector where he should absolutely *not* be. The Prince's face wasn't so recognizable he'd be immediately identified—an unintended result of his reclusion—but if he opened his mouth in the wrong place—and he would—or to the wrong person—and he would…

Kullen grimaced. *Shekoth, take it!* He couldn't let Jaylen get into even worse trouble because he lacked the common sense and street savvy to guide himself back to the Palace. And if he wanted to find the Prince, there was only *one* place he could think of to go.

He wended his way through the broad streets of the Stacks. Where most of the city had streets cobbled or laid with pavers, the Stacks was nothing more than mulched wood pulp. They produced most of the city's stone materials—a sign made evident by the nearly permanent cloud of dust swirling in the air—but those doing the producing found it more beneficial to sell than to use for the gentrification of their neighborhoods. Even at this late hour, work sounds drifted through shutters thrown wide open. The chop-chop-chop of towering windmills made the possibility of hearing any footsteps trampling through alleyways impossible.

Kullen scanned the many establishments in search of the familiar sign. He finally spotted it on a small wooden board hanging outside a nondescript, single-story, wooden building. Had he not known what to look for, it would've easily gone missed—only someone with knowledge of what the two yellow rings placed side by side meant would give it a second thought. To everyone else, it appeared wholly unremarkable. But Kullen was someone who knew, and the sight brought a rare smile to his face.

He did not enter the building but instead, slipped through the narrow passage between it and its neighbor, an equally plain-looking structure—either an oversized shed or undersized storehouse joining a particularly quiet part of the Stacks. Kullen's broad shoulders made it a tight fit, and he found it slow going, sidling along in the cramped space. It took him the better part of two minutes to cover a mere twenty yards, but to his relief, the opening widened into a circular courtyard perhaps five yards across. Four sets of stairs descended to four doors that rose no higher than his belt. Each bore the same symbol of two golden rings set side by side. Set inside the rings, however, were painted items: a ruby-red gemstone, a pair of black iron cogwheels, a pile of black powder, and an elaft—a brass-horned instrument with three strings and four ivory keys.

Kullen's search for Prince Jaylen led him straight to the door depicting the cogwheels. Kneeling at the base of the steps, he rapped on it with his knuckles. The *clank, clank* of vibrating brass echoed in a hollow space beyond. A moment later, vertical slits like dragon eyes opened in the two golden rings, pulling the painting into its recesses.

"Who is goink theres?" came a small, tinny voice from within.

"Talonfriend," Kullen answered without hesitation.

"Hmmmmmmmm." The muttered syllable stretched on for nearly ten full seconds before falling silent. "Talonfriend, it is beink?"

Kullen said nothing; the question was just the typical manner of speech and required no response.

"What is beink wanted?"

"I've come to speak with Vlatud."

"Hmmmmmmmm." Again, the dragged-out word.

Kullen couldn't see the one to whom the voice belonged. Cleverly hidden, far back from the door as they were, they used some sort of reflecting glass device Kullen couldn't comprehend, to examine him from the depths of shadows. But he did, however, recognize the voice.

"Come on, Stib," he said, fighting to control his frustration. "It's important. And urgent."

"Urgent, it is beink?" asked Stib, yet another rhetorical question. "And if busy, Vlatud is beink?"

"He'll see me." Kullen's jaw muscles clenched. "I'm here on Wymarc-sire's business."

"Wymarc-sire?" The word came out in a high-pitched squeak. The vertical slits slammed shut, and the door let out a hurried, cacophonous clatter of locks and groaning mechanisms. Despite the racket, it opened smoothly, sliding into a slot in the wall.

The emerging figure resembled a human, but only in the manner with which a horse resembled a wolf. Stib's head barely came up to Kullen's chest, and he squinted up at Kullen with eyes that shone a pale orange in the dim moonlight. When he shook his head, his long, pointed ears and drooping nose flopped back and forth. His green hair, however, didn't move but stuck three inches straight up into the air and remained stiff as a dragon's spine.

Like all of his kind, he wore loose-fitting woolen clothing. Stib's was a light taupe. The hems were stained due to its length and the muddy nature of the Stacks. He wore one long, dangling earring from his left ear that bore a bronze chain, connecting it to a ring within his nostrils—barely seen since his nose flopped about like a flaccid cock.

"Why you is not sayink that first?" demanded Stib. "Trenta always welcomink Wymarc-sire business." He waved a stubby four-fingered hand for Kullen to enter. "Come, come. Vlatud is seeink you now."

Kullen didn't bother thanking Stib; the Trenta cared nothing for words of gratitude, only tangible demonstrations of material value. And anything "Wymarc-sire" gave Vlatud in thanks for his assistance here would be equally divided amongst every one of the Trenta who aided in the providing of said assistance.

Kullen assumed a near-crawling position on his hands and knees just to clear the doorframe—not the most dignified entrance, but one he had long suspected was intentional, a means of reminding human visitors of whose world they were entering.

Beyond the doorway, a tunnel rose to twice Stib's height. Just tall enough that Kullen could stand and walk, though he had to bend nearly double to avoid scraping his head on the wooden ceiling.

A few paces away from the door, a comfortable-looking Stib-sized stuffed armchair sat next to a human-sized three-legged wooden stool the Trenta was clearly using for a table. A brass bowl no larger than Kullen's cupped palm held a few slices of dark-colored fish—onyx shark, a favorite of the Trenta—swimming in olive oil, vinegar, and green herbs. Smoke still rose from a long-stemmed cornhusk pipe, filling the tunnel with the aromatic scent of spicy *exarai* leaf.

If Stib was annoyed at the disturbance, he didn't show it. Instead, he led Kullen in wordless silence deeper into the tunnel and down a steeply declining wooden ramp. The path descended in a tight spiral deep into the earth beneath Dimvein—at least thirty or forty feet, though Kullen didn't know for certain.

Legend had it that the Trenta had always been around. No strangers to the underground beneath the city, they'd gone unnoticed for decades until a proper sewer system was put into place. A short skirmish had broken out, but the Trenta were crafty little buggers, employing steam-powered weaponry the Karmians had never before seen. Held at bay, a long standstill, Emperor Lasavic finally extended a friendly hand, vowing to leave the Trenta in peace so long as they kept to themselves and made no waves.

Centuries later, many of Dimvein's residents still had no clue these wonderful creatures existed just below their homes and workplaces.

The descent ended abruptly at two brass doors, both perfectly identical. As always, Stib led Kullen through the door on the right. Where the left-hand door went, Kullen could only speculate, but he'd done so often. His best guess was that it opened into the rest of the Trenta's underground dwelling. More caverns, tunnels, and chambers hollowed out from the very stone beneath the city and, possibly, beyond.

The room within was exactly as Kullen remembered it from every one of his previous visits: the walls themselves were crafted of pure brass—assuming one could call brass pure. Small round rivets marked wide, curved panels that stretched in a dome shape, ending in a cylindrical tube that hung down just above Vlatud's desk.

The desk itself was modest but well-crafted—also brass. Across from it was only one other piece of furniture: a chair made for a human, molded from iron. Kullen never missed the subtle distinction designed to remind Karmians of the difference between the races.

"You are waitink," Stib instructed, pointing toward the iron chair.

"Of course," Kullen said with a nod.

Stib didn't wait to see if he complied, merely retreated from the room and shut the brass door behind him.

Kullen took a seat, stifling a grimace as he settled into the chair. Despite it being larger than the Trenta's chair, it was still *just* too small and short for him. Just as the room was *just* too cold and the ceilings *just* too low. Another Trenta trick to put human visitors on the back foot, get an upper edge in negotiations. The Trenta took pride in their reputation for cutthroat cleverness.

Kullen was all too glad he didn't have to do business with the Trenta. The "little folk," as he'd grown up hearing them called in the poorer sections of Dimvein, had a crude grasp of the Imperial tongue but could talk circles around even the savviest merchant and best-educated solicitor. Fortunately for him, the Trenta held "Wymarc-sire" in the highest esteem. Like all those before him, Wymarc kept up Lasavic's bargain with them. They never attempted to haggle with whoever he sent to them, and in return, he always rewarded them in peace and abundance.

He settled in for the wait. As usual, to the Trenta, "now" meant "when we are good and ready." He sat for just long enough to feel frustration growing in his belly but not quite long enough to be properly annoyed or take offense.

The brass door slid open, and another Trenta entered, this one wearing a ragged, roughspun hooded robe of a thoroughly uninteresting dull brown.

"Be forgivink me the delay," said Vlatud in a voice that held not a shred of apology. "Trenta business important, but not important more than Wymarc-wise business."

"Of course," Kullen said, stuffing any trace of irritation down deep. "What's the word on the streets?"

Vlatud pulled back his hood to reveal bandages swathing him from head to toe. Only his shining orange eyes remained unwrapped, and they were fixed on Kullen's face. "Much word, much word. Interestink events takink place in night."

That was an understatement. The events at the shipyards were just the latest in a long string of "interestink events" that had transpired of late. The attempted destruction of the Refuge. The capture of Prince Jaylen. The fire in the fighting pit. Magister Branthe's death. The discovery that a high-ranked Orken was conspiring against the Emperor.

"Tell me what you know," Kullen said, "and I will tell you what you don't."

The gleam in Vlatud's orange eyes brightened. "Talonfriend is beink a part of it?"

Kullen gave him a nonchalant shrug that he *knew* didn't fool the sharp-minded, sharp-eyed Trenta. "Perhaps."

From beneath Vlatud's bandages came a sound like a half-yelp, half-cough. The Trenta did not laugh, but that was their attempt at simulating human laughter.

"Talonfriend is holdink trinket of value to Vlatud. Vlatud is beink interested." The little creature started unwrapping the bandages from about his head until his face was fully revealed. He had the same too-long nose and pointed ears as Stib, but his spiky hair was even longer and more unruly. And while Stib had skin to match his eyes, Vlatud was the color of a fresh bruise.

Kullen waited patiently—Vlatud might be interested, but he wouldn't be hurried by anyone, not even Talonfriend on the Emperor's personal business. Again, the Trenta was making him wait, a subtle reminder of who was in charge deep beneath the earth.

Finally, Vlatud had finished unwrapping his head and, bandages hanging loose about his neck, he padded over to climb into his brass chair. He didn't sit but had to remain standing on it to peer down at Kullen over his enormous desk.

"What is bringink Talonfriend here?" Vlatud asked, a keen look in his pale orange eyes. "He is comink for items or talkinks?"

"Talkings," Kullen said, using the Trenta's word for information. "You know what's happening in the Western Docks, yes?"

"Much, much." Vlatud rubbed his stubby-fingered hands together. "Magisters and aristocrats beink in troubles with Wymarc-sire's steelmen?"

Kullen nodded. "Steelmen"—the Imperial Scales—"came after all the excitement. After the fire that destroyed the *real* place of interest." He leaned forward. "An underground fighting ring where Magister Branthe was battling slaves for the amusement of those magisters and aristocrats."

Vlatud's bushy eyebrows waggled upward toward his green hairline. "Slaves, hmm?" He, at least, didn't drag out the musing syllable like Stib had. "Wymarc-sire forbiddink slavery, but magister disobey. Much punishinks?"

"Dead," Kullen responded, drawing his thumb across his throat. "By my hand."

The Trenta's orange eyes nearly bugged out of their head. "Talonfriend killink Wymarc-sire's magister?"

"After he betrayed Wymarc-sire, yes." Kullen cocked his head. "How much did you know about all of this?"

"Trenta not knowink," Vlatud said, visibly pained by the admission. "Some talkinks around city, but not knowink certain."

Kullen had assumed as much—had the Trenta known of Magister Branthe's activities, they would have sent word to the Emperor. Their loyalty to "Wymarc-sire" exceeded even their desire for the rewards he heaped on them—though perhaps that loyalty was so well-steeped in rewards that the two were inseparable.

No one had their ears to the ground in the Imperial capital quite like the Trenta. They had an entire subterranean city with many listening holes much smaller than the one currently above Vlatud. Additionally, they roamed the streets of Dimvein in the guise of lepers, their short stature easily mistaken for malnourished children when hidden beneath bandages and ratty cloaks. Few paid them a second glance. They existed beneath the notice of all in the city, even the poorest of the Embers-folk. Their keen ears heard everything, their eyes watched all, and there was little that went on in Dimvein they did not know.

Which went to show just how well Magister Branthe had guarded the secret of his conspiracy from all in the Empire. Kullen had only unmasked the treachery by coincidence, and even then, he'd learned of Branthe's role in it nearly too late.

Kullen smiled. "Then let me tell you what you do not know."

Vlatud's eyes gleamed bright, and he leaned forward, an eager look on his face. The Trenta valued a great many things—the gold and gemstones they worked into the finest jewelry, the intricate metal cogs, springs, and wheels that combined to craft complex clockwork machines, the wood and brass used to create instruments fit for the hands of the finest Imperial virtuosos—but held nothing in higher regard than information.

"Most valuable commodity," Vlatud said. "Talkinks."

"Indeed," Kullen agreed.

It wasn't just upon the Emperor's generosity to the little people that they built their fortunes—and they were rich—but upon the trade of whispers and secrets. He was about to give them something far better than gold or gems. What he brought to this particular negotiation gave him a distinct advantage, and he knew it.

Kullen told Vlatud as much as Emperor Wymarc would want him to share with the Trenta. Which, in this case, was everything. The Trenta would not use the information against the Emperor; on the contrary, they would use it to dig deeper and gather more intelligence that they would pass to Assidius, Turoc, or the Emperor himself. The more Kullen shared with Vlatud, the more likely it was his people could bring something of value later on. It didn't help solve his current problem but put the Trenta squarely in his debt.

Vlatud listened to every word out of Kullen's mouth with burning intensity. His long ears twitched, his nose quivered, and his fingers stroked the brass table, as if he used all of his senses to absorb the information. When Kullen finally finished, the Trenta let out a long sigh and leaned back against the chair, eyes closing. He took long, slow breaths, burning the details into his mind using some mental trick known only to the Trenta—a trick that ensured they never forgot a single thing they'd heard.

Kullen could've let Vlatud take his time; indeed, had this been any other situation, he would've let the full value of what he'd just shared sink in. But he was short on time. More precisely, *Jaylen* was short on time. Ezrasil alone knew how far into the wrong part of Dimvein the Prince had wandered, what manner of trouble he'd gotten himself into.

"I need to know if any of your people have seen Jaylen-sire." Kullen didn't waste words—better he was direct. "Magister Branthe took him last night, and though I got him out of the fighting pit, the Prince went missing afterward. Before the steelmen arrived at the shipyard. I need to know which way he might've fled, where he might've wound up."

Vlatud's eyes popped open. "I am findink Jaylen-sire quick." He turned away from Kullen and clambered up onto the high stone back of the chair, where he stood perfectly balanced to reach up. The tube above Vlatud's desk bore two hoses, a horn-shaped protrusion capping the ends. One, Kullen knew, was for listening throughout the region above, but the other would broadcast the speaker's voice throughout the entirety of the Trenta underground.

Vlatud pulled it toward his mouth. "Hear Vlatud, Trenta-kin. Talonfriend is searchink for Jaylen-sire. Gone missink from Western Docks. Any Trenta-kin be seeink him?"

Vlatud's brow furrowed, a wrinkle forming at the bridge of his long, drooping nose. For a long moment, silence echoed through the brass room. Then a small, tinny voice issued forth from the second tube.

"Belto be seeink Jaylen-sire," said the voice. "Seeink him with human-kin friends climbink into stinky-path. Belto be thinkink Jaylen-sire foolish for goink down, but all human-kin many foolish."

Kullen frowned. "Stinky-path" was the Trenta word for the sewers that honeycombed the earth beneath Dimvein. The little creatures despised the network of foul-smelling tunnels nearly as much as the Sniffers did. The stench burned their nostrils, and they were afraid of the predators they believed lurked in the shadows underground. Besides, as much as the Trenta had learned to live harmoniously with the Karmians, those sewers represented the loss of their homeland.

"What can he tell me about these human-kin friends?" he asked Vlatud.

The Trenta relayed the message through the speaking horn. A moment later, Belto's voice responded. "Human-kin like all human-kin. Running from grunters and steelmen, I be thinkink. Some hurtink. Jaylen-sire sleepink in arms of big human-kin."

Sleeping? Kullen's jaw muscles clenched. Or unconscious?

Mention of "big human-kin" set the hairs on the back of his neck prickling.

"These human-kin," he asked, a swirling in the pit of his stomach, "was one of them a woman with hair of Dragonfire?"

"Yes!" Belto answered when Vlatud passed on his message. "Pretty hair, for human-kin."

Kullen's heart sank into his shoes. Of all the trouble Prince Jaylen could get into, it was worse than he'd feared.

The Prince had fallen into the worst hands possible. If what the Trenta had said was true, he was being hauled away, unconscious, as a captive of the assassin who had murdered Magisters Estéfar and Perech.

Jaylen was now the prisoner of the Crimson Fang.

9
NATISSE

A weight dragged on Natisse's shoulders as she marched away from Uncle Ronan's rooms. She'd expected to feel better after giving him a piece of her mind. She'd been wrong. She felt only empty and miserable. Shouting at Uncle Ronan had done nothing to erase the hurt burned into her heart.

Fatigue weighed heavily on her, but she could find no rest. Not yet. She had one last thing to deal with.

Two things, it turned out. Outside Jad's room—what had become the infirmary of late—a small crowd had formed. Leroshavé, L'yo, and Haston spoke in hushed tones, casting furtive glances toward Jad's door and fingering their weapons.

"What's going on?" Natisse demanded as she marched toward them.

All three rounded on her. "Is it true?" L'yo's voice was hard, sharp edged. "Is that the *Prince* in there?"

Natisse's jaw muscles clenched. "And if it is?"

The trio exchanged glances. "All we've done," Leroshavé began, "it's been about bringing them down, but here you've brought—"

"It's been about taking down the aristocrats," Natisse said, cutting him off with a slash of her hand. "Punishing the people who have used their power and privilege to take advantage of those who have none."

"And no one more so than the Yildemé-damned Prince!" Leroshavé shot back, performing the sign of his goddess over his heart at the use of her name. Fire blazed in the Brendoni's dark eyes. "If anyone can be accused of taking advantage of power and privilege, it's him and his grandfather!"

Natisse met the smaller man's gaze unwaveringly. She knew his story—he'd been born into captivity, the son of hostages taken during the Emperor's subjugation of a Brendoni attempt at revolt. Indeed, he might have been a noble or princeling himself had his parents not made the mistake of raising swords in open rebellion against an Empire backed by the power of dragons and a superior military force. He'd never spoken of the fate of his parents—not to Natisse, at least—but she surmised they'd died in service to the Emperor. Not *slaves,* exactly, but forced servitude was merely thralldom by another name.

"You want to go in there and what?" Natisse asked, raising an eyebrow. "Put a dagger in an unconscious young man? A young man Jad has worked so hard to save?"

Leroshavé straightened, hand gripping the hilt of his dagger. He said nothing, but judging by the look on his face, Natisse suspected he'd given it serious consideration.

"So you think he deserves our help?" L'yo demanded of her. A scowl darkened his face, and there was no trace of his perpetual smile. Now, it was a frown, one part disgust, one part concern. He had as many reasons to hold a grudge against the Emperor as anyone born into the Embers. Even before Golgoth's destruction, when it was the Imperial Commons, it had been little more than a slum, barely livable on the best of days. "We just give him what we have and send him on his merry way? Asking him politely not to reveal our location to his grandfather and the horde of soldiers at his command?"

Natisse turned her glare on the man. "Yes," she said, her voice hard. "I do think he deserves our help. And when the time comes that he's strong enough to stand on his own two feet, we'll figure out what to do about him."

Leroshavé and L'yo looked ready to snarl a retort, but before they could, the door they'd been eyeballing flew open, and a huge figure appeared in the doorway.

"None of you is touching him," Jad rumbled. Blood painted him from head to toe—crimson fresh from the Prince's wounds layered atop old, crusted streaks that marked the guards he'd beaten to death in the fighting pit and shipyards. He looked a truly monstrous creature, nightmarish and feral, his eyes ablaze with determination. "You want to lay a hand on the Prince, you go through me. Is that clear?"

Leroshavé and L'yo took one look at him, and both backed down.

"Of course, Jad," they mumbled in near-perfect unison.

Haston had remained silent throughout the exchange, a look of wary reluctance on his face. He was no killer, Natisse knew. He'd be worried about the fallout of their holding the Prince, certainly, but he wouldn't be championing any attempt at harming the young man. He actually appeared *relieved* by Jad's intervention.

"Come on," he said, plucking at Leroshavé's sleeve. "Better we get something to eat before Nalkin and Tobin give the Orken all our supplies."

That sufficed to distract the eternally hungry Brendoni. L'yo cast one glance at Jad before following the other two up the corridor toward the common room.

Natisse and Jad stood silent as the trio took their leave.

"You think they would have tried it?" Jad rumbled once their comrades were around the corner and out of sight.

Natisse looked up at the big man. Worry creased his fatigue-lined face. His hands twitched, shaking with either anger or fatigue—likely both.

"No," she said, shaking her head. "But it's a good thing you made certain of it before they did anything regrettable."

Jad grunted and stepped back into the room.

"How is he?" Natisse asked, following him.

"He'll live," Jad said, then added. "I think."

"He'll live," Sparrow said from where she knelt next to the cot upon which lay the unconscious, pale-faced Prince Jaylen. The slight girl was busy wiping the young man's face with a damp rag. Her hands were scarlet stained to the forearms, and fresh blood soaked into the Prince's cot and puddled on the floor beneath. "We got his wounds stitched up in time. Though, he lost a lot of blood."

Natisse let out a relieved breath. "Thank you. Both of you." It felt as if a fraction of the weight lifted from her shoulders. Knowing that the Prince would live through the night gave them options. Still, she had no idea how to get Prince Jaylen back to his grandfather, but at least they'd bought time to figure it out.

"Garron helped, too," Sparrow said, now looking up from her work.

Natisse turned to the room's other cot, where tall, rangy Garron leaned heavily against the wall. He was breathing hard, face almost as pale as Jaylen's, etched with pain. The bandages swathing the stump of his left arm were soiled with fresh blood—the Prince's, she hoped. His wounds had only just begun healing, and he was a long way from being back in the fight. Yet the sight of him sitting upright lifted her spirits.

"Glad to see you've been putting lazybones here to work," Natisse said, giving Garron a grin. "You won't earn your keep lying around on your arse all day long."

"I'm perfectly… happy to lie… around on my arse," Garron said through labored breaths. "Especially after… that."

Natisse eyed Jad. "That bad?"

Jad gave her a grim nod. "Had to cut open the cauterized flesh. Organ beneath ruptured and was bleeding bad. I got it under control, but it was a close thing. He'll probably sleep through the night. Maybe all day tomorrow, too. Better that way. He needs plenty of rest just to get back on his feet. Food, too." He looked to

Sparrow. "Can you fetch him something to eat? Broth'll do. Some for Garron, as well."

"I can fetch my own damned food," muttered Garron, beginning the arduous effort of pushing himself to his feet. He, too, had lost a great deal of blood before the Gryphic Elixir sealed up his flesh. Even that marvelous potion couldn't fully restore his strength for him, hence the food and rest.

Sparrow rose anyway and went to help Garron. At first, he waved her away, insisting he could stand on his own. But he was off-balance and too weak to push himself upright with just one arm. Finally, with great reluctance, he accepted Sparrow's proffered hand.

"Come on," the petite young girl said, slinging Garron's sinewy right arm around her shoulder. "I'll walk with you."

"I'm not dying," Garron growled. "Ezrasil's bones! You lose one arm, and people think you're bloody useless."

His protests lacked any real substance. Natisse and Jad both chuckled, then stepped aside to clear a path for Sparrow and Garron to hobble out the door and into the corridor.

Again, Natisse and Jad stood in silence—what was there to say?

Natisse watched the pair depart. Jad fixed his eyes on the sleeping Prince Jaylen. When Natisse turned back, she found Jad scrubbing the back of his right hand with the palm of his left. It started small at first, but Jad's efforts quickly grew more determined. And more frustrated when the dried blood refused to wipe away.

"I can get you some water—" Natisse started.

Jad seemed not to hear her. He stampeded toward a bucket sitting in the corner of the room, dropped to his knees, and plunged his hand into the filthy water with a loud *splash.* He set about scrubbing his hands with a fury that stunned Natisse. Bloody water sprayed everywhere: the walls, the floor, Jad's tunic, breeches, face, and arms. A low, animalistic growl rumbled from the big man's lips, rising to a moaning groan.

Natisse's heart leaped into her throat as she realized his shoulders were shaking. He was *weeping*. Sobbing and moaning and frantically trying to cleanse away the blood from his flesh... and the stain from his soul.

"Jad!" She darted forward, knelt at his side, and threw her arms around his huge shoulders. "I'm here, Jad. I'm here." She held onto him as tightly as she could, poured all her strength into clinging to him. It felt like trying to wrangle a tornado—he was twice her size and three times her weight.

Yet she clung to him anyway, held him firm and refused to let go. No matter how hard he thrashed in his efforts to scrub away the lingering traces of death marring his flesh, Natisse forced herself to hold fast.

Until finally, Jad crumbled in her arms. Like an enormous mountain eroded by a river, his broad shoulders collapsed, his head slumped, and he tipped so far forward his great blocky head nearly dipped into the now red-tinged water within the bucket. Jad's shoulders shook as he wept into his hands—hands still wet and dripping crimson.

"It's okay, Jad," Natisse whispered into his ears. "You're okay."

"No!" The word was a great sough blowing from Jad's lips. He lifted his head, turned to face her. "No, I'm not. Don't you see?" Pain bit deep into the lines of his face. "I became *him* again. All this time, I've tried so hard to change, but it all came back. *He* came back."

He. Jad was speaking of a version of himself that had beaten two youths to death in vengeance for their killing the puppy that had been his only friend and companion—a monster that Jad had spent the years since trying his best to avoid letting off its leash.

And this was all her fault. She'd been the one to coax that beast out of him. Desperation had led her to it, but determination and stubbornness played their roles too.

The mission above all, she thought. But at what cost?

"He did," Natisse said softly. "And because of him, we're alive. All of us. You, me, Uncle Ronan, the Orken, everyone. *He* saved us, Jad. *You* saved us."

"I nearly killed you!" Jad shouted the words. "With these hands, Nat." He held them up before his face, glaring with hatred and revulsion. "I felt your throat in my grip, and there was a part of me that wanted to keep on. To keep squeezing and squeezing and squeezing until you broke like all the rest of them did. To hear your screams."

"Yes, there *is* that part of you, Jad." Natisse finally released her hold on his shoulders and now took his giant face in her hands. "But there's that part in all of us. You think I didn't want to do that when I watched Ammon being tortured to death? When Baruch died that night? If I'd had their killers' throats in my hands, I would have squeezed, too. Until I wrung the life out of them and then some for good measure."

Natisse's heart broke for the man, for the guilt consuming him. Jad's soft-spoken demeanor concealed a deep wellspring of rage—rage he fought stubbornly to control. Yet he'd unleashed it last night. At *her* request. This pain he felt, the torment wracking him, that was on her.

"But you won, Jad." She gripped his face tighter. "He didn't win. Not in the end. *You* won. You took back control before you killed me. And you saved his life." She twisted his head gently so he could see the Prince lying on the cot beside them. "That's who you are, Jad. You are a healer. A protector. *My* protector." She leaned forward until her forehead rested against his and spoke in a low voice. "That's why we all love you. Why we all need you."

Jad's eyes closed. Though his shoulders no longer shook, fresh tears slipped from beneath his shut eyelids. Yet he was growing calmer, the frenzy that had consumed him subsiding.

"I'm sorry, Jad," Natisse whispered to him. "I'm sorry I had to ask that of you. That I had to put you in that place. I swear on my life that I will never—"

"Don't make that oath." Jad cut her off. His eyelids popped open, and his big, dark eyes fixed on hers. "I know you won't ask it of me again, not unless you have no choice."

He pulled back, sitting upright to gaze down at her. "But you're right. I won. I beat *him.* It was close, but I won, Nat." A glimmer of triumph sparkled in his tear-rimmed eyes. "And if I have to beat him again, I will." His hands reached up to envelop hers, still clasping his face. "Because tonight showed me that I can't just sit here in the Burrow and let you all face the danger just because I'm afraid of becoming *him* again."

"We don't need you out there, Jad," Natisse said, shaking her head. "I can handle it. And with Nalkin and L'yo back—"

"You do need me, Nat." Jad's voice was gentle yet firm. His great jaw muscles tensed beneath her hands. "You need me to be more than just a healer. You said it yourself. The Crimson Fang needs a protector." He let out a long breath. "I'm not a killer—at least, I don't *want* to be. I'll never be as ruthless as Uncle Ronan tried to make me. I don't have that strength of spirit the same way you do, the way Baruch and Ammon did. But I can be there as a shield. For you. For them. For the cause. In any way I can. Whatever you need from me."

Natisse swallowed and threw her arms around his neck. "Thank you, Jad." She knew how much this was costing him and loved him all the more for it.

His arms were like old tree branches as they encircled her and pulled her close. They remained that way for long moments. Neither spoke, but no words were needed. Everything important had been said. For the first time since Baruch's death, Natisse felt something more than cold, icy claws tearing at her insides.

The mission above all, perhaps. But without these few… without Jad, there would be no mission.

10
KULLEN

Mere days earlier, Kullen had mocked the Crimson Fang as a hoax—or, if they had truly existed, nothing more than rabble-rousers seeking to stir up discord in Dimvein. Assidius had believed otherwise. The Emperor's trusted Seneschal and spymaster had tortured one of the Crimson Fang's members—a dispossessed aristocrat by the name of Ammonidas Sallas—and the man had refused to break even under Arbiter Chuldok's ministrations. He'd merely repeated the rallying cry for which he had given his life: blood for blood.

Even then, Kullen might not have given the Crimson Fang a second thought. Until the night Magister Perech had died not two paces from where Kullen was plotting his own assassination of Magister Taradan on Perech's pleasure barge. The red-haired woman had driven a dagger in the magister's corpulent body, killing him on the spot, and fled to a rowboat she and her companions had waiting. There, Kullen had fought the woman *again*—and taken nasty wounds from that strange whip-like blade she wielded—and nearly died when the *other* Sallas brother had dragged him overboard to perish together among the onyx sharks.

After that, Kullen could no longer write the Crimson Fang off as a nonthreat. Assidius and Turoc—the Orkenwatch's Tuskigo—

had done more digging into their insurrection and the assassination of various Magisters, leaving Kullen free to focus on his own missions for the Emperor. Yet fate had set their paths to cross again, he and the woman. Not hours earlier, in the fighting ring, Kullen had, after a fashion, fought alongside the Crimson Fang. His battle had been to protect Prince Jaylen while the red-haired woman and her hulking companion fought to rescue the grizzled soldier—General Andros—from Magister Branthe's fighting pit. He'd saved the red-haired woman's life, and she'd saved his in return. That was the last he'd seen of her. He had been so busy hustling Jaylen to safety and hunting down Magister Branthe that he hadn't spared her a second thought.

If only he'd paid closer heed to the threat she and her companions posed. They had Prince Jaylen—unconscious, perhaps even wounded—and Ezrasil alone knew what they intended to do with him. If, as Assidius believed, their goal was to destabilize the Empire and overthrow Imperial rule, murdering the Crown Prince was certainly a quick path to success. Emperor Wymarc was too old to sire new heirs. He'd have no one to pass the Karmian Empire on to when he passed from this world. Five, ten, even thirty years from now, it didn't matter. Jaylen's death spelled the eventual downfall of Imperial rule and order.

One thing brought a small measure of comfort to Kullen's soul. If the Crimson Fang did intend to kill the boy, they likely wouldn't have gone through the trouble of transporting him through the sewers.

Unless they meant to make a spectacle of him. Kullen shuddered at the thought.

"What can you tell me about these people?" he asked Vlatud. "Where can I find them?"

"Vlatud not knowink human-kin," Vlatud answered, again a pained look on his face. To the Trenta, admitting ignorance was akin to confessing to a crime of the highest magnitude. He spoke into the horn once more. "Belto knowink?"

"Belto not knowink," came the response. "But he be askink Trenta-kin. Findink answer for Talonfriend."

Vlatud turned back to Kullen. "We waitink. Not much time, I be thinkink. Belto speak quick with Trenta-kin." He gave Kullen a sly look, a curious light shining in his pale orange eyes. "But Vlatud wonderink about grunters with human-kin."

"Grunters?" Kullen asked. The word hadn't even left his mouth when he figured out its meaning.

And it made his blood run cold. Fear sent him surging to his feet. "The Orkenwatch had them? Or were hunting them?" The Crimson Fang could very well use Jaylen as leverage to compel the Orkenwatch to let them go—or merely slit his throat and leave him to bleed out while they fled into the sewers.

"Not big grunters." Vlatud shook his head, setting his ears and nose flopping. "Little grunters. *Ghuklek.*"

Kullen looked at the Trenta, confused. What was Vlatud talking about? There was nothing little about the Orken, especially for creatures as diminutive as the Trenta. And those last guttural syllables out of Vlatud's mouth made no sense to him. A name? Some Trenta word he did not know?

He waited for Vlatud to translate, but the purple-skinned creature just peered down at him from his perch atop the brass chair's high back.

Against his better judgment, Kullen admitted the truth, throwing up his hands. "I do not know anything about little Orken-kin. But you're *sure* it wasn't the Orkenwatch?"

"Belto is beink sure," Vlatud said, "so Vlatud is beink sure."

Kullen let out a relieved breath and slumped back into the uncomfortably small chair. Though the fear had passed, his worry and the burden of exhaustion remained, growing suddenly heavy. He was tired—so bloody tired!—but had no hope of resting. Not until he had found Jaylen.

"Wymarc-sire be wantink to know about grunters," Vlatud told him. "*Ghuklek* in Dimvein beink big fuss."

Kullen nodded. "I'll pass it on." Whenever he got back to the

Palace with Jaylen in tow, which was appearing less and less likely to be anytime soon.

"I find interestink you not be knowink of grunter presence here," Vlatud said, a wry smile on his face. "Seems Vladtud be givink Wymarc-sire valuable information."

Kullen groaned inwardly. He nodded. "Help me find the Prince, and I guarantee you'll be rewarded greatly."

The brass trumpet over Vlatud's head gave a tinny ringing, a sound like a distant bell chiming, and Vlatud reached up to pull it down again.

"Belto is findink little knowinks," came the voice from within. "But Irkal be tellink Belto he is seeink human-kin in Ember-place, and Throst be seeink in One Hand-place."

Kullen frowned. The Embers and the One Hand District. Precisely the sort of place where the Crimson Fang would be able to pass unnoticed among the poor and common merchants of Dimvein. Outside of Thanagar's protective dome, no one in the Embers would give them a second glance, and they'd have plenty of narrow alleys and maze-like back streets to get lost in. The ever-present hubbub in the One Hand District would more than cover their movements, doubtless provide them with supplies.

At least that narrowed down Kullen's target location. The sewers beneath Dimvein would give the Crimson Fang a way to traverse the city unseen by the Orkenwatch and Imperial Scales, but they'd have to resurface somewhere. They'd have some sort of hideout or stronghold where they felt safe. He just needed to find it to find Jaylen.

"Thank you," Kullen said, in his relief forgetting the Trenta's disdain for empty words of gratitude. He did remember a moment later when Vlatud's face creased into a growl, and he bared sharp, pointy teeth.

"Thanks not reward?" Vlatud asked, but it wasn't a question as much as a reminder.

Kullen quickly held up a hand. "Wymarc-sire will ensure you are rewarded properly. You have but to name your desire."

That settled Vlatud instantly. His expression lost all trace of antipathy and took on a greedy visage. Not the sort of greed common to men like Magister Deckard, but eager excitement of a magpie spotting a shiny object. Like magpies, it was in their nature to collect things of worth, to hoard trinkets that held immense value to them—and often to them alone. The Trenta had come to appreciate gold and gemstones because *human-kin* found value in them, but they were as likely to hunger for a rusted dagger or a broken leather boot as for a chest filled with marks.

A smile broke out on Vlatud's face. "Vlatud is wantink reward of dragonrum."

Kullen raised an eyebrow. The Trenta abhorred alcohol, and to his knowledge, Vlatud had never touched the stuff. Liquor—especially liquor as valuable as Dragonfire rum—was either used for a commodity with which to bargain elsewhere or, more often than not, put to work in some of the Trenta's craft.

"How many bottles?" he asked.

Vlatud held up both hands, splaying his six fingers and two thumbs wide. "This many. Enough for buildink great firink-engine."

Kullen pursed his lips. Eight bottles of Dragonfire rum was a reasonable price to pay, especially in light of what he'd learned from the Trenta. But it was the mention of "great firink engine" that set his mind racing. He'd seen the Trenta demonstrate some of their "engines" for Emperor Wymarc—machines capable of turning a stone mill or spinning carriage wheels for as long as they were fed wood or coal. Or, it appeared, Dragonfire rum. No telling what that thing would do. And, in truth, he wasn't certain he wanted to find out.

Since the early days when the Trenta's steam machines had stalled the attacks of Karmians numbering ten times that of the little people, only a few of the Trenta's constructions ever made their way into Dimvein. And that had been at the Emperor's personal request to the Trenta smiths and craftsfolk. Their gemsmithing, goldsmithing, and simple clockwork mechanisms were highly prized and affordable only to the wealthiest Imperial citizens. Yet every time he saw some demonstration of their skill at artifice, Kullen couldn't help feeling slightly apprehensive at the thought of what creations they hid deep beneath Dimvein. Creations capable of *destroying* Dimvein, perhaps?

Whatever the case, it wasn't truly Kullen's problem. Not unless Emperor Wymarc *made* it his problem.

"I will pass your request on to Wymarc-sire," Kullen said, inclining his head. Whether the Emperor gave them the desired reward or offered them something else was up to him.

"Vlatud is beink satisfied." The little Trenta hopped off the chair back and onto the desk, padding across its surface to thrust out a four-fingered hand to Kullen. It was yet another gesture foreign to the Trenta, but they had adopted it in their dealings with the human-kin above. Kullen took Vlatud's bandaged hand and shook it firmly but gently.

"Good." Vlatud nodded and climbed down from the desk. He headed toward the door, pulled it open, and beckoned for Kullen to follow him. "Vlatud is showink you out."

Kullen followed the little Trenta up the ascending spiral ramp. Vlatud took five steps for every two of Kullen's, but his stubby legs made the ascent with ease. Burdened as he was by fatigue, concern for Jaylen, and the myriad questions that had arisen since the events of the previous night, Kullen struggled on the way up. Sweat dripped profusely from his back and brow, his breathing far too heavy for his liking by the time he and Vlatud reached the doorway out.

There, Stib sat in his stuffed armchair, smacking his lips and splashing one hooked, stubby finger in the oil-and-vinegar mix, all that was left of his meal. Stib didn't bother acknowledging Kullen and Vlatud. With their business concluded, the human-kin wasn't worth his notice, and the Trenta wasted no words between one another. Neither did Vlatud address his fellow Trenta but just pushed the door open for Kullen.

Kullen dropped to his hands and knees once more to crawl

out. There was no bidding farewell or promising to see each other soon. The door merely closed behind Kullen's departing form, sealing the Trenta back up in their safe little hidey-hole.

Kullen climbed the four stairs back up to the circular courtyard in a single step. A glimmer of the sun's rising tickled the horizon. Though the wind was light, it brought with it a cool chill and the scent of bacon sizzling somewhere in the distance. Kullen's stomach growled. He had no time for sleep, no time for eating, and no time to waste.

He squeezed himself back through the narrow gap between the two buildings that served to conceal the Trenta's existence from all but those in the know.

His mind worked at the problem, trying to piece together what he knew. Which, in truth, was too damned little. The Crimson Fang had Jaylen—that much was certain. Where to find them, though, he had no idea. The One Hand District was far too large to search thoroughly in a day—even three days—and he could spend a lifetime wandering around the Embers and get nowhere.

No, he had to find a way to further narrow down his search area. Or better yet, speak with someone who would know exactly what he was looking for and where to find it.

He'd come to the Trenta because they were the best source of information on most of Dimvein. But when it came to locating some*one* in the Embers, he knew exactly where he needed to go.

11
NATISSE

A hiss escaped Jad's lips, and a wince flashed across his huge face.

"Oh, sorry!" Natisse pulled back. She'd forgotten the wounds Jad had sustained in their battle just hours earlier. He'd borne the pain in his usual stoic silence, more concerned with tending to the bleeding Prince than his own injuries. "Get that coat off, and let me take a look at you."

"I'm fi—" Jad began, but Natisse cut him off by clapping a small hand over his big mouth.

"None of that." Natisse tsked and shook her head. "Ezrasil and the others, between you and Garron, I'm not sure I can handle any more of this. Now, unless you want me dragging you to Serrod's, you'll do what I say and get that coat off."

Jad raised an eyebrow. "Drag me… to Serrod's?" His tone said it all. Their size and strength differences rendered her threat impossible to actually carry out.

"Fine. Then perhaps I just poke and prod until I spot the blood?" Natisse pretended to jab a forefinger at the point where the dagger had pierced his shoulder.

"Okay, okay!" Jad shied away, gently thrusting her back with one huge hand. "I yield." He began shrugging out of his coat, grumbling, "Bedside manner that'd make Serrod seem pleasant, I swear!"

Natisse gave him a grin and helped him to remove the heavy black greatcoat he'd worn in his disguise as Lady Dellacourt's manservant. Dried blood remained crusted to the garment from collar to hem, but there were patches that still glistened wetly, whether from his injuries or his ministrations to the Prince, Natisse couldn't tell.

He'd lost the necktie in the scuffle—likely removed it himself so it couldn't be used as a restraint—and torn two of the four buttons on his black velvet vest. Worse, the starched white shirt beneath was ripped at both shoulders, cut where the guardsman's dagger had pierced him, and soaked through with red.

Natisse sucked in a breath through her teeth. "Dragon's piss, Jad!" She had to peel the shirt away from where weak scabs glued it to his skin. "If I'd known it was this bad—"

"But it's not," Jad rumbled in a soothing tone. "Hurts like a dragon kick to the balls, don't get me wrong. But the dagger missed everything vital."

A quick examination of the wound proved Jad's assessment correct. The dagger had cut to the bone but avoided severing connective tissue or lacerating the top of his lungs.

"Damned lucky," Natisse said, shaking her head.

"Don't feel much like it, but yeah," Jad nodded. "Could've been far worse. For all of us." He gave her a meaningful look that made it clear which of "us" he was most concerned about.

"That's battle for you." Natisse tried to sound nonchalant, shrugging dismissively. "Plenty of danger anytime sharp things soar about."

"Natisse." Jad's voice was low, like distant rolling thunder. "We both know how close you came. If not for whoever that was fighting next to the Prince, you might be standing before Binteth and Ulnu right now."

Natisse turned away to hide the flush of red rising to her cheeks and set about gathering up needle and cat-gut thread. She *had* come too damned close to meeting a grisly end. The giant Joakim had come within a breath of crushing her with his bare hands. Had it not been for the mysterious man in the hood—the same man who killed Baruch—she'd be lying dead in the sands right now.

"How's Garron healing up?" Natisse asked, turning back to him with a too-bright smile.

"Quit trying to change the subject," Jad said, rolling his eyes.

"What's the good of talking about it?" Natisse threw up her hands. "I nearly died, you nearly died, we all nearly bloody died. But we didn't. And we're here now. So what more is there to talk about? It's not like the *next* battle is going to be any less dangerous."

"Hmmm." Jad's tone was musing. "That's not necessarily true *now*, is it?"

Natisse frowned, confused. "What do you...?" She trailed off, suddenly understanding. "Oh."

What Jad hadn't said spoke volumes. Natisse could only meet his gaze for a few seconds before she dropped her eyes.

"On the bed," she ordered, pointing to the cot Garron had just evacuated. "Easier to do this there than kneeling on the floor."

Jad rose without a word of argument, though he issued a little growl of pain. He knew she was trying to evade this subject, too, but wasn't going to press her. Yet.

Natisse waited for the big man to climb onto the cot—which protested beneath his prodigious bulk—and settled in behind him. With one leg planted on the floor and the other bent at the knee to support her weight on the bed, she stooped over the deep wound in Jad's shoulder and set to work with needle and thread.

Silence was a welcomed companion for the next few moments. Natisse didn't need to wonder what Jad was thinking; she could feel the curiosity emanating from his skin, setting every hair on his broad back and neck quivering with tangible energy. She tried to hold her peace and focus on the task at hand, but eventually, she could take it no longer.

"Damn it, Jad, what do you want me to say?" she demanded.

"I didn't say anything."

"No, you didn't. And that was more than enough. So out with it. What do you want to hear?"

"As much as you can," Jad answered in a gentle tone. "The truth. Even if you don't understand it all, telling me what you know is a start."

Natisse blew out her cheeks, expelling a long breath.

"I..." She found herself oddly hesitant. Not because she didn't trust him—this was *Jad,* after all. She didn't fear he would judge her, either. She just didn't know if she could trust herself. How could she, after what she'd done? A lifetime spent hating dragons and the power they represented, only to seize that power for herself the first chance she got? What did that make her?

Jad's huge head turned toward her, and he studied her from the corner of his eyes. "The truth, Natisse. Whatever that may be."

Natisse let out a sigh. "Ulnu, curse it!" She shook her head. "I don't even know... I don't really understand..." She swallowed, tried again. "It's a bloody dragon, Jad!" The words, disjointed though they were, burst from her lips.

"A dragon," Jad repeated. "The magic? The fire? It's a dragon?"

"That vial," Natisse said, heat rushing to her cheeks, "the one I found on the sands with the Gryphic Elixir. The one I thought might save the Prince's life."

"The one that you touched said 'ouch,' then instantly burst into flames?" Jad asked. "That vial?"

"Yes, that vial!" Natisse couldn't help feeling frustrated—mostly at her inability to get out the words. She fought to push past the fear. If anyone deserved the truth, it was Jad. And after her anger at Uncle Ronan for keeping secrets, there was no way she could do the same to him.

"There was a needle on the cap," she continued, "and when it pricked my finger, a bit of my blood mixed with the dragon blood inside the vial."

The words sounded so strange coming from her lips, yet they were the truth as she understood it.

"Wow," Jad said under his breath.

"Then I was dragged out of my body into this world that was all fire." It was as if a spigot had opened. Once she'd begun, she couldn't stop. "Crazy place, flames and lava and burning everything. And then there was this bloody great dragon. Golgoth, 'Queen of the Ember Dragons,' she called herself. And she told me that she could see inside me, that she could see my mind was filled with fear and caution, that I wouldn't abuse her power."

Everything was coming out in a jumble, the hammering of her pulse muddying her memories. Yet she didn't stop. Couldn't stop.

"She told me the fire that killed my family all those years ago belonged to her mate, Shahitz'ai, she called him. And said that he would trouble this realm no more, whatever in Ezrasil's name that means."

Her fingers darted quick as her tongue, sewing the wound, distracting herself from the insanity pouring from her mouth.

"And then, crazy as it sounds, she offered me her bond. Said she wanted me to be her *bloodsworn*. Or she was going to be my *bloodsworn*." She couldn't recall the words exactly, not that it mattered. All that mattered was the fire blazing in the core of her being. Dragon's fire. Magic. Power she could no more understand than whatever made Uncle Ronan a Lumenator. "And just like that, I was on fire. But it didn't hurt. No, it was like it came from inside me. Like *I* was the fire. I know it sounds ridiculous, but—"

"No." Jad's voice was soft, kind. He turned to face her fully. "It doesn't sound ridiculous, Natisse." He placed one huge hand on her forearm. "Certainly not something I understand—sounds like you don't really, either—but not ridiculous. Just…" He trailed off. "Shite, I don't know what to say."

Natisse's heart sank. Though she felt better for having gotten the truth off her chest, she found herself dreading the next words out of his mouth. Would he see her the way all the Crimson Fang saw those aristocrats who wielded magic and power—as *enemies?*

"I don't know, either." Her hands stilled, the needle and thread falling from trembling fingers that had grown suddenly numb. "I don't know why I did it. Why I took her bond. All I know is that when she offered it, I couldn't say no. Something inside me *had* to do it. Like I needed it. Every part of me needed it. I can't explain it."

"You don't need to. If anyone understands it, it's me." Jad looked down at his huge hands, flexing and relaxing his fingers. "Tonight, you saw what these hands can do. That's no magic, but that's a power all its own. And it's a power I've had for years. I've always been stronger and bigger than everyone. " He lifted his eyes to meet hers. "And the thought of being smaller or weaker terrifies me, Natisse. I can't imagine life any other way. If I didn't have it and someone offered it to me, I'd take it in a heartbeat."

"But what does that make me, Jad?" Natisse's voice held an edge of desperation and fear. "All this time, the Crimson Fang has been punishing the aristocrats and Magisters who've done exactly what I did tonight. Taking power—the power of their dragons—and using it for their own ends. Does that make me like them? Or..." She struggled to say the words echoing in the back of her mind. "Or worse than them? Because I've spent my life hating them, and now I've become the thing I hate?"

"Never!" The vehemence in Jad's voice surprised her. Jad took both her hands in his. "Do you suddenly have a craving to use the magic to become powerful or wealthy?"

"No," Natisse said, shaking her head.

"Are you going to stop doing what you can to help people who are less powerful than you, who need your help?"

"Of course not!"

"Then that's all that matters." Jad squeezed her hands and

released them, lowering his own into his lap. "Power doesn't change you, Natisse. Just what you do with it."

At those words, a mountainous load seemed to lift from Natisse's chest. She felt as if she could breathe again, and her heart slowed to a steady rhythm.

"You promise?" she asked, her voice barely above a whisper.

"Promise." A big smile broke out on Jad's face. "You're still the Natisse we all know and love. Just… more so, now."

"What does *that* mean?" Natisse cocked her head.

Jad gave a wry chuckle. "Ask anyone else, and they'll agree that you've always been a fiery one. Now you've got the actual fire to prove it."

"Bastard!" Natisse slapped him playfully on the arm—the very same arm she was just halfway through stitching.

Jad let out a hiss of pain and shied away.

"Sorry, sorry!" Natisse scooped up the thread and needle and finished putting in the last stitches. "There. Good as new."

Jad craned his neck, but the enormous musculature of his shoulder obstructed his view. "You won't be offended if I have Sparrow double-check it for me, will you?"

"Don't make me hit you again!" Natisse growled in a tone of mock anger. "Or, maybe I should just call fire right now and burn off your eyebrows for you. See how funny you are without eyebrows, eh?"

"It's just, I've seen your cloak—your stitch-work there."

Natisse raised the back of her hand in playful threat.

Jad held up a placating hand. "Fine, fine. I'll trust you did a suitable job."

"You take your 'suitable' and shove it right up—"

"That's no way to talk to your patient," Jad said, cutting her off. "You might be worse than Serrod."

"You're getting off easy." Natisse poked him in the ribs, careful to avoid a pair of bruises marring his bare torso.

Jad still grimaced. "Sure doesn't feel like it." He looked down at his chest and stomach. The dagger thrust to his shoulder was the worst of the wounds he'd sustained. He raised his gaze to her, his expression suddenly serious. "We both got off easy, Natisse. Next time—"

"Let's just pray there's no next time." Natisse climbed to her feet. Though the burden on her soul had lightened, her body felt suddenly drained, her eyelids heavy. "Now, if there's nothing else, I'll head out. Gotta check on the Orken before—"

"No," Jad said, his voice firm. "I'll check in on them. You get some rest."

"Jad—" Natisse began.

"You're half-asleep already." Jad clucked his tongue, once again in full "mother hen" mode. "You've done enough for tonight. Let the rest of them handle it. I'll make sure they've got it under control. You go. Sleep while you can."

Natisse lacked the strength to argue. "Thanks," she said, giving him a little nod.

She turned away and made for the door, but Jad's voice stopped her.

"Natisse."

She glanced over her shoulder to find Jad had risen and moved toward the small wooden desk that stood at one end of the makeshift infirmary. She turned back to face Jad, but he said nothing, simply continued rummaging through whatever objects he kept stored within the desk's lone drawer.

After long seconds, Jad turned back to her and held something out in one huge hand. "Here."

Natisse studied the object. The simple leather thong didn't look like much, but her eyes widened as she recognized the pendant in Jad's palm. A small, round green rock set within a network of finely wrought iron. No fancy jewel, this, but a simple river stone that had caught Natisse's eye.

Her gaze darted up to meet his. "You kept it?" she asked. "All these years?"

"All these years." Jad nodded, a smile on his lips. "I'll never forget the day you gave this to me. My thirteenth birthday. Said you and Ammon and Baruch had put together all your coins to have it made. Just for me. The first gift I'd ever gotten."

Natisse's heart swelled. It had been a simple gesture, a way to welcome Jad during his first weeks as a member of the Crimson Fang. They'd all known the story of what happened to him, and the gift had been *her* idea. She'd forgotten about it long ago. Evidently, he hadn't.

"Take it," Jad said, fumbling at the knot that secured the leather loop.

"It's yours," Natisse protested.

"Not the stone." Jad shook his head, scrunching up his huge face in concentration as he struggled to loosen the small knot with his huge fingers. "The thong. Use it to hang the vial around your neck."

Natisse's eyebrows rose. Instinctively, she drew out the vial from the pocket where she'd tucked it, and sure enough, the golden cap had a small loop through which to string a necklace.

"Aha!" With a triumphant look, Jad held out the now-untied thong to her. "That way, you can keep it within easy reach. Just in case you need to, you know, use the dragon magic. However that works."

"Guess I'll have to start figuring it out now, won't I?" Natisse grimaced, taking the gift. "Golgoth hasn't exactly been overflowing with helpful tidbits on how to use it." She set about stringing it through the loop on the vial's cap.

"What about Uncle Ronan?"

The question froze Natisse. Then the ice gave way to burning anger. "No!" She shook her head defiantly.

"He *is* a Lumenator," Jad said. The tightness in his voice told Natisse exactly how he felt about learning that particular secret the way he had. "Maybe he can—"

"I said no." Natisse fixed him with a baleful glare. "I don't trust him. Because he's not actually Uncle Ronan. Whoever he is, I don't want him to know about this. Not yet."

Jad looked ready to argue, but she drove on.

"And I don't want the others to know, either." Natisse held his gaze, her tone serious. "I'm not ready to tell them. Not until I know a bit more."

"You're angry at Uncle Ronan for keeping secrets, but you're doing the same with the others?"

Jad's words were spoken in a gentle tone, but the question stung.

"This is different," she said.

"Is it?" Jad cocked his head. "I'm snuffed with him, too, Natisse. But this is *exactly* the same thing."

"No, it's not!" Natisse felt the heat rush up from the pit of her stomach—from the wellspring of Golgoth's magic blazing inside her—and set her face burning. "He lied to us because he didn't trust us. I'm not telling the others just yet because I have no bloody idea how any of this works. I just need to figure it out a bit more. Then I'll tell them all everything. I swear."

Jad regarded her with a solemn look. "The longer you keep this to yourself—"

She shook her head all the harder, stepped closer to him, and gripped his huge forearm with one hand. "I haven't kept it to myself. You know."

"I only know because I watched it happen," Jad said, sorrow in his eyes.

She couldn't argue. She knew it was true. If he hadn't seen, she would've kept it from him as well.

"You're right. But that doesn't change the fact that I'm glad you know. You... you're my confidant. If anything... weird happens, you'll know. I promise. And it won't be long before I tell the others."

"Promise?"

"Promise. But let me get a handle on this, understand it a bit more. If that means I have to talk to Uncle Ronan, so be it." Though she said the words, they were for *his* benefit alone. She had no intention of trusting Uncle Ronan anytime soon. Especially not with something of this magnitude.

Jad's face softened, and he relented. "So be it," he said quietly. "But just remember how you're feeling right now about Uncle Ronan's secrets, and know that's what your secrets will do to the others."

"I will," Natisse said, nodding. "But thank you. For everything."

Jad reached up to pat her hand. "For you, Natisse, always."

12

KULLEN

Daylight had just begun brightening the eastern horizon as Kullen crossed the Mustona Bridge on his way to the Embers. This was the place where Thanagar's protective dome ended. It was unclear whether it was simply the natural point at which his power dwindled or where the dragon had thoughtfully chosen to end his protection, thereby leaving the people of the Embers responsible for Prince Jarius's and Princess Hadassa's deaths to fend for themselves.

The early-morning crowds filling the One Hand District hadn't yet grown unbearable; the noise still barely above a low hum as tired merchants opened their shops and stalls, unloaded wagons, or sipped steaming mugs of *caqo* to perk up before the day's commerce kicked off in earnest. Kullen found himself wishing for a mug of his own—the dark, bitter brew would wake him up, help him shrug off the fatigue weighing on his limbs.

First, however, he had more important matters to attend to.

The borders of the One Hand District quickly approached, and Kullen again felt the prickling sensation on the back of his neck as he stepped through Thanagar's translucent dome of protection and out into the Embers. The smell struck him like a slap to the face. Atop the usual reek of rot, abandonment, and decrepitude was a thick, acrid odor of smoke.

Kullen's gaze strayed to the sooty cloud hanging over the Embers. The fires at the Refuge had been put out—or, more likely, burned out—but the stink persisted. A reminder of what had nearly occurred the previous night. And that no one outside the Embers cared.

Kullen quickened his steps, hurrying through the last few streets separating him from the ruined carcass of what had once been his home—his, Hadassa's, and countless more orphans and foundlings over the decades. All of which had been taken in by

Mammy Tess and Mammy Sylla—now gone to whatever afterlife awaited a servant of goodness—and given a home far better than they could find on the streets.

Now, only charred beams, crumbling brick, and a mountain of ashes remained. Not a single Imperial Scale was in sight. They'd never venture this far into the Embers. It wasn't their problem if a building burned down.

The Embers-folk had come out, however. Scores of raggedly dressed men and women gathered around the Refuge, bringing what blankets, clothing, and food and drink they could spare. The thirty or so orphans who had weathered the attack on the Refuge were now being tended to by good-hearted, well-meaning people, all of whom had benefited from the kindness and generosity of Mammy Tess. The rest of the Refuge's surviving staff—a pair of women who assisted Mammy Tess in taking care of the children, the white-haired and stoop-backed groundskeeper, Voyles, and the old one-armed bricklayer Mammy Tess had brought in to help with upkeep—stayed close by the children.

Kullen couldn't recall the man's name. A problem he would need to remedy. Each and every soul who'd devoted themselves to that place deserved better than they'd received. Knowing one's name was a small thing, indeed, but great achievements were nothing but a series of small things.

Of Mammy Tess herself, Kullen saw no sign. He frowned. He'd expected her to be with the children, watching over them like a mother hawk. But she was not among those gathered outside the Refuge.

Kullen slid through the crowd, heading toward the woman he'd saved from Magister Branthe's hired grunts. He didn't know if she'd recognize him—she'd been in shock, terrified by the ordeal—but of them all, she appeared to have sustained the fewest wounds and burns.

He was mere paces away from the woman when movement amongst the ruins of the Refuge caught his eye. In the rear of the burned-down building, a single structure remained standing.

Small, squat, built of weathered stone, the chapel alone had survived the blaze. The door was ruined—he'd instructed Umbris to break it in—but the walls still stood, and only a few scorch marks stained half-standing columns.

He meandered into the courtyard. He'd spent so many long hours there, often wishing to be anywhere else. He could nearly recall verbatim the morning prayers Mammy Sylla had led them in. Not just to Ezrasil, either. The Refuge was a place for all. Before they were allowed to cross the threshold into the chapel proper, they were to ensure their foul deeds were cleansed by any and all gods.

Now, standing there amidst the rubble and ruin, Kullen would've done anything to hear Mammy Sylla's prayers.

Perhaps one day.

What amazed Kullen was that anything was still standing. It was as if time stood still around him. There was no threat to Jaylen's life here, no Crimson Fang tearing his fingernails off, no grand treason from a thousand different nobles. Here, there was just peace.

As he walked, his ankle twisted where the stone pavers had been cracked. He swore, catching himself on one of the columns. Bending to examine what damage might've been done, he spotted something strange. Black and blue, hard-cut stone—no, not quite stone… blueish something peered out at him from beneath the dust. He knelt and swept the dust away. The mineral, or whatever it was, practically sparkled.

It was unlike anything he'd ever seen. Digging his fingernails beneath the paver closest to him, he strained. It gave way, and more of the mysterious blue element gleamed through. It wasn't a solid layer of the stuff, intermixing with the natural stone beneath the courtyard, but it was curious.

"Kullen!"

Kullen quickly replaced the stone and covered the blue with dust.

Mammy Tess emerged from the chapel. Knowing her, she'd

likely spent time in prayer—though to which of the gods, Kullen didn't know and had never thought to ask. Now, she emanated an air of perfect calm and peace that contrasted sharply with the chaos and wreckage surrounding her.

He rose. He'd forgotten about his ankle, but it twinged only slightly as he headed straight toward her. Lucky for him, he had no time for injuries. He climbed over charred timbers and picked his way along a path someone had cleared through the ashes to the chapel.

A smile broke out on Mammy Tess's age-lined face. She enveloped him in a fierce hug, and Kullen hugged her back in relief. Finally, she pulled back and regarded him from arm's length.

"You came back, my Kully." Her voice was serene, and her expression showed no hint of the sadness that had been there the previous night when she watched her life's work torched to the ground. She'd always found such solace in her prayers, even in the darkest stages of her life. Kullen had often envied her that. "I didn't expect to see you again so soon. Protecting the Empire always struck me as a demanding job, enough to keep even you too busy for such frequent visits."

Kullen couldn't help smiling. He'd feared a rebuke—she'd looked at him with such horror the night he'd killed Magister Deckard's bully boys to stop them from burning down the Refuge—but apparently, she'd come to terms with what he'd become, what the Emperor had crafted him into.

"Never too busy for you, Mammy," he said. "Especially not at a time like this."

"Come, follow," she said, leading him back into the wreckage. Kullen fell into step beside her. His heart plummeted as they stepped into what had once been the Refuge's kitchen. His mind flashed with visions of Quelly, the best cook he'd ever known, dead beneath a table that was no longer there.

Though Kullen knew Mammy Tess was far from okay, she exuded strength.

"We'll have this mess cleaned up in no time," she said. "You'll see." Her eyes remained bright despite the pall of smoke hanging over everything. "The Refuge doors will open once more."

"I know," Kullen said quietly. "The Emperor is aware of what happened here. I'll make sure he sends enough coin to rebuild. It'll be better than ever."

"Thank you, Kully." Mammy Tess patted his arm, a motherly gesture that had irritated him as a youth but now brought a lump rising to his throat. He'd nearly lost her last night. All of the Embers had. It had been a close thing, but—

"I know you didn't come all this way just to check on me," Mammy Tess said, eyeing him. "I don't have much, but tell me what you need, and I'll do what I can."

Kullen smiled. Always sharp, the woman was. "Information, Mammy. About the Crimson Fang, if you have it."

Mammy Tess frowned, wrinkles forming on her forehead. "I know them. A few of them, at least. Good people. Kind, generous. In large part, they're why we could still keep our doors open before…this."

Kullen raised an eyebrow. That wasn't the response he'd been expecting. "I need to find them."

"Why?" The question held no trace of suspicion, merely calm curiosity.

Kullen considered how to answer. Finally, he decided on the truth. "They're holding Prince Jaylen captive."

"Captive?" Mammy Tess shook her head. "That can't be. Doesn't sound like them, not at all."

"But it's true," Kullen insisted. "I have it on good authority that the Prince was last seen being carried away unconscious by members of the Crimson Fang."

"Surely, they found the poor boy in that condition and are seeing to his well-being," Mammy Tess said.

"We could hope for that to be true," Kullen said. "Either way, one of my duties to the Emperor is to protect the Prince, so I need to find him, get him back to the Palace. In one piece."

Mammy Tess laid a gentle hand on his arm. "If they have the Prince, I'm sure it's for good reason. They're good people, the Crimson Fang."

Kullen didn't bother arguing with her. She couldn't possibly know everything they had done, how much blood they had spilled. *Aristocratic* blood, it was true, but those were only the victims he knew about. There was no telling what other lives had been ended in the name of their insurrection against the Emperor.

"I need to find the Prince," he told her again. "Which means I need to find them."

"I can't help you with that," Mammy Tess said.

Kullen raised an eyebrow. "Can't, or won't?"

"Can't." Mammy Tess's lips pursed together in the frown of displeasure he'd seen every time he'd been caught sneaking sugared biscuits from the kitchen. "The only times I've seen them is when they visit me here. A nice young man named Ronan, sometimes with his beautiful daughter."

That caught Kullen's attention. "That daughter of his… she have red hair?"

"Fiery as Mammy Sylla's." Mammy Tess's eyes glistened. "She's a quiet one. Reserved. But oh, so pretty. Never did catch her name. I always had the sense she carried a great deal of pain—deeper than just her scars—but she seemed kind enough. So was the big one… oh, what was his name?" She tugged at her lip. "Lad… no, that's not right. Gad? Ah, Jad! That was it, Jad! The biggest heart of anyone I've met. Gentle giant, as they say."

It couldn't have been the same big man that had been with the red-haired assassin at Magister Branthe's fighting pit. That fellow had been covered from head to toe in blood, crushing skulls and breaking limbs while roaring.

Gentle like a mad dragon.

"Then there was the other young one," Mammy Tess was saying, talking as much to herself as to him. "Cute as a button, she was. Sparrow, I think Jad called her. Only met her the once.

Needed a lot of fattening up, so I sent a pair of meat pies back with them that time."

"Back where?" Kullen asked. "You don't know where they went? Where they came from?"

"Best I can tell you is that they came from that way," Mammy Tess said, pointing toward the One Hand District. "Left that way, too."

Kullen suppressed a grunt of frustration. He'd hoped Mammy Tess could tell him more about the insurrectionists. Their names wouldn't prove much use—they were probably assumed to hide their real identities—and unless he stumbled across a "big man with a bigger heart" or one of a million girls who were "cute as a button" and "in need of fattening up," his chances of finding the Crimson Fang were no better than they had been hours earlier.

Mammy Tess's statement about the Crimson Fang being kind and generous struck Kullen like a switch. Then again, he thought after a moment's contemplation, it was smart for any form of rebellion to gain the support of the commoners. Marks—likely stolen from the aristocrats and magisters they'd killed—would go a long way toward generating goodwill toward their cause.

Still, he wasn't fully out of options just yet.

"How are the kids?" Kullen asked.

"Doing well, despite the circumstances," Mammy Tess answered, glancing over her shoulder at the small group that'd gathered just outside of earshot.

"That's good. I've been hearing murmurs that cases of Aching Fever have begun to crop up throughout the city. Especially bad here in the Embers."

"Thankfully, the gods have spared us any of that for the time being."

Kullen nodded. "Think any of the runners are up for a job?"

Mammy Tess's gaze slid past him, shifting toward the group of children huddled in front of the wreckage of the Refuge. "They've had a rough night, Kully. Better they get some rest rather than run around the city."

Kullen nodded. "I understand. But having something to do might help take their minds off what happened last night. Especially the older ones." Ezrasil knew that if he'd been in their place, he would have welcomed any of the odd jobs and tasks for which the people of the Embers hired the children of the Refuge. Any form of work would serve to distract from the fire and terror.

Mammy Tess considered that, then dipped her head to the side. "I'll ask. You want them to ask around about the Crimson Fang?"

"Yes," Kullen said. "I need a location, someone I can talk to. If, as you say, they've got the Prince for good reason, then they'll have no trouble with me taking him back to the Palace." And if *he* was right and the Crimson Fang intended to use Jaylen as leverage —or to cut his throat outright—he'd need to be in position to strike first.

"And if they find what you're looking for?" Mammy Tess asked.

"Deliver word to the Apple Cart Mead Hall. Tell them to pass word to Tavernkeeper Dyntas. He'll know how to reach me."

Mammy Tess nodded. "So be it. Let me get a good breakfast in them first, though."

"Of course." Kullen smiled. He reached into his cloak and drew out the largest of the purses he always carried around Dimvein. Marks could open doors, loosen tongues, or entice watchful eyes to turn away. Now, it would fill the bellies of hungry children— and, he hoped, begin the rebuilding process.

"Here," he said, pressing the clinking purse into her hands. "I'll make sure the Emperor sends more."

"Dear, sweet Kullen." A huge smile broke out on Mammy Tess's face, and she squeezed his hands. "Mammy Sylla was right about you. Always said you were good, deep down to the core." She pulled him toward her and stood up on her tiptoes to kiss his forehead. "And you keep proving her right."

Kullen blushed, heat rising in his cheeks. He couldn't imagine Mammy Sylla saying such things—she'd always been the one to scold him for his admittedly many misdeeds, and no one could scold quite like her. She had a tongue sharper than a dagger when she got going.

Mammy Tess pulled her hands from his and, patting his arm as she passed, headed back to rejoin her little flock of children and staff.

Kullen stayed where he was a moment longer. This place had meant so much to him. To Hadassa, too. Even after she became Princess Hadassa, she still loved the Refuge. Visited it every chance she could. To the people of the Embers, it was a sanctuary, a safe haven, a place to have their wounds tended to, to find a listening ear and kind word, and whatever scraps of food could be spared from the kitchen.

But what value had it held to Magister Deckard that he'd been so determined to either buy it outright or burn it to the ground? What could Magister Branthe's words "the Refuge is the key to everything" have possibly meant?

As much as he wished he could stay all day, recalling the good times spent behind these now-broken walls, he couldn't.

He spun on his heel. "Mammy Tess?" he called out, hurrying to catch up with her.

She hadn't gone far—age had slowed her movement to a sedate waddle—and turned to regard him with a curious look.

"Did Magister Deckard ever say *why* he wanted the Refuge so badly?" he asked. "Why it was valuable enough he'd spend a fortune—or do this?" He gestured to the ruins around them.

"He didn't," Mammy Tess said, shaking her head. "I never understood what he saw in it. All I know is that I never intended to sell. And never will."

Kullen smiled. "He should have known better!"

"Damned right."

So, what was it? Kullen shook his head. His gaze flittered back to where he'd twisted his ankle, to the black-blue lying just beneath the surface of the courtyard. Had Branthe known something no one else did? Kullen had spent half a lifetime in that place, yet this was the first time he'd seen anything to suggest it was more than what met the eye.

He considered returning to the spot, carving out a fragment of the blue stone with his knife, and seeing if Serod or Vlatud could shed more light on it—but Jaylen's life was more important at the moment.

All Kullen knew was he was gaining more questions than answers, and time was running out.

13
NATISSE

Natisse strode from Jad's room with a much-lightened step. Their conversation hadn't gone quite as expected, yet she felt better for it. His reaction to her admission of what had occurred with Golgoth gave her hope that perhaps the others would understand, too. Once she understood it enough to explain it to them, of course.

On her way out, she passed Sparrow returning from the common room. The petite young girl carefully carried a small wooden bowl filled with steaming soup. The smell set Natisse's stomach rumbling; she couldn't remember the last time she'd eaten.

"Where's Garron?" Natisse asked, surprised to find Sparrow alone.

"He wasn't quite ready to get back in bed yet," the young girl answered, looking up from the near-overflowing bowl in her hands. The expression she wore told Natisse of her fear of being reprimanded for letting the injured man stay out of bed. She added, "Stayed in the common room talking and drinking with the others."

Natisse couldn't help a little smile. "That's good, right? That he's up and around."

Sparrow nodded, clearly relieved. "Best thing to get him back on his feet, Jad says. Though I don't think he'll last long. He was already looking a bit gray after the first drink. I'll go back and fetch him in a few—"

"Natisse!" A voice echoed through the corridor, followed a moment later by Athelas hurtling around the corner at a run, his handsome face skewed. "We've got a problem."

Natisse summoned what little energy remained in her and turned to face the man. "Problem?"

Athelas pulled up short in front of her. "We're running out of food," he said, a look of extreme concern on his dirt-stained features. "Nalkin's given nearly everything we've got to the Orken. We've nothing left but crumbs." He patted his stomach, which Natisse had yet to see him fill. The man had a virtually bottomless appetite. Between him and Leroshavé, no food in the Burrow was ever truly safe. "Nowhere near enough for me, much less the rest of you."

"So run out and fetch some more," Natisse said.

"That's the problem." Athelas shook his head. "Most of what we took off Magister Perech went to the people. Everything we stocked up is pretty much gone—will be gone after the Orken are through."

"So go buy more," she said slowly, not having time for such trivialities.

"With what, my good looks? We're short on coin. Abysmally."

Before Natisse could reply, the door behind her opened, and Jad, once more dressed in his simple brown tunic and trousers, emerged.

"I'll sort it out," he told Natisse. "You go."

"Jad—" Natisse began.

"I said I'll sort it." Jad's huge hand rested on her shoulder, and he propelled her gently *away* from Athelas in the direction of her room. "There'll be bigger problems that need dealing with soon enough. Rest. Healer's orders."

Natisse didn't try to protest. She felt only relief that she *didn't* have to deal with this particular issue—a minuscule detail when compared to problems like what to do about the Orken or Prince Jaylen. At the moment, her brain was too thick with wool to think clearly. Jad was right. She'd need all her faculties sharp to figure out those much grander issues.

And so she complied, marching off down the corridor.

"Now, Athelas," Jad said, "let's see what we can do about getting more…" His rumbling voice trailed off as he headed in the opposite direction.

The moment Natisse's door latch *clicked* shut behind her, sealing her in the peaceful silence of her small room, the full weight came crashing down atop her. Her body was drained, her spirit exhausted, her mind all but numb. She took a deep breath and crossed the room to her small chest of drawers.

She bent and opened the bottom-most drawer, pushing aside scraps of fabric she'd use to repair torn and frayed clothing. From there, she pulled a splintered shard of wood—the only remaining fragment of the day Shahitz'ai had destroyed her life. Carefully, she let her finger trace the edge of the wood. It didn't bring her any additional peace. What had she done? How had she allowed that creature's mate to *bond* with her?

She replaced the wood, closed the drawer, and stood. It took all her remaining strength just to stumble the last four steps and collapse into her bed.

So much had happened over the last few days—*too* much. First Ammon's death, then Baruch's. Garron's loss of his arm, Haston's near-fatal injury at the hands of Magister Perech's guards, and Uncle Ronan's capture and fight in Magister Branthe's slave pit. She'd nearly died herself, more than once. In truth, the mysterious man in the hood was the only reason she was alive.

And, she realized with a start, *he* was the reason she was now *bloodsworn* to Golgoth.

Pieces clicked into place in her mind. Both the vial of Gryphic Elixir and the vial containing the Ember Dragon's blood she'd found lying in the sands could only have come from him. That pouch from which they had fallen could only have been his.

A swirl of conflicting emotions seethed within her chest. Anger over Baruch's death, yet gratitude that he'd saved her life for no reason she could comprehend. Confusion, suspicion, and worry over the vial. How had he come into possession of it? And would he come hunting it? She was safe in the Burrow—he'd *never* find his way through the maze of lightless underground tunnels, past all the gnashers and uglier monsters lurking in the dark—but would she be in danger the moment she left? The Orkenwatch and Imperial Scales were already threat enough. Now she had to worry about some strange, unnamed killer coming after her head?

All because of this… this… power!

She pulled the vial out from where it hung beneath her shift, suspended from Jad's leather thong. Aside from its gold cap, it appeared otherwise wholly unremarkable. The blood within gave away nothing to hint at its true nature. It was simply… blood.

And yet, so much more.

Natisse didn't consciously move her thumb toward the cap; indeed, she only registered the movement when she felt the needle-prick pain piercing her flesh.

A flood of power erupted within her. Bubbling, churning, overflowing like an eruption of lava from a volcano, it surged up from where it had settled within the core of her being and threatened to burst free. She felt the fire sizzling through her nerves, begging to burn free of her flesh. She couldn't stop it any more than she could hope to control it. It terrified and thrilled her in equal measure, drawing her toward it with an inexorable allure.

Have you need of me, bloodsworn? came a deep, resonant voice.

Natisse heard it not with her ears but echoing in her mind. The sensation was so strange, the booming timbre so foreign, that she almost threw the vial away from her. Not that it would do much good. The magic churned faster, the fire burning hotter until she felt she would be consumed alive from within. And yet there was no pain. Only power… so damned much power!

"*Do you summon me?*" came the voice again. Golgoth's voice, somehow reaching her from the Fire Realm where they had spoken face-to-face only hours earlier. How, Natisse didn't understand. There was so much about this magic she couldn't begin to comprehend.

"Summon… you?" The words, spoken aloud, came out in a croaking rasp. The faint sound of a terrified child.

"*Do you summon me?*" Golgoth repeated, emphasizing the word.

"N-No," Natisse stammered.

"*Then for what purpose do you call on my power, little human?*"

Natisse felt the dragon's simmering anger within her.

"I…" She could find no words. She had no desire to use the power of Dragonfire. And yet, she had embraced the bond without hesitation, without full knowledge of what she was accepting.

Swallowing, she forced herself to speak. "I want to understand. To understand what it means to be *bloodsworn* to you." That, at least, was somewhere to start. Perhaps if she could wrap her head around their bond, it would provide a solid foundation for everything else to come.

"*The bond of blood tethers us to one another,*" Golgoth explained, though Natisse couldn't tell if the thunderous growling held a tone of irritation, frustration, or something else. She didn't exactly have experience in the subtle nuances of conversing with dragons. "*I exist on a different elemental plane of reality from yours, a realm of fire. It sustains me, just as I am its embodiment. In order to manifest into the Mortal Realm—your realm, little human—I must be bound to a human. To you.*"

Natisse tried to understand. The part about the Fire Realm she could certainly comprehend; she'd been there, stood within the flames, felt the blistering heat. As for the rest…

"Why do you *need* to be bound?" Natisse asked.

"*To manifest into your physical realm, there must be connection to something within that realm. Humans are the only creatures with force of spirit—what you call 'souls'—to provide a connection strong enough to bring us from our realm to yours."*

Natisse chewed on that. "And what happens if you aren't bound? Are you trapped in the Fire Realm?"

Yes, Golgoth said. *"Condemned to know only* one *existence forever."*

The answer surprised Natisse. "You don't *want* to live in the Fire Realm?"

"Not only *in the Fire Realm,"* Golgoth corrected. *"Here, nothing truly changes. There is only ever fire, hunger, destruction. I ask you, little human, would you* want *to experience nothing else for an eternity?"*

That, at least, made sense. "So having a bond with the Mortal Realm lets you come into our world. A world where you can experience… more?" She didn't quite know how to phrase the question.

Golgoth seemed to understand. *"Yes,"* the dragon growled in her mind. *"Day and night, light and dark, cold and heat, hunger and satiety—all of these exist in your realm. It is a place of balance and contrast, where one thing offsets another. For every blazing fire, there is the cold absence of heat. For every death, there is life. So much to experience, good and ill in equal measure."*

Natisse scowled. "Well, that's just not bloody true!"

The dragon's confusion echoed in her mind. *"I do not understand."*

"There is no equal measure of good and ill," Natisse said, anger drowning her curiosity. "You said it yourself. You have been *bloodsworn* to vile men for longer than you care to remember. Men who sought to use your power to their own ends. Tell me, how many *good* men have you been sworn to?"

"A fair point, accepted well," Golgoth rumbled.

"Nothing in this life is fair!" The words burst from Natisse's lips. "That's the whole problem with it. There will always be those like your old *bloodsworn* who want to bring about death and destruction. And they are always the ones who have the most power."

"Until now, little human. It is you who wields my power now." The

dragon's words took the wind out of Natisse's sails, and an angry retort died half-formed on her lips. *"That is why I chose you for my bond. Because you are different from them. I offered it willingly, and I and my power are yours to summon when needed."*

"How exactly do I do that?" Natisse asked. Finally, she'd worked her way up to the question she'd intended to ask. "And once I summon you or your power, how do I control either one?"

"You do not CONTROL me!" Golgoth thundered with such force it threatened to shatter Natisse's skull from within. *"I am in thrall to no one, no man's slave."*

"That's not what I meant!" Natisse felt the dragon's rage and disgust echoed within herself. "I've spent most of my life fighting *against* slavery in all its forms. That's the last thing I'd want for you. I just…" She drew in a long breath. "I'm just afraid of what might happen if your power gets *out* of control. And if I can't *control* it, I can't *use* it, not if I risk hurting others."

"Ahh," Golgoth mused, her anger fading. *"I believe I understand. These are the nuances of language."*

Pressure mounted inside Natisse's head, and she *felt* the dragon's eyes burning into her soul from across whatever vast void separated them.

"You fear the fire," Golgoth said, her voice slow and deep. *"You fear its power, the destruction it can bring."*

Natisse didn't hesitate in response. "Yes." Her hand shot automatically to the thick, stiff burn scars marking her neck, shoulder, and upper arm. "I've seen—and felt—firsthand what it can do."

"Alas, I cannot teach you to control the power. I am simply its source, the conduit between you and the elemental forces of the Fire Realm. It is you *who must gain control yourself."*

"How?" Natisse asked.

"That is for you to discover yourself." Golgoth's voice was firm but not unkind. *"It is unique to all who have shared my bond. But I tell you this: the power is within you, was within you before ever we met. Our bond has simply unlocked it and allowed you to harness it. How you go*

about tapping into that power will determine your control and how much you are able to access."

Natisse's thoughts whirled. "Shekoth's icy pits, couldn't you be any more cryptic about it?"

"Seek the fire within yourself, little human. Find its source, and draw it out." Golgoth's voice began to fade, growing fainter in her mind. *"All you need do is share your blood with me, and I and my power are both yours for the asking."*

That made everything about as clear as mud in Natisse's mind.

"Wait!" She sat upright, hands reaching out as if she could seize the dragon and keep their connection from being cut off. "That can't be all you can tell me!"

"For now, it is, little human," Golgoth said, so quietly the dragon's booming rumble sounded barely above a whisper. *"We will speak again when you summon me into the Mortal Realm."*

The thought nearly knocked Natisse flat onto her back. "Summon you… what?"

But there was no answer from the dragon.

14
KULLEN

Kullen wrestled back his frustration—he felt the urgency to locate Jaylen *soon* but could do nothing but wait—and tried to wash it down with a long pull of *caqo*. The hot, bittersweet liquid slid down his throat and sent energy coursing through his veins. The rush was nowhere near as pronounced as an alchemical Navapash draught, but the taste was far better and the after-effects far less vicious.

He took a bite of his food, a hot, savory Cargiway pudding. He'd never been to the region of Cargiway, in the far eastern reaches of the Empire, but he approved of their tastes. However, as decadent as the puréed meat might've been, it took effort to swallow with the worry roiling in his stomach. Swordmaster Kyneth had beaten into him the importance of sustenance, especially after long days of marching and fighting. After last night, Kullen felt as if he'd just slogged across the entire Karmian Empire without a splash of water.

The chill of the Shadow Realm had left his limbs, but the sense memory lingered. Though the rising sun had begun to warm the day, Kullen found himself huddling deeper into his cloak, pulling the thick fabric tight about himself to preserve his body heat. The *caqo* and pudding warmed his belly but couldn't drive the ice fully from his soul.

Fortunately for him, he had no reason to move from his comfortable perch in the heart of the One Hand District. He'd all but exhausted his resources and avenues of investigation. He had no desire to return to the Palace and admit failure to the Emperor—and *especially* not to either Turoc or Assidius. Not yet, at least. He would swallow a generous helping of humble pie if, and *only* if, Mammy Tess's little eyes and ears found nothing by nightfall.

He had come to the busiest section of the One Hand District for two reasons. First, it was where Dyntas would relay anything brought to him. Kullen hadn't seen sign of either Sumaia or the blue-and-white-cloth-covered basket that was Dyntas's signal that he had information to pass on. It was too soon, but he held out hope that the Apple Cart Mead Hall proprietor's daughter would show up before long.

Second, it was here that the Crimson Fang's slogans appeared in the thickest concentration. Every second wall bore either the words "Blood for Blood" or a swooping, curved line that bore a crude resemblance to a dragon claw—both splashed on with cheap crimson paint. If they were confident enough to display their insignia here, he supposed they would feel safe in this busy section of the marketplace. All the better chance of him spotting the red-haired woman, the giant of a man whom Belto was convinced had been carrying Prince Jaylen or any of the others he'd encountered on the rowboat fleeing Magister Perech's pleasure barge.

And the fact that Witta, the owner of the small stand adjacent to the Mead Hall, brewed the best *caqo* in Dimvein didn't hurt.

He drained the last of the under-sweetened brew and contemplated fetching a second. He could use the warmth, but too much fluid and the undeniable call of nature might very well pull him away from his perch at precisely the wrong moment. With a sigh, he set down the pewter mug and settled back into as comfortable a position as he could manage while hunching his shoulders and keeping his head down.

From his pocket, he pulled a blank parchment. Now was as good a time as any to document his findings from last evening while it was still fresh. He scribbled the names of every Magister and aristocrat present in Branthe's underground cavern, doing his best to not forget a single one. While Captain Angban could be trusted, it was not something Kullen was willing to leave to the hands of others.

He wrote a name, then looked up, careful not to spend too long with his investigative eye away from the streets. When finished, he folded the parchment and tucked it away. He lifted his gaze fully to the hustle and bustle of the One Hand District from beneath the hood of his dark cloak. There was nowhere in the city like it. Whereas the Upper Crest held only the nobles and their ilk, and the Embers housed the destitute, the One Hand District had something for all. It wasn't uncommon to see one of the Magistrates on a stroll, longing for a moment outside of their day-to-day lives.

Though they would never be caught without their surrounding regiment of guards. The One Hand District was named such for a reason. Even as he sat, Kullen could identify at least three thieves. They were one slip of the finger, one bump of the shoulder away from losing a hand for their crimes. But for some, that was simply their way of life. As it has been said: one must steal to eat, must eat to live.

On the far end of the avenue, a Brendoni priestess stood bellowing morning prayers. They couldn't be heard from so far away, but Kullen knew the words. He'd heard them enough. He had no aversion to their ways—he held no regard for any deity, in truth—and it appeared more than just her dark-skinned brethren found comfort in her words. Men and women of all backgrounds stood around her, repeating the mantra while just a short walk to their left sat a gathering of Navapash missionaries, determined to convert the capital to their ways.

And who would stop them? The Imperial Scales were out in full force, devoted only to upholding the law of the Empire, and no law prohibited the gathering of believers of any of the Empire's many religions.

Still, most wandering the extensive bazaar were there for one reason: to trade coin for goods. And there was no place in the city to find such a wide variety of offerings.

"Sacrificial animals!" cried a man wearing dirt-stained clothing. He passed Kullen, looking up at him with hopeful eyes only to turn away at the look of disgust he found there in Kullen's returned gaze. A string of livestock traipsed along behind him, no clue they were facing their last day alive for the whims of some fanatic or another.

Kullen sighed. It wasn't his business, and he wouldn't let it be.

A ruckus to his right caught Kullen's attention. A few child-sized figures wearing the bandages and cloaks of lepers hobbled through the crowd. Merchants, aristocrats, and commoners alike gave them a wide berth. None looked too closely at the tattered cloth wrappings and ratty garments—indeed, most averted their eyes and made the hooked-thumb-and-pinky-finger warding sign against Kleanna—who was ironically both the goddess of disease and festivals.

Kullen shook his head. *If only they bothered to peer beneath the façade,* he thought wryly, *they'd be in for a shock of their lives.* A mere fraction of Imperial citizens knew the truth: they shared the streets not only with the enormous Orken but also the diminutive Trenta, a race far older—both to the Karmian Empire and the greater world of Caernia—than they.

The hours seemed to drag by at an interminable pace. Before Kullen knew it, the sun was reaching high noon—and still no sign of Sumaia. That worried him. If Mammy Tess's runners could find nothing, he'd have no choice but to return to the Palace. And face whatever consequences awaited him there.

That sat ill with him. He had no fear of the Emperor's wrath—he would understand what Kullen had done and why—but had no desire to inflict greater suffering on the monarch. Wymarc had lost his beloved son and daughter-in-law years earlier. Last night, he'd learned his most trusted adviser—and, truth be told, his only friend—was behind the plot to undermine his Imperial rule. Jaylen was all he had left.

Thoughts of Magister Branthe brought back everything *else* that had transpired over the last few days: the scrimshaw hinting at collusion with the Blood Clan pirates, the note bearing the name "Red Claw"—though whether that identity belonged to Magister Branthe or another, Kullen had no idea—the former soldiers hired to kill Magister Issemar and guard Magister Deckard.

And what of the army Kullen had seen gathered behind Magister Branthe's walls? In his rush to reach the Emperor, he'd forgotten to make mention of that amassed force. What had Branthe intended to do with those men? They, too, had been former soldiers, loyal either to the Magister's coin or his reputation as former General of the Empire.

Kullen made a mental note to bring it before the Emperor upon his return to the Palace—by Ezrasil's grace, with Prince Jaylen in tow. He'd also speak with the monarch about sending funds, laborers, and materials to rebuild the Refuge. The Embers needed the Refuge desperately.

Making a post-script to his thoughts, he added speaking to him about the Lumenators' magic as well. If anyone knew what in Binteth's frozen prick had happened back there, it would be him. After all, it was Thanagar who granted the Lumenators their power. Surely previous Black Talons bonded with Umbris had experienced something similar.

A chill ran down his spine. Was *that* what had happened to Heshe? Umbris refused to speak of the former assassin, and Emperor Wymarc had offered little in the way of detail as to how the man ended up trapped in the Shadow Realm.

Kullen decided it was time to ask Umbris for more details. Even if the dragon didn't know how the Lumenators' magic interfered with their bond, Kullen might be able to glean some useful tidbit from whatever had happened to Heshe.

He reached for the vial hanging at his neck but hesitated with his thumb hovering over the golden cap, uncertain.

"You must rest before calling on my power again," Umbris had told him.

Did that include communicating through their mental bond? He found himself reluctant to try it, lest that link to Umbris's presence in the Shadow Realm somehow lead to his being dragged back into the void.

No, he decided, lowering his hand onto his lap once more. Better he spoke with Umbris in person. He had to call the Twilight Dragon into the Mortal Realm soon, regardless. He'd have no chance to get out to the Wild Grove Forest for a while yet, but there were plenty of large and deserted properties sizable enough to accommodate a summoning.

He climbed to his feet and strode to Witta's bar. The portly, white-haired woman looked up from serving a mug of *caqo* to one particularly jewel-bedecked noble lady.

"Another cup, love?" she asked in the thick Lanercostian brogue.

"Later," Kullen said, handing back his empty pewter mug. "Do me a favor and keep an eye out for a pretty girl carrying a basket, will you?"

Witta raised one wispy white eyebrow. "Not likely to see one of those around here, is it?" Her tone held a mocking edge, and she gestured toward the nearby bustling market, where close to a dozen young women who adequately fit the description wandered among the stalls and carts.

Kullen grunted. "Basket'll be covered with a blue-and-white cloth."

"Ahh, well, that narrows it down a tad, aye?" Witta fixed him with a grin. "That'll cost you a mark. Mug of *caqos* included."

Kullen passed her three marks. "Flag her down and keep her here until I return."

Witta stared down at the coins, her vivid green eyes wide. "For that, I'll drag every lass in the One Hand District over by the ear and tie them to me cart, if'n that's needed."

"It's not." Kullen chuckled. "I'll be back in a few minutes." He waggled a finger at her. "No dragging or tying, Witta."

"Aye, aye!" The old woman dismissed him with a wave of her gnarled hand. "I'll find yer girlie for ya."

Satisfied, Kullen hurried away from the *caqo* cart. The butcher shop where he bought the applewood-smoked pork shoulder Umbris loved so much was just one street north. He could buy the meat, visit with Umbris, and return in a quarter hour, easy.

A bell on the door jangled when he entered Krok-Rok Butcher Shop. Behind the counter, a long, slender, Brendoni man stood, thick knife in hand.

"Pork?" he said, recognizing Kullen.

"Pork," Kullen confirmed.

Krok-Rok—a name Kullen didn't believe truly belonged to the man—was one of few words. For as long as they'd known one another, their exchange was similar. He retreated behind a pale yellow curtain only to return a minute later.

"Don't know what you do with so much," Krok-Rok said, lugging the pork shoulder over his own.

"I'm a man of simple tastes," Kullen responded as he always did. He tossed down his payment, received the hunk of meat, and exited without another word.

Turning onto the next street in search of a place to meet with Umbris, he spotted a familiar sign.

"Serrod, alkemyst and heeler," it read in poorly written Imperial.

Kullen contemplated, then headed toward the shop. The *caqo's* effects were wearing off, and if he had to spend the rest of the day and night hunting down the Crimson Fang, he'd need to stay awake and alert. A few of Serrod's Navapash draughts would do wonders to stave off fatigue. He could procure a few more healing potions, too. No telling how his rescue attempt of the Prince would go. He had no more Gryphic Elixir—he'd lost that potion along with the dragonblood vial he'd taken off the pile of ash that had been Magister Deckard back in the fighting pit—but Serrod had a few potent remedies that could work wonders just the same.

The entry room was longer than it was wide, both sides lined with display cases containing everything from empty flasks to rare flower petals. Serrod was in the business of goods and services. A product of the Embers, he knew what it meant to provide one with the means to take care of one's self. If a customer preferred to make their own potions—and they had the know-how—Serrod would provide the elements needed from all over the Empire.

A thick staff hung from one wall, crested with colorful feathers from a bird Kullen didn't recognize. Below it, three masks, lined up in a row.

Kullen took a few steps forward, following a path worn into the age-old wooden floor. Kullen wrapped his knuckles on the counter.

Moments later, the umber-skinned Brendoni alchemist bustled out of the back room. The half frown, half scowl that eternally lined Serrod's face relaxed a fraction as he recognized Kullen—likely his *best* customer. Being the Emperor's personal assassin lent itself toward a high demand for all manner of poisons, tonics, and alchemical concoctions.

"Must be a reason you're darkening my door," Serrod said. "Don't got no love potions. Looks like that's what you're needing."

Kullen gave a small chortle. "Navapash draughts, healing elixir, smoke orbs, and…" He contemplated. "Why not throw in a few bottles of alchemical fire, just for fun?"

Serrod snorted. "Careful with those Navapash draughts," he warned, his frown once again deepening. "That shite'll wreck your guts. Kidney stones and stomach ulcers. Mix it with the wrong thing, and you'll be seeing sideways for a week."

"Lucky me, I know a good alchemist in case that happens,"

Kullen said, giving the man a smile that had little more effect than a fly bite on a dragon's tail.

Serrod just rolled his eyes. "Don't touch nothing," he snapped, then hustled out of the main room and into the back from whence he'd just emerged.

Kullen chuckled inwardly. He was all too glad he'd never had cause to come to the Brendoni with any serious conditions or injuries. He could only imagine how dreadful the grumpy healer's bedside manner would be.

He had no need of Serrod's warning not to touch anything. None of the bric-a-brac held any interest to him, and everyone who visited the alchemist knew to be wary of his more volatile concoctions. Serrod's shop had burned down thrice in one year, always due to some experiment gone wrong or unstable mixture of ingredients that had no place being combined.

He did, however, find the masks to be quite fascinating. Kullen knew very little of the Brendoni practices. He knew of their goddess and the priestesses throughout Dimvein but had never stepped foot in their temples. He appraised one of them closely, wondering what meaning they held.

After he was satisfied, he straightened his back and returned to the counter, tapping his fingers in a rhythm only he knew, impatient.

He opened his mouth to call out to Serrod. That was when he saw it.

Small red letters had been painted onto the wall in the short hallway leading to the alchemist's back room. Kullen didn't know about the Brendoni religious practices, but he knew their written language. All Black Talons were required to have a working knowledge of all seven languages represented in Dimvein. And there, written on the wall in the native script of Brendoni…

Eight letters that, when translated into the Imperial tongue, spelled out the words "Blood for Blood."

The motto of the Crimson Fang.

15
NATISSE

Natisse tossed and turned. Exhausted as she was, sleep did not come easy in the wake of her conversation with Golgoth. A maelstrom of emotions filled her mind—confusion, doubt, anxiety, anger, dread, and more she couldn't put a name to. Even after she managed to finally drift off, she found no peace.

She dreamed of fire.

The gold and scarlet flames ravaged her flesh, seared her eyes, and burned her throat and lungs. Only now, she could *see* every terrible thing.

Her father, screaming for her to run. Her mother, struggling in Joakim's grasp, kicking weakly and fighting for breath that would not come. Two children—her brother and sister, one older than her, the other younger—lying dead on the trade road. And above it all, eyes of hideous gold watched the carnage, and mighty red wings spread wide as a gaping, fanged maw belched a column of fire.

Natisse woke with a cry. Sweat drenched her from head to toe, soaked her sheets, turned her thin blanket sodden. Her heart hammered such a frantic beat she feared it would tear free of her chest. Every fiber of her being trembled with fear—fear and fury.

She understood, then. Understood why she had so easily taken on Uncle Ronan's mission and come to hate the dragons. Even if she hadn't remembered it then, it *had* been a dragon who killed her family. An Ember Dragon under the control of some nameless aristocrat but at the command of Magister Branthe himself.

She remembered that day, clear as if she had just lived it. She and her family had been among a caravan of slaves being transported to Dimvein—from where, she couldn't recall, but it didn't matter. One of any town or village within the Karmian Empire. She and everyone else she'd known had been rounded up, clapped in chains, and sent to the Imperial capital to be sold.

Only they hadn't reached Dimvein. Magister Branthe's men—among them the giant Joakim—had attacked the caravan and killed everyone, slaves and slavers alike. Not because the Emperor had commanded an end to slavery. No, the Magister had done it for his own reasons.

The words echoed from Natisse's memories, haunting her dreams. *"Tell your master what will happen the next time he tries to bring slaves into our city."* Magister Branthe had shouted those words from atop the back of his mighty bronze dragon. Natisse didn't know to whom they were addressed—had the bastard left one of the slavers alive to tell the tale—for she had seen nothing but fire and death. She'd had no choice but to flee or share the fate of her family.

She'd chosen the only option one so young had: she fled, grabbing up that small scrap of wood as if it would defend her against a bloody dragon.

And her decision made perfect, terrible sense now. She hadn't taken on the bond with Golgoth because she craved power. She'd done it for the same reason she had spent a lifetime hating dragons: from fear of being powerless.

That day, she'd been helpless to stop her parents being killed. Helpless to do anything but flee in terror. Helpless, too, to stop suffering in poorer Dimvein, to do anything when Golgoth's fire turned the Imperial Commons into nothing but embers and ruin.

She'd spent every year since pushing herself to—and beyond—her physical limits every opportunity she got, never truly knowing why. But now she knew. Now she understood the truth.

She *never* wanted to be powerless like that again. Whatever she had to do to protect those she loved, whatever weapon she had to wield, she would do it gladly. Steel, Dragonfire, or that Ezrasil-damned stick, it mattered not.

With that realization came serenity. A quiet peace washed over her, lulling her back into dreamless, restful sleep.

When she finally awoke, it was not with a start or jolt but slowly, calmly. Rested even. Her eyes opened to the darkness of her quarters, and she sat up in bed, heart beating so steady a rhythm she wouldn't have felt it if she hadn't been trying. Her lungs worked in measured breaths. She rose and dressed at an unhurried pace, pulling on clean clothing and boots, strapping on her lashblade and daggers. Gone was the heaviness that had plagued her the previous night. Her anger at Uncle Ronan remained like a hot coal glowing in the pit of her belly, but talking with Jad and Golgoth had led to the clarity she now felt.

She was still a long way off from truly understanding everything that her *bloodbond* with the dragon entailed, but this was a good place to start. She'd have ample opportunity to delve into the rest in the days to come.

The hallway outside her quarters was bright, illuminated by oil lamps hanging from sconces set into the packed earth walls, but empty. Natisse frowned. How long had she slept? Were the rest of the Crimson Fang asleep as well? Finding out would be the first step. Then she'd have some tough choices to make—regarding Prince Jaylen and the Orken both.

She stopped at the door to Jad's room-turned-infirmary and pushed the door open as quietly as she could. Inside, only a single candle stood on the table on the desk. The flickering light shone on two figures. Prince Jaylen still lay pale faced and unconscious—or sleeping, Natisse hoped. Sparrow sat in the chair between the two cots, eyes closed and chin resting on her chest. She still held a cloth in her hand, a bowl of filthy water resting on the ground between her feet. Sweet girl, she'd drifted off while tending to the Prince.

But where was Jad? Natisse's gaze wandered to the second cot, which stood empty against the wall. And Garron, for that matter?

She found the latter seated outside the training room door, sharing a quiet drink and conversation with Haston. Although to be fair, Haston was doing most of the talking, while the laconic Garron handled most of the drinking. Both had sustained wounds and appeared the worse for wear, but neither were the sort to let injuries slow them down. As was evidenced by Haston's presence at Magister Onathus's shipyards the previous night, and Garron's efforts to help Jad and Sparrow tend to Prince Jaylen's wounds.

Garron, back to the wall so he could see down all three corridors, spotted Natisse first. A tight, tired smile broke out on his rangy face. "Sleeping Princess awakens, I see."

Natisse scowled. "Call me princess again, and you'll find out whether or not the fact that you've got just one arm stops me from tearing off your other and beating you over the head with it."

Garron just chuckled and shook his head. "And here I thought most people woke up after a full night's rest in a *good* mood."

Full night? Natisse raised an eyebrow. "I was out that long?"

"Six, seven hours," Haston said, shrugging. "Jad swore that if any of us woke you, we'd answer to him. You can imagine we all took that threat *very* seriously after…" He trailed off. What had started out as a joke quickly turned dark.

Every one of the Crimson Fang had heard the tale of what Jad had done to the bullies who murdered his puppy all those years earlier, but most simply saw him as soft-spoken, studious, and inclined to the academic and healing pursuits—traits that had made him invaluable to their mission. Haston and Athelas had come face-to-face with the grim reality the previous night. Doubtless, word had spread among the others.

"Bit early for wine, no?" Natisse asked.

"You think me a drunk?" Garron asked. "*Caqo,*" he added, lifting the goblet.

"Where did you get that?" she asked, wondering if there was more where it came from. She'd kill for a cup.

"Tobin found a stash," he said. "Fine lad, he is." Then he extended the goblet to Natisse. "It's my second cup. Here, finish it off."

"You sure?"

Garron just gave her a look.

"Thanks," Natisse said, taking the goblet and sitting beside him. She took a long sip of the still-warm *caqo*. Energy coursed through her like lightning. She let her head fall back against the wall and sighed.

"Good, huh?" Haston asked.

"Like Ezrasil's bosom," Natisse said.

Haston smiled.

After a moment, Natisse asked, "So, where is Jad? He wasn't in his quarters." She glanced past the pair to the closed door into the training room. "He in there, tending to the Orken?"

"No," Garron said with a shake of his head. "He took Leroshavé and L'yo to the One Hand District. Said he needed to pay Serrod a visit for a few more potions while the others handled the supplies."

Natisse couldn't help noticing that *both* of the men with Jad had been the ones most vocal in their desires to finish off what Magister Onathus's guards had begun. The big man had been smart enough to get them out of the Burrow and far away from Prince Jaylen… just to prevent them from doing anything stupid in his absence.

Garron gestured to Haston. "Haston here picked the pockets of the fine aristocrats pissing their breeches in terror when everything was going to shite last night."

"So I did!" Haston beamed proudly. "Marks enough to replenish our supplies and feed the Orken for a month, I got!"

Natisse gave him an approving nod. "And the others?"

"Uncle Ronan left a few hours ago," Garron said with a grunt. "Didn't say where he was going or what he was doing. Not that he ever does."

Natisse's jaw muscles clenched. Garron and Haston didn't know the truth about Uncle Ronan—those secrets were known to her and Jad alone. She'd damned well make sure they all found out in due time. She'd just have to be ready to share her secrets at the same time, too.

"I just sent Nalkin to get some rest a half hour past," Haston said. "Tobin passed out three, four hours ago. Athelas is still recovering from his wound, so he's been resting since he returned."

Natisse nodded. "How are they doing?" She gestured to the door with a thrust of her chin.

"All quiet inside." Garron grunted, shrugged the shoulder of his one good arm. "They've been fed, given what supplies we can find. Except…"

Natisse raised an eyebrow. "Except?"

Haston shot Garron a look that said *what are you doing?* but Garron ignored it. "Except what's in Baruch and Ammon's quarters. We didn't want to touch their clothes and blankets yet. Not until you had a chance to go in there."

The words struck Natisse like a blow to the gut. She opened her mouth to ask why they thought she wanted anything to do with that room, but the words died on her lips.

In truth, she'd given no thought to the small chamber the two brothers had shared since the day they joined the Crimson Fang. She'd pushed it from her mind completely, treating it as if it didn't exist at all. A way to protect herself from the sorrow that she feared would overwhelm her when she accepted reality.

She swallowed the lump rising in her throat. "I'll deal with it in a bit. First, I need to speak to them." She nodded a head toward the training room.

"Good luck with that," Haston said, shaking his head. "None of them seem much in the mood to talk. And that after we saved their asses!"

That surprised Natisse. "They wouldn't even talk to Uncle Ronan?"

"Don't think he's tried." Haston's eyes narrowed slightly. "Only time I saw him was when he buggered off a few hours ago."

Natisse felt her fists clenching at her sides. Of course Uncle Ronan was being secretive. He'd spent decades lying to every one of the Crimson Fang, concealing his identity—*both* of his identities, as a Lumenator and General bloody Andros—from them.

"Worth a try of my own," she said, forcing herself to sound calm. "Worst that can happen is they'll ignore me, too."

Haston swept a lazy gesture toward the door. "Have at it."

Nodding to the two, Natisse stood and pushed into the training room, leaving the goblet of *caqo* on the ground beside Garron. He quickly scooped it up and set to drinking again.

The vast, high-ceilinged room was large enough to fit at least two hundred people—closer to three hundred of the abnormally small Orken creatures. All of them had huddled against the only wall that held no weapons racks, though a quick glance at the racks revealed none of the swords, daggers, spears, and other armaments had gone missing. Not a martial people, these Orken? Natisse wondered. Or merely too overcome by the ordeal they'd clearly suffered to do more than collapse.

They *had*, however, managed to push the training dummies into a half-hearted defensive barrier between themselves and the chamber's lone door. The Orken had also arranged themselves in three concentric half circles: the children at the innermost with their backs against the wall, the mothers in the middle, and the aged males and females at the exterior.

A few Orken heads perked up at her entrance. Evidently, not all of them had fallen asleep, but the creatures had possessed the presence of mind to set some form of watch rotation. Among those who stirred was the one who'd first spoken to her in the cage. Urktukk, that was his name.

Natisse strode toward the wizened, gray-haired Orken, and he climbed laboriously to his feet amidst a chorus of popping joints and creaking bones. A few of the other creatures, most stooped by age, joined Urktukk in taking up what might've been considered a defensive stance, as if expecting Natisse to attack.

Natisse spread her hands wide and raised them high to show they were empty. "I come in peace." She was careful to speak in a quiet voice; no sense awakening the sleeping children. "I just want to speak."

She knew Urktukk, at least, understood her. To her relief, the Orken translated her words to the rest of his people. They didn't sit back down, but they lost their hostile glares.

"We owe gratitude, Ketsneer," Urktukk said, repeating the gesture he'd given to Uncle Ronan: pressing one hand to his forehead, the other to his throat, and bowing at the waist. "For free us. And bring us to *Kha'zatyn*."

"About that," Natisse said, raising an eyebrow. "What is that, exactly? *Kha'zatyn?*"

"I not know the word in your tongue," Urktukk said, shaking his head. "But for *Ghuklek*, home. From stories. Not seen for long time. But still home."

Natisse tried to make sense of that. "This—" She gestured to the vast room around them. "—was your home?"

"Many time past." Urktukk's expression grew grave. "Not for many time. But *Ghuklek* remember." He tapped a finger against his temple.

"And *you're* the *Ghuklek?*" Natisse asked.

"Yes." Urktukk gestured to the people huddled behind him. "*Ghuklek.*"

Natisse frowned. "Not Orken?"

Urktukk's face drooped, his expression darkening. But this wasn't the perpetual glower that graced the faces of every Orken she'd ever encountered. No, this was a bone-deep sadness, sorrow far more profound than she could understand.

"Not Orken," he said, dropping his head. "*Ghuklek.*"

Repeating the name didn't make its significance any easier for Natisse to understand, but it seemed Urktukk's grasp of the common tongue was as limited as her knowledge of the Orken, or *Ghuklek*, or whatever in Ezrasil's name these things were. Orken, and yet not, Uncle Ronan had said. No more helpful than Urktukk's explanations.

So, instead of chasing an answer she doubted she'd get from this old Orken, she opted for something she felt more certain he *could* give her.

"Why were you there?" she asked. "In the cages? What did they want from you?"

Urktukk's expression morphed from sorrowful to stubborn in the space of an instant. His lips curled back to reveal jagged yellow teeth in a savage snarl far more akin to the Orken than his gold-hued skin or bottomless black eyes.

The rest of the Orken responded with equal ferocity. Though they carried no weapons, they extended their long, claw-like fingernails and dropped into a wary, ready crouch.

Natisse showed no sign of fear—her lashblade sat looped on her belt, within easy reach should these creatures make the mistake of attacking—nor made any outwardly aggressive move. She simply remained still, her face calm, gaze locked on Urktukk.

"We mean you no harm," she told the old *Ghuklek*. "You are safe within these walls. No one will hurt you nor your young. I simply wish to understand why you were locked up in those cages so I can figure out the best way to get you far away from whatever threatens you and your people."

She didn't know if Magister Branthe or the high-ranked Orken at his side was behind the *Ghuklek*'s captivity. Not that it made much difference to them—the creatures had suffered, regardless of whose orders had imprisoned them—but it would dictate what manner of precautions they'd have to take to get these creatures safely out of Dimvein.

If Magister Branthe or one of his co-conspirators—Baronet Ochrin or Magisters Onathus or Perech—were to blame, the *Ghuklek* had nothing to fear. But if that Orken had orchestrated their incarceration, the Crimson Fang might very well have a serious problem on their hands.

Long seconds passed before Urktukk relented, lowering his hands and standing up straight once more. "No harm," he said, inclining his head. *"Tuskigo'lek* gave his word. Your word, too, *Ketsneer?"*

"You have my word, Urktukk." She met his gaze steadily. "I swear to all the gods and on my life that I mean the *Ghuklek* no harm. And that I will do everything in my power to get you away from Dimvein or wherever you and your people will be safe."

"Safe." Urktukk's face creased into a grimace at the word. "*Ghuklek* never be safe."

Natisse frowned. "Why not?"

"For reason we were in cage." Urktukk rolled up the left sleeve of his ragged coat—one of Jad's old cast-offs—to reveal a bandage wrapping his forearm to the elbow. With slow, precise movements, he began unwinding the cloth.

He'd barely removed a few layers when a soft, golden glow began to shine through the bandages. Natisse's eyes widened as she recognized it.

She'd seen it more than enough these past days, poured over the wounds of injured and dying men she cared about. She thought about the vial of the Gryphic Elixir she'd found in the fighting pit just paces from the cages where these poor creatures had been held captive.

"*Ghuklek* never be safe for reason of our blood."

16
KULLEN

Kullen's eyes narrowed at the letters painted on Serrod's wall, his mind racing.

What in Binteth's horns is that doing here?

A memory sprang to his mind: emerald-green fires blazing to life in Magister Branthe's fighting pit. Alchemy that could've come from few places in Dimvein. Serrod's wasn't just *among* those few—the Brendoni was the one to which Kullen would have first come were he in the market for such a concoction.

A loud *crash* from the back room caught Kullen's attention, drawing him reluctantly from his musings. Was someone back there with Serrod?

No, the alchemist was alone. Alone, and—judging by his angry muttering—clumsy enough to have dropped some glass vial or jar.

When Serrod emerged from the back room a few moments later, the Brendoni wore a heavy scowl. Grumbling in his native tongue, the front of his filthy shirt, apron, trousers, and boots were splashed in vivid-pink spatter that reeked of rose water and embalming fluid.

"Anything else?" Serrod snapped, setting down the assortment of items Kullen had requested. "And if you say 'yes,' better make certain it's *truly* important. That mess back there don't have thirty seconds before it sets into something egregious. If I don't get it off the floor now, it'll never come off."

"Yes," Kullen said, his voice hard. He pointed with one rigid finger. "You can tell me about that."

Serrod's scowl deepened at Kullen's response. Muttering, he turned in the direction Kullen indicated, then froze as he spotted the source of Kullen's inquiry.

"It's nothing," he said, a little too hastily. "Just an old Brendoni axiom, one my old teacher—"

"Serrod." Kullen stepped up to the counter, reached across, and seized the alchemist's collar too quickly for the man to avoid. "Look at me," he said, pulling Serrod close.

The swarthy Brendoni had no choice but to turn to face Kullen.

"Don't feed me dragon piss and call it wine," Kullen growled, his blazing eyes mere inches from Serrod's. "I read Brendoni just fine."

Serrod's dark skin paled, eyes going wide as dinner plates. His wire-brush brows nearly graced the peak of his balding skull, and those thin lips pursed tightly, vanishing beneath his gray wisp of a beard. "I-It's nothing, l-like I said," the alchemist began. "Just—"

"Where can I find them?" Kullen demanded. "The Crimson Fang. Tell me now." He made no move to draw his weapons, added no further threat to his words beyond the inescapable grasp with which he held Serrod in place. But the alchemist had sold him enough tricks—most of them clearly put to violent purpose—to know how dangerous Kullen was.

"I don't know!" The words came out in a half wail, half shout of protest. Serrod shook his head. "I swear it. They always come to me, but once they leave, I got no idea where they go."

Kullen eyed the man, watching every minute detail of Serrod's face for any hint of deceit. He saw none. Serrod was an abysmal liar, even for a Brendoni.

To his surprise, Serrod continued speaking. "But even if I knew, I wouldn't tell you." The alchemist's jaw took on a stubborn line, a defiant tone in his voice. "Not after what they done for me."

"And what, pray tell, did they do for you?" Kullen snarled.

"Nothing less than saved me!" Serrod tried to push Kullen away, but Kullen refused to relinquish his grip on the man's collar. "I fled Brendoni to get away from cruel men, only to find crueler men here. Everything I had, I dumped into this place and would've lost it. Yet they intervened." The light of zeal blazed in Serrod's dark eyes. "They're trying to make the Embers—make all of Dimvein—a better place. All the places where the Emperor is failing his people, where Thanagar's light don't reach, and none care for the people, that's where they'll always find a home. So even if I did know where they were, I wouldn't betray them. Not for nothing."

"And should I rouse the Orkenwatch?" Kullen asked quietly. "Have you hauled away to the Palace dungeons?"

Serrod paled even more, if that were possible, but did not relent. "Then I'd suffer in ignorance. I know nothing!"

After a long, silent moment, Kullen released his hold.

"So be it." He scooped up the collection of alchemical creations before Serrod could stop him, dropped a purse of coin on the counter, and strode from the shop. The bell gave an angry jangling behind him, and a Brendoni curse followed him out into the streets.

Kullen's stomach clenched. He regretted his actions, wished he hadn't been forced to do that. Serrod was prickly, and he'd be cross with Kullen for a long while yet. All the gold Kullen had left in that purse would do little to repair the damage he'd just done to his longstanding relationship with the alchemist. He'd have to find his supplies elsewhere in the coming weeks—perhaps months.

But he'd done only what was needed to find Jaylen. Not that it had come to much good, but it *had* been necessary. Just knowing the Crimson Fang frequented Serrod's for their alchemy needs gave him hope. Once he finished with Umbris, he could find a nearby vantage point allowing him surveillance of both the primary One Hand District markets and the alchemist's shop. Even if Mammy Tess's runners failed to discover anything, he suspected the Crimson Fang would require a visit to Serrod's soon. They were bound to be wounded after their fight in the slave pit. That one grizzled old warrior—General Andros, if Magister Branthe was to be believed—had taken a vicious battering.

Kullen hurried away from Serrod's, moving along the streets until he came upon an old, rundown cannery that had clearly been abandoned for months, perhaps more. The door was locked, but a well-placed boot shattered the cheap iron hinges. Kullen pushed into the empty building, moving through the wreckage of shattered crates and barrels. The stink of fish still rotted in the air, and the barrage of flying insects made breathing a chore. Finally, he came upon a space large enough for his purposes.

This time, when he reached for the vial hanging at his neck, he didn't hesitate to press his thumb onto the golden needle.

Come to me, he told Umbris through their bond. *I've brought you a treat.*

A cold chill passed over him, starting at his head and slowly working its way downward. His head grew light, sending pins and needles through his limbs. The room spun though his feet stayed planted where they were. Tendrils of shadow spilled in from his periphery, coalescing into one great mass of inky darkness.

From that epicenter of night emerged the Twilight Dragon, yellow eyes gleaming brighter than the few shafts of sunlight streaming through holes in the crumbling roof.

"Your favorite," Kullen said, tossing the pork shoulder to the ground before the dragon. "Though Krok-Rok forgot the plum glaze today."

Umbris gave a low growl in his mighty throat and pounced upon the meat like a hound devouring a treat.

"Not too sweet," the dragon said in Kullen's mind. *"Perhaps it is better this way."* After a few more powerful chomps of his massive jaw, which ripped the meat to shreds between razor-sharp teeth, the dragon gave one nod of his huge horned head. *"Yes, much better this way. No more plum glaze."*

A wry grin split Kullen's face. "You got it, boss."

"Boss?" Umbris's golden eyes lifted to fix on Kullen. *"What is this word?"*

Kullen opened his mouth but stopped, the words dying on his lips. How could he explain the colloquialism in a way the dragon could understand?

"It is like *Honorsworn*," he said, referring to the concept he'd used to explain his relationship with Emperor Wymarc, "but the bond does not always involve honor. Simply acceptance of another's requests and will over one's own."

"*Hmmm,*" the dragon mused, chewing loudly on the last scraps of meat not yet torn to pieces in his maw. "*And you say I am your boss?*" Umbris asked.

"Not exa—"

"*Yes,*" Umbris said, lowing his great head and baring his fangs at Kullen in a great dragon smile. "*Yes, I like this. Boss. Boss. Umbris Kullen-boss. It has a nice sound to it, do you not agree?*"

Kullen met the dragon's gaze. Umbris's golden eyes twinkled with far more humor than one would expect from such a predatory creature, and his mirth shook the ground beneath Kullen's feet.

"I'm not going to call you that," he told the dragon.

"*Would you not?*" Umbris asked, lowering his head close to Kullen—so close Kullen could feel the heat whuffing from his nostrils. "*Even if I demanded it?*"

"You know what they say, Umbris." Kullen frowned at the enormous dragon head hovering mere inches from his own face. "If you have to proclaim yourself the boss, then you're not really the boss at all."

Umbris snorted a puff of steamy air at Kullen, but the humor remained sparkling in his flaxen eyes. "*Then you must call me boss of your own accord.*"

"Exactly." Kullen placed a hand on the dragon's sharp, horned nose and pushed it away playfully. "Which I'm never going to bloody do again. So better be happy with just *Bloodsworn*."

"*I will give it time,*" Umbris said, resisting Kullen's push the same way an over-active canine would. "*You will accept I am your boss. There is no other who would save you from the hungry jaws of onyx sharks. Or the creatures of the Shadow Realm.*"

That sobered Kullen up quickly. All playfulness drained from his mind, replaced by the memory of the void's chill.

"Tell me you've given that more thought," Kullen said, frowning. "How the Lumenators' magic could affect our connection so strongly. Has that *never* been a problem for any of the humans you were once *bloodsworn* to?"

"*It has not,*" Umbris said. "*They, like you, remained in the shadows, far from the light. This is the first time your human magic has clashed so violently with my power.*"

Kullen hesitated. He knew how Umbris felt about the matter, but he *had* to broach it anyway. If not, he might find himself untethered and lost in the Shadow Realm once more. And there was no telling if Umbris would save him in time, if he could fight off the effects as long as he had.

Summoning up the courage, Kullen asked the question. "And what of Heshe?"

The Twilight Dragon's head snapped up and back, his tail curled around him, and the claws on his forepaws and wings thrust outward, as if preparing to fight. The violent reaction surprised Kullen—almost as much as the searing anger he felt through the bond with Umbris.

"*I have told you before, Kullen Bloodsworn, I will not speak of him.*" All trace of banter had vanished, replaced by immense fury, more than Kullen had ever felt from Umbris in all their years together.

"Forgive me, Friend Umbris, but why not?" Kullen stared up at the rearing dragon. "What is it that you are so afraid o—?"

"*I am not afraid!*" Umbris thundered in his mind. The force of the voice sent Kullen staggering back a step, set his head pounding. "*I fear nothing. Neither man nor beast.*"

"Fine." Despite the pain, Kullen wouldn't back down. He couldn't. His life hung in the balance. "If not fear, then what?" He forced himself to retake his ground, stepping forward. "Why won't you talk about it?"

"*Because if I speak of it,*" Umbris growled, teeth baring, "*then the pain returns.*"

That surprised Kullen. "The pain… of losing him?" He recalled how much Umbris had suffered in the wake of losing his former bond—of Inquist's murder. Yet the dragon's suffering had eased after he took on a new bond. "Surely your pain diminished when you swore to a new human? Isn't that how it works? The bond is broken when your human dies, but—"

"*You do not understand,*" Umbris said, dropping low onto his haunches, head between his forepaws. "*You cannot.*"

Kullen felt the dragon's anguish—not just physical pain, but emotional turmoil far beyond anything he'd felt before.

"I want to try," he said, reaching a hand toward the dragon. "Help me understand."

He half expected Umbris to pull back, to retreat further into the shadows. But the dragon merely stared up at him, sorrow and grief dark in his golden eyes that now seemed a fair bit less brilliant.

"*The bond was never fully broken.*" Umbris's voice in Kullen's mind sounded muted, surprisingly small for such a great beast. "*When Heshe was taken, his flesh became shadow and everything that tethered him to the Mortal Realm was destroyed. But I am a being of the Shadow Realm, and so here, in this place, I can still feel him. Feel what he has become. What the Shadow Realm and the creatures lurking here have turned him into.*"

Kullen's eyes widened. He still remembered the terror and horror that had nearly overcome him as he was dragged deeper into the Shadow Realm, when the void strove to consume him and assimilate him into just another scrap of its nothingness. Yet he had experienced it only in part—his flesh had never succumbed to it, only his soul.

Whereas Kullen was a specter while traversing the Shadow Realm, Umbris remained as real and complete there as in the Mortal Realm. He possessed a tangible physical form capable of feeling even in the void. Kullen couldn't begin to imagine just how much the dragon suffered by *feeling* the thing that Heshe had become. Had the former Black Talon been one of those faceless creatures sinking icy claws into him, rending at his flesh, devouring him?

"Is that how you found me?" he asked, his voice now quiet, too. "Did you... sense Heshe and use him to find me?"

Umbris growled, a low, dangerous sound that Kullen took for acquiescence.

A lump rose in Kullen's throat. Had the dragon been human, he might've thrown his arms around it and embraced it as a means of comfort. But Umbris's scales and horns would make that a dangerous proposition. Besides, dragons didn't express their emotions the same way humans did. Umbris might've mistaken it for aggression, especially in the fragile state with which he now found himself.

And so, Kullen placed both hands on the dragon's great nose and knelt. *I am sorry, my friend,* he said silently through their bond, pouring every shred of gratitude, love, and compassion he could summon into the thoughts. *I am sorry you feel that pain. And that you had to feel it again for me.*

Umbris tilted his head forward until the horned ridge between his huge eyes rested against Kullen's chest. This was the dragon equivalent of a fierce embrace.

"For you, Kullen Bloodsworn, I would endure a great deal more. Few humans with which I have shared my bond have endeared themselves to me as you have." The dragon remained silent for long moments, but Kullen felt the emotions radiating through their bond, and the intensity nearly brought tears to his eyes.

"Heshe's fate was a folly of his own choosing," Umbris finally said, rumbling low in his throat. *"I warned him against overdrawing on the bloodsurge, but in the end, he could not resist the allure of the Shadow Realm's might. It consumed him, and in so doing, made him a part of it, a creature of shadow and oblivion. It is why I have endeavored to dissuade you from following in his footsteps. Last night, when you were lost to me—though it was only for a heartbeat—I suffered that grief all over again. I do not think I could bear* another *loss, another bloodsworn consumed by the Shadow Realm."*

"I swear to you, that won't happen to me." Kullen poured every shred of certainty he could muster into the words. "I will not put myself at risk. Not for my own sake, but because I would not bring you pain, my friend."

"You are good and kind, Kullen Bloodsworn," Umbris said, rising. He shook himself like a wet dog. *"It is good to be your boss."*

Kullen shook his head and smiled. "Until we meet again, Friend Umbris." With a thought, Kullen sent Umbris home, back to the Shadow Realm where he and Heshe would once again be reunited, whatever that truly meant.

17
NATISSE

Natisse's jaw dropped. Their blood! There was no mistaking its color. She'd never seen anything its equal anywhere. None of the countless alchemical potions Serrod concocted came close to matching the lustrous golden glow emanating from the blood—both fresh and dried—on Urktukk's forearm.

None but Gryphic Elixir.

Even then, she'd encountered only a few vials over the years, but the distinct coloration and seemingly magical radiance the elixir emitted was unmistakable.

"Your blood," she repeated the words aloud, struggling to make sense of the evidence before her eyes. She lifted her gaze to Urktukk. "They wanted… your blood?"

"Yes," the *Ghuklek* said, his wrinkled, leathery face growing somber. "Blood used for magic. Healing magic."

That confirmed the notion that Natisse hadn't wanted to entertain.

"Alchemy," she croaked. "In Gryphic Elixir."

"Do not know name," Urktukk said, winding the bandages to cover up his wound once more. "But know its effects. Effects *only* for humans, not *Ghuklek*. Not Orken."

Natisse's mind raced. "So you're saying a human was the one who put you in that cage?"

Urktukk shook his head. "No, Orken. Only Orken capable to find us in *Cak'morg'lek.*" At Natisse's blank look, the old *Ghuklek* tried again. "Great Forest of…" He trailed off, a frustrated look on his face, then finally settled on *"Cak'morg'lek"* once more.

"Wait." Natisse frowned. "Are you talking about the Riftwild?"

"Yes, that is human name!" Urktukk nodded eagerly. "Rift… wild. Human name. Good name."

Natisse tried to make sense of that. The Riftwild had once been called the Great Lashtrye Woods, a vast forest that dominated the ancient borders between the early Karmian Empire and the Kingdom of Trill. That was before the darkness enveloped the land, that unholy, dark magic that left the city with its name: Dimvein. The forest had rotted away, leaving husks of what once thrived there. The wildlife all but scattered—those that weren't turned to ash.

Much of it remained hearsay. As to the truth of the matter, all Natisse knew for sure was the evidence pointed to there once being vast woods, and now deep chasms filled the region like scars. Only the bravest of adventurers dared travel there. And when they did, reports of feral creatures with the faces of men and the bodies of everything from spiders to goats filled the taverns. Most of it sounded embellished or downright fabricated, a result of too much drink and need for praise.

The Kingdom of Trill no longer existed; Emperor Trelayne, Wymarc's great-great-grandfather, had obliterated the Trillians for refusing to bow their knee to the Empire. Two hundred years earlier, however, the Hudar Horde's invasion of the Karmian Empire had pushed the borders back a hundred leagues. Now, the Riftwild was deep within Horde territory.

But what interested Natisse more was the Riftwild's proximity to the Korpocane Caverns from which it was said the Orken had first emerged long ago. The caverns stood at the very heart of the

Riftwild, protected by uncrossable rifts within the earth said to be so deep one could not determine their depths and so wide it would require a day's travel even if a bridge could be constructed.

"Orken, and yet not," Uncle Ronan had said.

Natisse had only to look at the *Ghuklek*, and it was clear they shared heritage with the Orken. Their skin had a golden hue far richer than the yellows, greens, and browns of the Orken. Too, they were far shorter—standing just over *half* as tall as the smallest Orken—and lacked the bristling beards and heavy musculature that characterized the Orken people. Yet, still, they shared similar features.

The lore said that human men had entered the Korpocane Caverns millennia past and emerged as Orken. Had some been turned into *Ghuklek*? Or were the *Ghuklek* a form of creature neither fully Orken nor human? Whatever the case, one thing stood clear in Natisse's mind: an *Orken* had taken them from the Riftwild and brought them to Dimvein. An Orken had ventured deep into Horde territory and returned with scores of captives. The Hudar Horde didn't tolerate trespassers; any Imperial citizens, be they Orken or human, caught on the wrong side of the border suffered agonizing torture and death atop a wooden stake.

"When?" Natisse asked. "How long ago were you taken from the Riftwild and brought to Dimvein?"

"Taken three moons past," Urktukk said, anger darkening his aged face. "In human city days. Not know how many. But many. Enough for blood to collect."

Natisse's eyes widened. "They collected your blood?" She looked from Urktukk to the rest of the *Ghuklek*. "From all of you?"

"Children first." Urktukk's fists clenched at his side, his shoulders squaring as if ready for battle. "They say child blood most… potent. Then men. Women last. Women be taken for other things. Awful things. Then they return, not as they were. Two times they come. Humans come, but follow orders of Orken who take us."

The same Orken who'd been standing next to Magister Branthe, of that Natisse had no doubt. A high-ranked member of the Orkenwatch, one with power enough to venture away from Dimvein and travel to Hordelands—no doubt taking a force of Orken with him to defend against Hudar attack and to aid in the rounding up of the *Ghuklek*.

The journey to the Riftwild took the better part of three weeks on horseback. Orken didn't ride, but they could match a horse's trot with ease. But if Magisters Branthe, Onathus, Perech, or any of their other co-conspirators had decided to aid in the effort, a dragon could cross that distance in a day, perhaps two. And that would solve any problems regarding the rift-crossing.

All this information made Natisse's head spin. However, in truth, the knowledge did her little good—Tuskthorne Keep was the only place where she could find intelligence on the movements of the Orkenwatch, and she'd have a better chance of sprouting dragon wings herself than getting the Orken to talk. But it *did* clarify at least the nature of the threat to the *Ghuklek*.

Magister Branthe might be dead, but the Orken who'd worked with the bastard still lived—and knew the *Ghuklek* still lived, too. Doubtless, the brute would attempt to track them through Dimvein. The Crimson Fang's use of the sewer tunnels had saved their asses now, and the *Ghuklek* would be safe in the Burrow for the moment, but Natisse and her companions would have to be smart about their next steps. Getting this many *Ghuklek*—at least eighty, likely closer to a hundred—out of the city under the Sniffers' noses would prove a monumental challenge.

That brought to mind another question she'd been too tired to ask the previous night.

"You knew about this place," she said. "*Kha'zatyn*. How? Have you been here before? Before we were here?"

At that, a shatter-toothed smile broke out on the old Orken's face. "*Kha'zatyn* known to all Orken and *Ghuklek*. We its builders."

Natisse's eyes widened a fraction. "You built this?" She stared at the high-vaulted ceiling rising over her head, the packed earth walls, the solid steel doors. Her eyes strayed toward the hidden passage through which Uncle Ronan had slipped out to meet his contact in the tunnels—tunnels she hadn't known about, but Urktukk had.

"Fathers' fathers' fathers' fathers' fathers built it," Urktukk said. "Many seasons past. Built for human Tuskigo'lek." He raised his hands with the proud look of a craftsman displaying his finest tools. "Our people create ways through darkness. Find and make paths where are none." A sly smile split his lips, further revealing jagged teeth. "Secrets only know by us. Many, many secrets. Many lost. Forgotten by Orken, but *Ghuklek* remember. *Kha'zatyn* remembered." He gestured to the vast chamber in which they stood. "Never see *Kha'zatyn* before now, but stories past from father by father's father by father's father's father."

Natisse stared at the old *Ghuklek*. It sounded an awful lot like he'd just said his people had crafted the hidden tunnels and secret ways around Dimvein. She couldn't imagine the mighty Orken digging underground—they excelled at the ways of combat and war but had never, to her knowledge, shown an aptitude for anything else—but the notion of the diminutive *Ghuklek* burrowing beneath the ground made sense. Their large black eyes, sharp talon-like fingernails, and thick skin certainly made them suited to the task.

"One last question," she said, struggling to digest everything she'd learned. "Why would the Orken do this to you? The *Ghuklek* and Orken clearly share heritage. Why do that to their own people?"

Again, Urktukk's face darkened, and he gave a sad shake of his head. "*Ghuklek* not Orken. Orken hate *Ghuklek*. Cast out from Orken home. Make us live in the hot and bright, outside safety of earth, stone, and dark. Name us *Ghuklek*."

The word meant nothing to Natisse, but to Urktukk and all those around him, it seemed to carry great shame.

"Orken only want give humans *Ghuklek* blood," Urktukk said grimly. "Or kill *Ghuklek*."

Natisse's fists clenched. "We're not going to let that happen," she said. "We'll make sure you get back to your home in the Riftwild. Somehow." It was certainly a tall order—just getting out of Dimvein was challenge enough, then they had to cross hundreds of leagues of the Karmian Empire and sneak the *Ghuklek* into Hordelands.

"You have *Ghuklek* gratitude, *Ketsneer*." Urktukk placed his hands on his forehead and throat and bowed to her. To Natisse's surprise, the other *Ghuklek* did likewise. Surely, it was merely to imitate Urktukk's gesture more than anything, but they appeared genuinely respectful.

Natisse returned the bow with a nod of her own, though she kept her hands firmly at her sides. "Until we figure this out, your people are safe here. We'll make sure you have food, clothing, blankets, everything we can provide. It won't be much, but it'll certainly be better than that cage."

"Better than cage, yes." Urktukk's lips parted in a grin. "Much better."

Natisse turned on her heel and strode toward the door without a backward glance. Haston and Garron both shot her curious looks as she emerged, but she was too lost in her own thoughts to pay them much heed, much less answer questions. Her conversation with Urktukk had given her a great deal to think—and worry —about.

Chief among them was the involvement of a high-ranking Orken. The Orkenwatch was a very real, very serious threat, even on the best of days. Uncle Ronan had trained the Crimson Fang to steer well clear of their patrols at any cost. Yet now, it was possible the Orkenwatch would be hunting *them.* At least one Sniffer had her scent, that much she knew. It was said that a Sniffer's nostrils never forgot. Not even a lifetime and a thousand leagues would suffice to erase that sense memory from a Sniffer's mind.

That was a problem she couldn't afford to take lightly. If the Orken had Sniffers hunting the *Ghuklek*, there was an honest chance they'd be tracked down as soon as they left the Burrow. Yet they couldn't keep the *Ghuklek* here indefinitely. That was no less imprisonment than the cage they'd just been trapped in. Kinder, perhaps, with no one draining their blood, but a prison all the same.

Had Baruch and Ammon been alive, she would've conferred with them over a problem of this magnitude. But they were gone. Uncle Ronan would know what to do—or, at the very least, they'd have attempted to figure it out together. Yet the thought of talking to Uncle Ronan both nauseated and infuriated Natisse. She couldn't just look at his lying face and pretend nothing had happened. Even *she* couldn't push down her emotions that completely. Not yet, at least. Given time, she'd process things and come to grips, perhaps find a way to forgive Uncle Ronan. But time wasn't on their side. Not with the Orken hunting the *Ghuklek*.

Garron would certainly have valuable insight on the matter, as would the rest of the Crimson Fang. At the moment, the rangy man appeared relaxed, drinking his *caqo* and chatting with Haston. Ezrasil knew he'd had few enough pleasant moments since losing his arm. Doubtless there would be fewer still in the difficult days to come. She decided to let him enjoy Haston's company; she could speak with him about the matter of the Orken involved in Magister Branthe's conspiracy and the problem of the *Ghuklek* at a later time.

She sought out Jad in his room but found only Sparrow, still dozing at Prince Jaylen's side. Everyone else was asleep or absent from the Burrow.

Looks like I'm wrestling with this on my own, she thought.

But the sight of the door at the far end of the hallway brought back Garron's words from earlier.

We didn't want to touch their clothes and blankets yet. Not until you had a chance to go in there.

For now, she had something else to wrestle with, and she'd put it off far too long.

Moments later, she stood before Baruch and Ammon's old quarters as she had done so many times before. This time would be different. Neither of them would be there to greet her, only the ghosts of memories past.

18
KULLEN

Kullen hurried back to the One Hand District marketplace. He'd intended to be gone from his perch for just a quarter hour, but between the events at Serrod's and his conversation with Umbris, things had dragged on. A glance at the sun told him he'd been away for the better part of an hour. Hopefully, not so long that Witta had gone home or forgot she needed to keep Sumaia until he returned.

Pushing through the crowded square, past the shouting hawkers, he made a beeline straight for Witta's cart. To his relief, the old *caqo* seller was still very much in business, howling at the passing market goers in her heavily-accented and occasionally indecipherable brogue, extolling the virtues of her brew. Many of the claims were highly suspect—Kullen doubted a steaming cup of *caqo* could wake the dead or warm even Ulnu's frosty heart, as she asserted with full confidence—but no one could argue that Witta's mugs were the largest and tastiest in the One Hand District.

The old woman didn't let up her patter even when she spotted him approaching.

"—finest cup in all of Dimvein, nay, the Empire! Why, e'en Emperor Wymarc hisself—ain't seen the lass—swears by my *caqo*.

Gets his royal arse out of bed—been watching but naught hide nor hair yet—and he wouldna start a day of judging ye fine folk without it."

Kullen nodded his thanks and continued on past without slowing. He didn't know whether to be pleased he hadn't missed Sumaia or frustrated at the lack of information. Noon was an hour gone, and he'd come no closer to locating Prince Jaylen.

He swallowed his impatience and forced calm over himself. The Crimson Fang hadn't taken Jaylen just to murder him quietly in a back alley. Though every one of the Magisters they'd killed had been eliminated without fanfare—Magister Estéfar, killed from afar while sitting in Magister Iltari's skybox at the Court of Justice; Magister Perech had tasted steel on his own pleasure barge—events at Magister Branthe's slave pits had shown him another side of the insurrectionists.

They were carrying out some form of mission—"the mission above all" had been some of the only words tortured out of the mouth of the captured Baronet Sallas before his execution—and had thus far operated with a surprising degree of efficiency. One might almost call it *military-like precision.* If they'd wanted the Prince dead outright, they would likely have slit his throat and be done with him back in the slave fighting pit or shipyards.

No, if the Crimson Fang had the Prince, it was with purpose in mind. Ransom, perhaps, a bargaining piece to compel the Emperor to heed their terms. Or for some gruesome spectacle, a public execution, or torment to rival the treatment given to their own compatriot. There would be whispers and rumors spread about *before* they put their nefarious plans into motion. Kullen would just have to be prepared to move fast when the time beckoned.

He'd much rather track them down *beforehand,* though. With any luck, he'd spot them in the One Hand District—either stocking up on foodstuffs or paying Serrod a visit.

Ducking into an alley off the largest and busiest market square,

Kullen climbed up the rough stone walls of a three-story structure and onto the roof. From the top of the Merchants Guild, he gained a vantage over the whole of the One Hand District. He could even see Heroes Row in the distance, the massive statues of the lionhearts of old reaching toward Thanagar's dome. He had little trouble picking his way along the timber-framed slate rooftops to a spot where he could look over both the market and the street outside Serrod's alchemist shop.

There, he settled to wait.

The bright sun burned hotly upon both him and the tiles, giving him the feeling of being baked in one of Dyntas's ovens. It also aided in bringing his exhausted state to the forefront of his troubled mind. His eyelids felt like lead weights hung from each, desperate for respite and relief through sleep. With effort, Kullen shook himself awake. He slapped his face a few times just to be certain. He had Serrod's Navapash draughts tucked away, but he'd rather not use them unless no other choice was given him. Once their effects wore off—and they always did, far too quickly—he'd be utterly drained. Better a bit sluggish and sleepy than unconscious. He found himself wishing he'd stopped at Witta's for another *caqo*.

He watched the bustle below, men and women from all corners of Dimvein. It truly was a sight to see from so high. Brendoni women carried heavy pots filled with grains and oils upon their heads. Merchants, fat from their price gouging during the dry season, promised the best quality and finest goods. The smells from the many eateries wafted up to him, including the Apple Cart Mead Hall's smoked pork loin. Why hadn't he stolen a nibble from Umbris?

Watching only employed a fragment of Kullen's attention. While his mind instinctively sorted through the visual details he absorbed, he occupied it with the one thing he'd put off contemplating since the previous night.

General bloody Andros, eh? He had never met the man in person

—the General had been disgraced and tried for treason while Kullen was but a child. However, like every other young lad growing up in Dimvein, he was familiar enough with the legend of the man.

General Andros, Hero of Blackwater Bay. Savior of Kollick. Conqueror of Hudar and Defender of Dimvein. From the mightiest military commander to accused traitor. This last had apparently been Magister Branthe's treacherous doing.

Rumor held that the man had hanged himself in Halfvale, the village of his birth. He'd been dirt-poor and a nobody before his days in service to the Emperor and died in equal ignominy.

But Assidius had dismissed that as nothing more than speculation. Kullen wouldn't have lent it much credence until he'd seen the man himself standing in Magister Branthe's fighting pit. Far older and lacking any hint of the golden aura poets, bards, and storytellers had ascribed to him, but still very much alive.

Alive and, it seemed, involved in the Crimson Fang.

Leading it, more likely, Kullen reasoned.

A man like General Andros wouldn't follow anyone short of the Emperor himself. Perhaps not even him, after what the Emperor had done, accusing him of treason. It wouldn't matter that Magister Branthe had falsified the evidence leading to General Andros's trial. That knowledge had come too late to stop the man from suffering humiliation, being stripped of his rank and title, and declared a public enemy by the Empire he'd championed for his entire military career.

Was it any surprise that he had now taken up arms against the Empire? Kullen could understand that much, at least. The Crimson Fang's existence and purpose began to take on new meaning in light of that realization.

The good news, at least, was that a man like General Andros wouldn't just slit the Prince's throat. He was too clever a strategist and tactician to do something so wasteful. What General Andros intended with Jaylen, however, remained a mystery. There was no doubt the man had plans for the Prince. But what in Shekoth's icy bloody pits was it?

Kullen found himself muttering a silent prayer to Cliessa, goddess of fortune. He'd need her help if he was to have any chance of—

His prayers were answered almost as soon as they had formed in his mind.

So surprised was Kullen that his jaw dropped. His eyes locked onto the man. It couldn't be!

And yet it was.

There was no mistaking the enormous frame, shoulders as broad as an ox, head big as a gryphon's, and towering height. Gone was the blood from the previous night. In place of cestuses, the man's hands were filled with two canvas sacks. He'd traded the costly black overcoat for dull brown trousers and a gray tunic. But it *was* the same man, the giant who'd fought in the pit beside the red-haired woman and General Andros. The one whom Belto had seen lugging the unconscious Jaylen into the sewers.

Kullen's heart leaped into his throat. He fought the urge to spring to his feet right then and rush in with drawn steel. He could take the giant, of that he had no doubt. He wouldn't even need Umbris's power—Swordmaster Kyneth had dedicated countless hours training him to best the toughest of Orken. But killing the man would bring him no closer to unearthing the Prince. And fighting here in the One Hand District would certainly draw the wrong kind of attention. There were far too many Imperial Scales present; they could tie him up, give the Crimson Fang brute a chance to flee.

No, his best play was to watch from afar and track the man back to his bolt hole. Once Kullen found the Crimson Fang's stronghold, he'd take his time, plan an attack that promised safety to Jaylen *first,* and the meting out of the Emperor's justice on the insurrectionists second.

Kullen leaped a gap between buildings, bringing him closer to the giant of a man while still staying far enough out of range as not to be seen. He moved low, using the low roof walls for cover. When the giant stopped, so too did he.

The man knelt, lowering his bags to the dusty marketplace ground. A dozen street rats surrounded him in an instant, smiles plastered across their dirty little faces. Kullen was too far to know for sure, but he believed he recognized one of them from Mammy Tess's Refuge. Yes, it was the one Kullen had introduced to the orphanage, Sanjay. The boy stood the closest to the kneeling man, hand outstretched.

One after another, the Crimson Fang member reached into his bag, producing a small, wrapped package, and placed it into their hands.

The children jostled around joyfully, exclaiming to one another in loud voices, celebrating the gift. What was it? Food? Coin? Something else? Kullen wouldn't find out. As quickly as they had descended upon the man, they were gone into the folds of shoppers in the bazaar.

The big man rose and continued onward. Kullen rose and followed from above. His heart leaped when he spotted a second, smaller figure sidling up to the first. An umber-skinned Brendoni fell into the giant's shadow without hesitation, and the two moved through the throng with purpose. Kullen couldn't be fully certain, for that night had been chaotic at best, but the smaller man bore a strong resemblance to the Brendoni who'd been on the rowboat fleeing Magister Perech's pleasure barge with the red-haired assassin.

Kullen withheld his internal roistering as he pressed forward from one rooftop to another until he followed them to the end of the market. On his final leap, he timed it so he'd land, feet planted against the wall, grasping the roof's ledge. Then he kicked off backward, gaining a handhold on a windowsill facing the alley. With one final jump, his feet touched the grime-covered ground.

He wasn't entirely sure where he was, but through the mouth of the alley, he could still just see the Brendoni. Using the shadows for cover, yet not daring to enter the Shadow Realm, he followed, pausing only as they approached the door to a ramshackle old warehouse. As soon as the door shut behind them, he bolted across the street and slid into place outside, back to the wall. He listened intently for any sounds from within. Silence greeted him.

Frowning, he considered his next move. Burst in prepared for a fight? Sneak in? After a moment's contemplation, he chose a third option. Subterfuge and deceit had served him before.

Pulling up his hood, Kullen hunched low in his cloak and shambled toward the door, swaying violently. He had no time to buy a bottle of cheap wine to pour over his clothing; instead, he broke into a raucous, off-key sea shanty, singing at the top of his lungs.

Whence did the sailor man come
Full of wine and a bottle of rum
Legs like straw but a heart for fun
Whence did the sailor man come

Still singing, he slammed hard into the door. It burst open to reveal an empty space filled with refuse, piles and piles of debris and trash across the full expanse of the place.

Kullen fought the urge to abandon the pretense. There could very well be eyes watching him from the shadows all around, perhaps crossbows loaded or swords unsheathed and prepared to strike. He had to keep up the façade until he was certain he was alone or until he lured the Crimson Fang out of their hiding places.

Whence did the sailor man come
Smelt like salt and a bucket of chum
Eyes of glass and a head gone numb
Whence did the sailor man come

He stumbled from corner to corner, searching for the two who'd entered only moments before him, but found nothing. No back door, no window left ajar—not a window in sight, in truth. Just thin wooden walls. Using them as if to stay steady, he ran his hands along the walls, searching for a secret hatch or anything that might lead elsewhere. He found nothing, not even footprints.

His heart sank, and he couldn't stop himself from growling a curse.

The Crimson Fang had given him the slip. The two men had somehow vanished, and Kullen had lost his only chance of finding Prince Jaylen.

19
NATISSE

The room was small.

Natisse had always felt cramped every time she stepped into the chamber; perhaps that was why she'd always insisted Baruch came to *her* room on those cold, lonely nights when they'd wanted to share each other's company.

She'd asked him about it once when they lay tangled in her bedsheets. His answer surprised her.

"You spend a couple of months living on the streets of the Embers," he'd said with that wry grin she'd found so charming, "and you'll find the closer the walls are, the safer you feel."

"That I get," she'd retorted, poking his bare, muscled chest with one sharp-nailed finger. "But don't you get sick of sharing such a small space? Don't you want a room of your own?"

"We *had* rooms of our own, once." His expression had grown suddenly serious, his eyes taking on a distant, pained look. "Grand rooms across a grand hall from each other. So grand that neither of us knew the rest of the house was on fire before it was nearly too late."

He'd told her how Ammon had awoken first, recognized the danger, and forced through the flames consuming the hallway to reach his room.

"That day, we swore we'd always stay close together," Baruch had said in a solemn tone. "Until we had someone else to look out for us."

He'd fixed her with an intent look, and she hadn't missed the significance of the words. She'd brushed it off at the time, though. Made a joke out of it, something about wanting privacy for the strenuous activities they'd just engaged in. He'd laughed, and that had been the end of it. Now, however, Natisse couldn't help wishing she'd taken it—taken *him*—a bit more seriously.

Baruch and Ammon's room was exactly as she remembered it from the last time she'd entered, nearly a year earlier. Ammon had been as meticulous in his personal hygiene and cleanliness as his sword work. Natisse knew without looking that every clean outfit he owned still sat folded within the wooden trunk at the foot of his bed. His boots and shoes were always clean and lined up against one wall, next to the small wooden rack with three pegs for his two favorite rapiers and long main gauche parrying dagger.

Baruch had never quite lived up to his brother's strict adherence to tidiness—a fact that brought Ammon more grief than he typically voiced aloud. Baruch's clothing lay scattered around the foot of his bed or slung over his trunk, his boots haphazardly arranged in a messy mirror image of Ammon's.

They'd come away from the wreckage of their lives as Baronets of the House Sallas with nothing and had accumulated little more in the years since: a few weapons—every one of them painstakingly maintained, a task for which Baruch had never needed encouragement—a half-dozen changes of clothing, and only a few trinkets of little value to anyone, save the two brothers.

Tears welled in Natisse's eyes as she ran a finger carefully along the wooden shelf that spanned the wall between the brothers' beds. An army of small metallic figurines stood at attention. Proud cavalrymen on horseback. Infantry carrying shields and swords, spears, and axes. Archers with bows raised and lifted to the sky, ready to loose their nocked arrows. Officers shouting orders or studying an imaginary battlefield through a spyglass.

How she'd teased him—*both* of them—for the toys. The playthings of children, she'd mocked. Baruch had just smiled and accepted the jokes in his usual good humor. Ammon had grown serious but remained silent. Until the day he'd taken Natisse aside and told her the true meaning of the toy soldiers. Soldiers, much like them, had been the last gift given to the brothers by their parents, destroyed among everything else they'd lost in the fire that ruined their lives.

After that, Natisse's jests stopped. She'd gone out of her way to help Ammon find and collect more of the soldiers to add to Baruch's collection. Every time, the look of sheer delight that lit up his face warmed her heart. The gift she'd given him on his last birthday had been the prize of his collection: two generals with high-plumed helmets crafted from tin scraps. General Andros and General Tyranus, the metalsmith had told her—the two greatest heroes of the Empire within the last century.

Now, the sight of those generals tore at Natisse's heart, and her anger flared. She refused to give in to that feeling, but pushed it down, buried it deep, and cast a veil of ice over it. This was her moment to mourn the brothers who had meant so much to her. Ammon had received a funeral of sorts, but Baruch's death had gone unmarked by any ceremony or commemoration. Not because the rest of the Crimson Fang didn't care—on the contrary, every one of them had loved, respected, and admired the brothers in their own way—but because the mission had demanded they continue on.

The mission, she thought grimly. *It's over, and yet it's not.*

They'd freed the slaves, destroyed Magister Branthe's fighting pit, and killed the aristocrats behind the cruelty. That wouldn't put an end to slavery in Dimvein forever—wicked, greedy men would always find a way to profit off the suffering of others—but for the moment, the Crimson Fang's grand objective had been accomplished. Now, all that remained was to see the *Ghuklek* safely back to their home in the Riftwild… and then what? What came next?

Once, she might have looked to Baruch to answer that question. To *be* her answer to that question. A life together wouldn't have been so bad. But that was not to be. Not anymore.

Natisse moved to sit on Baruch's bed. The rope undergirding creaked beneath her weight, the mattress sagging gently beneath her. She fought the urge to lie down; if she did, the memories of the few moments of quiet she'd spent here with him would overwhelm her. Instead, she scooted backward until her back rested against the wall, then drew her legs up beneath her. Lifting his pillow—a case stuffed with old clothing—she buried her face into the soft wool and finally allowed herself to mourn.

His smell filled her nostrils; such a strong, masculine scent, a combination of his natural musk with a hint of the sandalwood oil he'd occasionally applied to his dark hair. It brought tears to her eyes, and she let them flow. Let them soak into his pillow, which she hugged to her chest.

She didn't howl or sob or rage—that was never her way—but bled a silent flow of sorrowful tears alone in the quiet of the room. She felt a rush of emotion in the pit of her stomach. Not her own, but Golgoth's. The dragon sensed her pain, empathized with her grief. Such a strange response from a creature she had spent her life hating. One more among the many surprises she'd discovered in recent days.

Baruch would have *loved* to explore the nuances and complexities of her bloodbond with Golgoth, to test the limits of whatever magic the dragon gave her. He'd always possessed an endlessly curious nature; in truth, that was what had drawn her to him in the first place. Where she'd seen the world through the hard, often cold eyes of one who'd suffered—and suffered she had—he'd never truly lost a sense of childlike wonder. He'd grown into a man, mature and thoughtful, yet could find pleasure in even simple things. Like the toy soldiers, the stories of General Andros, or his favorite meal of cottage pie washed down with bitter ale.

She shoved her hand into the pillow. Her fingertips grazed

something, and she pulled it out, sitting upright at the sight. She chuckled softly, but that only made the tears come quicker.

That stupid hat.

He'd been wearing it the day they'd met. It was silly and yet so perfectly suited to Baruch. For years he'd worn it, the floppy, velvet brim now frayed and filled with holes. Natisse hated it, begged him not to wear it, had even bought him replacements, but he'd refused to retire it until Uncle Ronan told him its bright red color drew too much attention.

She'd never known he slept with it so closely every night, hid it inside his pillow. She hugged it tightly to her chest. Why had she made him feel so foolish for wearing something he loved so much? She'd give anything to see him adorned with it one last time. Anything in the world.

She gave it one last squeeze, then returned it to its place within a pillow that would never be used again.

She burned every trace of him into her mind. His scent, which had already begun growing faint, washed away by her tears. The lingering memory of his hand on her arm, her face, her body. The smiles and laughs they'd shared, their mutual grief over the loss of Ammon, their kindred determination to complete their mission.

Eventually, her tears dried up. The grief remained like a hollow in the pit of her stomach, a wound raw and far from healed, but the sorrow diminished. That was the way of sorrow, she knew. It ebbed and flowed like the tides of Blackwater Bay. But as long as she remembered Baruch—remembered the man he'd been and how much he'd meant to her—he would never truly be gone.

Wiping her face clean, Natisse pushed off the wall and climbed to her feet. She set the pillow down on the bed and set about folding Baruch's blankets, gathering his clothing and boots. Once done, she did the same with Ammon's belongings. This proved only marginally easier. Though it brought no tears—she'd cried for the older Sallas brother enough—she still struggled to swallow the lump rising in her throat.

Finally, she had everything she could carry in her arms. Yet she did not haul it away. Not yet. Instead, she took a moment to pause and look over the room one last time. They were gone but not forgotten. Their clothes and bedding would be given to the Orken, but Baruch's pillow would stay in the small chamber, and its grand tin army would remain as well.

The world was a worse place without the Sallas brothers in it. She would miss them dearly, but—

"I hear you talked to the *Ghuklek*." Uncle Ronan's voice echoed through the small room.

Startled, Natisse spun, dropping half the clothing and blankets in the process.

Uncle Ronan stood in the open doorway, his expression grave, the lines on his face deeper and more pronounced than ever.

"I did." Natisse bit off the words—angry both at him and her own skittish reaction to his presence. She knelt quickly to hide the flush of her cheeks and set about collecting the items she'd dropped.

"So you know their secret," Uncle Ronan said.

Natisse didn't look up at him, couldn't bring herself to.

"Their name, *Ghuklek*. It means 'great shame' in the Orken tongue." Uncle Ronan's voice was solemn, subdued. "They are outcasts from their own people. Treated as freaks and aberrations because they are smaller and weaker. Until the power of their blood was discovered thirty years ago. Then they became little more than a commodity."

"Blood that heals," Natisse said, moving slowly, fearing what she would say and do when she stood up and looked Uncle Ronan in the eye once more. "Blood used in the Gryphic Elixir."

"Not used *in* it. What you know as Gryphic Elixir is, in truth, *Ghuklek* blood. Nothing else."

The words sank home like a dagger driven into Natisse's gut.

"You knew that," she said, each word forming on her lips with great weight, "and yet you took it. Used it on Garron and Athelas." Now she lifted her head to regard him. "You drank blood."

"I did." Uncle Ronan's face hardened.

"You knew that people were harvesting blood from the *Ghuklek* and using it to produce Gryphic Elixir, yet you went out of your way to procure some." Though she spoke quietly, her statement was a hurled accusation.

"I did," Uncle Ronan said, stiffness in his posture, tension etched into his face. "It's not ideal, but we do what we must to survive."

"You do what you must to survive." Natisse forced herself to rise and drew herself up straight. "Is that what you are taught in the Emperor's army, General Andros?" She spat the name. Each syllable dripped venom.

Uncle Ronan winced but nodded.

"It is." He didn't back down beneath her tangible anger. "I have done what I can to stop the harvesting of *Ghuklek* blood, but once the deed is done, I'd be a fool to pass up using such a resource. It saved Garron's life, and Athelas's, and mine."

"Yes, it did." Natisse felt the rage building within her. She fought to control it, to trap it beneath the icy calm that had always been her refuge in times of turmoil. But it was a losing battle. Every thundering beat of her heart set the fire blazing brightly. It was only a matter of time before—

"It's kept us alive thus far, Natisse," Uncle Ronan said, "and because of it, we've managed to complete our mission."

Those words shattered the last of Natisse's restraint.

"The mission?" She roared the words with a power that shook the room, set the floor beneath her feet trembling. Golgoth's power. "Look around you! Look at where you are standing. Whose room this is. And you talk to me about the mission?"

Uncle Ronan actually took a step back, his steely gray eyes going wide.

"They died for your precious mission!" Natisse unleashed the power surging within her—not the fire, but the dragon's fury. "They died for your Ezrasil-damned lie!"

Uncle Ronan took another step back, as if driven to flee by the force bleeding off her. Natisse pursued him. She would give him no option to retreat.

"You're a fangless coward. That's what you are!" Natisse stormed out into the hallway, bulling down the corridor while Uncle Ronan—the once-great General Andros—gave ground before the tempest of her rage. "You have had every chance to speak the truth, to let us in on your secrets, and every time, you've chosen to build lies atop lies!"

Through the red haze of her anger, Natisse saw the faces at the end of the hallway—Haston's and Garron's—turn toward her. Both men rose, their eyes fixed on the unfolding scene. Natisse didn't care. They deserved to know the truth.

"Tell them!" she roared at Uncle Ronan. "Bloody tell them the truth. Tell them who you really are! What you've done all these years while convincing us that we're fighting for some noble cause. Blood for blood, that's what you always told us. But whose blood have you really spent your life shedding? Certainly not your own! That's not what a general does, is it? You sit at the rear of the fight and command your armies to march into battle and die for your cause."

Uncle Ronan tried to regain his balance, to summon some retort, but Natisse's blood was up, and she had the power of a dragon backing her.

"And what exactly is that cause?" Her shout rang through the corridors with such force chunks of earth tore loose from the hard-packed ceiling. "What is the *real* cause beneath the façade you've so carefully built all these years?" It didn't matter that she'd already gone over this; she could hold herself back no longer. "Tell them, Uncle Ronan. Tell us all. But for once in your deceitful fucking life, Tell. The. *Truth!*"

That last word thundered down the corridor so loud it might have come from Golgoth's own throat. The power bowled Uncle Ronan backward, and he tumbled head over heels. Even Haston and Garron staggered and clutched the wall for support.

At that moment, Jad barreled around the corner. He took in the scene at a glance.

"Natisse!" His deep, rumbling voice cracked like a whip. "What are you doing?"

"I'm tearing off his mask!" Natisse didn't back down, but she didn't turn the force of Golgoth's magic on the big man. "I'm showing everyone who he really is. No, that's not right." She snarled down at Uncle Ronan, who was struggling to his feet. "I'm making *him* show us all."

"Like this?" Jad asked. His face was grim, his eyes filled with worry—worry for *her*. "Is this the best way to—"

"It's the *only* way!" Natisse felt the fire burning along her skin, begging to burst into life. Her wellspring of anger was as deep as Jad's, only she took no pains to conceal it. Not anymore. Not when she had Golgoth's power at her command. "He's concealed the truth from us all these years. He'd never have told us if we hadn't found out. But now that *we* know, it's only fair that everyone else knows." Then she spun once more on Uncle Ronan. "Tell them all your dirty little secret, you husk of a man."

The corridor was suddenly filled with people. Nalkin burst from her room, sword half-drawn, her eyes fixed on Natisse and Uncle Ronan. A yawning Tobin and half-asleep Athelas stumbled out of their shared quarters, awoken by the commotion. Behind Jad, Natisse spotted the swarthy Leroshavé, still carrying a crate heavy with supplies they'd procured from the One Hand District. They all deserved to know the truth—a truth that had led to the deaths of Ammon and Baruch.

Natisse fixed a baleful glare on Uncle Ronan. The grizzled man had risen, collected himself, and now braced himself like a soldier meeting an enemy charge. But with Golgoth's fire burning through her veins, she was far more dangerous than even the Horde cavalry.

"No more lies," she snarled. "The truth, or I walk." She stabbed a finger toward the rest of the Crimson Fang. "But first, I tell them what you've been hiding. I guarantee they'll all join me."

Uncle Ronan met her gaze with surprising calm—the composure of a general accustomed to life on a battlefield—and drew himself up to his full height. "You want the truth? So be it!" He rounded on the rest of the Crimson Fang. "Here is the truth. I am—"

A cry of pain suddenly rang out from the direction of the common room. Natisse was moving before she realized it. Clothes and blankets flew from her arms, and she charged past Uncle Ronan at a dead sprint, hand dropping to her lashblade.

She barreled around the corner before Jad and Leroshavé even registered the sound. Then she was past the pair, racing toward the two figures illuminated in the torchlight spilling through the Burrow's open front gate.

One was L'yo, hand hovering a finger's breadth from the belt knife sheathed on his hip.

The other, however, the one holding the razor-sharp tip of a long, slim dagger to L'yo's throat, sent a chill down Natisse's spine. She'd recognize that dark hooded cloak and the man beneath it anywhere in the Empire.

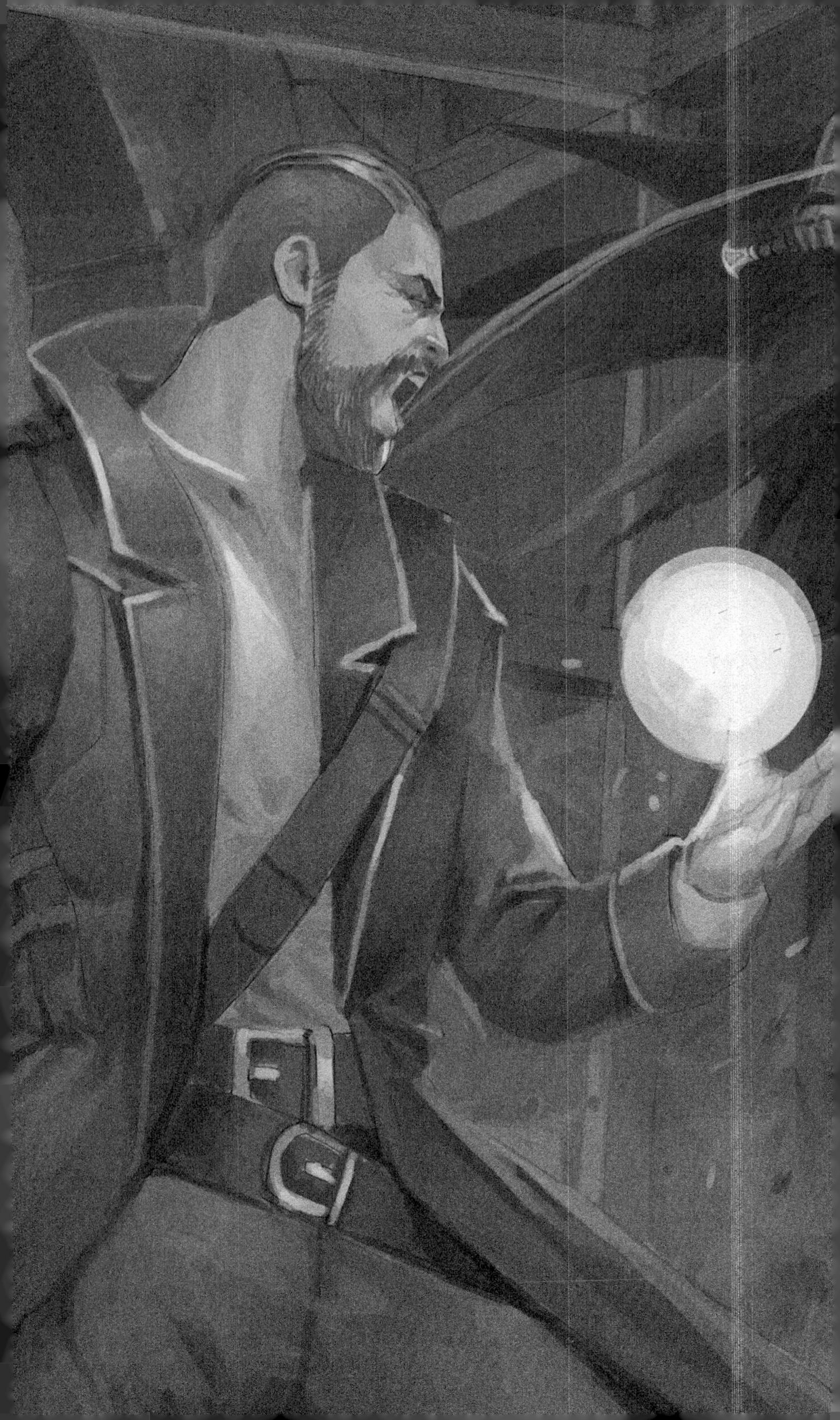

20
KULLEN

The creak of a door echoed through the seemingly abandoned warehouse. Instinct sent Kullen darting into the corner shadows. Only once he'd slid out of sight did his conscious mind register the thought that had prompted him to *hide* rather than flee or fight.

A man appeared, oddly out of place in the decrepit building. He had the look of a fighter—an upright bearing in his posture that belied the simplicity of his attire, a lightness to his step as if he floated on the balls of his feet, and the wary eyes of one accustomed to combat—though he wore no sword Kullen could see. No weapons save for a small belt knife. That knife, however, bore the threat of a weapon more than a tool for eating.

Kullen had lost the two Crimson Fang men he'd been tracking, but there existed a possibility, however remote, that this man was also one of General Andros's insurrectionists. The sack of vegetables and fruits he hauled on his back was more than one man alone could eat. Enough for a small force of rebels hiding somewhere in Dimvein, perhaps?

The man gave a quick look around, forcing Kullen to duck deeper into concealment. Yet from his position, he had a clear view of the man striding toward a pile of debris near the structure's southern wall. The man took a knee, then fondled a nondescript metal canister lying among the rubbish. Something beneath the floor gave a *click* loud enough even for Kullen to hear. A moment later, the entire heap of trash began to shift, sliding slowly and smoothly aside.

Kullen's jaw dropped. A hidden entrance that led *underground?* No wonder the Crimson Fang had proven so damned hard for Assidius to locate. The Seneschal's network of eyes and ears around Dimvein—and the entire Karmian Empire—had failed because they'd been looking in the wrong place.

A grin broadened on Kullen's face as he watched the man produce a torch from among the rubbish, light it with a firestriker, and descend the staircase that the hidden trapdoor had opened to reveal. Cliessa had blessed him *twice* today.

Kullen's pulse quickened, and he fought the urge to hurry after the man. Only once the pile of debris slid shut, once again sealing the stairway down, and a full thirty seconds had elapsed, did Kullen emerge from his hiding place. Moving on silent feet toward the pile of rubbish, he followed the example displayed to him, kneeling and repeating the man's movements as best he could. Inside the nondescript metal canister, his fingers closed around a small, familiar-looking brass ring. A gentle tug unlocked the hidden mechanism with the same loud *click*. Kullen spotted the hidden caster wheels and metal frame upon which the seemingly ordinary rubbish had been piled. A clever design, one he'd only found by Cliessa's guiding hand.

He slithered down the steps and found himself in the deepening shadows of an underground tunnel. The walls were unremarkable, as were the floors and ceiling. The only feature of note was a small brass ring—identical to the one inside the canister—jutting from the hard-packed earthen wall. Kullen pulled and as he'd suspected, the trapdoor above rumbled shut.

An oppressive, all-encompassing darkness enveloped him. To his relief, Umbris's dragon-eyes activated only a heartbeat later. Yet there was no light at all to see. Not so much as a glimmer or flash in the choking obscurity. The man he'd followed down into the secret tunnel had vanished, torch and all.

Kullen cursed silently but remained calm—he'd seen only *one* way forward from the stairs, a single tunnel running deeper into the earth beneath Dimvein. He'd given his quarry a full thirty-second head start. If the passage was as mazelike as Kullen's own hidden tunnels, the man could be a few hundred paces away but around enough bends in the path that the torchlight would be fully obscured.

Drawing in a deep breath, he groped blindly for the walls. He didn't have far to reach. The tunnel was barely two paces across, just wider than the length of his extended arms. His fingers quickly found the cool, damp earth, and Kullen began his steady advance through the darkness.

He hadn't been in pure, unbroken darkness for as long as he could remember. Not even the hidden passages that opened into the Palace dungeons were totally lightless—there were occasional apertures that allowed the rays of the sun or moon to illuminate their depths.

Yet in the years before he'd taken on the bond with Umbris, he'd trained with Inquist, the Emperor's former Black Talon, in the assassin's arts. Stealth, subterfuge, misdirection, the art of tracking people and animals alike, deceit, the martial arts, and, of course, moving through all manner of terrain: muddy swamps, boggy moors, gravel-strewn walkways, even glowing hot coals. Picking his way through the darkness of the tunnel and feeling his way along the impressively smooth walls and floor was far from the most difficult thing he'd accomplished.

It took all his self-control to maintain a steady, cautious speed when a voice in the back of his mind screamed at him to hurry. He would lose his target, the voice shrieked, and once he did, he'd have no way to find Jaylen and no way out of this place. He'd be trapped down here forever, condemned to fumble his way through darkness until hunger, thirst, or, more likely, one of the predators said to lurk in the darkness beneath Dimvein ended his life.

But control himself, he did. He'd dedicated his life to knowing the moment for wary prudence and when to strike at full speed and with overwhelming force. Right now, he needed to keep a level head and make steady progress in finding his target. First, he had to grow accustomed to the rhythm of feeling his way forward, the sliding of his feet across the hard-packed earthen floor to sense any pitfalls or traps.

It took a few minutes, but finally, Kullen allowed himself to hasten. He let muscle memory take over; Inquist had set him to navigate a similar environment, a specially-built maze beneath the Palace—one he now used regularly—and refused to let him eat, sleep, drink, or rest until he performed up to the Black Talon's high standards. Weeks of wandering those twisting, turning corridors hungry, cold, and exhausted had trained Kullen well.

The tunnel turned to the right perhaps a hundred paces down, and hope stirred as the passage brightened. His *human* eyes would never have spotted the faint glow from around another bend fifty yards ahead, but Umbris's dragon-eyes were far more sensitive to even the tiniest scintillation. Now able to see the way forward—dimly, but enough to be certain there were no traps or yawning abysses into which he might fall—Kullen broke into a silent run. Every heartbeat brought him one step closer to his quarry. A strange, dull sound roared in from ahead. By the time he reached the next turn—an intersection with two passages branching off to the right and left—the light had grown bright enough that Kullen no longer had need of Umbris's magical vision.

He peered around the squared corner. In extreme juxtaposition to the cramped tunnels he'd just traversed, a high-ceilinged cavern greeted him. The man stood upon a stone bridge approximately thirty feet long and three feet wide. Rushing water echoed from below, so loud that Kullen could hear little else.

The man stopped before the massive door, tossed his torch into a basin, and set his burden down. Fishing around his pocket for what Kullen suspected was a key of some sort, though he couldn't see it from his place in the shadows, the man then set to work opening the lock, twisting back and forth as if releasing hidden mechanisms or traps.

Or, he realized with a sudden wrenching in the pit of his stomach, *arming* them!

Kullen scanned the way forward. Two hundred paces separated him from the man he followed. Two hundred paces that led across a path too narrow for two men to pass facing each other and crossed too-smooth ground toward a steel door that could only have been *built* there by human hands. It was no Trenta-made door; he knew that much. But whoever had constructed it had clearly anticipated an attack. What manner of defensive measures would be there to keep him out? What chance did he truly have of crossing that open space unseen and unassailed by defensive measures he couldn't perceive?

Kullen sucked in a breath. *There's no other way,* he thought grimly.

Even as the man hauled open the door, Kullen reached for the dragonblood vial at his neck and the dagger on his belt. He had only *one* means of reaching his target before the man disappeared and shut that enormous door behind him. One way to instantly evade any traps or countermeasures.

Time stood like a statue, everything around him slowing to a paralyzed crawl. The door slowly opened, revealing scant light within. The man bent to retrieve his pack.

Umbris, I have need of your powers, Kullen told the dragon through their bond.

Umbris's concern echoed in his mind. *"I warned you it—"*

I have no choice, Kullen answered resolutely, *nor any desire to return to the Shadow Realm again so soon. But my* honorsworn *needs my aid, and to help him, I must get in there.*

"I cannot guarantee your safety," Umbris said, but Kullen had known the Twilight Dragon's answer even before he'd asked. *"So*

be it," rumbled Umbris. *"One last time, but no more until you rest and recover properly."*

And there it was, that familiar power coursing through Kullen's every fiber. It was like the strength of a thousand men and a thousand swords. Icy heat flowed through his veins, and his vision shifted gray. His eyes locked onto the single patch of shadow behind the heavy steel door, which blocked the light of the oil lamp hanging on the opposite wall of the high-ceilinged room.

With lightning speed, Kullen's incorporeal form whisked from one end of the cavern, through the door, and into inky darkness. Cold whispers like the beating wings of ravens surrounded him. He braced himself for what he knew came next. He willed himself to return to the Mortal Realm before it was too late. Soulless eyes and barely recognizable humanoid figures swooped in all directions. One passed through him, feeling like a sharp blade. He sucked in a breath, wincing as fear dug at him like dragon's claws.

With one last final force of will, Kullen felt himself returning to the underground. It took a moment in the cool, dark tunnel before he realized it had worked. He was panting, nearly doubled over in pain, but he had no time to recover. The instant he materialized, the door began to swing shut. He broke into a mad dash, charging straight at the man. He did not strike out with his dagger—there was no need, given the heavy sack weighing the man down—but, instead, drove his shoulder into the man's belly hard enough to knock the wind from his lungs and hurl him backward into the earthen wall.

A cry of pain erupted from the man's lips, cut off abruptly as his back and head struck the wall. The heavy sack of produce fell from his hands and crashed to the floor, spilling out vegetables, fruits, and parchment-wrapped loaves of bread—not unlike that which Kullen had watched the big man distributing to street kids in the One Hand District. Despite the surprise and jarring impact, the man had the presence of mind to fumble for his belt knife.

Quick as a flash, Kullen brought his own dagger up and pressed its tip to the man's throat.

"Don't move," he snarled, his voice low and menacing. "Twitch a muscle, and—"

Movement flickered in the corner of his eye, and Kullen's head swiveled. Two figures came racing around a corner. The first he'd recognize anywhere. That blazing red hair was unmistakable, as was the fiery look in the eyes that fixed on him. Even as she charged him, her hand was drawing a long, rapier-thin blade from a sheath at her hip. The same blade, he knew, that had cut him deep the night he faced it on the boat fleeing Magister Perech's barge.

The second figure, too, he knew. The grizzled man who'd stood in the center of the fighting pit, facing off against Prince Jaylen to fight for Magister Branthe's pleasure. General Andros.

A hard, cruel smile split Kullen's lips. He'd found the Crimson Fang. They would give him what he'd come for, or he'd kill them all and step over their stiff, silent corpses to take it.

"Where is he?" His words bellowed through the tunnels with far more force than he could summon on his own. Umbris's power backed him, lent him strength.

The man at the end of his dagger had the audacity to move. His hand came up and slapped aside Kullen's wrist, sending his knife hand flying wide. But when the man made to draw his belt knife, Kullen was ready for it. He swung his free hand around in an open-palm slap that *cracked* against the side of the man's head and struck his ear. The effect was instantaneous—the man dropped like his legs had been cut out from beneath him and hit the floor with a loud *thump*.

A roar of fury warned Kullen of an impending attack, and he swung around in time to see the whip-like blade darting toward his right eye. Instinct alone saved him in that moment. Even as he leaned back, his right arm came up to deflect the razor-sharp tip of the strange weapon. Instead of carving his flesh, the whip-sword deflected off Kullen's leather bracer and gouged a furrow into the hard-packed earth wall beside him before the woman could recover.

In the half second it took for the woman to retract her blade, Kullen dropped to one knee, snatched the belt knife from the disoriented man, and hurled himself toward the woman. His short knives could never hope to match the whip-blade, but if he could get inside her guard, he could disarm her and—

The sword snaked toward him so fast, Kullen had just enough time to throw himself against the wall to evade. Still, it drew a line of fire along his shoulder and upper arm. He rebounded off the wall, hard, momentarily dizzy, but momentum carried him forward within striking range of the woman. He struck out with the stolen belt knife, swiping at her sword arm. She pulled back with impressive speed, spun, and drove an elbow at the side of his head. Kullen blocked the blow with a forearm and drove a punch at her midsection. When she shuffled backward for the inevitable dodge, he hooked her back foot with his and pulled her legs out from beneath her.

She fell with a shout of fury that slammed into him with near-tangible force. He actually staggered backward, and before he could recover, the grizzled General Andros was wading into the fray. He swung a heavy longsword in tight, vicious strokes, a soldier's fighting style, highly efficient on both the battlefield and narrow back alleys.

But Kullen had spent his life training to fight *all* manner of opponents—Orkenwatch, Imperial Scales, soldiers, Hudarians, Blood Clan pirates, even the gryphon-rangers of the Griviane Range. He recognized General Andros's tactics and countered each strike before they had a chance to land. Deflecting, dodging, and countering with brutal force, he struck the old soldier's elbows with the pommel of his knife, kicked out one knee, and pistoned a closed fist into General Andros's chin. The man floundered backward, swiping at the air around him frantically with his sword.

"Where is he?" Kullen roared again. The question was aimed at the off-balance General Andros, the red-haired woman—who was even now springing to her feet and searching for an opening to slip past her commander to strike.

A half-dozen more men and women appeared in the corridor behind the pair: the giant and the swarthy Brendoni from the market; a stern-faced woman carrying a drawn sword and fixing a worried look on the man behind Kullen; a scrawny-looking beardless youth, and a man so ordinary-looking he wouldn't have stood out from a pile of dragon-shite; a rangy man with only one arm and a pale face, and at his side, a compact, fierce-looking man who'd been on the rowboat the night of Magister Perech's death.

Kullen fixed them *all* with a baleful glare, dropped his stolen knife, and drew two of his own daggers.

"Tell me where he is!" he demanded. "Or by Ulnu's bloody claws, I'll cut my way through every damned one of you until I find him."

His words seemed to freeze most of the Crimson Fang in place. Some blinked at him—confused or half-asleep, he wasn't certain. The huge man looked between him and the red-haired woman, his huge fists clenched and knuckles white. General Andros tightened his grip on his sword, and the woman pushed past her leader, whip-blade coiled and ready to strike.

One look at her face, and Kullen could tell she had no qualms about facing him blade to blade. She was good, far better than Kullen had given her credit for the night he'd leaped aboard her rowboat, but he was better. By far. And he had Umbris's power at his back. General Andros's strategic mind would do him no good against Kullen's steel. Their numbers might prove problematic, but should they choose battle—

"Kullen!" A weak voice echoed through the tunnel.

All eyes—all but General Andros's and those of the red-haired assassin—turned toward the sound.

It came from the passage from which the armed men and women had emerged only moments earlier. Standing there, pale faced and clearly in pain but very much alive, was Prince Jaylen.

21
NATISSE

The moment Natisse laid eyes on the assassin, she'd felt a rock-solid certainty that he was there for her. He'd saved her life in Magister Branthe's fighting pit, and she'd saved his in return. But as she'd told him, their debts were paid. She owed him only death—slow, agonizing death, preferably involving red-hot steel—for killing Baruch.

And yet, when he'd demanded "Where is he?" over and over, Natisse's certainty had fractured, then shattered. Why *was* he here? What did he want, if not to kill her?

"Kullen!"

At the sound of that word—that *name*—a change seemed to come over the dark-cloaked assassin in an instant. Natisse didn't turn, couldn't allow herself to tear her gaze from the dagger-wielding man who'd invaded their home, but she recognized Prince Jaylen's voice.

Just as the assassin did. His fury dissipated like a puff of smoke on the ocean breeze, his furious snarl transformed into a look that seemed to hold genuine concern.

"What did they do to you?" the assassin snarled.

"They did nothing." The Prince's voice grew stronger, and Natisse glanced over her shoulder just for a split second—long enough to see the young, pale-faced man hobbling forward. "Nothing short of saving my life."

"Saved…?" The assassin's frown deepened. His dark eyes flicked to Natisse, and it took all her willpower not to flinch beneath their burning intensity. "Why?"

Natisse heard the suspicion in his voice, read the mistrust in every line of his hard face. She opened her mouth to respond, but Prince Jaylen spoke first.

"They found me… bleeding… hurt badly… and…"

A sudden widening of the assassin's eyes was followed by a scuff of heavy boots.

"Damn it!" Jad cursed behind Natisse.

Natisse tensed, bracing herself for the assassin's charge. The man looked ready to rush her—no, rush *past* her to—

"He's unconscious," Jad's deep voice filled the tunnel. "Blood loss."

The assassin's wicked glare returned. "If you've harmed one hair on his head—" He made to advance, but Natisse shifted, interposing herself between the assassin and the rest of the Crimson Fang. She felt Uncle Ronan's strong presence at her side, bolstering her resolve. He'd recovered enough to join her in defense of the Burrow. At least he could manage to not disappoint in that regard.

"Stand in my way and die," the assassin snarled.

Natisse snapped her lashblade, unhinging it, letting the razor-sharp thongs lie inert on the ground before her.

"Stop!" Jad's shout forced everyone to a sudden stop. "Raise a hand against *any* of us, and he'll die."

The words surprised Natisse, but the assassin only growled low in his throat and braced his legs, clearly still intending to charge.

"Sorry, sorry!" Sparrow's voice echoed from the corridor leading to their quarters, and the girl's footsteps came charging around the corner a half second later. "I fell asleep, and when I woke, he was gone, and I heard a shout—oh!" The petite girl sucked in a sharp breath.

Natisse didn't need to glance back to know Sparrow's eyes had gone as wide as Athelas's favorite soup bowl, her face drained of color. She was fierce and tough, but the sight of drawn steel and an armed stranger in their midst was enough to startle even the older members of the Crimson Fang into momentary inaction. Only Natisse and Uncle Ronan had acted at the sound of L'yo's cry. Fortunately, Jad had recovered in time to intervene before the assassin resumed his onslaught.

"He's weak," Jad said, his deep voice firm, hard. "His wounds nearly killed him, and it was only by Cliessa's good fortune that he's still alive."

The assassin's face grew blank, his expression stony.

"What wounds?" he snarled. "What did you do to him?"

"We did nothing," Natisse snarled. "We *found* him like this."

"Look!" Jad called out. Natisse glanced back and found Jad had lifted Prince Jaylen's shirt to reveal the wound that had nearly did him in. "My words were no threat, assassin. If I don't tend to him *now*, he'll bleed out long before you can get him to a physicker. But I won't lift a finger to help him until I know you won't raise a hand against any of us. That's the threat."

"So be it." To Natisse's surprise, the assassin slid his weapons into the sheath at his waist. "Tend to him now."

"Not until you disarm," Uncle Ronan snarled. He waved his sword at the assassin's daggers. "Those and every other weapon you've got hidden on you, *Black Talon*."

The man raised an eyebrow, a look of surprise on his face. "I will relinquish none of my weapons, *General Andros*." He spoke the name with emphasis to match Uncle Ronan's pronouncement. "But I swear by my service to the Emperor that I will not draw them lest my life or that of the Prince's is threatened in any way."

Uncle Ronan bared his teeth. "You expect us to—"

"If you know what I am," the assassin said, his voice cold and terribly calm, "then you will know the oath I give you is not one any in my position would lightly break." He didn't advance, but he seemed to grow larger, his presence more forceful. "If you wish my weapons, you are welcome to come and take them."

Uncle Ronan actually took a half step forward.

"Enough!" Again, Jad's voice reverberated through the Burrow. This time, even Natisse, Uncle Ronan, and the assassin all turned their eyes toward him.

Jad knelt at the unconscious Prince's side, pressing a huge hand to the blood flowing from the re-opened wound. Sparrow was nowhere in sight—doubtless dispatched by Jad to fetch bandages or some herb or healing draught—and the rest of the Crimson Fang had formed a solid wall of glares and drawn weapons a few paces farther down the corridor.

"You want to keep your weapons? Fine!" Jad fixed a fiery stare on the assassin. "But if you break your oath, I'll let him die."

"So be it." The assassin inclined his head.

Sparrow raced back around the corner, a wad of fresh linens clutched in her hands. She slid to knees beside the fallen Prince and pressed the fabric against his wounds while Jad carefully lifted the unconscious young man into his huge arms.

The assassin shifted only slightly, but the action brought Natisse's head whipping around. The man advanced as if intending to follow. Uncle Ronan and Natisse both moved to stand in his way.

"Let him come," Jad said, a tone of command in his voice Natisse had rarely heard before. A strange aura seemed to come over him every time someone's life rested in his hands. The power of Naiera, goddess of healing, perhaps. "He has given us his word, and I have given mine. Let that be enough for now."

To Natisse's surprise, she actually found herself moving out of the way. Uncle Ronan was slower to act. His gaze fixed on the dark-cloaked man, his face creased with fury, suspicion, and indignation. Yet he, too, ultimately gave in and stepped aside.

The assassin looked between Natisse and Uncle Ronan for a moment, his gaze lingering on both as if taking their measure.

"I suggest you each pick a god and pray that boy survives," he said. Then, with a nod, he strode between them and marched after Jad.

The rest of the Crimson Fang took their cues from Uncle Ronan and Natisse, opening a path first for Jad and Sparrow to carry Prince Jaylen, then for the assassin to pass. All save Nalkin fixed the man with a mixture of angry, outraged, and apprehensive looks—which the assassin ignored.

Nalkin alone stayed planted. The stern-faced woman hurried past Uncle Ronan and Natisse to where L'yo leaned against the wall near the Burrow's entrance.

"Are you badly hurt?" she asked quietly, gripping her husband's arm.

L'yo muttered something and shook his head.

"Good." Nalkin gaped at the mess of fruits, vegetables, and bread that lay scattered around the man. "Then let's get this cleaned up before it's further damaged."

She bent to pick up the produce, and L'yo stooped to help, albeit more slowly. He didn't stray far from the wall—evidently, the assassin's blow had disoriented him more than he cared to show his wife and comrades—and swayed unsteadily every time he straightened.

"Dumast, take it!" Uncle Ronan's curse drew Natisse's attention back to the Crimson Fang's leader. He rotated his arms, wincing with the movement. The assassin's strikes had left no bruises on his elbows, but Natisse had sustained enough blows like that to know the pain resided within the bones.

"Binteth's jagged tooth, what just happened?" Natisse demanded. Her frustration flared, but it was a pale shadow of the rage that had gripped her and unleashed Golgoth's scorching power minutes earlier. She was angry, afraid for her people, worried. But her wellspring of wrath had died.

And there was something strange about Golgoth's reaction. The fire burning in Natisse's belly felt oddly diminished, as if the dragon no longer sensed a threat. From the man who had nearly killed her *twice* now?

That made no sense, but Natisse hadn't the time to consider it for the moment.

"Black Talon?" she asked, studying Uncle Ronan's face. "You know him?"

"Know him? No." Uncle Ronan shook his head. "But I know *of* him. I've known two of his predecessors, too."

Natisse waited, expectant. Uncle Roman seemed disinclined to elaborate, so she pressed the matter. "And? Who is he?"

Uncle Ronan didn't answer. Instead, he looked past Natisse. "Athelas, Haston, Leroshavé. Arm up and post yourselves outside Jad's quarters. Anything happens—should you hear a needle drop—I want you ready to fight."

"Yes, Uncle Ronan," Haston said, nodding. Athelas and Leroshavé both obeyed without a word, hurrying off with Haston to fetch *proper* swords to replace the compact knives they'd been wielding thus far.

Uncle Ronan turned to Nalkin and L'yo. "Get that food to the *Ghuklek*. Tobin and Garron can help."

"All the same," Garron said, his voice as gruff and dour as his scowl, "I'll be joining the others guarding Jad's quarters."

"Garron," Natisse began, "you've barely recove—"

Garron's dark eyes locked on hers. "If it comes to a fight in our home, I'm not bloody sitting out. No matter how many arms I lose."

"Go," Uncle Ronan said curtly before Natisse could protest. "Your sword is welcome."

Natisse's jaw dropped when Uncle Ronan turned on his heel and strode toward the Burrow's entrance—*away* from the armed assassin in their midst. She closed on the departing man, seized his wrist, and hauled hard, spinning him around.

"Where are you going?" she snarled.

"Out," Uncle Ronan snapped toward her. Clearly, he'd no more forgotten what had passed between them in the hallway than she had. An almost imperceptible blue fire flashed within his eyes. It was so quick, Natisse was left wondering if she'd imagined it. With that, he turned to stalk away.

Uncle Ronan's eyes might've given Natisse pause once. No longer. She'd lost all fear of him and whatever magic dwelt within him. All respect, too. Ever since she'd learned how long he'd been lying to her and all the Crimson Fang, how many Ezrasil-damned secrets he'd been keeping—this being just another reminder. Her earlier rage had faded but was not altogether gone.

"No!" She darted around him and drove a palm into his chest, hard enough to stop him in his tracks. "That's not good enough. Not anymore."

He opened his mouth to growl an angry retort, but she beat him to it.

"Where are you going?" she snarled again, taking a step closer to glare up at him. "You're abandoning us with an assassin inside our home. You give me an answer, damn it!"

"It's *because* of that assassin in our home that I have to leave," Uncle Ronan shot back.

Natisse frowned. "What does that mean?" She saw Uncle Ronan about to dismiss the question, to brush it off as he had so many other inquiries, expecting her to merely trust him. But those days were long over. "Explain that to me, now."

Uncle Ronan's jaw muscles twitched, his shoulders squaring as if prepared to fight, but Natisse didn't back down. She was too damned sick and tired of being played for a fool and kept in the dark.

Uncle Ronan seemed to realize that, to sense the new intractability she'd adopted. He knew how stubborn and determined she could be—he'd hammered that iron into her, after all—and so he *had* to know that offering anything but the answer she demanded would be wasting his breath.

He relented. "I need to know if he was sent for me, for you, or if, as he says, he's only here for the Prince."

Natisse cocked her head. "Why would he be here for either of us? And if he was, so what? There are ten of us and one of him."

"That is ten too few," Uncle Ronan said. "I've seen Black Talons fight before, watched them slaughter soldiers by the scores. He is just one man, and yet he is so much more."

His face hardened. Where Lumenator magic had just flared, now, a strange, unfamiliar shadow flashed in his eyes. It was *fear*, Natisse realized. The Crimson Fang's leader—and a former General of the Karmian Empire—was afraid.

"The Black Talon is no mere killer. He is the Emperor's personal assassin, and if he's come for either of us, then we are already dead."

22
KULLEN

Kullen paid the glaring insurrectionists no heed. His full attention was fixed on Jaylen, lying unconscious in the arms of the man called Jad. How young the Prince looked, a man barely out of his childhood years. Not much older than Kullen had been when Emperor Wymarc swore him into his personal service, but he'd lived a far softer and more sheltered life. Nothing had prepared him for the cruelty he'd endured at the hands of Magister Branthe. He'd come close to dying far too many times in the last day alone... and even now, looking at Jaylen's pale face, Kullen wasn't fully certain he'd pull through.

He hurried after Jad and his petite assistant into a small, earthen-walled room that housed two bloodstained cots, a chair, and a table upon which sat an assortment of herbs, spices, and vials.

Vials! Kullen reached into his pouch and drew out two of the healing draughts he'd procured from Serrod earlier.

"Here," he said, holding out the glass vials to Jad, who had set Jaylen gently down on one empty cot. "This could help to—"

Jad snatched the draughts from Kullen's hand with a grunt and nod, then turned back to his patient. A loud *pop* echoed in the room as Jad pulled the cork from the bottle, then the sound of pouring liquid.

Kullen tried to maneuver around Jad to get a better look, but there was no getting past those huge shoulders and broad back. He went the other way toward the foot of the cot, and there, had a clear view of the Prince's wound.

It was bad. Jaylen had taken a dagger or sword to the side,

lacerating organs and blood vessels. Someone, likely the giant, had attempted to stitch the wound shut, but the stitches had torn free, and the bleeding renewed.

"Tell me what to do," Kullen growled. "How can I help?"

Though he was no healer, he'd sewn up more than his share of wounds—his own. But he couldn't merely sit by and do nothing with Jaylen's life hanging in the balance.

"Just stay out of our way," Jad rumbled, a warning in his tone. "Sparrow and I have got this."

Kullen glanced at the young girl—Sparrow—who had plucked up a length of catgut thread and a sharp, hooked needle. She stood watching Jad pouring the contents of Serrod's vials onto the wound and down Jaylen's throat in equal measure. The former would slow the bleeding, but it was the latter that would accelerate the healing process.

"Needle," Jad said, holding out a hand without looking up from Jaylen.

Sparrow handed him both needle and thread. Nodding his thanks, he set to work stitching up the Prince's wounds.

Kullen had to hide his astonishment at the brute's skill. Some of the Palace's finest seamstresses would fail to match the dexterity and steadiness of his colossal hands. He moved quickly but carefully, sewing up Jaylen's wound with the tenderness of a tailor threading lace. It took him but a minute, perhaps two, to finish his work before he cut the thread with a pair of scissors the girl handed him. He spent the next long moments studying the Prince's face with a pensive frown.

Only then did he look up from Jaylen for the first time. "He'll live." He grunted in a manner sounding oddly satisfied. His blocky face turned to regard Kullen. "It was a close thing, but those draughts were the tipping point."

Kullen let out the breath he hadn't realized he was holding. An immense weight lifted from his shoulders, his worry draining away.

"Thank you," he said, sincerity in his voice.

Jad nodded. "I told you, we didn't do this to him. *Wouldn't* do this." He gestured to the Prince with one thick-fingered hand. "Only reason we brought him here was to save him. But he's no one's prisoner. As soon as he's strong enough, he's yours to take."

The words surprised Kullen. He'd come prepared for a fight—and he'd *gotten* one, no doubt about it—but the gentle giant's obvious care for Jaylen was far from what he'd expected. The man might be an insurrectionist, stirring up the Empire against its ruler, but this one small deed had shaken Kullen's certainty.

Mammy Tess's words echoed in his mind. *"The biggest heart of anyone I've met."*

"Jad, is it?" Kullen asked, careful to keep any hint of menace or threat from his voice.

The giant's blocky face hardened. "Jad," he confirmed, jaw muscles working. "This is Sparrow."

"Then you have my gratitude. Both of you." Kullen thrust out a hand toward the big man while regarding Sparrow with a soft smile. "Mine, and the Emperor's. That's his grandson you just saved."

Jad regarded Kullen's hand with a wary eye, then nodded and clasped it in his own. It wasn't exactly friendly—hard to be genial with the one who'd just tried to kill his comrades—but the big man's expression held a look of grudging acceptance. "Show it by leaving as soon as you can. And forgetting everything about us."

Kullen said nothing—he couldn't do the latter, and the former depended on Jaylen's condition—merely released his grip on the big man's hand.

"Come, Sparrow," Jad said, gesturing to the young girl. "Let's give our guests some space."

Sparrow's face set in a stubborn cast, but Jad's stern expression silenced whatever protest had been forming. Shooting a sharp glance at Kullen, she hurried toward the door and pushed it open. Outside, Kullen caught a glimpse of four armed men standing guard, swords drawn and faces hard. As expected. But they made no move to enter, merely stepped aside to let Sparrow through.

Jad followed Sparrow from the room and closed the door gently behind him, leaving Kullen alone in the room.

He breathed steadily for the first time since entering the room. Also a first, he registered the pungent smell of blood and healing concoctions of various sorts. The odor reminded him of Serrod's shop with a touch of mildew. The room was sparse but for the cots and a small ornamental statue upon a shelf to his far right. A few steps brought him before it, and he immediately recognized it. He lifted a hand, stroked the smooth wood. Dao, the god of healing and virtue.

All of these details washed over Kullen in a rush, the walls closing in around him and the world spinning. Adrenaline fading, exhaustion once again took firm hold of his mind and body. He managed to stumble over to the room's lone chair and sit before he collapsed. His legs felt like severed bowstrings, his head oddly heavy.

A maelstrom of emotions seethed within him. His relief at finding Jaylen alive clashed with the fear and worry over the Prince's dire condition. Not to mention the armed men standing outside this room. No telling if or when they would burst through the door. He'd killed one of their comrades only a few nights earlier. Just because they hadn't yet come for vengeance didn't mean they'd hold their blade for good.

He'd been so prepared for battle that he found himself at a loss for what to do now that the immediate threat had passed. Despite Jad's assurances that he would depart in peace, Kullen doubted General Andros was foolish enough to step aside and allow him to merely walk out of there with the Prince. Not when either one of them could report directly to the Emperor and reveal the Crimson Fang's location.

But none of that mattered at the moment. Jaylen was in no condition to travel, so Kullen wasn't going anywhere soon.

He leaned over the unconscious Prince. Jaylen's breathing was shallow, his cheeks pale, his face so listless. Were it not for the steady rise and fall of his chest, Kullen might've believed Jaylen dead. It had been a close thing.

"Don't worry," Kullen said into the empty silence of the room. "I'll watch over him." He spoke not to himself but to the Emperor and the memory of Jaylen's parents. Jarius and Hadassa had loved their son with every fiber of their being. Kullen owed it to them to keep their most treasured possession safe.

Reaching into his pouch, Kullen drew out the gold-capped vial he'd pilfered from Lord Branthe's corpse. It might've been his imagination, but it felt as if Tempest's blood stirred at the proximity to Jaylen, as if the dragon could sense its *bloodsworn*. Or some fraction of him. Kullen wrapped the gold chain around the Prince's hand and tucked the vial between his fingers.

"We'll both watch over him," he said quietly.

He had a great many fond memories of watching Jarius play with Tempest. The silver Wind Dragon had a sleeker, more avian-like body than Umbris or Thanagar, with broader wings perfectly suited for catching even the slightest updrafts and eddies in the air currents. How many times had Kullen and Hadassa stood enviously on the ground while Jarius soared among the clouds?

The bond between Jarius and Tempest had been no less fierce than the love the Prince had shared with his wife or his affection for his son. Jarius's death had nearly shattered the silver dragon, Emperor Wymarc had told him. Only the desire to protect his *bloodsworn's* son had kept Tempest anchored to the Mortal Realm through his immense sorrow.

Kullen sat back, leaning his head against the wall, his eyes moving between the sleeping Jaylen and the door. Or so he thought. Fatigue dragged at his eyelids, and his body grew heavy. As his breathing matched Jaylen's, sleep washed over him.

He must have dozed off because he started awake when the door latch *clicked*. He was on his feet, dagger half-drawn when he recognized the healer's hulking figure entering the room.

Jad gave him a pointed, scolding look but moved past Kullen without a word. Kullen glanced toward the door and, finding the armed insurrectionists outside making no attempt to rush him, sheathed his dagger.

He turned back to Jad, but the big man just gave a satisfied grunt and redressed Jaylen's wounds. A few moments later, the healer left without a word or a second glance at Kullen. Clearly, he had no fear of violence, not with the Prince's life on the line. That made *one* of them.

Kullen resumed his seat, but he didn't allow himself to relax. How long he'd slept, he didn't know. An hour, perhaps two? It was far from enough, but it would have to suffice.

"Ku... llen?"

The sound of his name brought Kullen's head whipping toward the cot where the Prince lie. Jaylen's eyes were open and clear, his skin a healthier shade of pink.

"What are you... doing here?" Jaylen's voice grew stronger with every word.

"I'm here for you," Kullen said. "I promised your grandfather I'd get you back in one piece." He gave the young man a wry smile. "Haven't failed yet, though you're not exactly making my job an easy one."

Jaylen's forehead scrunched up, a frown blossoming on his lips. "Why?"

The question confused Kullen. "What do you mean, why?"

"Why you?" Jaylen asked. "I thought he'd send Angban or Turoc or... or anyone else."

"Ahh," Kullen said, nodding in understanding. "I was the one who discovered what Magister Branthe had done. Thanks to Umbris, I could get there faster than anyone el—"

"No." Jaylen cut him off with a weak shake of his head. "Not last night. Now."

Kullen blinked, confused. The Prince knew of his duties as the Black Talon, of his loyalty to the Emperor. So why was he questioning—

"I can only imagine the lengths you went to in order to find me," Jaylen said. "But why? Why, when you hate me so much?"

The words stung Kullen like a blow to the face. "What?"

"I see it in your eyes, hear it in your voice every time you talk." The prince's eyes took on a steely edge Kullen had rarely witnessed before—at least not in *this* prince. "You despise me. And knowing that, I can't see why you would put yourself in this position, not when the Elite Scales and Orkenwatch would do. Even if Grandfather ordered you to, I—"

"I don't hate you." Kullen spoke the words before he realized them.

Jaylen's jaw clenched. "Of course you do. Maybe it's because you think my life is so easy compared to yours, or maybe you just don't like me for me. I've thought about it and never could figure it out."

"I *don't*," Kullen repeated. Looking at the Prince now, seeing that hard edge in his eyes, he was reminded of what Umbris had told him. And it suddenly made sense. "I don't hate you, Jaylen. It's just…" He let out a long breath. "You remind me so much of them. Of *both* of them. And of what I lost."

The Prince's eyes went wide. "What *you* lost? They were my parents!" The effort sent him coughing, wincing with the pain of it.

"And my friends," Kullen said when the fit ended. His words were so quiet they were nearly lost in the emptiness of the room. "More than just friends, really."

It felt strange sharing this part of himself with the Prince—who, in truth, he *had* disregarded and disdained for years, seeing him as a nuisance at best and a royal pain in his ass at worst. And yet, now that he had begun speaking, he found he couldn't stop. As if some part of him *wanted* to let someone else see this part of him that he kept so carefully hidden.

"Jarius wasn't just my charge to protect," Kullen said. "From the moment your grandfather brought me into the Palace, Jarius accepted me, even welcomed me. He became like the brother I never had. And your mother..."

He swallowed hard. Emperor Wymarc alone knew the truth, and perhaps not even the *fullness* of it. The monarch might've guessed—he was an intuitive, insightful man, after all—but he didn't know. Kullen had never spoken the words aloud to anyone.

"She's the only woman I ever loved." Until now.

Jaylen's eyes widened even more, going as round as one of Turoc's giant dinner plates.

"She and I were children together in the Refuge," Kullen said, staring down at his hands. "Orphans who Mammy Tess took in and brought up. I don't know when it happened—I couldn't have been more than ten or eleven—but she went from being my best friend, my *only* friend perhaps, to something more. I never got a chance to tell her, though. Before I could, she met your father, and that was it for her. For both of them. They loved each other, and I loved them both." He lifted his gaze to Jaylen. "And they loved you. With every breath in their bodies. I've never seen prouder parents. The three of you... you were perfect. Until..."

"Until the day." Jaylen's expression darkened. He was old enough to remember it all too clearly. "You weren't there."

"I wasn't." Kullen's hands balled into fists, his knuckles whitening. "I was with you that day. Teaching you the sword when I should've been at their side."

"Is that why you've hated me all these years?" Jaylen asked. "You blame *me* for your not being there?"

"No!" The vehemence in his voice surprised even Kullen. "No," he said, quieter. "I don't blame you. Not at all. I blame..." He shook his head. "I blame Magister Deckard, for it was *his* lust for power that led Golgoth to unleash her rage on Dimvein. I blame Magister Branthe, who I have cause to believe was the one who orchestrated their deaths. But you?" He blew out a breath. "No, Jaylen. I don't blame you. Nor do I hate you."

"I just remind you of them so much that it hurts." Jaylen seemed to finally understand what Kullen himself had only just realized.

"Yes," Kullen said, nodding slowly. "And it's not fair the way I've treated you all these years. So I'm sorry, my Prince." He said the words in a respectful tone, the tone he typically reserved for the Emperor. "I owe you—and them—better."

Jaylen grinned. "I'd say between your saving my royal person last night and being here now, you're well on your way to making up for it."

Kullen couldn't help a little chuckle. "Make sure to tell your grandfather that once I get you back to the Palace alive. He'll want to—"

His words were cut off by the sound of the door latch clicking. This time, he stopped himself from leaping to his feet and drawing weapons on the healer.

Only it wasn't the healer who strode into the room. The red-haired woman marched in with a determined step, chin held high, jaw set, and bright fires blazing in her eyes. She emanated a tangible aura of power, as if an inferno raged within her.

Kullen rose to his feet, prepared to meet an outpouring of fury. Yet, in that moment, he caught sight of something that chilled him to the bone.

Hanging around the woman's neck, suspended from a plain leather thong, was the missing vial of Golgoth's dragonblood.

23
Natisse

Uncle Ronan's ominous words had lingered in Natisse's mind long after he departed the Burrow. Try as she might to busy herself with other important tasks—feeding and tending to the injured *Ghuklek,* overseeing the restocking of supplies Jad and Leroshavé had purchased, and checking on L'yo—she couldn't shake the dread rising within her.

And it wasn't just the dread that had her on edge. Ever since she'd exploded on Uncle Ronan and Golgoth's voice echoed through her own, she couldn't stop shaking. It was only a slight tremor, but it unnerved her, made her feel... She wasn't sure what she felt. Anger? Frustration? Intolerance? All those things and more.

Eventually, there was no more to do. She resorted to stalking up and down the corridor outside Jad's room like a whitespine wolf on the prowl. The room where the Black Talon—apparently, the Emperor's personal assassin if Uncle Ronan could be believed—sat at Prince Jaylen's side. Just because he hadn't murdered them all yet didn't mean he *wouldn't*. Natisse felt as if they'd just caged a dragon, and only a few planks of wood separated them from certain death.

She wanted to storm into that room and confront him head-on. If he intended to kill them, better she took the fight to him. But she couldn't bring herself to do it. Not with Uncle Ronan's dire warning ringing in her mind. *"If he's come for either of us, then we are already dead."*

Hours passed—two, perhaps three—and still, Uncle Ronan did not return. Natisse envisioned him meeting with that nameless contact in the dark tunnels. Whoever the bastard was, she could only hope he had information of value.

Haston, Garron, Athelas, and Leroshavé watched her with worry written plain on their expressions. The four fingered their weapons, visibly nervous. Athelas and Leroshavé exchanged apprehensive glances with one another and eyed the door as if getting up their courage to storm in. Garron was as dour as ever, too smart and cautious to pick a fight unless necessary, especially against a man who had just disarmed L'yo with ease and fought both Uncle Ronan and Natisse to a standstill. Haston tried unsuccessfully to hide his unease. He stood guard but took up position against the wall opposite the door. Though the former thief could never be accused of lacking courage, he wasn't the sort to rush in like a hot-headed fool, either.

At some point, Jad entered the room to check on the unconscious Prince. Natisse fought back the instinctive worry surging within her. She didn't trust the Black Talon, oath or no. But she *did* trust Jad. He seemed unconcerned by the assassin's presence, outwardly treating the man like any other patient.

Yet she only breathed easier when he emerged from the chamber a minute after he'd entered, alive and unharmed.

"How is he?" she asked once he'd closed the door behind him.

"Sleeping, but better." Jad gave her a relieved smile. "Assassin had a couple of healing draughts. No Gryphic Elixir, but they helped."

Natisse winced at the mention of the substance she now knew was *Ghuklek* blood. Did Jad know? No, she decided, he couldn't.

"Best he sleeps for a while," Jad continued. "Though if he wakes up, it'll be good to get some broth in him. You hear anything from our guests, you let me know, and I'll send Sparrow with a bowl."

"Will do," Natisse said. He looked and sounded so calm—too calm, compared to the anxiety worming deeper in her belly. "Guests," he'd called them, as if they weren't the future ruler of the Karmian Empire and one of the most dangerous men alive.

She turned to march on, but Jad caught her by the arm.

"Natisse," he rumbled.

His tone got her attention. When she glanced back at him, she saw worry there on his face. Worry for *her*.

"You're not doing anyone any good stomping around," he said, pitching his voice low for her ears only. Which was silly, given that there were four of her comrades standing mere paces away, and Jad's deep voice carried. "Maybe you get some rest, or food. Anything's better than stalking up and down these halls like a mother krae bear and making everyone nervous."

"I'm going nowhere," Natisse shot back. She managed to keep a tight rein on her anger… barely. She wasn't mad at Jad—he was only trying to help—but the situation in which they found themselves infuriated her. They were just supposed to sit by and do nothing until the assassin who killed Baruch decided to finish what he'd started? "I'm staying right here until I know for sure what's happening." Until either Uncle Ronan returned or she had a *proper* conversation with the Black Talon. "One way or another, I need to know so we can be prepared."

"For what?" Jad asked.

"You know what!" Natisse snarled. "He's not just walking out of here and forgetting us. That means we need to come to some kind of arrangement, or…" She left the words unspoken.

"The Prince, too?" Jad cocked one bushy eyebrow. "After all I've done to nurse him back to health?"

"*I* won't be the one who forces that particular issue." Anger edged Natisse's words. "But if he gives us no choice, we'll do what needs to be done." She dropped her hand to the hilt of her lashblade—and found she'd been gripping it in a white-knuckled fist already.

Jad gave a half grunt, half sigh but said no more. What was there to say? Jad might be disinclined to violence, but she had no qualms about slitting that murdering bastard's throat should it prove necessary. For Baruch's sake, if not for the rest of the Crimson Fang's.

Releasing her arm, Jad headed down the corridor toward the room that had once been Baruch and Ammon's. Since his quarters had been converted into a makeshift infirmary, he'd used that room to grab a short rest between treating the Prince, the *Ghuklek*, and the Crimson Fang's injured.

Natisse watched him go, then resumed her prowling. She never strayed far from the door, her ears attuned to even the slightest sound from within.

Jad's words gnawed at her. She'd never shied away from killing, but only when it proved utterly necessary. Try as she might to tell herself that *this* was as necessary as it got, she couldn't believe it. Not truly. Much as she would relish the Black Talon's death—she owed Baruch that much—he hadn't *yet* shown any intention of killing them. His attack on L'yo had been intended to disarm and disorient. He'd taken Uncle Ronan down with nonlethal, incapacitating strikes. And though she had unleashed her lashblade against him, thinking back, she recognized the truth of his counterattacks. He'd gotten inside her guard not to put a dagger in her belly—he'd proven that much when he punched rather than stabbed her—but to stop her from cutting *him* open.

Even if she could stomach the notion of slaying the assassin, Prince Jaylen was a different matter. She couldn't raise a hand against a man in his condition. Even if that man happened to be the future ruler of the Karmian Empire. Doing so would make her as bad as every Magister, criminal, and bully boy the Crimson Fang had brought down. She would not abuse her skill, training, and newfound magical abilities in that way.

To her surprise, she sensed Golgoth's approval echoing through their bond. Could the dragon read her mind? More likely, she was feeling the fiery swirl of emotions in Natisse's heart. Whatever the case, the dragon endorsed her thoughts. That was, in great part, why Golgoth said she'd chosen Natisse.

So she couldn't just strike out at either the assassin or the Prince, even if their deaths meant her people would be safe. That left just one course of action. And action was precisely what she felt she needed. She was sick and tired of just waiting.

Jaw clenched, fire coursing through her veins, Natisse stalked toward the door to Jad's room.

"Step aside," she snapped, "but do *not* enter unless I call out for help."

"Natisse," Garron began, the worried look on his face deepening, "perhaps we should—"

Natisse stalked past, ignoring the rangy man. She shot a fierce glare at Haston and Leroshavé. They'd made their intentions toward the Prince very plain a few hours earlier, and she couldn't afford for them to burst into the room at the wrong moment.

"Stay!" she snapped.

The little Brendoni nodded hastily and stepped back. Natisse didn't wait to see Haston's reaction, just marched toward the door, seized the handle, and pulled it open.

Inside, the Black Talon sat in the hard-backed wooden chair next to the Prince's bed. It looked as if they had been talking, and her arrival cut them off mid-conversation. The assassin's head snapped toward her, and he rose instantly. It wasn't an abrupt scramble or startled leap to his feet but a fluid movement as graceful and nimble as a Hudarian twill bird in flight. One moment, he appeared relaxed and at ease; the next, he stood, his eyes locked on her.

She'd marched into the room, determined to demand answers. Only she never got the chance to speak. Before she could unleash the angry words forming on her lips, a dagger sprouted in the assassin's hand, and he was lunging for her. So surprised was

Natisse, that she didn't remember to cry out. Instinctively, she twisted out of the way of his bared steel and dropped her hand to her lashblade.

The Black Talon pursued her, silent and swift. His free hand clamped around her wrist, preventing her from drawing her weapon, and his dagger darted toward her neck. Natisse managed to get a hand up to catch his right wrist, and she gave it a savage wrench. It felt as if she'd just attempted to twist a steel bar and had about as much effect. Too late, she realized her strength was no match for his. She barely managed to backpedal, desperate to keep the razor-sharp blade from slicing into her flesh. The assassin pursued until her back met the wall, and the dagger was at her throat.

She braced herself for the inevitable pain, the icy chill of steel parting flesh, the warm spurt of blood gushing from her severed throat. It felt so foolish, dying like this. In her anger, she'd disregarded Uncle Ronan's warning about the Black Talon. Now, she would pay the price with her life.

Only death never came. The assassin kept the dagger pressed there against the supple flesh of her throat, but he made no move to cut. His eyes fixed not on her face but at her chest. That struck her as terribly odd. Odder still, his words.

"That does not belong to you!" he snarled. His gaze rose to meet hers now, and Natisse felt the urge to recoil from the inky blackness billowing behind his eyes. "Return what you stole, and I will not kill you here and now."

It took Natisse's whole mind to realize what he'd been staring at. Careful of the knife's sharp blade, she shifted her face downward at the gold-capped vial hanging from Jad's leather thong around her neck.

That surprised Natisse almost as much as the sudden ferocity of his attack. The anger that had been building within her erupted before she could stop it.

"And what of your oath?" she snarled. "Or does your word as the Black Talon mean so little?"

"I gave you my oath in good faith," the assassin snapped back. "But I am duty bound to protect the Empire from *all* threats, and what you hold is a threat far greater than you realize. Threat enough that *every* one of you will die if you do not return it to me."

What remained of the restraints containing Natisse's fury shattered in full.

This Ezrasil-cursed prick had dragged Baruch to his death in Blackwater Bay, trespassed upon their home, raised weapons to her and her family, putting the Crimson Fang at dire risk. And now, he dared threaten her. He *dared* threaten *her*?

She felt a tingle of power at her fingertips, white, hot, burning fire. With speed and strength far greater than her own—Golgoth's, some part of her mind understood—she shoved the assassin away. He flew backward hard enough to slam against the chamber's opposite wall with jarring force and crumple onto the wooden chair, shattering it. Though to his credit, he was back on his feet in a heartbeat, dagger still held at the ready, eyes blazing.

But Natisse burned with a fire of her own.

"You want it?" she snarled. Then, repeating the assassin's own words, she added, "Come and take it."

As if her threat gave permission to the dragon within, Golgoth's flames burst forth from her hands in a tumultuous golden wave.

24
KULLEN

Kullen's vision spun—and not *only* from his head using the wall like a springboard. The red-haired woman's impossible burst of strength had caught him off guard, but the sight of her hands bursting into flames stunned him motionless. But only for an instant. He threw himself to the side, fearing that fire would emulsify him. But when he looked up, he saw the golden tongues lash out and dissipate mere inches in front of her before returning to her clenched fists.

Impossible! They licked up her fingers, palms, and wrists. Her eyes—icy blue a moment earlier—now shone a deep scarlet, as if they, too, burned. He couldn't believe it, yet there was no denying the evidence his eyes offered.

The woman wielded Golgoth's power.

How? The realization boggled his mind. *I just killed Deckard last night!*

Then he realized what night it had been. The night of the blood moon, when dragons took on new bonds. Magister Deckard's death had freed Golgoth from her servitude, but instead of retreating to the Fire Realm, she had chosen to bind herself to this woman.

But why? Kullen could understand at least partly what Golgoth had seen in her. She was fierce, fiery, and driven. That much had become perfectly clear over their few encounters—more confrontations, really. But what was it about this woman that intrigued Golgoth so that she would willingly submit to the *bloodbond* so soon after earning her freedom from Magister Deckard's cruelty?

Curiosity blazed within Kullen—he wanted to know, to understand why this seemingly ordinary woman was special enough to compel the mighty Ember Dragon to accept the bond—but he had no time to consider it further. The woman advanced on him, clenched fists and eyes ablaze.

"Wait!" He raised his free hand to halt her and slid his dagger into its scabbard slowly so as not to startle her into attack. "There is no need for us to be at odds. Not anymore."

That seemed to confuse her. As well it should've. Had he been in her position, he wouldn't have understood why he went from threatening to kill her to sheathing his weapon in the space of mere heartbeats.

"That vial you wear," he said by way of explanation, "you know its purpose, its power?" Looking at the tongues of fire sprouting from her balled fists, she clearly did. "You bonded with Golgoth last night."

The woman's jaw clenched. "And so what if I did?" she snarled, every muscle in her body rigid, tensed for attack.

"If you did," Kullen said, careful to keep his voice calm, his tone neutral, "then by all rights, it *is* yours. Though you took it from me, by virtue of Golgoth's bond, it belongs to you now."

He saw the words sinking in, saw the moment she understood. The fires wreathing her hands shrank, then died without so much as a puff of smoke, and the smoldering embers in her eyes cooled. Something Kullen interpreted as relief flickered behind those crystalline eyes. Whether it was an understanding that their fight had come to an end or that the dragon's influence had left, he didn't know.

The former made sense only if she knew that he, too,

commanded the strength of a dragon, though he didn't think that was true. For if she believed she alone bore that power, she could've killed him without the slightest worry. The latter, however, Kullen understood with intimate clarity. The first time he'd tapped into Umbris's abilities, it had terrified him speechless. It had taken him years to learn to separate Umbris's thoughts and emotions from his own. Even now, he often found himself influenced by the Twilight Dragon.

The tension in her posture, however, lessened not at all. Nor did she lower her fists or relax her fighting stance.

"Just like that?" the woman asked.

"Just like that." Kullen gave a little shrug, careful to keep his hands well away from his weapons. "I do not claim to understand all there is to know about the dragonblood magic and the *bloodbond*, but I *do* know that you only access Golgoth's power because she wills it." He grimaced. "The last time someone attempted to force her into submission, her flames burned the Imperial Commons to embers. The fire that destroyed Magister Branthe's fighting pit last night was alchemical, not dragon-made. Therefore, it can only be concluded that Golgoth *chose* you."

The words were true, though why, he didn't know. But he damned well intended to find out.

She seemed surprised, her eyes narrowing and a furrow deepening her forehead. "How do you know this?"

Kullen let a small smile play across his face. So she didn't know. That left one fewer question in his mind. He reached beneath his shirt and drew out Umbris's vial.

"Because of this."

That sent the woman's eyes wide. She took a step back, her hand dropping to the whip-like blade at her hip.

"I have no intention of using any magic against you," Kullen said, his voice calm. "Nor raising my blades again." In truth, he'd merely uttered the threat intending to scare her into returning Golgoth's vial. The fact that she'd bonded with the dragon changed a great deal. His mission here had just taken an interesting new turn. "My oath still stands. As soon as the Prince is recovered, I will take him away from here."

"You expect to simply walk away?" the woman demanded. The fire in her eyes blazed bright once more, her jaw taking on a stubborn set. "You clearly know who we are, and now, where to find us. Surely you cannot believe we're fools enough to let you depart with that knowledge."

"No one could ever accuse General Andros of being a fool," Kullen said.

That elicited an interesting reaction from the woman. Instead of glowing with pride at the recognition of her leader's skill, mention of the legendary name actually seemed to make her *angrier.* Her scowl deepened, and she looked as if she wanted to strike him.

He didn't understand her response, but one thing he knew for certain: he couldn't antagonize her. Though the healer might've given his word that he and the Prince could leave, this woman clearly wielded power in the Crimson Fang's organization. She and General Andros had been first into the fray, and just having spent a few moments speaking with her, Kullen had no doubt her force of character made her a leader among her insurrectionists. Backed with Golgoth's power and the skill to use that vicious whip-blade, she was *not* an enemy he wanted to make at the moment.

Unfortunately, he felt confident that an enemy was exactly how she viewed him. He'd killed her comrade that night on the rowboat. He'd invaded her underground stronghold, hurt her people, and just threatened her. The fact that he'd saved her life the previous night couldn't begin to make up for it. It would take real work to change her perspective of him.

"I understand that you will not easily accept me at my word," Kullen said, "but I offer it anyway. I have no intention of harming you or your people."

"Or turning us over to your Emperor?" Her ice-blue eyes darted past Kullen toward the Prince. "His grandfather?"

Kullen glanced over his shoulder. Jaylen had found the strength to prop himself up onto one elbow but couldn't summon the energy to rise. He'd said nothing throughout the brief exchange; his face was still pale, his breathing shallow, and he clutched Tempest's vial to his chest, as if calling on the Wind Dragon for fortitude.

"The Prince has greater concerns to occupy his attention," Kullen said. "Chief among them, learning to one day rule the Empire. I'm certain he will be quite forgetful of anything that transpired after he sustained such a grievous wound." He tapped the side of his head. "Blood loss has a way of muddying recollections."

"Y-Yes!" Prince Jaylen stammered, giving a vigorous nod. "Can't remember a blasted thing that happened. Just collapsing in the night, then waking up here. Where here is, I haven't a clue!"

The woman pursed her lips in contemplation. Jaylen's words seemed to confirm Belto's story that Jaylen had been carried unconscious into the sewers. Only now, it appeared that had been with the intention of *saving* him, not kidnapping him to use as leverage against the Emperor.

"And what of you?" The red-haired woman turned icy eyes on him. "You know too much."

Kullen heard the underlying threat in her words. He didn't blame her.

"I do," he said, inclining his head. "But I am willing to strike a bargain with you."

The woman's eyes narrowed. "What bargain?"

"First," Kullen said with a grin, "a simple exchange. Of names." He pressed a hand to his chest and gave a little bow. "I am Kullen, Black Talon of the Karmian Empire."

The woman stared at him long and hard. Fraught silence stretched between them, the air within the room as tense as a drawn bowstring. One wrong word, one wrong move, and it would snap. He had to play this cautiously, slowly. He needed to get a better sense of who she was—not just the skilled, defiant rebel, but the woman beneath. He needed to understand what Golgoth had seen in her. Only then would he know what manner of threat she *truly* posed to the Emperor and the Empire.

After long seconds, the woman spoke. "Natisse."

Kullen raised an eyebrow. "I'd say pleased to meet you, Natisse"—he liked the way her name rolled off the tongue—"but I suspect that our past encounters have soured your opinion of me."

Natisse snorted. "Who knew that killing someone's friend was likely to make them hate you?"

Kullen hid a grin. Scornful words were far better than drawn weapons. Progress in the right direction.

"Prince Jaylen, you already know," he said, gesturing with a thumb toward the young man lying on the cot behind him. "And thus, our first bargain is concluded to the satisfaction of all. Leading us to our *second* bargain."

Natisse's eyes narrowed. "And what, pray tell, would that be?"

"Simple." Kullen now allowed the smile to show on his face. "I trade my silence in exchange for your allowing us to leave." He held up a finger. "*And* your allowing me to help you understand the power you now wield."

Natisse's expression had *almost* softened at the mention of his silence, but the latter half of his offer brought the hardness right back.

"You think I want your help?" she snapped. "Much less *need* it?"

Kullen raised an eyebrow. "Perhaps not the former," he said, "but I suspect the latter more than you realize."

It was immediately clear he'd chosen his words poorly. She took a step forward, every muscle in her body tensing.

"I do not know how familiar you are with the *bloodsurge*," he said quickly, "but I remember how overwhelming it felt when first I was learning the full extent of my abilities. There is a great deal to understand about the dragonblood magic, both its capabilities and its limitations."

That seemed to resonate with her. Her neck muscles relaxed. Though in noticing that, Kullen also noticed something else—scar tissue running from beneath her collar up to the lines of her chin and behind her ear. His immediate thought lent itself to believing she'd played with Golgoth's magic and suffered for it. But no, she'd only made the *bloodbond* the evening prior. This was an old wound.

"Go on," she said, pulling him back to the present.

He cleared his throat. "Again, I do not claim to be an expert in the ways of magic, but what I can explain, I will. In exchange, I offer my word that I will speak nothing of this place or your people to my Emperor." Unless the Crimson Fang's actions directly threatened the safety of the Karmian Empire or its monarch, he thought but left unsaid. His oath to serve Emperor Wymarc superseded all others—save, perhaps, for the vow he and Umbris had sworn through the *bloodbond*.

For a moment, he thought she might accept his offer.

"No," she said, shaking her head. "That is not an acceptable bargain."

Kullen's heart sank. "Then what do you—"

"I *will* let you both leave in exchange for your silence," Natisse said, stabbing a finger at him and Jaylen. "But that is where our deal ends."

Kullen kept his dismay carefully hidden and his tone neutral.

"So be it." He shouldn't have been surprised. After what had happened to her comrade, Baruchel Sallas, she had every reason to despise and distrust him. "I accept your counteroffer."

He held out a hand to her. She stared at it as she would a viper coiled to strike. Only after long seconds did she take it.

Her hand was warm. Too warm. She held it long seconds, and Kullen felt his own searing beneath its grasp. Umbris stirred within him as if in response to the threat.

It's okay, Kullen thought, directing the unspoken words toward his friend. *Steady.*

He met her eyes, saw the flicker of Dragonfire burning there. Despite what he'd said, he had no intentions of leaving the matter alone. Natisse had become too powerful for him to merely walk away. She commanded a dragon—and not just *any* dragon, but Golgoth herself! Alone, she represented a potentially serious threat to the Empire. But what if she were *not* alone?

Golgoth's wasn't the first dragonblood vial to go missing. More had been filched from the corpses of Magisters Iltari, Estéfar, Perech, Taradan, and Oyodan. Perhaps others neither he, Turoc, nor Assidius yet knew of.

If the Crimson Fang had them as well, there could be an army of *bloodsurging* insurrectionists hiding in these very underground tunnels. Much as he *hoped* Mammy Tess was a good judge of the Crimson Fang's character—she'd clearly gotten a good sense of the healer, Jad, or at least the part of him that *hadn't* been blood raging the previous night—he couldn't leave this place without a great deal more certainty.

"I'll stay only until the Prince is well enough to travel," he said. "But stay, I will."

And he would ensure they were no true threat to Emperor Wymarc. He would learn all he could about their purpose and plans. He would discover the motives behind the murders of these Magisters. If the answers satisfied him, his word would remain unbroken. He and Jaylen would leave and never speak of this place and its inhabitants ever again.

However, should their mission prove a danger to the sovereignty of the Karmian Empire, he would still leave, but the corpses of every last one of the Crimson Fang would remain as food for the rodents. And Natisse would be the first to taste his steel.

25
NATISSE

Natisse studied every inch of the Black Talon's face. It was handsome but hard, worn, and dark. Not only his exceptionally dusky eyes, but his black hair, beard, and cloak made him appear like a creature born of shadow itself. She watched the movement of the minuscule muscles around his mouth and eyes in search of any hint of deceit. Uncle Ronan had trained her to spot the signs.

She could feel the underlying tension beneath his outward calm. Not surprising, given that he stood surrounded by enemies. But there was more to it than that. More than likely, it had something to do with Golgoth.

He'd reacted so violently to seeing the dragonblood vial. Clearly, he understood the power it represented. Yet his mood had changed so suddenly, it left her reeling. His offer to explain the intricacies of the magic—*bloodsurge*, he'd called it?—came as a surprise. Even more surprising was the realization that the offer had been genuine.

She released his hand—a strong, callused hand, a fighter's hand—and stepped back.

"Even after I walk out of this place, my offer stands," said the Black Talon. Kullen. "*Bloodsurging* has its limitations and dangers.

Better you learn about them from me rather than finding out the hard way yourself."

Natisse had to stifle a snort of derision. She found it difficult to believe the magic had *any* limitations. Not when the Magisters wielded unchecked power—power derived from both their access to dragons and their immense fortunes.

"I'll be fine," Natisse snapped. She had no desire to be treated like a callow novice, especially not by *him.*

"I certainly hope so." Kullen gave her a small smile, far too confident for her liking. "All the same, if you have any questions, I will be here as long as the Prince is convalescing."

"So, hopefully, not too long." Natisse couldn't stop herself from spitting out the words. For all his apparent geniality, she couldn't shake the memory of his dagger pressed against her throat. Or that same blade protruding from Baruch's back. Whatever façade he donned, whatever masquerade of cordiality he affected, she would *never* forget what he'd done.

She felt the fire surging within her, anger fanning the flames of Golgoth's power roiling in her belly. But she'd be damned if she let him see the effect he was having on her. Turning on her heel, she marched from the room.

Athelas, Leroshavé, and Haston all jumped back as she emerged. The guilty expressions on their faces told her they'd been listening at the door. Fortunately for her, the doors were constructed by skilled hands, thick and not susceptible to eavesdropping—no matter how loud things had gotten. But, if, by some miracle, they'd heard what she and the assassin had discussed…

"Is Uncle Ronan back?" she demanded of Garron. He alone hadn't moved but stood leaning against the wall with a sword gripped lightly in his one remaining hand.

The laconic man just shook his head silently.

Natisse nodded. "Anyone need anything?"

"All's well, it seems," Haston put in. "*Ghuklek* are fed. L'yo and Nalkin are resting. Tobin's in the common room working on some manner of meal, if you're hungry."

Natisse was about to deny it, but her stomach chose that moment to issue a loud rumble. She couldn't remember the last time she'd partaken of anything more than crumbs or drink. She set off down the corridor, but not without giving her companions a stern glare and warning them, "No one enters."

"Sparrow came by a few minutes ago," Athelas said. "Brought some broth, but we figured it was best we keep her away for now."

"Where's she now?" Natisse looked between the four.

Garron nodded his head toward the common room.

"I'll send her in." Natisse skewered Athelas, Haston, and Leroshavé with another look. "But none of *you* goes in."

"You trust her alone with him?" Leroshavé scowled and toyed with the hilt of his sword.

"You trust *him* alone with her?" Haston added.

"He won't harm her," Natisse shot back, "and she, at least, I can trust not to try anything foolish that'll get her killed."

Athelas and Leroshavé both hung their heads, and Haston had the good grace to look ashamed. Garron just grunted and said nothing. Natisse didn't know what was going on in his head—she rarely did, and he rarely deigned to speak his thoughts aloud—but felt confident he wouldn't do anything foolhardy. Though he still had full use of his sword arm, his balance would be off, his strength depleted by the healing process. He'd be far from at full fighting capacity for a while yet.

Especially against him…

Natisse did her best to silently convey her thoughts to Garron. There was no need to embarrass the man. He was proud—and rightly so. Thankfully, he nodded, understanding. Trusting him to keep the others out of trouble, Natisse headed toward the common room.

Sparrow sat alone at one of the tables, a half-empty bowl of partially congealed broth sitting in front of her. Of Tobin, Natisse saw no visible sign, though she more than heard the clatter and clack of cookware echoing through the narrow door that led into the Burrow's kitchen.

Sparrow looked up at Natisse's approach and scrambled to her feet. "Jad said the Prince should have some broth. Get his strength up."

"Go," Natisse said, nodding. "You've nothing to fear from the Black Talon."

Sparrow appeared unconvinced, hesitating as she picked up the bowl.

"Trust me, Sparrow." Natisse was surprised by the confidence in her own voice. It was a strange certainty she felt—not only her own but Golgoth's, too—yet there was no doubt in her mind. "He won't lay a finger on you." He wouldn't offer to educate her in the ways of *bloodsurge* magic one moment and murder her friend the next. "Just go in, leave the bowl, and get out if you're not comfortable."

"I'll be fine." Sparrow lifted her chin resolutely. "Should I..." She paused. "Should I bring *him* some, too?"

Natisse considered that. "No need," she said, shaking her head. "He's neither our patient nor our guest."

Sparrow stared for a moment, still unsure.

"I'll finish yours, though," Natisse said.

"Right," Sparrow said, leaving her bowl and hurrying from the common room.

Before Natisse could move to take a seat or enter the kitchen, Tobin bustled through the door.

"Oh!" The slim young man stopped, startled by her presence. "I... er... I c-can... er..." He collected himself. "Y-You hungry?" He looked down at the paltry bowl of broth. "That... I'm sorry. I've got a s-stew on the s-simmer. Should b-be ready a-any time now."

Natisse nodded. "I'd love that. Thank you, Tobin."

The young man scrubbed a hand down his face, leaving behind a white streak of flour on his cheek, and blushed to the roots of his hair. "Sure-sure thing!" He rushed forward to remove the broth.

Natisse stopped him with a raise of her hand. "Leave it," she said. "I'm sure it'll be a great appetizer."

Tobin looked horrified at the thought but did as he was told. "Stew, c-coming right up."

He turned without another word to race back into the kitchen.

Natisse raised an eyebrow. *Well, that's new. Shouldn't be surprised, though, I suppose. Lad his age...*

She shook her head and took a seat at the table, sipping slowly at Sparrow's remaining broth. It was fine, if not good. Still warm. Salty and hit a spot Natisse didn't know needed hitting.

More noise came from the kitchen. Then, a loud curse.

Natisse snickered.

Tobin spent most of his time under the wings of Nalkin and L'yo—the pair, unable to have children of their own, had all but adopted him. He traveled with them on their missions away from Dimvein and generally stayed within their direct line of sight even when in the capital. The young man had a knack for getting into all sorts of trouble. Between his natural clumsiness, his too-innocent look, the perpetual stutter, and his tendency to say the wrong thing at the wrong time, he typically needed a minder watching over him.

Not so, Sparrow. The young girl was highly competent, skilled not only as a healer but a pickpocket and spotter. She had the savvy of one who'd grown up on the streets. Tobin had, too, though he'd never managed to grow much in the way of smarts. His eager willingness to help made him best suited to running the Crimson Fang's errands.

As if on cue, Tobin emerged from the kitchen carrying a bowl of thick stew. Which he promptly proceeded to spill when he tripped over his feet. Natisse hid a grimace and responded to his embarrassed apologies with kind, soothing words.

He quickly rushed back to the kitchen to fetch another. As soon as he was gone, Natisse's mind once again set to spinning.

For all her mistrust of the Black Talon, his offer held more appeal than she cared to admit. She understood so little of the power coursing through her. Golgoth hadn't exactly been forthcoming with advice or instruction on how to master her Dragonfire. The magic had bubbled up from within her with a force beyond her control. What if that had happened at another moment—in the middle of some Crimson Fang mission that relied on stealth or subterfuge? What use would she be to the mission if she couldn't gain some semblance of mastery?

Yet thoughts of the so-called "mission" only made the fire within her surge more out of control. They were Uncle Ronan's missions, Uncle Ronan's grand schemes. Only he *wasn't* truly Uncle Ronan. He had spent years lying to her face. Somehow, that made her hate him even more than she hated the assassin who had killed Baruch.

Tobin emerged from the kitchen at that moment. This time, he managed to set down the bowl in front of her without spilling too much of it. Natisse thanked him, which only made him blush all the deeper.

"I hope you l-l-like it."

Natisse handed him the nearly empty bowl of broth.

"If it's half as good as this…"

Tobin's face went red again. He smiled for the briefest moment before his face returned to a horror-stricken state. Then, he whirled and rushed back to the kitchen.

Natisse sighed and watched the door to the kitchen swing shut behind the young man. That could grow wearisome if allowed to persist. She'd have a talk with Nalkin about—

"Natisse." Uncle Ronan's voice echoed through the common room. "I'm back."

"So I see," Natisse snapped. The anger in her voice matched the fire burning in her belly, so she attempted to quash *both* by taking a long sip of the stew. Tobin might be far-from-useful on most Crimson Fang missions, but he had an impressive grasp of the culinary arts.

Uncle Ronan ignored her ill temper and sat across the table from her. She could feel his eyes on her, so she purposely fixed her own gaze on the stew. She wouldn't give *him* the satisfaction of seeing her anger, either.

Long moments passed while Natisse ate and ignored Uncle Ronan. His patience finally ran out.

"I spoke to my contact," he said, his voice a cold growl. "We're not in danger. The Black Talon hasn't been dispatched for us, only to retrieve the Prince for his grandfather."

Had he told her the same thing a week earlier, she would have merely accepted it at face value. Now, however, she couldn't help questioning *everything*. Who was his mysterious contact, and how did they have such thorough knowledge of the Black Talon's activities? She hadn't seen the man who Uncle Ronan had met, only knowing it was a man by the voice.

"Who is he?" Natisse asked, lifting her gaze to meet his. "This contact of yours in the Palace who seems to know the Emperor's every command."

Uncle Ronan's face hardened. "Natisse, I cannot—"

"Cannot tell me?" She slapped a palm on the table. "There seems to be a bloody lot you cannot tell me!"

"This again?" Uncle Ronan threw up his hands. "Will you not see reason? Surely you must understand why I didn't reveal the details of who I once was."

"No, *Uncle Ronan*," Natisse bit off the words like a curse. "I don't understand." She shoved aside the bowl roughly, slopping stew on her hands, and leaned toward him. "Explain it to me!"

Uncle Ronan ground his teeth, clutched the table so hard his fingers turned white. "Because General Andros is dead. Has been for decades. The name remains, but the man to whom it belonged died long ago."

Natisse's eyes went to the thick scar running along Uncle Ronan's neck. It looked an awful lot like a rope burn, truth be told.

"And what, you didn't tell me because you didn't think I needed to know?" She balled her fists in her lap, her arm muscles cording in fury. "You didn't think Ammon or Baruch or Jad or any of the others needed to know? Let me guess: Need to know basis?"

"That's right." Uncle Ronan's voice was so cold, so calm. He'd always been pragmatic; Natisse had long admired that about him.

Now, the cost of that pragmatism was a gulf yawning between them; one she wasn't certain could ever be bridged.

"And that's why I'm bloody angry," Natisse snarled. Fire surged in her eyes, and she fought to control it. She had no desire to burst into flames in front of *him*. "Because you made that decision for us and can't see why it's wrong."

She flung herself to her feet, but Uncle Ronan leaped up, too, blocking her exit. "Damn it, Natisse, enough of this!" His voice cracked like a whip. "We're still far from done, and I need you."

A million responses flooded into Natisse's mind, but instead, she chose silence. Uncle Ronan took that as a cue to continue.

"I've got a plan to get the *Ghuklek* out of Dimvein and back to the Riftwild. It's going to take every one of us to complete this mission, what with the Imperial Scales out in full force and—"

"You can take your missions and rot in Shekoth's pits!" Natisse marched straight at him, fully intending to go through him if necessary. "Every one of them is a lie. A lie you expected us to swallow without hesitation. But I'm *done* with your horse-shite missions!"

"They're not horse-shite," Uncle Ronan growled, his grizzled face darkening. "Every one of them serves a greater purpose."

"And what greater purpose is that?" Natisse demanded. "Is it all about regaining your power, General Andros?"

"General Andros is bloody dead!" Uncle Ronan roared so loud Natisse's ears rang. His face went suddenly soft, and his voice lowered to nearly a whisper. "I gave up being General Andros when the Empire I served accused me of treason and tried to hang me. Even though I was bloody innocent, it didn't matter. Not to them."

He stepped slowly toward her, and Natisse was suddenly struck by the power he emanated in his docility. Gone was the Uncle Ronan she'd known for so many years, and in his place stood a man who had once been the highest-ranked general in the most powerful nation in the world.

"You want to know the truth?" he said. "You want to be in the know? Fine. Sit down."

He didn't even wait to see if she would obey before returning to his own chair. She stared down at him for a beat before lowering herself.

"The Karmian Empire turned its back on me, Natisse. And it broke me. Even after I escaped execution, I lived in hiding for years, doing nothing, merely surviving. Until I saw what was being done to the people I'd dedicated my life to protecting. I saw their suffering, and the ones responsible for that suffering were not the Empire's enemies but its own people. The Magisters and aristocrats and those who called themselves 'betters.' So, I set out to right that wrong. The mission I've instilled in you hasn't changed since the day I first took it on alone. I have given my life—just like all of you—to bringing to justice those who abused their power in the name of avarice and cruelty. Not the Emperor's justice, for I saw all too clearly what that meant for those like me who were innocent. But *true* justice, Ezrasil's justice." He raised a clenched fist. "Blood for blood."

Natisse sat, stunned. The zeal in his eyes seemed genuine. Honest. His words hid no deceit that she could tell. Either he was speaking truly, or he had convinced himself it was true.

"Then why not just tell us that?" she demanded. "Why keep that from us? That, and the fact that you're a Lumenator?"

Her question struck a nerve. But rather than pulling forth the answer she wanted, it only drove Uncle Ronan to retreat.

"That, I cannot tell you," he said, his voice suddenly hard again.

"Then you are a fangless coward," Natisse spat. "And your precious missions will have to go on without me." She stood once more.

"Natisse, please," he said, his eyes pleading. "You can't turn your back on us now. The lives of the *Ghuklek* hang in the balance. We have too few swords to do what needs doing. Garron is far from recovered, leaving just you, Nalkin, and L'yo as the only capable fighters who—"

"No," she snapped. "I'm done. And nothing you say will change my mind."

Some fury burned deep inside of her, something that didn't feel natural, didn't feel… like her own. She stormed out of the room, fire burning in her throat, and left him alone. She wasn't sure this was the end of the Crimson Fang for her, but for now, she could stand no more.

When he's ready to be honest, I'll listen. If he's ever ready.

26

KULLEN

Kullen watched Natisse, the red-haired woman, stalk from the room. He had no trouble seeing why Golgoth had chosen her for a human bond-mate. Though she kept herself well in check, there was no mistaking the deep well of fire burning within her, anger simmering just below the surface, ready to boil over at any moment.

It was unfortunate really that Kullen had become such a convenient target for all that rage. It would make it more difficult for him to keep his eye close upon her without fear that her dagger would find its place there.

"You should not have done that." Prince Jaylen's voice was soft, but only due to his weakened state. Still, some of that arrogance Kullen had become accustomed to laced the words.

Kullen's insides leaped at the sound, though he didn't let it show externally. He'd all but forgotten the young man was still in the room.

"Done what?" he asked, turning to the Prince, cocking an eyebrow.

"Struck that bargain." Jaylen had summoned the strength to push himself up to a sitting position. From his expression alone, he might as well have been seated atop the Emperor's grand throne, not some ramshackle cot. "You cannot keep this from my grandfather."

"I can," Kullen said sharply, "and, if necessary, I will."

Jaylen's frown made his pointy nose appear downright razor-sharp, his forehead even blunter than usual. "You serve at the Emperor's pleasure and carry out his will."

"And his will happens to be getting your arse out of here as alive and intact as humanly possible," Kullen said. It took all of his years of training to restrain himself from snapping at the Prince. Instead of succumbing to annoyance, he opted to take the young man's growing imperiousness as a good sign—he was recovering from his wounds.

With effort, Kullen softened his tone. "All due respect, Prince Jaylen, but your grandfather trusts me to handle situations like this."

Jaylen opened his mouth, but Kullen didn't give him a chance to speak.

"Right now, there are two factors at play." He held up a pair of fingers in front of the young man's nose. "First, there is the matter of the Crimson Fang itself. Insurrectionists and seditionists, or so we've been led to believe." Mammy Tess's words had been playing over and over in his mind since he'd learned that the big brute had *healed* the Prince, not kidnapped him. "I don't claim to understand why they murdered all those Magisters, but it's growing abundantly clear there is more at work here than merely destabilizing Imperial rule. Were that the case, you would be far less talkative and far more dead at the moment."

That shut Jaylen up. His open mouth snapped shut, teeth clicking audibly.

"We are provided a unique position to learn more about the Crimson Fang... from within," Kullen said. He didn't bother glancing around. After his conversation with Natisse, he felt all but certain anything he said within these earthen walls would go unheard. This wasn't the Palace with all its spy holes and false walls to conceal listeners. Not even the Trenta's practiced ear could hear their exchange. And those beyond in the corridor would strain themselves to deafness before a single utterance snuck through the massive door. "Which ties in neatly with the *second* factor."

"Natisse," Jaylen said. "Her bond with Golgoth complicates matters."

Kullen had to admit the young man was as sharp as his features—at least enough to understand that without being spoon-fed. Perhaps there was hope for a future beyond Emperor Wymarc's death, after all.

"I don't know how closely her personal desires align with those of the Crimson Fang," he said, nodding. "Which means I cannot know to what ends she will use Golgoth. But more than that, it is clear she understands nothing of *Bloodsurging* and the true power at her command. That makes her both unpredictable and dangerous."

"So you want to get a better sense of her, see what she intends." Again, the Prince said it as a statement, not a question.

"Precisely," Kullen said.

"And that has nothing to do with her striking beauty?" Jaylen said with a wry smile.

Kullen dismissed the question without a response, continuing as if the Prince hadn't spoken. "If keeping her secrets allows me to get you back to the Palace alive *and* earn some small measure of her trust, then you know what your grandfather would do. What he would have me do."

It took a moment, but finally, Jaylen nodded. "You're right."

Kullen masked his surprise—those were the last words he'd expected out of the young man's mouth. He'd prepared himself for the inevitable argument, to eventually force the issue in some way. But Jaylen had come to understand the reason behind his actions with only minimal persuasion. That boded well, indeed.

"So what's the p—" Jaylen began, but at that moment, they were interrupted by the door grinding open. As always, Kullen kept himself outwardly calm, but internally, he braced for battle in case the four armed men standing outside had decided to rush in, or General Andros had given the order to attack despite the tentative bargain he'd struck with Natisse.

But it was just the wheat stalk of a girl, Sparrow, carrying a bowl of broth. She hesitated in the doorway, eyeing Kullen nervously. It only lasted a half heartbeat, then her expression grew resolute.

"Brought some food for you," she told Jaylen, striding toward him, determined not to meet Kullen's gaze. It didn't pass his notice that she also chose to ignore the proprieties of addressing the Crown Prince. She sounded a great deal like Serrod—all business, no fuss, though with only a fraction of the Brendoni's typical brusqueness. "Drink it all down, and if you're feeling up for it in a few hours, I'll see about bringing you something a bit more solid."

"Th-Thank you," Prince Jaylen said. "It smells wonderful."

Kullen was shocked to see the young man beaming shyly at the girl, a flush on his cheeks as he pulled the bedsheets up higher to cover himself. The prince couldn't be more than a year or two older than Sparrow, and he'd lived a far more sheltered life. Had he ever *spoken* to a lass without being under the direct supervision of an army of fussy chaperones?

"It's just broth," Sparrow said, seeming not to notice Jaylen's reaction. "Not the worst Tobin's ever made, but nowhere near his best. It'll give you strength, though."

"Then best I drink it down straightaway!" Jaylen said far too eagerly. He reached for the bowl with one hand while clutching the sheet to his chest with the other.

Sparrow handed him the bowl but didn't wait to watch him drink. Instead, she turned and marched from the room, studiously ignoring Kullen all the while.

Kullen concealed a smile with his raised palm. A youth such as this one, brought up on the hard streets of Lower Dimvein—likely the Embers, though perhaps the One Hand District—would carry that hard edge all the way to the grave. Not a kind life, certainly. Perhaps that was what had drawn her to the Crimson Fang in the first place.

That thought brought back what Kullen had learned about Ammonidas and Baruchel Sallas. The brothers had been the remnants of a minor aristocratic household, the only survivors of an attack intended to wipe out the entire House of Sallas. Dispossessed sons, doubtless forced to eke out a hard living on the streets of Dimvein.

Had *they* been drawn to the Crimson Fang for the same reason as Sparrow? Had the insurrection offered them the pretense of a home, a family, to replace those they'd lost? That was ever the way of things with such organizations. Men like General Andros collected the weak, downtrodden, and castaway to serve under whatever banner they flew, whatever dogma they espoused. People with nothing to lose rarely thought to look beyond the mission to which they had been "called."

Was that who Natisse was, too—another outcast General Andros had added to his collection? If so, she could very well have drunk deep of whatever doctrine the general spouted to recruit to his cause.

And what cause is that, exactly? Kullen wondered. *What does 'blood for blood' truly mean?*

From what he knew of General Andros—admittedly precious little—the man had ample cause to loathe the Empire he'd served and who he no doubt believed had betrayed him. Yet the fact that he hadn't killed Prince Jaylen outright suggested he might have a purpose beyond vengeance against Emperor Wymarc. Until Kullen learned more, he would never fully understand what drove Natisse. And that made her a greater danger to the Empire than enemies like the Blood Clan pirates or the Hudar Horde. At least with them, their motivations were clear—the utter destruction of the Empire in the name of power and conquest—so the Emperor could attempt to anticipate and counter their plans.

Kullen doubted he'd get a straight answer from General Andros. He'd likely get nothing beyond a dagger to the gut. The man had to know who he was, the threat he represented. Yet Natisse's willingness to bargain in the first place showed Kullen that *she* was his best path to uncovering more about this insurrection. His offer to help her master the *Bloodsurge* and comprehend the extent of her bond with Golgoth provided the perfect cover to remain close and dig deeper into this rebellion she helped General Andros brew.

The clatter of wood on hard-packed earth drew Kullen's attention to the Prince's cot. There, he found Jaylen had fallen asleep partway through drinking his broth. The bowl lay inert a foot or so away, a few chunks of stewed vegetables splattering the floor and walls beside the cot. However, judging by the small puddle, Jaylen had gotten most of the nourishing liquid down.

Kullen smiled. Better for him, the Prince slept. Not only did it save Kullen the need to defend or explain his actions to the callow young man, but with luck, Jaylen would awaken stronger. Hopefully, strong enough to endure the journey back to the Palace.

Kullen sat in the corner, crossed his legs at the ankle, folded his arms over his chest, and closed his eyes. Better he rested while he could as well. When the Prince awoke, things would grow a great deal more interesting.

Kullen awoke to the sound of shifting cloth and a quiet grunt. His eyelids popped open, hand darting to his belt. But it was only Prince Jaylen pushing himself slowly to his feet.

"Steady," Kullen said, standing and moving to lend the Prince a hand. "No need to rush it."

"Easy for you to say," Jaylen hissed through teeth clenched against pain. He hunched slightly over the wound in his side, unable to stand fully upright. He did manage to keep his legs from giving out, which was a testament to the boy's perseverance—another fine quality for an Emperor. "You're not the one whose life dangles from a Trenta's nostril hair."

Kullen raised an eyebrow. Where had the young man heard *that* expression?

"You've nothing to worry about, my Prince," he said, trying for a serene tone. "The Crimson Fang—"

"Could come through that door at any moment," Jaylen snapped. "They could very well change what little mind they have and decide that I'm better off to them dead than alive."

Kullen frowned. "I assure you, if killing you was the plan, you'd be dead already."

"So you say," Jaylen retorted, "but if it's all the same to you, I won't stake my life on the 'maybe' of an assassin."

Kullen released his grip on the young man and stepped back. Jaylen swayed but managed to hold himself upright by clinging to the hard-packed earthen wall.

"What is going on with you?" Kullen demanded. "Why the sudden change?"

"There's no change," the Prince said in a tone that said he might've been trying to convince himself more than anyone.

Kullen glared at him.

"I had a dream, all right?"

"A dream?" Kullen cocked his head.

Jaylen's face flushed a deep red—embarrassed but a bit angry, too. "Yes, an Ezrasil-damned dream!" Steel edged his sharp voice. "You might not believe it, but it's true. I saw them outside this door, waiting with chains and swords and murder in their eyes. And this is not the first time. Not at all. I've had other dreams before. Many of them. And they come true. And I don't want this one to—"

"Dreams that came true?" Kullen felt a sudden chill sliding down his spine. "What came true, Jaylen?"

Jaylen stared at him like an aurochs eyeing a prod. "There was a pit. In my dream. A pit with blood. Lots of it on the sand around me. Pain, too. Screams and shouts and darkness. Fire, too. Fire that burned me until I was a pile of ash. And that's exactly what happened last night. Except for burning to ash, everything else happened exactly as I saw it in my dream."

"They threw you in a pit?" Kullen asked. "In your dream?"

"Well, I didn't see that part," Jaylen admitted. "Not exactly. They were there, just outside that door, waiting with weapons. Then things... shifted. It happens like that—in my dreams. I'm one place, then another. But it's always connected. I had a... sense that they'd been the ones to deliver me into the pit." Jaylen looked up, his features hardening. "And if you don't believe me, that's just too bad. I'm the Prince, and I say we are going. Now."

Kullen's jaw dropped. He couldn't believe it. A long moment of silence passed between them until Kullen could finally find his voice. "You inherited your mother's gift."

Jaylen's eyes widened. "My m—" He sucked in a breath. "You knew?"

Kullen remained silent again. This was one more secret he'd never spoken of with the Emperor. Nor with Jarius. Hadassa had begged him never to utter mention of it. Jaylen's pleading eyes roamed over Kullen's face, desperate until Kullen could no longer ignore the boy.

"I did," he said quietly. "She was terrified the first time it happened. She dreamed that Ontas, one of the other boys in the Refuge, would die. Told me about it after they found his body floating in the Talos River. Just like she saw it in her dreams."

Jaylen's face paled. He grew more hunched, no longer standing straight and confident.

"Every time after that, she shared the dreams with me." Kullen summoned those memories from deep within his mind. He hadn't thought about it since the *last* dream she'd told him about.

"Right up until she had one final dream." He forced himself to smile through the pain still haunting him all these many years later.

"And... what was that dream?" Jaylen asked.

"She met your father."

There was a sense of relief that washed over the prince. Perhaps he'd expected something else, that Hadassa had predicted her own death and ventured into the Embers anyway. Kullen didn't voice it aloud, but he was sure she'd have done just that.

"I don't know if she never dreamed again or simply stopped telling..."

His voice trailed off as the realization hit him. There'd been a look of such sadness in her eyes the day she and Jarius had ridden out to bring aid to those affected by Golgoth's fire. All this time, he'd written it off as her empathetic nature, *feeling* the pain and suffering of the people of Dimvein. But perhaps it had been more. Perhaps she *had* dreamed of her own death and that of Jarius. Maybe even Jaylen's, which was why she'd insisted he stay within the Palace walls. They would never know now.

"Kullen?" Jaylen said.

Kullen's attention returned to the prince. "Right. Well, if you have her dreams, then we must take them seriously." Kullen stripped off his cloak and wrapped it around the young man's slim shoulders. "Lean on me, but if anything happens—"

"I'll watch your back," Jaylen said.

Kullen stifled a snort of derision. He'd been about to say, "Stay behind me and keep your royal pain in the arse out of my way." The Prince was in no shape to fight; he could barely walk unaided. Yet he merely nodded and said, "Good."

He helped Jaylen hobble toward the door, loosening his daggers in his sheaths as he went. He knew not the details of Jaylen's dreams—or just how far he could trust them—but he wouldn't take chances with the Prince's life. Though Natisse had agreed to his bargain and Jad had made his stance plain, there were others in the Crimson Fang, General Andros among them, who would doubtless be less than willing to let them merely walk out of there alive.

Kullen reached for the door and pulled it open. It appeared Jaylen had, indeed, inherited his mother's gift.

Angry eyes stared at them from the corridor—Crimson Fang members with weapons drawn, ready to use them.

"Leaving so soon?"

27
NATISSE

Natisse wanted to let out her anger on a punching bag, but the *Ghuklek's* scrutiny unnerved her. She could feel their amber-gray eyes fixed on her, watching every movement until she could no longer bear it. Throwing her sweat-soaked cloth hand wrappings into one corner of the training room, she stalked out into the corridor, passing Nalkin and L'yo without a word. The couple, set to watch over the *Ghuklek*, let her pass without a word.

Natisse stormed past Haston, Garron, Athelas, and Leroshavé. A shake of Garron's head silenced the question forming on Athelas's lips. The rangy man could see the storm brewing within her, and Natisse silently blessed him for holding back the others. They had no need to suffer the force of her wrath. They weren't the intended targets, but her last conversation with Uncle Ronan left her so furious that she doubted she could restrain herself from unleashing Golgoth's fire at him. Better for everyone that she just withdrew.

That was how she found herself in her quarters throwing everything she owned into a small leather knapsack. Not that she had owned much in the first place: a few changes of clothing, spare boots, a pair of plain daggers gifted her by Baruch, and a small wooden figurine of a cat she'd carved years earlier to improve her dexterity with a blade. Together with the lashblade she wore and the leather thong Jad had given her for the dragonblood vial, that was all her possessions. So little to show for her life. But then again, that had always been the point, hadn't it?

Everything Uncle Ronan had done had been for the sake of the mission. One task after another, all building blocks in his "grand plan"—a plan he hadn't deigned to share with them, instead, keeping them so focused on the day-to-day minutiae that she'd never thought of anything else.

Natisse slung the bag over her shoulder but hesitated before marching out of the door. What was there for her outside? Despite everything she'd lost—Ammon, Baruch, and Uncle Ronan—the Crimson Fang was still the closest thing she'd had to a home since her parents' deaths. There were people who still needed her. Or, at the very least, might be hurt by her leaving. Jad, certainly. Garron, perhaps. As for the others, she had no doubt her departure would affect them, though to what extent, she didn't know.

Did she dare leave, then? And if she did, where would she go? Her life was nothing outside these walls. She was no one beyond the loyal Crimson Fang killer into which Uncle Ronan had made her.

Uncertainty paralyzed her in place. Dread, confusion, and fear of the known rendered her motionless. For seconds, minutes, even hours? She couldn't bring herself to reach for the door latch and shove it open. Because the moment she did, everything she knew, everything she *was*, would all come to an end.

All because of Uncle Ronan—General bloody Andros!

Something drew her attention to the corridor outside her room. A sound, perhaps, like a door opening. A sensation, a wave of tension rippling through the Burrow. Maybe even Golgoth's magical senses. Whatever it was, it snapped Natisse's momentary hesitation and spurred her into motion. She ripped open her chamber door and strode out into the passage beyond.

Just in time to see the Crimson Fang gearing up to attack Prince Jaylen and the Black Talon.

In the span of a heartbeat, maybe less, she took in the scene: the man who'd called himself Kullen stood supporting the young Prince beneath the arm, facing off against her comrades, a dagger halfway from its sheath. Not all of them, she realized—Jad and Sparrow were absent—but Uncle Ronan stood at the head of a wall of swords, with Garron, Athelas, and Leroshavé on his right, Nalkin and L'yo at his left, and Haston and Tobin behind him. In his right hand, Uncle Ronan held a drawn sword and, from his left, dangled thick manacles.

The order to attack had not yet been given, but Natisse could see the words forming on Uncle Ronan's stony face.

"Leaving so soon?" she called out in a jaunty tone, striding down the corridor at a casual, unhurried pace.

All eyes snapped toward her. Kullen craned his neck over Prince Jaylen's shoulder for a better view of her.

"Trying to," he said, his voice cold and hard. "Seems your friends here have other ideas."

Natisse plastered on a too-wide grin. "That's because they didn't know I'm coming with you."

Surprise registered on every face before her, except the assassin. Though she knew his brain rattled with this idea, his outward visage stayed calm and collected.

"What are you doing?" Uncle Ronan growled, his expression darkening.

Natisse planted herself next to the assassin, squaring her shoulders to look Uncle Ronan dead in the face. "What's best for the Crimson Fang, of course. As I've always done." She kept her tone calm, but he knew her well enough that he would feel the chilly edge to her voice.

"Speak clearly," Uncle Ronan said.

"You heard me. I'm going with him. To help get the Prince here back to his grandfather." Natisse turned to favor the assassin with that sharp, saccharine smile. "And to make certain he doesn't betray us to the Emperor."

A calculating look entered the assassin's eyes as he weighed her words. Prince Jaylen hadn't yet recovered from his shock, nor had most of the Crimson Fang. Only Garron and Nalkin seemed to have their wits about them enough to realize there was more at play here than what was apparent at face value. Both pairs of eyes watched Natisse but occasionally flicked to Uncle Ronan.

"Natisse—" Uncle Ronan began.

Natisse cut him off with a shake of her head. "I've decided," she said curtly. "It's the only way I can figure we'll trust *his* word." She gestured to Kullen with her chin, then to Jaylen. "And the only way I can make sure to get the young Prince here safely aboveground without the gnashers getting him."

A small smile tugged at Kullen's lips. "A kind gesture," he said in a voice that stopped just short of sardonic, "but not truly necessary. As you've seen, I'm more than capable of—"

Prince Jaylen cut off the assassin. "Kullen, let her come. They saved my life. If this is what she needs to ensure her people's safety, then we owe her that much."

The ring of authority in the young man's voice surprised Natisse. Even more surprising was Kullen's answer.

"So be it, my Prince." He gave a little nod to the young man that, to some eyes, could have been mistaken as a bow, then turned to regard Natisse. His eyes took her in, head to toe. "Prepared to travel already, I see."

Natisse shrugged. "And for a great deal more, should you prove faithless to your word." She rested a hand on the hilt of her lashblade for emphasis.

Kullen just inclined his head and said nothing.

Natisse looked to Uncle Ronan, then past him to fix the rest of her Crimson Fang comrades with a stern glare. Many of them were trying to conceal their drawn blades from her as if ashamed.

"We'll be on our way, then," she said in a hard voice.

Haston, Athelas, Tobin, and Leroshavé all watched Uncle

Ronan as if for approval, but Garron, Nalkin, and L'yo seemed to understand what was going on. Natisse hadn't exactly kept her anger at Uncle Ronan secret, not since their shouting match in the corridor before Kullen's arrival. Anyone with ears and half a mind could tell something was amiss between them. The younger members of the Crimson Fang deferred to Uncle Ronan by default, but the older, wiser ones had formed opinions of their own.

To Natisse's relief, Uncle Ronan grunted and stepped aside. "Let them pass," he growled, fire blazing in his steel gray eyes. "If this is what Natisse believes is best—"

"I do." Natisse bit off the words. "For all of us." She fixed the Crimson Fang's leader with a baleful glare, and he met her eyes with stony calm. She could almost feel the anger rising within the man. She'd put him in a tough position. Should he argue, he would be all but admitting to ulterior motives. Jad and Sparrow had spent the bulk of two days tending to the Prince's wounds, and for what, if not his safe return behind Palace walls?

But if he stayed silent, he'd lose the upper hand—perhaps for good.

Natisse, for her part, was unsure what Ronan would do. Until late, she'd believed Uncle Ronan's interests were solely for the Crimson Fang and their mission. But now, would General Andros seize control for his own hidden agenda? And could she keep herself from tipping the pot and letting pour the truth, thus damaging the mission all on her own?

She broke off first. Better to leave before she said or did something from which there would be no return.

"Let's go," she said, gesturing to Kullen and Prince Jaylen to follow her as she marched through the wall of armed men and women facing her. Nalkin and L'yo moved first, and the others followed suit a moment later, stepping aside to clear a path. Natisse refused to glance back—she wouldn't give Uncle Ronan the satisfaction—but kept her gaze fixed straight ahead on the closed door to the training room.

She led the way through the Burrow, toward the heavy front gate leading across the Talos River to the secret entrance of the old warehouse. Before she passed the common room, however, a voice called out to her.

"Natisse!"

Natisse glanced back. A sleepy-looking Jad was rushing up the corridor, Garron at his side.

She stopped. "Wait for me by the gate," she told Kullen. "I'll need a moment to sort this out."

The Black Talon nodded. "As you wish." Despite his outward calm, the tension radiated off him in tangible waves, like heat rising from sunbaked stone on a blistering summer's day. He was right to stay wary. They weren't out of the Crimson Fang stronghold yet.

Natisse turned to face her two comrades. Her *friends*.

"What is it?" she snapped. "I don't have time—"

"You're really leaving?" Jad planted his huge frame directly in front of her. "Just like that? Walking away without even a goodbye?"

"I'm not *leaving* leaving," Natisse said, jaw muscles clenching. "Just accompanying them to ensure he holds to his word."

Jad gazed down at her. Something in his eyes said he knew the truth, that she was looking for an escape, a way to create time and distance and sort through the chaos of her thoughts.

"Dragonpiss!" Jad said finally. He shook his head. "You and I both know what's going on here, Natisse. If it was anyone else—"

"But it's *not* anyone else!" Natisse's voice cracked like a whip. "And if I stay right now, we both know what could happen." Fire surged in her eyes, coursing through her veins. She could no longer find that cold, detached place inside herself, for it had been filled with Golgoth's flames, and now she only felt the heat of those years worth of buried emotion. "But I will be back. I promise. I just need…" She let out a harsh breath. "I just need to get away from *him*."

Though Jad looked hurt, he understood and nodded. "Then I'm not saying goodbye. So you *have* to come back."

"I will," Natisse said, holding his gaze.

Jad took a few tentative steps backward before turning to walk away. Natisse stared at the big man's back as he went, fighting the urge to call out to him.

Garron, however, didn't move. He studied her face, evaluating her like a fine-cut gem. Long seconds passed in silence.

Natisse felt her frustrations mounting until she could finally bear it no longer.

"Garron—"

"I don't know what's going on," he said at the same time. "But whatever it is, you need to sort your shite out. And soon. Getting the *Ghuklek* out of Dimvein is going to be bloody difficult. Haston spotted Elite soldiers at the shipyards, and Uncle Ronan said he's seen the Imperial Scales and Orkenwatch out on the streets in increased numbers. What we did the other night has them riled up. It's going to take a couple of days to get this piss bucket in order and prepare to move the *Ghuklek*. So you take your time to cool down, get your head straight. Then, you get your ass back to us."

His tone was the sternest she'd ever heard. Garron hardly spoke, only when there was something worth listening to, and Natisse listened.

"You can't just run away, even if you're pissed at Uncle Ronan for whatever reason. We need you. Your help. Because without you, it's just Nalkin, L'yo, and me to make sure the others are safe if anything goes wrong. And those would've been shite odds even before this." He gestured to the empty space where his left arm had once been. "We *need* you, Natisse. All of us. Not for his missions. But because without you, our chances of surviving every day get a little bit worse."

He was right. There was no denying it. The Crimson Fang had suffered many losses, and she couldn't be yet another.

"I'll be back," she said quietly, forcing the words from her suddenly dry throat. "I'm not abandoning you. Never."

Garron nodded. "Good." He turned to go but stopped halfway. "Oh, and tell your new friends there we had no plans to hurt them. Uncle Ronan just wanted to make sure they couldn't hurt *us*, especially while we were dealing with the *Ghuklek*."

Natisse's mind flashed back to moments earlier, to the manacles in Uncle Ronan's hands. No surprise, the Black Talon had been prepared to fight. And that response could've been precisely why Uncle Ronan had intended to shackle the man in the first place and brought most of the Crimson Fang to lend a hand.

"Sure. I'll tell him," Natisse said.

Garron's demeanor abruptly shifted to the laconic man Natisse had known for so long. No more words, just a simple grunt as he continued on his way. She knew it had taken a lot for him to say all that. It proved she'd been right to steady her emotions and slow her departure.

But she was right to leave, too. For both her sake and that of the Crimson Fang.

With a heavy sigh—one that did nothing to release the churning in her gut—Natisse turned and followed Kullen to the front gate. She surveyed the tunnel walls as she went, considering all the hours the *Ghuklek* had put into this place and the treatment they'd received as a reward for their hard efforts. Was that just the way of things in the Karmian Empire?

It got her thinking toward her own legacy and her years of work she'd invested in the Fang. They were fighting for freedom for all, but some, apparently, already believed themselves as free as could be. Would history write them as the heroes or villains of this story? And to that point, were Uncle Ronan's machinations all that heroic to begin with? Was this a simple act of revenge on his part?

She spotted the assassin where she'd requested he wait for her. Curiosity marked his features now that they were alone.

"And that was?" he asked.

"Let's go," she said, ignoring his inquiry.

Whatever Kullen thought in response, he didn't say, simply nodded. "After you."

Natisse pulled the small brass ring to the right of the door and it rumbled open to the sounds of rushing water below.

"Impressive," Kullen said, admiration evident on his face. "How did you find this place? I've never heard of it before."

Natisse had no response to that—not unless she planned to discuss the *Ghuklek* with him here and now, and she had no intent for that. In truth, she'd never asked Uncle Ronan how he'd come to live in the Burrow. Merely accepted it as home, secrets and all.

Once again, she ignored the question. "Stay close," she told the pair. "Better for all of us you don't get lost in these tunnels."

"You sure about that?" Kullen asked. "If we do, your problems disappear with us."

"Kullen!" Prince Jaylen chided, shooting the assassin a scolding look.

Kullen just grinned wider. "You deny it?"

Natisse shook her head. "Had the Prince's death been the outcome we desired, we'd be having a very different conversation right now."

Kullen actually chuckled. "Fair point." He adjusted his grip on the Prince and nodded. "Lead the way."

Natisse grabbed an oil lamp hanging just beyond the door. Its light projected dancing shadows on the rough-hewn stone but vanished into the darkness below the narrow bridge.

Natisse cast occasional glances over her shoulder. Just to make certain she hadn't lost the Prince and his minder, she told herself.

In truth, the Black Talon intrigued her. There was more to the man than just the hardened killer she'd hated since the night Baruch died. She nearly stopped walking, hesitating a step while she pondered.

When had I stopped thinking of it as the night he was murdered?

She shook away the thought, deciding she hadn't. It was just a momentary stutter, likely due to exhaustion.

The assassin had said he'd come *just* to bring the Prince safely back to the Palace. He'd been honest about that much, at least. Had he been equally genuine in his offer to help her understand her new magical abilities?

No. That was another thought that must be brushed aside. This man *was* a killer. He was the Emperor's lapdog, his loyal dagger, and yes, Baruch's murderer. He was not to be trusted, no matter what honey-glazed words he spoke.

She dug deep, past Golgoth's burning flames, and reached for the icy depths of her inner being. She would show no warmth to this *Black Talon.* None at all.

Finally, they reached the ladder leading into the old warehouse above.

"Wait for the sign the coast is clear," she told Kullen. "Only then, follow."

She didn't wait for a response before starting the climb. As the refuse above slid to the side, she silently gazed into the wide building. On the rare occasion it wasn't empty, it was a drunkard or vagabond looking for shelter from the rain or elements. Tonight, there was nothing. Darkness hung thick in the air. Through the crumbled rooftop, a bare sliver of moon hung in the sky, all but blotted out by a dense layer of clouds.

"So what now?" Natisse asked, turning to the assassin and Prince. "He's in no shape to walk all the way back to the Palace. I've no coin to hire horses or a carriage. I take it you intend to flag down a company of Imperial Scales for an escort?"

"That won't be necessary," Kullen said, a sly grin on his face. "We have a better means of transportation."

Natisse tilted her head in confusion. She started to speak but went suddenly mute as the assassin reached his hand beneath his tunic. A moment later, where nothing but shadow had been, the air swirled and oscillated, giving form to a massive bloody dragon.

28
KULLEN

A cruel part of Kullen genuinely enjoyed Natisse's violent reaction to Umbris's presence.

To be fair, *he'd* responded much the same the first time the Twilight Dragon stepped out of the shadows before him. Hard not to considering Umbris's size, the fiery shine of his golden eyes, enormous razor-sharp fangs, and the sleek purple-black shimmering of his scales.

However, to her credit, Natisse didn't quite cry out or even leap back. She merely stiffened, hissing in a sharp breath. Her hand slid for her whip-sword. A fighter's reaction. Kullen's estimation of her rose another notch.

"Natisse," he said, trying and failing to conceal the mirth in his voice, "meet Umbris. Umbris, this is Natisse."

"Natisse," Umbris said through Kullen's mental bond. Aloud, the dragon's rumble sounded threatening, loud enough to set the warehouse walls shaking. Not something this dilapidated old place could withstand much of. Natisse's fist locked on her weapon's hilt, and the blade was halfway out of its sheath before Kullen gripped her arm.

"He's not going to harm you," he said, keeping his voice

composed. "But if he thinks you're threatening me, that might change. Quickly."

Natisse froze, every muscle in her body going rigid. Slowly and with visible effort, she released her weapon and brought her empty hand up to show the dragon she held no threat.

"I know this one," Umbris said in Kullen's mind, his rumble taking on an angry tone. *"Hers is a smell I will not soon forget, seeing she was among those who threw you to the onyx sharks."*

That's not exactly how it happened, Kullen shot back. *She was there, yes, and tried to kill me, yes. But to be fair, she clearly thought I was trying to kill her.*

Umbris's huge yellow eyes narrowed, and he lowered his giant horned head to get a better look at her. Natisse flinched but managed to hold her ground, jaw muscles tight as spun wool and spine stiff as a spear.

"She reeks of Golgoth," Umbris said. *"I can smell the Queen of the Embers' fire in her."*

Kullen nodded. That saved him from having to explain the situation to Umbris, at least. *We'll be keeping an eye on her for a while,* he told the dragon. *Just to make certain she poses no threat to my Honorsworn.*

"Very wise." Umbris growled low in his belly, his serpentine head circling Natisse to examine her from all angles. *"She is dangerous, this human."*

Kullen had to hide a smile at that. Even before Natisse had bonded with Golgoth, she'd been one of the deadlier opponents he'd faced. That whip-blade of hers was a truly mean weapon, and she wielded it with skill he'd quickly learned to take seriously.

"Is he… going to do anything?" Natisse asked, the hint of fear in her voice barely audible. "Or just gawk at me all night?"

"He's just sizing you up," Kullen answered. "I'm pretty sure the fact that he hasn't yet eaten you is a good sign."

The words, intended as a jest to help Natisse relax, only made her warier. Kullen could see her muscles coil, ready to fight or flee.

"Umbris will be conveying me to the Palace," he explained quickly. "Prince Jaylen will likewise be traveling on Tempest."

"Tempest?" Natisse asked.

Even as the word left her mouth, a gust of wind whipped through the warehouse's crumbling roof. Yet this was no ordinary wind, drifting along aimlessly, but a magical vortex that swirled and danced with a mind all its own. For it *was* a mind.

Fragments of silver flecked the air, seemingly at random, until the form of a long, slender dragon appeared beside Umbris. Where Umbris was thick with girth and raw strength, Tempest looked as if he could blend with the air itself in a heart span. Bony appendages that always reminded Kullen of the ageless tree branches in the Wild Grove Forest where he, Jarius, and Hadassa would frolic as youths jutted out at his side. Thin, nearly transparent, sinewy wings hung like drapes from them. It was a wonder they carried the dragon at all.

Long, jagged scars peppered the Wind Dragon's body, revealing patches of thick hide where scales should've been. Tempest had seen battle many times, and it showed.

Kullen made a point not to stare at Natisse, but from the corner of his eye, he saw her take a slight step backward.

"Tempest!" Jaylen gave a relieved cry and stumbled toward the silver dragon. He only managed a few steps before his legs crumpled beneath him, and exhaustion dragged him down.

Tempest's head darted low and slid beneath the young man, catching him as he fell. Jaylen's arms wrapped around the dragon's neck and held tight.

"I thought I'd lost you!" Prince Jaylen whispered into Tempest's ear.

Tempest puffed cold air from his nostrils. So cold, in fact, Kullen had to fight to suppress a shudder. He knew the dragon was communicating telepathically with Jaylen and let them have their privacy.

"Are you two intent upon bringing this place down atop us?"

Now, looking upon her fully, Kullen enjoyed the sight of

Natisse watching the prince and his dragon. Wonder and curiosity sparkled in her eyes. Her mouth hung open in an intriguing "O" shape, and her icy blue eyes glimmered in the light emanating from Umbris's golden ones. Harsh reflections of Natisse's oil lamp bounced from Tempest silver scales all around the room.

When she finally tore her gaze from the dragon and prince to look at him, Kullen gestured encouragingly. "Go ahead," he said. "There is still space enough to summon Golgoth." He studied the warehouse with a critical eye. "I think." Last time he'd come face-to-face with the Ember Dragon, she had towered high above Magister Deckard's three-story staircase. It would be tight, but perhaps, if she remained low, she could squeeze in as well.

"Summon... Golgoth?" Natisse asked, incredulity in her voice.

Kullen nodded. "Yes."

A look of confusion, uncertainty, and doubt flitted across her features.

"Or," Kullen said, "you could ride Umbris with me." He glanced to the Twilight Dragon. "With his permission, of course."

Umbris gave a low growl that sounded menacing but, in reality, signaled contemplation. *"You trust her not to stab you in the back?"*

She hasn't yet, Kullen responded. *I'm willing to play out the wager and see how far I can take it.*

"Ride Umbris," Natisse repeated the words woodenly as if unable to comprehend them. "You're sure?"

Kullen nodded. "It's quite enjoyable—if you don't mind the heights. Or the freezing wind. Or the speed. Or the sharp scales prodding parts best left unprodded."

By now, Jaylen had carefully clambered atop Tempest's back—more accurately, he'd clung to the Wind Dragon's neck with all of his strength while Tempest lifted him into position. He sat hunched behind the dragon's neck frills. His face pale and lined with fatigue, but his eyes shone with boyish enthusiasm.

"You'll love it. I promise," Jaylen said, grinning down at Natisse.

Kullen shimmied up Umbris's scales and settled into his usual spot on the Twilight Dragon's back, then turned and reached a hand down to Natisse. "It'll get us to the Palace faster than a horse or carriage. Get you back to your people quicker, too."

After a long moment of hesitation, Natisse accepted his outstretched hand. He lifted her with little difficulty. She was lean and clearly well-muscled beneath her simple clothing, and her strength combined with his aided the effort. He aided her in settling comfortably on Umbris's back—which, it turned out, was directly behind him.

"Wrap your arms around my waist," he said, "and whatever you do, don't let go."

"Why in Shekoth's pits would I let gooOOOOO!!!" Her words rose to a shriek as Umbris bounded into the air. At Kullen's instruction, of course. Natisse's arms snapped tight around his ribs—hard enough to bruise, he suspected—and her fingertips dug into his abdomen.

The One Hand District shrank beneath them. Kullen squinted against the rush of wind, letting the freedom of flight minister to his weary soul. No matter how many times he'd ridden Umbris, it was still awe-inspiring to watch the clouds, the sun, and the moon grow closer and closer until they nearly brushed Thanagar's dome.

In many ways, Kullen envied Natisse. For all the terror he'd felt his first time flying, the exhilaration had far outweighed it. Indeed, it had taken him less than one heart-pounding minute to lose his fear—*most* of it, at least—and give in to the thrill.

Natisse, for her part, didn't cry out once. Her fingers nearly tore his clothing and the skin beneath, but she had a tight rein on herself. Far more fearless than he'd been on his first flight. His estimation of the woman rose yet further.

And, he reasoned, *if she's holding on for dear life, she won't have a free hand to put a dagger in my back.*

"Then allow me to make it a bit safer," Umbris said, reading Kullen's thoughts.

Before Kullen could think to respond, Umbris sent them into a steep dive. Kullen smirked when it failed to have the effect his dragon friend had expected. Natisse still remained collected and as calm as could be expected under the circumstances.

Her offer to accompany him to the Palace had been beyond perfect. He'd wanted to keep her close, to watch and learn more about her to better understand what she would do with her newfound power. At the time, he'd worried that she would use it to further the Crimson Fang's ultimate objective—whatever in Ulnu's frozen ball sack that was. Now, however, he wasn't so certain.

There'd been no missing the confrontation between her and General Andros. It had gone beyond mere disagreement into outright hostility, possibly even hatred. Perhaps there was some vulnerability to exploit, some weakness he could use to gain the woman's confidence and learn more about the insurrectionists. Alone, she might eventually grow less defensive, more likely to open up to him.

The first time Natisse showed any sign of nerves was when Tempest, Jaylen straddling his neck, swirled around Umbris so close, the air chilled by a dozen degrees.

"Careful with him!" Kullen shouted to Tempest.

In response, Tempest straightened into an undulating line.

Kullen felt a surge of relief at the sight of the boy. The Prince would find no fiercer defender than the Wind Dragon beneath him. There were few threats in Dimvein—indeed, in the entire Karmian Empire—capable of getting to Jaylen now that he was reunited with Tempest.

And yet, Kullen couldn't help feeling a flicker of pain, too. In the pale moonlight, Jaylen's resemblance to his father grew stronger. He recalled the last time they'd gone flying—him on Umbris's back, Jarius riding Tempest. Hadassa had insisted on joining them. Stubborn as ever, even though she *hated* heights, she'd argued until Jarius had no choice but to relent.

What a night that had been—like old times, in the days before

Hadassa became Princess and Kullen adopted the mantle of Black Talon. Three friends, all appellations and duties forgotten, laughing and soaring high above Dimvein.

A fortnight later, Jarius and Hadassa had been killed. Lost to Kullen, to Tempest, to Emperor Wymarc, and the Karmian Empire.

In the distance, the Palace crested the horizon. Even from such a range, Thanagar's sturdy frame could be spotted atop his favorite tower, tail wrapping it like a slithering serpent. Closer and closer they came, and with the approach, Natisse's grasp on Kullen constricted. He could almost feel the heat radiating off of her. He thought to reassure her but knew the words would do little to ease her mind.

They passed the Upper Crest and crossed over the Palace walls. Thanagar stirred. The great beast's reception contrasted sharply with Kullen's last visit to the Palace. The dragon raised its enormous head and let out a roar, but even Kullen could hear the joy in the booming, thunderous bellow. All of Dimvein heard it.

Kullen brought Umbris into a tight, spiraling dive, banking hard and pulling up just above the Emperor's personal garden. There, he saw a handful of figures standing in a ring of torchlight. Emperor Wymarc stood at the front, flanked by Turoc on his right side and Assidius on his left. Behind him, a ring of Elite Scales formed an honor guard. There was no need—up here, so close to Thanagar, the Emperor was utterly untouchable—but Kullen suspected his violent entrance two nights past had prompted Captain Angban to increase security.

The ground shook as Umbris landed amidst the flowering plants. Tempest, in contrast, landed soft as a breeze, lying low for Jaylen to disembark. Which he did, immediately falling into the waiting arms of his grandfather. Wymarc clutched the young man to his chest and held him with all the strength of elderly arms. Tears of relief streamed down his age-lined cheeks, soaking into the young man's rough-spun tunic. Kullen turned away to give the

Emperor a moment of privacy and focused on helping Natisse down from Umbris's back.

"Watch the scales," he told her. "They can be nasty."

Umbris puffed.

"No offense meant, friend," Kullen said with a smile. "You're just a dangerous weapon to soft flesh."

Natisse leaned in tentatively toward what passed for the dragon's ears. "Thank you," she said so soft Kullen almost missed it. Then, she turned to accept Kullen's outstretched hand.

She looked quite the sight, he had to admit. Her windswept sanguine locks fluffed like a lion's mane. It was a good look on her. Her icy blue eyes sparkled with the light of a thousand stars.

"Kullen." Emperor Wymarc's strong voice demanded his attention. With effort, he tore his eyes away from the red-haired woman and turned to kneel before his monarch.

"My Emperor," he said in the tone of respect he *only* espoused when addressing the monarch in public.

Emperor Wymarc's hands gripped him by the shoulder and pulled him to his feet, then embraced him in a fierce hug.

"Thank you!" he hissed into Kullen's ear. "You brought him back to me."

"Always, Majesty." Kullen was unused to the monarch showing such outward gratitude toward anyone. For him to do so with Kullen, with the Elite Scales and others present—especially Assidius—he must've been truly perturbed by the potential loss of his grandson. It was unsettling to see him this way.

Emperor Wymarc pulled back and turned away from Kullen, looking once again toward the Prince. Two of the Elite Scales now supported Jaylen, who had grown even paler and now shivered as if chilled—or feverish.

"Get him inside!" Emperor Wymarc barked, snapping his fingers to the Elite Scales. "All of you, take him to his chambers and summon the Imperial Physicker at once."

"Yes, Imperial Majesty!" came a unified response.

One by one, they turned on their heels and stomped from the

gardens, leaving Kullen and Natisse alone with Wymarc, Turoc, and Assidius.

Kullen took note of Turoc—the golden, rune-etched rings in his beard, in particular. The man who'd attacked the Refuge had noted gold rings in the big, ugly Orken's beard who'd been in league with Magister Branthe. And Kullen still carried in his pocket the trinket he'd found on Magister Branthe's corpse—a sign that one of the highest-ranked members of the Orkenwatch was in on the conspiracy of traitors.

"When Captain Angban conveyed your message," Emperor Wymarc was saying as Kullen turned back to him, "I feared the worst. I am elated to find your word to be true. I must admit, my fears gained their hold on me, and I had irrational moments of doubt in you."

"Understandable," Kullen said. "Under the circumstances."

Emperor Wymarc's eyes slid past Kullen, and a curious expression blossomed on his face. "And who, pray tell, is this?" he asked, looking straight at Natisse.

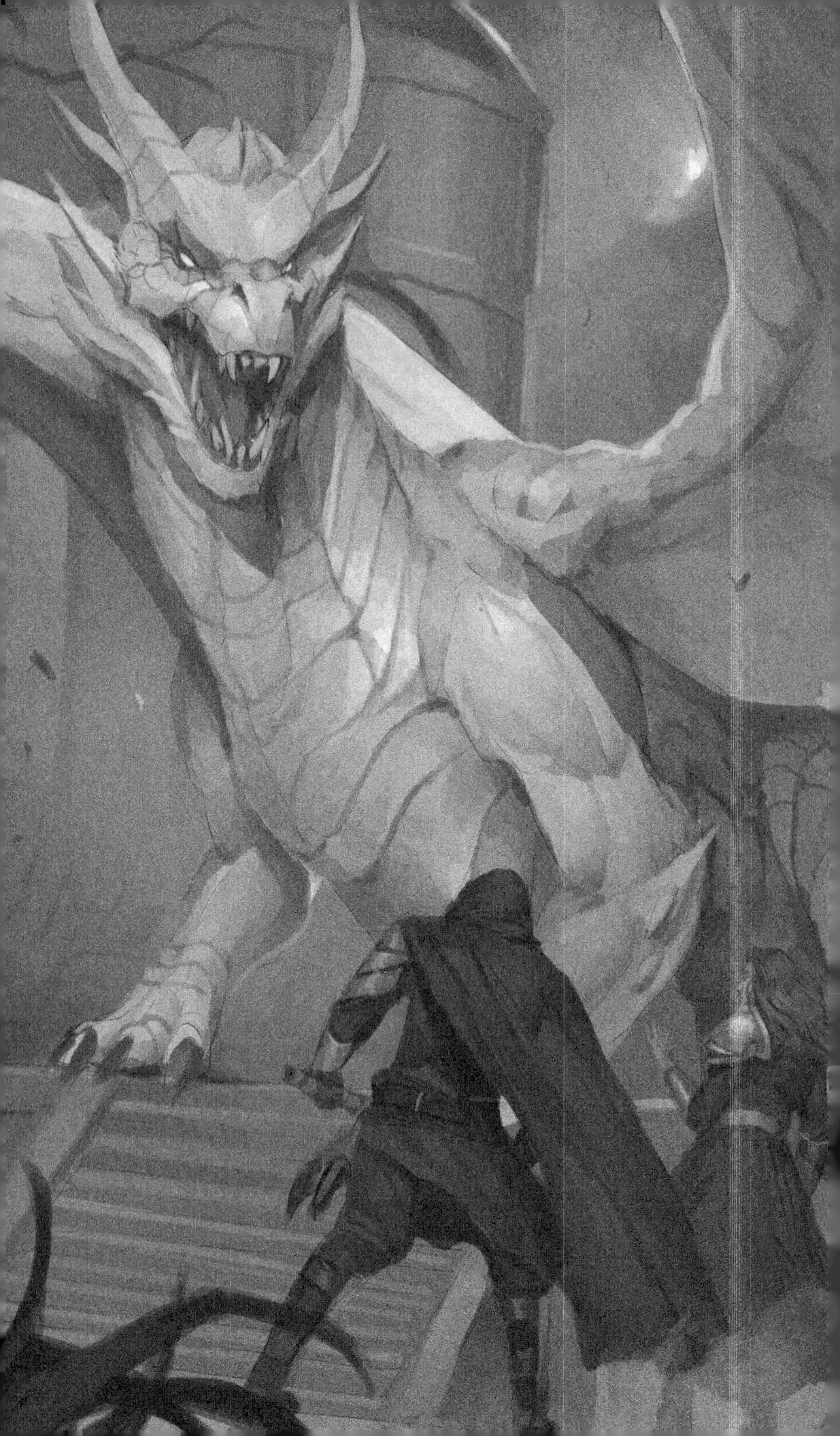

29

NATISSE

Natisse's head spun. Coming literally face-to-face with a living, breathing dragon had unnerved her, and the heart-pounding, breathtaking dragon-back ride through the night had been as terrifying as it was exhilarating. Now, she stood in the Imperial Palace itself. She couldn't decide who to stare at: the ferocious-looking Orken brute looming large before her, the monstrous bulk of Thanagar, the so-called Protector, just a few strides away, or the Emperor himself.

Thanagar's size stole her breath. She'd thought Kullen's dragon —the assassin had called him Umbris—was heavily muscled, and the wingspan of the Prince's serpent-like dragon, Tempest, had impressed her. But this creature before her dwarfed the other dragons by magnitudes. Soul-piercing red eyes seemed fixed on her—though, perhaps, the beast was eyeing Kullen. Either way, it emanated raw, oppressive energy.

The Orken, too, was a truly impressive specimen, even among his own kind. He, however, seemed to pay her no mind, his dark eyes locked on Kullen, watchful, wary. Though he made no move for the enormous two-handed sword strapped to his broad back, Natisse had no doubt the giant creature would wade into battle bare-handed to defend the Emperor. The fact that he was focused on *Kullen* rather than her intrigued her. Did the Orken view the Black Talon as a threat?

But the one who intrigued her most of all was Emperor Wymarc. She'd never seen him up close—the monarch rarely deigned to venture outside the Palace, preferring to keep himself removed from the suffering of his people. What she saw now bore little resemblance to the image she'd painted in her head.

The tyrant had clearly once been a powerfully-built man, but time and the cares of the Empire had worn away his strength, left him, somehow, diminished. The lines on his face were far deeper than she'd expected, and there was a pronounced weariness to him as he clung to his grandson and wept. *Wept*! She found the sight terribly disconcerting. Terribly... *normal*. As if he was just another aging grandfather relieved to see his beloved child alive. In the face of that, she found it difficult to remember that this age-worn man was the ruler of the most powerful empire in all of Caernia.

But she remembered soon enough when the Emperor turned his gaze on her. "And who, pray tell, is this?"

There it was. She saw it in his eyes. A sharp intelligence, keen insight, and the ability to peel back the layers to examine what was beneath the surface. He studied her the way Uncle Ronan did, a look that threatened to unmask her true identity before she could summon the words to speak.

To her surprise, Kullen came to her rescue. "A new friend I made in my hunt for the Prince."

"Friend?" Emperor Wymarc asked. His eyes never left Natisse, but the sharp smile forming on his lips was clearly directed at Kullen. "Since when have you made friends anywhere, Kullen?"

"You wound me, Majesty." Kullen mimicked a dagger thrust to the heart. "Kullen the Amiable, they call me."

A snort from behind the Emperor drew Natisse's attention. For the first time, she spotted the lean man standing in the giant Orken's shadow. Dark hair, black as the lands beyond Thanagar's dome, a pointed goatee, sharp eyebrows, deep-set brown eyes, and whip-thin frame put the man at odds with his surrounding fellows.

"You have something to add, Seneschal?" Kullen's voice was hard as pounded metal.

"Not as such," the man said. His words had a strange sibilant quality to them as if hissing from a serpent's tongue.

"Leaving aside what 'they' call you, amiable or otherwise," Emperor Wymarc said, ignoring the exchange, "I'll admit surprise to find you keeping the company of others." The Emperor's wary gaze drilled holes into Natisse. She knew that look—judgment, unabashed judgment. Finally, he shifted his focus away from her and settled on Kullen. "More surprising is that you brought her here."

"I didn't have much choice," Kullen said, shrugging.

Shrugging… To the Emperor! Natisse's mind boggled. She'd never imagined anyone would be so brazen with the Imperial monarch.

"We were in a bit of a hurry to return Jaylen back in one piece," Kullen continued, not noticing her astonishment. "I figured you wouldn't mind her seeing your precious garden. Call it payment in exchange for her assistance in returning your grandson."

The words confused Natisse. The notion of payment had never entered her mind, not once. Ulnu's bloody claws, she'd have settled for merely letting the Prince and his minder walk away without bringing the Orkenwatch down on the Crimson Fang. Yet here they were, standing in the Emperor's "precious garden," and Kullen had—thus far—kept his word not to reveal her true identity to the monarch.

"I'm just glad we could deliver him safely, sir," Natisse said. That felt—and judging by the scowl on the thin-faced, goateed man—terribly insufficient, so she added, "Er… Imperial Majesty." She didn't know if she ought to bow or curtsy, so she did neither.

A ghost of a smile tugged on Emperor Wymarc's lips. "And what is your name? 'New friend of Kullen's' seems an awful mouthful."

Natisse's eyes darted to Kullen and found him looking at her, waiting. For what?

For her to speak, she realized. To give her name—or some other—to the Emperor of her own free will.

Again, he surprised her. All she could do was stammer out. "N-Natisse, Imperial Majesty."

"Natisse," the monarch repeated, testing the sound. "A beautiful name. Meaning 'flame of the gods' in Old Imperial, yes?" He glanced over his shoulder at the slim man.

"Indeed, Your Imperial Radiance," said the one Kullen had called "Seneschal." "Though it could also be interpreted as 'divine fire' or 'inferno of the exalted ones,' depending on the characters used to scribe it."

"Indeed. Indeed," Emperor Wymarc seemed to consider that, then smiled wider. "Whatever its meaning, it is a good name. And fitting for you." He grabbed a lock of his own thinning hair as if to demonstrate his meaning.

"Thank you, Your Majesty," Natisse said, simply because she knew not what else to say.

"If you don't mind, Eminence," Kullen spoke up, "there are a few matters that require your personal attention. As soon as possible."

"Of course." Emperor Wymarc nodded. He glanced at Natisse, his eyes questioning.

"Some of it concerns her, Majesty," Kullen said, his voice oddly calm. "Best she is here while we discuss it."

And there it was. Any aspirations Natisse had entertained that Kullen wouldn't betray her died, snuffed out by his words. He had her cornered, surrounded, at the mercy of an Orken and the world's most powerful dragon. All he had to do now was reveal her true identity and divulge the location of the Crimson Fang, and there would be nothing she could do to escape the inevitable capture, imprisonment, and doubtless torture. The Burrow would be raided, and her people—

"Natisse was instrumental in helping me locate your grandson," Kullen said, "and getting him to a skilled healer who very well saved his life." He shot her a glance that appeared casual but which she realized held a warning to hold her tongue. "She came across Jaylen while he was fleeing the chaos of Magister Branthe's fighting ring. Your grandson had gotten free before Captain Angban arrived, but I trust that the good captain had the scene buttoned up tight and did a thorough job of identifying every aristocrat present?"

Emperor Wymarc looked to the Seneschal as if for confirmation. "Assidius?"

"The list is thorough, indeed, Divinity," the goateed man said, bowing low. "I suspect a few managed to flee before the Scales were on-site, but—"

"I made sure to identify everyone I saw there *before* it went up in flames," Kullen said. Reaching into his cloak, he drew out a folded piece of parchment and offered it to the Emperor. "If this isn't evidence enough to arrest and prosecute those who slipped through Captain Angban's net, I will be more than happy to pay them a visit personally. Punishment must be meted out for their involvement in Magister Branthe's treacherous slave ring."

Natisse struggled to mask her surprise. He spoke about the slavery with a poisoned tongue, as if his hatred for their actions rivaled even her own.

With a nod, Emperor Wymarc took the parchment and handed it to the Seneschal without a glance of his own. "Good work, Kullen. Everyone you identified will be dealt with appropriately."

Natisse's surprise gave way to fear. Had he included *her* name on that list? Jad's? Uncle Ronan's? But if his intention was to betray her, he could've done so a thousand times over. He was certainly fast and skilled enough to disarm her, remove her dragonblood vial, and incapacitate her if he so chose. No, the more Natisse considered it, the more likely it seemed that he was actually keeping true to his word.

"The Black Talon spoke the truth, and he will honor it," Golgoth whispered into her mind.

It startled Natisse to hear the dragon speak so clearly. Once the shock settled, she tried a response. *How do you know?*

"Just as I knew you would be my next Bloodsworn. Your heart is true and honest, as is his."

Something tugged at Natisse's insides—a longing, urging to be present with Golgoth bodily. It twisted her gut in a fashion not dissimilar to how she felt when thoughts of Baruch entered her mind. She didn't like it.

"You said matter*s*." Emperor Wymarc's voice drew Natisse's attention back to her surroundings. "What else?"

"I told you of the assault against the Refuge," Kullen said. "But I paid them a visit, and from what I could tell, no Imperial aid has been dispatched to facilitate the repairs."

Emperor Wymarc's face drew into a frown. "Is that so?" He turned a dire glare on the rat-faced man behind him. "Assidius? Did I not command you to see it sent this morning?"

"You did, Radiant Majesty," Assidius answered, cringing. "But as I consulted the Imperial Treasurer, I was informed that taking out the sum necessary to effect such repairs would greatly diminish Your Imperial Greatness's capacity to maintain the flow of food and supplies into Dimvein. What might help the Embers would harm much of the rest of the city."

"All due respect to the Seneschal," Kullen said in a voice that held little respect at all, "as Natisse will agree, the Refuge is the only thing standing between the poorest of Dimvein and certain death by starvation, exposure, or illness. I have it on good authority that cases of Aching Fever have begun cropping up around the Embers. Which makes the need for the Refuge all the greater. There is a chance that others *may* suffer should you spend the meager sum needed to repair the damage. It is an absolute certainty that the Embers *will* suffer if the Refuge is not rebuilt with all haste." He spun to Natisse. "Do I speak out of turn?"

She'd been surprised to hear her name mentioned, and even more so when he looked to her for confirmation. This was the first she'd heard of the Refuge being attacked or destroyed. She had no idea what made him believe she knew *anything* about the orphanage, but he wasn't wrong.

"Kullen speaks the truth, Your Majesty," Natisse said. She had to force the words out, but as she spoke them, she gained confidence. This, at least, was a subject about which she knew a great deal—the suffering of the Embers' people. "I've spent most of my life in the Embers and the One Hand District, and I can say with absolute certainty that many people in Dimvein depend on the Refuge for food, clothing, shelter, healing, education, and, of course, the care of the children abandoned on the streets—of which there are far too many. Failing to rebuild the Refuge in the wake of its destruction would be as bad as telling the people of the Embers they are worthless, useless."

Only *after* she'd finished did Natisse realize that last might have been a step too far. She'd heard Uncle Ronan's anger echoing in her words. Yet they hadn't been an exaggeration. Already, most of the Embers-folk felt as if the Emperor cared nothing for them. The Imperial Scales and Orkenwatch certainly conveyed that sentiment. They had far too loose a concern for the rampant crime, seemingly considering the Embers's people expendable. And she couldn't even recall the last time the Royal Physickers spent the afternoon tending to the many ailments of its citizens.

Emperor Wymarc's expression grew grave. He stroked his white beard for a long moment, his gaze fixed on her. He seemed not to have been offended by her tone—to be fair, the aghast expression on the Seneschal's hatchet face showed outrage and offense aplenty for all of Dimvein.

"See it is done, Assidius," the Emperor finally said. He turned to the man with a hard look. "At once."

"Imperial Maj—"

"At once, Seneschal." The Emperor's voice never rose in volume, but still thundered with a note of command. "We must do everything in Our power for all Our people. Even those of the Embers."

Those words stung Natisse, but she understood his meaning.

At least, she thought she did. It wasn't so much a slight against the Embers as a needed reminder to the Seneschal.

"As you say, Divine Radiance." Assidius bowed deep and turned to go, but Natisse caught the dark look he shot at Kullen—with a little venom to spare for her, too.

"Another thing, Majesty," Kullen continued, not waiting for the Seneschal to fully depart. "The night I flew here to warn you of Magister Branthe's treachery, I spotted what looked like an army marshaling behind his walls. Have they been rounded up and disarmed?"

"Unfortunately, I have little good news to offer in that regard." The Emperor frowned. "As soon as you brought word of Magister Branthe's deceit, I dispatched the Orkenwatch and a company of Elite Scales to secure his mansion. The Orken saw signs of a small force—perhaps two or three hundred strong, but by the time they arrived, the gathered men had vanished. To great effect, it seems." He turned his gaze on the giant Orken, who had, until now, remained silent, his expression an impassive mask of stone. "Your people have turned up nothing, Turoc?"

"Nothing, sir." The Orken shook his head, and the motion set the gold bands in his beard jangling. "Search, we have, through entire city. Even underground and in sewers, much to dismay of Sniffers. But continue we will, not stopping until they are being found."

Kullen muttered a barely audible curse under his breath. Natisse was just doing her best to keep up with everything being discussed. She still didn't know why Kullen had kept her on hand for the conversation—perhaps to prove he had no intention of betraying her?

"Good." Emperor Wymarc nodded, then turned back to Kullen. "Anything else to report?"

"Just this." The Black Talon reached into his cloak and withdrew a vial identical to the one Natisse wore around her neck—blood-red contents, golden cap, and all. He held it out to Emperor Wymarc. "Isaax."

The single word seemed explanation enough for the Emperor. His shoulders slumped noticeably. He took the vial between thumb and forefinger and eyed it with forlorn sadness.

"Oh, Carritus!" He let out a sigh, running his thumb along the vial's smooth glass curves.

For the first time since they'd arrived, Thanagar moved. His long neck slithered down toward them. Natisse held her breath. The dragon's snout stopped an inch from the vial, and he let out a soft groan. Soft for a dragon. In truth, it made the leaves around them shiver. Natisse herself couldn't suppress her own shudder.

The Emperor recovered, though not fully. "You have done well, Kullen." He nodded to the assassin, then to Natisse. "And you have Our gratitude for your assistance in rescuing and protecting my grandson."

Natisse began to speak when the Emperor continued.

"However, I will need to speak with Kullen alone. I am sure Turoc would be happy to keep you company for a short while."

The Emperor turned to Turoc, who nodded.

Fear tightened around Natisse like a corset.

"Of course," she said, swallowing hard.

Wymarc grabbed Kullen by the arm and ushered him away from Natisse and Turoc and deeper into the gardens.

Natisse took a small moment to consider her predicament, surrounded by dragons and Orken—alone. And Kullen off with the Emperor. What did they need to discuss? Was the Emperor suspicious of her? Had he recognized her name somehow? Had her admitting to spending her life so close to the potential known whereabouts of the Crimson Fang let the Emperor onto something?

She would only have to hope Kullen stayed true.

All the while, the tightening of her gut persisted, the presence of Golgoth within her pressing and growing stronger.

She took a cautious step forward, and Turoc fell in behind her. The perfect position to drive his blade through her spine.

30
KULLEN

"I have a new mission for you," Emperor Wymarc said when he'd drawn Kullen out of earshot of Turoc and Natisse. Well, Natisse, certainly. Orken had keener ears than a bloodhound. But the Emperor knew that, so if he'd chosen to speak within Turoc's hearing range, it meant he wanted only to keep his words from the unfamiliar woman Kullen had called his "new friend."

"Does it have something to do with Red Claw?" Kullen asked, raising an eyebrow. He hadn't forgotten the name he'd seen signed on the scrap of parchment taken from Magister Deckard's fireplace. He had once believed it might be Magister Branthe, but when he'd asked the dying traitor, the magister had refused to divulge the one behind the identity. Which, in a way, led Kullen to believe there was another hand pulling the strings—if not controlling Magister Branthe.

"Assidius has turned up nothing to indicate who this mysterious 'Red Claw' might be." Emperor Wymarc shook his head, a frown twisting his lips. "Were it anyone else, I might suspect willful ignorance or deliberate obfuscation. But not Assidius. If he has not found anything yet, either he will in time, or there will be nothing to find."

Kullen held his peace. He had never liked Assidius, but more than that, there was something about the unctuous, obsequious man that kept Kullen from ever fully trusting him. Just because Emperor Wymarc held the Seneschal in the highest confidence, that wouldn't stop Kullen from suspecting him. Privately, of course. The Emperor had made it clear that he and Assidius were to work together for the good of the Empire.

"As for the *other* matter you brought to me that night," Emperor Wymarc said, his eyes flicking to Turoc, "Assidius has begun digging. But he must tread with care, for it is a sensitive matter."

"To say the least." Kullen's jaw muscles twitched. The Orken, proud warriors all, wouldn't take kindly to being suspected of treason. Assidius would have to dig with a featherlight touch or risk stirring up outrage among the Orkenwatch. Such accusations could lead to an insurrection amongst the beasts. Kullen always suspected they were just waiting for an opportunity all these years. And who would stop them—Captain Angban and his Elite Scales, who Kullen could take five-to-one?

Given everything that had happened in the last few days, that was one problem Dimvein could ill afford.

"The nature of this new mission is no less delicate," Emperor Wymarc said, his expression growing serious, "but it is one to which I believe you are best suited."

"What is it?" Kullen asked. Alone with the Emperor, he had no need for formalities. "Who's the target?"

"That is what I expect you to find out." Emperor Wymarc's lips pressed together, wrinkles forming at the corners of his mouth and eyes. "Assidius has received word of an… affair taking place tomorrow evening, but it is no more than a front, an excuse to gather potential buyers for a great auction. One where, according to Assidius, the missing dragonblood vials will be sold off."

Kullen's eyebrows shot up. "He's certain?"

"As certain as he can be, given its location." Emperor Wymarc fixed Kullen with a meaningful look. "It's taking place on Pantagoya."

Kullen hissed in a breath through his teeth. "Of course it'd be there!"

His memories of Pantagoya were far from fond—on the contrary, he'd nearly died every time he stepped foot onto the floating pleasure island. A haven of scum and villainy in all its forms, though cleverly concealed beneath a façade of gold, silver, silks, and crystal. There were few places on Caernia that could rival the wickedness of Pantagoya.

"Get there," Emperor Wymarc said, his tone somber. "Buy, bribe, talk, or kill your way into that auction. Whatever you have to do, just get in. Retrieve the dragonblood vials at all costs. Find out who is behind the auction, and *convince* them to reveal how they've been stealing all the vials from the dead Magisters."

Kullen grinned. "I can be quite persuasive, Majesty." He tapped the hilt of his dagger. "Tongues will wag, and, if necessary, heads will roll."

"Only as many as are needed." Emperor Wymarc shook his head. "The last thing we need is to anger the Pantagorissa by messing up her home. The Empire has prospered from our mutually beneficial arrangement these last ten years."

"Understood." Kullen nodded. He glanced over his shoulder to where Natisse stood in Umbris's shadow, staring between him, the Emperor, Turoc, and Thanagar with an utterly unreadable expression on her face. The sight of her brought back the memory of the night they'd first met on Magister Perech's pleasure barge. That gave him an interesting idea.

"Any reasons I can't bring my new friend with me?" he asked the Emperor.

Emperor Wymarc cocked his head. "You think that's a good idea?" He might not know who Natisse was, but he knew Kullen and trusted his judgment.

"I'd certainly have an easier time gaining access to these festivities in her company," Kullen said. "And she can more than play the part." He hadn't so much as noticed her among the dilettantes and fops until *after* she'd put a dagger in Magister Perech. Though, he must admit, that was a surprise considering what he knew of her now. She should've stood out amongst them like a bright, shining star amid the blackest night.

Emperor Wymarc studied Kullen, then Natisse, then Kullen once more. Kullen met the monarch's gaze levelly. He didn't *need* Natisse's help, but he did want to keep her close, learn more about her. This gave him a chance to do precisely that. He could at least extend her the offer; surely there was something on Pantagoya the Crimson Fang wanted badly enough that she'd consider accompanying him.

"So be it." Emperor Wymarc gave a little nod. "I defer to your expertise, Black Talon."

Kullen gave a little bow. When he straightened, he caught sight of Thanagar. Standing so close to Umbris, it was almost as if the Great White glowed with the radiance of pure light. That brought back the memory of what had happened two nights past when the Lumenators' light clashed with Umbris's Shadow Realm magic. If anyone could help him make sense of it, it was the man *Bloodsworn* to Thanagar, the presumed source of the Lumenators' gift.

But the chance for inquiry escaped. Before he could speak, a high-pitched voice cut through the quiet of the garden.

"Imperial Majesty!"

Kullen and Emperor Wymarc both turned to see a young pageboy rushing toward them.

"F-Forgiveness, Radiant One," the boy stammered, somehow managing to bow deeply without slowing his run, "but I've been sent to fetch you. The Royal Physickers are concerned over the Prince, and they need Your Grace's instructions on how to proceed."

"I'll be there momentarily," Emperor Wymarc said.

Kullen stifled his worry for Jaylen. Jad had done a good job of dressing and stitching his wounds. No doubt it was just the natural fussiness inbred into physickers like Rassad and Erasthes.

The young man slowed to a stop before the Emperor. "The Royal Physickers impressed upon me the urgency of this situation," the pageboy said, clearly nervous. "Their precise words were 'Summon the Emperor here with all possible haste.'"

Emperor Wymarc's face paled.

"Go," Kullen said quietly. "I'll report back as soon as I can." He could speak on the Lumenators' magic upon his return. "We'll find who's behind the missing vials, Majesty."

"Thank you," the Emperor said, but the words came out in a croak. He turned and hurried away with the pageboy, leaving Kullen alone.

The Emperor marched toward Natisse, spotting Turoc's wide nostrils wafting the scent of her, imprinting, ensuring that should there be reason, he'd be able to locate her. Turoc may not have been a Sniffer, but all Orken had an acute sense of smell. The Tuskigo grunted and followed the Emperor, as was his royal duty.

Kullen approached Natisse. She hadn't spoken much—not surprising, given that she'd just come face-to-face with the Emperor, the commander of the Orkenwatch, and Thanagar himself in the space of a few minutes—but what little she'd said had impressed him. There had been genuine conviction in her voice, and she hadn't been afraid to speak her mind, even to the Emperor.

As he grew closer, he saw the pain wracking her features. She held one hand to her belly and stood hunched, if not bent at the waist. He knew all too well what she was experiencing, though she did not. Whether she realized it or not, she needed his help. And he had an idea that would likely benefit them both. Now, it all hinged on whether or not he'd built up enough trust with her that she would oblige him his request for company to Pantagoya.

"You up for another ride?" he asked, gesturing to Umbris, who had settled down on the grass, eyes shut. Tempest was nowhere in sight, dismissed from the Mortal Realm once his *Bloodsworn* had left the gardens. "Best we depart before we overstay our welcome.

And I've got something I want to show you. If you're up for a short journey out of Dimvein."

Natisse looked up. She did her best to straighten her posture and cocked an eyebrow. "That doesn't sound at all ominous," she said, a sharp edge in her voice—though more of humor than anger. "You're not planning to toss me off Umbris's back over the ocean or dump my corpse into the Wild Grove Forest, are you?"

"Not at the moment." Kullen chuckled. "To be fair, if I had any such intentions, I'd just let Umbris eat you."

Those words groused Umbris from his rest. The Twilight Dragon raised his head slightly, parted his lips, and showed long, serrated teeth.

"She has not enough meat on her bones to make for a satisfying meal," Umbris said. *"Though she looks tasty enough for a snack."*

Judging by the look of horror on Natisse's face, the dragon had spoken plainly into both their minds. Kullen stifled a laugh.

Climbing onto Umbris's back, he reached down to help Natisse up. This time, she didn't take his hand but climbed up behind him with admirable dexterity.

"Just know that if I plummet, you come with me," she said, settling into place and grasping his waist tightly.

"As you say, good lady." With a laugh, Kullen gave Umbris the mental command to fly.

Thanagar watched them leave with rapt attention. Once they'd cleared the Palace walls, he rewrapped himself around his favorite spire, and those glowing red eyes went dim behind closed eyelids.

"Where are we going?" Natisse asked.

"Wild Grove," Kullen said. "But don't worry, I have no intention of leaving your corpse."

"Ah, well then, consider my fretting at ease."

They traveled the rest of the way in silence, listening to the *thump-thump* of Umbris's giant wings. At least once, Kullen sensed Natisse's growing discomfort, knowing she had precious little time left before falling fatally ill. She would need to summon Golgoth, and soon, if she wanted to keep her insides on the inside.

Kullen found the clearing below and brought Umbris in for a smooth landing. The forest was dark and foreboding to most, but for Kullen, it was a welcome change to the ever-present light of Thanagar and his Lumenators. As an assassin, the darkness was a retreat.

With Umbris in the Mortal Realm, Kullen had no access to the dragon's magic and thus was as blind as Natisse. But he had no need of magic for what he had in mind.

"What are we doing out here?" Natisse asked, more than a hint of worry in her voice. "I'm not going to lie, despite your claims otherwise, this feels a great deal like the sort of night that ends with one of our corpses being left in the forest."

"I brought you here to show you what you can do," Kullen said. "Or, more accurately, to give you a safe place to find out for yourself what you can do."

Her grip on him tightened. He couldn't see her face but could imagine the concern festering there. They both slid down, landing softly in the plush grass.

You may return home, friend Umbris, Kullen said through his mind.

A patch of shadow, darker than all the rest of the near pitch blackness, blossomed before them, and Umbris stepped through into the Shadow Realm, leaving Kullen and Natisse alone in the woods. The darkness immediately dispelled before Kullen's dragon-eyes, bringing each tree trunk, each leaf, into vivid clarity.

Now that he could see her, the pallor and the weakness etched onto her normally vibrant and beautiful face, his concerns for her were confirmed.

"Come, let me guide you," he said. "We're nearly too late."

"I told you," Natisse said, her voice hard, "I don't need your help."

Kullen heard her words, but they were lost beneath the pain in her tone.

"I'd like to offer it anyway." Kullen kept his voice calm, careful not to make any sudden movement that might startle her. "I know what's happening to you, what you're feeling. Your bond with Golgoth, you can sense it weakening, can't you?" He didn't wait for her to answer. He *needed* her to understand the danger she faced—it might be the only way she'd trust him enough. "If you don't let me help, you *will* die."

31
NATISSE

"*Die?*" Natisse spat the word, unable to hide her annoyance. She couldn't believe she'd been foolish enough to agree to accompany the assassin with no idea of their destination. Now, she was deep in the Wild Grove Forest in the middle of a cloudy night with barely a hint of pale moonlight visible.

And the pain…

Fire coursed through her, but it was unlike the raw power she'd felt at Golgoth's urgings. Something far more than fear of being alone with dragons and assassins and emperors. This was something agonizing. Her nerves were ablaze. Could Kullen have been telling the truth? If left unchecked, would Golgoth destroy her from the inside?

Momentary panic gripped her at the thought. Had she been tricked?

Kullen advanced on her, and Natisse's hand dropped to the hilt of her lashblade. If he intended to harm her, he'd find she was no easy target. The Black Talon and his pet dragon were in for the fight of their lives.

"Do your worst," she snarled, drawing the blade, wincing as a stinging in her ribs nearly doubled her over.

"I have no intention of doing anything." Kullen's voice was far too calm for Natisse's liking. He hadn't yet made a move toward his weapons—not that she could see—nor ordered his dragon to snap her up, but that didn't mean he wouldn't. "But you need to know the danger you face."

"Right now, the only danger I see is you," she shot back. Though she knew it was a lie. Additionally, she couldn't *see* Umbris, couldn't feel his bulk nearby, but that didn't mean the dragon wasn't crouched and ready to spring.

"That's because you don't understand the full extent of the *Bloodbond*. Or the peril that access to Golgoth's magic brings."

"Explain," she growled.

Though she couldn't see Kullen's face, Natisse felt the assassin's tension slackening.

"From what was told to me when first I bound myself with Umbris," he said, "the *Bloodbond* does more than act as a tether from your consciousness to that of your dragon. It also ties the Mortal Realm to theirs—in your case, the Fire Realm."

Natisse frowned. That was simple enough she could understand. And that perhaps began to explain the agony stirring within her.

"The dragons' power is fed to us through our bond," he continued. "It's why you can summon the flames."

She didn't bother telling him that she hadn't *summoned* anything. The magical fire had sprung into existence without her conscious thought or control.

"Think of it as two ends of a conduit," Kullen continued. "On one side is you, on the other is Golgoth. The bond is the channel that connects you two and allows you to access the power of the Fire Realm and allows Golgoth to materialize in the Mortal Realm. Over time, however, the bond between human and dragon weakens. Should it break, you will become untethered from Golgoth, but the conduit between the Mortal and Fire Realms will remain. All of Golgoth's power will come spilling through into the Mortal Realm." He paused a moment. "Using you like a portal."

"Me?"

Kullen nodded. "Without her magical resistance to help you control it, that power will tear through your all-too-mortal body and burn it from the inside out."

Natisse's throat clenched shut. She couldn't breathe. Memories of her past flooded her: fire, flames, destruction. She'd felt that torment before, the day Dragonfire killed her family and scarred her flesh. Only, by the assassin's words, this would be worse by leagues. She wouldn't simply suffer burns; she would be utterly consumed.

"What must I do to keep the bond strong?" she asked, fighting to stay calm, or at least appear that way. Her legs were quaking, stomach muscles twitching. She went to speak again, but her legs gave out.

Kullen caught her before she fell. "You must summon Golgoth into the Mortal Realm," he said, a note of urgency in his voice. "And soon, before the bond is severed completely."

"How?" she gasped.

"Reach out to her," Kullen said. "Locate her presence through your bond, hear her voice, and summon her to you."

"Just… like that?" Every breath caught, the words feeling like hot coals on her throat, as if the fire burned the air within her lungs.

"Golgoth chose you." There was a note of encouragement and affirmation in Kullen's tone. "She *wants* you to be her conduit to the Mortal Realm. Whatever she saw in you, it was enough that she bound herself to you. Even now, she can feel your pain and wants to help. So let her."

The words surprised her. But they shouldn't have. He was bonded to a dragon, too. He had to know what she was feeling. He could doubtless sense his own dragon's thoughts and feelings, much as she could sense Golgoth's. And he was right. The moment she turned her attention inward, the dragon's presence loomed large in her mind, drowning out the fire raging within her veins.

Golgoth! Natisse called out to the dragon, though not with words. *Golgoth, I summon you!*

Golgoth stirred. Natisse wasn't sure how to explain it, even to herself, but the dragon moved closer, like it was drawn by her mere thoughts.

She felt feverish. Darkness crept in around her eyes and, with it, cold sweats. Then, where the night had been dark, empty, and quiet, suddenly, an enormous figure materialized in a burst of flame that set the very air ablaze around her. A pillar of brilliant red-gold fire ten paces across shot fifty feet upward into the starless sky. Instinctively, Natisse threw up an arm to shield her face. Heat washed over her, searing her lungs and prickling her skin, wicking away the sweat from her brow. Only to die a moment later.

Natisse lowered her hand, and her jaw hung limp as she stared at the creature towering over her. Golgoth rivaled Thanagar in size, a mass of rippling muscle and monstrous power.

Natisse had seen Golgoth before, but that was in the Fire Realm, where the beast was enraptured by flames. Here, in the dense, cool forest, she loomed over even the trees, her body a magnificent crimson where before, her vibrancy had been lost amongst the reds, oranges, and golds of the other plane. Those two long horns curving off the top of her head could skewer a whole squadron of the Emperor's men and still have room for yet more.

But it was the eyes that held Natisse riveted. A mighty inferno blazed within the brilliant golden orbs, with hints of crimson edging the flames. They shone like the sun, burning nearly as hot. Yet there was no denying the gleam of intelligence and wisdom, gathered over centuries—perhaps millennia—of life. And the power! So much power, raw and untamed, a fury that seemed ready to pour forth from the dragon's maw with force enough to destroy the world.

Natisse heard a sharp intake of breath beside her. Kullen had fallen back a step, and in the light leaking from between the scales on Golgoth's enormous body, his face looked pale, a glimmer of fear sparkling in his eyes. He held up one hand like a shield between him and Golgoth's burning eyes, and the other rested on one of his daggers.

Golgoth stared down at the assassin, and Natisse could feel the dragon's ferocity blazing through their bond. Yet there was no animosity aimed at Kullen. Merely… acknowledgment? A strange sense of familiarity she hadn't expected.

"You know each other?" she asked aloud.

"We've met," Kullen said, his voice strangled.

Golgoth rumbled a low growl, her enormous muzzle opening to reveal the glow of Dragonfire churning deep in her belly.

"It is he who freed me from my enslavement," the Ember Dragon said in Natisse's mind. *"But that will not stop me from turning him to ash should he threaten you, Bloodsworn."*

Natisse considered that. A part of her ached to give Golgoth the order to unleash her Dragonfire in vengeance for Baruch's death. But that would do her no good. There was still too much about her *Bloodbond* with Golgoth and the magical abilities it conveyed that she needed to understand.

"He is no danger to me," Natisse responded through their mental bond. To her surprise, she found she actually believed it. He'd had every opportunity to betray her to the Emperor and his pet Orken, but as far as she could tell, Kullen had kept his word. *"The moment that changes, you're more than welcome to eat him."*

Golgoth snarled and lowered her head until it hovered mere inches from Kullen's face. The assassin flinched away from the heat waves rolling off Golgoth, and a snort from the dragon's huge nostrils pushed him back a half step. Yet he didn't cringe or shy away from Golgoth's enormous eye—easily twice the size of his head—glaring furiously at him.

"So what now?" Natisse asked aloud.

"Now," Kullen answered with only a *hint* of fear, "you return her to the Fire Realm so we can practice using your fire magic."

Natisse was about to ask how exactly she went about that, but

Golgoth's voice echoed in her mind. *"Should you wish it, I will see you again soon, Bloodsworn. Just give the thought to release me."*

Before Natisse could help it, the command entered her own thoughts, and a sudden rush of power ravaged her. But this time, there was no pain. She sensed a renewed vigor, fresh strength coursing through her veins with so much force, fire sprang from her hands.

Golgoth was gone, leaving just a charred mess of grass where she'd just been.

Kullen grinned. "Maybe I should've said 'practice *controlling* your fire magic.'" He eyed the flames licking upward from the tips of her fingers. "It'll do you no good if you can't summon it at will or if it flares up at the wrong time."

Natisse tried to step away from her own hands. It was foolish, but the fear gripping her at the sight of it left her brain foggy. She could think of nothing but that day when her parents were torn out of her life, burnt to ash, along with all the others.

"H-How do I control it?" she asked, her mouth suddenly dry.

"What does it feel like?" Kullen asked. "When your hands burst into flames when we were in your underground stronghold, what were you feeling?"

Natisse tried to recall what had been going through her mind at that moment. "Angry," she said.

"And afraid?" Kullen asked.

Natisse's temper flared, as did the flames streaming up from her palms. "I'm not afraid of you!"

Kullen raised his hands. "I had just threatened to kill you and your people. Anger is to be expected, but over the course of my life, I've learned that anger is often a defense mechanism to conceal something we perceive as weakness. Hurt, vulnerability, fear." He shrugged. "Trust me, I've lived with anger long enough to know what I'm talking about."

Natisse raised an eyebrow. "What do *you* have to be angry about?" She couldn't help the sharpness of her tone. "Someone stole your sharpest dagger or tore your finest cowl?"

To her surprise, Kullen didn't respond with irritation or annoyance as she'd expected. Instead, his expression just grew somber.

"Or killed my only friends in the world."

The stillness of his voice sucked the breath from Natisse's lungs almost as much as the words themselves.

"I'll tell you something few others still living know," he continued. A shadow of pain darkened his near-black eyes, and she saw the sorrow written there. "The woman who everyone in Dimvein knew as Princess Hadassa was just Hadassa to me for most of my life. Growing up together in the Refuge as we did, she was the closest thing I'd ever had to family."

That surprised Natisse. Natisse hadn't known much of Princess Hadassa—the woman had died years earlier, when Natisse was around Sparrow's age. Or Prince Jaylen's age, she supposed. But her humble origins as a lowborn citizen of Dimvein had been public knowledge. Indeed, the marriage between a commoner and Prince Jarius had earned the Imperial family the love of Dimvein and the Empire at large.

But to learn she'd been raised among the orphans Mammy Tess took in at the Refuge shocked her almost as much as learning the assassin's own story.

"Prince Jarius, too, eventually. For years, since the day they died, I've barely contained my fury with Magister Deckard for his part in what happened. His greed and thirst for Golgoth's power are what led to the destruction of the Embers. But the Emperor never allowed me to seek vengeance. Which made me hate Deckard all the more."

He fixed his gaze on her. "But all that hate and anger was just another way to protect myself from having to confront the pain of knowing that the two souls I loved most in the world were gone. Dead. And worst of all, that I had to somehow go on living without them." He tapped his chest. "So yes, I know anger. Just as you do. And I know what lies beneath. What it's hiding, and why."

Natisse was so intent upon Kullen's story, she'd hardly noticed the clearing had become even darker. The only light seemed to be her—

"Look at your hands," Kullen said, still in that quiet voice.

Natisse looked down, and her eyes spread wide. The fires were virtually extinguished, with only a candle-sized flame burning on the tip of her right forefinger.

"How did you—?" She cut off, her mind racing. "I did that?"

"When your anger died," Kullen said, nodding. "Or, when you were no longer focusing on it, so too did the flames."

Natisse stared at the little orange tongue sprouting from her fingertip. "So it's anger that controls it?"

"Maybe," Kullen said, rubbing his bearded chin with a rough hand. "Or maybe any strong emotion. Next time you're deliriously happy, see if fire burgeons from your hands. If not…" He shrugged. "Anger's certainly the easiest one to call upon."

Natisse couldn't argue that. She had a great deal to be incensed over.

Something he'd said tugged at Natisse's mind. "You said Golgoth had been bonded to Magister Deckard before me?"

Kullen nodded. "What of it?"

"I always thought only those of aristocratic blood form the bond," she said. "But if you really were raised in the Refuge, then you're no more a magister than I am."

Kullen frowned. "I've never considered that." He spent a moment contemplating the question—or, as it turned out, communing with his dragon. "From what Umbris tells me, anyone can be chosen by a dragon. Blood means nothing to them, only the… *takenth.*"

"The what?" Natisse asked.

"As he explains it, the best translation I can deduce would be soul or spirit. Perhaps our character or our hearts."

Natisse struggled with that one. "What have I in common with Magister Deckard that Golgoth would choose both of us?"

"That's a fine question," Kullen said. "One best suited to be asked of her, don't you think?"

"I..."

A low rumble emerged from somewhere within Natisse. Golgoth's internal voice was becoming more familiar and easier to bear. *"My former master was not always the man he'd become,* she said. *Let that stand as a warning—absolute power corrupts absolutely."*

Kullen waited patiently as Natisse listened. It was an odd characteristic for the man who'd killed Baruch. He was thoughtful, caring, and she hated him all the more for it.

"But I have seen within you something he did not have," Golgoth continued. *"Something I had promised myself I would identify in my next Bloodsworn."*

And that is? Natisse asked, concerned for what she might learn of herself.

"Restraint. A love for those beneath your station."

"There aren't many beneath my station," Natisse said within her mind. She felt her lips pull into a smile and couldn't help feeling a flicker of relief. She had spent so long hating the aristocracy—men like Magisters Estéfar, Perech, and Onathus—that she couldn't stomach the idea of *being* one.

And that fit with what Golgoth had said when first their bond had been formed. The Ember Dragon hadn't mentioned bloodlines or nobility but chosen Natisse, believing she wouldn't abuse her fire magic.

"Now that you have been chosen," Kullen spoke cautiously, "it's important that you maintain the bond. To do that, you have to summon Golgoth once a day."

"Every day?" Natisse's eyebrows shot up.

"Every day." Kullen nodded. "It's easier for me with Umbris. He's small as far as dragons go. I've got warehouses around Dimvein where I can bring him from the Mortal Realm without stirring suspicion. Or, if I need to travel anywhere at night, he's invisible to most human eyes in the darkness. As for you..." He shook his head. "It's going to be bloody hard to find anywhere in Dimvein large enough to contain her. Certainly not in that underground fortress of yours." He chewed on his lip. "We'll work on it."

His casual tone of voice and the way he said "we" so easily surprised Natisse. "You're going to *help* me?" she asked.

"If you'll let me," Kullen said, smiling. "I told you, my offer is genuine. There's a lot to learn about *Bloodsurging*. I had help when I was first bonded with Umbris. I've got some *friends* back in Dimvein who owe me a favor or three. Maybe they've got something sizable."

"You have friends?" Natisse said. Kullen started to protest but stopped when he spotted the grin on her face.

"I do," Kullen said with a nod. "And as I've seen, you do as well. We will speak with mine unless one of your fellows in the Crimson Fang has access to magic—"

"No!" The word echoed through the open air, sending small critters into a frenzied scurry to hide.

Kullen raised an eyebrow, and Natisse cursed inwardly. Only a dense fool would miss the significance of such an abrupt overreaction, and Kullen was neither.

"No," Natisse said, quieter this time. "There's no one in the Crimson Fang who can help me."

If Kullen thought anything of her response, he let it slide. "Then I'd be honored to share what I know, help you understand *Bloodsurging*. The more you practice and learn, the easier it will be to control your powers. And use them more fully. Like this!"

Kullen reached into his cloak. The air whipped around them, and somehow, the woods became so much darker, Natisse wondered if everything had disappeared. Then, the pale light of the moon returned, and Kullen had vanished.

32
KULLEN

Kullen materialized a few paces behind Natisse, deep in the shadows of the walnut trees where he usually summoned Umbris. He stood there for a few moments, enjoying Natisse's confusion as she spun about, eyes darting. The fire on her fingertip flickered out entirely, and the little glade was plunged into darkness.

Perfect, he thought, grinning.

"Don't think." His words echoed through the gloom, causing Natisse to whirl toward him. Silent as night, he shadow-slid across the clearing and spoke again from behind a thick walnut tree. "Feel. Feel the power within you."

Again, Natisse spun, and Kullen changed positions again. He needed to get her heart pounding, to play into the instinctive anxiety most people held toward the darkness and the unknown it concealed.

"Fire wants to burn free," he said, pitching his voice low. "Let it. Be the conduit that brings it from the elemental realm of fire into—"

Twin flames sprang to life not five paces from where he stood. Natisse's eyes blazed with their own inner light, as red-gold as Golgoth's eyes, and the firelight cast her face in a fierce contour.

"Hah!" Grinning, Kullen stepped out from the shadows. "Beautifully done."

Natisse's wild expression darkened to a scowl. "Was that really necessary?"

"I don't know." Kullen shrugged. "But it worked."

That only made Natisse's flames burn brighter; the fire in her eyes blaze hotter.

"Look, I don't know much more about this fire magic than you do." Kullen turned his palms upward. "Umbris connects me to the Shadow Realm, a place vastly disparate to the Fire Realm Golgoth inhabits."

"Oh, is that what you did just there?" For a moment, curiosity peeked through Natisse's anger. "Moved through the shadows? Used it to hide you from sight?"

Kullen's eyebrows rose. She'd taken to her new magical abilities and expanded her understanding far more quickly than he had all those years ago.

"Sort of," he said, waggling one hand back and forth. "Best way I can explain it is that my body *becomes* shadow. When I *Bloodsurge*, it's as if I partially leave the Mortal Realm and step into the Shadow Realm. I can exist in both places at once, though it takes effort to travel between them."

"You travel?" Natisse's eyes sparkled with genuine curiosity, and the flames sprouting from her hands turned from an angry crimson to a cool, whimsical gold.

"Shadow-sliding, I call it." Kullen nodded. "Handy in my line of work. I'd be a pretty damned useless assassin if I sprouted fire."

Natisse glowered down at her hands. "Any advice on how to get rid of the flames once they're here? Calling them into existence felt easy, but now that they're burning free, it's like they don't want to go out."

Kullen considered that. With Umbris's shadow magic, he merely had to *will* himself back into corporeal form. Maybe that could work for her, too?

"Try imposing your will on the fire," he said, attempting to sound as if speaking from experience. "Compel it to obey you."

Natisse focused on her hands, a furrow appearing on her brow. She seemed to hold her breath while concentrating all her effort on the flames. To no effect.

"Nothing's happening," she said, looking up at him.

"Try again." He kept his tone and expression encouraging. The more she felt he was on her side, the more easily she would start trusting him. That had been the whole point behind his telling her the story of Hadassa and Jarius. "This time, really focus."

"What do you think I've been doing?" Natisse snapped. The flames returned to their deep, violent crimson.

Kullen ignored her retort; she was frustrated, as was to be expected. Ezrasil knew he had struggled to master his own Umbris-granted ability.

"Try again," he repeated. "But call on Golgoth to lend you her will. She is the Queen of the Ember Dragons, a being of pure fire. If anyone knows how to control it, it would be her."

Again, Natisse's forehead furrowed, and she bent all her focus on her burning hands. Long seconds dragged on, and still, nothing happened. Sweat pricked her brow. Her jaw muscles clenched, and every muscle in her spine seemed to go rigid as if she exerted every shred of effort.

Kullen was about to recommend they try a different approach, but the words died unformed on his lips when the flames snuffed out in a wisp of smoke.

"Hah!" Natisse crowed. She held up her hands to him. "I did it!"

"So you did." Kullen beamed, though, in the darkness, he knew she could not see him. "And it was well done."

"What next?" Natisse asked, excitement in the question. Even as she spoke, flames sprang up on her palms and fingers once more.

"Next?" Kullen raised an eyebrow. "Don't you think you should practice that a bit more?"

Natisse shook her hands, and the fires extinguished instantly.

Damn, she was learning fast. It was as if control of fire came naturally to her—far more naturally than mastery of shadow had come to him.

"Okay," he said, drawing out the word. "Let's try a lesson I heard Jarius learning when he was younger." He strode toward her, though careful to keep his hands well away from his weapons. "A way to help you channel the fire, to control it."

"What do I do?" Natisse asked, eagerness in her voice. A tiny flame flickered to life in the palm of her hand, casting a small globe of illumination that lit up her excited face.

Kullen came to stand directly in front of Natisse. "To be honest, I don't know much about this one, but maybe it'll work for you." He considered how best to explain the concept he'd never tested for himself. "When Jarius was first learning how to manipulate Tempest's wind magic, he liked to use a solid object to help him visualize the currents of wind and his control over them. For him, it was a sword. He would wave it about him while he worked the magic, using the wind like an extension of the blade. He said it gave him something to focus on and direct the power. Maybe that'd work for you." He glanced down at the weapon on her belt. "With that."

Natisse followed the line of his eyes. "My lashblade?"

"Yes." Kullen had to admit that was a much better name than "whip-sword."

Natisse drew it slowly, almost hesitantly, watching him all the while. Kullen forced himself to remain calm, keep his expression impassive. This was intended as the ultimate demonstration of his trust in her. She held a bared weapon while he stood empty-handed. If she turned it on him, he'd have no chance to defend himself. She was certainly more than skilled enough to kill him.

When she didn't cut him down, Kullen continued as if nothing of great importance had just occurred.

"Focus on the blade," he said in a voice far calmer than he felt. Indeed, his heart pounded just a bit too fast, and sweat trickled down the small of his back. "Get a sense of weight, its heft, the solid feel in your hand." Clearly, it was a weapon she knew well, which hopefully made the task more facile. "Use it to direct the magic. Not *into* the sword—that could damage the steel—but around it. Picture the tongues forming a sheath to encase the weapon in fire."

Natisse bent to the task, her forehead wrinkling ever so slightly in concentration. It didn't take long before the fires sprang to her hands, but this only served to singe the hilt's leather wrappings. Growling a curse, Natisse extinguished it.

"Again," Kullen encouraged.

Her second attempt proved no more successful. Nor the third or fourth.

In a way, Kullen was more than a little relieved to find that this, at least, was proving more difficult. He'd have felt a downright dunce had she mastered it so quickly.

"Try it different this time," he said. "Move the sword around, and use the air currents to help you control the fire."

"That makes no sense," Natisse snapped. "Air will just make it *harder* to control."

Frustration was clearly getting the better of her. And, Kullen guessed, exhaustion as well. She had been playing with the fire magic for far longer than Kullen could use his own shadow magic. If she hadn't yet reached her limitations, it wouldn't be long.

"Fire craves air," he said, "feeds on it." He'd burned down more than a few structures, all belonging to the Emperor's enemies. "Without air, the fire starves and dies. Too much air, and the fire is snuffed out. But with just the right amount, it grows from a small blaze into a firestorm."

Natisse slowly swung the blade back and forth. When nothing happened, she hastened. Soon, she was flailing the weapon around like angry bees were attacking her, and she was desperate to get away.

"Focus," Kullen said. "Control it. Don't let it control you."

Natisse let out a frustrated grunt, and fire suddenly exploded into life along the whipping blade, but instead of a controlled burn licking at the steel, it burst outward in a flaming halo, setting the nearby trees ablaze.

Kullen's hand darted into his shirt, and he jammed his finger onto the cap of the dragonblood vial. *Umbris, come to me!*

The Twilight Dragon materialized from the shadows, of which there were suddenly far fewer as the inferno spread.

Help me put out the flames!

Umbris didn't need two tellings. He went to work, beating his wings hard. However, instead of sending forth great gusts of wind as Tempest would've done, darkness began to swallow up the flames.

Kullen caught a glimpse of Natisse's face. She stood wide-eyed, almost paralyzed by the sight. He couldn't know her thoughts, but some great darkness hovered in her mind, and he could see it in her eyes.

That surprised him almost as much as her natural affinity for fire magic. Or perhaps, that might *explain* how easily the element responded to her. Sure, her red hair danced like flames when she moved. And clearly, her temper was fiery, but it was more than that. He'd seen the scar tissue on her arm and neck—clearly, she'd been touched by flames, and they'd left their mark on her mind as well as her body.

Perhaps that was what Golgoth had seen in her. The dragon's fire had destroyed a massive swath of Dimvein, killing thousands in the process. Kullen had felt Golgoth's pain, shame, anger, and remorse over what her flames had done. But someone like Natisse —someone with a healthy fear of fire—would be far less likely to unleash its destructive power lightly.

Finally, Umbris had managed to extinguish the forest. It wasn't a pretty sight. Husks of age-old trees stood, crumbling to the earth. Embers still floated on the air, dithering toward the charred ground.

Thank you, Friend Umbris, Kullen said before releasing him back to the Shadow Realm.

"I-I'm sorry," Natisse said, face flushed and shame in her eyes. "I don't know what happened. It just—"

"I know what happened." Kullen plastered on a grin. "I thought it was somehow a good idea to practice fire magic in the middle of a bloody *forest*."

Natisse tilted her head, clearly unsure how to read him

Kullen chuckled to lighten the mood. "Next time, we'll go somewhere far less flammable."

"Next time?" Natisse's eyebrows rose.

"You're going to keep learning, aren't you?" Kullen asked but didn't wait for an answer. "So yes, there will be a next time. If you're up for it."

She only stared at him, and Kullen was suddenly struck by her natural radiance. She practically glowed as brightly as her *Bloodsurge*. She was beautiful. But it wasn't the soft, delicate beauty of a costumed and perfume-drenched noble lady. Her life had made her hard, but that hardness served to sharpen her allure.

Kullen hadn't known anyone who challenged his stony facade like this since Hadassa. They were both gorgeous, strong, willful, and determined. And perhaps they shared a bit of that fiery temperament as well.

He smiled to himself. Perhaps learning more about Natisse and the Crimson Fang would prove a far more enjoyable task than he'd anticipated.

33
NATISSE

Something about the way the assassin looked at Natisse brought a flush of heat to her face. She tried to tell herself it was the after-effects of the fire, but in reality, it was the approval she felt from him. He seemed genuinely pleased by the progress she'd made, almost as excited by her results as she was. Despite his claims, the Black Talon had proven to be a surprisingly good instructor, far more lavish with his praise than Uncle Ronan, Garron, or Ammon had ever been.

A warm glow filled Natisse, and for once, she knew it wasn't Golgoth's fire burning in her belly.

"One last lesson for tonight," Kullen told her with a grin. "Provided you're up for it."

Natisse was surprised by the question. More surprising, however, was the exhaustion she felt. It went beyond just the fatigue of physical exertion. She knew that sensation well, having always pushed herself to the limits of her capabilities in every training session, working harder and longer than every one of her Crimson Fang comrades.

She felt oddly stretched and thin, drained of energy beyond anything Uncle Ronan's most grueling training had ever achieved. In that moment, she wanted nothing more than to lie down and sleep for a week. This weariness went bone-deep—or perhaps deeper still, to her very soul. What had Umbris called it? *Takenth?* That seemed as fine a word as any to describe something she barely understood.

But she just nodded. "I'm game if you are."

"Something simple." Kullen bent to pick up a twig from the ground and held it out to her. "Help me get a fire started. Without burning down the forest, of course."

Natisse shot him a glare and snatched the stick from his hand. That only made Kullen smile wider. He was actually laughing as he strolled around the clearing, collecting more kindling for a fire.

Once again, Natisse found herself exhausting through her remaining stores of strength, both physically and mentally. These new powers would take some getting used to. Small sparks danced at the tip of the twig, and even such a small exertion left her feeling like she'd just swam across Blackwater Bay.

By the time she managed to catch the twig alight, Kullen had a small pile prepared. Soon, they were sitting in front of a merrily burning blaze, basking in the warmth and light.

In the quiet, Natisse surveyed their surroundings. She couldn't recall the last time she'd been this far outside of Dimvein.

"What is this place?" she asked, glancing over to the assassin sitting across the fire from her. She had the sense this wasn't his first visit—he'd flown straight here from the Palace. This deep into the Wild Grove Forest, there would be plenty of privacy for him to summon Umbris. But the look on his face told her there was more to it than that.

He remained silent for a long moment, his brow furrowed as he stared into the fire. "It was our place," he said, his words so quiet, the gentle breeze nearly carried them away.

The pain on his face and in his voice was so raw, so deep that Natisse could almost feel it. She didn't press the issue. If he wanted to speak, he would, and if not, it would do her no good to force an answer.

But answer he did. He lifted his eyes from the flames and fixed her with a piercing gaze. "The Prince, Princess, and myself. Every chance we got, we'd sneak out of the Palace and come out here." He swept a hand toward the darkness behind Natisse. "We built a shrine like the Mosleon used to. Our own little marker to remember the past."

Natisse glanced at the pile of stones. It *could* be a shrine of the crudest sort. Nothing as monolithic as the mountain-sized rocks the ancient Mosleon had assembled for purposes known only to them and lost to time, certainly. Precisely the sort of thing children would build.

"Do you mind if I ask you something?" Under normal circumstances, Natisse would have just bulled ahead and demanded an answer. Yet something about the moment—the darkness of the secluded forest glade, the calm of the night, the soft glow of the fire, and the fact that he'd essentially just saved her life and given her greater insight into her newly discovered powers—made her approach the matter delicately. She genuinely wanted to know and suspected her forthrightness might cause the man to clam up.

Kullen inclined his head. "Ask."

"You said you grew up in the Refuge, yes?"

Kullen nodded without a word.

"How does a young man from the Embers end up not only serving as the Emperor's personal assassin but also feeling the bond of a family with the Crown Prince himself?"

"You find it odd that a man with no other connections or loyalties might make the ideal assassin to serve at the Emperor's pleasure?" Kullen's voice held a note of sarcasm.

"No." Natisse shook her head. "But there's a vast chasm between serving the Emperor and calling his son 'friend'."

Kullen chewed on his lip, his expression, contemplative. "It certainly didn't start out that way," he said. His words came slow, every one weighted and measured. "At the beginning, it was merely an excuse to explain my presence in the Palace. Who better to serve as the young Prince's boon companion than the lowborn youth who had saved his life?"

Natisse's eyebrows shot up. "How'd that happen?"

Kullen's forehead knitted. "Pretty much exactly as you'd expect," he said, shrugging. "Foolish young Crown Prince gets sick of life cooped up behind the Palace walls, sneaks out, and gets himself in way over his head on the streets because he's utterly unprepared for what is *real* life for the people who don't have an army of servants to care for them."

"And you really saved his life?"

"I didn't know who he was at the time," Kullen said. It almost sounded as if he was making an excuse of it. "Just saw a scrawny, too clean kid my own age about to get stabbed by a pair of muggers who saw him as the easy mark he was. Besides, I owed those pricks for beating and robbing some of the younger children from the Refuge. Only *after* the Emperor himself showed up at the Refuge at the head of an army of Elite Scales had I found out what I'd done."

"The Emperor entered the Embers?" Natisse asked, incredulous.

"That day, the Emperor said he wanted to reward me personally for a great service I'd done. And before I could ask what exactly I'd done, who pops out of the Imperial carriage than the same scrawny kid?" Kullen grinned wryly, as if at a fond memory. "My reward turned out to be a life in the Palace—first as Jarius's training companion, then as the Emperor's Black Talon."

Natisse absorbed everything he'd just shared with her. A surprising amount, she had to admit. In a way, it made it easy to understand his implacability in his efforts to retrieve Jaylen. The Prince was all *he* had left of the two people he'd loved and lost years earlier.

"So, let me get this straight," Natisse said, carefully constructing her next sentence. "Your reward was for the Prince to use you as a practice dummy?"

Kullen laughed. "Sounds that way, doesn't it?" He shook his head. "It ended up quite the opposite for a long while. Jarius suffered many fine bruises at my hand before he finally learned how to defend himself."

"And you never got in trouble for hurting him?"

"Again, the opposite was true," Kullen said. "It was as if Emperor Wymarc wanted Jarius to learn his lesson within the Palace walls so he would never again need the protection outside the Palace walls." His words slowed toward that last bit. And slower still. "Had I done better, perhaps…"

"I'm sorry," Natisse said. The words left her mouth, and she nearly tried to reach out to catch them. This man, the Emperor's Assassin, was the one who killed Baruch, and she was feeling sorry for him?

"Do you mind if I ask *you* something?" Kullen asked.

The question caught her off guard, almost as much as the hesitance in his voice.

"You can ask," she said. "Doesn't mean I'll answer."

Kullen smiled. "Fair." He leaned forward, wrapping his arms around his knees and clasping his hands. "Who was he to you? The man who tried to kill me—"

"Tried to kill you?" Natisse snapped. How dare him?

"I'm sorry," Kullen said, leaning back. "You must understand my perspective."

"Oh, I do?" Natisse asked. "Pray tell, what perspective is there other than you jumping onto my skiff, attacking us unprovoked—"

"Unprovoked?" Kullen barked. "You were killing noblemen!"

"So were you!" Natisse shouted back.

"I aimed my strikes with purpose, never hitting anything vital. Your friend would have survived had he not dragged me into shark-infested waters."

"That's a lie," Natisse said, though she wasn't sure. "You dragged him…" Her words trailed off as she recalled the night. "I don't know what Baruch was to me, not really. I know he loved me, but it was—"

"Complicated?" Kullen asked. He nodded. "I know the type."

"The Princess?" Natisse asked, suddenly putting it all together.

"It's funny," Kullen barked a bitter laugh. "The very man I saved ended up being the one to take from me the one thing I cared most about in the world. And I couldn't even blame him for it."

Those words resonated within Natisse as if she'd been a struck bell. She watched the assassin, the one she'd saved and who had saved her. The one who took Baruch from her. The one who was doing his job, faced with the impossible task of confronting the Crimson Fang at work.

"*Go*," she heard Baruch's final words. *"The mission..."* And that was it before he grabbed the assassin and dragged him into the icy Blackwater Bay.

Kullen sucked in a deep breath. "I had no desire to see anyone die that evening. Well, except Magister Taradan. And you... you were after Perech. Did you—did the Crimson Fang—know about the fighting pits?"

Natisse shook her head. "We weren't entirely sure what was going on, not yet. But we had our suspicions."

Long moments of silence passed between them. The fire crackled. Soft bird noises surrounded them. She stole a glance every now and then at the man who claimed he'd meant Baruch no true harm. Could he have been telling the truth?

Her eyes drifted to the flames, and her hand instinctively drifted to the scars on her neck and arm.

"What did that to you?" Kullen asked.

The question made her pause. That day wasn't something she spoke of lightly, but neither was Baruch. Now that the dam had burst, what did it matter? His question held no judgment, condemnation, or scorn, only curiosity that seemed genuine. Despite her initial reaction, Natisse found herself speaking.

"Dragonfire," she said, biting off the word as the memory flashed before her eyes. "An Ember Dragon by the name of Shahitz'ai, acting on Magister Branthe's orders, attacked the caravan with which my family and I were traveling. I alone survived the attack."

She hadn't recalled the truth until the night she faced the flames and Joakim's snarling face up close. Since that moment, she'd had no chance to tell the story to anyone—not even Jad. It felt odd sharing it with Kullen. Yet after these last moments of transparency between the two of them... right.

He nodded, understanding in his eyes. "Is that why you and your people attacked him at the fighting ring? Vengeance for what he did to you?"

"No!" Natisse felt the word burst up from within her. She didn't understand why, but for some reason, she wanted him to know that it wasn't just petty revenge that drove her. "The Crimson Fang doesn't seek vengeance, only justice. Justice for the people who have been trodden into the mud, abused, and enslaved by men who wield their power and wealth like weapons against those who have none of their own." Her fists clenched, and she had to fight to keep the flames from springing to life on her hands. "The Crimson Fang exists to correct the balance, to redistribute the power so that everyone has it in equal measure. From the poorest Embers-born beggar to the Emperor you serve, there must be equity for all."

She heard the words—Uncle Ronan's words—and though she did not believe the man who'd spoken them, she believed their *meaning* and the intention behind them.

"So you think everyone should have equal wealth?" Kullen asked, raising an eyebrow. "That the Emperor should open his coffers and pass out his gold to everyone in the Empire?"

"If that is what it takes, yes." Natisse nodded emphatically.

"And what happens after that?" Kullen leaned forward so the fire highlighted his features. "Once everyone has all the gold they need, who will work the land to produce food, or sail the boats that bring in fish, or quarry the stone used to build?"

Natisse's lip curled up into a snarl. "It almost sounds like you believe that the Empire is best off with the wealth being held by a select few—those with the right *blood* or *titles.*" She poured a generous helping of scorn into the words. "Not what I'd expect from someone who's lived on the streets of Dimvein and seen the suffering among the Embers. Then again, perhaps you've enjoyed a cushy life in the Palace for so long that you've forgotten what it's really like down in the gutters."

Kullen didn't rise to her bait. "I haven't forgotten," he said, shaking his head. "But I am not so arrogant as to believe I know the best means of running an Empire. That is a job for the Emperor, not a gutter-born man like myself."

"And that is precisely why the Empire has existed for so long," Natisse snapped. "Because men like you don't bother to take responsibility or to stand up for what is right."

"Or," Kullen shot back, "because I believe Emperor Wymarc genuinely cares for his people—*all* his people, as you heard for yourself tonight—and acts in their best interest. Just as the Empire has done since the days it first brought light and magic to Dimvein. Look around you, Natisse. Is it dark?"

Natisse hesitated. "Yes."

"Thanagar's dome keeps it from utter darkness," Kullen said. "Imagine not being able to see your hand in front of your own eyes."

"I don't need a bloody history lesson!" Fire blazed in Natisse's belly, and the flames of their little campfire reached toward her, as if she called them to her. She was tempted to let them—she could put a bit of fear into the assassin—but that would get her nowhere.

With effort, she controlled herself. She's spent many long years mastering the art of shoving her emotions down into the cold, icy depths. However, this time, it was difficult to find that place. Perhaps it was merely in her mind, knowing that Golgoth's magic was so close, the thought of cold became a foreign concept. She sucked in a breath and buried the feeling. As soon as she did, the campfire returned to its natural form.

"After everything I have seen," she said, her voice tight but her anger restrained, "I cannot believe that the Empire's current inequity of power and wealth is 'best' for anyone except those who possess it. The Crimson Fang and I are willing to risk our lives to balance out the scales. Because of that, we have been labeled criminals."

"I'm pretty sure the whole 'murdering Magisters' had some part to play in that," Kullen said. His words sounded humorous on the surface, but there was no mirth in them.

"But when *you* do it, it's the Emperor's will?"

"That's exactly what it is." Kullen squared his shoulders. "I'm a servant of the Empire just like the Orkenwatch and Imperial Scales. Only my service is dealing with the problems that can't be solved publicly or through official channels." He threw up his hands. "I know why I'm doing what I do. I know the reasoning behind the Emperor's decisions, and I respect and trust the man enough to carry out his will free of guilt. Can you say the same?"

Kullen might as well have thrown a dagger. Had he asked the question days earlier, Natisse would have responded without hesitation. But everything she'd learned about Uncle Ronan had shattered the trust built over a lifetime. She had no idea who he was or what he *truly* wanted. She had no idea if the words out of his mouth were truth or just more lies. And she'd lost all respect for him because he was too much the coward to tell her the truth.

Natisse could almost feel the color draining from her face. Her throat was dry, and words simply wouldn't come.

Kullen stirred, though she didn't see his movements.

"It's late," he said, his tone brusque, "and using your magic as much as you have is bound to have taken a toll on you."

Natisse stood, brushing herself off. "Don't you worry about me."

Kullen held up his hands. "It's the truth. I can only *Bloodsurge* a handful of times before I risk damaging both my body and my bond with Umbris. I know no more about the limitations of your powers than you do, but I can tell you that you need to sleep. A full night of rest will suffice to restore your strength, and only then can you safely access your magic."

Natisse let his words sink in. It was true, the exhaustion she felt wasn't normal. But could the Black Talon be trusted?

"Fine," she said. "Let's get some sleep." She lay back on the grass, placing her balled-up cloak beneath her head like a pillow. She listened to Kullen also settle in. Her heart pounded within her chest.

"Good night," he said.

Natisse acted as if she hadn't heard him. He didn't utter another word. Eventually, Natisse nodded off.

34
KULLEN

Kullen awoke with the rising sun. That he awoke at all, he took as a good sign. After the end to their conversation the previous night, he'd half expected Natisse to stab him in the belly or cut his throat. Or, perhaps, summon Golgoth to rip him apart or immolate him.

But he remained unharmed. And, it appeared, un-abandoned. Natisse still lay curled up with her cloak beneath her head, her back firmly to him. Though nothing remained of their fire but dull gray ash, tangible waves of heat rolled off her. Angry at him still, even in her sleep.

Kullen didn't know why he'd shared so much of himself with her. He'd spoken of Jarius and Hadassa in a way he hadn't with anyone else, not even Emperor Wymarc. Perhaps fatigue from a too-long day or the soothing warmth of the fire had dragged it out of him. He'd gone well beyond just telling her enough to earn her trust. And it had paid off. She, too, had given him a glimpse into her soul.

But only for a few minutes, until he'd cocked it all up, asking questions about her friend. The one she clearly saw as murdered by Kullen's hand. All the progress he'd made since leaving the

Crimson Fang might very well have been undone with just a few sharp, hasty words.

No. He would not accept that. He may have lost ground, but there had to be a way to rebuild what was broken. He contemplated it for a few minutes, letting the rising sun warm him and the sounds of the Wild Grove Forest calm his soul. It had been years since he'd spent the night here—not since he, Jarius, and Hadassa were much younger—but he'd always loved the peaceful quiet of the woods. Especially when he had a protector to keep the predators at bay.

Thank you for watching over me, he told Umbris through their mental bond. He didn't look toward the stand of oak trees, but he could feel the Twilight Dragon in the shadows as surely as he could feel his own arm or the grassy ground beneath his back.

"I am reminded of days long past," Umbris told him. *"Happier days, when you laughed and smiled more. There are too many days when your mind is filled with shadows dark enough for even me to hide in."*

Kullen's eyelids flew open. *Was that... a joke?*

The barking sound of Umbris's laughter echoed in his mind. *"It was. And yet, it was not."* The dragon's thoughts grew serious, somber. *"You have been without companions for too long, Kullen Bloodsworn. Perhaps this one, given to the fire as she is, may bring some light to your soul."*

Kullen raised an eyebrow. *She'd definitely be happy to set this mortal coil alight,* he said. *By Binteth, I'm surprised I haven't burst into fire already the way she glares at me.* He did not know the full extent of her magic, but the more control she gained over Golgoth's flames, the more careful he'd have to be not to anger her.

He didn't hear Umbris's response, for, in that moment, Natisse sat bolt upright. No quiet stirring, no groaning as if groggily awakening from a deep slumber. She went from inert to fully alert in the span of a heartbeat. Her eyes fixed on him, and Kullen could feel the heat radiating off her rising in temperature.

It was still dark, and with the fire extinguished, Kullen could have use of his dragon-eyes. He quietly requested Umbris return to the Shadow Realm now that his protection was no longer needed. No sooner had the request been made than Kullen felt his eyes shift, and things came into noon-day clarity.

He sat up slowly, turning to face her. "I'm sorry."

The hard words he'd seen already forming on Natisse's lips went unspoken. One corner of her mouth twitched, and her eyes narrowed a fraction.

"You're *sorry?*" Her voice was hard, cold, and held a note of disbelief. "For what, exactly?"

Kullen drew in a calming breath. Clearly, she had no intention of making this easy on him. But he *had* to try to patch up what had been broken the previous night.

"I intended no offense when I brought up Baruch, nor when I asked if your attack against Magister Branthe was driven by vengeance." He spoke quickly to forestall the anger rising visibly to her cheeks. "I believed I was doing my job that evening on the barge. To the Empire, the Crimson Fang stirs up strife and subverts Imperial rule." Kullen raised his hand as Natisse rose to speak. "It's possible we see things with the wrong lens." She glowered but let him continue. "For that, I am sorry."

Natisse didn't offer a response, but she didn't bite his head off either. Kullen considered that permission to continue.

"I sought to kill Magister Deckard because of what happened to Jarius and Hadassa. His actions led to their deaths. I've spent years wanting him dead, and I finally got it. Vengeance is a motivation I can understand, but in my assumption, I did not take into account that you and your people might not be driven by the same things as me. And that rightly angered you. For that, I am also sorry."

He had managed to get through the apology without interruption, though Natisse visibly wrestled with angry retorts. She'd proven herself possessed of admirable restraint on more than one occasion—the fact that he'd walked out of the Crimson Fang's lair without bloodshed was largely her doing—but he knew some things were impossible to control. His anger and hatred for

Magister Deckard had certainly driven him to actions cool-headed logic might have forestalled. He should've extracted information *first,* then killed the fat bastard after.

"There is nothing I can say that will make up for what happened to your friend, Baruch," he said.

"I—"

Finally, her composure shattered.

"What *happened?*" she snapped the word, leaping to her feet. Her hand dropped to her lashblade instinctively. "Nothing *happened* to him. You killed him. Put a dagger in his back right in front of me."

"I know." Kullen held up both hands, showing they were empty. He kept his calm, looked up at her looming over him. He needed her to see he was no threat. "I did. Just like you or he would've done to me. Like you *tried* to do to me."

Fire roared in her eyes, but her lips pressed into a tight, furious line.

"We were both doing what needed to be done that night," he repeated. "I was hunting the assassin who killed Magister Perech, and you were fighting for your lives. But for the death of your friend, I can only continue to apologize."

Natisse said nothing, her face flushed a deep red. Kullen half expected her to burst into flames right then and there or to draw her lashblade and cut him down. But she remained frozen by her rage and torn by indecision—whether to kill him or accept his word.

She opted for a sound halfway between a snarl and grunt. Her hand did, however, release the hilt of her lashblade.

Kullen saw the opening—the tiniest fracture in the hard stone walls she always kept around herself—and seized it. "Last night, when I asked about your fear of the flames, it wasn't to anger you or to judge you. On the contrary, I wanted to understand you so I can help you."

"Help me?" Natisse growled the words. "Help me how?"

Kullen rose gracefully to his feet, never taking his eyes off her. "Help you find the balance between respecting and fearing the power." He held out his hands, palms up. "Think of it like the two pans of a scale. On one, there must be an innate understanding of the magic's potential. What it is capable of, and what you are able to achieve with it at your command. What you did last night is just the beginning. Only with time will you, working in concert with Golgoth, come to understand your true limits."

Natisse's eyes narrowed. "But if I am afraid, it will stop me from achieving my full potential, is that it?" The words dripped a measure of scorn. "You sound like every man who ever stood across the training hall from me."

Kullen had to suppress a grin. That didn't surprise him—just as it wouldn't surprise him to learn that she'd ultimately defeated every one of them.

"Yes," he said, "but that's not all." He hefted his other hand, raising the opposite side of his invisible scale. "Fear imposes limits on what you can do, which can be both good *and* bad. It will stop you from overusing the ability and—in your case, quite literally— burning yourself out. Just as I told you that I can only shadow-slide a few times before I must rest, you, too, have limitations. Fear will keep you from crossing that line once you discover what it is."

He paused to let the words sink into Natisse's mind. Her expression had changed from infuriated to contemplative, her lips quirked into a thoughtful frown.

"But," he said, holding up a finger, "fear can also stop you from reaching that line, from pushing its boundaries. It can interfere with your mastery of the magic and cause you to lose control. When that happens…" He gestured to the blackened glade. "The price of your fear may be paid by others as well as yourself."

Natisse's face hardened. She looked as if she wanted to say something, perhaps hurl the words back in his face, but she remained silent and pensive.

Kullen could see he was getting through to her. Now he had to go one step further, to put himself at risk once more. It was the only way he could repair the damage done the previous night.

"I found that out the hard way, you know." He spoke in a quiet voice. It wasn't just for show—dwelling on the memory was about as painful as running on a broken foot. "My fear cost someone else dearly."

Natisse's eyes widened a fraction.

"Who was it?" she asked. Her tone held no scorn or derision, merely curiosity. And more than a little empathy, Kullen was surprised to find. "What happened?"

Kullen had to force himself to speak. He hadn't *intended* to share this piece of himself when he awoke this morning, yet now that the moment had come, he knew it was the right thing to do.

"When I first bonded with Umbris, I labored for months to master the skill of shadow-sliding." Kullen could still feel the old, familiar frustration. In truth, it had never left him. He still felt it from time to time, though he'd grown adept at burying it down deep and ignoring it... mostly. "Nothing I did would work. I would feel myself drawn toward the Shadow Realm, but something would always stop me just before I entered. I could sense the shadows, could feel the pull on my body and mind, yet there was always some barrier blocking my entrance."

Interest had replaced the anger sparkling bright in Natisse's eyes. She leaned forward, fully engaged in his story. His *true* story.

"One night," Kullen continued, "I finally thought I cracked the code, and I tried to show Jarius what I could do. I stood on the precipice of the Palace rooftop and attempted to jump to the shadows of the gardens below. But all I succeeded in doing was plummeting to near death. Jarius tried to catch me using his own wind magic. He saved me from breaking my neck and very nearly shattered his own back in the doing, falling six stories onto a firecherry tree."

Natisse sucked in a breath, her hand rising to her lips.

"But that's not all." Kullen shook his head. "Instead of helping him, I ran and hid like the terrified youth I was." His cheeks burned hot at the memory. "I stayed hidden for three days until the Emperor himself found me tucked into a pantry behind the kitchens. But instead of having me flogged—as I assumed he would—he brought me to see Jarius, assuring me that he would live. Then he sat me down and told me the truth of why I had failed. He'd wanted to let me figure it out for myself, but the time had come for me to know. And do you know what he said?"

"What?" Natisse asked, interest tangible in her features.

"That I was so afraid of being invisible that I would never succeed until I conquered my fear."

"I don't understand." Natisse frowned. "How could anyone be afraid of being invisible? Especially someone training for your line of work."

Kullen shook his head sadly. "Not *physically* invisible. Metaphorically. Invisible like every other orphan and street rat who grew up in the Embers. Someone unseen by the world except to despise or mistreat. Meaning nothing to anyone, merely existing in the world."

Kullen's throat went dry. He pulled a small skin from his belt and sipped, then offered it to Natisse. She waved it away, still waiting.

"I was afraid that if I truly stepped out of the Mortal Realm and into the Shadow Realm, I would have nothing left to return me to my body. No connections strong enough to keep me from vanishing altogether."

Kullen paused again. His eyes began to water at the memory. Lowering his head, he pressed on. He knew he must. He had to expose this side of him to her if he hoped to earn her trust for what was to come next.

"And that day, instead of sitting by his injured son's bedside or tending to the affairs of the Empire, Emperor Wymarc spent time ministering to me, inquiring about my life in the Refuge, offering his own stories of his days as a soldier. He led me to secret places known only to him and Jarius. He *showed* me that I wasn't invisible to him. Or to Jarius. For when I went to see the

Prince, he smiled and laughed and told me he was just glad I hadn't gotten my fool self killed. He didn't hate me because my actions had endangered his life, but he cared. He *cared*, Natisse. For me—an orphan, a nobody. And that was the first day I stepped into the Shadow Realm. Because I had something to bring me back. *Someone* to keep me tethered to the Mortal Realm."

Natisse said nothing, but Kullen could see his story had made its impact, had tapped into something deep within her—though what, he didn't truly know. Not yet. He knew too little about her to see what aspects had resonated with her. Perhaps the part about his being an orphan taken in by the Emperor. From her account of her family's deaths, she might've been similarly taken under General Andros's wing.

Whatever the case, her anger toward him had diminished. Certainly not died—she might never look past his part in the killing of her friend—but forgotten for the moment.

He gave her a small smile. "All that to say, fear can save you from overusing your abilities *and* stop you from utilizing them to the fullest. Locate the source of that fear, face it, and push past it. Once you can do that, you will have control."

Natisse nodded slowly. "I understand." She looked down at her hands.

Kullen remained silent for long moments, giving her space to consider his words. And, with luck, open up to him as he'd done with her.

But Natisse just sat with her own thoughts, and the quiet stretched out between them.

Kullen didn't force the issue. It would do no good. He could be patient. He *had* to be if he hoped to build the necessary trust between them. The previous day, circumstance had thrust them together. Now, he had to keep her at his side to learn more about her to determine whether or not she posed a threat to the Empire.

"I've been given another mission by the Emperor," he said finally.

Natisse looked up. "Mission?" She cocked an eyebrow. "A target to kill?"

Concern visibly washed over her. She scooted back an inch, her hand falling to her hilt once more.

Kullen shook his head. "Not you," he assured her.

Her tension shrank, but her hand stayed put.

"A number of dragonblood vials have gone missing," he said. He studied her expression carefully, watching for even the slightest hint that she knew anything about it. Either she was *very* adept at hiding the truth or totally ignorant of the missing vials, for her face revealed nothing. "Rumor has it they're going to be auctioned off on Pantagoya."

Natisse's eyebrows shot up. "Pantagoya?"

"Tonight. Ever been?"

Natisse shook her head.

"Want to see it for yourself?"

Surprise flickered across Natisse's face. "You'd take me? On an Imperial mission?"

Kullen ignored the hint of contempt in her voice. "I told the Emperor you'd come in handy getting the job done. Considering the charade you put on for Magister Perech, was my assessment wrong?"

That brought a ghost of a smile to Natisse's lips. "Not at all." It faded a moment later, replaced by the shadows that had appeared at each mention of her friend, Baruch.

"You spoke of the Crimson Fang's purpose of correcting the balance," he said quickly, "of redistributing wealth among those who need it most. Well, I can say that the Pantagorissa's guests will be among the richest in the Empire—and far beyond—so I'm certain there will be plenty of wealth readily available for redistribution."

"We're not thieves," Natisse said, a tinge of fire flashing in her eyes. Her fists clenched, jaw muscles pulling tight.

Kullen held up his hands. "Nor am I suggesting such a thing." Though, to be fair, stealing from the rich certainly fit the description of "theft." "But I have no doubt there is plenty that will be of interest to the Crimson Fang. In return for your assistance, I offer mine in return. Umbris is capable of carrying quite a princely sum in loot and anything else you might want transported."

Kullen couldn't read her. She stayed firmly transfixed. General Andros had done one thing well, he'd made his soldiers into granite.

Finally, where her visage showed no break, her words assured him. "Very well."

"Wonderful," Kullen said, rising.

"But only under one condition," she said, holding up a finger. Kullen froze halfway to standing. "And trust me when I say it's *not* one you're going to like."

35
NATISSE

Natisse had to admit Kullen was far less infuriated by her demand than she'd expected—at least outwardly. She thought she heard the occasional mutter coming from his seat, but the splashing of the oars and the whistling of the ocean wind carried his words away.

She watched him bending his back to the oars. The black jacket she'd insisted he wear to complete his disguise strained against the thick muscles of his upper back and shoulders. He'd spent the last hour rowing without respite, maintaining a steady stroke that displayed his impressive strength and endurance.

Oh, they could certainly have hired a rower to convey them from the fishing village of Tauvasori out to the floating city of Pantagoya. Indeed, Kullen had offered to put up the coin—it was his mission for the Emperor, after all. Yet Natisse had insisted on doing it *her* way. Lady Dellacourt was wealthy enough to afford the comfortable, sturdy skiff that now sliced through the rising swells and gentle troughs of the Astralkane Sea but not so flush with Imperial marks that she could afford an entire entourage. Just herself and her manservant—a role Kullen played in place of Jad—and the small fortune in gold she intended to spend in the gambling houses of Pantagoya.

Kullen had stared long and hard at her, suspicion written plainly in his eyes. But she had stubbornly maintained her position: if he wanted her help, he would allow her to play the role to which she felt best suited.

"Besides," she'd argued, "if all eyes are on me, no one will look at you twice when you slip away to fulfill your goals."

After that, Kullen had acquiesced to her demands as she'd hoped he would. She had only pushed for her way as yet *another* test. He'd proven himself admirably flexible when Natisse herself would've fought and disputed were she in his place. This was *his* mission, after all, yet he was amenable to her plan. Admittedly, it was a good plan—even he'd said as much—but she couldn't imagine relinquishing the reins in a situation like this to anyone else without damned good reason. Baruch and Ammon, she could trust. Uncle Ronan, too, at least *before* recent events. Jad, Garron, Nalkin, perhaps even Haston. But a total stranger? One she wasn't certain she could trust? She doubted it.

In a way, that spoke volumes about the man paddling before her. Clearly, he possessed a great deal of confidence in his skills— and rightly earned, as she'd seen—and cunning. He'd acquiesced to her demands no doubt to ensure her compliance, yet he could only do so knowing full well that he could change and improvise to achieve his objective. That adaptability had made Uncle Ronan bloody effective in similar situations—and on the battlefield, according to the tales of General Andros.

The last time Natisse had been outside of Dimvein, she'd been but a girl. Her parents had still been alive and well. She'd never in her adult life seen the daylight sun with such splendor. Shrouded always by Thanagar's dome, its rays were weak and dull compared to the vibrancy of their glow out here on the sea. And the Embers —they suffered from Dimvein's curse, whatever that was. She was used to darkness or muted light, but this…

"Beautiful, isn't it?" she asked.

"Huh?" Kullen grunted as he pulled.

"The sun," she clarified. "It's been years."

"Ah, yes. Quite the sight. Wait until you see Pantagoya."

Natisse leaned back against the gunwale and stared upward. The sun, just vanishing behind the western horizon, splashed the heavens in a glorious array of gold, purple, and orange. Even now, stars began to sparkle to the east, the pale face of the growing moon appearing in the settling gloom. It brought a prick of sadness to Natisse's heart to see such beauty fade. Soon, the shadows would fall thick, but night rumor said it would never fully touch the ever-alive island of Pantagoya floating just a few hundred paces to the south.

"So it's true?" she asked. "It is always bright on Pantagoya?"

"More than you can imagine," Kullen said. "The Lumenators, in all their numbers, couldn't begin to compare."

The word dredged up thoughts of Uncle Ronan and his lies—lies she couldn't seem to let go. Why lie about such a thing? Why not share with the rest of the Crimson Fang that he had magical power to create light in the midst of darkness? What a help that would've been on countless missions in the past. She thought of all the times crawling through the tunnels with weak torchlight when all the while, Uncle Ronan could've lit the passages to blinding success.

"There she is," Kullen said.

The sound of his voice drew her attention to the horizon and the famed island. Even from such a distance, Natisse could hear the sounds of merrymaking and revelry. Shouting, cheering, laughing, and singing—mostly drunken and discordant—accompanied by myriad stringed and woodwind instruments. The throb of a hundred drums echoed across the sea, each distinct yet somehow combining into a single melodic rhythm as grand as the heartbeat of the legendary Kraken that had ruled these waters millennia past.

And the lights—by Ezrasil, more lights than even shone in Dimvein! Thousands of torches, lanterns, alchemical globes, bonfires, barrel fires, even tiny heartfires belched from the throats of *kinallen*, the minuscule two-legged cousins said to have been descended from dragons. These lights shone in every conceivable hue: deep crimson and gold joined by radiant white and festive blue-green, interspersed with flashes of pink and orange fireworks brightening the sky.

It was said Pantagoya never slept, and Natisse could very well believe it. There were easily fifteen or twenty thousand people crowded onto the floating city—a messy collection of docks, jetties, pontoons, and buildings that appeared to hover impossibly high above the water on spindly, stilted legs. Some structures sat atop boats, as if the vessels had been swallowed by the ever-expanding confusion of the pleasure island.

Natisse had never once desired to visit Pantagoya. The gambling, whoring, drinking, and fighting that ran rampant there held little appeal to her. Indeed, even now, she couldn't truly understand why she'd agreed to accompany Kullen. Pantagoya had wealth aplenty to steal, but had that been her sole purpose, she could've found easier targets in Dimvein. Less heavily defended targets, too, including the Imperial Palace.

As they drew closer, at least one in every five people she saw carried bared cutlasses and wore the breastplates displaying the skull-and-crossed-oar emblem of the Pantagorissa.

So why *had* she come? What had prompted her to accept such an absurd offer? She'd given it a great deal of thought on their dragonback ride from the Wild Grove Forest to the swamps just outside Tauvasori. Though she had found no satisfactory answer —yet—she *did* feel confident that she'd made the right choice.

Despite Kullen's words, Natisse hadn't yet brought herself to tap into the fire magic. She'd awoken eager for another day but seeing the damage inflicted on the forest when she'd lost control of her power had reignited her fears. She hadn't wanted to summon Golgoth yet, not until she could get a grip on the gnawing sensation in her belly.

And in truth, she felt as if Kullen was the key to that. He could train her in the ways of magic—he'd proven himself quite useful, helping her advance her mastery exponentially in just a few hours

—and did so with none of the expectations she knew she would feel from Uncle Ronan, Jad, and the rest of the Crimson Fang. Everything would change the moment the rest of her companions learned of her new capabilities. She doubted they would fear her —at least, not at first—but they would treat her differently. They would see her less as Natisse and more as a weapon to aim toward the Crimson Fang's enemies. The nature of the missions could very well change once Uncle Ronan knew what manner of firepower she could bring to bear.

Natisse wanted none of that. At least not yet, not until she could come to terms with it. She would return to the Crimson Fang—she had to, no doubt about it—but for at least tonight, she could lose herself in the distraction of a mission. She was always at her most confident and calmest when given something on which to focus her oft-troubled mind.

"Almost there," Kullen grunted, hauling harder on the right-hand oar to bring their skiff around. "Get ready, *Lady.*"

Natisse smiled at the sharp edge in his voice. So her demand *had* annoyed him. Good. She owed him far worse. His apology, though it had seemed genuine, wouldn't make up for Baruch's death. This was a form of retribution she could enjoy without negatively impacting their mission.

"You sure this will work?" Natisse asked.

"I'm sure," Kullen said. "Not my first time here."

"Why am I not surprised?" Natisse's tone was breezy, as befitted Lady Dellacourt. "This seems precisely the sort of place the Emperor's Black Talon might enjoy in his free time."

Kullen snorted. "Not for all the gold in the Imperial coffers."

Natisse raised an eyebrow, though, with Kullen's back to her, the expression was lost on him.

"Too much noise," Kullen said. "Too few shadows."

"Fair enough," Natisse said with a knowing grin he wouldn't see.

She fixed her gaze on the floating jetty to which Kullen was rowing them. Impossibly high walls were crafted out of wooden trees, the likes of which Natisse didn't even know existed. She spotted no joints, which meant each tree had to be taller than the Imperial Palace. And hundreds of them, side by side, as far as she could see until they curved upward in a dome. It reminded Natisse of Thanagar's protection, though one far more tangible.

Whatever this protected, it was important to someone. To answer her question, five men in the bright breastplates of the Pantagorissa marched through a narrow gate—a greeting party of stern faces, bared cutlasses, and officious-looking scowls.

"Just say the words exactly as I told you, and we'll be fine," Kullen said. "And for the love of Ezrasil, try not to set anything on fire."

Natisse bristled, then calmed as she heard the humor in his words. "No promises. Anyone gets too handsy with Lady Dellacourt, and the whole Pantagoya might go up in flames."

Kullen chuckled, leaning lower into his hunch and bending over the oars. With a few powerful strokes, he propelled their skiff the last few dozen yards to the jetty, then slid them free of the oarlock to stow them in the bottom of the boat. Snatching up the rope, he leaped lightly onto the end of the jetty and secured them to the post. It was all done so smoothly that the skiff came to a stop just before the rope pulled taut, without so much as a jerk or bump.

"My lady," Kullen said in a false guttural voice, extending a hand to her.

"Thank you, Yarlton." Natisse pitched her voice high and loud, emphasizing the genteel accent Baruch and Ammon had painstakingly taught her. She allowed him to help her out of the boat, then called, "See to my valise. Keep it close—at all costs."

"Yes, my lady." Kullen ducked his head and leaped back into the skiff to pluck up the leather satchel that had made the journey between Natisse's feet. The *clinking* from within the bag was audible; it held enough gold and jewelry inside to feed the Crimson Fang for a month.

"A small sum to prove ourselves worthy of the Pantagorissa's invitation," Kullen had said after procuring it from the Emperor's agent in Tauvasori. He'd said it lightly, as if the wealth meant nothing.

"My lady." The foremost of the Pantagorissa's guards spoke in a rough voice, his thick Brendoni accent a match for his umber skin. He didn't bow to her; indeed, rather than respect, he studied her with open suspicion. "And who, pray tell, might you be?"

"Lady Dellacourt of Elliatrope," Natisse said, extending a limp-wristed hand toward the guard.

He didn't take it, didn't even look down at it. "And what might you be wantin', Lady Dellacourt of Elliatrope?"

"Why, only the same thing everyone else who travels to this fine kingdom desires, of course!" Natisse snapped her fingers. "Yarlton, show him."

"Yes, m'lady." Kullen stepped forward and snapped open the valise's hinges to reveal its contents.

"I am told the Pantagorissa is hosting a truly special event this evening," Natisse said in the airy, fluttery tone she always hated but Baruch had insisted was popular among the Imperial aristocracy. "I have come with gold ample enough to—"

"Event's private." The Brendoni cut her off with an upraised hand. "You're welcome to explore the rest of the island, but I've no word of any Lady Dellacourt bein' on the guest list."

Natisse arched an imperious eyebrow. "Perhaps you should consult that list again, my good man." She looked him up and down. "Or, perhaps, go and fetch it. For if you read it closely, you would see—"

"I said, you *ain't* on the list." The guard took a menacing step closer. Though he didn't raise his drawn cutlass, his scowl was sharp-edged enough. "Time to be scootin' back into that boat of yours."

Natisse rolled her eyes heavenward. "Blessed Yildemé, and here I had heard so much about the Pantagoya's legendary hospitality." She clucked her tongue in disapproval. "Clearly, I can see the stories were greatly exaggerated."

The guard drew himself up to his full height. "This dock's reserved for the Pantagorissa's personal guests."

"We all know there's no list," Natisse said.

The guard didn't flinch. "Best you be on your way and off to any of the public landing points. Otherwise, you're in for a long, cold swim back to shore."

The four guards behind the speaker shifted slightly, as if preparing to execute their commander's threats.

Natisse sighed theatrically. "Very well." She sniffed daintily and brushed an invisible speck of dust from the hem of the bright blue dress she'd insisted Kullen procure for her disguise. "Milk and bread may spoil and mold, but replete is the belly filled with gold."

Upon hearing the words, an immediate change came over all five guards. The four rearmost backed down, and the leader's demeanor went from demanding to pleasant in a heartbeat.

"Very good." He actually smiled, revealing a handful of teeth punched as crooked as his flat nose. "Pantagorissa Torrine Heweda Eanverness Wombourne Shadowfen III welcomes you to her kingdom."

RED CLAW

36
KULLEN

"Could you not have spoken the words sooner?" Kullen hissed from where he marched behind Natisse.

"What'd be the fun in that?" Natisse whispered back. "Besides, a lady must always be memorable, yes?"

Kullen could *swear* she was grinning wickedly beneath the false smile she had plastered on the moment "Lady Dellacourt" stepped off the skiff. Bad enough she'd made him row the bloody boat for the last hour; now, she was entertaining herself at the Shieldbandsman's expense?

Kullen forced his expression to remain studiedly neutral as he moved in Natisse's wake, keeping his head low and demeanor humble as expected of a manservant. Too, he clutched the valise tightly to his chest—despite the two guards bringing up the rear of their small company, he knew that anything more valuable than a bent copper penny would draw the greedy eyes of the countless muggers, thieves, and pickpockets blending in among the noisy throng.

Chief among them, of course, were the armed and armored men who served in the Pantagorissa's Shieldband. The title reeked of pretentiousness to match the woman to whom they answered; in truth, the majority were little more than thugs and brutes paid to keep the peace on Pantagoya. However, they weren't paid enough to keep them from demanding extra compensation from every establishment that called the floating pleasure island home—or ripping it from the arms of the very people they were sent to guard.

Assidius's contact in Tauvasori had insisted that the password would gain them both entry into the Pantagorissa's private soiree and protection for the duration of their visit to Pantagoya. Provided they played nice. The moment Kullen shattered the Pantagorissa's peace to make his move against whoever was behind the theft of the dragonblood vials, the Shieldband would respond without restraint or mercy. He would be beaten to within an inch of his life, stripped of clothing, weapons, and valuables, and thrown off the island to die in the cold depths of the Astralkane Sea. If onyx sharks and worse didn't eat him first, of course.

He had no intention of meeting any such fate. Umbris's vial remained within easy reach should the need arise.

The Emperor's remonstrance echoed in Kullen's mind, however. Better for all of them if he could get off Pantagoya without drawing that sort of attention. Pantagorissa Torrine would be far from pleased by the appearance of dragons in her tiny water-bound kingdom, and she'd express her displeasure to Emperor Wymarc with all her usual stridence. The flimsy peace forged between the Karmian Empire and the diminutive yet ludicrously wealthy Pantagoya would shatter if the violence could be traced back to Dimvein.

Not that violence was foreign to Pantagoya. On the contrary, it seemed everywhere Kullen looked, fists swung, teeth flew, and blood flowed. Down what could be called an "alleyway" between two taverns built atop pontoons, three men tussled on the waterlogged, vomit-soaked wooden planks—until one of them slipped through a crack in the wooden structure and vanished into the dark Astralkane Sea with a loud splash. The shouts and jeers of those watching rose in a mocking chorus, accentuated a moment later by the screams of the unfortunate man. The myriad hungry predators that ruled the waters beneath Pantagoya fed quickly, and the agonized cries died off in seconds.

The two remaining combatants seemed not to notice the third's disappearance but continued punching drunkenly at each other. Kullen didn't see who won—a gambling house built onto the back of a moored two-masted caravel rose in front of them, blocking out his view. Yet aboard that floating structure, too, there were fights aplenty. A square had been ringed off with ropes, and in the middle, a handful of men and women in gaudy, tasseled costumes flailed and grappled with abandon.

Off to Kullen's left, an orchestra of off-tune fiddles, bagpipes, drums, flutes, and other instruments he didn't recognize filled the air with a discordant melody, and a boisterous crowd wielding overfull mugs lifted their voices in ear-splitting song. Half a dozen songs, in truth. Some sang in the Imperial tongue, others in Brendoni, and still others in the crude pidgin dialect native to Pantagoya. Among them, Blood Clan pirates and rough-looking, horsehair-clad men of the Hudar Horde joined in their own language.

Kullen's eyes narrowed a fraction. He hadn't been on Pantagoya in years—not since the Emperor had dispatched him to eliminate a consortium that had proven troublesome and threatened the Pantagorissa's rule on the island—but he didn't remember seeing more than a couple of Hudarians or Blood Clan on his last visit. Yet now, what appeared to be an entire ship's crew of Blood Clan pirates spilled out of a nearby tavern, carousing at full volume and lavishing attention on the dockside doxies with all the manners of a herd of stampeding wildebeest. The cacophonous clacking of the sea shells they braided into their unruly hair nearly drowned out the shouts rising from a quartet of pirates jousting with mops, brooms, and buckets.

The Hudarians had apparently commandeered an exarai leaf den across from the pirates, but their building was as silent and solemn as the Blood Clan was boisterous. Smoke rose up from the front porch, where half a dozen of them sat smoking from long pipes. Through the cloudy haze, dark eyes peered out. One of them had locked onto Natisse, and Kullen wasn't excited about the look that danced behind his gaze.

"Be ready," Kullen whispered to her.

"For?"

In that moment, the Hudarian rose and leaped down the small set of stairs, staggering toward them. His eyebrows—if they could even be spoken of as a pair—met in the middle, thick as a braided rope. He smiled as he approached. His teeth were filed into sharp fangs, as was common for the Hudarian warriors. When he spoke, it was barely discernible Imperial.

"I take," he said.

The guards stepped up from behind.

"Back to your den, beast," one said.

The Hudarian grunted. "I take," he said more emphatically, stretching a hand for Natisse.

Kullen moved with practiced speed, shifting the valise to one hand while the other grabbed hold of the Hudarian's wrist and bent it to near breaking.

The guards watched him work, wrenching the man's arm behind his back.

"If you desire to ever pleasure yourself again with this hand, I suggest you return to your fellows," he whispered into the Hudarian's ear.

The Hudarian spat something in his language. Kullen understood very little, but this word he knew.

Kullen smiled.

"That's a kind interpretation of what I truly am," he said. "Now, I'm going to let you go. If one foot steps out of line on your return, I'll keep my promise."

Kullen let the Hudarian go with a shove that sent him halfway to the exarai leaf den.

By now, the others on the porch had noticed the fight. They rose, but Kullen's new friend waved for them to sit.

"Impressive," one of the guards said.

"At least someone decided to protect my honor," Natisse said in Lady Dellacourt's voice. "Was there no safer route from the Pantagorissa's private dock?"

The Shieldbandsmen didn't respond except to push forward through the throng.

Finally, after a few more minutes of chaos, the Shieldbandsmen led them toward a set of wooden stairs that ascended to Pantagoya's second level. Ten more armed and armored guards flanked the solid steel gate barring entrance to the staircase.

"At least that means these foul creatures won't be following us," Natisse said.

Kullen cleared his throat. "Laying it on a little thick," he whispered.

"This way, my lady," said one of the Shieldbandsmen leading them.

Natisse flounced up the stairs with poise and grace even Swordmaster Kyneth would've envied. Anyone who saw her in the elaborate blue evening gown would certainly give her a second look—and a third and fourth, as Kullen had—because she was truly striking, even with her flaming red hair done up in a simple braid. Yet they would be looking at her beauty, never knowing how lethal she could be with the lashblade and daggers he'd helped her conceal beneath the dress.

Kullen had to admit she was playing the role of Lady Dellacourt far better than he'd expected. Clearly, she'd had practice. No wonder she'd gotten close enough to Magister Perech to put a dagger in him without drawing suspicion. Indeed, she'd vanished into the night with no one the wiser. No one but him that was. And he'd only spotted her by pure chance.

Then again, perhaps her beauty had been to her detriment that evening as well. She certainly knew how to steal the show.

He was certainly in good company, he knew. Perhaps in more ways than one. She might not be his equal in combat, but she could hold her own. Just as she could playing the role of haughty noblewoman. And her low-cut dress, neck adorned with sparkling silver, certainly would keep all eyes fixed on her while he blended into the shadows.

The stairs brought them to awe-inspiring views. Crystal chandeliers hung like icicles from a network of cables and ropes crisscrossing in the air above the buildings of the second level. Each one bore a hundred glowing alchemical globes and spun on their chains through some form of pulleys and gears invisible to view. The effect was like swimming just below a glittering sea while the sun shone from above. It was mesmerizing. But even that didn't steal from the spread of delicacies splayed out on tables carved from coral that lined the avenue. Lords and Ladies mingled around them, swirling between the tables and pecking from plates of all sorts of steamed, baked, and broiled sea creatures.

"Welcome to the festivities," the Shieldsbandman said.

"Charming," Natisse said.

They moved forward, their path taking them closer to the food.

"People eat these things?" Natisse whispered, gazing over her shoulder at the Shieldbandsmen keeping their distance by a few yards.

"Don't deny before you try," Kullen said, swiping a spindly urchin from the nearest platter. He took a bite, and the juices spilled down his chin. He then offered the remaining bite to Natisse, but her face scrunched in response. "A lady should have a palate refined enough for such things."

He pushed it closer, and Natisse took the bite. Something flashed across her face, a sadness. Something Kullen couldn't quite place.

"What is it?" he asked. "It's not that bad."

"Just… just a memory," Natisse said. Then she sucked in a deep breath, and Lady Dellacourt reappeared. "Now, let's enjoy ourselves, shall we?"

"As you wish," Kullen said.

Nearby, a delegation from the Caliphate of Fire, all neatly

trimmed beards and glittering nose rings, squared off over a game of *Surat* against a pair of fur-garbed Qilaqui. On one side, a jewel-hilted scimitar in a gold-and-silver-worked scabbard sat atop a heap of colorful Zahidi silks. Opposite, two tusks of the purest black ivory nearly as long as the ten-foot-long Surat table itself. Cards and dice flew back and forth, and the Caliphate men were clearly losing to the two tundra-dwellers, judging by the number of black-and-gold pieces they still controlled on the tiled board.

But the company of Shieldbandsmen led them unerringly past all of the ruckus on a straight path toward the enormous wooden structure that served as the beating heart of Pantagoya.

From Umbris's back high above the floating island, the Pantagorissa's Palace would've appeared like a six-legged spike-back turtle. The ovular wooden dome had once been the hull of eight Vandil longships, back when the Ironkin battled against the Kraken for dominance of the Astralkane Sea and the vast Temistara Ocean beyond. Four towers rose from the peak of the dome like the spines of a dragon's back—one for the Pantagorissa, one for her most hated enemies and prisoners, one for the priests of Abyssalia, the Vandil goddess said to have commanded the creatures of the sea. As for the fourth tower, Kullen had never learned its purpose—nor, it seemed, had anyone else. Yet all who knew of Pantagoya had heard the name of the Dread Spire spoken of in hushed, fearful whispers.

The "legs" were formed by six Vandil-style longhouses jutting out from beneath the dome. Each was rumored to be large enough to house a hundred men and horses, and the Pantagorissa had converted them into barracks for her Shieldband.

How Pantagoya remained afloat beneath the weight of such a monolithic structure was the subject of much debate among scholars around the Karmian Empire. Even Prince Jarius had attempted to conceive of a logical explanation—one that involved four enormous elephant crabs riding on the back of a mind-bogglingly vast sea turtle—which had earned him a hearty but loving rebuke from Hadassa—when she could stop laughing, that was.

Kullen didn't care how it was possible, only that it was to be their destination. The Shieldbandsmen led them straight toward the enormous gate set into the side of the Palace commonly referred to by Pantagoyans as "south." Directions of the compass held little true meaning on an island that rotated slowly as it floated along, so the Pantagorissa had merely decided which ends of her kingdom to name which, and the matter was settled.

"Here you are," said the Shieldbandsman, stopping just outside two gargantuan double doors. "Safe and sound."

His tone of voice left no doubt as to his expectations, though he held out one beefy, callused paw to make certain Natisse didn't miss his meaning.

Natisse stared down at the hand with a look of airy confusion.

Kullen cleared his throat and, reaching into a pocket, drew out a handful of Imperial marks. "You have Lady Dellacourt's gratitude for your assistance."

The Shieldbandsman eyed the gold coins disdainfully, as if he'd expected far more of them. But when the seemingly ignorant aristocrat didn't order her "manservant" to increase the gratuity, the guard grunted and pocketed his tip.

"Abyssalia smile on you both," he said, in a tone that suggested he hoped the goddess did something far more unpleasant than merely smile.

"And you, good sir!" Natisse called out, fluttering her hand in a cheerful wave that both acknowledged and dismissed the Shieldbandsmen at once.

Kullen hid a smile as he watched the scowling guards march away. Damn, she could play the role well!

"Funny, as a Brendoni, I'd have expected him to praise Yildemé," Natisse said.

"Pantagoya has no ties outside of Pantagoya," Kullen responded. "Abyssalia smile upon us," he mocked. "She hasn't so far; why would she start now?"

Natisse smiled. "Shall we?" She spread her hand toward the doors.

"After you," Kullen said. He pulled on the handle, a long, braided rope made of dried seaweed bound with bands of gold, and the doors opened with an ease that belied their size.

Bright light greeted them—brighter even than the grand room with all its many chandeliers. At first, it seemed to be coming from the walls themselves. But upon closer inspection, the walls were habitats for aquatic life the likes of which Kullen had never laid eyes upon. Creatures big and small, spiked and dotted with purulent bubbles, flitted just beyond the glass. Their main inhabitants, bioluminescent creatures reminiscent of a jellyfish, emitted the most brilliant glow Kullen had ever seen. They ebbed and undulated upward, then sank back down. Streams of light followed them, drawing wondrous patterns in the inky waters.

Together, they walked down a long hall, silent but for small gasps. Finally, they arrived in something far less extravagant but no less impressive. The décor aped every grand feast hall Kullen had seen in the houses of the Dimvein aristocracy, yet had a distinctly unfinished look and feel to it. As the island shifted back and forth with the tide, the walls creaked, and wooden planks separated, only to come back together again moments later. Shieldbandsmen stood at attention all around the room's perimeter. And here, it was clear, was where the true party was to take place.

"We're in," Kullen muttered into Natisse's ear. "Easy part's done. Now we've got to figure out what in Ezrasil's name to do next."

37
Natisse

Natisse couldn't help marveling at every strange detail filling the Pantagorissa's Palace. Having left the stunning grand room filled with sparkling gems and glowing lights, she'd expected something different here. But it was no less beautiful—just more... natural.

Seaweed climbed the walls like vines, crawling along the ceiling, hanging down. Their tips burned with fire but appeared to not be consumed by it. Something inside of her stirred at the sight of the flames, but she did her best to shove it down as she always had. Though, this time, it was not the same fear-driven panic. Instead, she felt compelled toward it, as if she could call upon its power to engulf the world.

In here, there were nobles aplenty, just as there'd been in the last room. But instead of eating and gambling, they were dancing around deep chasms in the floor that seemed to move and shift with the ebb and flow of the sea outside. It was as if the island itself was alive. As that thought passed through her mind, she focused on the walls. They expanded and contracted like lungs, as if they were breathing.

Such a place couldn't possibly exist—much less remain afloat—

yet here she was, surrounded by a bizarre challenge: all she'd thought of reality had been shattered.

Not only did the walls themselves seem to live and breathe, but upon closer inspection, creatures—she thought they were called barnacles—clung to every inch of the place. Octopi and squid hung from the ceiling like decor, and they, too, were dancing.

"What is this place?" Natisse asked, breathless.

Kullen didn't respond. Instead, he seemed fixed upon a collection of the wealthiest, most powerful people in Caernia.

But then Natisse realized Kullen wasn't watching the aristocrats. His gaze was firmly fixed on a gaggle of men and women dressed in leathers. Tri-corner hats sat crooked on their heads, hair flowing down that looked as if it hadn't been washed in a thousand years. Gold dangled from everywhere the body allowed dangling: the ears, the lips, the brows. One even wore golden hoops through the tough skin of their elbows.

"Blood Clan," Kullen said. "Pirates. The worst of them, it seems, too."

Pirates. Natisse had never seen the famed Blood Clan Pirates. Though now, she wished she could still say the same.

She'd thought the aristocrats of Dimvein possessed immense riches; yet even the gaudy finery of Magister Perech's pleasure barge and Magister Iltari's skybox paled in comparison to the excesses on full display everywhere she looked—even the filthy pirates.

It looked out of place amidst the natural beauty of the Palace—silk ascots and long coats on the men, precious gems, richly painted faces, and perfume so thick it made Natisse nauseous. But it wasn't just those from the Imperial Empire who'd gone all out to impress. Hudarian women wore their hair in tightly wrapped braids that sat upon their heads in a conical shape. It made Natisse's neck hurt just to look at it.

She'd never imagined so much wealth existed. Everyone bore enough gaudy finery to feed all of the Embers for a month. And it was all here in one place, within easy reach. Kullen had been right:

Pantagoya presented an incredibly tempting opportunity to carry out the Crimson Fang's mission of redistributing the world's vast wealth. If Sparrow, Leroshavé, Athelas, or Haston had been here to pick pockets and filch jewelry, they could've walked away from Pantagoya richer than half of Dimvein.

And yet, Natisse felt only the faintest desire to relieve these greedy bastards of their fortunes. Learning Uncle Ronan's true identity had shaken her faith in the Crimson Fang's existence and mission. Or, more accurately, the hidden reasons beneath the mission. She believed in their efforts to help the impoverished and destitute of Dimvein, those most affected by the greed and excesses of the aristocracy. But she couldn't stop questioning *why* Uncle Ronan—once a wealthy and powerful general himself—cared.

Standing here amidst so much opulence, she couldn't help wondering if Uncle Ronan truly cared at all. It could all be one more deceit to manipulate her and the Crimson Fang into helping him further his aims, whatever they might be.

"My lady?" Kullen spoke from her left side. Though he kept his voice low for her ears only, he was cautious enough to maintain their charade on the off-chance someone overheard him. "Are you well?"

"Yes, thank you, Yarlton." She pulled herself from her thoughts, snapping back to the pretense of Lady Dellacourt. "Just enjoying the company of my… peers."

Kullen kept his expression neutral, but she could see exactly what he was thinking. "Lady Dellacourt" couldn't afford more than a small skiff to convey her to Pantagoya; the small sum in gold and jewelry he carried in the valise clutched to his chest was an inconsequential amount compared to the vast fortunes on full display.

"Come, Yarlton." She lifted her head and beckoned for him to follow. "The rigors of our journey have left me thirsty."

Kullen snorted, though quietly enough only she heard it, and muttered something that might have been, "Said the one who did none of the work."

Natisse allowed the imperious smile to spread across her face as she drifted in a flutter of blue lace and frills toward the refreshments table. Which, it turned out, was actually two dozen or so long tables arrayed end to end and heaped high with enough food and drink to feed half of Dimvein.

Now, Natisse saw things she'd eat without protest, though she still didn't know what some of them were. What looked like goat or sheep simmering in a brown gravy really caught her eye. But then, just next to it, a rice noodle dish peppered with sliced carrot and onion in a creamy white sauce made her mouth salivate. And the breads... there were white breads, brown breads, even a mealy but moist-looking yellow cornbread. She didn't know where to start.

"Might I suggest the Brendoni hotcakes, my Lady?" Kullen said. "I hear it's best served with culberry jam and a dollop of cold cream."

Natisse was fiercely hungry—she hadn't eaten a proper meal since the previous day—but she knew if she allowed herself to gorge, she'd be far less useful for the mission. Thus, she picked sparingly at a crème-filled pastry.

A pyramid of crystal goblets filled with sparkling golden wine offered refreshment for her throat, parched from the salt air and the harsh, acrid exarai leaf smoke that had filled the lower levels of Pantagoya.

"What are we looking for, exactly?" she asked, using the gold-embossed rim of the goblet to hide her lips from any watching eyes.

"My contact didn't know." Kullen spoke from behind his hand, which he'd raised to politely cover his mouth as he ate a firecherry-topped cheese tartlet. "Everyone who should know already does. Which means we're on our own figuring it out."

Natisse sipped at her wine, then frowned at it as if displeased. "Pshaw!" She set the goblet down and plucked up another, this one filled with a rich, ruby-red vintage that smelled of plums. "That's not—"

"Is something amiss with my wine?" came a deep, rich voice from behind Natisse. "Or is Kolanthian icewine merely not to your liking?"

Natisse turned, expecting to find some pompous lordling or plump aristocrat. Instead, she faced a powerfully built woman who stood easily a full head taller than everyone around. Bony bleached-white spines from some deep-sea predator rose in a queenly frill from shoulders any blacksmith would envy, and jet-black hair framed a face tanned by sun yet still perfectly smooth and free of wrinkles or spots.

And what a face! Somehow sharp and delicate, angular and beautiful all at once, with piercing olive eyes supported by high cheekbones that accentuated the frown pulling down the woman's full, black-painted lips. Thick streaks of charcoal served to both highlight her facial contours and compliment the pitch-colored garment clinging to her muscular frame—a garment that appeared somehow a suit of armor and an elegant dress at once. Twin shadesteel cutlasses with midnight nabrine gemstones sat sheathed in black velvet-wrapped scabbards at her hips, and two braces of diamond-edged daggers crisscrossed her chest. But instead of detracting from the magnificence of the clothing and the woman who wore them, the weapons lent a breathtaking edge of menace and grandeur.

The woman stared at her with an expectant look, and only after long seconds did Natisse remember the question she'd asked.

"The wine is divine," Natisse said, though her tongue stumbled over the words. "If perhaps a bit too sweet when paired with the crème puff." She held up the pastry with thumb and forefinger, the other three dancing in the air above it.

The woman frowned down at the confection in Natisse's hand. "Indeed." She raised one strong, callused hand and tapped at her chin with her forefinger, upon which she wore a razor-sharp claw tip made of the same shadesteel as her cutlasses. After a moment, she snapped her fingers to the trio of similar-garbed men Natisse only now saw behind her.

"Ronolfo?" she barked.

None of the three men responded, but one turned and repeated the name in the harsh, resonant voice of a town crier. Within seconds, a fussy-looking man in a burgundy vest, as wine-stained as his too-red lips, hustled through the crowd toward them.

"Yes, Pantagorissa?" he said, bowing and scraping with well-practiced reverence.

"The Kolanthian icewine," the woman said in a curt tone. "It's too sweet."

Ronolfo straightened, his face, deathly pale and his mouth agape. No words ever left his lips. With a terrible swiftness that startled Natisse, the woman swept out her left-hand cutlass and severed the man's head from his shoulders. His head slowly tilted backward. Then the skin tore, and his head toppled off and bounced along the refreshments table until it came to rest in a bowl of thick red syrup. There it floated face up, eyes and mouth still wide.

His body crumpled to its knees, then toppled over into the table, staining the white cloth crimson as it slammed into the floor. A pool of blood seeped out from beneath the table, and Natisse had to move to avoid being overtaken by it.

"Tarothis!" Again, the woman snapped her fingers, and again the barking voice rang out through the hall. When the summoned man appeared—this one wearing a vest with far fewer wine stains—he stared in open-mouthed horror at the legs sticking out from beneath the tablecloth and the blood-stained wooden planks. Then he turned his attention to the still-dripping blade in the Pantagorissa's hand.

"Y-Yes, Pantagorissa?" Tarothis squeaked out, bowing so low his wispy brown hair and long nose nearly dipped into the pool of Ronolfo's blood.

"The Kolanthian icewine," said the woman again. "It's too sweet."

Tarothis gave a strangled sound like a mouse caught in a cat's paws. When he straightened, all blood had drained from his face and he eyed the bloody cutlass as if expecting it to carve his flesh next.

But the Pantagorissa just wiped the blade on his vest, leaving long streaks of gruesome crimson along the burgundy velvet. "See that the next vintage is less displeasing to our guests."

"Y-Yes, Pantagorissa. O-Of course, Pantagorissa." Tarothis didn't quite tuck tail and flee, but Natisse had never seen anyone make such a hasty retreat while still bowing and scraping with every retreating step.

The woman turned back to Natisse. "You have my apologies for your displeasure," she said, sheathing her cutlass as casually as if she'd drawn it to clean or test its edge. "I can personally vouch for the quality of the Bossiri Invecchiato in your hand. From my personal stores."

Natisse looked down at the all-but-forgotten goblet of wine she held. A drop of what might have been blood leaked down the fluted exterior, but she chose to ignore it and instead take a sip.

"Breathtaking," she said, and it was no lie. She was no connoisseur of wine, but the heady vintage with its deep, rich flavors of black cherry, plum, and spices she couldn't quite place set her palate dancing. "I can say, in all honesty, I've never tasted its equal anywhere in the world."

"Nor should you." A proud smile broadened the woman's face. "I had every barrel in existence brought to my Palace, killed the master vintner and all his apprentices, and burned the Bossiri vineyard to the ground. What you are drinking is without a doubt the finest wine in all of Caernia." She leaned forward until her face hovered just mere inches from Natisse's own. "And yet, somehow, *you* are even more breathtaking."

Natisse couldn't help the little flush of color rising to her cheeks, though the potent wine and an empty stomach certainly played a role. Yet she allowed it to show on her cheeks—as expected of Lady Dellacourt—and gave a pretty curtsy.

"You honor me." Straightening, she stared up into the woman's alluring olive eyes. "You mentioned 'my Palace.' It appears the stories I have heard of Pantagorissa Torrine Heweda Eanverness Wombourne Shadowfen III fall far short of doing you proper justice."

The Pantagorissa gave a throaty laugh, and merriment sparkled in her eyes. "Were you anyone else, I might be wary of such a flattering tongue. Yet I will admit I am quite interested to find out what more that tongue of yours can do."

This time, Natisse managed to keep from blushing at the innuendo. "I am at your service, Pantagorissa. In *any* way you might desire."

The woman quirked a perfectly trimmed black eyebrow. "And who might I ask is so readily offering their services?"

"Lady Dellacourt of Elliatrope," Natisse said, sweeping a deeper curtsy this time—one that offered a clear view down her dress's plunging neckline.

"Elliatrope?" Pantagorissa Torrine's lips tugged into a frown. "The name is not known to me." She snapped her fingers. "Saurmat?"

A short, bald, nervous-looking man appeared as if from thin air. "Pantagorissa?"

"Elliatrope?" she asked, without taking her eyes off Natisse.

"A minor city in the far western reaches of the Karmian Empire," Saurmat said, mopping at his forehead with a silken scarf. "Nothing of great interest to you."

"On the contrary," the Pantagorissa said, grinning wolfishly down at Natisse. "Quite a lot of interest." She dismissed the man with a flick of her shadesteel-taloned finger, and Saurmat vanished into the crowd as abruptly as he'd appeared.

One of the trio at her back—not the one who'd roared for the doomed Ronolfo—stepped forward and whispered into the woman's ear. Pantagorissa Torrine's right eyebrow rose and a look of interest flickered across her face.

"I see." Her olive eyes flitted past Natisse to where Kullen stood clutching the leather valise. Her smile widened, grew hungry, and she held out a hand to Natisse. "Come," she said. "Dance with me. I would hear more of Elliatrope and the magnificent lady it has gifted us."

Natisse heard the note of command in the Pantagorissa's voice —clearly, this was a woman accustomed to getting precisely what she wanted when she wanted it.

She shot a quick, sidelong glance at Kullen but didn't let it linger. Suddenly, she regretted her offer to be used however the Pantagorissa deemed fit, but this was the role she'd chosen to play, and perhaps this distraction would buy Kullen the time needed to snoop.

"I would be honored, Pantagorissa." She took the woman's hand. It was warm, strong, and surprisingly gentle despite its calluses and the flecks of Ronolfo's blood still splattering two of her fingers.

As she followed the Pantagorissa to the dance floor, she glanced over her shoulder. Kullen smiled and nodded. Perhaps they'd found their way into the auction after all.

38
KULLEN

Kullen struggled to keep his jaw from touching the ground as Natisse flounced out onto the dance floor hand in hand with Pantagorissa Torrine. Cliessa had clearly blessed them with her luck tonight. Kullen had expected Natisse to turn heads—he had to admit she cut a truly astonishing figure in that cetacean-blue dress, her fiery-red hair tied in a braid far simpler than the overelaborate coiffures—but this particular head far exceeded his wildest expectations.

Could it simply be that easy for her? he wondered. *A few smiles, a witty remark or three, and suddenly she's invited to the auction as the Pantagorissa's arm candy?* He could hope, certainly. But he wouldn't hinge the success of his mission entirely on happenstance.

Kullen allowed himself a moment to enjoy the pleasant sight of Natisse spinning around the dance floor. He supposed he shouldn't have been surprised to discover she was a fine dancer—she moved with the grace of a trained swordsman—but the more he came to know the ardent woman, the more he realized he had no idea the full extent of her capabilities. She had transformed into Lady Dellacourt so fully he would never have recognized her as the same hard, fierce fighter who'd killed Magister Branthe's guards in his underground fighting pit.

The moment ended when he realized he no longer stood alone by the refreshments table where Natisse had left him. The trio who had taken up station behind the Pantagorissa—all of whom displayed the gold-etched skull-and-crossed-oars of her personal, elite guard—now surrounded him. Two remained facing the dance floor, keeping an eye on their mistress. The third, however, the scowling, scar-faced man who'd roared in the voice of a drill sergeant, fixed Kullen with a hard stare. Though the Shieldbandsman said nothing, Kullen got the distinct impression the man was taking his measure—and Lady Dellacourt's by extension.

Kullen clutched the valise tighter and shifted nervously from foot to foot, as if discomfited by the scrutiny. He kept his shoulders hunched, and his eyes never truly lifted to meet the Shieldbandsman's. Better he appeared utterly uninteresting and unthreatening to the watchful elite guards.

Realizing the Pantagorissa's man would continue watching him as long as their mistresses shared each other's company, Kullen chose to ignore the black look of the guard and instead appraise the room around him from beneath his downturned forehead. If Natisse failed to secure an invitation as the Pantagorissa's invited guest at the auction, they'd require an alternate plan to gain entrance.

He nibbled at a roasted quail leg, though he barely tasted the perfectly spiced, tender meat. His attention was riveted on those sharing the vast chamber with them. Most were dancing, some were eating, and all were drinking… a lot. By and large, everyone seemed to be enjoying the festival without causing trouble.

But every few minutes, one of the serving men wearing the Pantagorissa's colors—darkest black and bleached skull white, with a hint of gold accent—appeared from a door at the northern end. These carried no food trays or barrels of drink like did their companions, nor did they mingle among the guests to offer refreshment. Instead, they sidled up to seemingly random people and exchanged a few brief words. What they said, Kullen couldn't possibly hear over the music—heavy drums and harsh woodwind instruments. Whatever it was, those who were thus approached were inevitably led through the doorway through which the servants had disappeared.

By the time the Pantagorissa and Natisse had danced to their second song, Kullen had witnessed seven guests conducted away in this fashion. One Qilaqui, an umber-skinned Brendoni, a trio of men clad in clothes cut into the latest style popular in the Karmian Empire, and two from the Caliphate of Fire, both of whom wore the ornate blues and golds of the wealthy religious state of Niazi.

A ghost of a frown played on Kullen's lips when the next servant to enter sidled up to a group of Hudarians who had sat silent and somber along the chamber's eastern wall. The two women in the party both wore colorful beaded robes and horse-hair headdresses that marked them as *Tabudai,* shamankas, and leaders of the Horde. The two men had to be father and son—one with steel-gray mustachios that drooped over his abundant, studded armored belly; the other with wispy facial hair but the lean, squat build of a man born to battle on horseback.

Kullen tried to hide his surprise. Were these the *Khorchai,* the Horde's chosen leaders? Two to command their warriors, two to bend the spirits to their will. That might explain why he'd seen so many Hudarians in the streets below.

The four somber-looking Hudarians followed the servant from the room. That couldn't be good. For centuries, the Karmian Empire had managed to prevent the Horde from getting their hands on dragonblood vials. Tonight could change everything... unless Kullen managed to retrieve the vials first.

Finally, another servant appeared at the start of the next song and headed directly toward the company of Blood Clan pirates Kullen had been eyeing. Presently, they engaged in a raucous drinking game that involved bared daggers, knucklebone dice, and copious amounts of phlegm. The servant managed to keep a straight face as he sidled up to the bloody, spittle-flecked pirates. Their departure was marked by the clacking of the gold chains weaved into their hair and a rousing—if off-key—chorus of "The Lusty Boatman Kissed My Loot," an old sea shanty favored among sailors around Caernia.

Kullen was again too far away to hear their response to the servant's quiet inquiry, but from his vantage point, he could see something golden flash in the hands of the smallest, leanest pirate in the group. A coin twice the size of an Imperial mark. The servant hadn't taken the coin, but it, accompanied with whatever words had been spoken, seemed the signal for which he had been looking.

Well, that bloody complicates things, Kullen thought, gritting his teeth. He studied the remainder of the Pantagorissa's guests—more than three hundred in this vast hall alone, and Ezrasil knew how many more elsewhere. Every one of them sported enough wealth to hold their own in an auction for something as valuable as a vial of dragonblood. For that reason alone, none of them stood out as likely targets. No way of knowing who else in this room might be carrying a coin, much less where they'd be concealing it.

His Black Talon training had included skills in picking pockets and pilfering worn jewelry, but it was only possible if he knew which pockets to pick or could see the rings, necklaces, bracelets, and earrings he intended to steal.

He considered his course of action. The chances of lifting a coin from one of the—apparently few—guests invited to the auction from among the crowd filling the hall were slim. He was unconfident the passcode given to him by Assidius's agent would suffice to gain access, either. He suspected the guests invited to the auction were given *different* code words with which to identify themselves upon their arrival to Pantagoya, along with these special coins.

At the moment, their success hinged entirely on Natisse. Turning his attention back to her, he found himself feeling optimistic. She danced with an abandon so exuberant it appeared truly genuine, even to him. Her ice-blue eyes sparkled with merriment as she laughed at some remark from the Pantagorissa, and a comely flush deepened her cheeks to a beautiful crimson to match her fiery hair. The blue dress seemed to swirl about her like the waves of the ocean. Indeed, she was a vision to set the imagination ablaze and the blood rushing.

The Pantagorissa clearly felt the same, for her strong, sun-bronzed face was aglow with delight, her olive eyes twinkling in response to Natisse's clear enjoyment of her company. She held Natisse's wrist lightly in one strong hand, but the other rested well *below* the proper and appropriate placement on her partner's lower back. The most powerful woman on the island—and one of the wealthiest in the world—seemed incapable of taking her eyes off Natisse, so thoroughly she was entranced.

Kullen's spirit soared. Clearly, he'd made the right choice convincing the Emperor to allow him to bring Natisse. As he'd surmised, she had proven herself an invaluable asset in his mission. All she had to do now was seal the deal and convince the Pantagorissa to keep her close.

A clever device on the northern wall used what Kullen could only imagine to be Trenta engineering to display a sundial without the use of the sun. Upon their arrival, the Shield-bandsman had said the primary festivities would take place in two hours—less than three-quarters of an hour off, now.

Come on, he silently directed in Natisse's direction. *You can do this.*

As if on cue, the song ended, the music fell silent, and all in the hall broke out into applause. The Pantagorissa stood at the center of attention, and she swept broad, grand waves to the crowd. Natisse breathlessly fanned herself with a hand in a great show of exhaustion and exhilaration from the dance.

Pantagorissa Torrine offered Natisse her arm, and Natisse took it with a whispered remark that had the Pantagorissa laughing and nudging Natisse with one well-formed hip. The two spoke with their heads close as Natisse allowed Pantagorissa

Torrine to lead her back to where Kullen and the elite guards stood.

"Yarlton!" Natisse called out to him, snapping her fingers in an imitation of the Pantagorissa's gesture. "Come." She offered no further explanation, merely turned away and headed toward the door at the northern end of the hall.

Kullen followed like the well-trained manservant he was pretending to be, hunched over the valise and hurrying to catch up to his departing mistress.

"Truly," the Pantagorissa was saying as he drew within earshot. "Formality serves a purpose, reminds all of my vassals and guests of the respect I am due. But a very select and special few may call me Torrine." Her hand wandered farther down Natisse's backside. "And you, my dear Atina, are among them tonight."

"I'm honored, Pantagorissa." Natisse turned a coy smile up to the woman at her side. "Torrine."

"I relish in the way it sounds on your lips," the Pantagorissa said. "After the night's grand event, we shall see what other ways those lips can make me relish."

"I believe you'll be pleasantly surprised." Natisse was clearly playing the role to full effect, but with such adroitness, Kullen *almost* believed it real.

He had to fall back as the Pantagorissa led Natisse through the door at the end of the hall under the time-telling device, and the trio of elite Shieldbandsmen pushed past him. Obviously, he hadn't passed the scowling guard's muster, but they only tolerated his presence because of his mistress's entanglement with theirs. This certainly *wasn't* the first time Pantagorissa Torrine had selected one of her guests to serve as suitable "entertainment." The woman had a reputation for being a notorious libertine. No surprise that the Pantagoya played host to every conceivable pleasure, entertainment, and vice known to man—and a few even Kullen wasn't familiar with.

They traversed a simple wooden corridor. The walls closed in, then expanded in synchronous movement that made Kullen think they danced to a song all their own. One large break in the floor had been repaired, four long planks lay side by side to create a makeshift bridge. It was old wood clearly salvaged from a seafaring vessel.

"Allow me, my dear," Pantagorissa Torrine said, taking the hand Natisse rested on her arm in her own hand to lead her across the creaking bridge. "No missteps for you tonight. It would be downright criminal to lose a morsel as delectable as you to my pets."

"Pets?" Natisse asked, managing a tone midway between curious and delighted. "You have puppies? Or a cat?"

Kullen had to hide his laughter. By Ezrasil, she danced the fine line between simpering and flighty with grace.

"I do," the Pantagorissa said, not bothering to contain her laughter. "But these pets have a few more teeth and tend to enjoy the company of those who fall into their water." She extended the forefinger of her free hand to show the razor-sharp shadesteel talon adorning its tip. "Or, perhaps I should say, enjoy the *taste?*"

Natisse gave a little squeak that could have signaled either fear or enchantment.

Either way, it delighted the Pantagorissa, who laughed even harder and pulled Natisse to her on the far side of the bridge. "But never you worry, my little bluebird. I will keep you close and safe tonight."

They passed three large porthole windows which showed little more than darkness over the sea before reaching a spiraling staircase rising up several stories. Kullen consulted the mental map he'd begun drawing of the Pantagorissa's Palace since first he entered the main doors. He suspected they approached the base of the Pantagorissa's private tower. For a moment, he worried the woman would pull Natisse up those stairs, but his perturbations were short-lived. The Pantagorissa's appetites might be legendary, but not even Emperor Wymarc had ever accused her of being less than dragon tooth sharp when it came to business and negotiations. She would certainly do her duties as hostess to this auction first, then enjoy her more carnal pleasures after the matter was settled.

They passed the first staircase and then another. This one was stained with blood. A pair of shackles lay open on the first step. A small moan drew Kullen's attention about ten steps up to where two men stood, chained to the wall, arms pulled so tightly he wondered how they were still connected at the shoulders. Each one bore cuts and bruises enough to render a man mad with pain. And here they were, displayed for any and all who passed to see. A warning of what was to come should anyone cross the Pantagorissa.

"This is our Worship Hall," the Pantagorissa said, stopping momentarily before two wide open doors. "We hold no god above another here. Any visitor to my Palace can pay homage to any deity they please."

"So close to the prisons," Natisse said softly.

"I believe they should be as close to their gods as can be," the Pantagorissa said, smiling. "It will make their journey into the afterlife that much quicker. I'm not a monster, after all."

Statues of every god Kullen had heard of and more lined the room. He recognized the nearly naked Yildemé, Goddess of the Brendoni, and a threesome intertwined beneath her statue in worship. Beside it—a rather strange neighbor—a rather crude-looking version of Ezrasil. Even Ulnu and Binteth, the twin demon gods, had their place. Beyond the familiar, the Quilaqui gods, Tatkret—god of night—and Sura—goddess of day, stood back-to-back.

Four members of the Caliphate of Fire stood before their spirit god, Abna Zufar, the one who rules the fire.

"What do you think, my lovely little bluebird?" Pantagorissa Torrine said to Natisse in a low, breathy voice. "Perhaps you'd like to pay the goddess homage with me later, hmm?"

To her credit, Natisse managed to both blush prettily and turn a look of wide-eyed innocence on the Pantagorissa. "I thought you and your people worshipped Abyssalia."

"We do." The tall woman leaned lower and whispered into Natisse's ear in a voice loud enough for even Kullen to hear. "But that doesn't mean we can't honor Yildemé for such beautiful additions to our mortal world, does it? Come. Let's continue."

She led them further into the bowels of the island and past the third tower. This was marked with statues and paintings of the sea. A globe hung like a lantern, as massive as it was terrifying. Tentacles wrapped it, and one large eye stared down at them. The Kraken in all its wondrous glory. A mural rose along with the stairs depicting the Vandil triumphantly sailing the stormy seas. Their ships were painted in lavish colors: red, gold, orange, and white. This would be the Temple Tower.

Yet still, Pantagorissa Torrine did not stop. Kullen's heart began to beat faster, excitement thundering in his chest. Could it be…?

They stopped before a giant door so black it looked as if it could swallow Kullen into the Shadow Realm. Six Shieldbandsmen stood before it, unmoving. Their eyes remained forward, not even acknowledging their presence—not even that of the Pantagorissa.

However, when she stepped forward, they all turned as one and hauled on the doors. It took all six pulling with all their strength and a ponderous chorus of groans and creaking wood.

When the door opened, Kullen saw only darkness. Then, the guards stepped in and opened a second black door, using the same strained effort. Beyond it was a staircase. Without Kullen's dragon-eyes, he wasn't sure he'd have seen it.

"Watch your step," the Pantagorissa warned. When she stepped foot on the first step, a line of brilliant flame erupted *within* the wood. It traced a path up the stairs in a wide circle. "It won't harm you," she said.

Kullen could see the trepidation on Natisse's face. Though, just as she had the whole night, she pressed onward. Kullen followed, enraptured by the fire that did not consume.

The Pantagorissa held Natisse tightly the whole way, ensuring that her treat didn't stumble and break an ankle. She paid no such mind to Kullen, nor did the guards that stomped on his heels.

When they reached the top, six more guards were posted at another door identical to the ones below. It opened to a thirty-foot-long corridor lined with blue-green alchemical lanterns. Despite the fire, the air grew cold around them. His skin pricked with gooseflesh. There was no doubt in Kullen's mind: this was the way to the Dread Spire. And it was so aptly named.

"Boreo, see Lady Dellacourt's manservant back to the common room," the Pantagorissa said to one of the Shieldbandsmen.

"Can he not stay," Natisse said, clearly trying to keep the panic from her tone.

"You will not need him. You are safe here with me. I was kind enough to give him those assurances."

Kullen bowed. "You have my gratitude."

"Of which, that means so little," the Pantagorissa said. "Come now, Atina, tonight, I will show you wonders the likes of which you have never dreamed." She bared her teeth in a wolfish grin. "First here, then in my private chambers. Tell me that pleases you, Lady Dellacourt." It wasn't a question.

"It pleases me, Torrine," Natisse said, returning the smile with a dazzling one of her own.

The Pantagorissa extended her arm. "Then let the marvels begin."

"Wait!" Natisse said. Kullen gritted his teeth, worried Natisse might spoil the whole evening and all they'd accomplished so far. She turned back. "Yarlton, my valise?"

Kullen let out a worried breath and stepped forward. He was met by the strong arms of the Pantagorissa's guards.

"You won't need it," Patagorissa Torrine said. "Besides, there's no way you have with you enough to merit your presence here at my auction. It was your charms that garnered my attention." Without another word, the Pantagorissa pulled Natisse forward, leaving Kullen alone with the Shieldbandsmen.

39
Natisse

Natisse's stomach lurched at the explosive shutting of the doors behind her. Until that moment, she hadn't realized just how comforting Kullen's presence at her back had been.

She was still far from trusting him—after everything he'd done, she didn't know if she ever would—but since the moment they'd stepped foot onto Pantagoya, she'd never once doubted he'd be there if the situation grew dangerous. And after seeing Ronolfo's fate, Natisse *knew* she danced along a razor's edge with the Pantagorissa. Such a mercurial, capricious person could go from enchanted to enraged between heartbeats. If the woman could so easily kill one of her own people, she wouldn't bat an eyelash at taking Natisse's head.

It hadn't only been once she had needed to steer Torrine's hand from her hips as they danced. She was handsy! It took all of Natisse's self-control not to reach down and feel the hilt of her lashblade hidden beneath her dress, just to reassure herself it was still there. That would draw the Pantagorissa's attention to the wrong thing. She wanted the woman fixated entirely on everything she found *pleasing.*

Natisse was surprised by the heat she'd felt rising within her veins since the moment she followed the Pantagorissa out onto the dance floor. She'd never experienced anything like it before. With Baruch, she'd felt a warming sensation deep in the pit of her belly. But the Pantagorissa exuded a raw animal magnetism that seemed to set every hair on Natisse's skin prickling, her heart racing, and sweat sprouting on her flesh. The only comparison was the blazing heat of Golgoth's magic burning in her soul.

Yes, Natisse could understand precisely why the woman held Pantagoya in her sway. Charismatic, commanding, charming, brutal when needed, and utterly in control of everything around her—she was everything one expected in a leader.

Nothing at all like Emperor Wymarc. She'd met the man just once and only exchanged a few words with him. His was a quiet dignity, a sense of self-confidence as understated as the Pantagorissa's was brashly put on full display. Even his immaculately tailored royal clothing had been far simpler than the gaudy armor-like dress clinging to the Pantagorissa's powerful frame.

And from the stories Kullen had told her, Natisse could understand why he chose to serve the Emperor. For all that she'd hated Wymarc and everything he represented, he had at least agreed to aid the efforts to rebuild the Refuge. He'd given his time and attention to a terrified young Kullen. Such action would certainly engender loyalty, while the Pantagorissa's rule was clearly built on fear.

How strange her life had become! She'd gone from hating Kullen for Baruch's death to *hoping* he found a way to rejoin her here and now—from despising Emperor Wymarc for what she'd seen as disregard for his people to positioning him favorably above the Pantagorissa. The ability to summon dragons and control fire magic seemed almost ordinary by comparison.

"Come, my lovely bluebird."

Oh, how Natisse hated that name. Like she was some weak thing, fluttering around at the behest of another.

The Pantagorissa's voice echoed through the hallway with

unnatural volume, caroming off the ebonwood planking and setting the sea-green fires dancing in their alchemical lanterns.

"Tonight, I promise you delights few others alive today have experienced." Her eyes sparkled with merriment and a generous portion of desire. "Precious few can boast that they visited not one but *two* of the Pantagorissa's towers. And most of those now dance with the winds and skies atop my Tower of Justice."

Natisse hid the shiver of fear that rippled through her and turned a coy smile up to the imposing ruler. "Is that to be my fate, then? From dancing in your grand hall to dancing atop this Tower of Justice?"

Pantagorissa Torrine laughed. "I always believed the ladies of the Karmian Empire preferred their lovemaking in a bed, but should the danger of shackles and manacles be more to your liking…" She shrugged. "There are chains aplenty in my Pleasure Tower, but those are made of gold and furs, not blood-stained iron."

"The night is young yet," Natisse said, waggling an eyebrow suggestively.

"It is, indeed." The Pantagorissa ran a strong hand down Natisse's back and wound around her hip—once again so close to the hilt of her lashblade that Natisse had to fight an involuntary stiffness in her posture. She covered it up by leaning into the woman and turning her body inward, so the hand on her hip returned to the small of her back. She leaned against the Pantagorissa and wrapped her arm around the woman's powerful waist.

"Now, I was promised wonders and marvels," she whispered, a coquettish smile on her face. "And yet, all I see is this hall. And you, of course." She reached up a hand to trace along the Pantagorissa's jaw. "Wonderful as you are, I came here for the auction. Even if I cannot join the bidding"—she allowed a look of pouty disappointment to flash across her face—"I would still like to enjoy the spectacle."

"An interesting choice of words." Pantagorissa Torrine beamed, her olive eyes bright with excitement. "I do not exaggerate when I say it shall be a spectacle unrivaled."

"Then let us not keep your honored guests waiting." Natisse slid out of the Pantagorissa's grasp to flounce along the corridor, turning and beckoning the Pantagorissa to follow, as if too excited to contain herself.

With a bark of laughter, Pantagorissa Torrine chased after her, heavy boots thundering on the loose planks underfoot. Natisse picked up just enough speed to give the woman a merry chase, but only for a few dozen paces. Then she slowed to let Pantagoya's ruler catch up and made a grand show of being out of breath. She slipped her arm into the Pantagorissa's and allowed the woman to escort her toward one final grand staircase.

Where the previous were black with what seemed to be harmless fire, this one burned like freshly lit flames. Natisse could sense Golgoth internally groaning in pleasure at the sight.

"These won't harm you either," Torrine said.

As they drew closer, skulls poked through the flames. As Natisse followed the railing downward, she saw they sat atop long human bones like those found in one's legs.

"Nothing goes to waste in Pantagoya," the Pantagorissa said. "The Tower of Justice feeds these halls with the bones of the damned."

Those words brought a chill even colder than the air.

Natisse cautiously stepped forward, memories of that fateful day when her parents were ripped out of her life flashing before her eyes. She was breathing heavily—and noticeably so.

"Do you not trust me, little bluebird?"

Natisse sucked in a breath meant to gird her heart and body. She nodded. "I do."

With that, Torrine led Natisse up the spiraling staircase past more bones and skulls. She was unsure, and it was difficult to tell through the crackle and whipping of fire all around her, but she thought she heard voices whispering just beyond the walls.

Toward the middle, Natisse slowed, but a tug from Torrine had her moving once more.

"Ah, here we are," the Pantagorissa said when they reached the top. "Welcome to the Dread Spire. Prepare yourself for the vision of a lifetime."

Natisse looked up at her, faking a smile again. "I've already seen that tonight."

"Oh, you truly are one of Yildemé's ilk."

Only two guards stood before this door. It wasn't large or heavy-looking, but the wood was carved in ornate detail. Everything from horned skulls and Vandil longships decorated its face. Torrine didn't even stop walking. The guards thrust the doors inward, and the entire room hushed.

A triangular room awaited them. Its walls were painted in the same impossibly black style as the rest of what Torrine had called the Dread Spire, and the walls all shone with the fire that didn't burn. From the floor to the pitched roof, ending in a wide glass ceiling, the flames coursed in equally spaced lines. If followed horizontally, they all led to a stage upon which stood an ensemble singing an eerie chorus.

Natisse stood in awe, first focused on the moon above, then her surroundings.

"Speechless, are we?" the Pantagorissa asked.

"It's… amazing."

The Pantagorissa smiled

"All rise for your honored host, Pantagorissa Torrine Heweda Eanverness Wombourne Shadowfen III!" a heraldic voice boomed through the chamber. The speaker was a pot-bellied, pox-faced man wearing the black, white, and gold livery of Pantagoya, standing behind the throne-like chair that stood upon the stage, high above any guest or singer.

At once, every attendee turned and nearly kissed the floor in a sweeping bow. Even the women did not curtsy. A fast assessment counted half a hundred people, not including the entertainment nor the workers. Faces both like hers and completely different filled the room. Natisse even recognized several who were downstairs with them just moments earlier. These were the chosen ones. Those with enough gold to bid on dragonblood vials.

Pantagorissa Torrine raised a hand in acknowledgment of the obeisance, then dismissed the crowd with a wave.

"Enough," she said, her voice flat, almost bored. "Rise."

Not a single soul disobeyed. Though some looked put out by the formalities—the Hudarian men and those garbed in leathers and gold in particular. The ones Kullen had identified as Blood Clan Pirates. Most, however, kept their expressions hidden and their postures respectful. They were in the Pantagorissa's domain, after all. None carried weapons that she could see, and just as she'd been forced to do, any manservants or bodyguards had been left without. That wasn't to say there were no weapons present. Twenty of the breastplate-wearing guards stood around the room, all armed with cutlasses.

Pantagorissa Torrine marched toward her throne, Natisse at her side.

At the center of the room, they passed a large bronze cauldron filled to the brim with sparkling water. Atop it lay a flat plane of glass that shimmered like the roiling waves of the sea. Etched around the rim were symbols and glyphs Natisse didn't recognize, but they spoke of some ancient magic. Any further inspection of the object was cut short as the Pantagorissa pulled her along.

Upon reaching the throne, she ushered Natisse to stand behind it, then turned to face the assembled throng. "I will not waste words on pleasantries. You have already enjoyed the comforts of my hall below, sampled my food and drink. Now is the time for business."

A new air came over the woman as she spoke. The genial, charming Pantagorissa vanished, and in its place stood the commanding ruler of Pantagoya, one of the wealthiest people in all of Caernia.

"You believe you are summoned here tonight for an auction." She inclined her head in acknowledgment. "And so you are. You know what is on offer, and I trust you all came prepared. Tonight, one and only one of you will walk away with the power to change the fate of your clans, tribes, nations, or caliphates."

Eager murmurs ran through the crowd.

"All of Caernia," she heard rise above the rest.

Natisse kept her expression carefully neutral, but inwardly nervous energy coursed in her veins. Even *one* dragonblood vial held enough power to decimate armies and raze cities to the ground. Yet from what Kullen had told her, multiple vials would be placed on offer tonight. The Karmian Empire had thus far maintained its dominance in Caernia due to it alone having access to dragonblood magic. That could very well change tonight unless she and Kullen succeeded in their mission.

A mission that appeared to have fallen to her alone for the moment. She had no doubt Kullen would attempt to reach her, but if he couldn't, she'd have to execute the plan on her own. A tall order, given that she stood surrounded by twenty armed guards, the Pantagorissa herself, and whatever tricks the auction guests had smuggled in. After all, Natisse had entered with her own lash-blade. She certainly wasn't the only one who would think of concealing swords and daggers beneath their dresses and coats. One look around the room, and she counted at least eighteen people who wore more than enough clothing to effectively hide weaponry.

"But that is not the only reason you are here." Pantagorissa Torrine's voice thundered through the Dread Spire. "No, I have graciously allowed my kingdom to play host to this auction because it allows me to show you the face of *true* power." She pointed to herself. "My face."

Whispers, murmurs, fearful all of them, rose from the congregation.

"For all the might of the dragons," Pantagorissa said over the din, "they are not the only creatures with the power to conquer. There are some even older than the beasts of flame and ice, fang and wing." She leaned forward, her voice dropping to a low growl. "Creatures that can destroy not just cities, but *empires!*"

A shudder ran down Natisse's spine. The muttering grew to a loud and confused roar.

As if on cue, a low chanting song echoed through the room, but it was not the onstage singers creating it. Rhythmic and dissonant at once, harsh yet soothing, the song reverberated through the tower-top chamber, setting the hair along Natisse's arms prickling. She *felt* the power in the pit of her belly, a power that grew as the song rose in volume.

Then five figures appeared at the head of the staircase. Each wore gauzy dresses of a different color—red, shining gold, brown, midnight black, and purest ivory white—to match the hue of their hair. The one in the crimson gown drew Natisse's eye. They could've been sisters, so similar in appearance and age they were. The black-haired, black-robed figure was barely a child, the woman with white hair and robes hunched and gnarled by the passage of years.

The five women strode down the aisle that had been arranged between the seated guests, their path leading directly to the bronze cauldron in the center of the chamber. One by one, they began to circle the cauldron in the same direction as the rising sun. The white-haired woman was the first to draw a weapon, a ceremonial dagger with opals and diamonds that glittered in the moonlight. Blacksteel flashed as she cut a small furrow into the palm of her left hand. That hand she placed atop the cauldron's glassy canopy, leaving a smear of blood behind as she continued circling.

The others followed suit, first the brown-haired woman, then the golden-haired, then the fiery-haired, then finally, the young raven-haired girl. Their blood soon mingled, leaving gory streaks atop the crystalline surface. With every step, their song rose in volume, the cadence quickening and growing in intensity until Natisse could feel it thrumming in her very soul.

Golgoth groaned again, but this time, there was no pleasure in it. Natisse felt it, the warning of something otherworldly, but she couldn't think to do anything. If she summoned Golgoth now, their entire charade would end, and that was not the plan.

Blood trickled down into the water. There must've been some aperture at the glass's center Natisse hadn't spotted. The liquid within the cauldron swirled like a storm, and the runes began to glow bright and hot. In a breath, it was as if the moon and the waters converged, and a beam of light burst forth blindingly.

It seemed the whole room began to spin, but it was just the runes as the cauldron sprang to life. Faster and faster it went until it raged like a whirlpool within the bronze basin.

The confusion of the room turned to panic, but the Shieldbandsmen stood at the ready, swords drawn, daring anyone to run. And where would they go? The only entrance was closed and sealed, several flights of stairs and the Tower of Justice between the crowd and any means of escape.

They were trapped in here with whatever this was.

"Behold," Pantagorissa Torrine declared in a grand voice that sounded terribly small in Natisse's ears. "The power of the Vandil, once believed lost to time, now reborn. And with it, Abyssalia herself will rise. And with her might, we shall conquer!"

There was a sudden and complete silence in the room as she finished speaking. The song ended. The beam, though filled with power, made no sound. There wasn't even the clatter of swords.

Then, like a thunderclap, something Natisse could only describe as a deafening heartbeat boomed and echoed throughout the room. And from within the moonlight, a gleaming eye opened.

40
KULLEN

Kullen stared in helpless frustration at the immense gate through which Natisse had just vanished. He couldn't follow her in that way, not unless he intended to fight past the Shieldbandsmen standing guard and those tasked with ushering him back downstairs. He had weaponry enough hidden beneath his clothes for the job—not to mention the drawn cutlasses just begging to be disarmed—but the Emperor's instructions had been very clear. He was to avoid breaking the Pantagorissa's peace at all costs. Stealth and subterfuge over bloodshed unless otherwise unavoidable.

"Move along," the Shieldbandsman said, giving Kullen a little shove.

Kullen bit his tongue and obeyed. Valise still clutched to his chest, he turned away from the doors and shuffled back the way he'd come, careful to keep up the Yarlton façade. Natisse had rightly believed that this was the best role for him. A servant abandoned by his master was far beneath the notice of the Shieldbandsmen and guests both.

Dutifully, he put one foot in front of the other, passing all the same fixtures, trying his hardest to ignore the moans of the prisoners as he passed the Tower of Justice. When they reached the room with the crystal chandeliers, he considered his best course of action.

"Wait here," one guard said.

"Or don't," the other added. "Don't give two shark teeth what ye do. Just don't ye be causin' trouble."

Kullen dipped his head slightly.

The jacket he wore was double-sided. He could turn it inside out, putting his elegant dress coat on the inside. Using the items he'd procured and stuffed within its pockets, it would be a simple matter to alter his appearance sufficiently as to be unrecognizable to the Pantagorissa's guards.

But there was still one glaring flaw: he had neither the golden coin nor the correct words to gain him entrance. If he tried and failed to talk his way past the guards, the Shieldbandsmen would doubtless pay closer attention to him, and he'd lose the cover of anonymity.

The more he considered it, the more he became convinced that he was better off finding another way to reach Natisse. Fortunately for him, night had fully fallen—indeed, midnight was just an hour off—and there would be shadows aplenty outside the Pantagorissa's Palace. All he needed to do was find somewhere to duck out of sight and into a patch of darkness, then shadow-slide up to the Dread Spire's peak.

It certainly wasn't the ideal plan with plenty that could go wrong, but it would have to serve. Natisse was only here because of him; he couldn't abandon her in the Pantagorissa's company. Besides, he needed to get close enough to identify the seller and retrieve the dragonblood vials being auctioned off.

He paid the party little heed. Any guests important enough to be participating in the auction would already be sitting in that tower-top. The Pantagorissa struck him as the sort who expected her guests to await *her* pleasure, not the reverse. That meant, now that she was there, the auction would begin at any moment.

Urgency hummed within his belly, quickening his steps. He needed to keep the vial from falling into the wrong hands—Blood

Clan, Horde, Caliphate, even the Qilaqui all would doubtless turn their newfound power against the Karmian Empire—just as he needed to identify the one selling it. *Both* tasks of equal importance that would grow exponentially difficult if he failed to reach the auction in time.

"You, Lady Dellacourt's man." A guard Kullen didn't recognize approached him. He must've recognized him from Natisse's company. "Come with me."

"Er, excuse me, but—" Kullen began, playing the role of nervous servant.

"No buts." The Shieldbandsman, a tall, dark-haired man displaying the swarthy skin of Hudarians mingled with the lean features of an Imperial, gripped him by the arm. "Not a request, either."

Kullen put up only token resistance before allowing the guard to whisk him away. To his dismay, he was dragged not out the front door but through a smaller side entrance used by the servants bearing trays of refreshment. The clatter of pots and pans, dishes, and sizzling grills told Kullen he was close to the kitchens, but his escort led him down another adjoining southbound passageway that ended at a plain-looking wooden door.

Within, a handful of men and women from all corners of Caernia sat or stood in tense silence. When the Pantagorissa said "common room," Kullen took that to mean the party room he'd just been in. But this… this complicated things.

Tables and chairs were arranged in small clusters, simple but not distasteful. Most of its inhabitants bore the look of servants and attendants, though the Hudarians had the broad shoulders, scarred visages, and callused hands of warriors. The Caliphate menservants dripped with gold-and-diamond jewelry, nearly as gaudy as their masters'. Only the Qilaqui were unrepresented in the room. Their culture disdained servanthood or slavery. Oh, and the pirates, since none of them would dare serve another of their kind.

"Wait here." The guard barked the same command, though this

time, it seemed final. Pushing Kullen into the room, he added, "There's food enough for the night, and the chairs aren't half-bad. Sleep if you want, or don't." His tone made it clear just how little he cared. "Don't give two shark teeth what you do. Just don't stir up trouble."

Odd that two different guards would use the same phrasing.

"You'll be summoned when your mistress is done."

"Forgive me," Kullen began, "but—"

The Shieldbandsman ignored him. "You step outside this room before you're called, and you'll enjoy a late-night swim. No one gives a steaming crab shite for what happens in here. But if someone turns up dead or broken, you'll have your mistress *and* the Pantagorissa to answer to."

Kullen had no doubt a swim would be the least of his worries in that situation.

"You need anything, find a way to live without it." The guard fixed him with a hard scowl.

"Including the... er... facilities?" Kullen asked, emphasizing the last word. "I'm ashamed to admit that I drank a bit more of your mistress's wine than anticipated, and—"

"Facilities are right there." The guard thrust a finger toward one dark corner of the small room. "You need privacy, you're outta luck. You fall in, you climb out, or swim as best you can. Best to keep your mouth closed if you can manage."

Kullen glanced in the direction indicated. There, a large crack had widened in the wooden planks that made up the flooring, and no one had bothered to repair or cover it up. Indeed, they'd used it quite cleverly.

"But—" He turned back to the guard, only to find the door slamming in his face with a loud *bang*.

Kullen spun toward his peers. Everyone looked utterly disinterested in his arrival, either carrying on conversations amongst one another or playing games of chance. They appeared as if this was commonplace, to be set apart from their *betters* while they were left to themselves for the evening. Even as Jarius's companion, Kullen had never been treated in such a way.

Then one spoke up, "Just settle in, boy. It's not so bad."

Kullen took a seat beside the man. He was well dressed but had the gaunt look of one who ate very little. Whether that was by choice or by station, Kullen couldn't say.

"First time attending the Pantagorissa's soiree?"

"I would hardly refer to this as attendance," Kullen quipped.

The man cackled. "Fonwin Guspas," he said, extending a hand.

"K—" Kullen caught himself nearly revealing his true name. He had to get his mind straight if he was to find success this evening. "Yarlton."

"Yes, well, this may not be the grand hall, but it's grander than most servant cells I've been stuck in."

"Cell?" Kullen asked.

"Ah, just a term of speech. Though, it does feel that way at times, doesn't it?" He looked around the room. "Especially for some of the others." His voice got quiet. "My master treats me nearly as well as his own family, but some of these… might as well be slaves. Some are, in fact."

Kullen took in the faces surrounding them. Upon this second glance, he noticed the dour expressions on nearly all but Fonwin.

"Lady Dellacourt treats me kindly as well."

"Lady Dellacourt?" Fonwin asked. "That's not a name I've heard. Pray tell, from whence does she hail?"

"Elliatrope."

"My word!" Fonwin asked. "Tell me, how is Lord Polcart?"

Kullen's heart leaped into his throat. He knew nothing of a Lord Polcart nor anything of Elliatrope. With no means of escaping this room, should he slip up—to a servant no less—both he and Natisse would find themselves in no better position than the dying men lining the walls of the Tower of Justice.

"Spare me a moment," Kullen said, grasping his stomach. "Nature calls. I'm sure you understand."

"Sounds like someone drank the water here without diluting it with a drop or two of Cultiquin." Fonwin laughed.

Kullen had no idea what the man was talking about, but he stood and made his way toward the corner of the room. Despite his best efforts, he could think of no better way to escape than the avenue the guard had unwittingly suggested. Grimacing, Kullen strode toward the fissure. It didn't smell too bad and appeared free of stains. Not the ideal means of escape, but he'd make do with what he could.

But not just yet.

"Ladies and gentlemen," he said, gaining everyone's attention. "No man deserves to be enslaved. Please, enjoy a parting gift from Lady Dellacourt of Elliatrope." He tossed down the gold-filled valise. It spilled open onto the floor, and immediately, the entire scrum of servants became one writhing pile atop it. Kullen had no real use for it now. The Emperor would just have to accept the loss as the cost of doing business on Pantagoya.

With a flourish, he stepped back and dropped through the opening. Light and sound became a distant memory as he plummeted. Barely a sliver of light poked through the singular opening above, and the clatter of servants disappeared. He could sense the churning waters below, knew it was filled with onyx sharks and worse, but he had no intention of joining them nor becoming their snack. Even as his feet left solid wood, he reached for his dragonblood vial and jammed his finger down onto the golden cap.

The needle pricked into his skin, drawing a minuscule drop of his own blood and mixing with that of Umbris. Time came to a grinding halt. Kullen was falling no more. The familiar sensation of being carried upon the wind greeted him, and an instant later, he was shrouded in shadow.

He could feel the drawing of the Shadow Realm, but having rested, he had no worries of being sucked in. A chill washed over his incorporeal form, and a burst of light cut through. He had reached the far end of the island, and the moon shone down upon the glittering sea.

The wooden underbelly of Pantagoya dripped with sea spray. Hundreds of ships lined the docks below. And yes, Kullen could see not just the great fins of hundreds of onyx sharks but also the slapping of tentacular appendages, the clawing of gold talons, the spray of geyser beasts. It seemed no oceanic threat was left unaccounted for in these waters.

This time, instead of focusing on the shadows—for they were plenty and not difficult to find— he reached out his senses for any source of light visible in the all-consuming darkness. In the far distance, a glimmer of light peered through, just big enough to be seen with his vision—a mere pinprick, but it would be enough.

With an effort of will, Kullen jettisoned himself toward the light source. Whereas most of the planking throughout the dome's foundation was tightly pressed like a ship, this one was just wide enough for Kullen to squeeze through. Soaring up through it, his form found shadow, and he was back inside.

He was solid again, a member of the Mortal Realm. A chill passed through him—a familiar feeling, though never an enjoyable one.

Timbers of a long-dead ship splayed out before him, and when he turned, he realized his mistake.

He'd emerged into a well-lit courtyard filled with the Pantagorissa's Elite Shieldbandsmen.

41
NATISSE

The eye within the cauldron blazed with radiant blue-white power, reminding Natisse of the midday summer sun glimpsed from beneath the water's surface.

The room was frenzied, everyone recoiling with cries of alarm —all save the Pantagorissa. Even Natisse herself had to fight against the instinct to retreat a step. She knew not what manner of creature the eye belonged to, but she could sense its might radiating from the cauldron.

The power thrumming within the room snapped the next moment, so abruptly and with such a violent backlash of force that a wind buffeted Natisse. The eye within the cauldron vanished, and the waters stilled. Yet, to all within the room, there was no doubt what they had just witnessed.

They had stared into the eyes of the goddess Abyssalia herself.

Though Natisse didn't believe Golgoth could use her eyes like windows, a sense of foreboding filled her belly. There was a fear, a trepidation, something powerful Natisse knew did not belong to her.

Such a thing *should* have been impossible, Natisse knew. Only the highest-ranking members of the priesthood could commune with the deities they served, and to her knowledge, the gods had never spoken—or stared back—themselves. They communicated in signs and omens, portents and auspices, which their priests interpreted to the people. Natisse had never doubted the gods existed but had certainly never seen such tangible proof of that fact.

Until now. Not the gods of her people, but the forgotten goddess of the long-dead Vandil.

Her mind boggled. She wasn't alone; all in the fiery chamber atop the Dread Spire sat stunned and wide-eyed. All save the Pantagorissa herself and the five priestesses still chanting and circling the cauldron. The bright amber light shining from the cauldron and its brazen frame had begun to dim, the power trickling from the room. Yet the memory of what they had witnessed was powerful enough to plunge the tower-top chamber into silence.

Pantagorissa Torrine raised her hands in a grandiose gesture. "You have felt the gaze of Abyssalia for yourself, the power she wields." She wasted no time on flowery speech; the demonstration had been more than sufficient. "Tell me, revered guests, how much is it worth to you to *command* that power for yourself?"

Shock rippled through the crowd. Even as her words fell silent, one of the fur-clad Qilaqui leaped to his feet and shouted something in his own tongue. An iron-haired woman in Hudarian horse hides barked in her language but was nearly drowned out by a call from a gold-bedecked man in the opulent silks of the faraway Caliphate of Fire.

"One million golden *talakh!*" he roared.

"A thousand chests of scrimshaw!" shouted a man in the pirate leathers. "Nay! A thousand thousand!"

"Two hundred of our finest horses!" The raven-haired *Tabudai* added her voice to the mix. "The Empire will kneel before the Horde at any cost, and—"

Her voice was drowned out as the other guests deteriorated into a frenzy of bidding. Each and every one in the auction was desperate to seize the power Pantagorissa Torrine had placed on offer—even if they had no idea *how* they would control it. Was the Pantagorissa selling the five priestesses? The cauldron? The tower itself? Natisse had no idea, and she felt more than a little lost. She'd gone from freeing slaves mere days ago to witnessing what could very well be the first step toward total upheaval of Caernia itself. Whoever walked away from this auction with the power of Abyssalia—a bloody *goddess!*—would gain control of a force mightier perhaps than all the dragons in the Karmian Empire or the combined armies of every fractious religious state in the Caliphate of Fire combined!

For all her uncertainty, Natisse felt compelled to do something. She couldn't let *anyone* wield a goddess as a weapon against their enemies. The Blood Clan pirates and Hudar Horde were the Empire's oldest rivals, at war since Emperor Lasavic first began building the Karmian Empire upon the foundation of a dozen battle-plagued minor kingdoms. The Caliphate of Fire, which occupied the continent of Othman on the far side of Caernia, hadn't gone to war with the Empire since the advent of dragonblood magic, but not one of the eight men and women who declared themselves "Grand Caliph" would hesitate to turn their eyes northward once they subjugated their rival states. Even the ice-bound Qilaqui might decide they would rather live in the temperate climes of the Empire rather than endure the brutality of the Nuktavuk Tundra on the far side of the Temistara Ocean.

Nor could she let it remain in the hands of the Pantagorissa. Even if the woman had no designs on conquest, Natisse had no desire to imagine the consequences of Torrine unleashing her cruelty on a challenger to her power, enemy, or servant in a moment of pique. With a simple blade, she had taken Ronolfo's head without a second thought; would she show any more restraint with the power of a goddess at her command?

Whoever wielded the goddess's power, the poor and powerless would suffer. No place in Caernia was without their own Embers. Regardless of how it had come to be, each land shoved their destitute and broken into their little corners where the rich and powerful would need not lay eyes upon them. They were always the first to die in any war for conquest or domination. Whole nations could very well find themselves enslaved by a new goddess-harnessing madman.

But Natisse could see no way to stop it from happening. She had no target at which to point her blade, knew of no item she could pilfer that would sway the building threat. The only possibility she could imagine was to kill Pantagoya's ruler *and* the Vandil priestesses. On that account, her odds were terribly slim. She could strike down the Pantagorissa, but the Elite Shieldbandsmen guarding her throne would react before she could eliminate the five women around the cauldron at the heart of the chamber. And even that might not suffice. Ezrasil alone knew who else on Pantagoya shared in the knowledge of what she had just witnessed.

For the first time in days, she wished Uncle Ronan was with her. She needed him—not just Uncle Ronan, but General bloody Andros. He'd know what to do, how to complete *all* the objectives before her. Or, at the very least, how to prioritize her next actions.

But he wasn't here. Nor were Baruch, Ammon, Jad, Garron, or *any* of the Crimson Fang. Not even Kullen, though she desperately hoped he wasn't far off. She'd have to take matters into her own hands and pray to all the gods that she survived what came next.

Surreptitiously, Natisse ran a hand down her side and reached into the false pocket on the front of her dress. Within, she felt the hilt of her lashblade pressed up against the whalebone corset savaging her ribs. The steel segments hung loose around her waist, hidden by the darker blue sash encircling her gown. The weapon would not be drawn easily, but she wanted it close at hand for when the moment arrived. She'd need to pull it free in a hurry—and if she shredded the beautiful garment in the process, so be it.

Running her fingers down the lashblade's hilt, she felt for the flat throwing knives Kullen had helped to tuck in concealed sheaths along the belly of her corset. The blades were short—

barely the length of her middle finger—but they would serve her purposes just fine. One quick thrust to drive the steel through the gaps in the Pantagorissa's bleached-bone frill and into the base of her skull, and Pantagoya would be in need of a new ruler. With Cliessa's luck, she could hurl it and the two remaining throwing blades to end the Vandil priestesses—deaths she would regret immensely, necessity or not—and draw her lashblade in time to fight her way past the Elite Shieldbandsmen to flee down the stairs. Not the best plan, certainly, but far preferable to any currently presented alternative.

Natisse sucked in a deep breath and slowly slipped the blade from its sheath. She had no fear of anyone hearing or seeing her—all eyes were locked on the Pantagorissa and the priestesses circling the cauldron, and the cacophony of the bidding could have drowned out the bootsteps of the entire Imperial army.

She slipped the blade free, but before she could strike, the Pantagorissa raised her hands.

"Wait, wait!" she called out.

Natisse couldn't see the woman's face but heard the mocking edge to her voice. All in the room fell immediately silent—save for the Qilaqui, who shouted one final bid—and still. Natisse froze, too. She couldn't strike… yet.

"On second thought," Pantagorissa Torrine said in a flippant tone, "perhaps we should put this on hold until later, hmm?" She brought her hand up to tap at her chin in a gesture of fake contemplation. "After all, you came here to bid on *another* item of value."

Scattered protests and a fair number of groans rose from the crowd, but the Pantagorissa paid them no heed.

"Come, Magister Morvannou," she said, gesturing to the crowd. "Let us see what you have to offer."

A man at the rear of the crowd stood from his seat, a decidedly uncomfortable look on his face. He was a sharp-featured man—all angles at the elbows, knobby knees, chin, nose, and cheekbones—with no more spare fat on his frame than spare hairs on the top of his nearly bald head. His spine curved like a bow when he walked, and Natisse had little doubt that below his fine gilded robes, the bones of his back would nearly pierce his skin.

"Er… thank you, esteemed Pantagorissa," he said, uncertainty in his thin, reedy voice. "Although, I would hesitate to—"

"Nonsense!" Pantagorissa Torrine snapped her fingers and pointed to the ground, a gesture reminiscent of a master commanding a trained hound. "Always save the best for last, they say."

"Certainly." Magister Morvannou barely managed to keep the disdain from his tone. His face, however, puckered as if he'd just eaten the sourest of green Brendoni grapes. He slid gracelessly through the rows of seats, jostling his neighbors, and hurried—if his painfully sluggish gait could be described as such—up the aisle in a flurry of bony limbs and flapping coats. The man looked as if he could keel over dead at any instant.

"I'll admit I, too, have some interest in the contents of your item," the Pantagorissa said, her words stopping just short of condescending. She lifted her gaze to regard the rest of her guests. "Bear that in mind as you place your bids now, for this may very well sweeten whatever you have to offer when we get down to the *real* auction."

Murmurs ran through the crowd, and the expressions of every man and woman present grew calculating.

Pantagorissa Torrine backed to her throne and took a seat.

"Atina," she said, motioning to Natisse with barely a glance over her shoulder. "Come, stand by my side and enjoy the show."

Natisse complied, moving around to take up position next to the Pantagorissa's throne.

The Pantagorissa snorted. "Come, come, little bluebird! That is much too far away!" She reached out one solidly-muscled arm to wrap around Natisse's waist and pulled her over the arm of her throne onto her lap. Natisse barely managed to keep from sprawling, giving a little moue of displeasure. Which only made

Pantagorissa Torrine laugh. "You didn't think I actually meant *beside* me, did you?"

Natisse smoothed down her dress and her expression, taking extra care her weapons remained hidden. Being manhandled was no better just because it was a woman doing the handling.

"You'll have to be more explicit with your instructions later tonight," she said, trying to play off her annoyance.

"You have my word that I will." The Pantagorissa placed a firm kiss on Natisse's neck, then sat back. "But first, let's have some fun, shall we, my pretty?"

All of this was said at full volume, much to Magister Morvannou's visible chagrin and annoyance. The Imperial aristocrat was clearly displeased at being upstaged by the Pantagorissa—first her offering of immense value, then her finding more interest in "her pretty" than his dignity and importance.

Yet he said nothing to the woman on the throne but instead turned to face the crowd of auction guests.

"Tonight, ladies and gentlemen, I have an item of exceedingly rare and immense value." His thin voice and unimpressive personage couldn't come close to the Pantagorissa's flamboyancy. He spoke as slowly as he moved. Indeed, he seemed like an invalid by comparison. A shaky hand reached into his coat and lifted out an object that he held over his head for all in the chamber to see. "A vial of dragonblood. But no ordinary vial, this! No, the blood within is imbued with potent and ancient magic that gives its owner the power to bond with and command the might of a great serpent. And not just any, but the mighty Andrun'dar, fiercest of the Mist Dragons himself!"

His attempt to pause for dramatic effect merely highlighted the quietness within the chamber, which accentuated the reediness of his voice. A polite cough and the clearing of a throat were all that cut through dull silence.

Magister Morvannou seemed put off by the crowd's detachment. He continued with diffidence in his tone. "Th-This vial confers to you the power to bond with and command the might of a dragon!" In his nervousness, it took him a long moment to realize he'd repeated himself. Sweat pricked on his brow, and he drew out a handkerchief to mop the perspiration from his forehead. "Andrun'dar was once commanded by Edran Shieldbreaker himself, and most recently, Magister Wa—"

But Natisse never learned the name of the dragon's former owner, for the Magister's words were cut short by the harsh ringing of alarm bells.

Kullen.

42

KULLEN

Time slowed to a crawl as Kullen took in the sight of the twelve Shieldbandsmen standing not five paces from him. Only two had their backs to him; the rest stared straight at him, and their conversations died instantly as they spotted him.

The light of the flickering torches filling the courtyard made it impossible to tap into Umbris's magical abilities. With no avenue of retreat and nowhere to flee, he had just one choice: attack.

"Bloody pits," Kullen said under his breath before reaching for his daggers.

He leaped toward the nearest Shieldbandsman, crying out "For the High Caliph!" though he looked nothing like the men who'd stood in the Pantagorissa's hall. He wore a black jacket cut in the Imperial style, and he was clearly lacking the glittering nose rings and copper-toned skin that marked the people of the Caliphate of Fire, but he banked on the misdirection to throw the guards into confusion. Confusion that he could exploit to fight free of the Shieldbandsmen and eventually, Pantagoya. He couldn't let Natisse get caught up in the violence from which he could no longer escape, so deflecting the blame elsewhere was his best recourse.

He drove the knife edge of his hand into the guard's neck, just beneath the flange of his square-topped half helm. The impact would never snap the spine, he knew, but he merely needed to render the guard inert long enough to snatch the cutlass from his sheath.

Even as he drew the curved blade free, the Shieldbandsman sagged on limp knees and fell forward onto his face in a clatter of steel armor striking stone. The guard directly in front of the downed man had no time to react before Kullen swung the cutlass at his face. The blow struck high to ring off the front of his helm, and the Shieldbandsman went down like a felled ox.

"For the High Caliph!" Kullen roared again and threw himself at the next batch of guards. They were the foremost of those standing between him and the nearest of the two passages leading out of the courtyard and into darker regions where Kullen could disappear. Behind them, only two Shieldbandsmen barred his escape—one stunned into motionlessness, his cutlass still in its scabbard, and the other leaping to his feet and bowling over the wooden camp stool where he'd perched his bulk.

The Shieldbandsmen directly in front of Kullen managed to clear their cutlasses from their sheaths and deflected his attack with practiced finesse. These, at least, had clearly spent ample time in the training field—not all of the Pantagorissa's guards were brutes and thugs, it seemed. Their ripostes nearly tore a hole in Kullen's throat, chest, and belly. Only his magically-enhanced speed and the training of a lifetime saved him from being cut to ribbons.

Still, it proved a damned close thing for three agonizingly long heartbeats. The world around him didn't hasten into crystalline focus—on the contrary, it seemed to speed up to a blistering, frantic pace. Steel whirred toward him from all sides, the light assailing his eyes, and momentary fear gnawed at his belly.

It took all of his skill and swiftness to stay out of the reach of the swinging cutlasses. He cut one guard deep in the leg, just above the knee, darted toward the second, a feint, then vaulted over an upturned chum bucket in the opposite direction. The third guard, caught by surprise, had a chance neither to bring up his sword nor dodge as Kullen barreled straight into him. The two went down in a tangle of limbs, but Kullen had anticipated the fall and half flipped, half somersaulted to come to his feet beyond the downed Shieldbandsman.

He stood—albeit shaken—calculating his next move.

"Kill the bastard!" came a cry from behind Kullen. He didn't glance back to see which of the guards had recovered their wits enough to shout out; he was too busy bull-rushing the two standing between him and escape.

One partially drew his cutlass but, upon seeing Kullen, abandoned his efforts and swung a vicious punch at Kullen's head. The mailed fist flew wide, the blow wild and uncontrolled. Kullen's own left hand drove a straight jab into the guard's throat. In the same motion, his right hand swept the cutlass up to slap the flat of the blade against the second Shieldbandsman's helmet. The *clang* rang out like the toll of an alarm bell, and the two men slumped in unison.

Kullen sprinted past the falling men, his eyes locked on the empty passage leading away from the courtyard. He braced himself in expectation of a rear attack. Should any of the other guards be carrying crossbows, he could very well find himself standing before Ezrasil at any moment. In a split-second decision, he raced away from the courtyard as fast as his legs could carry him.

He planted his feet firmly but with care, considering each plank bowed under his heavy steps. He took no note of his surroundings but for the darkness at the end of the path and ran toward it with all haste. He had no need to get away from the Palace or off Pantagoya itself—yet. He merely had to find someplace where the shadows were deep enough to conceal him fully. There, he could draw on Umbris's power and vanish into the night.

He turned the corner, hoping to find darkness, but it proved far more impossible than he'd anticipated. Everywhere he looked, torches and lanterns shone bright enough to turn the night nearly as bright as noonday.

The shouts of the Shieldbandsmen echoed behind him. A chorus of "Find him!" and "Bring that bloody bastard to heel!" filled the air, calling out reinforcements from every which way. Kullen knew he was running out of time—if the noise reached any of the guards ahead of him, his path forward could be blocked.

He slid around a corner, nearly running headlong into a cluster of four breastplate-wearing, cutlass-wielding guards. They were too surprised by his charge to raise their weapons, but their thick, brutish bodies offered Kullen an obstacle he couldn't merely bull his way through.

"Where ye goin', ye right bastard?" one guard growled, dropping his torch and drawing his cutlass.

Kullen kept running. When he was a man's length from the Shieldbandsman, he shoved off the ground with his left foot, planted his right on the wall beside him, and came down hard with a closed fist that pistoned into the soft flesh of the man's neck.

He rolled forward, coming up just behind the other three startled guards. Instead of stopping to wage war, Kullen dug deep and sprinted.

He glanced behind him to find at least two of the Shieldbandsmen were in pursuit.

These men weren't as slow as he'd hoped. Hands reached for him, clutching at his jacket, his sleeves, his arms, but he slipped free and raced forward without slowing. However, the warning shouts of "Get him!" were now close on his heel as new guards joined in the chase.

Ulnu, take it! Kullen's heart raced, and anxiety clutched his stomach tight. If he couldn't escape, he was done for. There was simply no way he could take on *all* of the Pantagorissa's guards, not to mention every armed man who'd accompanied the Blood

Clan, Hudarians, Qilaqui, and Caliphate auction guests. He'd be cornered and butchered before long—or, worse, thrown into the dark waters beneath the floating island, where the deep sea predators would feast on him long before Umbris could whisk him away to safety.

As he ran, he put space between him and his pursuers by merit of his speed alone. Onlookers from taverns, brothels, and exarai leaf shops watched as he passed. However, the bored expressions told him this type of thing was commonplace around these parts.

Finally, he reached the end of the row of shops and cut a hard left. More establishments filled to the brim with drunkards and revelers greeted him, but with the lead he had on the Shieldbandsmen, they'd be none the wiser if he darted down one of the many alleys and into shadow.

Kullen dove into the first one he passed. He jammed his thumb onto the golden cap of his dragonblood vial. Power flooded into him like lightning. In an instant, he was one with the night, hidden from any mortal eyes. Fog rolled around him, always there but never seen. He waited, watching as his tail blew past him, calling out in confusion. One stopped and peered into the alley, but he would never find what he was looking for.

Grays and blacks danced amongst the harsh white that was the light beyond the alley, but Kullen stayed still. He heard the whispering voices, the creatures, the lost souls trapped within the Shadow Realm growing ever closer. They were desperate to claim him to their kingdom. He knew if he tarried too long, they would find him. He'd shadow-slid several times in the past few minutes, and they sensed his weakness. He also had the inkling that because of what happened at the shipyard, they now knew his scent, wanted him all the more.

If shadow had taken root in his soul, it would call the creatures of the void to him like a beacon. But he had no time to dwell on the matter. Escape first, mission and retrieving Natisse second. He could worry about the Shadow Realm later.

Once all signs of the Shieldbandsmen were passed, Kullen turned toward the Pantagorissa's Palace. From here—from anywhere, really—he could see the Dread Spire. The moon shone down upon it, glinting off its wet dome. He spotted a patch of clouds covering one quadrant of the rooftop. With a quick slide, he leaped toward it, letting the air carry him formlessly to his desired location.

The whispers grew louder. He could almost feel the claws rending his flesh, and a hot wave of anxiety passed over him.

With a thought, he noiselessly materialized, crouching in place on the north end of the Palace dome. His boots skidded on the sharply slanted roof, but he found the seams, dug in his toes and fingers until he finally found purchase. Only then did he let out the breath he'd been holding.

Far, far below, the shouts and cries of the Shieldbandsmen rang out. They couldn't possibly realize their prey had *escaped*—perhaps they'd merely assumed he'd slipped between one of the many cracks in the deck and fallen into the dark, icy waters of the Astralkane Sea.

To them, his end would've been the same as capture. Either way, Kullen had no desire to wait around to find out.

On his way up to the roof, he'd gotten a good look at the top of the Dread Spire. There were no windows in the sides of the tower-top, nothing at all to allow him entrance into the cylindrical chamber. He couldn't accept the fact that the room was fully enclosed. Otherwise, what was the point of building a chamber at the top of a tower? Still, from what he'd seen, there was only one possible way in: from above.

He clambered up the steep slope as quietly as he could manage —no sense alerting those beneath him to his presence—and breathed a sigh of relief as he reached the roof's zenith. There, the sharp-topped peak had been cut away and replaced with a circular skylight.

Cautiously, Kullen peered through the aperture. Below him, Pantagorissa Torrine stood with her hands upraised, speaking to a crowd of seated guests—all those Kullen had seen in the Palace's grand feasting hall earlier. Natisse stood many paces behind the grand throne, her expression fixed, and one hand tucked into the pocket of her dress where Kullen had helped her conceal her weaponry.

That spoke volumes. Natisse had proven herself clever enough to *only* draw her weapons if absolutely necessary.

The entire room was aflame, yet no one stirred as if alarmed. It struck Kullen as strange but didn't let his mind linger on it too long.

Kullen eyed the glass that served as the only barrier between him and his goal. It appeared solid, nearly as thick as his thumb and anchored well in the bronze frame. It would not be easily broken. Had he the proper diamond-tipped blades and no fear of being overheard by those below, he could have cut his way through—albeit with a great deal of patience. But he felt all but certain time wasn't on his side. If the Shieldbandsmen spread the alarm across Pantagoya, the auction would be over before the dragonblood vial ever appeared.

A moment later, however, Pantagorissa Torrine beckoned to the crowd, and a nervous-looking man in Imperial clothing stood. Kullen's eyebrows nearly touched his hairline.

Magister Morvannou?

He knew of the man… barely. Morvannou was a minor aristocrat, affluent enough to afford a residence in Dimvein but far from the wealth and power of Magisters like Branthe, Deckard, Taradan, or Iltari. Indeed, it was doubtful he even knew any of those men whose dragonblood vials had gone missing.

So how in Binteth's taloned claws did he get his hands on a vial? Ezrasil knows he's not powerful enough to have one of his own. Indeed, if he had, he'd have attempted to use it himself.

The man's presence could only mean someone *else* was behind the theft of the dragonblood vials. Perhaps the same "Red Claw" who had directed the actions of Magister Branthe's conspirators, the soldiers who'd attacked Magister Issemar, and the high-ranking Orken who'd been in league with the traitors.

He watched Magister Morvannou shuffle his way to the front of the room and take up position in front of the Pantagorissa. A moment later, Natisse moved to stand beside the throne, only to be roughly dragged onto the Pantagorissa's lap.

A fury Kullen wasn't proud of made its way into his heart. He ground his teeth but held himself in check. Just a little longer, until he knew for certain…

There!

Magister Morvannou withdrew from his pocket an object Kullen would recognize anywhere: a gold-capped glass vial filled with blood-red liquid.

He had confirmed his target.

Not a moment too soon. Even as his eyes lit on the vial, a thousand ship-bells tolled out across Pantagoya.

Kullen cursed.

The Shieldbandsmen had raised the alarm.

So much for the stealth option, he thought grimly.

He had *seconds* before the auction below ended, and both Magister Morvannou and Natisse vanished—the former into whatever nook and cranny he could find to cower in, the latter hauled way by the Pantagorissa to the safety of her fortified tower.

Umbris, I have need of you, Kullen thought.

Before the words had fully formed in his mind, the great Twilight Dragon stepped out of shadows that were not formerly there and onto the rounded rooftop. His legs slid ever so slightly before he caught himself and proudly stood beside Kullen.

"Hello, Friend Kullen."

"Umbris, would you be a pal and break this glass for me?"

Something like a smile appeared on the dragon's face.

"With pleasure."

Umbris's massive tail whipped upward and, with the sound of a rushing torrent, crashed down, shattering the skylight into a billion small shards that rained down upon the Pantagorissa's affair.

My gratitude, Kullen said in the same thought that sent Umbris back to the Shadow Realm. Kullen glanced down just long enough to see Natisse's eyes on him before he leaped into the newly formed hole and directly into the center of the party.

43
Natisse

The ringing of the alarm bell brought everyone in the tower-top chamber to their feet—including Pantagorissa Torrine. Natisse had just time enough to leap off the woman's lap to avoid being shoved off.

The sharp ring of the Pantagorissa's cutlass being ripped from its sheath cut through it all. It was as if every little move the woman made stopped time itself.

"Ullred, Lloyden," the Pantagorissa snapped, drawing her cutlasses, "go and find out what the bloody—"

In that moment, a resounding *crash* echoed through the chamber, and a hailstorm of glass and wooden splinters peppered down from above. Natisse looked up just in time to see a dark figure drop directly onto Magister Morvannou. The elderly Imperial aristocrat crumpled to the floor in a limp heap, and the dragonblood vial flew from his hands to skitter beneath the seats of the assorted guests.

Such was the chaos that even with the torrent of jagged glass, few aside from Natisse noticed; all eyes were fixed toward the entrance as if expecting to see an army charge up the stairs to assault them. Only the Pantagorissa and the guards nearest her throne joined Natisse in watching the dark-coated man who had made such a violent entrance.

Natisse's heart leaped, relief flooding her as she recognized the familiar black jacket. He'd gotten a cutlass from somewhere—likely taken off one of Pantagoya's guards—but his back was to her and the Pantagorissa, his gaze fixed on Magister Morvannou's now-empty hand.

Which was how he failed to notice Pantagorissa Torrine drawing back her right-hand cutlass for a decapitating swing.

Natisse acted without thinking. Her hand dipped into her pocket, and she whipped the lashblade free from its hiding place, shredding her dress in the process. Yet she didn't care—all that mattered was keeping the Pantagorissa from landing that attack on Kullen's exposed neck.

The segmented blade darted forward like the tongue of a striking serpent to coil around the Pantagorissa's right wrist, hand, and the grip of her cutlass. Natisse hauled on her lashblade with every shred of strength she possessed. Though she could never hope to match the Pantagorissa's immense power, surprise aided her efforts. Her pull caught the woman off-balance and dragged her right arm backward before she realized the danger. Razor-sharp steel sliced deep furrows into her outstretched limb, tore the cutlass from her grip and brought the towering woman spinning halfway around.

A roar of pain and fury exploded from the Pantagorissa's lips. Her eyes darted about wildly, searching the room for whoever had attacked her. Only when Natisse brought the lashblade snapping back to her side did the movement draw the stalwart woman's gaze.

"You?" she roared, fury flushing her face. "You dare break my peace?" She whipped her right hand at Natisse, spraying droplets of the blood gushing from her arm. "You dare strike me?"

The Pantagorissa spun a full circle, swinging her left-hand cutlass around in a whirling arc of steel. The bared muscles on her arms bunched like corded ropes, and Natisse knew that parrying the powerful blow would shatter her bones or blade—or fail to stop the attack completely before it separated her head from her shoulders.

Instead, Natisse dropped into a low crouch, and the cutlass whistled above her head, blade missing by a finger's breadth. Natisse's dress tore further, and the corset sent agony shooting through her imprisoned ribs, but she had no time for pain. She lunged upward and thrust the lashblade forward—right toward the Pantagorissa's throat. She hadn't intended to kill the woman, but in the heat of battle, her body acted on instinct.

With impossible speed, Pantagorissa Torrine twisted her head aside from the path of Natisse's strike. Instead of tearing cartilage and blood vessels, the keen edge of the lashblade laid open the left side of her face—jaw, cheekbone, temple, and scalp. The Pantagorissa unleashed another furious roar and chopped down at Natisse. Natisse had no choice but to throw herself to the side, deftly avoiding the descending cutlass. She felt a tug on her leg as the blade parted the torn strips of her flimsy under-gown, barely missing flesh.

But her frantic leap carried her away from the Pantagorissa's throne and into the swirling chaos that now gripped the towertop chamber. Many of the guests had turned to flee, others to fight, and still, others stood paralyzed by confusion and fear. The stampede of bodies fighting to escape the chamber swamped the Pantagorissa's guards and kept them hemmed in against the walls of the circular room. That wouldn't last long, Natisse knew. But with no other way out—

A hand seized her arm and spun her roughly around. Natisse slashed the lashblade up and across diagonally in a motion meant to disembowel the Pantagorissa or whatever guard had laid hands on her. But the blow crashed into the curved edge of a cutlass.

Only then did Natisse recognize the face before her.

"The vial!" Kullen roared. "You can't let her get away with it!"

The words barely registered through the rush of blood filling Natisse's ears.

Kullen had no chance to explain. His eyes widened a fraction as he saw something over Natisse's shoulder, and he darted past her, raising his blade as he went. The *clang* of steel dangerously close to her left ear jarred Natisse's nerves.

But Natisse couldn't spare the second to glance behind and see how close she'd come to death. Five guards had formed a defensive circle of steel around Pantagorissa Torrine, and three more rushed toward her and Kullen from both sides.

Natisse stepped to her right and sent her lashblade whipping around in a horizontal arc. The steel segments extended to their full length, glinting in the moonlight streaming through the shattered roof, and the tip swept across the throat of the nearest guard. Blood fountained from the torn flesh, and the man's half-formed shout cut off in a wet gurgle.

The second guard was fortunate enough to be just out of the lashblade's reach, but the third guard coming from Natisse's left took the full impact on the side of his head. Steel struck sparks on his helmet, then dragged across his chest. He went down in a bloody, tangled heap of limbs, sprawling unconscious atop Magister Morvannou's prone form.

"I'll kill you!" Pantagorissa Torrine raged from amidst the circle of her guards. "I'll tear you limb from limb, break every bone in your pretty body, and—"

Natisse didn't hear the rest. She was too busy fighting for her life as the surviving guard hurled himself at her, joined a moment later by a fourth cutlass-wielding enemy. All of Natisse's skill went into weaving a blurring wall of steel around herself to keep the blades from striking true.

"On your left!" came a shout from behind Natisse. Instinctively, she retracted the lashblade into sword form and brought it swinging around to attack the guard on her right. In the same moment, a dark shape hurtled past her to bury a cutlass into the eye of the guard attacking from her left.

The guard howled as he died, but Kullen was already on the

move, pulling his brain-covered blade free to charge the knot of guards encircling the Pantagorissa.

"The Hudarian!" he shouted over his shoulder. "A woman. Scar on her left cheek. She has the vial!"

Only then did the meaning behind his words register in Natisse's mind. He'd come here to retrieve the dragonblood vial on the Emperor's command, and *that* was his sole focus. He had no idea of the threat the Empire faced from the goddess Pantagorissa Torrine had intended to auction off.

Indecision tore at Natisse. She couldn't just leave Kullen to fight the Pantagorissa and her guards single-handed, but if the Hudarian with the vial escaped, the Horde would gain a weapon of terrible power to wield against the Empire. That was, indeed, a threat she couldn't ignore. She could tell Kullen about Abyssalia and the Vandil priestesses once they survived this chaos.

And so, despite the instincts that screamed of her abandoning Kullen, she turned and raced toward the stairs with expert precision.

The mission above all. Ammon's words echoed in her mind. Kullen could take care of himself.

Natisse dashed between the two guards, who were still half-dazed after being caught in the stampede, and charged down the staircase. She met a blockade of fleeing men and women who'd never likely raised a blade in their lives but to cut their finely prepared meals. The raucous cries were deafening and disorienting, but she clawed her way through the throng, desperately searching for the four Hudarians that had been sitting in the tower-top chamber mere moments earlier.

The magically burning stairs made it all but impossible to see where she was going. She used the wall as a brace point and cared little for who she sent tumbling. She vaulted over the fallen, taking the steps several at a time before reaching the platform below.

Breath suddenly filled her lungs as the press of cowards thinned. A few of the fastest-moving guests raced down the corridor ahead of her—including, Natisse saw, the Blood Clan pirates and the four Hudarians.

Natisse followed them down the hall, shoving aside any strays who got in her way. Screams of protests and curses followed her, but her intent was singular: stop the Hudarian and recover the vial.

They made a turn just beyond the Tower of Justice. By Natisse's recollection, that would put them within the worship hall.

Behind her, the Pantagorissa's guards had been caught flat-footed, and now they, too, were being swept away and pushed back beneath the tide. Natisse wasn't sure if that was a good sign. She was outnumbered, and though she'd just attacked their mistress, they would be hard-pressed to put her indiscretions above the theft of such a valuable item.

Above it all, the alarm bells clanged out the warning. What they signaled, Natisse had no idea, but she turned into the Temple Chamber and immediately spotted her quarry. A cluster of eight Blood Clan pirates, now armed with cutlasses taken from the dead, came bursting through the door at the far end of the worship hall, and in their midst, behind their guard, the four Hudarians.

Including the raven-haired woman with the scar on her left cheek. She stood, panting and scowling, clutching the dragonblood vial to her chest as if it were her own child.

44
KULLEN

Kullen breathed an inward sigh of relief as Natisse turned and ran from the tower-top chamber. He had to trust she'd retrieve the dragonblood vial from the Horde woman. He couldn't leave until he and Magister Morvannou had shared words—likely at the edge of his favorite dagger.

Which meant the task of covering her flight and keeping the Pantagorissa's guards fully occupied fell to him.

His stolen cutlass knocked aside a slashing cut from a Shieldbandsman's blade, and he drove a punch straight into the man's face. Cartilage *crunched* beneath his knuckles, and the guard's nose splashed a bloody mess against his cheeks. Even as the man staggered backward, Kullen drove his boot up between the fork of his legs. Air rushed from the Shieldbandsman's lungs in a pitiful half groan, half gasp, and he went down mewling like a newborn babe.

"You bastard!" Pantagorissa Torrine's deep voice thundered off the chamber's circular walls. "You'll pay dearly for breaking my peace. You and your *mistress* both!"

Kullen rounded on the woman, who stood amidst the only guards remaining in the rapidly emptying room. Blood streamed down the side of her face and poured from her arm, bone exposed as she clutched it to her chest. Yet fire blazed in her eyes, and she strained against the grasp of her Elite Shieldbandsmen, clearly intending to attack him with the naked cutlass carried in her left hand.

"Mistress?" Kullen snorted a derisive laugh. "I would rather open my throat than serve that simpering whore who calls herself a *lady.*" He allowed his voice to slowly change, layering on the thick, unmistakable accent of the Caliphate. "She is merely a tool, as are you. Pawns in the High Caliph's game. Now, I claim this power in the name of Abdul Haamid el-Tahir, Eternal Flame of Sadek, Champion of the Truth Faith, and rightful ruler of all Caernia!"

Pantagorissa Torrine's eyes narrowed at the name and its accompanying myriad of honorifics. No one other than a true believer would speak thus of the High Caliph of Sadek, the smallest and poorest of the religious states comprising the Caliphate of Fire. Nor would the Sadekhar hesitate to resort to such treachery to obtain the dragonblood vial—their *hasasyin* were renowned throughout Caernia. The fact that Kullen was clearly *not* from the Caliphate only gave her a moment's pause.

"The High Caliph has erred gravely today," the Pantagorissa snarled. "He has made an eternal enemy of Pantagoya. An enemy that no more forgives than forgets."

Kullen bared his teeth in a zealot's smile and hefted his cutlass. "You will carry the memory of the Caliph's enmity into the blazing fires of eternity, where the *djinni* will feast on your screams and torments."

He loosed an ululating cry and charged the small cluster of guards around the Pantagorissa. Only six stood between him and the wounded woman—had he truly intended her death, he could have taken her down with a throwing knife from across the circular chamber. But this was all a show, a farce put on for the Pantagorissa's benefit. Anything to deflect suspicion from Natisse —and, by extension, the Karmian Empire, as per Emperor Wymarc's command.

And so, like a wild shrieking spirit of the deserts, he hurled himself at the Elite Shieldbandsmen, cutlass swinging and shouting, "For the High Caliph!"

He struck with reckless abandon—or so he made it look to the guards surrounding the Pantagorissa. His blade bounced off breastplates, batted aside his enemy's weapons, and thundered against helmets. He didn't hesitate to draw blood, but his strikes always stopped short of fatal. He had no need to kill the Pantagorissa or her Shieldbandsmen, merely—

"We must go, my lady!" shouted one of the guards, dragging Pantagorissa Torrine backward.

"No!" The Pantagorissa's furious roar echoed above the deafening clamor of Kullen's blade battering at the Shieldbandsmen's armor. "He cannot be allowed to—"

"Captain, *now!*" The first guard seized the Pantagorissa by the left arm, and another of his companions lifted her bodily from the floor. The two of them carried the struggling, shouting woman away from Kullen, circling around the strange-looking bronze cauldron in the heart of the chamber.

The rest of the Shieldbandsmen, seeming to understand what their comrades were doing, increased the ferocity of their attacks, pressing Kullen hard. Kullen added his own enraged shouts to the tumult, howling the few Sadekhar words he'd picked up over his many years as Black Talon but allowed himself to be forced backward. He gave ground without seeming to, letting the Shieldbandsmen barrel him out of the Pantagorissa's path of escape. As he retreated, he purposely aimed his steps toward Magister Morvannou. The Imperial aristocrat had awakened and now struggled to rise. Kullen *accidentally* heel-kicked him in the face, sending the Magister sprawling again.

"Go!" came the shout from the Pantagorissa's guard. Kullen caught one last glimpse of the pair hustling down the stairs, their monarch hoisted onto their shoulders, and Pantagorissa's frenzied, bloodthirsty scream echoed through the stairway as she disappeared.

Kullen loosed another baying cry, as if incensed at the sight of his quarry vanishing. He unleashed a flurry of blows that pushed the four remaining Shieldbandsmen back and drew blood from a dozen minor wounds on their faces, arms, and legs. Now it was their turn to give ground—indeed, they all but turned and fled the moment they could disengage their cutlasses. Kullen could have easily cut them down, but he hadn't come here to kill random guardsmen. He screamed out a torrent of Sadekhar words—a nonsensical jumble of numbers, colors, and the names of desert animals—that chased the fleeing men down the stairs. He, however, did not move. There was no need. He had what he'd come for.

Partly. He ground his teeth. His plan to render Magister Morvannou unconscious by dropping onto his head had worked to perfection, but he hadn't counted on the aristocrat losing his grip on the dragonblood vial. Now, his hopes hinged on Natisse succeeding at retrieving it. Or at least keeping sight of the fleeing Hudarians long enough for him to finish his work and catch up with her.

Flames of some magical design danced all around him, but there was no heat. It reminded Kullen of the Lumenators' globes— the same, yet... so different.

Spinning on his heel, he stalked toward the again-unconscious Magister. He had no fear of attack—the Shieldbandsmen would doubtless take up position on the stairs and wait for him to come to them. More would likely watch the Palace roof from below just in case he attempted to escape the way he'd entered. He had hours to put the Magister to the question before the Pantagorissa ordered her guards to assault the chamber and capture or kill the Sadekhar assassin.

But time was a luxury he could ill afford, not with the dragonblood vial in the hands of the Hudarians.

He seized Magister Morvannou by the collar and slapped the thin-faced man awake. The aristocrat let out a little shriek of terror and pain as his eyes opened and met Kullen's hard, grim visage. He tried to shrink back, but he was already prone with nowhere to go.

"Look at me," Kullen growled down at the terrified aristocrat. "Look into my eyes, and tell me what you see."

"Y-Your eyes?" Magister Morvannou sniveled. "I don't—"

"Do you see your death?!" Kullen roared. "Because when I look at you, all I see is a corpse. A man who planned to betray his Empire by selling their most powerful weapons to their enemies." He knelt at the aristocrat's side and bent until his face hovered mere inches from Morvannou's. "A man who has been sentenced to the Emperor's justice, and *mine* is the hand that will deliver it."

The magister's eyes flew wide, and a babbling torrent of protestations poured from his lips.

Kullen could make no sense of the words, so he slapped him once, twice, three times. Not hard enough to draw blood or render him unconscious once more, but with sufficient force to silence the jabbering.

"Shut your cock gobbler, and listen well, you spineless prick." Kullen fixed the aristocrat with a baleful glare. "The Emperor is not without mercy."

"Mercy!" The word burst from Magister Morvannou's lips. "Please, mercy!"

"Tell me what I wish to know, and you may yet escape the blade."

Magister Morvannou latched onto that, and hope sparkled in his eyes. "Anything!"

Kullen hid a grin. Men like Magister Morvannou felt powerful when surrounded by guards and the proof of their wealth but folded like dried straw in the face of any *true* threat.

"Who are you working for?" he asked.

"Working for?" Confusion flitted across Magister Morvannou's face. "I don't—"

Kullen cut off his words by cuffing him across the face with the hilt of his cutlass. "Lie to me, and you'll taste steel next!"

"It's no lie!" shrieked the magister. Tears of pain and fear welled in his eyes. "I'm working for no one."

"So the sale of the vial was *your* idea?"

"Yes!" he blathered in a wailing cry. "I-I mean, no."

Kullen narrowed his eyes and brought the bloody edge of his stolen cutlass to the man's throat. "Choose your next words with care. They may well be your last."

Magister Morvannou swallowed, his throat bobbing dangerously close to the sharp edge against his neck. "I am working for no one." The words poured from his petrified lips. "But the sale of the vial was not my idea. Not really. I received a note, you see? The morn one day past, outside my mansion. There was a small wooden box. Yes, yes, and a hand-written note informing me that the contents within were a gift and that the auction had been pre-arranged and the Pantagorissa was waiting for me. All I needed do was arrive and sell off the vial. The proceeds of the sale were mine to keep so long as I did as instructed."

"Instructed by whom?" Kullen snarled. "Who were the note and box from?"

That had a strange effect on Magister Morvannou. His lips pressed into a tight line, his jaw muscles clenching.

"Who?" Kullen pressed the blade close enough to provide a shave, just hard enough to draw blood.

"Red Claw!" Magister Morvannou wailed.

Kullen's stomach clenched. There was that name again. Red Claw, the one who'd orchestrated Magister Branthe's conspiracy, who'd conspired with Magisters Deckard, Iltari, Taradan, and Issemar to weaken the Emperor's power by selling to the Blood Clan pirates supplies desperately needed by the people of Dimvein.

"Who is he?" Kullen demanded.

"I don't know!" Magister Morvannou started to shake his head, then thought better of it as the cutlass's edge cut deeper into his supple flesh. "I've never met the man, I swear!"

"And yet you follow his instructions?" Kullen narrowed his eyes.

"Whoever he is, he has always been a friend to me," the magister babbled. "Gifts, lucrative business contracts, opportunities for investments." His voice took on a plaintive, whining tone. "Times have been hard. My House has only survived these last years because of him."

Kullen snorted in derision. That certainly made him the perfect asset, a whipping boy who would do anything the mysterious "Red Claw" asked of him. He had no choice.

"There is nothing you can tell me about him?" Kullen demanded. "Nothing at all?

"I swear, that's all I know!" Magister Morvannou squirmed beneath Kullen. Sweat streamed down his pale, whip-thin face and the smell of urine rose from his britches. "I would tell you if I could, but—"

"Then you serve no purpose. Not to either me or the Empire." Kullen removed the cutlass from the Magister's throat and lifted it high over his head in a dramatic display of impending violence.

The exaggerated pantomime had the intended effect.

"Wait!" Magister Morvannou shrieked, raising one hand as if to ward off the blow. "Waaait. Please, wait. I-I don't know who Red Claw is, but there is someone who might. The one who saw the vial and note delivered."

Kullen quirked an eyebrow, but the cutlass remained motionless above him. "Who?"

"A-An Orken," the magister said, mild hope flittering behind his widespread eyes. "One of high rank bearing the golden mark upon his beard."

45
NATISSE

Natisse cast aside the tide of dismay rising within her. She'd be damned if she let the Horde escape with the dragonblood vial. She'd heard all the stories of the attempted invasion of Dimvein by the combined might of the Blood Clan and Hudar Horde. Indeed, they'd come dangerously close to succeeding. Armed with ballistae and their own magic, the united armies had sailed into Blackwater Bay, and only the bravery of General Andros—Uncle Ronan—and his hand-picked battalion had carried the battle in the Empire's favor.

The *next* battle might go differently if the Horde and pirates commanded a dragon of their own. From what Uncle Ronan had told them, the Imperial army was spread throughout the entirety of the Karmian Empire, keeping the peace in the subjugated territories like Hudar and Brendoni and hunting down Blood Clan wherever they could be found. And being a time of peace, the army was just not what it once was. Many were allowed to return home to their families, take up their trades once more. Regiments had been disbanded. Funny, no one thought that peace only came by the presence of a strong arm.

But could the same be said for the Empire's enemies? The Horde had proven a fractious people, Hudar a hotbed of insurrection and rebellion that necessitated a sizable Imperial armed residence. The Blood Clan seemed to always find new hidey-holes into which they'd disappear, and Natisse had no doubt they'd continued fostering their armada. The day might not be far off when the savages made another attempt to strike a blow against the Empire.

Which made it imperative that she retrieve that dragonblood vial. Despite what she thought of the Karmian Regime, it was her home. Any attack upon the Emperor would result in a new—and possibly better ruler—but an attack upon Dimvein would result in many wasted lives. Good people. Her people. She couldn't let such a power fall into the wrong hands. Everything she'd done, all the years she'd dedicated in service to the Crimson Fang's mission, had been to prevent precisely that. Her targets now might not wear aristocratic robes, but they were no less a threat for it.

She stared down the pirates, each wearing an arrogant smirk as if to goad her into attack. She didn't plan to disappoint them. Sure, they out-armed her, but only one held a crossbow. And sure, it was pointed directly at her, but she knew her limitations—and strengths.

Natisse immediately dropped into a crouch, whipping out one of Kullen's throwing knives. With a swift flick of her wrist, the blade closed the space between her and the cohort. It drove so deeply into the man's face that not even a glint of metal remained. A stray bolt shot upward harmlessly, and he collapsed.

This drew a fury-filled cry from his fellows. They dug in heels and prepared for a defense. But not all of them. Three turned tail and accompanied the Hudarians through a rear passage and were lost to darkness.

Natisse swore. She would have to make quick work of the remaining four pirates before she could reengage the chase.

"Come on," she growled. From a crouch, she sprinted toward them. At the last second, she changed course, drawing her lash-blade and swiping up at the flaming outstretched claw of Binteth's statue.

The claw dropped to the wooden planks, and to her satisfaction, fire erupted and spread quickly. The pirates scrambled to get away from the inferno, but one slipped through, determined to tear Natisse apart.

She pulled her blade back to a solid form in time to block a cutlass attack. But that opened her up to receive a left hook. She went with the momentum of the hit and rolled to her right, accepting it as a glancing blow. When she came up, she did so with an attack of her own, slicing at the pirate's calf muscle. He hobbled forward, nearly falling onto his face. With the advantage, Natisse drove her sword tip through the pirate's unarmored back.

It went straight through, getting stuck in the wood below. It cost her precious seconds, but she pulled the blade free and started after the Hudarians. However, when she spotted the exit, the fire had nearly blotted it out. That old fear rushed back to her, the day her parents were taken, and her life began its spiraling descent into chaos.

She knew what needed to be done. If she lost the Hudarian with the dragonblood vial, all of Dimvein could suffer that same fate.

Golgoth's power churned within her. Images sprang unbidden to her mind. Though these were not memories of her past, they were visions directly from the dragon's mind. There was fire, yes. But so much more. Ships firing large bolts, men in uniform aflame, screaming for their lives. She felt Golgoth's pain as she took a bolt to the side, as a wide swath of bluish-white light that looked eerily similar to Lumenator magic created a shield against her. She crashed into the light, crumpling to the sea below. Flashes of memory brought an unfamiliar face to mind though it was clear, this was her former master, dying at the hands of the enemy. The Hudarians.

The rush left Natisse breathless. Golgoth had been there, had joined into the battle, and nearly died because of it. The Queen of the Embers had lost her *Bloodsworn* that day. The memories of that suffering, the raw agony of sorrow as the bond was violently severed, threatened to drag Natisse to the floor. And yet the power, too, amplified her every sense and flooded her with Golgoth's determination.

Fire blazed in Natisse's veins, propelling her to bring up what remained of her dress. Covering her face, she dived through the licking flames. There was no heat. There was no pain. Distracting as the blaze was, it was no different from what she assumed to be Vandil magic that lit the stairs and main room of the Dread Spire.

To her left, the pirates were still falling over one another to keep out of harm's way. But as soon as they saw her unharmed, they gave chase through the back corridors.

The fight had taken too long, and as Natisse turned, she no longer spotted the Hudarians and their pirate protectors. She ran, putting every remaining ounce of strength she had into it. With pirates behind her and her target ahead, she pushed. Her feet flew with impossible speed—speed she could never have imagined or demanded from her body. This was Golgoth's power burning within her, fueling her. A power as terrifying as it was exhilarating.

Someone stumbled into her path, and she barreled through them without slowing. The impact hurled the person—she saw not who they were or what they wore—off their feet to vanish from her field of vision. A *thump* and cry of pain resounded through the corridor. Natisse spared a moment's pity for whoever she'd bowled over, but it was tempered by the sheer exuberance at the energy coursing through her.

Now she understood how Jad felt. Such raw might was both titillating and terrifying. She could see why he was afraid of what he'd do when he lost control. Within her seemingly stewed enough power to rend a man's flesh and bone with naught but her bare hands.

Light flashed at the end of the hall, and when she reached it, she spotted her quarry fleeing toward the second tower—the Pantagorissa's personal sanctuary. Natisse summoned the power from deep within her, commanding it to flood her veins, and poured on another burst of speed. She had to catch up to the fleeing Hudarians and Blood Clan before they reached the main Palace hall, packed with hundreds of guests enjoying the Pantagorissa's feast and revelry. If they reached it ahead of her, she might lose them—and the dragonblood vial—forever.

Sweat poured off her in puddles, but it did little to slow her. She navigated the uneven planks like she'd impressed their placements upon her mind. She could see each step before she took it, almost like a vague memory.

Golgoth's rage seared within, a sizzling, erupting power like nothing she'd known. It urged her—coerced her even—to go on. It was beginning to be too much. Her head was swimming, arms and legs tingling. This feeling, she could revel in it forever. Caution crept in like a mouse, reminding her of Kullen's warning. He'd tried to tell her what this would be like, how easily one could give in to the temptation. Even as she ran, shame washed over her in a torrent. How would she be any different from any of the evil men who came before her? She would need to learn to temper these desires for more power.

The Hudarian woman and her entourage were growing weary, whereas Natisse was not. They had slowed considerably, giving Natisse the chance to close the gap. She could see them clearly now. Turning back, one spat a curse.

"Use my power," Golgoth urged in her mind. *"Beckon me. Summon the flames, and let us end this threat with fury."*

Her mind filled with images of what that would look like. Fire erupting from her hands. The Hudarian and her pirates' remains left charred and smoking on the spot. But once again, those visions mingled with the recollection of her parents and what Shahitz'ai had done to them.

"I can't!" she shouted, not bothering to keep it bottled up within her mind.

"You can and must," Golgoth said. *"They cannot get away. They cannot wield such a potent weapon."*

"Nor can I," Natisse said, still running. "I must… be… different."

"… find the balance between respecting and fearing the power."

She heard Kullen's words dancing in her head.

"I can't," she said again.

Kullen's words repeated over and over again. Before she could even fully process them, Golgoth roared within her, and vitality, fresh and new, burst from a well inside.

"Stop!" The word roared from Natisse's lips with force enough to send the tightly-clustered Hudarians and pirates to the ground as if struck from behind by a giant's fist, tumbling head over heels. One, the elder of the Hudarians, rolled with the fall and came to his feet, spinning around in a fighting stance. Natisse was on him in a flash, lashblade whipping out at his head. The leather-skinned man ducked beneath the strike and lunged for her with outstretched arms.

Natisse had no chance to snap her lashblade back or evade the Hudarian's grasp. Strong arms wrapped around her waist, lifted her from her feet, and slammed her to the ground with bone-crushing force. Natisse's breath exploded from her lungs, yet with it came a gout of fire—purest dragon flame! The Hudarian screamed as his hair, beard, and horse-hide clothing caught ablaze. Releasing Natisse, he batted in vain at the flames now consuming him.

Squirming out from beneath the struggling man, Natisse surged to her feet. Her lashblade, still extended in whip form, hung in a long, loose coil, but as Natisse snapped it back into the solid blade, a Blood Clan pirate charged her in a thunderous cacophony of hammering bootsteps and clacking shells. Natisse barely managed to evade the swipe of the cutlass, and the follow-up blow cut a shallow gash along the back of her left arm.

With a growl of pain, Natisse leaped backward and spun in a graceful pirouette any ballerina would envy. The movement was far from practical in close-quarters combat, but with a gap opened between her and her enemy, it gave Natisse ample space to swing the whip-like lashblade. Segmented steel closed around the pirate's neck. With a hard yank on the weapon, Natisse sawed his head free of his shoulders.

Two more Blood Clan had found their feet, and Natisse engaged them with her lashblade pulled back into sword form. They were good with their cutlasses, light on their feet, and accustomed to the uneven planking of ship decks—decks doubtless like those used to build the entirety of Pantagoya. But they had never faced a weapon quite like Natisse's, nor one who'd trained for years to wield it. Natisse cracked the lashblade forward like a whip to bury the tip into one pirate's eyeball, then swung it around to open a ragged tear in the other's chest.

A Hudarian's ululating war cry echoed from just behind her back. Natisse couldn't spin to meet the attack; every shred of speed and skill went into hurling herself into a forward dive meant to evade the inevitable blow. Something slashed the air where her head had been a half second earlier, catching the nib of her tight braid.

Natisse landed in a forward roll, rising to her feet and whirling to strike out blindly with the lashblade. She *felt* more than saw the blow strike. Flesh parted like straw beneath the scythe, and warm blood spilled from a ragged tear in the belly of the young male Hudarian warrior.

A shrill scream of rage emanated from the young Horde shamanka. Her eyes locked on the dying man, and horror twisted her face. His lover, perhaps? Natisse didn't bother to find out—she seized the opportunity to reach her left hand for one of the slim, flexible throwing blades hidden among her under-dress and hurled it at the Hudarian woman. The cry cut off in a gurgle as the dagger buried in the woman's throat. Crimson gushed from the wound to stain the colorful beads hanging from the front of her ceremonial garments.

From the corner of Natisse's eye, she saw the raven-haired Horde *Tabudai*—the one with the vial!—staggering to her feet and racing for a door at the end of the hall. One of the surviving

Blood Clan pirates bent to help her while the others engaged Natisse.

"No bloody way!" Natisse bellowed. Without hesitation, she drew another throwing knife and hurled it at the pirate in front of her. The woman batted it aside contemptuously—exposing her midsection to Natisse's thrust, which buried a foot of lashblade into her gut. Screaming, the pirate dropped her cutlass and fell to the side, clutching at the wound in her belly.

"Halt!" came the cry from a Shieldbandsman from behind who'd just caught up to the action. He was immediately joined by three others, but Natisse had no intention of waiting around for them to fully arrive.

She burst into a run, charging through the door in pursuit of the fleeing pirate and *Tabudai*. One throwing knife remained. She pulled it free and waited for the opportune time to fling it, but her quarry was too sporadic in their movements. They weaved and bobbed, all the while never slowing. Finally, Natisse saw her opening and took it. She whipped the blade forward with as much strength as she could manage while maintaining her accuracy.

It struck home with a *thwack-squelch*. The pirate was out of the way, and the Horde woman stumbled onward, alone and weaponless. Without her guard keeping her focused, the Hudarian couldn't keep pace. Natisse caught up in half a dozen steps and brought the *Tabudai* down in a flying tackle.

The weathered old planks cracked beneath their weight. As they rolled, one bowed so deeply, the two of them plummeted a foot. Natisse punched down at the woman's throat in an attempt to end things quickly, but her fist never found its mark as the flooring gave way completely. They crashed downward. Natisse's stomach flipped, and she watched the *Tabudai's* face go from enraged to terrified.

Only seconds passed, but it felt like days as they fell. When they slapped down on the sea below, it felt like landing on solid ground. It slammed her in the face, punched her in the gut, and knocked the air from her lungs even as it closed around her, ice-cold water burying her. The shock paralyzed her for a moment and caused her to suck in a breath. Still tangled with the Hudarian, she couldn't tell up from down, and if she didn't figure it out soon, she'd drown.

She was breathless and desperate to orient herself. By now, the *Tabudai* had released her grip on Natisse, and she was clawing her way through the water. Nothing gave Natisse the slightest sense of direction. The darkness was all-encompassing.

Then, a tiny glimmer of light shone as the *Tabudai* swam. Her leg moved, and it was there. Moved again, and it was gone. Natisse pushed with all she had toward that little shining bit of hope. She rushed past the Hudarian, sparing not even a moment for her.

Her vision began to blur, her brain screaming out for air. And not a moment too soon, she breached the surface and coughed. The waves dragged her down again. Then she realized it wasn't the waves but the Hudarian woman grasping at her leg. Natisse forced her head above water, sucked in a lungful of air, then dived back down.

There it was, floating from its chain: the dragonblood vial. Natisse grabbed it, then planted her boot on the Hudarian woman's face. Just as she was about to shove off, Natisse's enemy was torn free by something large, something terrifying. She couldn't quite see it, but the Hudarian was gone in an instant.

Natisse broke for the surface, trying to wrap the vial around her wrist as she swam. Her face felt the night air. Her lungs tasted it too.

Then something cold and slick wrapped around her leg, squeezed tight, and dragged her under the water's icy surface.

46
KULLEN

"You expect me to believe an *Orken* played messenger?" Kullen snapped. "And not just any Orken, but a commander of the Orkenwatch?"

"Y-Yes!" Magister Morvannou said. "Er, I mean, no." He swallowed and tried again. "What I meant was the Orken was present to ensure it was delivered, but he, himself, did not deliver it."

Kullen narrowed his eyes. "Explain."

"Esseldon—the captain of my House guard—he spotted the Orken at the same time that Nahall found the note. Alone, which he thought was odd, given that the Orkenwatch always move in a patrol. Esseldon was going to approach him and find out why he watched the mansion, but the Orken slipped away before he had a chance."

"So he didn't get a good look at the Orken?" Kullen demanded. "This Captain Esseldon of yours, he couldn't identify the Orken beyond the color of the bands in his beard?"

"Identify him?" Magister Morvannou frowned. "How could he? Damned things all look alike! Brutes and beasts, the lot of them. That silly affectation of wearing gold or silver is nothing more than an attempt to pass as human, when they're—"

Kullen slapped him with his left hand, hard. "Focus, you old prick!" He had no desire to hear the aristocrat's ranting—a sentiment he knew was shared by more than a few of the Empire's wealthiest. "I asked you a question."

"Qu-Question?" Magister Morvannou swallowed and blinked, his fear-numbed mind visibly struggling to recall exactly what Kullen had asked. ""Er... yes... right! No." He shook his head. "Captain Esseldon couldn't identify him." He wisely kept any further tirade to himself.

Kullen pondered the information. If the magister had nothing else of value to offer—

"Oh!" The aristocrat's eyes flew wide. "There's this!"

He fumbled in his coat—now rumpled, torn, and stained with his own blood—and produced a small, round silver disc etched with runes.

"This was in the box with the vial," he continued, holding it up in front of Kullen's face. "I don't know what it does, but the note from Red Claw told me that if I encountered any obstacles conveying myself and the vial to Pantagoya, to bring this to Tuskthorne Keep and present it to the Orkenwatch. That there would be those who knew what to do to ensure my safe arrival."

Kullen snatched the coin-shaped object from the magister's slim fingers. It didn't look like much—like an Imperial mark, though a fraction larger—yet he knew exactly what it was. He had one just like it.

Sliding the silver disc into his pocket, Kullen lowered the cutlass and rose to his feet, taking a step back from the prone man. "You have the Emperor's sincerest gratitude for your cooperation."

Magister Morvannou stared up at him in wide-eyed surprise, his mouth agape. He'd gone from facing certain death one moment to being *thanked* in the next, and his mind clearly struggled to keep up with the sudden shift. It took him long seconds to collect himself enough to shimmy to his feet.

Magister Morvannou licked his lips nervously. "So the Emperor's mercy—"

His words cut off in a gurgle and a spray of blood as Kullen whipped the cutlass across his saggy old throat.

"Is reserved for those who deserve it," Kullen told the dying man. "Not traitors who would seek to arm his enemies."

Magister Morvannou fell to his knees, hands clutching frantically at his torn flesh in a vain effort to stanch the torrent of blood sheeting down the front of his robes. Crimson bubbled between his fingers, dribbled from his lips, and stained the wooden planks at his feet. With a wet, gargled gasp, he toppled forward to land with a *splash* in an ever-widening puddle of his own life.

Kullen sneered down at the corpse. Magister Morvannou had died a fool, pawn of Red Claw, and coward to the end. Unfortunately, he'd also died without yielding much useful in the way of information. Kullen was no closer to identifying the mysterious entity behind the conspiracy. At best, he'd received further confirmation that at least one of the high-ranking Orkenwatch was involved.

And something the aristocrat said bothered Kullen. He'd spoken of receiving a box with the vial—not vial*s*. So where were the rest of those taken off the dead magisters? Kullen didn't know which of the vials belonging to Perech, Taradan, Iltari, Estefar, Oyodan, and all the others who'd died recently had turned up here. But it was just *one*. The others had vanished—gone to auction somewhere else, or disseminated to "Red Claw's" trusted co-conspirators?

He needed to get his hands on that vial, needed to know which dragon it summoned and which dead aristocrat to credit it to. Otherwise, he had no way to backtrack its movements arriving in Magister Morvannou's hands to when it had first gone missing—and thus no way to discover who else was complicit in the treachery.

Kullen pricked up his ears at the sound of heavy, booted feet rushing up the staircase. The Pantagorissa had ordered the attack far faster than he'd expected. Enraged as she was, she had no intention of letting the "Caliphate assassin" escape.

Kullen concentrated, trying to count the footsteps. At least a dozen, judging by the clanking of armor and thunder of heavy hobnailed boots on the wooden stairs. Armed with only a cutlass and wearing a jacket far more fashionable than defensive, he'd have a bloody hard time weathering the assault. Surely, the first of *many* the Pantagorissa intended to throw at him.

But he held no designs to wait around to cross blades with the Shieldbandsmen. He raced to the chamber's south-facing wall and turned his gaze up to the aperture Umbris had broken into the tower-top roof and pressed his thumb onto the vial's golden cap. Along with the slight pain in his digit came the closeness of his dragon friend.

Lend me your power, Umbris!

"Receive it, Friend Kullen."

In the span of a heartbeat, Kullen was airborne, his wispy form darting toward the shadows beyond the oddly burning room. As he fluttered upward, his very essence seemed to be tearing away. At first, he worried he'd miscounted his slides, and the Shadow Realm was claiming him for good. However, once he cleared his mind, he realized the pull was more of a gentle drawing of his shadow toward the cauldron in the middle of the room. It was unlike any power he'd encountered before. It lacked the fire and ferocity of the dragonblood magic, yet there was an inexorability to it, a force as timeless and enduring as the ocean itself. It didn't rip and tear as he'd first thought. Instead, it was patient, drawing him toward it in creeping increments. It coaxed him with the gentleness of a lover, but its power was undeniable.

Kullen pulled free of the power and slipped up to the roof, where he once more took on flesh and bone. The lingering effects of the Shadow Realm remained chilly and numbing deep within his core, but the magic from that cauldron, too, left its mark on his soul like salt from the sea breeze clinging to a ship's hull.

He stared down through the broken skylight at the unassuming brazier. Though Kullen didn't know what it might be, he had no desire to leave such a power in the hands of the

Pantagorissa. She might be allied with the Empire for the time being, but such things had a tendency to change with the unpredictability of the ocean's shifting tides.

Umbris, come to me.

The sky split open, shadows and light expanding to make room for the Twilight Dragon as he stepped through the slit between realms.

"Have you ever seen something like that?" Kullen asked aloud, pointing down at the cauldron.

Umbris appraised it, his reptilian brows knitting together in thought. Finally, he snuffed and shook his head. *"Never. But its power..."*

"Indeed," Kullen said. "Unlike anything else."

"Not unlike anything."

Kullen stared up at him, the question evident on his features.

"In the Shadow Realm, there is something I've felt like it. Something I cannot explain. I dare not venture close to it. It stands alone, a pillar of light in the midst of grays. The power is undeniably alike. Not even the shades will suffer its presence."

"Can you destroy it?" Kullen motioned with his head toward the one here on this plane.

Umbris glared down at it. His reaction was one part pain and one part reverence. Then, his lips peeled back in a snarl.

What was this thing if its likeness was present in the Shadow Realm? The question would remain unanswered for the time being, for the bootsteps of many guards grew louder, accompanied by a shout of "Bring him down, lads!" echoing up the staircase.

Break it, now! Kullen commanded through their mental bond.

"With pleasure," Umbris growled. The dragon dove down through the open chasm of the roof. Then, spinning in mid-flight, the dragon whipped his tail. The tentacular appendage connected with the brazier and sent it soaring across the room and into the far wall, where it exploded in a spray of water, glass shards, and twisted bronze.

It was as if some magical tie had been severed. The pull from the cauldron—one Kullen had barely recognized as still being present upon the rooftop—had dissipated.

Umbris! Back! Kullen shouted as he saw the Shieldbandsmen's shadows dancing in the threshold of the room. The Twilight Dragon returned, and Kullen leaped onto his back. *Up!*

Without hesitation, Umbris sprang from the roof, propelled thirty paces into the air by his powerful hind legs. His wings snapped out and caught an updraft of heat rising from the myriad torches, lanterns, lamps, and fires burning below. Within seconds, they were streaking toward the cover of wispy clouds drifting low in the night sky.

Kullen cast one glance back, just in time to see torch-and-cutlass-wielding Shieldbandsmen flooding the now-empty tower-top chamber. He smiled at the mental image of their dumb, confused expressions when they inevitably found their prey vanished. Not climbing out the new hole in their roof and down the side of the tower, but *disappeared* like smoke on the wind. Or, in his case, the shadow of night beneath the slowly rising sun.

"Hah!" he let out a single grunting laugh. That had turned out better than he'd expected. Worse, too. His smile faded. He hadn't yet gotten what he'd come for. He still had to locate Natisse and retrieve the dragonblood vial.

At his silent urging, Umbris circled back toward the floating island.

Torches seemed to swirl like fireflies, dotting the island and all its many establishments. Chaos reigned on Pantagoya. The guests had spilled from the Pantagorissa's Palace and flooded through the streets of the common levels. Their fear and confusion were palpable and had spread throughout the rest of the floating island. Everywhere, Kullen could see fights breaking out both between the common riffraff and guards. As things escalated, fires broke out. Inns, brothels, gambling halls—and to Kullen's pleasure, the exarai leaf den where they'd been accosted earlier—were up in flames.

He could hear the cries from a dozen languages filling the night. Everything from spat curses to terror-filled howls. People fell—or were tossed—to their icy deaths in the sea below. The waters churned like a hot spring as creatures of all shapes and sizes found their night's meal.

Kullen swept his eyes across the island. But it was no use. Amongst the torches and roaring infernos, Natisse's bright red locks wouldn't stand out as usual.

Find her, Umbris!

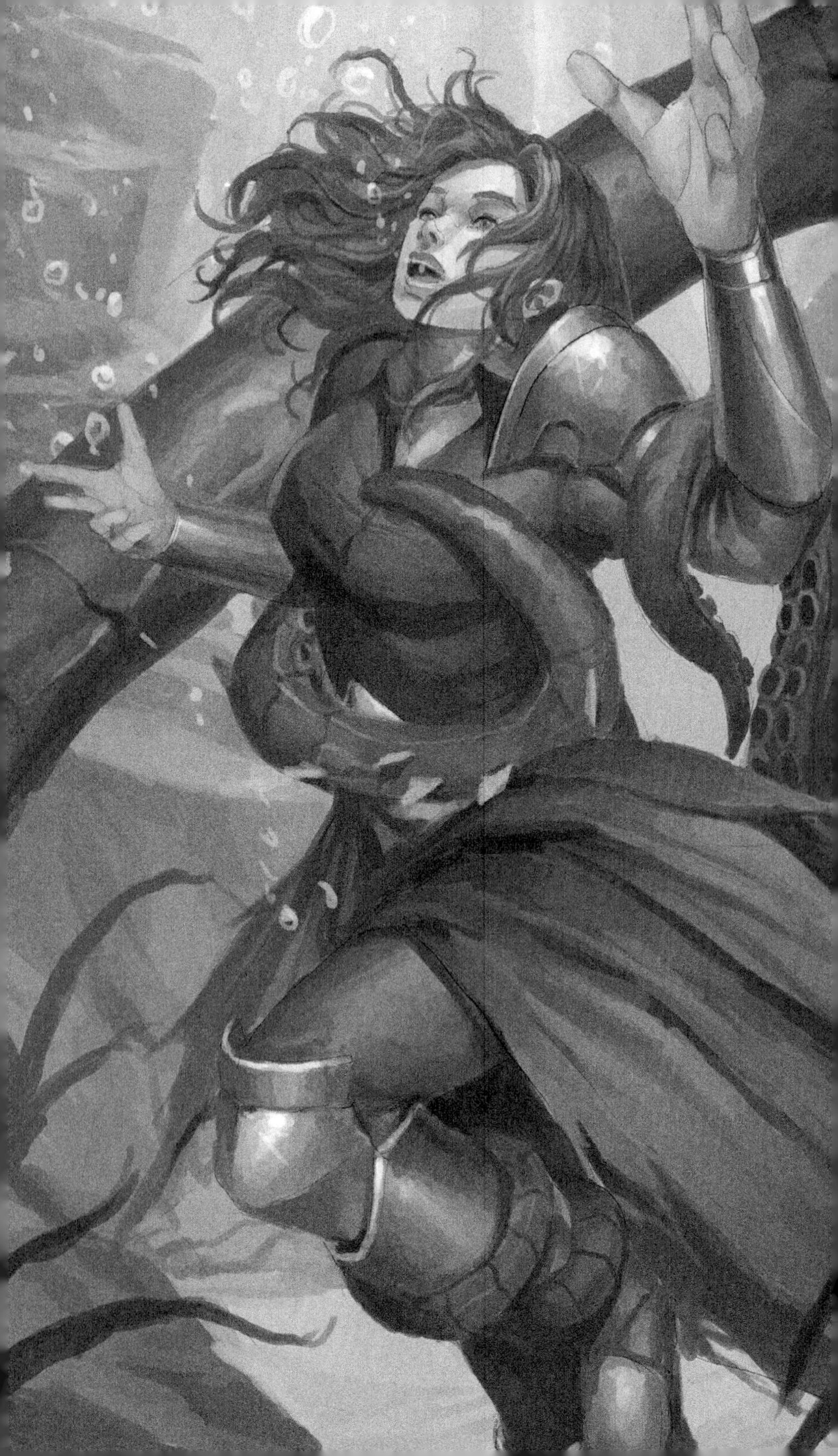

47
Natisse

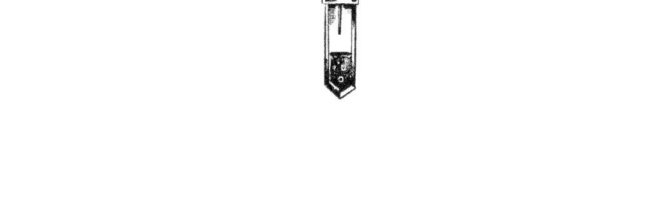

Panic gripped Natisse as inescapably as the powerful, supple limb encircling her right leg. She kicked frantically with her left foot, but it had no more effect on whatever creature was dragging her down than a mouse biting a dragon's paw. It took all her willpower not to relinquish her grip on the lashblade or dragonblood vial to claw her way back to the surface.

"Use my power!" Golgoth thundered in her mind.

Natisse wanted to scream—she doubted even *magical* fire could burn underwater—but forced her jaw to clench tight against the instinctive fear swelling within her. She had to remain in control, had to fight the terror. If she didn't fight, she *would* die.

The dragon's voice came again. *"Summon me to the Mortal Realm! I can save you, but you must call for me."*

Natisse scanned her memories of that night in the woods with Kullen. How had he instructed her to summon Golgoth? She'd done it, but in the tumult of battling for her life in the cold sea, her mind was blank.

She acted on instinct and thought the words, *Come to me, Golgoth!*

Power drained from her as if a dam had been opened. The cold of the ocean water pierced her body like a thousand icy daggers. Yet no dragon materialized in the water before her.

Golgoth! she screamed mentally, knowing she only had seconds left before she'd be forced to suck in a lungful of salt water. Darkness threatened to subdue her. She could almost hear Ezrasil's voice beckoning her into the unknown. Pressure built behind her eyes, her nose, and her insides felt as if they were going to burst.

Then it came, like the winds of a hurricane rushing toward her, bringing with it a surge of heat that warmed the ocean in the space between heartbeats.

Her eyes opened, and through the water's murk, she saw the enormous flame carving a path through the water in her direction.

In the fire's light, she got her first glimpse of the creature who would've claimed her as dinner. One pale white eye stared up at her with no emotion. If it had a second eye, Natisse didn't know, but this one took up the fullness of what she would call its face. It had sallow flesh pockmarked with scabby brown splotches. Three spikes of some fashion protruded from each side of its eye. There was no mouth to speak of, but she had no doubt wherever it was, it was filled with sharp teeth.

Her hopes were answered when the fire reached it. Its head, which was also its body, reeled backward, revealing a giant maw buried beneath its undercarriage, nestled betwixt eight writing tentacles.

It shrieked, a sound louder than the pressure building all around her from the water's weight. Those teeth would have shredded her into chopped meat before she could have given protest. It took her a moment before she realized the beast no longer had hold of her. Vast, lithe arms rippled toward Golgoth's approaching form as the sea monster eagerly grasped for a larger meal.

Yet this was no mere prey, but a predator the likes of which Natisse was sure this ocean held none of.

Golgoth's enormous muzzle split open, and a jet of brilliant yellow-gold fire erupted from within. The pillar shot toward the tentacled creature and struck it head-on. The impact sent it hurling downward, nearly dragging Natisse with it and the bubbling, boiling water.

Then Golgoth's huge wings encircled Natisse, and she felt herself being dragged along through the water at a terrifying speed. Together, they moved faster than any bolt—faster than she'd ever thought it possible to move.

Her eyes shut tightly, and she breached the surface. Water exploded around her. Somewhere within, she knew air surrounded her, but still, she didn't breathe. She couldn't. The flight had her stunned, paralyzed, gripped.

Then, her body told her she could wait no longer, and Natisse sucked down greedy gulps of air, coughing and vomiting salty, icy water. When her eyes opened, fear found her once more. Where was Golgoth? She was soaring through the air, the great Crimson Dragon nowhere in sight. It was as if she was suspended there, a hundred feet above the sea. Then, she began to plummet. The waters rose up quickly. She braced for impact, but Golgoth's bulk rushed up beneath her at the last possible instant, and Natisse was swept up onto the dragon's scaled back. The contact with the dragon's steel-hard scales jolted what little breath Natisse still held in her lungs, but she managed to cling onto Golgoth's spines for dear life.

Up and up, Golgoth took her until all she could see were the wisps of clouds prancing around them. She collapsed forward, wrapping her weary arms around Golgoth's neck. She lay there for long minutes, struggling to catch her breath, to slow the frantic beating of her heart. How close she had just come to death —not just once, but easily half a dozen times in a matter of hours? Yet she had never felt so alive in her life. The power coursing through her, the exhilaration of the fire blazing in her veins, the wind rushing past her as the dragon—*her* dragon!—cut through the night sky over the Astralkane Sea.

Golgoth's great wings beat at the air, propelling them forward at such velocity it didn't feel real. Not even when flying with Kullen on Umbris's back had they traveled with such swiftness. Natisse should've been terrified, she knew. Would have been mere days earlier. Yet now, she felt only elation.

The euphoria passed quickly, however. Wind rushed across her soaked clothing, chilling her to the bone. A bizarre smarting permeated her entire body—reminding her of raw, ragged skin healing from a burn wound. Almost as if Golgoth's fire had scoured her veins and left them acutely hyper-sensitive to every minute sensation. She hadn't the strength to lift her head from Golgoth's back. The exertion had left her far more drained than even the most punishing of Uncle Ronan's training sessions.

Natisse's felt her eyelids growing heavy, a sluggishness settling over her mind and a weight dragging at her body.

Well, at least I know how Kullen survived the onyx sharks, was the last thought that flitted through her mind before exhaustion claimed her.

Natisse awoke to star-lit darkness and rushing wind. She experienced a terrifying, dizzying sense of disorientation at the absence of close-packed earthen walls to shield her.

She jerked upright and immediately regretted it. Every muscle in her body shrieked in protest, and she winced at the sting of a half-dozen wounds she hadn't previously observed. None were serious, but all sent twinges racing through her with each movement.

She regained control of her wits slowly and started to remember the events on Pantagoya. She'd fallen asleep on Golgoth's back—for two, perhaps three hours, judging by the first gleaming rays of blue brightening the eastern sky.

She peered over the scaly, sharp-spined ridges of Golgoth's

spine. She could see only snatches of ground below her. They had returned to the shores of the Karmian Empire, leaving the Astralkane Sea and Pantagoya far behind.

Where are we? she asked through the mental bond. Speaking aloud would be a waste of effort, for the wind would no doubt carry away her words.

"*Passing over Yalethi Province,*" Golgoth answered. "*We will see the walls of Dimvein before sunrise.*"

Natisse let out a long breath, relieved. She was all too glad to be back on dry land, far away from the Pantagorissa's floating domain. After what she and Kullen had done—

Kullen!

Instinctively, she glanced over her shoulder. A foolish act, she knew. Even with the rising sun and pale crescent moon to cast light, the chances of spotting Umbris were infinitesimal. The Twilight Dragon's dark purplish-black coloring blended with the shadows far too well.

She could hear nothing save the rushing wind and the beating of her pulse in her ears. She felt nothing but wasn't certain if she ought to be able to.

Did he get out? Natisse asked. *Did you sense him or Umbris?* It still felt odd, communicating without forming words, but she was slowly growing accustomed to it.

"*I did not,*" Golgoth rumbled back. "*But I felt your spark growing faint and feared you might be injured, so I carried you back to land in case you weakened further. By the time I came to understand that you were merely exhausted, it was no use returning for him. Either he survived and escaped, or he did not. We can do nothing to affect the outcome now.*"

Natisse felt an instinctive pang of guilt twisting in her belly. The Crimson Fang would *never* have left anyone behind. Kullen might not be one of her comrades, but she had agreed to aid him in his mission. She should have made certain he got out alive before fleeing.

Yet she *had* succeeded. Looking down, she found the dragonblood vial's chain still wrapped tightly around the numb fingers of her left hand. She'd fallen asleep gripping it and her lashblade both. Cold, wind, and fear hadn't robbed her of at least that instinct.

What now? She racked her brain, trying to decide what to do. She'd stopped the vial from falling into the hands of the Empire's enemies, as Emperor Wymarc had commanded his Black Talon. Yet something told her that Kullen wouldn't just let her *keep* the vial he'd been sent to retrieve. She'd been bonded to Golgoth, and only her death could sever the bond. After what had happened back on Pantagoya, Natisse suspected Golgoth wouldn't allow that to happen lightly. The dragon had channeled magic through her body even though Natisse had been unable to summon it of her own accord.

But Kullen knew where to find her. He could track her down in the Burrow—hopefully with a less unfriendly welcome from the rest of the Crimson Fang—and she could give him the vial there. After that... well, she didn't quite know what happened next. She did, after all, command the Queen of the Ember Dragons. That was a power Natisse suspected Kullen wouldn't want unleashed against the Emperor any more than the vial Magister Morvannou had intended to auction off.

It was decided: the best thing she could do now was return to the Crimson Fang. At least there he could find her. If he'd survived, that was.

He survived, she told herself. *No way the Pantagorissa and a handful of her guards took him down. Umbris wouldn't let that happen.*

The guilt at leaving him still nagged at her. In equal measure, however, was the guilt born of knowing she had almost failed to retrieve the dragonblood vial. It had been too damned close. The Horde and Blood Clan had *nearly* escaped because she had hesitated to use Golgoth's power.

She tried to tell herself that it had been out of necessity. Kullen had impressed upon her the importance of maintaining tenuous peace between the Empire and Pantagoya. The fact that she'd attacked and seriously wounded the Pantagorissa certainly didn't help matters. But if she'd called on Golgoth's Dragonfire, a woman as cunning as Pantagorissa Torrine was said to be would immediately see Emperor Wymarc's hand in the attack. After all, it was common knowledge that only the most powerful in the Empire commanded dragons. She'd chosen not to tap into the dragonblood magic out of caution. And her caution had served her well.

But the thought rang hollow in her mind. She knew the truth. Could see it as clearly as she could see the red-gold light shining through the cracks in Golgoth's scales.

Fear had held her back, not prudence.

How do I do it? she asked, wrestling against the shame flooding through her.

"Do what?" Golgoth answered.

Find the balance. Natisse struggled to put into words the turmoil roiling in her belly. *You chose me for your Bloodsworn because you believed my fear would prohibit me from abusing your power. Yet you saw what just happened. My fear very nearly cost me—and countless others.* Her conversation with Kullen from the previous night came back to her unbidden once more. *How do I find the balance between respecting and fearing the power?*

"Hmm." Golgoth rumbled deep in her belly, her tone pensive. For long seconds, she remained silent save for the occasional thunderous beat of her great wings. *"To you humans, fire is both a thing to fear and cherish, yes?"*

Natisse considered that. *It is. The same fire that warms our homes and cooks the food we put in our bellies could just as easily kill us if out of control.*

"There is your answer, then." Golgoth snuffed through her nostrils, sending a plume of sulfurous smoke rising to be carried off by the wind. *"You control the fires you build. So, too, you must control the fires within you."*

Natisse frowned. *But how?*

The dragon made it sound so easy, but she was a creature born of fire, her magic innate. Natisse had only just begun learning how to co-exist with it, much less master it.

"Precisely the way you have your entire life." Golgoth said it as if it was the simplest thing in the world, a concept even a squalling babe—or whatever dragon called their young, if they had any—should understand. *"You channel it, direct it where you want it to go, corral it to stop it from spreading, shield it to stop the wind from extinguishing it, feed it when you wish it to grow hotter, and starve it to let it die out."*

The concept certainly sounded simple enough, but Natisse could see no practical way to apply the dragon's words. *But how?* she asked again. *How do I do all that?*

"With your will." The fires in the core of Golgoth's body glowed brighter, radiating greater warmth and lighting the night sky in a crimson-and-gold halo around them. *"Your will is the fuel, the shield, the corral, and the channel. I chose you because I saw the strength of your spirit. You have the heart of a dragon, even if your body is frail and human. Use it to control the fire, and you will become its master. Otherwise..."*

The dragon let the words hang in the silence of Natisse's mind. There was no need to finish the sentence. The raw tenderness of Natisse's veins was proof enough of what would happen if the magic coursed through her unchecked. Golgoth had saved her life but, in so doing, had damaged her spirit or soul or whatever channeled the dragon's power. Holding it back and in, allowing fear to almost kill her and forcing the dragon's hand to keep her alive... if she permitted that to happen again, it could have dire consequences.

She wanted to be rid of her fear—how desperately she wanted it, had wanted it for as long as she could remember—yet the memories of the day her former life ended consumed by Dragonfire would not so easily be shaken free of her mind. Confronting the giant Joakim had given her a measure of control over the instinctive terror, but then she'd felt the *Bloodsurge* of fire within her, and it all came billowing back.

How would she manage to be any better than Golgoth's former masters if she feared the very thing that would grant her freedom? Perhaps in time, she would learn. But for now, only one task remained. She needed rest.

48
KULLEN

Kullen circled in the sky above Pantagoya, fighting not to cede to the worry gnawing at his gut. He desperately hoped Natisse had gotten out of the tower without difficulty, caught up to the fleeing Hudarians, and retrieved the dragonblood vial. But if not, he had to be ready to shadow-slide down and find her among the chaos in the—

Then he felt it: a familiar rush of power, a sudden thrum of energy expanding outward with such force it strained the fabric of the world around it. Though unmistakable, it was faint, distant, coming from far below him.

Yet there was nothing faint about the blazing fires that sprang to life all around the Palace. It seemed as if every torch, lantern, lamp, and building fire suddenly flared to ten times their size and heat. But rather than exploding upward in a sky-high pillar of crimson-and-gold flames, it was sucked downward. Every light for a hundred paces around the enormous tortoise-shaped structure was snuffed out in a heartbeat, and a vast swath of Pantagoya plunged into total darkness.

That could only mean one thing: Natisse had summoned Golgoth. Not into the Palace—which meant she hadn't been corralled by the Shieldbandsmen or cornered by her enemies—but *beneath* it, into the cold, dark waters where the Pantagorissa's hungry "pets" lurked.

Kullen's heart leaped into his throat. He knew all too well the terror of facing that endless expanse of icy-cold blackness alone, knowing he had mere moments to live before something ravenous marked him as a toothsome morsel. Umbris had saved him from becoming a feast for the onyx sharks. He had to hope Golgoth could arrive in time to save Natisse from a similar fate—or, perhaps one far worse, for Paliantra alone knew what manner of creatures dwelled in the depths of her sea.

He strained his eyes, scanning Pantagoya for any sign of the enormous red dragon—and, he prayed, the woman who commanded it. Hope flooded over him as he spotted a figure of fire-edged shadow breaking the surface a quarter league to the south of the floating pleasure island. He didn't need Umbris's eyes to recognize Golgoth's bulk or the fiery red visible through the cracks in her scales.

With a mental command, he sent Umbris hurtling away from Pantagoya and in Golgoth's direction. He had to make certain Natisse had escaped unharmed—*and with the vial, of course*, he added hastily.

But before he'd covered even a fraction of the distance, Golgoth set off toward Imperial shores at blistering speed. The Ember dragon's mighty wings beat at the air, catching an updraft that sent her soaring sharply upward to vanish into a wispy bank of clouds.

Kullen urged Umbris to climb, too. Perhaps he could spot Golgoth in the pale moonlight, draw the dragon's attention and convince her to slow her flight—but when he broke above the cloud cover, the skies were empty save for the crescent moon and the glimmering stars. He saw no sign of Golgoth.

Can you catch up? Kullen asked.

"*Even if I were to strain with all my might,*" Umbris told him, a hint of irritation in his deep, rumbling voice, *"I could not close the distance. The Queen of the Embers flies with the urgency of hungry wildfire."*

Kullen ground his teeth, cursing under his breath. He was glad, certainly, that Natisse had escaped alive; if she'd died, Golgoth's bond to the Mortal Realm would have been severed, trapping her in the Fire Realm. But why was she in such a hurry to rush off and leave him behind? He'd been convinced they were gaining ground. After the night spent in the forest glade and everything they'd discussed over the last day, he'd actually believed they might've begun forming an alliance—perhaps even friendship.

But Natisse clearly thought different. Maybe she *always* had, merely hidden it from him. Too well. Had she really come along on this mission merely to get her hands on *another* dragonblood vial? That would give the Crimson Fang control of two dragons. Kullen didn't know which dragon the second vial belonged to, but Golgoth alone was threat enough.

Was I really such a fool? The question played over and over in his mind as Umbris sped through the darkness after Golgoth. They'd never catch up with the Ember Dragon, but Kullen would reach Dimvein shortly after Natisse. He'd have more than time enough to track her down and retrieve the vial before the next blood moon.

But what if she didn't know that the blood moon was the *only* time when dragons accepted new *Bloodsworn*? She might attempt to push one of her comrades to form a bond, and the results could be disastrous. Not just for whatever insurrectionist of the Crimson Fang attempted it—including General Andros himself!— but anyone else in the vicinity. The destruction of the Imperial Commons had been the result of just such a mistake.

She wouldn't do that, he tried to tell himself. *She's smarter than that.*

She was smart, no doubt about it. Yet she was also driven, determined. Golgoth's magical fires had only amplified whatever burned within her soul. If the Crimson Fang was planning something, some new offensive against the Emperor's rule, she might have seen Kullen as the perfect tool to use to acquire a truly powerful weapon.

His mind raced, his heart twisting in his stomach as he wrestled with the latest turn of events. He *wanted* to believe he'd seen the truth of her, that in the short time he'd spent around her, he'd come to understand her, at least partly. That all of her drive truly *was* in the purpose of championing the poor and destitute of Dimvein. That she cared more about helping those who needed the Crimson Fang than seeking to destabilize the Imperial rule—like, he suspected, General Andros did.

But how else could he explain her fleeing so abruptly? Once she had the dragonblood vial in her possession, she no longer had need of him.

The more he considered it, the murkier the situation grew. He couldn't believe he'd been *so* wrong about her, but he had to admit it didn't look good. He'd have to track her down and ask her face-to-face. Come what may, he would know the truth.

Fortunately for him, he knew exactly where to find her. His reception would be far less cordial—doubtless, the Crimson Fang would be prepared for him this time—but if she *had* made off with the dragonblood vial intending to use it against the Empire, all their preparations would be in vain. He had no doubt he could take down the motley bunch he'd faced in her underground stronghold. His *true* challenge would be facing off against General Andros, the giant healer with the ham-sized fists, and Natisse herself, backed by Golgoth's power.

But that was a matter for *later*. First, Kullen had to return to the Palace and report the outcome of his mission to his monarch. He'd uncovered information of great import that Emperor Wymarc needed to be apprised of.

Chief among them was the matter of Red Claw. Magister Morvannou's story compounded his growing belief that Magister

Branthe *hadn't* been the one behind the moniker. The now-dead Branthe certainly would have been in a position to draw Magister Morvannou deeper into his debt with lucrative business dealings and lavish gifts. Yet it was highly unlikely he'd been alive when the vial arrived at Magister Morvannou's mansion—under the watchful eye of the traitorous Orken.

And there was simply no way Magister Branthe could've organized the auction on Pantagoya himself. Pantagorissa Torrine had a deep well of hatred and a long memory, and it was a matter of public knowledge that she'd sworn to kill Magister Branthe on sight after he'd had a former lover of hers—a Brendoni whose name Kullen couldn't remember—killed over some business dealings gone awry.

Finally, it was Magister Branthe's reaction to Kullen's mention that had shifted suspicions elsewhere. *"Soon,"* the dying man had ranted, *"a new power—a terrible, all-mighty power—will rise and, with it, bring about a new age the likes of which this world has never seen."* That sounded a great deal like the ravings of a man with a minor enough role that the grand conspiracy would survive his death. Certainly, he was an important pillar of whatever nefarious plan was underway, but there were others to continue it. Perhaps even one to whom he answered: Red Claw himself.

No, Kullen felt more and more certain that Red Claw was someone else, a figure commanding even Magisters and high-ranking Orken from the shadows. There were few alive today who wielded such power. Assidius immediately sprang to Kullen's mind, but Emperor Wymarc was convinced of his loyalty. Turoc, perhaps? The Orkenwatch Tuskigo commanded the most powerful cohesive martial force in Dimvein. The Imperial Scales answered to him—indirectly, of course—and even the Elite Scales treated Turoc with deference. For all his outward brutishness, Turoc had proven himself clever and cunning. A truly dangerous combination of brains and brawn.

Or perhaps there was another as-of-yet-unidentified person

pulling the strings. Brighter minds than Kullen's would have to figure it out. All he needed do was report his findings to the Emperor and accept his next mission, whatever it might be. When the time came that the Black Talon was sent to dispatch the true "Red Claw," Kullen would be ready.

Take us home, Umbris, Kullen said through his bond.

Without a response, Umbris did as asked. He took to the sky, moving upward until shrouded in the clouds and shadow. He moved with such speed it made their boat trip appear as slow as a slinkab worm just born from the river.

They flew high above Tauvasori, the town with which Kullen had chartered said boat. From such a height, it was nothing more than a dot on a golden-brown landscape. Further out, he could see miles of farmland, field after field of wheat and corn as far as the eye could see. Knowing it wouldn't be a scenic trip, Kullen decided it was a good time to rest—something he hadn't allowed himself to do very often as of late.

He leaned forward, laying his head against what might as well have been cold steel. Umbris gave a soft groan—a soothing sound as if to bid Kullen a good night's sleep. A sleep that took him before his mind had time to ponder what he would say to the Emperor upon their arrival in Dimvein.

Perhaps that was a good thing.

Kullen awoke as they passed through Thanagar's dome. The feeling was always so otherworldly, making his heart leap. Warmth spread through him like fire, and he popped up to a sitting position on Umbris's back.

"Are you rested?" came through Kullen's mind.

More so than I've been in long days, Kullen told him. *Straight to the Palace.*

The sun hadn't yet fully risen, but the obscuring shadows were fast receding. They had little time to spare before anyone below could gaze up to see Umbris's vast silhouette against the muted sun.

Kullen glanced back at the Embers below, still lost in the darkness of the region, hoping to see some sign of Natisse there. Alas, luck wasn't with him. He cursed himself for trusting someone who had never shown the slightest bit of loyalty to the crown. Now, he'd have to face the Emperor, knowing it was his lack of good judgment that allowed the dragonblood vial to fall from the hands of one enemy into the waiting arms of another.

Umbris slowed as the Palace neared. Thanagar, wrapped loosely around his favorite tower, perked his neck up. He slowly uncoiled himself, stretching as if his sleep had been disturbed. He let out a bellow—not quite a roar, but perhaps a yawn.

Umbris hovered just within the Palace walls, close enough for Thanagar to know their intent to land but with enough distance to pose no threat. The great White Dragon rose on beating wings and met them in the air.

"What business have you here?" Thanagar asked within Kullen's mind.

Kullen knew Umbris heard it as well, but it was his duty to respond.

Speaking telepathically to a dragon not his own was no easy task. He focused with great effort upon Thanagar before forming the words in his mind.

I have completed a task for the Emperor. I am returning with news.

"For your sake," Thanagar said, *"I hope it is more than news you have returned with."*

Kullen held his response, dipping his head slightly in deference to Dimvein's guardian.

Where can I find him? Kullen asked.

"He is in the Throne Room. I have let him know of your arrival."

Thank you, Kullen said, swallowing hard.

Thanagar swept aside, granting them passage and permission

to land in the Palace Garden. Umbris pressed forward. As they passed Thanagar, the White Dragon's presence sent a wave of nausea passing through Kullen. It was not often Kullen had need to return to the Emperor empty of hand and devoid of victory.

49
NATISSE

Any fear Natisse might have felt at flying through the air miles above Caernia had all but vanished by the time Dimvein's lights came into view on the southern horizon. Night had not yet broken, and Natisse felt oddly at peace alone in the dark with the cool wind on her face and the heat of Golgoth's body beneath her. Up here, the world was quiet and peaceful, with only the clouds and her thoughts for company.

For a few moments, she felt calm, both mind and soul. But it would all come to an end soon. She *had* to return to the Crimson Fang, and that meant coming face-to-face with Uncle Ronan. Her jaunt with Kullen had been a welcome distraction, but now she had to confront the truth of her reality—the lies she'd been told, the man she'd never truly known, and the burden of deciding what came next for her.

Everything had changed in the last weeks. Starting with Ammon's death, then Baruch's. Learning the truth of Uncle Ronan as General Andros. Bonding with Golgoth and learning to command the dragon and her fire magic. What did she want now? To pursue Uncle Ronan's missions—missions she wasn't certain she could truly believe in, not until she learned more about the man behind them—or to leave the Crimson Fang, do something else with her newfound powers? What that something might be, she had no idea. Until this moment, she'd never entertained the possibility that she could exist outside the Crimson Fang.

Countless possibilities lay before her—so many choices, she felt paralyzed by indecision. She needed to speak to someone she could trust—with Baruch gone and Uncle Ronan... well, no longer Uncle Ronan. That left just Jad. She owed him answers about her newfound abilities, too. After everything she'd learned from Kullen and Golgoth herself, she had a better understanding of the dragonblood magic. Enough, she hoped, that she could explain the matter. Knowing Jad, the simple words of advice he'd offer would provide her a clearer understanding of how she felt about her unique predicament. She always felt better after talking with him.

The sun had fully risen, but now, entering Dimvein, all she saw was murky darkness below. Husks of trees and creatures of the dark scurrying within them—the contrast between where she'd been, and home was jarring. Yet, still, she'd take the Embers or the One Hand District over that lawless floating island any day.

Thanagar's dome loomed in the distance. She'd just begun to pass over the homes of outsiders, those who chose to live in the wilds beyond. She wondered what it would be like to live within the Empire, yet so far removed from the Palace that Wymarc's heavy hand never came crashing down. Pay the taxes, stir up no trouble, and live a life free from the Orkenwatch and the worries of the city.

But no. That wasn't her. She thrived amongst the people, and the people needed Natisse and the Crimson Fang. *The old Crimson Fang,* she thought direly.

Finding a place to land was a difficulty Natisse hadn't considered. Kullen had spoken of properties within the city large enough to hold the dragon, but of their location, Natisse was unsure.

Golgoth, bring us to rest in the glade, she said through her mental bond.

Golgoth snorted and banked hard to the left. Natisse's stomach flipped as the Ember Dragon took them into a sharp dive downward and flipped again as she leveled out. Her giant paws touched down with a particular grace Natisse hadn't truly expected. There was no loud, thunderous slam. No dirt and dust kicked up. It was as if the dragon were as elegant as a galler bird come to find solace in the Emperor's garden.

She carefully slid off Golgoth's back, groaning as a sudden rush of blood sent pins-and-needles sensations through legs she hadn't realized were numb.

Thank you, she said.

"You are a worthy flight companion," Golgoth responded. *"It has been many years since I have had a human on my back. My gratitude is yours for making it a pleasant experience."*

Natisse smiled, but it quickly turned to a frown. *Magister Deckard?*

"Never once did we fly together," Golgoth admitted. *"His fear of falling, his lack of trust in me was evident. I was no more than a tool for him. A means to an end. It is why I chose you, Natisse, and why I am glad you chose me."*

As Natisse stared into her dragon's eyes, a sense of overwhelming sadness flooded her. How lonely must they be? For so many years, Natisse had painted them as the very picture of brutality when, in fact, they were nothing more than an extension of human hands.

Yes, Natisse choked out. She cleared her throat. *Yes, we will have to do this often.*

Golgoth dipped her head low, and Natisse stretched out her hand to touch the beast's nose. it was warm to the touch but not hot. They stood there a moment before Golgoth spoke once more.

"Do you have further need of me? I should rest."

"Oh, I…" Natisse started out loud.

"You need only grant me permission to return to the Fire Realm."

Concentrating harder than she probably needed to, Natisse issued the command, but nothing happened.

"Think of it less as an order and more as your blessing for my departure," Golgoth told her.

Natisse considered the words and realized she was, indeed, thinking more like Uncle Ronan than she cared to admit. When Uncle Ronan gave a command, the Crimson Fang dropped everything and obeyed. This was not like that. Golgoth was not truly Natisse's to control.

Golgoth, thank you for your companionship, she said through their bond. *Rest, and we shall see each other again soon.*

In an eruption of flame, the dragon disappeared, leaving no sign she'd been standing there in the grassy glade just seconds prior.

A sudden jolt coursed through Natisse. Though she didn't summon fire from her hands, she felt within her the ability to do so. She bit back a hiss of pain. The magical fire burning in her veins felt like a torrent of hot water rushing across scalded flesh. *Bloodsurging,* as she had on Pantagoya, left her nerves raw, ragged, and tender with every movement. The weight of fatigue dragged on her. She hadn't gotten nearly enough sleep to recover from her magical exertion, apparently.

First thing I do back in the Burrow is rest, she thought, then amended. *Scratch that, second thing. After talking with Jad.*

Jad would have some kind of soothing remedy to offer, perhaps even a concoction to help her fall asleep faster. The sooner she rested and recovered, the sooner she could deal with the tough choices that lay ahead.

The trek back to the One Hand District was long, but her legs could use the stretch after her flight. She avoided the Lumenators' light, the Orkenwatch patrols, and interaction with the seedier of Dimvein's citizens who chose to embrace the evening hours by traversing the back alleys and scaling to the occasional rooftop.

Glancing around to be sure no one was watching, she slipped into the underground tunnels through a grate in front of Golden Arms, a blacksmith who must've had a tremendous amount of pride in his work, judging by his prices. Splashing down in the mire, she had far less fear of gnashers or the other creatures that lurked there—not with Golgoth's fire at her command—but she'd risked her life enough for one day. From a basin tucked into a small alcove, she pulled one of Garron's torches. The man had them hidden all over the city, and for that, Natisse was glad.

She stared down at her hand. It appeared as it always had, but with a thought and a fair bit of concentration, a small, dancing flame erupted from her fingertip. She touched it to the torch, and light illuminated the tunnel.

Thank you, she told Golgoth as she extinguished the flame. By crediting the dragon, she felt as if she'd never allow herself to become consumed by the power. After all, it didn't belong to her. Not truly.

Memories of the previous night's events echoed through her mind. Chief among them was the sensations she'd felt facing that enormous eye burning within the cauldron. She'd never have believed it had she not witnessed it herself, yet there was no denying the experience. The Vandil priestesses could summon the attention of Abyssalia—and through them, the Pantagorissa might very well command the goddess.

After all the years she'd spent hating Emperor Wymarc and everything he represented, she knew the truth: Abyssalia was a threat far beyond anything Natisse or the Crimson Fang could hope to deal with. It fell to the monarch and all the power he wielded to protect the Empire against this danger whenever it came to their doorstep.

She felt certain Kullen would track her down—he'd want to reclaim the dragonblood vial they'd gone to Pantagoya to steal—but when, Natisse had no idea. And she had no desire to wait around to find out. Better she get word to the Emperor another way: through Uncle Ronan's "contact" in the Palace.

Even if that meant facing Uncle Ronan?

Natisse was too tired to navigate the complexities of their new dynamic, to figure out which fraction of what he'd told her was truth or lies. She could deal with that after a night of rest. But she *would* talk to Uncle Ronan if it meant he'd get word to the Emperor. Perhaps she could also get word to Kullen that she'd returned to Dimvein with the vial. That would likely bring him, and *he* could relay the information to the Emperor. He'd been there, after all. Even if he hadn't seen the enormous burning eye in the cauldron or felt the power humming through the room, he knew exactly what manner of enemy Pantagorissa Torrine had the potential to be. He'd treat the matter with the requisite urgency and relay her message to the Emperor personally.

The thought of seeing Kullen again brought an odd sense of lightness to her tired body. She'd actually *enjoyed* infiltrating the Pantagorissa's party beside him. She'd felt surprisingly safe with him at her back, knowing his skills and dragonblood magic would be turned in her defense should the need have arisen. He'd adopted the role of Yarlton the manservant adroitly. In a way, it reminded her of all the times she'd played Lady Dellacourt and enjoyed the company of Baruch's Baronet Charlati.

A pang of guilt stabbed her belly. She shouldn't be thinking—or feeling—this way about Kullen. He *wasn't* Baruch. He'd killed Baruch, a fact for which she ought to hate him. Yet he'd spoken the truth when he said that he'd just been "doing what needed to be done that night." There was no doubt in her mind that she, Baruch, or any of the Crimson Fang would have put a dagger through him and tossed him to the onyx sharks to secure their escape from the pleasure barge. "The mission above all," and he'd have been just one necessary casualty in their war against the corrupt and vile Magister Perech.

So how could she truly hate him? She might never forgive him for killing Baruch, but she could understand how necessity had led to such an outcome. Even her anger felt somehow hollow in the face of his sincere apology.

She brushed the thought aside. Now wasn't the time to be thinking on such matters, not when there was so much to do. First, she'd have to get Uncle Ronan to send word to the Palace. That meant confronting him, no matter how much she wished it were otherwise. Then she'd have a long talk with Jad, sound him out on how best to share the truth of her dragonblood powers with the rest of the Crimson Fang. After that, a bath, a meal, and a few hours of sleep to replenish her energy—both physical and magical. She could worry about the Black Talon later.

Besides, there was still the matter of the *Ghuklek* to be resolved. The Crimson Fang had freed them from Magister Branthe's slave pit, but they still had to be conveyed across the breadth of the Empire, through Horde lands, and back to the Riftwild. That would be no easy task, even with a small group, but there were over a hundred of the Orken-kin to transport.

Thinking about that, at least, gave her a semblance of clarity. It didn't matter that she'd only rescued them due to a mission given her by Uncle Ronan—she genuinely *cared* about seeing the freed *Ghuklek* home. It was the right thing to do. And so she would do it. To make sure her friends—Garron, Haston, Jad, Sparrow, Athelas, and all the others—survived to return home once it was done. Backed by Golgoth's power, she stood a better chance than ever of seeing this mission through to successful completion.

Her harried pace slowed to a meandering stagger.

What if Kullen didn't search her out immediately upon his return to Dimvein? What if he went first to the Palace and reported to the Emperor, gave a full account of their time together?

She'd left him behind, flown away from Pantagoya without a backward glance. She'd been unconscious, but he couldn't possibly know that. Had she been in his position—watching him flee with the very dragonblood vial they'd gone to steal—she would've instantly suspected him of treachery or betrayal. Would he perceive it in that light? Would he see it as her pilfering the vial and the power it conferred upon its owner for the Crimson Fang?

Natisse's heart raced despite the fact she was nearly standing still. That burning sensation within elevated, causing sweat to pool under her eyes, between her breasts, and slither down her spine.

She started up again, this time running through the tunnels, no concern for her weariness and fatigue. She needed to reach Uncle

Ronan, had to make certain he sent word to the Palace with all haste. She wanted to believe Kullen would honor his word to guard her secret—he had thus far, hadn't he?—but couldn't hang the safety of her comrades on the hope that he was as decent a man as he appeared to be or that he would reciprocate that trust in light of the appearance of Natisse's perfidiousness.

She hadn't wanted to tell Uncle Ronan about the dragonblood vial she'd taken off the Hudarians—no telling what he'd do with so much power in his hands—but she had no choice now.

Worry gnawed at her gut at the thought of his inquiries. He'd ask her how she got her hands on it and how she recognized it. He would know, somehow—he always did—about Golgoth. And once Uncle Ronan knew, there would be no way to keep it from the rest of the Crimson Fang.

In that moment, everything would change forever. She'd harbored so much hate over his lies. Was she not guilty of the same crime? Her comrades—not all, but some, certainly—would never look at her the same. She was no aristocrat, yet she wielded the power of a dragon just like the very Magisters the Crimson Fang had loathed.

Jad would understand. Garron, too, she hoped. As for the others…

She let out a slow sigh.

Whatever happens, happens.

Come what may, she had withheld the truth from them long enough. Only honesty in the truest form could save them from what might come.

She was close to the Burrow now. Just a couple more turns until she reached the bridge over the underground portion of the Talos River with the Burrow's large door on the other side. Her heart felt like the stampeding hooves of a thousand horses within her. Blood rushed to her head, leaving her dizzy.

But something felt… off. She couldn't quite put her finger on it —not until she came around a bend in the underground passages and her torchlight shone on a lumpy, misshapen heap in the middle of the tunnel. Natisse's eyes widened as she recognized the hairy head, powerful limbs, and six-foot-long stinger-tipped tail lying lifeless on the hard-packed earth. Foul-smelling black blood puddled around the creature, and the stink filled the corridor—it was what had alerted her.

She slowed, heart hammering.

A gnasher, dead? Here?

It took just one look at the creature to recognize what had killed it: a great slash had cut its skull in half, splattering its brains on the wall. Such a forceful blow and she could think of only one man capable of such destruction.

Jad…

Worry had fully gripped her now. With each new step, she feared she'd find another corpse, one belonging to Sparrow or Tobin.

Then she caught sight of the remnants of another gnasher. Smaller, this one, barely half the size of the one lying dead behind her. A youngling. And then another. Skulls crushed, bellies gutted, one with a puncture wound that transfixed its body from its arachnid forehead to just beneath its scorpion-like tail.

Blessed Ezrasil! What had happened here?

She followed the death, careful but hastened by the sight of bloody bootprints leading…

She turned the corner and saw the markings leading across the bridge and to the enormous entrance to the Burrow. The gate was thrown wide, and blood—not ichorous black, but a deep crimson—stained the ground around it.

50
KULLEN

Captain Angban was apparently expecting him—warned, most likely, by Emperor Wymarc through Thanagar—for the Elite Scale ordered his men to step aside and let Kullen enter the Emperor's Throne Room with only the barest hint of suspicion etched into his expression. Kullen fought the urge to flip the Captain a jaunty Blood Clan salute; no sense antagonizing the man at the moment when he was just doing his job.

From the first time he'd stepped into the Throne Room, Kullen had understood why Jarius had hated it so much. It was garishly opulent with the gilded columns, colorful paintings of Emperors past, and the stark white walls. Each step Kullen took echoed from wall to wall, slapping back and forth to create a disorienting effect upon his ears. Not the kind of place an assassin ever wanted to find himself.

Jarius had said the enormous chamber, with its grand gold-and-silver throne, reminded him of the crushing weight of responsibility that would one day rest upon his shoulders. Even the idea of having Hadassa on an equally opulent throne at his side—a notion she'd dismissed every time he raised it—had never sufficed to make him want the burden of rule.

At the moment, it was all but empty, save for the six people on the far side of the vast chamber. The line of citizens come to present their complaints, requests, and petitions to the monarch wouldn't be allowed in for another hour. Emperor Wymarc had evidently sent all his Elite Scales from the Throne Room; indeed, the only extraneous individuals were the two liveried Imperial attendants who stood a respectful five paces back from the wheeled chair sitting at the base of the grand dais.

Emperor Wymarc sat on the stairs, speaking in a quiet tone with the chairbound Prince Jaylen. At the monarch's side stood the mighty, hulking Turoc, black beard bristling and golden bands resplendent. Assidius had assumed his position seated behind Emperor Wymarc, and his were the first eyes to lift at Kullen's ingress. Sharp eyebrows raised toward his dark hairline and thin, chapped lips pursed in a look that could've been either contemplation or disdain.

Kullen glided noisily across the marble-tiled floor. He looked far from presentable, he knew, in his bloodstained black jacket, hair a mess, face screaming of lack of sleep. But he didn't care. Nor would the Emperor. The monarch had to maintain outward pretenses of decorum for his populace, but in private, he relaxed enough that he'd take no offense at Kullen's disheveled state.

"Sir." Turoc's deep voice boomed out in the Throne Room, and he descended a single step in a chorus of jangling armor as if taking up defensive positions between the ruler and the approaching Kullen.

Emperor Wymarc looked up from Prince Jaylen, and his gaze found Kullen. A flash of worry darted across his face, but he smoothed it over in a heartbeat and adopted a regal smile.

"Ahh, Kullen." The aging monarch reached out a hand to Turoc to help him stand. It was accomplished with a great creaking and popping of joints, but once upright, he again became the calm, commanding Emperor. "You have returned."

Had it been anyone else, Kullen might have snorted a derisive response. But he merely inclined his head respectfully and said, "I have, Majesty."

Assidius rose with far more ease than the Emperor, but his gaze never faltered from Kullen. His expression left no doubt as to his thoughts on Kullen's appearance—or perhaps his existence in general—but he wisely kept them to himself. After their last scolding by the Emperor, he had to know better than to show his disdain openly.

"Was your journey a success?" the Emperor asked, the lines on his face deepening.

Kullen cocked an eyebrow and glanced pointedly at Turoc and Assidius.

Emperor Wymarc nodded. "They know why I dispatched you to Pantagoya."

"As you say, Majesty." Kullen inclined his head. When he straightened, his expression tightened. "There were... complications, I'll admit, but yes, the journey was a success."

"Complications?" Assidius hissed in his sibilant voice. "Of what nature, precisely?"

Kullen was tempted to ignore the question, but he, too, had taken the Emperor's chiding to heart. "I discovered the identity of the person auctioning off the dragonblood vial, as instructed."

"Vial?" Turoc rumbled. "Only one?"

"Only one," Kullen said, keeping his voice carefully controlled. "And I was unable to learn which of our recently deceased Magisters it belonged to."

Emperor Wymarc's eyes narrowed. "By your tone, I take it you do not have it with you?"

Kullen winced at the scolding tone. "I do not, Majesty. My companion—"

"The woman from the garden?" Emperor Wymarc's eyebrows shot up. "*She* has it?"

"I believe she does," Kullen said. Or, perhaps better said, he *hoped* she did.

He detailed what had transpired: the Pantagorissa's revelry, the guests from all around Caernia being led up to the Dread Spire for the auction, and his interrogation of Magister Morvannou.

"Morvannou?" Emperor Wymarc glanced at Assidius. "Is he the one whose debts to the Imperial coffers were due to be collected next month?"

"One and the same, Divine Majesty." The Seneschal's lip curled upward in disdain. At least this time, it wasn't aimed at Kullen but at the dead aristocrat. "I had already begun preparing the encumbrances to seize control of all his assets, knowing full well he could not afford to pay. But if he succeeded in selling the vial…" He trailed off, turning to Kullen. "And you say there were both Blood Clan *and* Hudarians in attendance at this auction?"

Kullen nodded. "And they were the ones who snatched up the vial in the chaos and scarpered with it. While I was occupied with Magister Morvannou and the Pantagorissa, I dispatched my companion to retrieve it."

"So where is she?" Turoc demanded, the enormous muscles of his arms rippling. "This companion?"

"We were separated in the commotion," Kullen said truthfully. No sense lying about *this* part, at least. "But she managed to make it off Pantagoya, and I will be meeting up with her soon to retrieve the vial."

"Yet you are not *certain* she has the vial?" the Emperor asked, his eyes narrowing.

Kullen forced himself to remain calm. "I am not, Majesty. But she would not have abandoned the mission until its completion." That was the Crimson Fang motto, after all. *The mission above all*.

"And you trust her?" The Emperor took a step closer, his gaze piercing to Kullen's core. "You trust her with such power?"

"I do, Majesty." The words surprised him almost as much as they appeared to surprise Assidius.

Truth was, he knew far less of her than he might have liked. He didn't trust easily, but something about Natisse made him *want* to believe that she was the person he'd glimpsed that night in the Wild Grove Forest. That beneath the mask of the Crimson Fang, she was the driven, determined fire spark who wanted to help Embersfolk and the commoners of Dimvein. That it was empathy and genuine compassion that drove her, not rage and enmity for the wealthy aristocrats she and her fellow insurrectionists had assassinated.

"Interesting." Emperor Wymarc folded his arms across his chest and tapped a finger against his lips. "What do you think, Jaylen?" he asked, turning to where the Prince sat in the wheeled chair at his side.

The question seemed to take the young man by surprise, but he recovered quickly and drew himself up to his full seated height. "I believe that if Kullen is certain of her, then we have no reason to doubt him." A small smile played across his lips, brightening his pale face a fraction. "I am only here and alive today because of him. His actions have earned that much of Our trust… er, *my* trust, at least."

Emperor Wymarc nodded gravely to his grandson, but he was smiling as he turned back to Kullen. It seemed the Prince had passed some sort of test unknowingly.

"Very well," the Emperor said, dismissing the matter with a wave of his hand. "Your priority will be to rendezvous with your *friend*"—he added a bit of extra emphasis on the word, accompanied by a mischievous twinkle in his eyes—"and retrieve the vial. Once you have it, return it here, and we will ascertain which Magister it belonged to, and that will narrow down the parameters of *your* investigation." This last was said to Turoc.

"Yes, sir," the huge Orken said, bowing to the Emperor. "Simpler matter to find one who stole dragonblood vials it will be with this information."

"I take it your efforts thus far have come up empty?" Kullen asked, careful to keep any hint of scorn from his voice. The Tuskigo of the Orkenwatch was among the proudest of a race of proud creatures. He wouldn't respond well should he feel Kullen was mocking his failures.

"No suspects yet," Turoc said, baring his fangs in a frustrated growl. "Vials gone missing by magic, almost. No one sees nothing, hears nothing, knows nothing." He raised a huge fist and clenched it, as if crushing a fly in his palm. "But someone sees, hears, and knows. Orkenwatch will find out who."

Mention of the Orkenwatch brought to Kullen's mind what Magister Morvannou had told him. Could the Orkenwatch be "failing" to find anything because someone—Turoc himself, perhaps—preferred the truth remained hidden? Magister Branthe's conspirator could be stymying the investigation or burying anything uncovered by the lower-ranking Orken assigned to the matter. Kullen *might* have to get involved himself. With the Emperor's permission, certainly, and likely Assidius's assistance.

But first, he'd have to retrieve the vial from Natisse. Knowing the identity of the dragon to whom it belonged would point him in the direction to start investigating. More than that, he just needed to make certain she *had* recovered the vial—or lost it in the Astralkane Sea. If the *Tabudai* had escaped with it, the consequences would be dire.

Speaking of the *Tabudai*...

"I must say, Majesty, that the presence of the Blood Clan and Hudarians together on Pantagoya was a cause for concern." Kullen had given it some thought during the flight home from the floating pleasure island. "We stopped them from getting their hands on a dragonblood vial, but the fact that they were invited *at all* is worrisome. Though they were stripped of the majority of their wealth in the aftermath of their last attempted invasion, clearly they have amassed enough to make their bid at the auction appealing to the Pantagorissa."

The Pantagorissa's Palace had been filled with exorbitantly wealthy men and women from around Caernia, but Kullen had seen *only* serious players invited to the Dread Spire. The Blood Clan and Hudar Horde couldn't have gotten into that tower-top chamber without significant wealth at their command.

"In light of what we learned about Magister Issemar and Deckard's dealings with the Blood Clan," Kullen said, "I fear the

Empire's oldest enemies are marshaling their strength against us once more."

Emperor Wymarc's expression grew grave. "I, too, feared the same the moment you mentioned their presence." He looked to Assidius. "Have your assets among the pirates and Hudarians told you anything that might confirm this suspicion?"

"They have not." The Seneschal opened the ledger he always carried clutched in his spidery fingers, flipping through pages as if searching for something important. He stopped at a seemingly random page and read the neatly printed, infinitesimally small words written there—myriad letters, numbers, and symbols Kullen couldn't begin to understand. "I have received plenty of the usual reports of Blood Clan ship sightings in Empire-controlled waters—both by the Imperial navy, merchant vessels, and fishing craft—but none anywhere near the Hudarian shores. Yet if there is any conspiracy against Your Divine Majesty afoot, I will uncover it at all costs."

"Thank you, Seneschal." Emperor Wymarc nodded to Assidius. "I am confident in your abilities and cunning. Nevertheless, I will not allow Our Empire to be caught unawares." He looked to Turoc. "You already have a great deal on your plate, Tuskigo, but allow me to burden you with one more task."

"What you want me do, Sir?" Turoc asked, a proud grin spreading over his face. It looked more like he was baring his teeth in preparation for a battle.

"Speak with Commander Arithas of the Imperial Sappers Corps," Emperor Wymarc said, his tone somber. "Relay to him my request for a full assessment of Dimvein's sea-facing defenses. Tell him I'll be expecting it by tomorrow night."

"Yes, sir." Turoc bowed. "See it is done, I will."

"Your Grace?" Kullen said as a means of requesting his leave from the Throne Room.

"One more thing before you depart," the Emperor said. "What of the Pantagorissa?"

This part, Kullen had been hoping, could've been avoided. He'd practically started a war between the Island and the Caliphate of Fire. Should things escalate, it could cause trouble for the Empire. Though, the monarch had told Kullen to stay discreet at all costs.

When Kullen didn't immediately respond, Wymarc added, "Will we have any problems with her?"

Kullen shook his head, "No, sir. I threw her off the scent."

Assidius eyed him suspiciously but kept his comments silent.

"Excellent," Wymarc said, retaking his throne. "You three have work to do. Leave me with my grandson."

"Yes, sire," Assidius said, obsequiously bowing.

Turoc grunted and started down the stairs. Kullen watched him as he went, wondering if those golden bands represented anything more than his rank within the Orkenwatch. Was this Orken part of the solution or the traitorous problem?

51
NATISSE

Natisse's heart lurched, and a dagger of fear drove into her gut. She made a mad dash toward the open doorway, drawing her lashblade. Golgoth's fire blazed within her, a surging volcano of power that threatened to burst free of her chest, and it took all her self-control to fight it back down. She couldn't lose control again. Not when there were *her* people potentially in the path of the dragon's flames.

She vaulted the small puddle of blood filling the entrance, spotting the discarded crossbow bolt with its crimson-stained head lying nearby. One of the Burrow's traps had been sprung and taken down an enemy. But just one out of Ezrasil knew how many. Natisse strained her ears but could hear no sign of fighting, no shouts or clashing steel or racing footsteps beyond her own. Everything within the Burrow was silent and dark.

Halfway between the entrance and the common room, Natisse spotted a familiar sword lying on the ground. L'yo's favorite broad-bladed Catallon shortsword. Blood stained its sharp edge and upswept point. Yet there was no sign of the man himself that Natisse could see.

A short distance away, Nalkin's twin belt knives were embedded in a small round buckler, the daggers buried a finger's depth into the wood. Strands of dark brown hair stuck to the spot of blood on the rounded tip of the buckler's steel boss. Nalkin's longsword was nowhere in sight, but Natisse knew the woman wouldn't have parted with her favorite blade without a fight.

The common room was dark, still, and quiet, nothing remaining of the lamps that always burned within save shards of shattered glass and a glossy pool of oil sloshed across the floor. By the light of Natisse's torch, she could see the wreckage of the room where she and the Crimson Fang had shared countless meals. The wooden benches were splintered, the tables cracked, crockery and dishes abandoned with the food half-eaten. The door to the kitchen hung on one hinge, but the fire in the oven had guttered to lifeless gray ash.

Natisse wanted to call out, to shout for her comrades, but dared not. She had no idea what lurked in the darkness deeper in the Burrow. Who had done this? Had the Imperial Scales or Orkenwatch tracked the Crimson Fang to their lair? Magister Branthe's guards? The Elite Scales? Some other enemy she didn't yet know? She might've laid the blame at Pantagorissa Torrine's feet, only it was impossible. Natisse herself had only just returned after a direct flight from Pantagoya, but unless the powerful leader of Pantagoya had some means of traveling faster than Golgoth, there was no way the woman could've done this.

Who, then?

Natisse raced away from the empty common room and pitch-black kitchen, running toward the intersection of corridors a short distance away. Her stomach bottomed out at the sight of the Training Room, visible through the shattered double doors. The *Ghuklek* were gone, as was every single weapon and armament that had been resting neatly racked against the wall. Only the straw-filled dummies and the hanging heavy-bags remained.

Natisse cut sharply in the opposite direction and down the corridor leading past all of the Crimson Fang's quarters. The first door—the room Tobin and Athelas shared—hung ajar, and the light of Natisse's torch shone on scattered clothing, overturned cots, and shattered furniture. The door opposite was shut, but Natisse shoved it open without hesitation. Nalkin and L'yo's room had been overturned as well, but the wooden table, two chairs, and frame of the extra-large bed they shared remained undamaged, though a blade had slashed apart the straw-tick mattress and the stuffing was ripped out by whoever had searched it.

Room after room showed the same scene of chaos and destruction. Blood was smeared across the wooden frame of Haston's door. Garron's longsword was buried halfway into Leroshavé's door, evidence that he'd at least *tried* to stave off the attackers. Sparrow's room, across from Jad's room-turned-infirmary, was in a similar state as Nalkin and L'yo's, and half of the daggers the young girl kept hanging on a bandolier next to her door were missing.

Someone—likely Sparrow—had attempted to clean off the stains left by Garron and Prince Jaylen's blood, but the bucket of red-tinged water with its scrub brush had been kicked over in the same struggle that destroyed the room's two cots. Natisse splashed her way through the puddle and charged through the open doorway to her room. It, too, had been ransacked.

That left just *one* room to search: Baruch and Ammon's, or, more recently, Jad's.

It had been difficult to spot through the mess, but as Natisse slowly inched her way down the hall, she spotted the trail of blood again. With Jad's room being at the end of the hall, the last door on the left, there was precious little to distract from that crimson stream.

Please, she prayed, desperation swirling within her. *Please, let him be—*

A quiet groan reached her as she hastened toward the door. Using her shoulder, she didn't even stop, just burst into the room, torch held high, and her heart somersaulted in her chest as she spotted the figure lying on the floor. Not the hulking, powerful frame she'd hoped to see. No, this was a tall, whip-thin man wearing the plain clothes of a manservant or scribe.

"Dalash?" She all but shouted the name. She threw herself to one knee beside the fallen man and turned him over. A gasp escaped her lips as she caught sight of the wetly glistening mess of blackened scarlet on his belly. Hideous loops of pallid, pink intestinal coils slipped from a gaping wound across his abdomen. Though his organs appeared intact, a vast plash of blood spread out from where he lay, reaching nearly to the bed that had once belonged to Ammon at the far end of the room.

Natisse recoiled. "By Ezrasil!"

"Na... tisse?" Dalash's voice was weak—so terribly weak—his face utterly devoid of color. "Is...that... you?"

"It's me, Dalash!" Natisse regained control of herself and, sheathing her lashblade, snatched up a blood-soaked cloth—the remnants of one of Jad's shirts—that had fallen away from Dalash's wound.

Judging by the trail of blood, he had dragged himself all the way from his room, one door over, into Jad's. Perhaps to search for the healing remedies Jad always kept handy or merely to escape his attackers. Yet the fact that he was alive at all staggered Natisse. Dalash had never been a strong man, but somehow he'd clung to life for...how long? Hours, at least, based on the freshness of the stains splattering the Burrow.

"Na...tisse!" Dalash repeated the word and reached for her with one sanguine hand. "You... you..."

"What happened, Dalash?" Natisse demanded, clutching Dalash's attenuated fingers in hers.

"I... came... back," Dalash said, each word clearly a struggle. "Came... to help. Extri... cated... myself... from Perech... house. But... I came... to..." His strength failed him, but he managed to sweep a hand toward the wreckage of the room.

"Who did this?" Natisse pressed. "Who attacked us?"

"Orken... attacked." Dalash swallowed, pain creasing his face. A faint whimper escaped his lips, and tears streamed down his eyes. "Took... the others. Sniffer... led them here... stabbed me... left me… for… dead." This last was spoken in a voice so faint Natisse could barely hear him.

"But you're not dead!" Natisse spoke with all the strength and conviction she could muster. She gripped his hand tight. "You survived this long. Your wound isn't too bad. You've just got to hang on a little longer. Jad's got supplies, potions, elixirs, bandages. We can keep you alive. Patch you up and—"

"No." The word escaped Dalash's lips in a ghost of a breath. Looking frailer than ever, he fixed his cloudy eyes on her face. "Just… stayed… long enough… to tell you…" He swallowed, coughed, and swallowed again. "Tell… you…"

His eyes stared forward, aimed at Natisse, but she knew they no longer saw her face. His mouth hung limply in the act of speaking, and the hand that worked so hard to keep his insides where they belonged fell inert to his side.

Natisse sat alone in the silence, staring down numbly at Dalash's body. For that was all he was now. The man she'd known for years—who had taught her to read and count sums and chart a map—was gone. Slaughtered by the Orkenwatch. Butchered like cattle and left to die in darkness.

Her mind wandered back to the day she'd met the man. He'd sat behind his desk, face buried in some ledger or journal. He hadn't even looked up when she entered. She could still remember the sound his feathered pen made as it scratched against parchment.

"Natisse, is it?" he'd said, eyes on his writing.

She'd only been a child at the time. Perhaps ten, eleven summers old. She'd nodded, but even at that age, realized the man wasn't looking and said, "Yes, sir."

He'd placed his writing tool down gently, then folded his hands and looked up at her. "There are three kinds of people in the world, Natisse. Do you know what they are?"

Natisse had wracked her brain, hoping to be able to provide the right answer to his question, something to impress this man who was to be her maths and words teacher. She pondered saying something witty like "The kings, the nobles, and the rest of us," but he gave the answer before she could respond.

"Those who can count, and those who can't."

She'd stared, puzzled for long seconds before Dalash smiled.

That smile. She'd never see it again.

Inside, rage was boiling like a pot left over an open flame. Flame. For so long, it had been her enemy. But now…

She threw her head back in a primal roar that came from somewhere so deep, she wasn't sure she'd ever tapped into it before. Fire burst forth, not just from her hands but from her chest, her mouth, and even her eyes. The entire room glowed with red-hot flames. Steam rose as her tears crossed through them, the pressure built within her chest. It became harder and harder to breathe. She felt a small bit of comfort within and recognized it as Golgoth.

This went on for Ezrasil knew how long, until finally, she had nothing left to give. Despair, fatigue, and exhaustion won out, and the flames receded, leaving her alone in a room forever blackened by her rage.

52
KULLEN

Kullen remained silent until the grand doors to the Throne Room closed behind Turoc and Assidius. He couldn't risk the Tuskigo overhearing the *other* matter he needed to discuss with the Emperor.

But as he turned back to face the monarch, he found himself confronted by Prince Jaylen. The young man could barely stand, and he leaned heavily on his grandfather, yet his face shone with a pride to match Turoc's as he took a shaky step forward and thrust a hand out to Kullen.

"I never did thank you properly for saving my life," the Prince said, his voice oddly regal despite the pallor of his exhaustion-lined face. "I know Grandfather sent you to find me. But you risked your life for mine, orders or no. I will not soon forget it, Kullen."

Kullen took the young man's hand and gripped it firmly. It reminded him so much of Jarius's—not the regal, princely man who'd fathered a son and stood to inherit the Karmian Empire, but the gangly, brash youth who Kullen had saved on the streets of Dimvein. Given how Jarius had turned out, one had to believe there was hope for Jaylen. This act of expressing gratitude, unnecessary as it was, certainly proved a step in the right direction.

"If it's all the same to you," Kullen said, letting a wry grin play across his face, "I'd rather not have to do it *too* many more times before you take the throne. Much easier to guard your back with a cohort of Elite Scales to do the real work, you understand."

Jaylen laughed. "Understood." He shook Kullen's hand, strength in his grip, but that seemed to drain the last of his stamina. He sagged back into his wheeled chair as if his legs could no longer support him.

Emperor Wymarc snapped his fingers at the two attendants standing near. "See the Prince to his chambers."

The two liveried men hurried forward—one to grasp the handles of Jaylen's wheeled chair, the other with a blanket to drape over the Prince's shoulders as if he was a child taken ill with fever. Jaylen was too weak to protest, however. He merely nodded once and gave in to the attendants' ministrations. Emperor Wymarc squeezed his grandson's shoulder with visible concern and affection before he was wheeled away.

"How is he healing?" Kullen asked the Emperor without taking his eyes off the departing Prince.

"Slowly," Emperor Wymarc said, concern in his voice. "Chiefly because he refuses to remain abed. Sound like someone else you knew?"

Kullen chuckled. "His father hated inactivity even more than he hated Scholar Ryneck's theology lessons. Said it felt like he was dying a slow death, having to rest when there was so much to do."

"I wish I could say his son was a better patient, but my chirurgeons have already petitioned a half-dozen times for permission to chain him to his bed." Emperor Wymarc shook his head wryly. "But he will heal. Thanks to you."

Kullen shrugged and opened his mouth to say something dismissive.

But Emperor Wymarc spoke before he could. "You, and your friend, Natisse."

The words, coupled with the sharp look in Emperor Wymarc's

steel-gray eyes, twisted a dagger in Kullen's belly. What did he know? What had Jaylen told him? The Prince had agreed to keep the matter of the Crimson Fang a secret, but how well could he hide the truth from his grandfather, the Emperor?

"How much do you know?" Kullen decided to get the question out in the open.

"Not nearly enough." Emperor Wymarc's jaw muscles clenched, the lines at the corners of his eyes deepening. "Jaylen says he cannot tell me more than he already has—that Natisse was instrumental in helping you keep him alive and returning him to safety. That I 'trust you to handle situations like this.' Those were your words, he said."

Kullen nodded. "They are. And I believe you do, or am I wrong?" He arched an eyebrow.

A scowl tugged the Emperor's lips downward. "If you have not told me, clearly you have your reasons. But I must know: does this Natisse pose a threat? Especially now that you believe she is in possession of the dragonblood vial?"

Kullen considered his answer carefully. In truth, he didn't know *what* to think about Natisse. They'd been working well together right up to the moment she took off on Golgoth and left him behind. If she'd gotten it in her head that the vial she'd—*hopefully*—recovered could serve the Crimson Fang's mission in a greater capacity than gaining control over her own *bloodsurging* by working with him, things could turn ugly in a hurry.

But he wanted to believe there was another explanation. He hoped there had been other mitigating factors leading to her disappearance into the clouds with the vial. And he fully intended to track her down and put the question to her.

"She won't be an issue, Majesty," Kullen said. One way or another. Either she handed over the vial willingly, or he took it—and Golgoth's vial—from her and put an end to the threat of the Crimson Fang.

"Good." Emperor Wymarc's expression smoothed, and his

shoulders relaxed in visible relief. "Now, what else have you *not* told me? Something to do with the Orken traitor, I take it, else you would have brought it up in front of Turoc."

Kullen stared at the Emperor. The man was too damned insightful for his own good sometimes. Or maybe just for Kullen's good. He relayed everything he'd learned from Magister Morvannou: the delivery of the dragonblood vial with the note signed "Red Claw," the Orken watching the mansion, and the silver disc the dead aristocrat had been given in case of difficulties. He drew out the token and held it up for the Emperor's assessment.

"This is not the only one of its kind I've run across," Kullen said, his tone grave. From his pocket, he produced the disc he'd taken from Magister Branthe. "I found its match in the possession of Magister Branthe."

The Emperor's eyes widened a fraction. *"Kharag?"* He, too, knew what the coin-like objects were used for. "There is no doubt, then, that one of the goldbands is in league with our enemies. But which?"

"That I don't know, Majesty." Kullen pocketed the trinkets. "Yet. I intend to find out as soon as bloody possible."

"How, exactly?" Emperor Wymarc's eyes narrowed. "Assidius's investigation has turned up nothing implicating Turoc, Ketsneer Bareg, or any of the Arbiters. Admittedly, we have only had confirmation of such treachery for a few days, and Assidius must tread lightly in this matter. But unless you intend to talk your way into Tuskthorne Keep and search the goldbands' rooms for yourself…" He trailed off, his expression falling. *"No!"*

Kullen shrugged. "Can you think of any means more efficient for identifying the traitor?"

"I certainly can't think of any more efficient way of getting yourself killed!" Emperor Wymarc grimaced. He rested a hand against his throne as if he'd fall otherwise. "You said it yourself, at least one Sniffer has your scent, and the moment Turoc realizes you entered his chambers—"

"He won't, Majesty." Kullen tried to sound far more confident than he felt. The idea hadn't had time to take root and blossom into a full-blown plan, but in truth, it was the best way he could think of to *quickly* uncover this threat. There would be no need to worry about Blood Clan or Hudarians if Red Claw's plans to weaken the Emperor and destabilize the Empire succeeded.

He drew out the *Kharag* he'd taken from Magister Morvannou. "This gets me into Tuskthorne Keep. With a bit of alchemical help, I'll be in and out without anyone—not Turoc or his Sniffers— knowing *I* was there."

The Emperor looked ready to protest, but Kullen drove on.

"We have to know for certain, Your Grace." His voice was firm, hard as iron. "Even if we don't take action against the traitor, knowing *who* they are is the first step in unmasking Red Claw and putting an end to this conspiracy before it does serious damage to the Empire. Risky as it may be, this may very well be the best— and certainly the quickest—path to the truth."

"I don't like it." Emperor Wymarc spoke in a reluctant tone, yet after a moment, he nodded. "But you're not wrong." He stroked his long, white beard in thought. "You're sure you can pull it off unnoticed?"

"No," Kullen said, shaking his head, "but I've still got to damned well try. This is what the Black Talon is for, after all."

Frown lines creased the Emperor's forehead. He turned and climbed the dais to his throne, sat, and stared hesitantly at Kullen.

"So be it," he said finally, letting out a long breath. "Do what you must to find this traitor among the goldbands." He looked up to the ceiling. "May Ezrasil's justice guide you to the truth and Cliessa's fortune shine brightly upon you."

"She hasn't done thusly so far," Kullen jested. "I must've fallen out of her favor."

The words had the intended effect, bringing out a slight chuckle from the Emperor. "Then may she at least bring you safely out of there alive and unharmed."

"Your Grace," Kullen said, bowing, then turning to leave the Throne Room.

Alive and unharmed sounded like a fantasy. He'd settle for alive and with answers.

53
Natisse

Brilliant tongues of gold and crimson fire consumed Natisse's dreams. She heard herself screaming, felt the searing agony as the flames washed over her. She could do nothing but watch in helpless horror as the blaze consumed her parents. The man with hair a fierce red to match hers, the woman whose features bore such a strong resemblance to Natisse.

But their faces vanished, replaced by *others*. Jad, with his blocky features and broad-shouldered frame, tried to shield the petite Sparrow. Haston and Athelas, Nalkin and L'yo, Tobin and Leroshavé. Garron, sword held in his one good hand and face set bravely as he battled the flames in vain. Uncle Ronan, wielding his Lumenator magic to no avail against the searing heat.

They died again and again, and Natisse was powerless to stop it.

She awoke screaming, clawing at the air with empty hands. Darkness hung thick about her, and for long moments, she could not remember where she was or what had happened. All she knew was the laboring pulses of her heart and the savage ache permeating every fiber of her being.

Panic clutched at her throat and constricted her lungs. She scrabbled at her bed, trying to drag away the bedsheets choking the life from her lungs. But she wasn't in her bed—or *any* bed. Only cold, hard-packed earth greeted her fingers. Until she felt something softer, waxy, cold as ice.

Then she remembered. She jerked back, sucking in a hissing breath, recoiling from the corpse. Dalash's corpse. Left there to die by the Orkenwatch who had raided the Burrow. She didn't know how they'd found out the way to the underground stronghold—her fault or that of one of her comrades—but at the moment, it didn't matter. All Natisse cared about was striking back and striking back hard.

No, she told herself, fighting to regain control. It couldn't be about vengeance. Ezrasil knew how badly she ached to unleash Golgoth's fire and destroy Tuskthorne Keep and every one of the bastards who'd attacked her home and hurt her friends. But she couldn't. Golgoth wouldn't let her, she knew without question. And that wasn't who *she* was either.

She drew in a deep breath, then another. Her heartbeat slowed, the tremor in her hands subsided, and she could once again think clearly.

The Orken had taken the Crimson Fang—and, possibly, the *Ghuklek* who had been holed up in the Burrow's training room. But not *all* of the Crimson Fang. Natisse had escaped by sheer virtue of being elsewhere at the time. That meant there was a chance she could find and free her people.

No easy feat, she knew. She had no idea where the Orken held their captives—Tuskthorne Keep to be subjected to the Arbiters' cruelty like Ammon or the cells in the Emperor's Palace—but either way, it would be bloody near impossible to infiltrate either to free her people undetected.

Impossible or no, she had to try. She couldn't allow Jad, Sparrow, Garron, and all the others to end up like Ammon, tortured to death in the Court of Justice as a public spectacle. Back then, she'd had nothing but her lashblade, crossbow, and companions of the Crimson Fang for support. Now, she had a dragon, the Queen of the Ember Dragons herself. Golgoth might not permit her to wield the fire magic with the intent to destroy, but Natisse doubted the dragon would let her come to harm—or die—when the power she wielded could save both her and her people.

Natisse turned her attention inward, feeling the knot of power swirling like a whirlpool of lava in the pit of her belly. In her rage, she'd drawn too much power, overexerted herself to the point of passing out. Her nerves felt even more raw and ragged than before. But Natisse *could* access the power. It still existed within her, ready to be summoned through her bond with Golgoth. That gave her a weapon far more potent than the entire Crimson Fang —even Uncle Ronan's Lumenator magic.

Gritting her teeth against the inevitable pain, she called a flame into existence. A spark sprang to life in the palm of her upturned hand, barely more than a wisp of crimson-and-gold fire, enough to light up the room. The room that had belonged to Baruch and Ammon, then Jad, and now served as Dalash's final resting place.

She stared down at the slim man lying cold and silent on the earthen floor. The involuntary burst of fire had singed his clothes and hair but left his skin untouched. He was a mess of blood and pain, his face contorted by the agony of the wounds that killed him. She couldn't leave him like this.

With effort, Natisse rose to her feet, every muscle sore and heavy. She had no idea how long she'd been unconscious, but it was far from enough to replenish her strength after the exertions of the previous day. She couldn't afford to rest, however. Exhausted as she was, she had no hope of sleeping while her friends were held captive. She had dedicated her life to freeing the enslaved; now, she had to put all of her training to use liberating the people who mattered most to her.

But first, there was one thing she *had* to do. She knelt and slid her arms beneath Dalash's body. Though slim, he stood nearly a head taller than she, and his body was limp and oddly heavy in death. She struggled to lift him from the ground. His clothes were torn and burned, his body crusted with dried blood, and his limbs hung loose. It took her far too long to wrestle his lifeless form onto her shoulders. When she stood, her legs trembled with fatigue, and her back threatened to bow under the weight.

Golgoth! she called to the dragon through their bond, desperate. *I need your strength.*

"It is yours," came the Ember Dragon's answer.

A rushing torrent of life pounded through her veins, burning with the heat of Golgoth's flames. She had to be careful to limit the flow for fear of inflicting worse damage, but she summoned enough to stiffen her spine and bolster her resolve as she carried Dalash's body through the Burrow's dark, silent corridors. She was alone save for the tiny spark of fire she cradled in the palm of her right hand, her left clutching Dalash's body on her shoulders.

The quiet was eerie. Even on the laziest of days, Jad could be heard tinkering, or Athelas's laugh would echo down the halls. But now? Nothing. Not even the squeak of a titmouse.

She carried her friend out the Burrow's main entrance and onto the narrow path alongside the Talos River. There, she stopped and lowered Dalash into her arms. She wanted to speak, to say a few final words for the man, but hadn't the strength to hold him up. So she merely released him to the waiting arms of gravity. He fell away and vanished from her sight. Long seconds of silence passed, then there was a *splash* from far below.

Images sprang to Natisse's mind, memories of when she and the others of the Crimson Fang had stood in this same spot and bid farewell to Ammon. Though they'd had no body to relinquish to the river, it hadn't mattered. They had merely wanted to honor their fallen comrade.

There had been no ceremony for Baruch—they'd been far too busy in the days since—but Natisse had already said her goodbyes the day she cleaned out his and Ammon's room. Now, she alone would honor Dalash until such a time as the rest of the Crimson Fang could join her here.

Please, let him be the last, she prayed, though to which god or goddess, she didn't know. Nor did she care. She cared only that *one* of the deities listened and answered her supplication. *I can't mourn anyone else. I've already lost too much.*

She stood there, eyes closed, listening to the sound of the river rushing far beneath her. The noise was oddly soothing, calming her racing mind and slowing her heart.

The situation was grim, certainly, but not entirely hopeless. Not as long as she was free, had breath in her lungs, and Golgoth's magical fire in her belly. The Orkenwatch attack had to have happened during the night, perhaps as early as the previous evening. That was time enough to get the new captives into cells, but they might not yet have begun the questioning and torture. That meant Natisse had a chance to get them out *before* they suffered worse—or died at the Arbiters' hands.

She wouldn't do it alone. She had Golgoth for backup. Every one of the Crimson Fang had been prepared for what to do in the eventuality of capture and torture. They would be attempting to free themselves, she knew with utter certainty. All she had to do was get to them and lend them her power—*Golgoth's* power—to break free.

And *if* it came to it, she would call on Kullen for help. He owed her. After all, *she'd* been the one to come away from Pantagoya with the dragonblood vial. She could trade it for his assistance or use it as a bargaining chip to negotiate with the Emperor for their release.

She dipped a hand into the innermost pocket of the underdress Kullen had purchased specially crafted for her in Tauvasori, and relief flooded her at the smooth, cold touch of glass beneath her fingertips. Just to be certain, she drew out the vial and held it up to inspect it in the light of her magical spark. It appeared identical to Golgoth's vial in every way she could tell. It emanated no power, gave no indication that it was anything more than what it appeared to be. To the vast majority of the world who had no idea what it was, the vial could pass for any alchemical potion or even a mere piece of jewelry.

But Natisse knew the power it represented. People had died

for this. At her hands, in truth. She had no idea which Magister the vial had belonged to before it ended up in Magister Morvannou's possession, but if it had come from one of her victims, then she was partly to blame for it nearly falling into the hands of the Empire's enemies. Now, it was her duty to keep it safe until she could return it to Kullen—and, in so doing, use it to secure the release of her friends.

She felt oddly secure in the knowledge that Kullen *wouldn't* abuse its power—he'd already proven himself trustworthy and judicious in his use of Umbris's magic, even against his enemies—but until she could get it to him, she had to make certain no one else could find it.

Though every fiber of her being protested, she forced herself to return to the bloody ruins of the Burrow. The signs of violence and destruction pained her, reminded her that it was *her* friends who had bled and died, but she strode resolutely on past the chaos. All the way back up the hall to step over the puddle of Dalash's blood and enter Baruch and Ammon's old room.

She knelt beside the bed that had once belonged to Baruch, then felt along the wall until she found the loose stone she sought. It pulled free with only a little effort, revealing the hidey-hole Baruch had carved out years earlier. Natisse reached inside and was rewarded by…

A ring?

She lifted it from its place and inspected it closer. The gold band gleamed as if it had been bought only recently, a crimson jewel rested between upturned prongs. She pondered over its meaning only a short while, unable to bring herself to think of the truth of what such a ring would imply. In her mind, she told herself it was nothing more than something Baruch had stolen and kept for himself.

Despite her internal resolution, a tear formed unbidden. She wiped it away quickly and returned the item to its secret place. There, it would remain Baruch's little secret forever. Or until such a day came when Natisse could bring herself to consider the real possibility that Baruch's love for her was greater than even she had imagined.

Beside it, she slipped the dragonblood vial. No one would know it was there, and it would remain safe until such a time as she could return for it.

With that done, Natisse sucked in a deep breath. It was time to find the Crimson Fang, but she couldn't just walk up to the Palace doors and ask to see them. Besides, she wasn't even convinced that's where they would be. Tuskthorne Keep seemed more likely.

She had no time to waste searching. But she knew someone who might know. Once she had that information, she could better know how to free them. She was only certain of one thing: she *would* free them. She was their only chance.

54
KULLEN

Kullen decided he would wait until nightfall to approach Tuskthorne Keep. After leaving the Palace through the hidden sewer tunnels, he'd gone straight to the Apple Cart Mead Hall for a quick meal, drink, and change of clothing in his room. There, too, he collected the alchemical supplies he'd need for the task ahead.

He forced himself to sleep, though not without difficulty. He couldn't stop playing over every moment he'd spent with Natisse, reliving every conversation they'd had. Nothing leaped out at him. He'd missed no signs of deceit, and she'd given no indication that she intended anything other than precisely what she'd said.

So where had it gone wrong? Had she been planning to flee with the vial, or had it merely been fortuitous happenstance that led to it being delivered into her possession?

He wanted to know—by Ezrasil, he was *dying* to track her down in the Crimson Fang's underground lair and find out for himself, face-to-face—but answers would have to wait. He could put it off until after he identified the traitorous Orken. A high-ranking Orkenwatch commander plotting against the Emperor was a far greater threat than the Crimson Fang could ever be. No telling how deep or widespread the conspiracy ran, how far into the city's Orken protectors the mutinous cancer spread, how many were, even now, working to undermine Imperial rule from within.

And so, Kullen fought to push thoughts of Natisse from his mind. If she'd deceived him, he'd deal with that in due time. But he'd needed to rest and recover his strength—both physical and magical. He could very well find himself in need of his *bloodsurging* to escape Tuskthorne Keep undetected.

He'd managed to snatch a few hours of fitful sleep and awoke feeling only marginally less fatigued. But it would have to be enough, he told himself as he dressed in the elaborate aristocratic outfit he'd chosen for the job. He left his head unadorned, shoulder-length hair pulled back into a tail behind his head. He even decided a shave was in order, but nothing too jarring. He dragged the blade around the edges, a mere cleanup. Upon his back, he donned a long coat, split in the rear, and falling to his knees. It was striking enough for the nobles to appreciate but not garish enough to call attention to him. Black—as was his custom—with silver filigree swirls only noticeable in the right light. His vest matched, though instead of black, it leaned toward the darkest of blues. Midnight blue, he believed the tailor had called it.

As he pulled on his shin-high boots, he cursed the aristocracy for their fashion, wobbling a bit in the heels before taking up his silver cane to do the work before him.

Night had begun to descend in earnest over Dimvein when Kullen entered The Stacks and turned up Martial Row, the broad avenue pouring directly into Tuskthorne Keep's single gate on the fortress's southern side. The ivory tusks bristling from its enormous tower seemed to glow in the last glimmers of daylight, vanishing over the eastern horizon—a stark contrast to the black stone that grew ever darker in the settling gloom.

Lamplighters set to work illuminating Martial Row, and shopkeepers and merchants lit lanterns to drive back the encroaching shadows. A pair of Lumenators marched at a stately, sedate pace up and down the broad avenue, balls of warm blue light hovering above their hands and adding to the glow brightening the darkness.

Kullen instinctively shied away from that light. The memory of what had happened when Umbris's shadow magic collided with the Lumenators' glow remained smoldering in his mind. Indeed, just the sight of that azure illumination brought back the ghostly remnants of a chill that had seeped into his bones as the claws and talons of the hideous, phantasmal creatures of the Shadow Realm dragged him ever deeper into the void.

He growled a low curse within his throat, aimed not at the Lumenators but himself. In everything that had transpired, he'd forgotten to ask the Emperor about the strange magic that brightened Dimvein—and which had nearly condemned him to a lightless existence in the Shadow Realm.

What else had he forgotten? He caught sight of a child-sized figure wrapped in leper's bandages racing up the street and was reminded of his conversation with Vlatud. Specifically, the Trenta's mention of "Wymarc-sire be wantink to know about little Orken-kin."

Then there was the matter of the Refuge—why Magister Branthe had wanted it so badly he was willing to offer exorbitant prices to buy it just to burn it to the ground when denied and kill everyone within. There was something important there, but Kullen had been too focused on his *other* tasks to remember to speak of the matter with the Emperor.

He resolved to address that failing at the first possible opportunity. When he returned to the Palace with the identity of the Orken traitor, he would raise his questions with the Emperor. As for the matter of Natisse…

He sighed. His reception among the Crimson Fang had been far from cordial last time. Whether or not they intended to use the dragonblood vial, he doubted they'd be any more welcoming on his next visit.

As Kullen drew within sight of Tuskthorne Keep, he straightened his spine, raised his head, and lifted his nose and chin into the air. He'd had plenty of practice mimicking the snooty manner with which all aristocrats comported themselves—as if they were somehow above the "riffraff," worthy of respect and fawning. For the task ahead, it was the perfect façade to adopt.

He marched toward the closed bone portcullis with a crisp, prim step, his heeled shoes and silver-tipped cane *click-clacking* on the cobblestones in front of the enormous black-walled Keep.

"I say, there, in the tower!" he called out in the most demanding tone he could muster. "Open up, says I!"

A sallow-skinned Orken peered over the crenellations above, staring down at him with bared fangs and slitted eyes.

Kullen banged his cane against the stones. "Open up at once!"

"Name?" growled the Orken. Fortunately for Kullen, it wasn't Garg, the one who'd been guarding the gate upon his last visit. He didn't recognize the Orken—and, it was immediately clear, the Orken didn't recognize him.

Precisely as he'd intended.

Kullen drew himself up to his full height and spoke in a curt tone. "Deonidas Morvannou, Magister of Dimvein." He added an offended edge to his voice, as if outraged the Orken didn't know his august personage at a single glance. "I have come to exchange words with your superior officer."

"Many of those, we have," grunted the Orken, clearly unimpressed by the aristocrat demanding entrance. "To which you wishing to be speaking?"

"I say, old chap!" Kullen stamped his foot angrily. "This is no way to treat a respected member of the aristocracy—whom, I shall remind you, you and your fellows serve! Mention not the lives you have built upon the wages of my taxed coin! Now open up this gate at once. I will not continue to shout like some commoner in the street."

The Orken gazed down at him for long seconds, disgust and annoyance written plainly on his brutish features—though it was difficult to determine if that was natural or due to the circumstances.

Finally, he grunted. "Wait there," and vanished.

Kullen stood, careful not to break character and be exposed by some onlooker he failed to notice. He fingered the silver pommel of his cane, shaped in the visage of a dragon's tooth. A moment later, a great rattling and clanking of ponderous chains echoed up Martial Row. The portcullis began to rise, revealing the Orken lumbering down the stairs from the battlements at a pace that could be described as "vexingly glacial"—meant in clear disrespect of the demanding "Magister."

"I do say, my Orken friend," Kullen called out to the slow-moving Orken, "this is quite the matter of urgency, something your superior will find intriguing upon hearing at once. But by all means, take your time. It's not as if the fate of the Empire hangs on my actions here or anything!"

His words and offended tone had no effect on the Orken whatsoever. The towering sallow-skinned creature continued descending the stairs, outwardly unhurried and sauntering toward Kullen.

"Now, see here!" Kullen snapped. "Surely you can hurry it—"

"What your business?" The Orken cut him off, his growling voice loud even from a dozen paces away. "Why you here?"

"As I have formerly said," Kullen said, pretending exasperation, "I have arrived with information of considerable import for your superior officer. If you will kindly show me in, I—"

"Which officer?" the Orken demanded. He was clearly in no mood to comply, his jaw set, his expression stubborn, and he folded his huge arms across his chest with a look that dared Kullen to test his patience. This was, after all, the *only* place in the city where humans—regardless of their noble status—could not simply demand entrance. Tuskthorne Keep had been gifted to the Orken by Emperor Veridius as "sovereign territory" and placed entirely under their rule. In that regard, Turoc—as Tuskigo of the Orkenwatch—was as close to a monarch as existed among Orkenkind.

"That is my business," Kullen said, his tone brusque.

"Then your business stay outside." The Orken shrugged his enormous shoulders. "You want in, you tell Drigka business. You want no say business, you no in." He sniffed, scratched at his nose.

Kullen huffed and puffed wordlessly, but it was all for show. He wanted the Orken to focus on what manner of man he was, not what he'd come for.

"Look here!" Kullen dipped a hand into his pocket and drew out the *Kharag* forcefully enough to nearly rip the fabric of his coat. "See this?" He held the silver coin-shaped token up before Drigka's eyes. "The entire point of this *thing* is to gain access without having to suffer the questions of imbeci—" He pretended to swallow the word. "Er… *meddlesome* persons who have no reasons knowing my business!"

Drigka's beady black eyes widened a fraction at the sight of the rune-etched silver coin, and he reached for it with a thick-fingered hand.

"Now," Kullen snapped, tucking the token back into his pocket, "allow me entrance at once! Or I shall make certain your superior hears of your rudeness at *great* length."

The Orken remained unimpressed by Kullen's sour temperament, but the sight of the *Kharag* had clearly tipped the scales in Kullen's favor. With a grunt and growled words in the Orken tongue—which Kullen had no doubt was a curse for the aristocratic arsehole—Drigka nodded and turned on his heel.

"Following me." He sniffed again, louder this time, and wiped his nose on his sleeve, dragging away a long line of yellow-tinted phlegm.

Kullen fell in step behind the Orken, hurrying to match the much taller creature's martial stride. He made a fuss over straightening his coat and vest. His cane and high-heeled shoes made enough noise on the cobblestone courtyard separating the outer wall from the Keep's high-arched gated entrance to draw more attention than he'd desired. Still, he kept his nose high and his eyes down.

More ivory tusks from a creature unknown to Kullen rose

twice the height of him on either side, creating a walkway from the front portcullis to the iron gate of the tower proper. Though the courtyard wasn't particularly large—twenty paces across in all directions—it was bustling with members of the Watch. Some sat with bowls full of gruel or stew, most engaged one another in various forms of training, from hand-to-hand combat to mock battle with sharpened sticks. One thing was certain, Turoc had a well-oiled machine at work here and a veritable army of his own.

The gate, which appeared as iron from a distance, Kullen realized was black wood. Its top and bottom were carved to sharp points, and even the bars bore thorny texture through and through. Though an Orken would be able to seize hold of it without breaking its skin, Kullen knew what would happen to human flesh should he decide to open it on his own.

Ten feet up, circling the tower, a thick strip of the same fashion wrapped the tower, ensuring no one would succeed in climbing its exterior to the arched windows above. That was if any man could manage to slip past the detection of the some half a dozen guards turned interiorly upon the yard. For a moment, he wondered if the Keep were better defended than even the Palace itself.

"Stand back," Drigka said to Kullen, marching him up the two steps.

They stopped just outside the gate. It was framed above and below by the enormous jagged-toothed maw of some great beast —possibly the same one who had offered its tusks throughout the aptly named fortress. It bore a passing resemblance to the Orken.

"Here." Drigka pointed to a round bone basin as wide as Kullen's arm was long, which sat atop a pedestal of the same spiked black wood.

Kullen eyed the basin, then looked back to the Orken. "Here, what?"

Drigka bared his fangs. "Dip fingers."

Kullen frowned. "Do what now?"

Instead of repeating his command, Drigka seized Kullen's free hand and forced it into the basin. The liquid within was not simply water, that much was clear upon first touch. Though the air outside was hot and humid, the contents of the basin were frigid and thick. Kullen pulled his hand back, and the slimy substance dangled from his outstretched digits. He affected an expression of disgust.

"Touch to forehead, cheeks—" Drigka stifled a sneeze and used his other hand to wipe the snot dripping from his nose down his beard. "—and throat."

Kullen stared at the Orken as if at a madman. But when Drigka began to move his hand with as little effort as a child manipulating the limbs of a marionette dancing on a string, Kullen slipped free of the Orken's grasp.

"I can do it!" he snapped, allowing outrage onto his face and into his voice. This time, the emotion required far less acting.

Drigka just stared at him, waiting for him to comply. Kullen did as instructed, hiding a grimace as the viscous fluid clung to his skin.

"Good." Drigka nodded, then hawked loudly and spat a massive gob of white phlegm into the basin. Covering one nostril and forcing air through the other, he added a hint of the snot running freely from his nose. A mischievous, fang-laden grin spread across his face while he watched Kullen. "Now you clean to enter Tuskthorne Keep."

Kullen allowed his jaw to drop in a pretense of horror. In truth, he'd known of the Orken's strange ritual—humans were required to "clean" themselves by daubing Orken spit onto their bodies, doubtless a way the proud Orken abased any who entered their territory—but "Magister Morvannou" didn't.

In a show of mock outrage, Kullen scrubbed his hand and the remaining Orken phlegm onto his jacket, but that only made Drigka's smile grow wider.

"Come." Drigka motioned for him to follow. "I—" The sneeze that had been threatening cut off his words. A wide spray of spit covered Kullen in a bath that would've saved him the trouble of dipping. Wiping his mouth and nose, Drigka continued as if it hadn't happened. "I take you."

"Er, that won't be necessary," Kullen said, using the cuff of his sleeve to wipe his eyes and mouth. He waved his other hand dismissively. "Merely point me in the direction, and I can see to my business for myself."

Drigka shook his huge head, a movement that set the silver bands in his beard to a jangling tune. "You no go Tuskthorne Keep alone. Drigka watch."

"Look!" Again, Kullen drew out the *Kharag.* "You know what this means. This comes from the very top, and with it, I am granted an audience—*private* audience—with your superior." He clucked his tongue loudly. "If he had wanted you to know his business, he would have informed you. But clearly, he does not want you involved. Do you wish to experience the ire of your betters?"

Drigka growled low in his throat. Indecision warred on his brutish face. Kullen wondered if he'd taken things too far with that last comment. Though the Orken had their pecking order, none would look kindly upon being denigrated by a human, regardless of his station. Their Tuskigo, Ketsneer, and Arbiters were not so much *chosen* as ascended to their rank by literally beating all challengers. Orken bearing the golden jewelry were the best, but not without experiencing continual challenge. One such as Drigka could decide to issue a contest of strength at any time, and should he succeed would earn the right to pluck golden bands from his competitor.

"And besides," Kullen said, his tone wheedling, "it seems like you're coming down with quite the ferocious cold, old chap. Best you look after yourself, yes?"

The proud Orken scowled and began to speak, but another ferocious sneeze cut him off. Thankfully, this time, he had enough presence of mind to aim it in the other direction.

"'True," Drigka admitted. "Drigka don't feel so well. You go inside. Do not dawdle. Find Tuskigo Hall to the right, all the way down. Make no other turns."

Kullen heaved an inward sigh of relief. His gamble had worked —the Orken was at least smart enough to know that Magisters wielded some influence within the Palace walls, and it was not in his best interest to anger one holding a *Kharag*.

And Kullen was smart enough to know that the riskiness of his plan had only just begun.

"Right-o, my friend," Kullen said. "And here, this might do you some good." He extended a handkerchief taken from his coat pocket.

Drigka scoffed at the offering, then turned and stalked away.

Kullen watched him go, then turned toward the black wood gate.

That's the easy part done, he thought.

Before arriving, Kullen had dabbled the contents of a small ampoule full of turpentine oil mixed with alchemical snuffdust over his hair and beard. That would sort out the Orken's keen nostrils. Drigka would certainly recall his vexatiousness, but would remember nothing of Kullen's scent beyond the pine resin used for the turpentine.

Now the real fun begins.

He took a deep breath, then stepped forward. As he passed through the now-open jawbone, he even looked behind him on instinct, waiting for the muzzle to close and gobble him up. It felt all too fitting.

Into the mouth of the beast.

55
Natisse

"Nothing?" Natisse had to fight to keep her voice from rising to a shout. It certainly wasn't Rickard's fault, but frustration was getting the best of her. "You're telling me you've heard *nothing* about an Orkenwatch assault or a slew of people hauled away in chains?"

"I says it like I hears it," Rickard said, running a finger under his pockmarked nose and over a pitch-black moustache. "And I ain't heared nothing about nothing like you're saying." He held out his gnarled, grime-covered hand to her. "But a promise is a promise, ey? One mark for telling you what I know?"

Natisse bit down an angry retort and plucked out a golden coin from her pouch. "You hear anything, you get me word fast!"

"Faster'n wet shite out a sick aristo's bunghole!" Rickard snatched the mark and bit down hard on it. Two decades living on the streets of the Embers and the One Hand District had taught him just how far trust truly went. Ever since a bad loan from some now-dead Magister had cheated him out of the small jeweler's store he'd once owned in High Reach, he had wandered the streets of Dimvein shouting about the treachery of the rich and powerful to everyone he passed. The fact that he was *always* out and about made him a good source of information for anyone with the coin to pay and the patience to endure his… unique temperament.

Natisse hurried up the street while his mouth was still busy testing her coin for authenticity. Tired, achy, and, worst of all, empty-handed despite hours of searching, she had no desire to put up with his tirades.

Ulnu's frosted horns! She cursed under her breath, jaw muscles clenching. Natisse was running out of places to look and people to ask.

She hadn't yet gone to the Refuge—Mammy Tess and her runners would likely be too busy rebuilding to have gathered much useful information—but she'd already tapped most of the Crimson Fang's contacts within the Embers and the east and south ends of the One Hand District. She had just Serrod left to visit before she had to *really* start casting a wider net. None of her usual informants seemed to have heard anything about an Orken raid or seen the Crimson Fang paraded through the streets in chains. The lack of bodies—besides poor Dalash—told her the Orkenwatch hadn't killed the others outright. But Natisse still needed to discover where they'd been taken for imprisonment or questioning.

Natisse trudged through the One Hand District, doing her best to blend in. As usual, vendors hawked wares, men promised the best the city had to offer, and suckers paid for subpar goods. Deep in the shadow of the alleyways, women of the night stood, beckoning forward any man who passed appearing as if he could use a good time and afford to pay for it.

Lumenators stood at intervals of half a dozen market stalls, casting their eerie glow in the darkening daylight. And everywhere, Imperial Scales wanting nothing more than to thrust some poor soul into the dungeons for something as little as stealing to survive another day.

In addition to the Emperor's guards, a small patrol of Orkenwatch loomed just ahead. Natisse gave them a wide berth, ducking down a side alley to circumnavigate the main marketplace square rather than risk drawing too close to them. She knew at least one Sniffer had her scent—was that how the Orkenwatch had tracked the Crimson Fang through the maze of underground tunnels, past the gnashers, and into the Burrow? Natisse couldn't shake that thought. Likely because of her, the Sniffers had found the Crimson Fang, but she'd been absent and escaped capture. Cliessa, goddess of fortune, was known to be kind to those she favored and played cruel tricks on those she deemed unworthy. If Natisse *had* done something—

No, she told herself, fighting the thought and the inevitable wave of acid it brought surging into the pit of her stomach. *No, this wasn't on me. It couldn't be.* She refused to give in to the feelings of guilt and shame; such misery wouldn't get her anywhere but might actually make the monumental task ahead of her even more difficult. She had to stay focused on finding information and locating the Crimson Fang. Everything else could wait until *after* she'd freed Jad, Garron, Haston, and all the others.

"Hey, beautiful," came a voice from behind her. Natisse spun, expecting to find trouble, but instead, saw only a lithe form wearing a sheer dress. "Looking for some fun?"

Natisse had pity for those who sold themselves on the streets. But for the grace of Ezrasil, she could've been one of them. She dug into her pocket and pulled a few silver marks. She strode forward and placed them in the woman's hand.

"Give yourself the night off and find something good to eat," Natisse said.

The woman stared down at the coins with appreciation evident on her face. "Th-thank you, miss."

Natisse smiled, then turned back and pressed forward toward her next destination.

She sucked in a breath as she caught sight of the Brendoni healer's shop. The front door had been kicked in, the brass knob snapped by a heavy boot, and the glass window front shattered. Despite her exhaustion, she broke into a run and burst into the small, cramped apothecary.

"Serrod?" she cried out. "Serrod, are you here?"

Worry thrummed in her mind. What had happened? Had the Orkenwatch or Imperial Scales somehow traced the alchemical fire in Magister Branthe's fighting pits back here? Was Serrod, even now, rotting in some dungeon or on an Arbiter's table, facing painful inquisitions—

A groan drifted from the back room.

"In here." Thank the gods, it was Serrod, but the healer's voice was weak and thick with pain.

Natisse vaulted the counter and darted through the compact doorway separating the front of the shop from the alchemist's personal quarters. Serrod lay on his own table—the same table where Haston had reclined only days earlier—pressing a cloth-wrapped poultice to the left side of his face. His right eye swiveled toward her, then widened in recognition.

"Natisse?" He tried to sit up but fell back with a moan and whimper.

"Serrod!" Natisse darted to the alchemist's side. "What happened? To your shop—and to you?"

Serrod was missing one of his front teeth, and there was a nasty slash over his right eyebrow. Yet it was the *other* half of his face that sent a chill through Natisse's veins. When the healer lowered the poultice, blood trickled fresh from two long gashes that ran from the top of his nearly bald head all the way to the stringy gray hairs that clung to the sides of his jaw. Knife work, Natisse recognized instantly. The wounds were deep and painful. Torture.

"The Orkenwatch." The Brendoni muttered the word through split, chapped lips, replacing the poultice over his wounds. "Came in here last night asking questions and not bothering with words."

"Questions?" Natisse's mind raced. "What sort of questions? Did they ask about us? About me? Or—"

"No." Serrod's jaw clamped shut. "I would never have said anything if I'd have known."

"Known what?" Natisse demanded, her voice rising to echo off the walls of the cramped room. "What did they want to know about, Serrod?"

"Not what. Who." Serrod's face went a shade paler. "The Black Talon."

The words sent a chill down Natisse's spine. "Black… Talon?" She frowned. "Why?"

"He's wanted for questioning." Serrod adjusted the poultice on his face, wincing at the fresh pain as he applied pressure. "They don't know who they're hunting, only that they're tracking his scent. Sniffer picked up his trace somehow, followed him here. They wanted to know what he was doing here and where he'd gone. I told them I didn't know, I swear. But the Sniffer said they'd picked up his scent again. That was when they left, and I passed out. Didn't wake up until a few hours ago—like this."

Natisse stared at the Brendoni in stunned disbelief. *Kullen* had been the one to lead the Orkenwatch to the Crimson Fang? That seemed impossible—he'd shown up nearly two days earlier, more than enough time for his scent to dissipate so thoroughly even a well-trained bloodhound couldn't follow it. But Sniffers had senses far keener than any hound. If they'd somehow picked up his scent, perhaps at Magister Branthe's fighting pit, that explained how they had made their way first to Serrod, then through the underground tunnel to the Burrow.

"Binteth's bloody teeth," Natisse swore.

How could she have been so foolish? She'd allowed trust to take her too far. This man, the Black Talon, Kullen—she'd watched him murder one of her closest friends. Then, she just… blindly followed him to Pantagoya while the Orkenwatch ransacked her home and abducted everyone she held true?

She shook her head. Someone would pay dearly for this. Someone would suffer for the pain that even now racked her chest.

"How are you here?" Serrod's question drew Natisse's attention. "When my contacts sent word that your people had been taken, I was afraid I'd never see any of you again." He gripped her arm with his free hand. "But tell me, how did you escape, and did anyone else get out with you?"

The question sent a fresh pang of guilt through Natisse's heart. If she'd been there, she might've been able to fend off the attackers —surely even the mighty Orken couldn't stand before Golgoth's power. If not that, she could have at least bought the Crimson Fang and *Ghuklek* a chance to flee through the hidden tunnels in the training room.

But that was folly, the rational part of her mind told her. Even with dragonblood magic at her command, she, too, could have been taken unawares or found herself overwhelmed by the Orkenwatch. Then, she'd be no better off, imprisoned alongside her companions, and there'd be no one to free the Crimson Fang. They'd all be rotting away in an Orken cell until their torture or public execution.

While she was free, the Crimson Fang stood a chance. She had to cling to that knowledge above everything.

"Did your contacts mention where they've been taken?" she asked, gripping the alchemist's shoulder. "Where can I find them, Serrod?"

"The information came from someone in the Stacks." The Brendoni's umber-skinned face—the half of it visible around the poultice—fell, his lips drooping into a frown. "He saw your friends being taken into Tuskthorne Keep."

A rock plummeted in Natisse's gut. Tuskthorne Keep? She'd considered that but truly hoped she'd been wrong. She had more chance of threading a dragon through the eye of a needle than getting in there. And even if she managed to enter, how in Shekoth would she escape?

"Thank you, Serrod," she said. She looked around the upturned and destroyed remains of his shop. "When this is all through, please tell me you'll reconsider our offer to house you in the Burrow? We could use your help."

She'd almost added, "and it's safe," until the vision of her home in a similar state flashed across her mind.

"My home is here," Serrod told her. "Just as yours is below. We both got our purposes, and mine stays topside."

Natisse nodded, placed a gentle hand on the man's shoulder, then turned and hurried away. She used the back door and rushed north along the streets of the One Hand District, through Heroes Row, and into the Stacks. Night had all but fallen by the time she drew within sight of Tuskthorne Keep.

For one brief moment, she entertained the idea of summoning Golgoth to the Mortal Realm and unleashing the Queen of the Ember Dragons against the Orken. That would show the bastards what happened to those who harmed her friends.

Before the thought had even fully formed, a bellowing *No!* rumbled through her mind. *I will never again be used in such a way!*

I know, Natisse said, fighting the surge of fire raging in her belly. *Nor would I abuse your power thus.* That was not who she was. She wouldn't risk the lives of countless Imperial citizens in the Stacks just to punish the Orken who had committed no crime beyond doing their job. To them, the Crimson Fang was an enemy to be dealt with as savagely as any other threat they faced in service to the Emperor. Regardless of how it felt, it wasn't personal. They had a task, and so did she. She couldn't afford to wage a new war against the Orken. If she did that, if she abused her magical bond with Golgoth, she'd be no better than the Magisters she'd spent years hating.

But she wasn't going to sit idly by and do nothing either. Not while the Orken held her friends captive.

One look at Tuskthorne Keep, and she knew she'd never get through their fortifications on her own. She couldn't fight her way past dozens of war-bred Orken—much less back out again. That left her only one option.

She ducked into a side street and slipped into the shadows under a corrugated overhang. There, amongst bales of hay and buckets of feed, she slipped the leather thong and dragonblood vial from around her neck. She'd need access to Golgoth's magic for what was to come. She could sense Golgoth's trepidation and did her best to soothe the dragon with her thoughts, assuring her she had no designs to utilize her powers destructively.

With deft twists, she tied her long red hair into a thick braid, concealing the slim glass vial of dragonblood within the knots and using the leather thong to secure the braid's end. She inspected the hasty hairdo, testing for any odd lumps that might expose its true purpose or its priceless contents. Satisfied, she turned her attention to the rest of her attire.

She stripped down to the trousers and undershirt she'd donned before departing the Burrow. Her outer coat and jacket she used to wrap up her lashblade and the daggers she'd secreted about her person. They would do her no good where she was going, but she'd want them handy when it was over. She buried the packages beneath the hay, hoping the owner had no intentions of moving it anytime soon. She'd have to risk the possibility.

Her transformation complete, she strode from the side street and made her way down the broad avenue that led toward Tuskthorne Keep. As she'd hoped, an Orkenwatch patrol was visible marching down the street—doubtless returning from their evening patrol.

"Hey, you!" she called out, breaking into a run. "You ugly bastard, I'm talking to you!"

The rearmost of the Orken turned at the sound of her voice. His brutish face creased into a snarling smile at the sight of her. Weaponless, she was no threat, she knew, but that only served to make them underestimate her.

"What you want, scum?" the Orken asked, smiling.

"I think I just saw your mother," Natisse said. The Orken's head tilted. "Then again, it might've just been a pile of horse shite."

The Orken's smile deepened to a scowl, and his huge flaxen hand reached toward the thick, iron-studded club hanging from his belt. He closed the gap between them, drawing his weapon free.

"I'm going to—"

Before Natisse could find out what creative and clever thing the beast intended to do to her, she leaped forward and drove her fist right into his jaw.

The others who had, until now, been watching in amusement descended upon her. Within moments, she was cuffed and dragged down the street. She kicked and screamed for effect, but inside, she'd gotten just what she wanted.

A free ticket into Tuskthorne Keep.

56
KULLEN

Kullen had been inside Tuskthorne Keep just once over his years as the Black Talon. Even now, it still felt like stepping into a foreign land. A dark, gloomy world lit by far fewer torches than illuminated the Imperial Scales' barracks and watchtowers. Orken eyes were far keener than that of the humans, capable of seeing through deep shadows without need for much light. Without Umbris's enhanced darkvision, Kullen might've stumbled blindly through the Orken fortress.

Thanks to the dragon magic, however, Kullen could see as clearly as if daylight filled the enormous tower that rose ten stories above his head.

He stood in an open chamber with the next useable floor two stories above. From the ceiling hung a chandelier of sorts, though not a single candle adorned it. Instead, what looked eerily like Orken skulls, tusks and all, were suspended from black wood and iron spokes. Draped through their open maws were ribbons of red and silver falling down like rain.

Two long tables with benches on either side ran from the front doors to the back of the room. Upon each, various weapons were arranged on cloth mats as if being used as cleaning or sharpening stations. On the northern and southern curvatures, staircases rose and disappeared beyond the ceiling.

Tuskthorne Keep stood three hundred paces in diameter—at least above ground. How wide or far it delved into the earth, not even Kullen's contacts among the Trenta could ascertain. The Orken guarded the secrets of their fortress with the same ferocity that they served the Emperor and upheld the law in Dimvein.

Guests to Tuskthorne Keep were few and far between, for the Orken did not dole out the *Kharag* lightly, nor were they inclined to invite humans into their "sovereign territory" en masse. Even Emperor Wymarc had only been invited within the fortress on a handful of occasions that Kullen knew of, and always at Turoc's invitation. The one time Kullen had been admitted into the fortress, it was in the company of Prince Jarius on one of the Emperor's rare personal visits to take part in an Orken ceremony they called Khal'vai—roughly translated to mean "The Integration of New Blood." There, he'd witnessed the promotion of Bareg, Turoc's *Ketsneer* and second-in-command.

On that lone visit, Turoc had led the Emperor and his small retinue—two Elite Scales, Prince Jarius, Kullen, and the newly-made Princess Hadassa—to the grand chamber that dominated the uppermost level of Tuskthorne Keep. That had involved climbing ten flights of stairs past hundreds of barracks-like quarters occupied by the warriors of the Orkenwatch.

Kullen had no desire to climb all that distance, not when he had Umbris's magic at his disposal. He only ascended the staircase to maintain the "Magister Morvannou" pretense for the handful of Orken filling the halls and the upper levels.

A squad of hulking, armored Orken clanked past him on their way down toward the ground—likely on their way for nighttime patrol duty. Each seemed to make extra efforts to shoulder him roughly aside with growls and muttered snarls in their own tongue. Kullen knew enough of the Orken language to recognize the curses directed at the "fetid littlekin." The combination of snuffdust and turpentine oil stung their keen nostrils and set one's eyes watering, earning Kullen a vicious glare.

He had no fear of being found out—Turoc was the only one who'd recognize him on sight, and Emperor Wymarc had promised to keep the Tuskigo occupied for the night. Not even Bareg was likely to make him out under his elaborate disguise. The Orken didn't bother to address him directly. There was only one way he could've gained entrance to Tuskthorne Keep, and the Orken respected the *Kharag* enough not to question him. Well, *most* Orken, excluding the nosy Drigka.

He continued climbing until the heavy bootsteps of the patrol passed through the enormous gated entrance, then glanced quickly around to make sure he was unobserved. Even single-minded as they were, they wouldn't dare show regard to Kullen. The only time he'd ever seen the Orken make eye contact with a human was when on official martial business or the word Emperor prefaced their name.

When he was confident no eyes were upon him, he reached into his cloak and jammed his thumb onto the cap of his dragonblood vial. With a familiar needle-prick of discomfort, he felt himself slipping into the Shadow Realm. Luckily, there was no lack of darkness to be found. With minimal effort, he shadow-slid up to the ninth level and materialized on the landing. Though his destination was the uppermost level, he had to cover his tracks—or, more accurately, mask any trace of his true scent. At least one Sniffer had a trace on him, and he couldn't risk discovery until he had what he'd come for.

From within his cloak, he drew out a glass vial no larger than his little finger, stoppered with a cork, and painted with the words "DO NOT OPEN!!!"—exclamations and all—in bright red letters. The liquid within was transparent, seemingly harmless, but the moment Kullen pulled the cork free, it felt as if a dagger shot up his nostrils and stabbed into his brain with such force he nearly blacked out.

The Snoutkiller potion Serrod had developed using herbs

found exclusively in his Brendoni homeland was aptly named. The alchemist had told him Brendoni hunters used it to mask their scent from predators. He'd prattled on about "temporarily paralyzing the olfactory nerves," which Kullen understood to mean it stopped desert lions—or Orken—from detecting his presence.

Kullen lacked the Orken's keen nostrils but one whiff of the stuff, and he had immediately lost any sense of smell. He splashed a few drops onto his clothing, boots, and on the floor around him. Any Orken who came within scent range of him would be stung by the same alchemy that had just disabled him. With his natural scent covered by turpentine oil and snuffdust, there would be no way for even a Sniffer to hunt him down.

He took the remaining stairs three at a time, allowing the few residual drops to trail him on the way. Any Orken who approached the uppermost level would have to pass through *two* clouds of Snoutkiller—enough to destroy their sense of smell for at least an hour or two, according to Serrod.

Kullen's mind wandered back to his last exchange with the healer. The Brendoni would likely be as furious as a tired dragon after their last exchange, but that was the cost of doing business. Either Serrod would hold that grudge forever, or he would accept Kullen's coin—and, he supposed, an apology—when next he needed to restock his alchemical supplies. Kullen could eat a bit of crow if it meant patching up his working relations with the best alchemist and healer in Dimvein.

The upper level was decorated with weaponry mounted in a seemingly random fashion. No wall space was left unused. Swords, axes, spears, glaves, warhammers, staves, maces, and whips surrounded him. He even saw quite a few things he didn't recognize, assuming them to be Orken designs outdated once the creatures learned the ways of blacksmithing.

Beneath each hung a rune-engraved bronze plate, no doubt displaying the names of the weapons or the Orken to which they had belonged—perhaps the Tuskigos and Ketsneers who'd preceded Turoc and Bareg. The sheer number of them was astonishing. If these were truly names, there were centuries worth of chieftains and champions immortalized in these chambers.

The door to the grand throne room stood ajar, and through it, Kullen glimpsed the enormous seat—little more than a block of stone carved into a lumpy, jagged shape barely resembling the seat of a king or leader—upon which the Orken Tuskigos had perched themselves since Emperor Veridius had gifted them Tuskthorne Keep. Behind it hung a long-disused, fading banner displaying the emblem of the Orken people: two white, curving tusks crossed over a black axe head on a field of blood-red and silver. That insignia hadn't been seen outside the fortress in centuries. Yet here, inside Tuskthorne Keep, it appeared as if the Orken still tried to keep their old ways alive—at least partly.

Kullen stepped through the threshold and under yet another skull. This one was larger even than Umbris's and carved from some sort of mineral, which had long ago formed into sharp-edged crystals that bore a striking resemblance to the creature whose fanged maw guarded the entrance to the Keep. Narrow eye slits were buried deep beneath a jutting brow and above sharp cheekbones that looked as if they could impale a man. Flared frills framed its lower half, reminding Kullen of the fans used to cool the Emperor in Dimvein's most humid seasons.

The Orken deity, perhaps? Kullen didn't know if the Orken believed in a god—he'd never thought to ask—but a creature so horrific in nature would certainly be the sort of predator they would hold in high esteem.

Whereas the Emperor's throne room was opulent and bright, the Tuskigo's was dank and drafty, dark and gloom-filled. Kullen felt a sense of foreboding as he crossed the black wood floor to the single door on the western wall.

That had to be his first stop—Turoc's task room. He *had* to know if the Tuskigo was the traitor or not. If the Emperor could count on his loyalty, that would—

Heavy footfalls from behind caught Kullen's attention. He turned to see a shadow moving behind the throne room's only other door. He had just enough time enough to reach for the vial around his neck and summon Umbris's power to transform him into shadow before the door opened and Bareg stepped out. There was nowhere in the Mortal Realm he could hide from the Orken's keen eyes.

Time slowed to a crawl and the Ketsneer's movements with it. Even still, Kullen knew he couldn't make it to the task room without drawing attention. That meant his only choice was to shadow-slide past Bareg through the still-open door behind him. He didn't know what awaited him there, but the passage appeared dark and empty.

Kullen acted without further thought, soaring through the air, catching each patch of darkness along the way. He materialized behind the Orken and pressed his back against the wall.

Heart hammering, he listened for any sign that Bareg had discovered his presence. The Ketsneer was the keenest Sniffer in the whole damned Orkenwatch. Kullen had never interacted with Bareg, but there was no doubt the Orken would recognize his smell as one which crossed Turoc's path on a regular basis. That would stir up suspicion.

He waited, silently counting to himself as a means of calming the blood pounding in his veins. Bareg stopped. But only for a moment and for reasons Kullen couldn't make out. Then, he lumbered off down the stairs, muttering and growling as he passed through the cloud of Snoutkiller potion.

Kullen let out a breath. *That was too bloody close!*

He waited for long moments until he no longer heard any hint of Bareg's presence. Still, he forced himself to move cautiously and quietly, slipping from his hiding place. He found himself in a nub of a corridor with three doors. He pressed an ear against the wood of the first, ensuring no one was inside. Then, he pushed as slowly as he could manage. Adrenaline pumping, he held his breath, expecting to hear the groan of hinges.

But Cliessa smiled on him. It was about damned time, too. The door opened and shut again without a sound, and Kullen let out the tiniest sigh of relief.

He turned to face the room. It was dark as sin save for a sliver of moonlight leaking in through an arrow-slit window on the northern wall. That was more than enough ambient light to allow Umbris's dragon-eyes to activate. The room lit for Kullen like he'd just stepped into an open courtyard.

It was time to suss out the traitor.

57
NATISSE

Natisse's Orken captors were far from gentle. She was kicked to the street, rolled onto her belly, her face crushed into the cobblestones, a boot driven into her spine, and her arms wrenched up and behind her back for the Orkenwatch to bind her wrists. By the time she was hauled to her feet, she bled from a split lip and a gash on her left cheek, her shoulders screamed in protest, and she could barely draw breath around the throbbing in her back. Had she not suffered a dislocated shoulder before, she'd have thought at least one of hers was. She rolled her neck as she hung limp between the two enormous gray-skinned brutes hauling her along—and it was only *partly* for show.

But her plan had succeeded, at least initially. She was hustled through the wide front gates, across training grounds, and into Tuskthorne Keep in short order.

The first thing she noticed was the darkness that prevailed like a shroud over the whole tower. In here, there were no candles or torches, no Lumenators or alchemical fires. Two long tables stood as the centerpiece below a massive structure she could only think to call an art sculpture crafted from bones and skulls.

Her captors dragged her through an arched stone doorway just off the round chamber, which led to one of two sets of stairs that both ascended to the upper portions of the tower and descended into the ground beneath the fortress. Uncle Ronan had insisted on gathering as much intelligence on the Keep's dungeon as possible —against an eventuality such as this—but few who'd spent time locked up here had emerged to bear witness. All the Crimson Fang had learned was that the cells were located five floors below the street level, carved from the very bedrock that served as the Keep's foundation. Not much to go on, certainly, but Natisse had no other choice. After what Arbiter Chuldok had done to Ammon, she couldn't let her comrades languish in the Orken's grasp for long.

Down the stairs Natisse was led—*carried,* mostly, her dangling feet barely scraping the stone steps—deeper into the bowels of the earth. Natisse let her head hang down, watching her surroundings from the corners of her eyes. She counted the steps that wended downward, paying special attention to the stone walls and their brass support beams—beams much like those she'd seen in the secret tunnel leading from the training room, she noted. Had the *Ghuklek* built Tuskthorne Keep, too? If so, it might be honeycombed with secret passages that could facilitate her escape. She tucked that thought away; it would come in handy later. For now, she devoted her scrutiny elsewhere.

Not that there was much to see besides passing walls and the occasional opening into chambers whose contents could only be guessed at. Down they went, further and further, until Natisse lost count. Her head throbbed, back ached, and her neck felt like it was about to snap.

Finally, the stairs ended at an enormous grilled gate made of black iron. Two heavily-armed and armored Orken stood on the landing outside the gate, with three more beyond. Natisse felt a little stab of worry. This obstacle would prove problematic at best, at worst, cut off her escape route. Doubtless, that was precisely why the Keep had been designed thus. The Orkenwatch had a straight path to depositing prisoners in their underground cells, but in case a prisoner dared to break free, they would have no way out.

The Orken hauling her down the stairs called out in their own language to the guards at the gate, who also answered in the Orken tongue. After a brief exchange that Natisse didn't understand, the Orken set to work opening the enormous iron portal.

The pair of Orken outside the gate wrestled a heavy beam out of its cradle and lowered it to the stone floor. Once they were done, two of the heavily-muscled brutes beyond the gate bent their enormous backs to haul at the handle of a winch anchored to a stone column in the center of the squared chamber. Great chains within the column gave a ponderous groan, and the gate began to rattle and rumble upward. It took fully half a minute of continuous effort to raise the massive iron gate high enough for the Orken to pass beneath the sharp-tipped spikes lining its bottom. The two who had worked the winch leaned against the column, breathing heavily and wiping sweat from their blocky brows.

Natisse was hauled over the enormous gate beam and dumped roughly onto the floor. She fell hard, gave a whimpering cry as if in pain. Which wasn't far from the truth. Her rough handling had left her with a fair crop of new bruises, scrapes, and aches to add to her exhaustion and the spent nerves from overuse of her dragon magic.

She lifted her head, wiped fake tears from her eyes, and stared up with a look of utter horror and shock at her surroundings. That seemed to amuse her captors even more.

The Orken she'd punched loomed large over her, fangs bared in a sneer—or snarl, she couldn't quite tell—and his dark eyes blazing. "She-human strike Orken," he growled in his thick accent, "break Emperor's law. Now she-human prisoned."

"Please!" Natisse begged, adopting her most terrified expression. "I-I know I shouldn't have, but I couldn't help myself. It's the voices, you see! The voices… in here!" She banged her hand against the side of her head. "They won't shut up. Won't stop talking, won't give me peace until I hurt someone. It's the only way.

They want blood and don't care whose I spill. It was the only way!"

The Orken stared down at her with a look of disgust written plain on his craggy, bearded face. Whether he understood her or not didn't matter—only that he saw her as weak and scared. Men in positions of power always liked when others cowered before them. The Orken might not be human, but she suspected they would share that particular trait with their frailer counterparts.

"Voices? Pah!" The gray-skinned brute straightened and growled something in his own tongue to the others, which earned a chorus of laughter. He shook his head. "Sit in cell, voices silent. Or spill your blood. Not matter to Orkenwatch. City peaceful again."

He barked something to the Orken who hadn't helped wind the winch. This one had skin a pale yellow and a sallow complexion but shoulders twice as broad as Natisse's. In response to the command, he sauntered toward her, clamped a strong hand on the back of her neck, and dragged her to her feet. She had no choice but to comply or risk her spine shattering.

"Go," the Orken barked.

He shoved Natisse out to arm's length and propelled her in front of him, pushing her down a narrow corridor that led out of the circular chamber and down a set of winding stairs. They descended one final floor before ending at a door of heavy oak beams banded with spike-studded iron.

"Stop," came the terse command, accompanied by a painful tightening of his grip on Natisse's neck. Natisse gave a little whimpering cry and cringed toward the wall as the Orken stepped past her to hammer at the door with his free hand. He exchanged a few words in his own tongue with someone on the other side, then the door was pulled open with a great rattling of locks and drawn deadbolts.

On the other side, Natisse caught sight of the ugliest creature she'd ever seen. Clearly, an Orken, for his face bore the bristling beard and heavy features of his kind, yet there the resemblance ended. Where Orken eyes were typically deep-set and black, his were a gleaming red and set into shallow sockets ringed with crusty black growths that looked like scabbed-over sores. His body had none of the impressive musculature of his race but was a blubbery mass of sagging flesh that spilled out of the leather harness and far-too-small loincloth he wore as clothing. His fingernails had been left to grow into long, hooked talons and his toenails were cracked and blackened by dirt. Strangest of all was his skin: a white almost as bright as Thanagar's pristine scales.

"She-human strike Shaggat," growled the Orken holding Natisse's neck.

"Struck Shaggat?" The question, spoken in near-flawless Imperial, issued from the white Orken's blubbery lips in a voice halfway between a croak and a sibilant whisper. He clucked his tongue and waggled one talon-tipped finger in Natisse's face. "A poor idea on the best of days."

"Voices. In here." Natisse's Orken captor rapped a knuckle sharply against her skull and spoke a few more words in the Orken language.

"I see." He dragged out the "s" sound for long seconds, sending an involuntary shiver down Natisse's spine. He crooked his raised finger, and the guard shoved Natisse forward into the room. Natisse stumbled and nearly fell, only barely catching herself by grabbing a fistful of the white Orken's fleshy skin. She expected her hand to come away wet, but instead, she was reminded of hard rough stone on a hot day. She recovered herself as best she could and stepped back.

The albino Orken clucked his tongue again. "Leave her with Gulma," he said, nodding. "Gulma will see she is settled in."

Natisse's Orken friend turned and marched out of the room without a backward glance. To her surprise, he didn't close the enormous door behind him.

"Yes," said the hideous white creature beside her. "Try it. Surely there can be no consequences?" He uttered a little giggling sound that sounded terribly odd coming from an Orken throat. He shook his head with visible mirth. "You are here to stay, a guest in Gulma's little kingdom until Gulma decides otherwise. There are three ways you will leave this place: headfirst into Gulma's treat pit or in irons to stand in the Court of Justice."

Natisse stared at him for long seconds. "W-What's the third way?"

"It doesn't matter," the Orken said, giggling again. "Gulma doubts you will prove innocent and be allowed to walk free." He ran a taloned finger down the side of her face. "You're guilty of *something*. Gulma will merely be the one fortunate enough to discover what. Once Gulma does…" He flicked a too-long tongue over his blubbery lips. "Let us say Gulma *always* does and leave it at that for now, hmm?"

Natisse had to fight the overwhelming urge to kill the monstrous thing on the spot. She couldn't act yet. She'd come all this way to find the Crimson Fang, and she wouldn't waste the effort just because of one menacing jailer.

"Come, come," said the Orken, wrapping his claw-like fingernails in the fabric of Natisse's tunic and tugging her along. "Gulma will show you your new home."

Natisse tried to pull free, but the Orken's grip was surprisingly strong, his strength impossible to resist without tearing her clothes. She whimpered and pretended tears, playing up the terrified, helpless act. If the Orken believed it or not, he didn't show it. He merely waddled along, blubbery flesh rippling with every step, and hauled Natisse deeper into the cells.

"Welcome home, little human," Gulma said, shoving her into an open cell,

Natisse hit the ground hard, skinning her knees and shins. She pushed herself up to all fours and crawled to her feet. She had seen the inside of plenty of cells. However, nothing could have prepared her for the stench she found here. It was made up of one stone wall and three others made of patinated bronze. Something wet stained the rear wall from the waist down, and she realized what the horrendous odor was.

Human offal coated the walls in thick grime. Upon closer inspection, she found there was no means to relieve herself nor the former "guests" who'd found themselves locked away. Scanning the cells around her, she had trouble seeing much, but if the Crimson Fang were present, it wasn't immediately evident.

"A woman!" a voice cried. Other voices rose in weary excitement at the proclamation. Natisse turned toward the sound to find a man barely older than her. He was skin and bones, sagging flesh hanging off his body like hung drapes. "And pretty."

A grin stretched across his face, showing brown and yellow teeth caked with what looked like years' worth of foul. His eyes were red and bloodshot, thick black bags beneath them.

"I'm Jarlth," he said.

"Shut your mouth, prisoner," Gulma barked, slamming his fist against the bronze bars and sending Jarlth skittering backward. Then, he turned to Natisse. "This one's been here twelve years. Don't you worry. He won't last much longer."

Something about the way Gulma spoke confused Natisse. It was an odd thing to notice under the current circumstances, but all the other Orken spoke in fragments of the common tongue. But Gulma spoke with proper sentences, like someone who had been taught. That thought fled from her mind nearly as quickly as it had developed as the giant, hideous, white-skinned Orken stalked toward her, brandishing his long claws like hooked blades.

She made a show of backing away but knew there was nowhere to go.

"Gulma sees what you're hiding under there." He slashed at her again and again, tearing away her clothing until she was stripped down to only her underclothes. "Truly, you struck one of our warriors without even a blade to your name? Perhaps you really are mad?"

Gulma giggled and raised his hand as if to go for her hair.

Until now, she'd been mostly playing the role of a frightened woman found on the streets of Dimvein. But now, knowing what was hidden beneath her fiery locks, she screamed and backed away, covering herself in modesty.

"Please," she begged. "I have nothing. You can see, I have nothing."

"I wouldn't say that," Jarlth commented from the next cell over.

"Gulma told you to be quiet!" Gulma shouted. "Now, you pay."

He started to turn to leave but eyed Natisse one last time with hungry eyes. Though, unlike Jarlth, there was nothing untoward in his glare. He licked his lips as if thinking she would make a tasty snack.

"Behave, and Gulma feeds you. Misbehave, and Gulma is always happy for more food." He rubbed a thick-fingered hand across his prodigious belly. "Gulma has questions, but Gulma will let you get acquainted with your new home. You will be Gulma's guest for a long time. " A queer smile peppered his lips. "The rest of your life, in fact."

With that, he turned and left, slamming the gate shut with a hard thunk.

"Now, you pay for not obeying Gulma," the white-skinned Orken growled as he entered Jarlth's cell.

58
KULLEN

Kullen closed the door behind him as quietly as he could and turned to inspect the room. One look at his surroundings, and he knew immediately to whom it belonged. None of the other commanders of the Orkenwatch would accumulate such a gruesome collection of paraphernalia like that he now saw—none but Turoc's favored torturer, Arbiter Chuldok.

The chamber had no bed, merely a messy collection of blankets lying tossed haphazardly against one corner with a straw-stuffed sack that might've served as a pillow. It was occupied chiefly with shelf after shelf of books, glass jars filled with fingers, tongues, and other body parts—human, Orken, Trenta, and creatures Kullen couldn't begin to identify—suspended in multi-colored alchemical liquids, and steel implements of torture. A complete human skeleton lay stretched out across the enormous metal table that occupied the center of the room. Foul-smelling wooden buckets stained with dark fluids Kullen didn't *want* to identify sat beneath the four drain holes at the corners of the table.

On the wall opposite the table's head, a large piece of yellowing parchment hung. Upon it were diagrams of the human body drawn with a steady hand. Flesh and skin were peeled back to reveal musculature and bones, with special attention focused on the points most effective in torture. Blood-red ink marked circles around the knees and inner thighs, the flats of the feet.

He turned his attention to the tray full of bronze tools. Kullen immediately recognized the handiwork of the Trenta in their design. Sure, the little furry folk were peaceful, but Kullen knew their proclivities toward information extraction at any cost. It made sense that they would have a deal of some sort with the Orken, even if they weren't exactly allies.

And the stink in the room was oppressive. With the door closed, only a hint of fresh air seeped in through the arrow slit that served as the chamber's window—nowhere near enough to carry away the fetid stench of rotting meat and moldering bones.

Kullen couldn't bring himself to search the room. Though he wouldn't mind connecting the Orken's head torturer to the Magister Branthe conspiracy, he doubted Chuldok would be in league with the Emperor's enemies. Not when Emperor Wymarc kept him supplied with a steady stream of victims to hone his iniquitous craft. Kullen had it on good authority that Chuldok was considered a freak even among his own people. While the Orken never hesitated to resort to violence, they saw the Arbiter's fascination for inflicting pain as a step removed from a warrior's brutality in battle. He had only risen to his place as an Arbiter because he relished the clash of weapons as much as he delighted in inflicting pain. When his blood was up, he was a truly fierce fighter that even Turoc would think twice about crossing.

It was also widely known that Chuldok had no aspirations toward Turoc's position as Tuskigo. With his focus being on agonizing Dimvein's people, he viewed leadership as an obstacle. Despite his likely prowess with any of the weapons mounted outside Turoc's throne room, he would never raise one against the Tuskigo in hopes of usurping the seat of power.

Kullen's face screwed up as he glared around the blood-stained room. He had no desire to sort through the chaos that cluttered every corner. Not yet, at least. He could double back once he'd searched Turoc's chamber first. The Emperor couldn't keep the Tuskigo occupied forever, and Kullen needed to be certain where Turoc's loyalties lay. That took precedence above all else. If Turoc *could* be trusted, he'd prove a valuable asset in weeding out the quislings. And if he was the traitor—doubtless their leader, for an Orken like Turoc would not take orders lightly from anyone beneath the Emperor—then Emperor Wymarc needed to know. Turoc's treachery would be a problem as monumental as the possibility of an attack by the Blood Clan and Hudarians.

Kullen cracked the door slowly, peering out into the corridor. No sign of Bareg or any other Orken. With relief, Kullen slid free of the foul-smelling room. He gave the other two doors in the truncated hall a glance and decided they would likely belong to Bareg and perhaps another of Turoc's trusted men. The raiding of their rooms could wait—Kullen's purpose today would be to rule out Turoc. Once he'd done that, all others were fair game.

He stepped out into the throne room and darted across to the door into Turoc's chamber. To his surprise, he found the door unlocked. Evidently, Turoc had no need to suspect his fellow Orkenwatch commanders of anything amiss. Either that, or he trusted his ability to rip them to shreds should they steal any of his few belongings.

Few was an understatement, to say the least. Turoc spoke only as much as necessary, a sentiment that clearly extended to his ownership of personal possessions. The closest thing to luxury in his chamber was a massive four-poster bed—large enough to support his enormous frame—with a straw-stuffed sack for a pillow. Otherwise, the room screamed martial austerity at its harshest.

Familiar armor stood on a pedestal in the corner of the room —a spare set, Kullen assumed. Beside it, several weapons of little note.

And yet, Kullen realized not *everything* in the room served Turoc's duties as Tuskigo of the Orkenwatch. Something caught his attention: a book, lying tucked beneath Turoc's pillow. Padding over silently, Kullen slid the book free and read the words etched into the fading leather cover.

Etchings of a Caliphate Slave: The Collected Works of Zafira Kamal. Kullen raised an eyebrow. He recognized the name—*everyone* who had stepped into the Emperor's Palace or half the aristocratic houses of Dimvein would. Zafira Kamal was a Caernia-renowned artist whose works had captured the attention of art collectors in every corner of the globe.

Kullen tugged open the book to a random page and stared at the simple charcoal sketches that had been painstakingly replicated within. Zafira Kumal, called "the Righteous Glory" by contemporary art historians, had somehow captured both the beauty and the cruelty of the hardships she'd endured while enslaved by High Caliph Azim Salah of Niazi. Her etchings depicted the best of humanity amidst the darkest of circumstances.

The image upon which Kullen gazed showed a woman huddling over her starving child, using her body to shield the youth from the sting of a taskmaster's whip. Tears and blood streaked the woman's face, yet there was a beatific look of maternal devotion and fiery determination. Just looking at the etching, Kullen could *feel* the woman's strength. There was no doubt that she would have endured the beating—even unto death —to protect her child.

Kullen flipped through a few more pages, taking in the etchings, each more heartrending than the last. A piece of paper pressed between two of the page leaves caught his eye. Drawing it out, he stared at the image depicted there. Not one of Zamira Kamal's, that much he knew for certain. The lines were too crude, the image of Orken, not humans.

Yet the suffering was no less real. A dozen Orken walked in a straight line, chained together like animals. Though the drawing was done with skill far inferior to the handiwork of Zamira Kamal, Kullen recognized the dead trees and craters marking the landscape as the Korpocane Caverns—the Orken ancestral home.

Kullen's eyebrows rose. It seemed impossible, but at the front of the line, an adolescent Orken who bore a strong resemblance to Turoc trudged. Had the Tuskigo himself scratched this etching? There were a few clumps of charcoal on the bed stand that suggested the possibility.

Kullen's lower lip hung limp. He had no trouble picturing Turoc carving through ranks of enemies with that enormous great sword he carried on his back, wading through streets running red with blood. Yet the image of the mighty Tuskigo sitting hunched over this tiny scrap of parchment and painstakingly sketching out the scene surprised him. Though it could never come close to the works of the Righteous Glory, the etching displayed unexpected talent.

Kullen took care to replace the book exactly as he'd found it and returned to his search. He didn't know exactly what he hoped to find—Turoc wasn't fool enough to keep damning evidence of treachery, much less leave it lying around in plain sight. But he had to try. There were only eight goldbands who might have been involved in Magister Branthe's conspiracy. Kullen had found the "Red Claw" note in Magister Deckard's office and the scrimshaw in Magister Issemar's mansion. Surely there would be *something* he could find.

He rifled through every nook of Turoc's task room and bedchambers, every chest, drawer, and hidey-hole. Frustration gnawed at his gut as he lifted the straw-filled mattress to find nothing but damp stone. Thus far, he'd only uncovered a hint that Turoc might be a reasonably skilled artist, but that did little to either absolve or implicate the Tuskigo.

A small, balled-up piece of paper fallen into the corner behind the bed drew his eye. It could be nothing more than trash, yet still, he stretched his arm until his fingers could grasp it. Pulling it free, he stood and unwrapped its hard contents.

Could it be a connection to Red Claw?

Something fell to the floor, shattering upon impact. A scrimshaw carving like those used as currency within the Blood Pirate's community. This was it… this was the connection he'd been searching for. Kullen bent to pick it up but stopped when his eye met the words writ upon the paper that had held the trinket.

On this, the ninth day of the third month, I, Emperor Stanislav Wymarc, honor thee, Turoc of the Orken peoples, as established Tuskigo of Tuskthorne Keep. It is with all my trust that I place upon you the freedom to rule in my stead in the ways of law keeping within my finest city, Dimvein. This is not a decision I have taken lightly. As my fathers and their fathers and their fathers' fathers have done for neigh on three centuries, I commission you as my hand of power.

Then, marked with the Emperor's seal, it was signed Emperor Stanislav Wymarc, lord ruler of the Karmian Empire.

Kullen's mind raced. The scrimshaw was damning in itself, but why had Turoc kept this for so long? Did it carry special meaning to him, or was it being used to house the proof of his betrayal, some kind of slight upon the Emperor?

His rumination was cut short by the sound of Turoc's door opening. Kullen rose and reached for his blades, but it was too late. In the doorway was a towering Orken figure. Somehow, the hulking brute had crept up on Kullen without making a sound. Kullen didn't get a chance to see who it was—his gaze locked onto the loaded crossbow aimed straight at his head.

He made a mad dash, leaping aside. It was no use. He'd been caught. The crossbow string loosed its missile with a *twang,* and Kullen knew no more.

59
NATISSE

Natisse drew in deep, slow breaths, fighting the instinctive worry and despair rising within her. She'd put herself in this situation intentionally, she reminded herself, knowing the risks and deeming them worthwhile if it led her to the Crimson Fang. Sure, she had no weapons, no armor, and nothing in the way of clothing beyond her simple undergarments, but she wasn't entirely destitute. Not as long as she still had Golgoth's vial.

With deft movements, she loosened the thong holding her braid tight, and slid the dragonblood vial free of her red hair. Slipping it over her head, she breathed a relieved sigh at the featherlight weight settling around her shoulders. Come what may, at least she could proceed with the confidence she wouldn't face it alone.

"I am here," Golgoth's voice echoed through their mental bond. *"You have but to ask, and my power is yours."*

The dragon's presence brought with it a sense of warm reassurance. She couldn't summon Golgoth—the dragon's enormous bulk would never fit within the narrow confines of Tuskthorne Keep—but the fire magic more than made up for her lack of weaponry.

I've come this far, she thought, rising smoothly to her feet despite the aches and pains in her body. *Now to find the others.*

A barely breathing Jarlth lay in a bloody mess in the cell beside hers, a simple reminder of what disobeying Gulma meant. She had no designs to stay put long. However, her plan faced one notable and immediate obstacle: she was locked in a cell from which there were no visible means of escape.

In the faint light of the lone cresset hanging in the corridor outside, she could see nothing that would offer her a way out. If the underground structure was *Ghuklek*-built like the Burrows, this particular cell had nothing that looked like the hidden passages Uncle Ronan had snuck through all those days ago. Natisse swept her hands across every one of the brass beams supporting the low stone ceiling but found no brass rings or concealed latches. It was certainly too much to hope that she would end up in the *one* cell that contained a secret of such value —if any such way existed at all, that was.

She turned her attention to the bronze bars that barred her escape. They were set too close together for her to slip through, though she could reach an arm out to feel at the locking mechanism that held the cell door closed. To her surprise, she recognized the design. It was Trenta-made, with the complex springs, mechanisms, and inevitable fail-safes that earned their locks a well-deserved, Empire-wide reputation for being uncrackable.

Ezrasil knew she'd spent time enough trying in vain to prove that reputation wrong. Countless picks, rakes, and jigglers had snapped in her fingers. The locks utilized some alchemical fluid that softened even the finest steel. Everything she and her fellows of the Crimson Fang had tried ended in failure. Even Haston, the lock-picking expert, could find no way through.

But something he'd said upon their last attempt flashed through her mind. Fresh off another frustratingly unsuccessful half hour, Natisse had thrown down her tools in frustration and attempted to kick the lock open. In vain, of course. The Trenta used a special bronze alloy—the secret of which they guarded with their lives—to make the mechanisms impervious to even direct impact.

"You could spend an hour battering at that thing with a ram," Haston had told her, shaking his head, "but you'll break the door frame before the lock cedes."

"Dragonpiss!" she'd growled. Then an idea had struck her. "Sod that! What about *Dragonfire?* Would that work?"

Haston had snorted and rolled his eyes. "Got a fire dragon in your back pocket, do you? Ulnu's tits, Natisse, if you're going to make harebrained suggestions, at least try to make them realistic, yeah?"

At the time, Natisse had been speaking of one of Serrod's alchemical potions—a potion much like the one she and Jad had used to burn down Magister Branthe's slave fighting pit. And yet, her notion felt far less harebrained at the moment.

She reached for the vial hanging at her neck, pressing her thumb onto the needle atop the golden cap. The slight prick sent a surge of hope through her veins as raw power flooded through her. Her surroundings practically glowed like hot coals, defining each element in stark contrast to the darkness.

Yet, as she felt it surging up within her, an image slammed into her. Fire, searing hot and gold-edged crimson, roaring past her to consume her friends. The dream that had haunted her sleep and awoke her screaming, now inundated her with hesitation and fear. The flames building in her belly were doused as if beneath a torrent of ice-cold water.

Pouring sweat and reduced to tremors, Natisse couldn't shake the memory of what had happened the first time she'd tried to wield Golgoth's power. She'd nearly burned down the Wild Grove Forest when the flames had exploded beyond her control. Visions of her parents, of Joakim, the man from her dreams and the shipyard... they tormented her into paralyzed fear.

What if she couldn't control the fire now? What if it burst outward from her again and swept down the corridor in a wave of destruction? The people imprisoned in the cells near hers—at least *some* of them innocents, no doubt—could die screaming, consumed by Dragonfire just as her parents had been. And if the Crimson Fang was somewhere nearby…

No! She stumbled backward on trembling legs. *No, I can't risk that.* She couldn't let that terrifying dream come true.

Fatigue—both physical and magical, compounded by the aches and pains inflicted by the Orken who'd arrested her—stole the strength from her limbs. She sat down hard on the floor, lying flat on her stomach to let the cool stone snuff out the last of the burning in her belly. Yet even the stone's chill couldn't dampen the flush of heat rising in her cheeks.

Kullen had told her to master her fear, yet here she was, a victim to it once again. Shame had become her cellmate, and it was a companion far worse than Jarlth could've ever been.

How long she lie there, wrestling with her guilt, she didn't know. She had no way to mark the passage of time beyond the slow beats of her heart. The steady *thump, thumping* of her pulse in her ears felt mocking.

She was right to be afraid, wasn't she? Her caution, born of her horrific past, was what had led Golgoth to choose her in the first place. The dragon had bonded with her knowing that Natisse wouldn't abuse the dragonblood magic, wouldn't do *anything* that could lead to destruction on a scale as grand as the fire that had leveled the Imperial Commons years earlier.

Kullen's words came unbidden to her mind. *"Fear imposes limits on what you can do, which can be both good and bad. It will stop you from overusing the ability and—in your case, quite literally—burning yourself out. Just as I told you that I can only shadow-slide a few times before I must rest, you, too, have limitations. Fear will keep you from crossing that line once you discover what it is."*

She had seen what happened when she lost control. That was what made her afraid—of herself and her lack of understanding of the magic. She had only *just* begun learning how to wield Golgoth's fire. That night in Wild Grove Forest, she'd started to feel better about her mastery of the raging torrent of power coursing within her. Right up until the fire had burst free of her grasp and wreaked terrible destruction.

Natisse couldn't let that happen. She had to find some way to use the fire in small measures, to prevent it escaping her control. Otherwise, it was a weapon far too dangerous to wield.

She rose from the floor, gathering her resolve, but the sound of heavy, slapping feet grew in the distance, accompanied by a thick sloshing. Natisse's mind raced, a desperate plan forming. She fell to her face on the ground beside the bars of the cell and curled up in a ball around her knees—both in a pretense of agony and to hide the vial hanging at her neck.

"Feeding time!" Gulma's sibilant voice whispered down the corridor. "Gulma has brought treats for his guests."

Natisse didn't move but let out the most piteous moan she could muster. It was a pathetic sound, weak and so faint she doubted human ears would have picked it up. But Orken had a keener sense of hearing. Gulma *had* to have heard.

Her hope was rewarded a moment later. "Gulma's new guest is hurting?"

The white-skinned Orken waddled closer to her cell and stopped just beyond the bars. Natisse could feel his gaze fixed on her but refused to move a muscle. She merely let out another whimpering groan.

"Hmm," mused Gulma, making a sickly sucking sound through his fanged teeth. "Perhaps the new guest is in need of Gulma's personal attention? Gulma did not intend to ask questions so soon—better for Gulma's guest to enjoy her new home without the comfort of food or water—but Gulma would not be happy if Gulma's guest could not answer Gulma's queries."

The Orken's leather harness gave a great creaking, and Natisse felt Gulma's breath hot on her back and shoulders. Though her skin crawled, she forced herself to remain still. No whimper this time. If he believed she'd passed out…

A clawed fingernail scratched a sharp, painful line down her back. "Wake up, new guest!" Gulma dragged out the last sibilant sound. "Gulma has—"

Natisse spun so fast, Gulma had no time to react before she seized his wrist and yanked as hard as she could. The Orken's blubbery face slammed into the bars between them hard enough that spittle sprayed from his mouth. His red eyes rolled up, and he sagged in a limp puddle of fat outside her cell. Natisse sprang to her feet but didn't release her grip on the Orken's wrist. She needed him to remain within her grasp so she could search him for the keys that opened the door to her cell.

Hope blossomed in her chest. Nearly obscured beneath the folds of sagging white fat, a bronze ring hung from the belt that secured his far-too-skimpy loincloth. She fought her instinctive revulsion as she lifted the flaps of his belly to tear the ring free. Only then did she release Gulma's wrist—she'd need two hands to work the lock.

The ring held easily half a hundred keys, all virtually identical. Natisse had no idea which one opened her cell but refused to let that daunt her. She set to work testing one key after another in the lock.

"What are you doing?" Jarlth groaned. She peered over her shoulder at him, but he was barely aware of his surroundings. As long as he stayed quiet, he would pose no true threat.

Click.

The sound set Natisse's spirits soaring. *Yes!* She wrestled with the door, straining against Gulma's bulk until she finally got it open wide enough to slip out.

"Wake up!" Jarlth shouted to Gulma.

"What are you doing?" Natisse growled.

Jarlth rolled to his side, staring up at her. "You don't leave if I don't leave." Then, at the top of his voice, he shouted again.

Gulma growled as he stirred. Natisse was uncertain what to do. She had no weapons to finish him off, and there was no way she could wrestle his corpulent bulk into her now-open cell. He was much too fat to bind him with his own harness—besides,

Natisse had no desire to touch his bare flesh any more than she wanted to put her head in a gnasher's maw.

She settled for the only thing she could do: she gave him a swift kick to the side of his head, then removed her undergarments and used them to bind his pudgy wrists behind his back. It wasn't ideal—the cloth was woven for comfort and softness more than durability, and she would now be running around Tuskthorne Keep stark naked—but at least she had one less thing to worry about.

"I don't know what you did to land yourself in here," she told Jarlth, who now looked at her with one part lust and two parts envy that she was free. "But you lost your chance at my mercy."

Jarlth begged. "Please, I would do you no harm." But his thirsty eyes at the sight of her nudity told a different story.

"I hope he takes his full aggression out on you," she said as she spun away.

Natisse hesitated for a single moment, torn by indecision and uncertainty. She had to find a way out *and* locate her friends—but which first? Much as she wanted to make certain of the former, the latter had to take precedence. She'd need the rest of the Crimson Fang as backup in case any Orken arrived to deposit more prisoners into Gulma's care. And with *all* of them working together, surely they'd have an easier time finding a way of escape.

She set off at a harried pace past Jarlth and deeper into the dungeon. Prisoners reached through the bars at her, some sharing Jarlth's sick proclivities and others desperate for a prison break. More, still, were asleep or unconscious and pity pangs stabbed at Natisse's heart. However, without knowing what crimes placed these men and women into the Keep, she had no way of knowing whether spending the time to free them would be better or worse for Dimvein.

One thing was sure, there was no sign of the *Ghuklek* who'd been taken from the Burrow nor the Crimson Fang themselves. Natisse's heart grew heavier with every step, the dim flames of her hope dying in the face of cold reality. More cells and no Uncle

Ronan or the rest. Where were they? Serrod had said he'd overheard talk of them being taken here. Were plans changed?

When she reached the final cell, the corridor ended. Her heart gave into plummeting. She stood before a five-foot by five-foot circular pit. Natisse skidded to a halt at its edge. Horror twisted in her stomach at the sight of its contents. Suddenly, she understood Gulma's mention of "treat pit."

Two dozen gnashers of all sizes and ages quietly gnawed away at piles of flesh-covered bones. She watched, horrorstruck, as they sensed her standing above. The babies turned first, cowering behind what Natisse assumed to be their mother. Then, the largest of the bunch turned on her and hissed. Soon, they were all scrambling in a flurry of limbs at the walls to get to her, but the sleek, smooth surface kept them from gaining purchase and escaping.

Natisse recoiled, her feet scrabbling at the hard-packed earth bordering the pit in instinctive fear. It hadn't been long since last she'd come face-to-face with a gnasher, and only Uncle Ronan's timely arrival had saved her. She had no Lumenator powers now, though her fire magic might work to drive the creatures back. Better if she stayed far away from the pit all the same.

She slowly backed away, feeling no different from those creatures desperate to escape their prison. What had she been thinking, getting herself arrested? There might've been a better way. She shook her head, then turned back in the direction of her cell. With no signs of the Crimson Fang, her efforts had been moot. Now, all that was left was to escape the most heavily-guarded place in all of Dimvein.

To make matters worse, a familiar heavy, slapping sound echoed from down the hall. She'd been a fool to believe her underclothes would do much to keep his muscles bound.

"Gulma will find you, little pet," Gulma taunted as he waddled down the corridor toward her.

60
KULLEN

Kullen awoke in immense pain. His head felt as if it had been split open by an Orken axe, and the entire left side of his skull throbbed with the force of a stampeding dragon. An involuntary groan escaped his lips. Light pierced his closed eyelids, painfully bright, but when he tried to turn his head away, he found he couldn't move. Something clamped down hard on his forehead and held his head fast. His arms and legs, too, were trapped within what felt like bands of steel.

Fear sent his pulse spiking, and his eyelids flew open. Orbs danced in his vision, but he took in what he could see of his surroundings at a glance: stone walls and ceiling, tables upon which lay bronzed steel and iron implements in neat rows, and Trenta torture devices. And on the wall before him, the same diagram of the human anatomy glared at him.

Three Orken stood just within his field of view. Two he recognized at once. One was Bareg, all lean muscles and too-wide nostrils. The Ketsneer still held the crossbow that had loosed the bolt—a blunt head, Kullen realized—that had rendered him senseless. Arbiter Chuldok's hulking frame and long, curving tusks were unmistakable even among his own people. So, too, was the look of eager excitement that brightened his face as he ran a thick, sharp-nailed finger across a pair of razor-sharp scissors.

The third Orken wore silver bands braided into his beard—a mid-level grunt of some sort, and, judging by the way he stood near the chamber's lone door, the one set to guard the room while Bareg and Chuldok set to work on Kullen.

"You awake," growled Bareg, his voice grinding in Kullen's ears like sand between metal plates. "Foolish human, you, creep into Turoc chambers. Think you outsmart Bareg. But Bareg outsmart you." He tapped his broad, wide-nostriled nose. "Recognize strange smell. Wrong smell. Follow smell to find you. Now you talk for Chuldok."

Kullen's mind raced. He wasn't in an ideal situation—strapped to a torture table, about to be at the mercy of Arbiter Chuldok's maltreatment, and, it appeared, utterly naked. His cloak, coat, vest, shirt, breeches, and boots had been stripped off. Even his undergarments had been removed. All of his belongings lay in a carefully folded pile nearby.

Including, he realized with a rush of fear, his dragonblood vial.

The gold-capped canister and its silver chain lay neatly placed atop his clothes, tantalizingly close yet *just* too far out of his reach. Without that vial, he had no way to access Umbris's powers directly. He had just the bits of magic available to him through their bond to facilitate his escape.

"No need to break out the toys," he said, trying for a jovial tone. "I'll happily answer any questions. You have but to ask!" He plastered on a wide grin.

Bareg stared down at him, black eyes cold and face impassive. "Who you?" he asked.

"Turoc's very best friend in the whole world!" Kullen beamed. "You know how much he loves surprises, and with his birthday just around the corner, I took it upon myself to plan a truly spectacular party." He gave a high, excited laugh as if the restraints on his head, wrists, and ankles didn't bother him at all. "Oh, the look on his face when he sees what I've got planned for him. I dare not reveal *all* the secrets of the marvels to come, but I can give you a hint—if you're interested. Hmm?"

Bareg's expression remained blank.

"Yes, I thought so." Kullen waggled his eyebrows and dropped his voice to a conspiratorial whisper. "It involves dancing bears, a feather duster, a deck of playing cards, and four scantily-clad virgins. But that's all I can say!" He pressed his lips tightly together and spoke from the corner of his mouth. "I will tell you no more. It would ruin the surprise, and our dear Tuskigo deserves only the best on his special day."

While Bareg's eyes were locked on his face, Kullen surreptitiously twisted his right wrist to test the manacle holding him restrained. There was just enough give that he could shift slightly, but it would be damned hard to slip his hand free without breaking any of the small bones. Which he would do if necessary, though only as a last resort.

The Ketsneer's face never altered, but his fist darted out and struck Kullen hard across the face. Though Kullen saw the blow coming, he could do nothing to evade it. The force set his ears ringing and his vision spinning. Through the blur, he saw Bareg leaning over him, bared fangs dangerously close to his face and throat.

"Not Turoc's birthday," snarled the Ketsneer. "Not until *Nodbrogsnacht.*"

Kullen stared up at the Orken, more than a little surprised. That wasn't the sort of thing he'd expect *any* Orken to keep track of—they didn't celebrate things the way humans did—but somehow he'd gotten the one Orken who did? Cliessa had exhausted all her care on him this night, it seemed.

"Little man lie." Bareg opened his mouth wider, giving Kullen a closer look at the two razor-sharp tusks protruding from his lower jar. "Little man need convincing to tell Bareg truth." He turned to look at Arbiter Chuldok and growled something in the Orken tongue.

"No convincing needed!" Kullen said, trying for the same jovial tone. "I'll admit you were *mighty* clever seeing through my ruse the way you did. Truly a testament to your intelligence, my Orken friend."

"Bareg not friend," snapped the Ketsneer. "Bareg and little man enemies. Little man thief, and Orken *crush* thiefs." He straightened and reached with one huge hand to clamp on Kullen's wrist. "Break hands, then feet, then knees, elbows, then *hrignuzz*…" He flicked at Kullen's manhood with his other hand. "Thief sent to Gulma for *ugboda* food."

Kullen flinched instinctively away from the assault on his most delicate parts. Being naked and in restraints wasn't exactly how he'd intended to spend the night. He had no desire to endure whatever Arbiter Chuldok had in mind for him, nor to find out what this "Gulma" was that Bareg intended to feed him to.

"You want the truth?" He dropped the genteel façade, letting his usual rasping harshness back into his voice. "The truth is that I was sent by the Emperor himself to investigate your Tuskigo." He fixed Bareg with a hard glare. "I am here on the orders of the Emperor all of you have sworn to serve, and by holding me prisoner, you are defying his royal will."

If Bareg believed him or felt even a hint of fear, his brutish face didn't show it. Arbiter Chuldok, however, appeared to hesitate. His hand stopped caressing his torturer's tools for a moment, and his eyes darted to Kullen. Though he hadn't spoken, Kullen knew he understood. His grasp of the Imperial tongue was impressive even by Orken standards.

Chuldok spoke a few words in the Orken tongue, and Bareg answered without taking his eyes off Kullen. Kullen could only make out a few words, just enough to understand the general thrust of their conversation. The Arbiter was asking if Bareg knew Kullen—either his features or his scent—and the way Bareg's eyes narrowed, Kullen suspected the Ketsneer *had* recognized something about him. Bareg leaned low over Kullen's chest and drew in a deep breath through his nostrils. The closeness to his bare skin set Kullen's skin crawling.

Bareg's expression hardened. When he straightened, he barked a few words in Orken. In response, the Orken who'd stood guard at the door hurried from the chamber.

Kullen stared up at Bareg. "You know my scent, don't you? You've smelled it on Turoc before. When he returns from the Palace."

"Many scents," Bareg said, a scowl deepening his boulder face. "Many, many scents."

Despite the Ketsneer's protests, Kullen saw the look of recognition in his eyes. Though the two of them had never come face-to-face before today, Kullen had interacted enough with Turoc that his odor would be recognizable to the Sniffer's keen sense of smell.

"You want proof that I am who I say I am?" Kullen looked between Bareg and Arbiter Chuldok. "Get Turoc down here. Or Seneschal Assidius. They'll both confirm my identity."

Much as Kullen hated the idea of needing the help of either Turoc or Assidius—that last set his stomach twisting in revulsion—his pride mattered less than the successful completion of the mission given him by the Emperor. He had seen the hidden bits of scrimshaw that proved Turoc's collusion with the Blood Clan pirates, a link to the same conspiracy that had involved Magisters Deckard, Branthe, and Issemar. Now, he just had to do whatever it took to get out of Tuskthorne Keep and bring word of his treachery to the Emperor. Even if that meant relying on the Seneschal or Tuskigo.

But even as the words left his mouth, he realized with a sinking heart he'd somehow said the wrong thing. Both Arbiter Chuldok and Bareg bristled, baring their fangs and growling in guttural Orken.

"He work with *Zadruzak?*" was the gist of Bareg's question.

Kullen had heard that one before—an Orken insult that referred to a particularly loathsome and slimy breed of serpentine reptiles that made their home in the Riftwild. There were few words Kullen could think of more disparaging.

Arbiter Chuldok's huge hands flexed, and he raised the scissors menacingly. "Truth he tells us, then he die," the Orken growled in his own tongue.

Kullen had no need to translate. He recognized the meaning behind the action: mention of the Seneschal had only turned them further against him.

But why? To all of the Orken serving the Empire, Assidius was just another of the Emperor's loyal servants. Turoc and the rest of the Orkenwatch commanders knew that he was the Emperor's spymaster, certainly.

Then, realization hit him harder than any Orken fist could have. *Of course!* He couldn't believe he hadn't seen it earlier.

They could have merely killed him outright—as was their privilege, given that he'd infiltrated their sovereign territory—but instead chosen to capture and torture him. They wanted something from him. Information. Answers. They wanted to know how much *he* knew.

Because it was not just Turoc who plotted against the Emperor. These two were also in on the collusion. His mind reeled at the implications. Just how many of the goldbands were involved? It seemed things were far more complicated than even Kullen imagined.

61

NATISSE

Cold sweat poured over Natisse. The closed doors of cells barred any escape to her right and left. With the gnasher pit at her back and the obscenely obese Gulma coming straight toward her, she was trapped.

Gulma hadn't bothered to wipe the blood leaking from the wound where his forehead had struck the bars of Natisse's cell. A thin line of crimson streaked down his face, droplets staining his sagging chest and belly. Indeed, he seemed more irritated by Natisse's flight from her cell than the injury to his person.

The ponderous Orken clucked his tongue. "Bad guest. Gulma gives you a home, and you want to leave Gulma before questions are asked? Bad, bad guest!" He waggled a taloned finger at her, which set his heavy jowls and thick flaps of arm skin wobbling. "Gulma must punish you."

Behind Natisse, the gnashers' hissing increased in volume, and she heard the skritching sound of claws scraping at stone. She risked a glance back and down into the pit where the hair-laden creatures leaped toward her with open maws and their multiple eyes, appearing ravenous. The stone walls were *just* too smooth and high to keep them from escaping, but Natisse's heart quickened, fear settling like a boulder in her belly.

"Don't worry, pretty ones!" Gulma called out in a singsong voice. "Gulma will soon have treats for you." His gleaming red eyes fixed on Natisse, roaming every inch of bared flesh. "Tasty, tasty human treats for Gulma's hungry darlings."

"Piss on that!" Natisse snarled, summoning every shred of defiance she could muster. She dropped the key ring and settled into a fighting stance, knees bent and fists raised. "Tell me where my friends are, and I'll consider letting you live."

Gulma stopped half a dozen paces away, eyeing her with a curious expression. His face showed no fear of her—and why would it, when she'd played the role of terrified, docile captive all this time? He merely cocked his head, his pointed ears twitching as if listening to some sound she couldn't hear.

"Friends?" the Orken asked, hissing the last letter like a serpent's rattle. "What friends?"

"The Crimson Fang." Natisse forced herself not to recoil from his hungry stare, to shield her body from his greedy eyes. "I know they were arrested last night. Where are you keeping them?"

"Keeping them?" Gulma blew out a mocking laugh that set his fat lips wobbling. "Gulma has not your friends. No Crimson Fang as Gulma's guests. Not anymore. Once the Emperor is done with them, he will surely send them back to Gulma for more questions." He ran his tongue over his teeth with a loud slurping sound. "Delicious, delicious questions. Gulma is good at asking questions. Gulma always gets his answers. In the end, all answer."

Natisse stifled a shudder, focused on Gulma's words. The hideous Orken had confirmed the suspicion that had begun growing in her belly. Her friends weren't here. "Not anymore," as Gulma had said. They'd been taken to the Palace dungeons. She'd come this way hoping to free them—too late. Now she was trapped here, alone, unclothed and unarmed, with nothing but her wits, fists, and dragonblood vial to get her out.

"Come, come," Gulma said, crooking his taloned finger toward her in a beckoning gesture. "Gulma will give you a chance to return to your new home quietly. Do that, and Gulma will only punish you a little. Do not..." The Orken licked his lips again and slapped his belly with his other hand. "Gulma must teach his guest to be more polite."

Natisse didn't budge. She'd spent time enough in that bloody cell. With her friends even now languishing in the Emperor's dungeons, there wasn't a damned thing that would keep her here.

"You want me?" she snarled. "Come and get me!"

Gulma clucked his tongue a third time and gave a disappointed shake of his head. "Bad guest," he said, his tone scolding. "Gulma will teach manners."

The Orken lumbered into motion like a vast ship leaving berth, slowly at first but picking up speed as he crossed the six paces toward her. Natisse ducked beneath his outstretched arms and drove two quick punches into his kidneys. The blows struck home with the precision she'd honed over years of training but had no more effect on Gulma than on the straw dummies. The Orken's enormous, blubbery belly rippled beneath the impact, dissipating the force of her strikes. Her hardest blow earned nothing more than a little grunt of irritation from Gulma and a hurt hand for her part. Then Gulma's huge, flabby arms were reaching for her again.

Natisse danced to the side, evading the Orken's grasp, but slammed into the bronze bars of the empty cell. She shoved off and swung a hard right hook into Gulma's face. The Orken just turned his head, so her fist bounced off his flabby cheek instead of shattering his nose. Before Natisse could recover, one thick arm wrapped around hers, trapping her in place.

She struggled to break free, but Gulma had Orken musculature beneath the heavy layers of fat. His free hand reached up to seize her wrist in a grasp as unbreakable as an iron vise. The arm he'd used to trap hers now slid around her shoulders, and his long, talon-tipped fingers seized her by the neck.

He brought his face close to hers, his fetid breath hot on her cheeks. "Must teach mann—"

Natisse bashed her forehead into his nose. This time, her blow landed true. His nose *crunched* beneath the impact and splashed blood across his left cheek. Blood gushed as if a spigot had been opened, seeping down his lips, chin, and splashing onto his chest and belly.

"Bad guest!" Gulma roared, pain in his cry. His arm clamped tighter around Natisse, pulling her closer, burying her face against his enormous chest.

She tried to pull away, fought to escape, but it seemed every movement only drove her deeper into Gulma's flabby folds. Sagging white flesh enveloped her, suffocating, choking the air from her lungs.

She couldn't help but recall being dragged beneath the waters below Pantagoya, watching as the light faded and the darkness of sleep crept in. In that moment, her need had been the same. She felt the weight of Golgoth's power rising within her, starting with a tingle, then burning deep in her bones. Unbidden and out of her control, fire roared to life, bursting out of every pore in her flesh. It was as if an alchemical bomb had detonated between Natisse and the Orken choking the life from her lungs. She was hurled backward to crash against the brass bars so forcefully, they bent beneath the impact. The air evacuated her lungs, and sparks swirled in her vision.

But the damage to Gulma was far worse. The blast of magical Dragonfire seared the length and breadth of his bare torso, burning through his leather harness and turning the skin of his upper body into a charred, blackened mess. Through the dizzying blur, Natisse saw the corpulent Orken staggering backward, battering at his burning flesh with thick, taloned hands. His screams filled her ears and rang off the dungeon walls and ceiling. Absently, she recognized the voices of prisoners cheering as their tormenter anguished.

And then, suddenly, Gulma was gone. His screams ended abruptly in a loud *thump* that set the ground beneath Natisse reverberating. Dazed as she was, she had no idea what had happened. Not until she managed to shake off the dizziness and climb to her feet. That was when she saw the pit's edge.

The hissing and yowling of the gnashers pierced through the blood rushing in her ears. She peered down into the hole and spotted a single patch of white beneath the swirling, frenzied, furry bodies. In an act of pure poetry, Gulma was being torn apart by his own creatures.

"Bad host," Natisse said, barely able to get the words out. She would have spat into the pit, but her mouth was too dry. Her throat felt as parched as if she'd just traveled across the harshest deserts in the Caliphate of Fire. There was nothing left in her. No strength, no energy, no vigor. Exhaustion was her last companion. She collapsed to her knees, falling onto her hands, panting and gasping for air. Her lungs felt scorched, her muscles drained. Fatigue set the world around her swimming and spinning wildly.

Golgoth had saved her. Again. The dragon's magic had come to her aid, bursting forth from her body with a force beyond her control. And in so doing, it had ravaged her again, leaving her a husk of her true self.

Natisse knew that this was not how it was meant to be. *She* was supposed to call the fire to her, summon and control it the way Kullen had tried to instruct her. But her fear of the fire—of the harm it could do—was interfering with her bond. Much more of this, and the power could burn her from the inside out. She couldn't keep this up. It felt as if years had been peeled away from her.

But she refused to give in to the physical and magical exhaustion. Not while she was still trapped inside Tuskthorne Keep and her friends were held captive in the Emperor's dungeons.

She racked her brain, trying to figure out what to do now. She still had Gulma's keys—they still lay where she'd dropped them—but even if she could open the door barring the dungeon's entrance, she'd still be dealing with all the Orkenwatch at the massive gate—a gate she had no way of opening on her own, even if she could somehow survive fighting *three* Orken alone.

There was no chance she could leave Tuskthorne Keep the same way she'd entered. But did any other way out even exist?

Even as the question formed in her mind, her eyes settled on a patch of darkness downward and at the far end of the gnashers' pit. It seemed impossible, and yet—

Can it be?

Natisse pushed herself to her feet and stumbled toward the nearest torch, swaying unsteadily with every step.

"Save us!" shouted one female prisoner. Natisse appraised the speaker, seeing dirty and matted hair atop a face so white and pale she appeared like a ghost. Sores grew on her mouth, her cheeks, and even around her eyes. Sunken and pitiable eyes. "Please, you can't leave us here! I've done nothing wrong. Nothing. I merely stole some bread so my children could eat. Please, miss. Please."

Natisse glared down the row of prisoners. The worry that she could be unleashing more criminals onto the streets weighed upon her chest, but she couldn't simply leave and do nothing. Besides, a bit of mayhem in the tower as the captives tried to escape could only help conceal her own flight.

Mind made up, she crossed the distance to where the ring of keys lay and scooped them up. She handed them to the woman. "Free your fellows. From there, it's up to you. It won't be easy, but perhaps your numbers will help."

"Oh, Ezrasil be praised," the woman sobbed. "Thank you. Thank you to the heights of heaven and the depths of Shekoth."

"Take it," Natisse said, pressing the keyring through the bars. "Take it and go. May Ezrasil be with you."

Hearing the clatter of metal against metal, Natisse returned to her plan, wondering if she'd be better off working with the gaggle of prisoners to dispatch the guards above and break free.

They don't stand a chance, she thought. *But better they try than rot down here.*

She lifted the burning brand from its holder and brought it back to the pit's edge. The gnashers were still occupied with Gulma's corpse—the Orken's frame had ample meat to feed even their voracious appetites for days—and only one looked up and hissed at the bright light in her hand. Heart in her throat, Natisse hurled the torch toward the inky black on the other side of the pit.

The torch landed on a patch of bare stone on the pit's ground, and the flickering light revealed the mouth of a tunnel leading out of the gnasher pit. For the first time since she'd broken free of the cell, hope swelled in her chest. The opening was too small for the largest of the creatures, the adults, but appeared to be sized for only the infant and young gnashers. Given the fact that the babies were akin in size to fully grown wolves, she had little doubt she could fit too.

Natisse couldn't believe that she was *actually* contemplating what felt like a truly insane scheme. But what choice did she have? None. When deciding between a horde of well-armed Orken warriors or hungry gnashers, Natisse knew which odds fell better in her favor.

Cliessa, she prayed, *smile on me now.*

Before she could reconsider, she lowered herself over the pit's smooth edge and began to climb down. She refused to ponder the consequences she could be opening herself up to but just kept climbing down, one foot and handhold at a time. She couldn't go straight down—not with all the gnashers tearing into Gulma's corpse—but circled around to the right, where the pit walls were a little more jagged, and the way down was easier.

With every new movement, she prayed the gnashers wouldn't notice her. They had a feast before them and the torch burning nearby. Hopefully, one small human clinging to the walls of their pit would be far less interesting than—

The rock face cracked beneath her foot, sending shards tumbling down. She heard the movement of gnashers below, hissing, clamoring for fresh meat. She tried to gain a new foothold but failed once, twice. Then, Natisse's hand slipped, a fistful of rocks breaking free. She screamed, swore, but it was no help. Despite all her protests, she felt herself falling. With nothing to grab hold of, she braced for impact. The only saving grace was the fall wasn't far, and it wouldn't be hard stone she landed upon, but still, it hurt. She felt sharp bones dig into her back and something jagged against her shoulder. She wished to lay there for long moments but had no time to give in to the pain.

She fought to stand, slipping on Gulma's rotted remains. The sound of her fall, the splintering of the bones, and now her struggles alerted every last gnasher to her presence. As one, they turned away from their feast of fresh Orken and whirled on her. Fangs bared, stingers flailing behind them, taloned legs brandished, they came for her.

With all her willpower, she tried to draw upon Golgoth's magic.

Golgoth, I need you.

But no answer came.

62

KULLEN

Kullen stared at the two Orken before him, suddenly seeing them in a new light. Magister Branthe's conspiracy hadn't just included *one* goldband—Bareg, Chuldok, and perhaps the rest of the Orkenwatch command were colluding with their Tuskigo against the Empire.

He fixed a baleful glare on Arbiter Chuldok, who held a pair of wicked-looking scissors and turned toward him. His golden eyes gleamed with a sense of elation at what he was about to do.

"So it's true, then?" He shifted his gaze to Bareg. "You *are* working with the Empire's enemies. You are turning traitor and breaking the oaths your people swore to Emperor Lasavic?"

"Oaths!" Bareg's lip curled up into a sneer, baring one curving tusk. "Sworn by Orken now dead. But us Orken living still held in chains. Living in prison of our own making." He thumped a fist against his chest. "Us Orken living now be freed."

Kullen frowned. "What chains? You are given a place of honor in Dimvein, treated with respect, and imbued with the power to carry out the Emperor's justice."

"*Emperor's* justice!" Bareg snapped. "Not Orken justice."

Kullen snorted. "Ripping out your enemies' throats with your tusks or snapping them in half—that sound like justice to you? Sounds like bloody murder to me."

"Because you are human." Arbiter Chuldok's deep voice echoed through the room. "Understand not the ways of Orken, do you. Warriors, the Orken are, strong and fierce, desiring free roam. Not lock life away in dark tunnels or serve another. Good, Emperor may be, but he is no Orken."

"And Orken not serve human." Bareg snapped. "Not for longer much."

Kullen's own face contorted into a wicked sneer. "You remember why your kind swore to serve the Empire, don't you?" His eyes darted between the two Orken. "Because the Hudarians, Trillites, and every other shite-sucking kingdom bordering the Riftwild saw you as monsters to be eradicated. Only the Empire treated you as equals. You think the Blood Clan or the Horde will let you live once they've conquered the Empire? Or will you end up in cages, fighting for their entertainment, or marching into battle as fodder for their armies?"

"Not matter." Bareg's jaw clenched, his face hardening. "Empire destroyed and Emperor dead, Orken free of oaths. Free to return home and live as free Orken. No chains of humans. Free to honor *Kith'meh'ga*."

"Even if that means fighting for your very survival?" Kullen demanded. "How long until the Hudar Horde marches on the Riftwild or sends an army to march into the Korpocane Caverns? Until they decide that you're too great a threat to allow to multiply and decide to erase you from Caernia for good? You would turn your back on the Emperor for *that*?"

"*Kith'meh'ga* demands it," Chuldok said, though his tone carried more hesitation than before.

"What is this Kith'meh'ga?" Kullen asked, curiosity at the second use of the word getting the best of him.

"Not what—who," Bareg said, drawing a closed fist to his forehead as if performing some sign or ritual.

Before Kullen could follow up on the mystery, the door

reopened, and the Orken who had left minutes earlier now returned, but not alone. He carried a small black-wooden cage with iron bars that contained a hideous creature Kullen had only heard about but never seen in person.

With a head bearing only the slightest resemblance to a wolf or lion, eight glowing yellow eyes drilled into Kullen's. A wisp of a tail, just beginning to grow, swatted the air behind it, occasionally drawing a thudding clank from the bars of its cage. It snarled, a pitiful sound coming from one so young.

A *gnasher*. And a baby one at that.

The Orken's arrival seemed to banish any last hints of uncertainty or doubt from the two Orken traitors. Arbiter Chuldok spoke to the Ketsneer in Orken—words Kullen didn't understand —and at a nod from Bareg, set down the tools of torture. He strode around behind one of the tables, leaving Kullen's field of vision. Bareg, however, turned to the Orken holding the caged gnasher and, to Kullen's dismay, tugged at the latch that held the iron doors shut.

Kullen had heard tales of the monstrosities that lurked in the darkness beneath Dimvein. Remnants of the Time Before, when the darkness prevailed throughout Dimvein. These creatures of ravenous and endless appetites used to roam free, but now, they were lost to the underground. Though this creature was barely as large as a buckler, there wasn't a part of it that couldn't inflict pain in magnitudes.

Yet Bareg showed no trace of fear as he opened the cage. Indeed, a grotesque expression that passed for an Orken smile split his brutish face and he began speaking to the hideous beast as one might to a small child as he reached for the creature.

Kullen's jaw dropped as the gnasher nuzzled its cheek against Bareg's thick fingers, much in the way a well-trained cat might. Bareg tickled the patch of fur above the beast's tail with one taloned claw, then pulled the gnasher out of the cage and set it gently onto his shoulder.

His smile grew crueler as he saw the expression on Kullen's

face. "Interesting creatures, *azuhka.* Fierce, hungry, dangerous to enemies. Like Orken. Also, can train *azukha* like hunters train bloodhounds." The Ketsneer stroked his thick-skinned hand along the fur-covered chest, setting its tail to flicking. "*Azukha* friends to Orken. But hungry. Always hungry. Not like Orken meat. Too tough. But human meat." He licked his lips. "*Azukha* like much human meat."

At that moment, Arbiter Chuldok reappeared in Kullen's field of vision, carrying a wooden bucket filled with some dark, viscous liquid that reeked of fetid blubber and old blood. His nostrils recoiled from the stench, but Bareg drew in a deep breath through his nose, closing his eyes as if in delight.

"This *Azukha* named *Mauhul*," Bareg said, petting the gnasher again. The creature rose to its hind legs, front paws scratching at the air in eager anticipation of the bucket's contents. "*Mauhul* spend time with you. Convince you speak truth."

Arbiter Chuldok dipped a finger into the bucket and raised it to drip the viscous fluid onto Kullen's chest. It sent a cold shiver down the length of him. It felt like he'd been doused in snow— slimy, foul-smelling snow. Bareg stretched out his arm and feet bearing claws that would've torn Kullen's skin upon touch padded down. Green-tinged saliva dripped onto the Orken's arm, but his lack of response told Kullen he didn't care.

At once, it leaped onto Kullen's chest, eyes glued to the spot where the liquid pooled. But it merely watched, tail flicking in excitement. Four of its eyes flittered to its master, then back. A tinny clicking sound rattled in the gnasher's throat, but it waited.

Patiently, it waited.

Kullen dared not move.

"This is not necessary," Kullen said. "I know nothing but a name. Just a name. We can stop all this madness and cast all thoughts of Red Claw from our minds."

Chuldok growled the words back to him. "Red Claw…"

Then, Bareg snarled a word in Orken, and the gnasher sank its fangs into the gooey mess on Kullen's chest. Kullen stifled a grunt as the teeth pierced his flesh, too.

"Hungry, hungry *Mauhul.*" Bareg's dark eyes glinted cruelly. "Hungry for organ meat and soft, juicy insides of human. Eat all the way through until appetite is satisfied." He barked a laugh Kullen had only heard from the most wicked of men. The Orken was relishing in Kullen's pain.

"*Kith'meh'ga* pleased," Chuldok said, raising his fist to his forehead as Bareg had. "But *Mauhul* appetite never satisfied."

So far, the gnasher had only grazed the surface of Kullen's chest, but he watched, eyes turned downward, waiting for the moment the beast grew tired of the bloody concoction and found a taste for him.

"You want me dead so badly," Kullen said, "why not just kill me now? Why go through the show of the capture and torture?"

Bareg reached out and ran a finger down the gnasher's spine. *Mauhul* stopped momentarily, letting the pleasure of the Orken's touch settle in. It made that rattling sound again. "Before, I interested in human found in Turoc room. Now, I need know what *Zadruzak* know. He send you to Turoc room. He know much things. Too much, maybe."

Kullen seized onto that. The traitorous Orken were right to be suspicious of Assidius. He already knew of the goldbands' involvement in Magister Branthe's conspiracy and had doubtless set his agents to identifying those responsible. Kullen had no love for the man, but even he could admit that Assidius was damned resourceful. The Seneschal had means of gathering information Kullen could only begin to understand.

"*Zadruzak* knows everything." Kullen met Bareg's eyes, keeping his voice calm. "Even now, he is preparing to send the full might of the Imperial Scales to round up every one of the Orken around Dimvein. Once that is done, the Elite Scales will be on their way here to arrest all of the traitors. The best thing you can do now is flee the city before you're *truly* clapped in chains and executed in the Court of Justice." He turned his gaze on Arbiter Chuldok. "You've had so many people strapped to your table of death. Now it's time for you to enjoy being the spectacle."

Arbiter Chuldok scoffed, but Kullen didn't feel scorn in it. He was afraid.

Bareg just gave that harsh, guttural sound that passed as laughter among the Orken. "Orken not run. Orken *fight.*" He thumped a fist against his chest. "Tuskthorne Keep never be taken in past, never taken in future. Orken kill every human dare to raise weapons. Orken are greatest warriors in Caernia."

"That may be," Kullen said, shrugging carelessly as if there wasn't a vicious killer with too many eyes perched on his chest. "But can you withstand the might of dragons? Thanagar alone could crush you. How many more dragons will respond to the Emperor's call?"

Bareg laughed again, then finished with a snarl. "Dragons? Pah! Orken no fear dragons. Dragons not reach us here."

Sadly, that was the truth. Kullen had no idea how far beneath Dimvein they were, but there were rumored to be a wide labyrinth of tunnels. He'd used them to enter the Palace, to convene with the Trenta, and to navigate the streets of Dimvein. He doubted even the Crimson Fang had seen the vast majority of the spokes and shafts throughout. No doubt, the Orken had their own underground network.

Bareg disappeared behind Kullen and returned a moment later with a leather device. He handed it to Chuldok—a muzzle. Before the Arbiter could move to affix it to Kullen's face, a last-ditch attempt to turn the odds in his favor spilled from his lips.

"The Palace already has Red Claw in custody." He spoke the words fast and sure, hoping they would land home and send the Orken fleeing.

Instead, Bareg broke into the most thunderous guffaw yet, doubling over with laughter.

"You talk too much," Chuldok said, strapping the muzzle over Kullen's face.

Then, Bareg raised the bucket of chum and poured the entire thing over Kullen. He said something in his language, and the gnasher returned to its meal.

Eventually, not even Kullen's iron will or the muzzle clamping his mouth shut could stifle the screams.

63
Natisse

Natisse tried again, reaching for the fire burning within her core, trying to draw it upward and expel it in a blast to push back the onrushing gnashers. Not so much as a spark materialized before her outstretched palm.

Golgoth! she screamed mentally.

She wasn't familiar enough with the *bloodsurge* to understand the full implications of her feelings, but she knew something was impeding her ability to connect with the Queen of Embers. A near-physical block pushed back at her, something she couldn't see, but the sensation of it butting up against her will was very real. And very terrifying.

Golgoth, please!

One last effort, she drew on every shred of strength in her possession in an attempt to call the magic to her. A single wisp of flames flickered into existence and winked out a moment later without so much as a hiss.

And still, the gnashers rushed toward her, fangs bared, claws outstretched, hungry eyes locked on her bare flesh. Not for the first time, panic rose within Natisse, threatening to freeze her in place. But she refused to merely accept death. Spinning, she darted toward the sputtering torch lying on the pit's rocky floor and snatched it up. It was not graceful as she twisted and writhed on piled bones. Skittering feet scraped across the ground behind her, and she felt the wind of the fast-closing gnashers. In desperation, she whirled on them and shouted with all her might.

"Back!" she roared, waving the burning brand before the gnashers. "Get back!"

The closest, barely an arm's length away, screeched and fell back before the torch's faint heat and light. From what Natisse knew of the gnashers, they'd once lived free in Dimvein's valleys and caves. Their eyes—all eight of them—not only preferred the darkness but required it. And now, in the gloom of the pit, her torch shone as a bright beacon of hope for her and a harbinger of destruction to them.

They reeled back, stinger-crested tails whipping behind them, front claws swiping with caution. Their hisses were frightening enough, but now, the largest let out a crazed, unearthly yowl. The bizarre sound shook her so greatly she felt as if even Golgoth would've paused upon hearing it.

The gnasher lunged forward, and Natisse barely evaded its lashing tail. By sheer luck and instinct, she managed to keep the torch between her and her would-be killer. They kept up their collective hissing, and others joined in the furious wails. But the fire kept them at bay.

For how long, though? Natisse had no desire to find out. The torch's oil-soaked rag couldn't burn forever. She had to get out of this pit before the gnashers overcame their fear of the fire or decided they could simply crush her en masse.

She took her eyes off the gnashers just long enough to peer over her shoulder. The tunnel was close—so close!—and just tall enough that she could enter it stooped low. It would be damned uncomfortable, but it was her only way out that didn't include battling angry Orken.

Waving the torch in front of her, Natisse backed toward the tunnel's mouth as quickly as she could without losing her footing.

The gnashers hissed and closed in but refused to draw within the torch's radius of heat.

Natisse felt the cold stone bump against her legs and fought to climb into the narrow passage while keeping the torch between her and the gnashers. Somehow, she managed it without falling or dropping the burning brand. Step by step, she retreated, bent nearly double at the waist but always keeping the torch outthrust to the full length of her arm. The fire's heat singed her face and hair, but the pain was far better than winding up gnasher food.

Yellow, gleaming eyes numbering in the dozens glared at her. Despite their wicked intentions, she could see sadness deep within at the loss of their snack. Several had already returned to Gulma's bulbous corpse while others still tried in vain to reach Natisse, hurling themselves bodily against the pit wall. Their long arms reached inward, but she was too deep now to be in any real danger—unless one of the babies dared break away from their pack and pursue.

Indeed, one tried. The smallest of the gnasher broodlings skittered after her, but a hissing screech from the mature one seemed to recall them. The last thing Natisse saw before she backed around a stony bend was the last of the creatures returning to feasting on what remained of Gulma.

After a harried breath, she turned and pushed her feet for all they were worth. The chill seeping down her spine had little to do with the cold within the passage; she'd come too damned close to dying back there. Her magic had failed her!

But why? How? The bond with Golgoth should've given her unrestricted access to the fire magic, and yet when she'd tried to call upon the dragon, it felt as if her call had gone unanswered—no, unheard. What had she done to anger Golgoth?

She was too busy trying to flee to entertain the thought fully, but she knew something was wrong. Then it dawned on her like the clarity of morning after a night spent too deep in the drink. Kullen had warned her that Golgoth would need to be summoned daily if her bond was to stay strong. How long had it been? At least a full day had passed since she'd summoned Golgoth into the Mortal Realm. Was *that* why their bond was weakening? Was she becoming untethered from the dragon? She couldn't summon Golgoth into Tuskthorne Keep—the Queen of the Ember Dragons was far too large—but she *had* to find another way to re-establish the connection, to reaffirm their bond. Otherwise, she could lose the dragon… which, if Kullen could be believed, would ultimately kill her.

But she'd die far sooner if those young gnashers favored hunger over obedience and caught up to her. Much as she wanted to stop, to devise a plan to beckon Golgoth to the Mortal Realm, she had to put a safe distance between her and the gnashers. The cold stone walls surrounding her only gave her one way: forward. To where, she had no idea, but she'd find out.

The tunnels were similar to those leading to and from the Burrow. Yet, she was familiar with those—knew the way as well as she knew her own skin. But here, she could find herself lost in an endless expanse of darkness, wandering until she starved or fell prey to some other creature lurking ahead. But those were *possible* threats; a very real danger lurked behind her. The gnashers wouldn't be long in stripping every last bit of flesh from Gulma's corpulent body. Once their appetites were satiated, they might come hunting her.

And so she ran. Pain rippled up and down her spine with every step—she'd jarred something when she fell, and the doubled-over position made it exponentially worse. She reached a hand behind her as she ran, pressing it to the source of the pain. When she pulled it back around, it was doused in scarlet. She gritted her teeth against the agony and pushed herself to keep moving, deeper into the tunnel. Whatever lay before her, she'd face it head-on. The only other option was to lie down and accept death, and Natisse would *never* entertain that notion, no matter how dire her circumstances.

Then she rounded a corner and caught a glimpse of light ahead. It was faint, flickering like the torch in her hand, yet it filled her with hope. She slowed her hasty, scrambling run, contemplating the meaning of the light's existence. It was a way out, but out into what?

Though it went against every instinct, she forced herself to set her torch on the ground. It had saved her life, but she needed the cover of darkness to approach whatever lay before her. Hopefully, if the gnashers decided to pursue her, the abandoned fire would hold them off long enough for her to get away.

She ambled forward, clinging to the shadows, bare feet padding noiselessly on the cold stone. Fear set her skin prickling, the hairs on the back of her neck standing on end. She was unarmed, naked, and the only advantage she'd counted on when getting into this mess was gone. She had no faith in her ability even to summon Golgoth's magic. But she refused to give into despair. She'd been trained better than that—trained to fight until her last breath. "The mission above all" had been the Crimson Fang's watchword. Right now, the mission was survival and escape. Her friends were elsewhere, and she had to break free of Tuskthorne Keep so she could help them.

The light grew as she drew closer. To her surprise, the low tunnel ended at what appeared to be a surprisingly large chamber —at least twenty feet tall, easily fifty paces wide and long. A handful of lit torches sat in holders around the vast room, casting just enough light for Natisse to see within.

At the chamber's center stood an enormous block of dark-colored stone—black or a violet as deep as Umbris's scales, though she couldn't quite tell in the dim illumination. The mass stood easily half as tall as the room itself, roughly five paces wide and two thick. Against the light gray stone surrounding it, it stood out like a patch of night itself, but how it had gotten there, Natisse couldn't tell. The only three doors she could see were normal-sized—albeit large enough for even the largest Orken to enter, yet far too small to allow entrance to such a vast chunk of rock. And as strong as the Orken might be, it would take half of the Orken-watch to move the monolith.

The room reminded her a great deal of the Burrow's training room: crude training dummies of leather-wrapped stone and wood, suits of armor from every corner of the Empire and beyond, and dozens of weapon racks lining the walls, fitted with long spears and pikes, double-headed axes, great swords, and all manner of armaments crafted for the enormous Orken. Her heart leaped as she spotted a rack of Orken "daggers"—what would be a short sword to a human—a few paces away from where she crouched within the mouth of the tunnel.

That in itself struck her as odd. There was nothing separating her from the rest of the extensive chamber beyond a six-foot-tall fence of hammered brass. She could easily see herself climbing over it or merely using the large gate set into the fence. But if *she* could escape with so little effort, so could the gnashers. Did the chamber's occupants know that? Did they realize that the other end of their tunnel connected to a pit filled with hungry, flesh-eating monstrosities?

Movement at the far end of the room spurred Natisse into action. She darted out of the tunnel and scaled the fence with the speed of a sailor clambering through rigging. She had just time enough to dart toward the weapons rack she'd chosen and snatch up an Orken "dagger," then duck for cover behind one of the leather-wrapped stone dummies.

Flickering torchlight combined with guttural conversation coaxed Natisse's heart into a rapid thrum. She peered out from behind the cover of the dummy, and her face paled. There was no mistaking the ten hulking forms of Orken trooping into the vast chamber. Though they all had a similar look to her eye, there was no mistaking the one she'd punched. None wore the recognizable armor of the Orkenwatch, but they carried weapons on their belts and strapped to their leather harness.

She was still in Tuskthorne Keep. Or, better said, still *beneath* it, only in a different part of the vast underground network of tunnels rumored to honeycomb Dimvein.

She retreated behind the dummy as more torches were struck,

and the Orken trudged nearer. She fought the rising dread and took deep, calming breaths. It wasn't her lashblade and had not nearly the range, but at least she had a weapon. The firm grip of the leather-wrapped hilt in her hand gave her a measure of confidence. She could fight. It wouldn't end in her favor—one short sword against ten heavily-armed Orken—but she wouldn't be taken captive easily. And if she could attack with the element of surprise, she might take a couple down, balance the odds a bit more toward favorable. She'd just have to time herself to strike out when they drew close to her place of concealment.

The voices grew more raucous but didn't seem to be getting any closer. She considered peering out again but thought better of it. Then, a loud hiss filled the chamber, followed by a loud rhythmic drumbeat like horse hooves against cobbled roads.

When curiosity could no longer be restrained, Natisse spied out from her hiding place. Nine of the Orken stood clustered a short distance away from the block of stone. Three held long, white lengths of what appeared a great deal like bleached bones. With them, they pounded a rhythmic beat on tambours capped with taut hide drum heads. The tenth stood with his back to the stone, arms spread wide. At his feet lay an axe with a burning head and a few chips of stone.

Natisse frowned, confused. She got an explanation a moment later when one of the assembled Orken stepped toward a brass brazier and dipped the head of his axe inside. When it emerged, it dripped and glistened wetly in the torchlight. The Orken holding the torch touched the flame to the axe head, and instantly, it caught alight with a sibilant wheeze. The flame burned a bright, angry red, illuminating the face of the Orken clutching it. It danced in his eyes and glinted on his saliva-coated fangs as he brought his arm back and whipped it forward to send his axe hurtling toward the Orken standing against the stone.

The axe soared end over end before *clinking* off the stone beside him and bouncing away, taking a few chunks of the dark rock with it. With a closer view, Natisse could now make out the true nature of the rock. Though it was black, veins of light blue coruscated through it in the light of the smoldering axes at its base.

Her jaw dropped, mesmerized as, one by one, the remaining Orken took turns dipping their axes into the liquid—some sort of oil or alchemical fuel—setting them aflame and hurling them at their comrade. Some of the throws struck dangerously close to the Orken's head. One actually took a chunk of flesh out of his shoulder, while another collided with the stone and spun away so near that his bristling beard caught alight. Yet the Orken never shied away, never flinched. He stood as still as the monolith behind his back, arms spread wide, fangs bared, and face hard.

The onlooking Orken roared in approval, patting the thrower on the back and cheering the next one on.

While the nine went to collect their weapons—some still wreathed by flame—the tenth Orken bent to gather the chunks of stone that had been chipped off the enormous block. The others helped him muster up every sliver they could, then, as one, they hauled the shards toward a basin on the far wall. As they neared with their flaming weapons and torches, Natisse spotted something she hadn't seen previously. The wall was covered in the stones, varying shades of black and blue assembled to create an elaborate mural.

The sight took Natisse's breath away. Though it was crude and lacking the elegance of something found in the Palace or even Pantagoya, it was gorgeous in its own right. She stared at it, transfixed by the shimmering stone. But what was it? Did it depict some scene she couldn't parse together? Perhaps it was something to do with their mysterious religion. Although Natisse found all faiths difficult to comprehend, the Orken held so many secrets, she didn't even know what god they swore allegiance to. She could surmise there was some intent behind the design, but what exactly, was lost on her.

Two of the Orken stayed behind. They took turns cutting one another on the arm and allowing their blood to drip into a second basin. One stirred its contents while the other slathered it onto the backs of the newly chipped stone and pressed them onto the wall to add to the confusing pattern.

The Orken who'd stood facing the thrown weapons directed the effort, and the others complied with his instructions. More axes were thrown; more chips fell, and within time, the image expanded. Through it all, the drumbeat never stopped.

The throws were intentional—both to pass as close to the standing Orken as possible and to chip away bits of stone from the block. Blue sparks scattered from the stone as blades struck, sending a new pile downward. One by one, the remnants were painstakingly placed upon the wall.

Natisse had seen enough. Much as the Orken's strange game—or ritual—intrigued her, she had more pressing matters on her mind. Chiefly, finding a way out of the chamber before more Orken arrived or the others decided it was time to use her hiding place as weapons training.

The Orken "artists" were working at the far wall, near one of the chamber's three doors. The second door was just a short distance to the right of the Orken, which left just the door nearest Natisse. With their attention fixated on their endeavor, the Orken's attention elsewhere, Natisse took advantage of their distraction to sprint toward the door, slipping through with deft stealth.

Once inside, she took a moment to exhale and gather her wits. The corridor was long and empty, not an Orken in sight. Short sword in hand, she bolted.

Please, Cliessa, she prayed as she raced down the tunnel. *Please let this be the way out.*

64

KULLEN

Being chomped on by a gnasher youngling was—as far as tortures went—certainly not the worst Kullen had expected from the Orken. But it came damned close.

Kullen had once heard of a culture long gone that had been masters of the craft. They knew just how far they could go, drawing pain from their victims without killing them. It was rumored they would make small incisions upon every inch of a man's flesh, then douse them in vinegar to let them writhe. Days later, when the wounds were healed, the process would start again. Week after week, month after month, a man would suffer this violence until he finally fell to the agony or gave into the demands of his captors. Either way, Kullen was sure the man saw Shekoth shortly after.

With that scenario in mind, he found himself pleased this would at least end quickly—albeit, painfully. Each bite from the gnasher's long-toothed jaw felt like daggers being dragged across his skin. It took small nibbles, never digging in too deeply, as if savoring the flavor.

The muzzle clamped tight around his mouth, suffocating him, and he could barely draw in breath enough to scream. Yet through the agony, he clung to a single thought: the traitorous Orken wanted answers. Just as the example of the man murdered by a thousand small cuts, his torment would end when they deemed him broken enough to answer. His greatest fear, however, was that these tormentors wouldn't let him die. They enjoyed the sight of his misery.

Arbiter Chuldok's beady black eyes shone with the fascination of a mathematician puzzling over a particularly engrossing and complex problem, his expression rapt as he took meticulous notes in a book with a blood-spattered leather cover. A fresh bucket of whatever gooey substance now soaked Kullen had been brought in, and occasionally, Chuldok paused in his writing to dabble drops of it onto some new patch of flesh he wanted the gnasher to feast on.

Bareg, too, seemed intrigued by the torment, but his eyes were fixed not on Kullen but on his pet monstrosity. His expression reminded Kullen of a proud parent watching an infant take their first steps or speak their first words. Occasionally, he growled a command to Chuldok—Kullen's agony-numbed mind couldn't begin to translate the Orken tongue—doubtless instructing the Arbiter in his torture.

One thing he did catch, however, was the incessant mentioning of that mysterious word: *Kith'meh'ga,* each time accompanied by the raising of a fist to their foreheads.

Kullen fought to cling to his sanity and conscious thought, though his vision wavered and his mind instinctively reached for the blessed escape of unconsciousness. He had to stay alert through the anguish, had to use the few tools at his disposal to turn the situation to his advantage. The moment he succumbed to the pain, he would truly be at the mercy of the Orken who now held him prisoner.

That didn't stop him from screaming as if demons from the deepest of Shekoth's icy pits were devouring his soul. In truth, it was only *partly* for the Orken's benefit. He needed to put on a show for them—needed to convince them he was on the verge of breaking—but there was no need to fabricate the distress. Kullen had never been flayed alive, but he imagined this was what it felt like. Only the knowledge that he was screaming because *he* chose to, not because their tortures made him, kept him on the right side of sanity through the ordeal.

Finally, at some point—it might have been minutes or hours—the torture blessedly stopped. Bareg emitted a chittering sound in a skilled approximation of the gnasher's own and reached a hand out for the youngling. The creature lifted its crimson-soaked muzzle from its bloody banquet and skittered up the Ketsneer's arm, leaving a long streak of wet red along the Orken's stony flesh.

Bareg growled something, and Arbiter Chuldok vanished behind Kullen. A moment later, the muzzle lifted free of Kullen's face. At last, he could breathe! He sucked in ragged breaths, throat raw from screaming. He tasted blood from biting his tongue and cheeks.

Kullen panted. Blood rushed to his head, making him dizzy. He was sweating, and the sting of it in his wounds was great, but it all melded together. Though the gnasher had stopped, he could still feel phantom bites gnawing at his chest. Yet he stubbornly refused to give in to the throbbing agony that seeped into every fiber of his being. He couldn't, not yet. He had to remain conscious long enough to give the Orken what they wanted—and get from them what he *needed.*

He wept, alternately blubbering like an infant and mewling like a drowned cat. The smile on Bareg's brutish face widened… telling Kullen the Ketsneer believed the charade.

Chuldok laid the muzzle at Kullen's banded feet and stroked his long gray beard. He stared at Kullen for a long moment, drinking in his emotions. Then, he hefted the journal again and scratched something anew.

"Please!" Kullen moaned, shaking his head weakly. "Please, no more. No more." His voice, hoarse from screaming, came out fragmented, cracking every third word. "I'll tell you. Tell you everything… you want to know."

Arbiter Chuldok made a note in his little book and spoke to

Bareg in Orken, something to the effects of "Pitiful human broke quickly." The torturer, too, was buying Kullen's farce.

"Anything!" Kullen strained against his bonds, arching his back to thrust his stomach upward as if he could somehow break free of the restraints by sheer force.

Bareg and Chuldok didn't bother holding him down; they knew as well as he that the bands locked around his wrists, ankles, and forehead were impervious to his struggles. He was trapped, at their mercy, and seemingly terrified. Precisely the sort of prisoner who would prove compliant and offer little resistance.

The Ketsneer moved to stand at Kullen's side, tapping a sharp-nailed finger against a patch of shoulder the gnasher *hadn't* yet gnawed on. The pain was exquisite and extensive. Every nerve in his chest fired simultaneously, and Kullen let out another shriek that was only partly pretense.

"You say *Zadruzak* knowing everything." Bareg took his time forming the words, gradually increasing the force of his tapping until his claw-like fingernails began to puncture Kullen's flesh. "What everything he know?"

"Everything!" Kullen moaned. "I told you, he knows—"

Bareg cuffed him across the face, hard enough to set Kullen's vision spinning. "Tell what everything!"

Kullen blubbered and hollered like a man possessed, but at a vicious glare from Bareg, lowered his cries to a dull whimper. Despite the pain, he had to fight to hide a smile. Now it was *his* turn for answers.

"He knows about the bargain the Magisters made with the Blood Clan," he said, each word tearful and spoken in a voice of utter misery. "Issemar, Deckard, Branthe, all of them."

Through the charade, he kept a close eye on Bareg's expression, watching to see how the Ketsneer reacted to his pronouncement. There was *something* the Orken wanted to know, some secret he needed to make certain Assidius hadn't yet uncovered. His reaction to Kullen's "extracted confession" would spell the difference between more torture and the reprieve of death. He hoped.

Bareg sneered. "What more?"

Kullen supposed he shouldn't have been surprised that the Orken didn't react to that revelation. Days had elapsed since the Magisters' deaths—time enough for the *Zadruzak* to uncover any hint of treachery.

"He knows that one of the Orken delivered the vial to Magister Morvannou just a few days ago." He whimpered, snuffled loudly, and shook his head.

"You already a liar," Bareg said. "We catch you tell lie. How us know you not just guess?"

Time to try a desperate gamble. "And he knows you played a role in the disappearance of the other vials."

Something in Bareg's face told Kullen he'd struck the mark. The faint tightening around the Orken's eyes and the twitching of his jaw muscles suggested that his wild hypothesis hadn't been far wrong. It certainly explained how so many of the dragonblood vials had gone missing—according to Turoc, that was. The Tuskigo could simply have reported them missing and pocketed them himself to facilitate whatever he and his traitorous underlings were planning.

"B-but, that's not all!" Kullen continued before Bareg could respond. He needed the Orken to believe he was a treasure trove of information, one now unlocked and available to spill their enemy's secrets until empty. Not only would that forestall the Ketsneer from ordering his execution, but it gave Kullen a chance to turn the interrogation back on Bareg without the Orken realizing it. "Th-there's more. So much more, I swear, and I'll tell you everything, just please, please, keep that thing away!"

He pretended to shrink back from the gnasher perched on Bareg's shoulder, jerking his wrists wildly in panic. His fearful expression brought a new fervor to the Ketsneer's face.

"*Mauhul* is hungry but patient. Patient his master, too." Bareg leaned lower, so the little monstrosity's tail whipped a finger's breadth away from Kullen's face. Bareg's beard dangled, tip tickling Kullen's exposed chest. Such a small touch sent agonizing stings through his torn flesh. "Tell more, and *Mauhul* will wait."

"I will, I will!" Kullen wailed, shaking his head frantically as if it could clear away the hideous image before his eyes. "I-I can tell you he also knows about your interest in the Refuge. Th-that you were the ones who insisted on the attack a few nights ago. That it was urgent and that—"

Bareg bent closer, fangs bared as if intending to tear out Kullen's throat with his teeth, and seized Kullen's jaw in a vise grip. "How you knowing this?" he snarled. "All men die in fire. You cannot know, unless…"

Kullen saw the calculating look in his eyes, saw the Orken beginning to piece together the impossible. If Bareg had his people watch the attack from afar—just as they'd watched Magister Morvannou before the auction—he might've seen a dark-cloaked figure rush into the burning Refuge. He hadn't consciously considered that Kullen could've been that person, but the expression on his face made it clear the Orken's mind had begun unconsciously figuring it out.

Kullen swore inwardly.

"M-my contacts!" he said, his voice a strangled gasp in hopes of deflecting the Ketsneer's suspicion. "I have them all over the city. A beggar—one who sits outside the Refuge. Saw the men coming and heard them talking. Talking about the 'big ugly Orken'—"

His words died in his throat as Bareg's grip tightened around his neck.

"H-h-his words!" he gasped. "Not mine."

The Orken's clenched fist loosened enough for Kullen to barely rattle out his last words. "—An Orken, calling the shots, saying it was urgent."

Bareg closed his fingers around Kullen's airway again. They exchanged stares while Chuldok continued scribbling in his book, occasionally grunting. A very real fear rushed over Kullen. He had little else to share, and if it wasn't enough, that damnable beast would be gorging on him once more. Already, his vision was blurring, the edges black, and his mind was on the verge of losing consciousness.

Finally, Bareg released his grip, and Kullen gasped. He moaned and coughed piteously, but Bareg silenced him with a hard, open-palmed rap across the face.

"What more?" the Orken demanded. "What *Zadruzak* know of plans for *Ur'khat?*"

It took Kullen a moment to comprehend Bareg's question. The Orken word "*Ur'khat*" was unfamiliar to him, but the way Bareg said it with such reverence reminded him of how they'd both spoken *Kith'meh'ga.* This was something of great importance. But with this word, no fist raised to their foreheads. No, this was something else. He was talking about the Refuge.

Kullen tucked that bit of info away in case he made it out alive. He recalled Magister Branthe's words that the Refuge was "the key to everything."

But why?

"That's all!" Kullen said. "Only that, nothing else. I swear." As he said this last, he purposely darted his eyes away from the Ketsneer, looking instead to the side. It was a small twitch done purposefully. Any interrogator worth their salt would know it was an indication that their quarry was lying.

Chuldok's response—a deep-throated growl and the slamming of his book—told him he was right. This Orken wasn't just some brute who reveled in causing others pain. He was smart.

"Lies!" Bareg dug his fingers painfully into Kullen's jaw. "Speak, or feed *Mauhul.*"

"I-I swear, I've told you everything I can!" Kullen pled, his voice utterly pitiful.

"But not all you know." Arbiter Chuldok spoke clearly in the common tongue. "There is more. You tell it, or there be more pain."

Kullen looked between the two Orken, summoning a look of

utter desperation. "Please!" he said, his voice barely above a whisper. "I-I can't. My family. He'll kill them all."

"Kill them worse than Orken can?" Bareg sniped. "They be brought here and fed to Gulma's pets. Be fed to Gulma even. You will be made watch as they scream and die. Then you die. Filling bellies of *Mauhul* family."

Kullen wept, thrashing in frustration, but he didn't speak.

Bareg snorted through his thick nostrils and growled to Arbiter Chuldok a single word in Orken: "More."

Chuldok raised the bucket, tilting it just above Kullen's man parts.

"Wait!" Kullen screamed. "Wait, just wait! I will tell you, I swear. B-but, I need the Tuskigo's word that my family will be protected. Because once I say it, the Seneschal will kill me."

"We kill you, too," Bareg growled. "Human on Orken land. No one miss little human."

"Turoc will," Kullen protested. "He's the one who ordered me to come here. Said he was going to offer to keep my family safe if I told him what I just told you. That, and the one thing that will get me murdered and dumped into the deepest, darkest hole in the ground if the Seneschal ever learns it passed my lips."

This was another massive gamble on Kullen's part. It wasn't an implausible story—certainly, the Orken had their own network of eyes and ears around Dimvein, people who traded information for the Orkenwatch's added "protection" and goodwill. Kullen was staking his life on the assumption that Turoc was the leader of this treachery. If so, he'd have made such a deal with one of Assidius's chief spies. If Kullen was right—and gods and devils, he hoped he was—Bareg would return to Turoc with the information, and then, there'd be proof enough of his mutiny to put the Emperor to action against Tuskthorne Keep.

Bareg softly pet the gnasher on the chin. "You tell me. I tell Tuskigo. He decide you live or die." He leaned in close to Kullen's ear, beard smothering him. "But you tell first."

Kullen turned away, trying to breathe without sucking in

Orken hair. "I will only say it to Turoc," he said, and let out a little whimper, as if terrified of what was to come. "Please, bring him here so I can tell him. And my family—"

"Turoc trusts his Ketsneer," Bareg said. "You tell me as good as you tell him."

"Perhaps Turoc trusts you," Kullen said. "But I don't."

"You no talk," Bareg snapped, "your family die. And you die, too."

Then, without a word exchanged between them, Chuldok dumped more of the viscous bloody ooze onto Kullen's thigh. The gnasher didn't wait for instruction this time, just leaped off Bareg's shoulder and set to eating.

Kullen's chest had been manageable, but now, with the beast so close to his most tender parts, Kullen let out a very real, very pain-filled cry.

65
Natisse

Natisse had barely stepped through the door and closed it silently behind her when the sound of heavy booted feet echoed up the corridor ahead. Her pulse quickened, sweat pricking on her palms. She couldn't retreat, not with the Orken playing their strange game in the chamber behind her. The only chance she had of escaping lay before her. But there, too, awaited discovery and recapture.

Optimism surged within her as she spotted an adjoining passage just a dozen paces ahead. Without hesitation, she took off at a mad dash toward it and hurled herself around the corner. Not a moment too soon. The bootsteps grew louder, the clank and clatter of weaponry now audible as the Orken rounded a bend farther up the underground corridor.

Natisse took quick stock of her surroundings. The passage in which she now stood ran straight for a few paces before ending at a door.

Fear lent wings to her bare feet as she sprinted toward the open door and dove into the shadows beyond and what appeared to be some form of storeroom. There was no way out, but at least she had a chance of hiding. The scent of musty canvas and dried grain hung thick in the storeroom, accompanied by the familiar tang of the oil used for weapons maintenance. Natisse ducked behind a large wooden barrel, hunkering low in the shadows and trying to ignore the greasy feel of the oil against her palms, back, and feet. She fought to control her breathing for fear the hammering of her heart would give her position away to the approaching Orken.

The bootsteps grew louder, so loud Natisse feared they were headed for the very room in which she'd concealed herself. She tightened her grip on her stolen weapon and braced for the inevitable clash when she was discovered. Judging by the sound, there had to be at least three, maybe four Orken in the patrol. If she was damned lucky, she might take a couple down and evade the rest. The oil seeping from the barrel and coating her skin could very well give her an edge to escape their grasp.

But for how long? Tuskthorne Keep would be filled with warriors of the Orkenwatch, all armed with sharp weapons and an even sharper razor sense of smell. It wouldn't take a Sniffer's keen nose to follow the scent of oil through the still air of the underground tunnels.

Her stomach clenched, anxiety sending a tremble through her hands, but Natisse fought to remain in control. Come what may, she would fight to her last breath. The Crimson Fang was counting on her.

As she waited, listening to the Orken boots, they softened. Then, in the distance, she heard the sound of a door open and close. They'd joined their fellows in the mural room. Natisse nearly wept in relief. Her shoulders slumped and her knees gave out. For a moment, she remained kneeling on the oil-slicked floor behind the barrel, drawing in deep, gasping breaths. Cliessa had been with her again. But she couldn't count on the goddess's favor forever. Luck had a way of turning at the worst possible time.

She had to find her way out of the bloody underground tunnels and out into Dimvein. Once above ground, she knew she could lose the Orkenwatch.

Be with me a little longer, she prayed to the goddess. *Just until I'm out of here.*

Natisse had never been a firm believer in the gods or put much store in prayers, but in her current situation, she had nowhere else to turn. Her newfound magic was failing. Her comrades were imprisoned. She was alone in unfamiliar tunnels, surrounded by a horde of enemies. The gods—or a miracle of truly divine proportions—were her only hope of survival.

Drawing in a deep breath and steeling her nerves, Natisse rose and slipped out from behind the barrel. She spent a moment studying the storeroom—in the dim torchlight leaking through the open door, she could see little beyond the barrels, bulging sacks piled high along the far wall, and a shelf filled with odds and ends. No weapons or useful items. Nothing to facilitate an escape.

Slithering out of the storeroom, she padded back the way she'd come toward the primary corridor that led away from the grand chamber. A quick peek in both directions revealed the passageway was once again empty, no Orken in sight or earshot. Stolen shortsword-sized dagger in hand, Natisse set off up the tunnel in the direction from which the Orken had come.

The oil slicking the bottoms of her bare feet made movement difficult. She had to step carefully to avoid slipping on the smooth stone floor. But she couldn't move *too* slowly for fear she would stumble across more Orken, or her absence from Gulma's cells might be discovered. She counted herself fortunate that the gnashers had thoroughly consumed Gulma's corpse—and in so doing, covered up any traces of her assault on him. Only the Orken who had marched her down the stairs or saw her enter the dungeon would note her absence.

A horn sounded in the distance. Cries of alarm and screams in the Orken tongue lingered in the air. She wondered how long it would be before the tower was flooded with escapees. She pushed forward and toward the outcries. Fatigue settled over her, and the edges of her vision blurred and darkened. Between her treatment at the hands of Gulma, what felt like hours of anxiety in the mad dash to escape, and her lessening bond with Golgoth, her exhaustion was compounded tenfold. Every step made her wince at the pain within her veins. It felt as if she'd been burned from within, and until she rested, her physical ailments would only slow her down.

Human screams now mixed in with the Orken cries. She could only hope they stood a chance by merit of sheer numbers. But more than that, she hoped they would cause a long enough distraction for her to find a way out. Ahead, a pair of Orken barged through a side door. She didn't wait to see which direction they would choose before slipping into another storeroom. Piles of weapons filled the space, nearly floor to ceiling. Big ones. Orken made for Orken use.

There were arms enough here to start a war. She hid herself behind a rack of spears and waited again, listening. Daring to peek through, she watched the two Orken hurry by. One was much like the others—powerfully built, brutish, with sloped shoulders, a dark, bristling beard threaded through with silver rings, and craggy features. The sight of the other, however, sent a shiver of instinctive fear rippling down Natisse's spine. She didn't recognize him, but she would know the over-small tusks and the thick nose with its too-wide nostrils anywhere.

A Sniffer! And, she realized, not just *any* Sniffer. This one had gold rings threaded through his beard. That could only mean he was one of the high-ranking officers of the Orkenwatch. He'd have earned his rank through his ferocity in battle, the keenness of his nostrils, and cleverness.

She ducked, listening as their sound faded. It seemed her luck had held a little longer. The Sniffer was too occupied in conversation with his underling to notice her. Indeed, the pair of Orken slowed not at all as they passed her hiding place. That's when she realized her good fortune in being coated with oil. With the coast clear, she decided to search the room. She thumbed through axes and hammers, swords and shields. Knives of varying sizes and shapes were stacked in one box, while another was filled with maces and clubs.

Finally, she spotted something of note. She reached into a crate and tugged free a long spike-tipped bullwhip. Maybe it wasn't a lashblade, but this, she could use. Wrapping it around her shoulder, she pushed back into the hallway. She'd only gone half a hundred feet before hearing something that stood out amongst all the commotion from upstairs.

A man's scream unlike any she'd heard before. It sounded as if he was being skinned alive. It was coming from down a short, unguarded corridor with three doors. Natisse risked a glance around the corner when the screams amplified and a door whipped open. An Orken emerged from the centermost of the three doors, carrying with him a wooden bucket filled with some dark, viscous liquid Natisse didn't recognize.

She peered past him into the room from which he emerged. It was small, no different from the storerooms she'd previously been in, but this one was brightly lit, not a shadow in sight. Then, as the Orken dragged the door shut, she saw him: Arbiter Chuldok, the very bloody shite-sucker who'd murdered Ammon.

And in the center of the chamber, strapped to a table with metal bands binding his limbs, was a familiar figure. Beaten, bloody, and bruised, but there was no mistaking the lean, tautly muscled form of Kullen, the Emperor's Black Talon.

66
KULLEN

Kullen could feel his consciousness fraying, his iron will cracking after Ezrasil knew how long the tortures had continued. Even *he* couldn't hold out against such pain forever. Yet he could do nothing but lie there and endure it.

He retreated into a fragment of his mind he'd been trained to use in circumstances such as these. Madam Shayel had been in charge of shaping young Kullen's mental capabilities, hardening his resolve, and ensuring no matter what was done to him, he wouldn't reveal anything of value. As Jarius's companion, it was no secret he was at risk for capture by enemies of the Crown. Who wouldn't want to get their hands on someone with potentially confidential information about the happenings within the Palace?

So, there he resided, deep in the recesses of his mind, where no amount of pain would coax him to speak any words but those he chose to. Until, blessedly, a knock sounded at the door. It didn't echo through the small room, but it cracked like thunder. The wooden door rattled beneath the pounding of a heavy fist so loudly Kullen heard it even through his screams and suffering. Both Arbiter Chuldok and Bareg turned away from their grisly amusement and looked to the Orken standing guard.

"Who is?" growled Bareg in his guttural language.

The guard opened the door to reveal another Orken, this one nearly as tall and powerfully-built as Arbiter Chuldok, but with silver beard rings. At the newcomer's entrance, Bareg moved away from Kullen and hurried to hear the cause behind the interruption.

Bareg's eyes went wide. The two Orken spoke in voices too low for Kullen to hear through the terrible sound of gnasher fangs tearing at his flesh. He did, however, have the presence of mind to note the look of concern on Bareg's face. It seemed luck had found him once more. Cliessa had devised a plan dire enough to draw the Ketsneer away from his amusement. And not a second too early—Kullen didn't know how much longer he could endure *Mauhul's* hunger.

To his relief, the gnasher actually turned away from feasting, its eight eyes fixed on its master. Its stinger swayed like a pendulum as it waited. Kullen gladly accepted the reprieve, heaving heavy breaths. He was finding it more and more difficult to need to fake the anguish.

Bareg growled something to the Orken, then turned back to Arbiter Chuldok. "I return soon," he snarled. "See he ready talk."

Arbiter Chuldok saluted the Ketsneer. "He will talk. Not doubt it one second."

Kullen chose that moment to let out a pathetic, moaning whimper. "Please," he rasped, his voice hoarse from screaming. "Please, no more."

Bareg gave Kullen a cruel, leering grin. "Give answers. You talk, you have chance of life. You silent, you certain die."

"I... can't!" Kullen pretended to weep. "My... family."

"He will talk," Chuldok said, cracking his huge knuckles.

Bareg nodded and grunted to the Arbiter, then hissed a single harsh, sharp syllable. The little gnasher leaped off Kullen's chest and lighted on the Ketsneer's arm. Gently, almost tenderly, Bareg returned his pet monstrosity to the small cage and shut the door. "*Mauhul* still hungry," he told Kullen. "Very, very hungry."

With that, he turned and walked out of the room in the company of the Orken who'd come to fetch him, leaving Kullen alone with Arbiter Chuldok, the Orken guarding the door, and the caged gnasher.

Kullen knew it wouldn't last long, but he greeted the respite like an old friend. Jolts of sharp, stabbing pain coursed through his torso and legs. A sensation as if lightning struck him time and time again mixed with the sting of a hive full of hornets rested on him without break. Though he knew he could handle anything Chuldok threw at him, his body shuddered, convulsed even, due to the shock it had been put through.

Arbiter Chuldok stood over him, his brutish face a cold mask as he slammed shut the little crimson-stained notebook in his hands. His dark eyes roamed Kullen's bare flesh, drinking in the gnawed, mangled scraps hanging from bone, the blood seeping from hundreds of teeth marks mixing with the macabre concoction he'd been using to egg the little beast on.

He looked down at the empty chum bucket, then barked something to the Orken guard who responded by retrieving the bucket and leaving—presumably to refill it.

"What now?" the Arbiter asked once the door was closed. "Yours is choice. We not need to wait for Ketsneer return. You speak with me now, the pain end now. You wait, you protect *Zadruzak* secrets…" He sucked at his teeth. "More pain. Much more pain."

"Please," Kullen begged. "Water. Just a sip. Then I'll tell you everything, I swear."

A smile tugged at Arbiter Chuldok's face, pulling his lips back from his long, razor-sharp tusks. "Wise choice. Pain is not necessary with compliance, yes?"

"Yes," Kullen said, his voice a weepy whine. "I comply. I swear it!"

"Some water, have you shall then." Arbiter Chuldok tucked the notebook into his thick, blood-stained leather overalls and turned away from Kullen, searching among the myriad items arrayed upon his torture table in search of the promised drink.

That was when Kullen *finally* made the move he'd been planning since the moment he awoke strapped to the torturer's table.

He'd bloody well had enough—Ulnu's frozen tits, he'd had enough the moment Bareg set his freakish pet to feast on his flesh! But it would've been foolish to attempt escape with *three* Orken present. Chuldok alone outweighed him by nearly double, the Orken's strength far superior to his. Unarmed, heavily injured, and fully naked, Kullen had just one weapon left to him: the element of surprise.

Bareg had caught him sneaking into Turoc's chambers and believed him a spy. Kullen's mention of Assidius had all but confirmed the Ketsneer's conviction, and Kullen had done his best to play up the role. Bareg's certainty that he was one of the Seneschal's eyes and ears in Dimvein prevented the Orken from considering any other possibilities—including the chance that he was the Emperor's Black Talon.

The Orken had tortured him much as they would an informant or spy, and Kullen's pretense of weakness had concealed from them his *true* strength. That tiny deceit had kept them from breaking him or inflicting any truly debilitating damage. They'd been so focused on loosening his tongue they hadn't bothered to consider taking his hands, shattering his feet, or killing him outright.

And that mistake would be their undoing.

The moment Arbiter Chuldok's gaze shifted away, Kullen extended his fingers and hauled against his bonds with every shred of strength he possessed. All of his thrashing and straining theretofore hadn't merely been for show—he'd felt the mingled blood and the viscous liquid trickling down his arm, and used his violent jerking to channel the flow to his wrists. Now, the slime was just enough to counteract the manacles' grip on his limbs.

Pain flared through both thumbs as the lowest knuckle bones fractured against the restraints, but this was just a fraction more suffering amongst a body full. Yet he embraced it, for his hands slid free of the restricting bands.

Kullen had no time for hesitation or uncertainty, only decisive action. He was too far from any weapon, but his hands were weapon enough. His right fist punched out at the nearest weak spot on his enemy's enormous body: Chuldok's groin. A shock rippled through him when his broken bones took the impact, but he bit down and endured it.

Something *popped* beneath his fist, and Chuldok's body folded into itself a moment later. A terrible, howling groan escaped the Arbiter's lips as he collapsed, all strength sapped from his limbs. His huge frame landed in a splash of blood and chum. The impact set the table shuddering, but it was built strong and sturdy.

Kullen fumbled at the iron band holding his head, trying to pry it open. He couldn't find any latch or release trigger, but again, slathered some of the lubricous fluid from his chest over his forehead and managed to twist his neck just enough to slip free. His powerful torso muscles flexed, and his body curled upward, arms extending toward the manacles holding his feet bound. They were equally thick and impossible to break, but they had no lock holding them shut. It took the work of but a second to throw them open.

That second was all the time he could afford. Impossibly, Chuldok's head lifted from the floor and his dark gaze burned hatefully toward Kullen. His huge clawed hand reached up in search of Kullen's leg and sank talon-like fingernails into the meat of Kullen's calf.

Kullen roared, equal parts pain and rage, and used that leg to kick out at Chuldok's face. His bare foot crashed into the bridge of the Orken's nose and snapped Chuldok's head back so hard the back of his skull bounced against the metal table that furnished his torture devices. His grip on Kullen's leg weakened just enough that Kullen could pull free. Flesh tore and hot blood streamed down Kullen's ankle and foot, but Kullen was free—free of his bonds, of the Arbiter's grip, and soon from this Shekoth-damned torture chamber.

He sprang to his feet and hurled himself toward the pile of his clothing. His hands reached for Umbris's vial—one more drop of blood, and he would have power enough to match the Orken's strength.

He never made it. A hand closed on his ankle and the power of a bear trap held him fast. His grasping fingers missed the hem of his dark cloak by a hair's breadth, and then he was being dragged backward. Chuldok's fingers raked at his calves, clawed their way up his legs, the Arbiter's bulk crushing him to the ground.

Desperation surged within Kullen. The moment Chuldok gained a position of advantage, his superior weight and strength would end the fight swiftly and decisively in the Orken's favor. Kullen's *only* edge here was his speed. That, and the copious amounts of slippery blood and goo on his body.

He writhed and twisted in the Arbiter's grip, and his legs slid free. Chuldok's fingers raked his flesh but could find no solid purchase. With strength borne of blind terror, Kullen squirmed loose of the Orken's grasp and tried to roll to his feet. He just needed to get clear of Chuldok's reach long enough to attain the dragonblood vial and—

A roar of rage burst from Chuldok's lips, and the Arbiter's huge figure hurtled up off the floor in a violent surge of energy and raw strength. Kullen reacted instinctively, throwing himself to the side to evade the Orken's grasping arms. Too late, he realized that he'd made a mistake. His dodge had sent him *away* from the vial that would be his salvation. Now, Chuldok's hefty frame stood between him and his best—only—chance of escape.

Judging by the triumph etched on Chuldok's face, that had been precisely his intention. He knew exactly what the vials could do—or as much as any Orken entrusted with the Emperor's knowledge could know—and had correctly deduced that his best odds at recapturing or killing his prisoner would be to cut him off from the dragonblood magic. Even if he hadn't yet figured out that Kullen was the Black Talon, he was smart enough to recognize true peril.

Arbiter Chuldok rose to his full height, cracking his neck and fingers, stretching away the effects of his fall and casting down the embarrassment at being tricked. Those black globes set deep into his face gleamed eagerly of cruelty and pure joy. This Orken loved torture, but he reveled in war.

"Come," he growled, extending his hands wide in a taunt. "Just you and me, it is." He nodded his head toward the door. "Freedom is there. You want be free, you go through me."

"It doesn't have to be this way," Kullen said.

"Your fear fuels me," Chuldok replied. "Your fear make me stronger. Let Chuldok see what you can do."

Kullen slowly rose as well, cautiously watching the Orken for deception. "Right. Well, your little pet just chewed holes into me. I'd hardly call this a fair fight."

"Haven't you been told?" Chuldok grinned. "Life not fair."

Chuldok lunged for Kullen, both arms outstretched as if aiming to place him in a crippling hug. Kullen dropped low, avoiding the grasp, and spun on one knee, elbow leading the way right into the Orken's belly. Chuldok, not expecting Kullen's swiftness, hesitated a second too long in turning back toward his prey. Kullen kicked at the back of the Orken's knee. It wouldn't cause much damage, but it sent him momentarily to the bloody stone floor.

Quickly, Kullen slipped around, putting the torture table between them—and as it so happened, the table containing Chuldok's torture implements within his grasp. Chuldok stood and leaped over the table, torso first. Kullen reached back and grabbed the first thing his hand touched: a small but sharp scalpel. As the Orken's hands wrapped Kullen's waist, he drove the scalpel downward into the fleshy meat of Chuldok's shoulder and twisted.

Chuldok roared, twisting away wildly. If Kullen hadn't released his grip on the knife, he'd have gone with him. Instead, he picked up another makeshift weapon. This time, a blunt hammer.

Meant for the Orken to use with one hand, it was large enough for Kullen to wield as a heavy warhammer. He swung for Chuldok's head, but the Orken evaded. The force of his blow shattered the table into shards. As it collapsed, it took Chuldok with it.

"Your fun over," Chuldok growled, rolling clumsily to his feet.

In one deft movement, he charged Kullen, ramming his shoulder into his injured chest. Explosions of pain tore through him. The torture devices went soaring as they crashed into the metal table and into the stone wall behind it. But Kullen kept hold of the hammer. He lacked leverage, but used the stores of strength left to him to beat down on Chuldok's back. He missed several times, but finally, managed to hammer home, driving the scalpel so deep into the Orken's shoulder it disappeared within folds of fat.

Chuldok dug his talons into Kullen's back and tore them forward, shredding skin. Kullen screamed and slammed the hammer again and again until, finally, the Orken lost his grip and he was able to slip free. He staggered toward the door.

"No!" Chuldok growled. "We finish this."

But Kullen had no intention of leaving. Not without Umbris's vial, which he could still see set upon nicely folded clothes in the opposite corner.

"I'd never think of it," he said. Then, he broke into a mad dash to his belongings, only to be met by Chuldok's firm grip on his ankle once more. His legs flew out from beneath him and he slammed face first into the ground, writhing and twisting to break free. He felt the Orken's other hand on his calf, dragging him further away from his salvation.

With his free foot, he shoved against the upper hand, but Chuldok's grip was too tight. Still holding Kullen's leg, the Orken rose. Kullen felt himself becoming disorientated as his whole world turned upside down and he was dangling.

"Like catching fish," Chuldok commented, laughing. "You fight good. But not good en—"

Kullen twisted at the waist, then snapped back, bringing the hammer around and into the side of Chuldok's knee. Bone shattered with a sickening *crunch*, then both he and the Orken were falling. Kullen landed on his head and the room spun. But he couldn't waste any time. A primal scream covered up all sound. Chuldok grasped at his shattered leg. Kullen staggered, but rose.

The Orken growled something in his language. Kullen might've been able to piece together the words, but he didn't care —they would be Chuldok's last, and the final words from a disgusting wretch like him weren't worth remembering.

Kullen dragged himself over, dropping the hammer and picking up a large pair of pliers. A thick bone jutted out of Chuldok's thigh. Barefooted and angry, Kullen stepped on the leg, twisting it the opposite direction. Confusion and contempt painted the Orken's features.

"Tell Binteth I said hello," he said as he grabbed hold of one of Chuldok's tusks and pulled with all his might. The bone tore out from the root, and blood went up in a geyser. Chuldok's head lulled back, eyes rolling as if the bringer of so much pain couldn't handle any more.

Kullen was reaching for the other tusk when the door swung open. The Orken guard stood there, taking in the scene. His newly-filled chum bucket crashed to the ground and he pulled two medium-sized axes from his belt.

67
Natisse

Natisse's hopes of escaping Tuskthorne Keep had hinged on divine intervention or the arrival of a miracle. Seeing the Black Talon not twenty paces from where she crouched could have been either. There were few people she'd rather have at her back in this place, few people with whom she stood a better chance of sneaking or fighting past the entire Orkenwatch.

Except for the tiny, insignificant little detail that he lay strapped to an Orken torture table, even more helpless than she at the moment. She had no idea how he'd ended up here or what had happened to his dragonblood vial, but one thing was certain: he'd need her help just as much as she needed his. Only together could they achieve what had thus far proven an impossibility.

Then the door swung shut behind the departing Orken, cutting off her view of Kullen. She pulled back, careful to remain out of sight of the brute carrying the bucket. There was nowhere to run, nowhere to retreat.

Fortunately, the Orken wasn't heading toward her. Instead, he opened the right-hand door and descended a staircase within. He didn't bother closing the door behind him, so Natisse could hear his heavy bootsteps echoing on the stone stairs. The sound diminished but didn't quite fade away. She heard the splash of muck accompanied by a disgusted grunt and a few harsh Orken words.

Then came *another* sound, this time from within the room. She didn't quite know what to make of it—it might have been a shout of anger or a roar of pain, but far quieter than the screams that had echoed through the corridors minutes earlier. What fresh torment was Arbiter Chuldok subjecting Kullen to now?

She ached to leap from her hiding place, race down the hall, throw the door open, and cut Kullen free of his restraints. Better to fight than remain crouched here like a wounded gazelle in a den of lions. If she could cut down the Arbiter, all the better. After what he'd done to Ammon in the Court of Justice, Chuldok deserved to taste the steel of her stolen dagger or a whip around the neck.

But that would be pure folly, she knew. With no way of knowing how many more Orken remained inside the chamber, she'd be hurling herself into a battle with the odds stacked far too heavily against her. Even just *one* Orken would prove problematic enough in her current unclothed and barely armed state.

Had the Orken who descended the staircase truly departed, she might've risked it. But his grunting, muttering voice drifted up toward her, accompanied a moment later by his heavy boots striking against the stone steps. He was returning from wherever he'd been dispatched, far too soon for her to have any real chance of rescuing Kullen.

Yet.

She gritted her teeth and tightened her grip on the dagger. When the Orken opened the door, she'd use the opportunity to peek within the torture chamber and take stock of the room. If there were only *two* Orken—the one hauling the bucket and the accursed Arbiter Chuldok—there might be a play to be made.

If she'd been able to call on Golgoth's magic, she might've considered bursting into the room and setting the Orken ablaze with Dragonfire. But after her recent… frustrations, she couldn't count on it.

Golgoth, where are you?

The dragon was gone, as if locked behind a solid steel door, no longer responding to her command. She'd have to find another way.

Perhaps she could retrace her steps to the first storeroom, fetch a small amount of the oil. If she spread it across the floor just outside the door, it could trip up the Orken guard and bring him to the ground long enough for her to finish him off.

She shrank back against the wall as the Orken reappeared up the staircase, bucket in hand. The brute pricked up his ears as another roar—deeper, angrier, this time—sounded from within Arbiter Chuldok's torture chamber. A cruel smile slowly spread across his lips and low, guttural laughter rumbled in his throat.

He lumbered toward the door and pulled it open, then stopped abruptly, his huge frame filling the doorway. For a moment, he stood frozen, as if pinned in place by an invisible hand. Then he let out a furious growl and reached for the two axes hanging on his belt.

Somehow, Natisse *knew* that the time had come. No more skulking or clinging to the shadows; she had to act. With speed born of desperation, she barreled around the corner and sprinted up the corridor toward the Orken's enormous back.

Time slowed to a crawl around her. Her legs moved as if through mire, yet she still felt the fires blazing within her, infusing her body with vitality and fueling her mad dash. The gap between her and her target closed at a glacial pace, but suddenly, it was as if she had blinked and arrived. The Orken had just dropped his bucket and pulled his weapons when Natisse reached him. Without hesitation, she drove her stolen weapon up and into his back.

Though a mere dagger by Orken standards, the blade was as long and heavy as a human short sword and sharpened to a razor's edge. The well-forged steel parted tough Orken hide and the muscle beneath, scraped against bone, and tore through soft tissue. A half grunt, half gasp escaped the Orken's lips and hot, dark blood gushed from the wound, splashing all down Natisse's legs. The brute instinctively twisted as if his body recoiled from the steel, trying to evade the blade even now piercing his organs. Natisse shoved with all her strength, driving the dagger deeper, deeper, deeper until the crossguard struck the Orken's spine.

Something crashed into the side of her head—the Orken's elbow—and rocked her, sending her staggering against the stone wall of the corridor. Blood slicked the handle of the weapon and she lost her grip on the blade. Even as she fought to recover her balance and slow the spinning in her head, she braced her legs in preparation to evade or dodge whatever blow the Orken unleashed at her.

But there was no need. The elbow strike had been instinctive, the Orken's training and reflexes attempting to bring down his killer. By the time Natisse found her feet and her vision coalesced, the Orken lay facedown on the ground, writhing in a far-too-large puddle of his own blood, his huge hands fumbling in vain for the hilt of the weapon protruding from his back. He hadn't the strength to lift his head, to meet the eyes of the woman who'd gutted him like a fish. Indeed, in a matter of seconds, his struggles ceased and his arms fell slack by his side. His face settled into the crimson pool beneath him. One last breath escaped his lips, spraying a mist of blood, and then he was still.

She panted, her breath burning in her lungs. Kullen stood there holding a bloody tusk.

Natisse held up her own hands. "Hey, whoa!"

He blinked at her, a look of utter confusion on his face. His eyes dropped from her to the Orken lying dead at her feet, then back up at her.

"N… Natisse?" His voice came out in a hoarse croak.

"Yeah," she said, surprised by the relief she felt at hearing her name from his lips. "It's me."

Kullen scrubbed a hand over his face and blinked again. "Ezrasil's hairy arse, so it bloody is!" He lowered his scarlet-stained hands and stared at her. "What in Shekoth are you doing here?"

"Glad to see you too," Natisse shot back. She couldn't help herself. "Remind me to bail your sorry arse out more often if this is the kind of gratitude I get."

"Bail my ass out?" Kullen arched an eyebrow. He pointed down at Chuldok. "I'm sorry, do you not see *this*? It's safe to say that I have this situation firmly in hand."

Then, Chuldok roared, springing to life, but Natisse didn't miss a beat. She unwound the whip from where it was looped around her shoulder, and flung it out. It wrapped around the Orken's neck until the spiked tip buried itself just below his pointed ear. Then, with a scream from her toes, she yanked. Blood showered the room as the spike tore the flesh from his face and opened the great veins in his neck. Hardly recognizable, Chuldok collapsed, dead even as he hit the ground.

"Firmly in hand?" Natisse said.

She stalked forward. Her grim satisfaction at seeing the Arbiter who'd tortured Ammon receive his just reward was tempered by a still dire situation.

"I suppose your timing was as close to perfect as a fellow could ask for. So yeah, you have my thanks for, as you say, bailing my ass out."

"There. See?" She folded her arms across her chest. "Was that so hard?"

"I mean, a little." He shrugged, but there was a ghost of a smile on his lips. "Now that you've been properly thanked, maybe you answer my question and tell me what you're doing here? Like that?" His dark eyes dropped from her face and he raised a curious eyebrow.

It took Natisse a moment to realize he was looking at her body —her very *naked* body. Her current posture accentuated the parts she preferred to keep concealed from the majority of the world, and a flush of heat raced to her cheeks. Especially because he, too, was utterly naked. The blood covering him—some of it still seeping fresh from deep wounds on his chest—failed to hide the parts of him she found herself both eager and hesitant to look at. Interesting, well-proportioned parts, the sight of which only made her already burning cheeks flash hotter.

Yet she refused to let him see her embarrassment. "Find me some clothes," she said, giving him a coy grin to conceal it further, "and I'll tell you all about it."

68
KULLEN

Kullen paid the uttermost attention to every word out of Natisse's mouth—largely out of interest, but also because it served to keep his eyes fixed on her face rather than roaming the rest of her. And what a rest of her it was! Her figure proved far more stunning and shapely than even the deep blue evening gown she'd worn to Pantagoya had revealed.

She'd clearly endured a lot in the last night and day since last he saw her, however. Her eyes had a gaunt, hollow look to them, her skin appeared both oddly pale and flushed, almost feverish. She radiated a furious intensity that rolled off her like tangible waves of heat. An assortment of cuts and bruises marred her, accompanied by streaks of Orken blood and dark splotches of something truly foul smelling.

He had to admit her recounted tale was impressive, even by his standards. From her finding her home destroyed to her willing imprisonment to escaping Gulma—a name that now made sense—to fleeing the gnasher pit to finally finding him here, she had endured a great deal and somehow come out alive. That was more than Kullen could say for the vast majority of those who entered Tuskthorne Keep in chains. And through it all, she'd somehow managed to remain in possession of her dragonblood vial. Indeed, it was the *only* thing she'd had on.

The torture room was light on spare outfits, so Kullen and Natisse had to make do with what little clothing he'd been wearing. His vest and coat served to cover her upper body, and she somehow turned his tunic into a pair of makeshift—if slightly breezy—trousers. Kullen let her have the garments gladly. The pain in his chest would have made wearing any of them utter misery.

The high-heeled boots, he left where they were. They'd prove too noisy and would serve him poorly should he need to run. He settled for pulling on his own pants and cloak with its two hidden pockets and the pair of "surprises" he'd tucked away in case of emergency. He wasted a single moment wishing for daggers, a sword, *anything* more effective than the silver-handled cane that he'd carried into the tower. But even that weapon, simple as it was, would be better than facing the Orken empty-handed.

But it was only when he slipped the chain holding Umbris's vial over his head that he *truly* felt once more in control of the situation. He'd rarely felt as helpless as in the last hours, and not only because he'd been bound to a table in the heart of Tuskthorne Keep. How long since he'd last been without his connection to Umbris's magic? In truth, he couldn't remember.

"*You're injured.*" The sound of the Twilight Dragon's voice in his ears alleviated Kullen's most immediate concerns.

Just a few minor abrasions, Kullen responded, a hint of levity in the response.

"*You need rest.*"

I first need to get bloody out of here, Kullen said.

When he looked to Natisse, he was surprised to find her staring at him, her face tight and her gaze piercing.

"What?" he asked, raising an eyebrow.

"Did you know?" Her words came out clipped, hard.

"Know what?" There were an awful lot of things he *ought* to have known before tonight—chief among them the complicity of

Turoc and possibly his *entire* command cadre in Magister Branthe's treachery—but wasn't certain which she was referring to.

Natisse's jaw muscles clenched. "That the Orkenwatch raided my home and killed and imprisoned my friends? And that it was *your* scent the Orken followed straight to us!" Her eyes flashed and she took a menacing step toward him. "I'm supposed to believe that wasn't your plan all along?"

Kullen frowned. "My scent?" His mind raced. He'd been entirely focused on tracking the giant Jad and his smaller Brendoni companion, but there was absolutely no way he'd have missed an Orken patrol following on his heels. Then again, he realized, a Sniffer could follow a smell hours—possibly even days—later. If the Orken who'd nearly caught him the night of Lord Issemar's murder had been leading the pursuit, the keen-nosed bastard might very well have pursued his redolence through the still, stale air of the underground tunnels.

"Ulnu's icy tits!" He raised both hands. "I had no idea about your friends, I swear. Nor did I have anything to do with it. I promised I would keep your secret, and so I have. Not even the Emperor knows the truth about you." His frown deepened to a scowl. "Nor did he say anything to me about a raid on the Crimson Fang when I saw him earlier this morning."

A thought nagged at the back of his mind. "When exactly was the raid? How long ago?"

Natisse seemed to consider the question. "Late last night," she finally said, "while I was returning from Pantagoya."

Kullen chewed on her answer. He'd arrived shortly after her—no more than an hour, he guessed—and gone straight to the Palace. Turoc had been at the Emperor's side. He *might* not have reported the assault on the Crimson Fang because there hadn't yet been anything to report. It wasn't uncommon for the Orkenwatch to mete out the Emperor's justice *first,* then inform the monarch of their actions after. Turoc typically maintained rigid enough discipline to avoid any punishments too excessive—broken bones and the occasional split skull, but no outright executions or mass bloodshed. If Natisse's assessment was correct, the Orken assigned to the task would've been marching their prisoners away while Kullen was delivering his news to the Emperor.

Or, it could merely be that the Tuskigo had other plans for the insurrectionists he'd arrested, and deliberately chosen to keep the truth from the Emperor. That last was equally likely. Bareg had implicated his commander in their schemes. There was no telling how deep and wide the Orken's treachery spread, what machinations were at play behind the scenes.

"Emperor Wymarc had no reason to keep it from me," Kullen said, his fists clenching, "which leads me to believe he didn't know about it."

Now it was Natisse's turn to narrow her eyes. "You expect me to believe the Orken acted on their own? That *they* were the ones who wanted the Crimson Fang locked up, not the Emperor?"

"It's a distinct possibility." Kullen ran a hand through his hair, remembering too late it was coated in blood and chum. "The whole reason I'm here in Tuskthorne Keep is because I uncovered evidence that the Orken are working *against* the Empire. They were in league with Magister Branthe, and had a hand in the attack on—"

"Wait, Magister *Branthe*?" Natisse said the word so forcefully it caught Kullen by surprise. "I saw one of the Orkenwatch commanders standing next to the Magister the night we destroyed his slave fighting ring."

Kullen's eyebrows shot up. "You're certain it was a goldband?" he demanded. "You saw them?"

"I saw them." Natisse nodded once, her expression darkening. "Giant bastard, gold bands in his beard. No doubt about it."

"Did you get a good look at him?" Kullen asked. "Could you identify him?" He had to fight the instinct to seize her arm in his eagerness. "Was he the same Orken you saw at the Palace?"

Natisse's brow furrowed in concentration. She took a long moment to consider the question, then shook her head. "I don't know."

"How don't you—" Kullen began.

"The one beside Magister Branthe was wearing a hood, okay?!" Natisse's voice rose to an angry shout. "I couldn't get a good look at his face; I just saw the beard with the gold bands, and I know that he was a big one." She hesitated, then threw up her hands. "It could have been, though. That one at the Palace was certainly large enough."

Kullen's mind raced. "And it wasn't him?" He thrust a finger toward Arbiter Chuldok's corpse.

"No," Natisse snarled the word. "Trust me, after what he did to… to my friend in the Court of Justice, I'd recognize him anywhere."

Right, Kullen thought. *That poor bastard on the table was one of the Crimson Fang.* Baronet Ammonidas Sallas was his name, brother to Baruchel Sallas who Kullen had killed leaving Magister Perech's pleasure barge.

"And I know it wasn't that Sniffer who was in here, either," Natisse continued. "He's too small to be the one I saw beside Magister Branthe."

"That rules out Bugrash, too, then." The salt-and-pepper-bearded Arbiter who served as whatever passed for chief-of-staff among the Orkenwatch was the only goldband shorter than the Ketsneer. "Leaving just Turoc and three others."

Given what Kullen had found in the Tuskigo's chamber, he felt more certain than ever that Turoc *was* involved in—or, more likely, leading—the conspiracy. Had *he* been the Orken at Magister Branthe's side? If so, Kullen had just missed seeing him the night he'd gone to rescue Prince Jaylen.

"Glad to hear I'm helping you solve *your* problem," Natisse said, her voice once more growing tight. "But that doesn't solve mine. I'm no closer to finding my imprisoned friends than I was before I got myself captured. If anything, I'm bloody farther than ever."

"Maybe not." Kullen voiced the thought aloud before he could reconsider. "If your people *aren't* locked up here in Tuskthorne

Keep, the only other place they can be is the Palace. And I just so happen to know a secret way into the exact part of the dungeons where they'd be held."

Suspicion flared on Natisse's face. "And you'd free them, just like that?"

"Under normal circumstances, no." Kullen shook his head. "But look around, and you'll see this is damned far from normal. Neither of us can make it out of here on our own, which means we *have* to work together. But more than that, I need to make sure that the Emperor knows what I found about the Orken traitors. So help me get word to him, and I swear I'll do everything in my power to convince him that your assistance in the matter is worth liberating your friends."

Though his promise surprised her, she still appeared unconvinced.

"And if that doesn't work," Kullen said, "I'll take you to them myself and help you free them." The Emperor would be furious at him, but once Kullen explained the situation, Wymarc *might* be brought around to his way of seeing the situation. If not... well, Kullen could always use the matter of the dragonblood vial to sway his opinion.

He felt reasonably certain that Natisse had retrieved the vial from the *Tabudai* and brought it back to Dimvein with her. No doubt it was tucked away someplace she believed to be safe from the world. Now wasn't the time to ask about it. Kullen had no chance of finding it on his own; he needed her to either hand it over to him, or lead him to it. He still held out hope that he'd been correct in his assessment of her, and she *hadn't* merely used him to get her hands on a powerful weapon with which to arm the Crimson Fang. But if she had, he'd need to keep her trust long enough to recover it, as he'd promised the Emperor.

"I can live with that," Natisse said.

"Good," Kullen nodded, surprised by the relief he felt. In a situation as grim as the one in which he found himself, he could think of few people better suited to fight at his side than the woman who'd come damned close to killing him not long ago. A woman who now wielded the power of the Queen of the Ember Dragons and could summon Dragonfire potent enough to burn an Orken to cinders in a heartbeat. Natisse was a powerful tool to have at his disposal and, as much as it pained him to admit it, his best chance of getting free of Tuskthorne Keep and back to the Palace in one piece.

And he supposed he wasn't entirely unhappy to see her.

Kullen began collecting whatever he could from the Arbiter's torture implements that might offer him an advantage.

"There's one more thing," Natisse said. Kullen could sense trepidation in her tone.

"What is it?" he asked, pocketing two small stilettos from the fallen weapons.

"I might've set the entire dungeon free."

Now he stopped and turned toward her. "That was you?"

She nodded.

"Then I suppose I owe you greater thanks than I'd even known," he said. She gave him a questioning look. "The only reason I gained the advantage over our faceless Arbiter here was that your careless action pulled the others away and left us alone."

"Careless?" Natisse snapped.

"Well, sure," Kullen said. "Now the entirety of the Orkenwatch is on high alert." That earned a frown from Natisse . "But they also may be too distracted to worry about us." He smiled. "Fine work, my lady."

Natisse had just begun responding—likely something snide and cutting—but her words were truncated as a familiar chittering caught his attention. His head snapped toward the noise, just in time to see a shattered cage and two fur-covered limbs clawing out from beneath Arbiter Chuldok's bulk.

Kullen barked out a curse and leaped over the dead Orken, landing on his left foot and driving his right heel down on the baby gnasher's head as it squirmed free of its entrapment. Mauhul exploded in a spray of ichor. Kullen spat and growled a curse at the little creature whose fangs had been responsible for so much torment. "Good bloody riddance!"

Natisse stared at him with a curious glint in her eye, but he shrugged. "I hate gnashers. Come on," he said, gesturing toward the door. "Time we vanish before Bareg returns or anyone else discovers their dead comrades."

"You'll get no argument from me," Natisse said, nodding. "I've no more desire to hang around than you do."

69
NATISSE

"Let me guess," Natisse said, shooting a glance over her shoulder at Kullen as they hurried from Chuldok's corpse and the room in which it had been abandoned. "You've got no bloody idea which is the way out."

Kullen gave her a wry, strained smile. "Up." He emphasized by pointing a finger toward the low ceiling.

Natisse snorted. "*Real* helpful."

Kullen's grin broadened. "I live to serve." The mirth quickly vanished from his face. "I was unconscious when they hauled me here. Woke up in that room. No idea how deep underground we are. You?"

Natisse nodded. "Five floors at least." She paused at the intersection where she'd hidden and stared in both directions. She could either continue deeper into the tunnels on the same trajectory she'd been headed after fleeing the Orken artists, or head back the way she'd come in the hopes that it somehow led out. After a moment's consideration, she turned to Kullen.

"Hard to tell where all the commotion is coming from," Kullen commented. "Everything echoes."

"That Sniffer friend of yours went *that* way." She gestured toward the tunnel that had led her here. "What are the odds he was heading up and out?"

Kullen frowned, then shrugged. "He'd be heading toward the dungeons—or at least toward wherever the prisoners had made their last stand."

That was a grim thought. Had they been better off in cages, or free to choose their own means of death? Who knew, perhaps a few had even managed to slip through the Orken defenses and even now stood in the freedom of Dimvein's streets. If that were true, she could only hope any who had were worthy of being sprung.

Kullen glanced down both corridors, shaking his head. "Might as well give it a try. Chances are we'll find a path out, one way or another. And that way..." he pointed in the direction she'd come from, "... won't be filled with a battle between Orken and prisoners."

That was precisely the conclusion Natisse had reached. "Come on, then." She set off down the tunnel. She moved far quicker now that she had clothing. There was something about running naked that had caused her to take extra care, as if a thin layer of cotton would matter in the grand scheme of things. "Sooner we make tracks, the sooner we're out of here."

Or dead, hacked to bits or torn apart by the Orken they'd inevitably encounter. But she kept that thought to herself.

Their bare feet made little noise as they padded along. In truth, the only sound echoing through the corridor was the occasional *swish* of Kullen's cloak or the faint grunts of pain escaping his lips.

Natisse fought the urge to glance back at him. She wasn't exactly certain how to process her emotions at the moment. She felt marginally better—he was unbound, armed with a plethora of small weapons and one big hammer. He was also clothed—a fact over which Natisse found both gratitude and disappointment—ready to fight at her side should the need arise. Her chances of escaping had just risen steeply for the better.

And yet, seeing him had reminded her whose fault it was that she was down here in the first place. Because of *him,* the Orkenwatch had found and raided the Burrow, killed Dalash, and hauled the rest of the Crimson Fang away. He'd insisted he knew nothing of the assault, and though she was inclined to believe him—he'd appeared so genuinely surprised by the revelation—that didn't diminish her anger over his role in her current predicament.

She had to remind herself of his promise to help her. After all, he hadn't yet broken any of the promises he'd made—not to her knowledge, at least. Though it took a supreme will of effort, she forced herself to trust that he'd keep this one, too.

And if not? Natisse's jaw clenched. If the time came that he double-crossed her or failed to uphold his end of the bargain, she'd deal with him the way she'd intended to the night they locked blades on the skiff. Only this time, she'd make sure to finish the job.

That thought sat oddly ill at ease in her stomach. She was surprised to find herself *hoping* Kullen would be as good as his word. The idea of killing him held far less appeal than it once had.

What's wrong with me? She scolded herself. *He killed Baruch!*

The protest felt hollow. That night in Wild Grove Forest, with just a few short words, he'd stolen the fire from her belly and the venom from her tongue. Baruch's death, though tragic, had been the unhappy result of the Crimson Fang's mission and the Black Talon's loyal service to the Emperor. Natisse found it hard to continue hating Kullen—any more than she could the onyx sharks who'd finished the job.

Orken voices snapped her from her thoughts.

"Shhh," Kullen said. "Over here."

The passageway, like all those dug around Dimvein, was rough walls and ceiling. Only the floors were smoothly carved. Kullen pulled her into a crevice to their left that was barely large enough to fit one of them, much less both.

Kullen winced as she pressed up against him and she grew acutely aware of Kullen's proximity to her. Even bloody and battered, he emanated a warm, calm aura, appearing far more composed and in control of himself than she felt.

His smell, despite the blood and whatever else had been slathered on him, brought a sense of serenity over her. Unlike all the Magisters smelling of perfumes and flowers, Kullen had a certain musky appeal—someone who had done real work with his hands. Granted, most of that work had been murder. But who was she to judge? Blood aplenty stained her own hands.

Natisse peered out. It seemed at least half of those who had been throwing axes and building the mural were heading their way in a hurry. She tucked her head back in.

"There's too many of them," she said. "If they see us, we're as good as dead."

Kullen made a low, animalistic growl.

"Hold me tighter," he said.

"I hardly think this is the time—"

"Now!" he whispered.

She gripped him tightly around the waist, pressing her cheek to his bloody chest. Then, her stomach, heart, and all the rest of her insides plummeted to her feet and she felt herself twirling and whirling like she was caught in a rushing whirlpool. She wanted to scream but dared not.

The next thing she saw was utter darkness. She couldn't even feel Kullen anymore.

"Just keep holding on in your mind," he told her. "Don't let go."

Panic swelled within her, but she did as he said, willing her body through her thoughts to hang on. A great surge of unseen wind rushed by her as if riding horseback at breakneck speeds. It didn't stop for long moments. She heard monstrous sounds all around her, teeth clacking and creatures moaning. Something brushed up against what would have been her foot and she let out a small yelp. Then, finally, the world filled in around her again and they were standing precisely where they'd just been. They hadn't moved at all!

They still stood entwined with one another. Natisse felt his hot breath on the top of her head and remained motionless for long moments after. It wasn't reluctance to move away from Kullen's steadying presence, she told herself. She just had to be certain that all was clear before they continued.

It was Kullen who moved first. They separated and he stepped back, opening up space between them. "That was too bloody close," he hissed.

"I'll say." Natisse found her throat strangely dry—definitely from the fear and anxiety of the moment and nothing else, she decided. "What in Shekoth's pits was that?" Her breaths came in heaving rasps as if she'd run laps around the Palace.

"My *bloodsurge*," Kullen said. "We entered Umbris's domain, the Shadow Realm. For you, without his direct aid, it would have been nothing but darkness."

"You don't say?" She smirked. "Unfortunately, that was the easy part."

Kullen arched an eyebrow. "Explain."

She told him about the room that led to the gnasher pit, where the Orken had indulged in their strange ritual of bravery and artistry.

"Much as I'd like to say it'll be empty, that wasn't all of them who we just escaped." Natisse shook her head.

"Great," Kullen said. "How many more?"

"At least as many," she asked, face grim. "Can we 'whoosh' past them?"

"It was difficult enough traveling with you without the threat of enemies in the room."

"Thanks," Natisse said with a note of sarcasm.

Kullen laughed. "It's not that. Simply sliding through the shadows is a precise art—one that took many years to master. You added a lot of weight, which made navigation through the Shadow Realm challenging."

"Thanks again," she said, smiling this time. "But… navigation? We didn't move."

"Even when standing still, the shift between the Mortal Realm and the Shadow Realm is tricky. I have to constantly fight to keep my incorporeal form from drifting away."

"So, no whoosh?"

Kullen shook his head. "No whoosh. At least, not together. We'll need to explore other options."

Natisse smiled.

"And you're smiling because…?" Kullen asked.

"I have a plan."

She told him the idea that had formed in her mind. With every word, his eyebrows inched higher up his brow.

"Audacious and half-mad." He grinned. "Not usually my style, but it just might work."

"If it doesn't, we're in serious trouble." It was no exaggeration. Their luck had held out thus far—they'd avoided one run-in, and left behind two corpses, but with every step they took, their odds of a violent encounter increased. The best they could do was plan for the worst.

"This way," she said, running back a short distance until they reached the storehouse. Once inside, she said, "Cut open and empty out the sacks. We'll need the canvas."

Kullen nodded. "Got it." He set to work with the stolen stilettos, slicing away at the stacked pouches with abandon. Soon, streams of golden kernels of corn, dark husked rice, and spelt grain of deep, earthy ochre were piling up all around them.

Natisse set to work prying open the nearest barrel of weapons lubricant. She'd need far more than the thin trickles that had seeped through the wood and soaked into the floor. While she waited for Kullen to bring her the canvas, she used the Orken dagger to pry loose the nails holding the lid staves together.

"Here," Kullen said, handing her shredded strips of canvas from what looked like five or six sacks.

"Perfect. Now see if you can break that lid apart, too." She gestured with her dagger to the next barrel over. "The more kindling we have, the better."

"Shame we don't have any flour," Kullen said, with a rueful

grin. "When ground into a fine-enough powder, it catches fire quite nicely." He mimicked an explosive burst with his hands. "Hot enough to do some real damage at best, shock and awe at worst."

"We'll make do with what we have anyway." Natisse set to work wrapping strips of canvas around the lid staves she'd pulled apart while Kullen dismantled another. The canvas alone weighed far too little to throw, but wrapped around the wood, it made a half-useful projectile. Doubly so if she dipped it into the oil and set it ablaze.

"Think you can control Golgoth's Dragonfire enough for this?" Kullen asked. "I'm sure you've been practicing, but it's not going to be easy just to light *one* on fire at a time without catching all the others ablaze."

"I'll figure it out." Natisse found the lie a difficult one to tell. She turned her face from him, focusing her attention on the torches that would serve as her initial source of fire. These, she could rely on, but whether or not her bond with Golgoth was strong enough for her to do her part, she was unsure. "But know that if things get really bad, if we're outnumbered and in serious trouble, the chamber is large enough to summon Umbris." She glanced over at Kullen. "He'll make quick work of them, though at that point, there'll be no way we get out of here without the alarm being raised. And something tells me the Orken would care more about a dragon in their midst than putting down a rebellion of prisoners."

"If we're at the point where we need Umbris," Kullen said with a grimace, "then we're in a pit full of gnashers."

"Not funny," she chided.

"Take heart. You stand beside the Emperor's own Black Talon. Nothing shall bring you harm, Lady Dellacourt." He swept a bow to match his tone of mock gallantry.

Natisse shook her head. "You'd better not be treating this as a joke. We've both been through a great ordeal already. I don't believe six on two are very fair odds."

"Not for them. You're right. You said there were only *three* doors in and out of that room, right?"

Natisse nodded.

"Good." Kullen said. "The fewer possible entries for reinforcements, the better. First, we try for stealth—traditionally—but if things get hairy, I'll draw their attention toward me long enough for you to make a run for it. I'll be right behind you. I'll shadow-slide to your location once you reach it. With any luck, we'll be able to lock the chamber behind us, trap the Orken inside."

Natisse feared Kullen wasn't feeling the gravity of their situation. Those Orken in there were not just big, they were well trained in throwing their axes with great precision. If even one of them spotted Natisse darting across the cavern, they'd not hesitate to launch one in her direction. At least the monolith wasn't a moving target…

Natisse dunked several canvas-covered staves into the oil at once. She offered a handful to Kullen, but he shook his head.

"I'll need my hands free for this," he said, hefting the great hammer. "I'll tell you something, perhaps I've misjudged the value of blunt weapons all these years. This one packs quite the wallop."

"I'll stick to the pointy kind," Natisse quipped.

"To each their own. Now, are we ready?"

They shared a hesitant look. She was entrusting this man—who had not long ago been her enemy—with her very life. A moment of guilt passed, leaving Natisse wondering if she should tell him the truth about her last two attempts to summon Golgoth but decided it would do no good. If he went in there anything other than confident, it could cost them in dividends.

"Things are about to get dicey," she said instead.

Kullen let out a breath. "Let's do this."

"Lead the way, assassin," Natisse said, grinning.

Kullen preceded her out the storeroom door, following her back toward the end of the hall.

Bootsteps behind them hastened their pace.

Kullen swore. "Looks like our distraction is over."

The pit in Natisse's stomach turned over at the realization that the return of the Orken so soon meant the prisoners had been unsuccessful. She'd be shocked if they weren't all dead.

Natisse slowly opened the door, careful not to make a sound. Together, they slipped in and closed the door behind them. Kullen mouthed something to her and pointed at the steel bar positioned vertically beside the door. Catching his drift, she lowered it, placing it securely within two eyeholes on either side of the door, locking it.

Once done, they maneuvered to the left and toward a row of axe-throwing targets.

"How many?" Kullen asked.

Natisse peered out. Much to her dismay, the chamber was far from empty, but still, there were fewer than she'd expected. She counted three and told Kullen as much. They stood with their backs turned on them, surrounding the gated tunnel leading to the gnasher pit.

Kullen gestured for her to go first, marking the next movement with a pointed finger. In the dim torchlight of the room, there was something odd about his features, as if he was already becoming one with the darkness. But she thought little of it. After all, his dragon was the Lord of Darkness as hers was the Queen of Embers.

She crossed to the start of the straw dummy line, moving low to the ground and minding every step. When she turned back to Kullen, his whole body contorted into something somewhere between light and shadow. Then, with a crash and clatter of the giant hammer and the rest of his pilfered torture implements, he slumped to the ground.

In an instant, every Orken in the room spun to face them.

70
KULLEN

Kullen had no need to transform into shadow, not when he could merely call the shadows to surround him, to blur the edges of his physical form just enough so that he'd be harder to spot.

But as time ground to a near stop, and the magic heeded his call, he could feel something amiss. An involuntary chill ran through his body, yet this was not a thing he felt in his flesh. No, this cold pierced to his very *soul.*

He knew it instantly: the icy void of the Shadow Realm was unmistakable, a bite sharper than the harshest winter, utterly devoid of life yet filled with the hunger to devour him and every living thing, to consume all until nothing but darkness and emptiness remained.

Umbris's roar of fear and fury echoed in the back of his mind, and suddenly Kullen's eyes snapped open. He lay facedown on the ground, head throbbing, limbs locked up and frozen. Yet the sound of his dragon's call had dragged him away from whatever edge his soul had been hurtling toward.

Something gripped his arm hard. A hand, attached to an arm he thought he recognized. A woman's face hovered above him. "…

happened, but you'd better get your arse up because we're about to have company!"

Kullen blinked, his mind slow to register the familiar features. Natisse, concern filling her eyes. She was hauling him to his feet, but only for a moment, then she loosened her hold on him and spun away with a wordless shout.

Only then did Kullen notice the Orken barreling down on him with drawn weapons.

The sight of bared steel did wonders to clear the fog from his addled mind. He was still reeling and weak from whatever that was, but he knew how to respond to the clear and present danger. The axes in the Orken's hands could cut him and Natisse down in a single blow.

Natisse roared, waving pitiful weapons—a makeshift torch in one hand, a short sword-sized dagger in the other—at the charging Orken. That was all the distraction Kullen needed. His body acted of its own accord and his hands flashed forward. He dropped the hammer, and his fingers found and released the twin stilettos he'd borrowed from Chuldok's torture chamber. One buried fully into the throat of the foremost Orken, the other driving deep into the second Orken's right eye. The first stumbled and fell to one knee, dropping his sword and clutching at gurgling blood. The second barreled right through his kneeling comrade and went down in a sprawling, ragged heap at Natisse's feet. Neither rose—one was already dead, the other dying from a torn windpipe.

Natisse appeared just as startled as the two Orken. So surprised, in fact, she barely remembered the *third* Orken until it was nearly too late. The huge mustard-skinned bastard vaulted his companions' corpses and swung his huge axe at Natisse's head.

"Watch out!" Kullen shouted. He reached for his hammer, but he'd be too late, he knew.

Whether it was his warning or merely Natisse's fighting instincts that saved her life, Kullen didn't know. All he saw was the blur of steel through empty air as Natisse dropped into a low crouch, then struck forward and up, driving her short blade into the Orken's groin. A pitiable groan exploded through the room, accompanied by a gush of dark blood from the ragged tear. The Orken collapsed, dragging the weapon from Natisse's hand. He managed just one word—a harsh, guttural command in the Orken tongue.

"Attack!"

For a moment, Kullen wanted to laugh. There were no Orken left standing to carry out the dying brute's last order.

His laughter died on his lips as four dark shapes sprang up from behind the gate around which the Orken had been clustered. Gnashers, but these were no younglings like *Mauhul*. They weren't quite fully grown, but their bodies were rippling with raw muscle. Eight hideous eyes—the largest two of a deep copper color, the remaining six black as night—fixed on him and Natisse, and with a hissing sound like the clashing of enormous teeth, the gnashers launched themselves through the air toward them.

Binteth's balls! Kullen darted to the side, barely evading the faster moving of the gnashers, who landed where he'd been standing a heartbeat earlier. Had he been caught beneath the creature's bulk, he'd have been crushed to the ground *and* impaled by its two powerful forelegs and likely its stinger-tipped tail.

Kullen brought his hammer around in a wide arc. It connected with the gnasher's side and rebounded hard enough to send him reeling backward. He used the momentum to keep moving, running as fast as his feet could carry him. He had no chance of surviving a clash with gnashers armed with a blunt weapon. He needed speed. He needed *real* weapons.

Fortunately for him, he was surrounded by precisely that.

His desperate dash carried him toward one of the swords that had apparently fallen from one of the wooden racks lining the chamber walls. His path brought him past an oddly swirling and glowing wall—stone artwork that felt very out of place in Tuskthorne Keep, but he had no time to examine it closely. It was all he could do to scoop up the blade—what the Orken wielded as a hatchet, but which for him was a two-handed axe—and swing it and himself around to strike at the gnasher he sensed hurtling toward his back.

Once again, Cliessa's fortune was with him, and the attack, driven by blind instinct, struck true. He was beginning to feel as if he owed the goddess a sacrifice or an offering of some kind. The fine steel head sheared through both the outstretched gnasher limb and the stinger-tipped tail lashing for his face, sending both flying in a spray of sickening bile-green blood. The gnasher let out a wailing, hissing cry and skittered backward, the sound of its three remaining feet like the clatter of bones. Kullen wanted to pursue and finish off the monstrosity while it was off-balance, but two more gnashers were already leaping atop him. He was forced to dive into a sideways roll to evade their snapping, venom-edged jaws.

He came to his feet, nearly stumbled over one of the fallen Orken, but managed to right himself in time to duck a swiping tail and twist out of the path of a gnasher lurching forward to bite at him. Its fangs so close brought back memories that resulted in a stinging sensation in his chest, but he forced himself to ignore it. He could deal with his wounds if they survived. Swinging the axe upward, he buried it into the underside of the creature's jaw. The gnasher emitted an ear-piercing shriek and darted in retreat. Before Kullen could pull his axe free, the wooden haft was ripped from his hands.

Once again weaponless, he sprinted away from the third of the gnashers. Too slow. The creature was upon him in a moment, its huge leg batting him off his feet with the force of a charging bull. Kullen flew through the air and crashed against the wall, then collapsed atop another rack of weapons. The black wood crumbled beneath him—and in so doing, saved his life. As he and the assorted axes, swords, and spears clattered to the ground, the gnasher's spike-tipped tail punched a hand's breadth into the wall just above him. There was an audible *crunch* of collapsing chitin, and the creature let out a wailing hiss.

That hiss turned into a full-throated howl a moment later. Fire seemed to engulf the entire rear portion of the gnasher, and its hairy body caught alight in the space between heartbeats. The creature stumbled back and to the side like a drunken sailor, swatting at the air with its four powerful legs in a vain attempt to put out the flames. Its eyeballs popped with a terrible sound akin to boiling mud, and when it finally gave way, its legs curled up beneath it in the way a dying spider's did. All the while, its injured tail lashed about until it, too, gave one final twitch and lay still.

Kullen stared slack-jawed first at the dead gnasher, then at Natisse. She was breathing heavily, bleeding from a pair of cuts on her left cheek and another on her right bicep, but she held two of her makeshift torches before her as if they were a fiery shield.

The gnasher that had gone after her was down, too. Burned to a crisp, the fine hairs covering its bulbous body still smoking and charred.

"Good… thinking," he managed, his breath catching in his lungs.

"Yeah," Natisse panted, lowering her torches. "You're welcome." She glanced toward the gate where the gnashers had emerged, and her face darkened. "That's not the last of them, you know. There could be more coming at any moment."

"More Orken, too." Kullen grimaced. "We got lucky here. But I don't want to be around when our luck runs out."

"Nor do I." She looked back to him, her expression grim. "What exactly happened to you back there? One moment you're standing, right as rain, the next, you collapse and knock over enough weapons to alert everyone in the Keep that we're here!"

Kullen frowned. "I… I don't know." He instinctively reached for the dragonblood vial around his neck but had to stop himself from drawing on Umbris's power. "When I called to the shadows, that's when I felt it."

The shivering fever returned, setting his vision spinning.

"Felt what?" Natisse demanded.

"The Shadow Realm." He swallowed hard. "I don't have time to explain it all now." In truth, he didn't even understand it himself. "But something about this place is muddling my magic. Trying to drag me permanently into the Shadow Realm."

He looked around the chamber, trying to make sense of it all. Dead Orken and gnashers lay about in a scene of death. Destruction in the form of broken weapons racks and crumbling walls joined them to turn the room into chaos. When his eyes fell on the strange mural adorning the wall where he'd been standing, he remembered the odd sensation that had come over him. He'd felt nauseated, disoriented, as if sickened by reality rippling around him. It made no sense—how could inert stone elicit such a reaction—but it *had* happened. He hadn't just imagined it.

"That!" He gestured toward the wall, racing across the chamber toward it. He slowed as he approached—even from five paces away, he felt sickness coming on. The feeling was faint, like the warmth emanating from a candle on the opposite side of a vast room, yet there was no mistaking it. "Something about this stone…"

Only after he said it did he realize he'd voiced the words aloud. He felt foolish for sharing the truth with Natisse—his training as Black Talon had taught him to *never* reveal any weakness that could be turned against him—but he hadn't been able to help himself.

"What about that one?" came Natisse's question from behind Kullen.

Kullen turned to find her pointing at a strange fixture at the center of the room. All black but for thin veins of glowing blue cast its center into near pitch darkness. He hadn't given it much thought, but looking at it now, it appeared to be of the same make as the mural.

"When I came through here last," Natisse explained as Kullen approached the obelisk, "the Orken were taking turns standing by the stone, while their comrades threw axes at them. The stones that chipped off the block went up onto the wall." She gestured toward the unfinished artwork by the door. "Some strange Orken game or ritual, it seems."

Kullen had no words. His attention was riveted on the stone. The small shards fixed to the wall had emanated a bizarre, disorientating distortion effect that set the world around him rippling like heat rising off a hot road under the summer sun. But as he approached the two-story block, it seemed to waver, shimmering like precious jewels. Nausea gurgled at his stomach.

"Take care, Friend Kullen," Umbris said.

What is it?

"I do not know," Umbris admitted. *"And that alone is reason to be cautious of it."*

Give me your eyes, he told the dragon through their mental bond. There was light enough in the chamber that he could see clearly, but not enough for Umbris's vision to activate on its own. With dragoneyes, Kullen could see the world in an entirely different spectrum. Perhaps they could—

Umbris immediately granted Kullen's request. Sucking in a startled breath, Kullen viewed the stone as his dragon would. No longer did it appear the inert lump of ordinary rock, but it had blossomed to life. The thin veins of blue transformed to a red-hot burning blaze surrounded by vast expanses of blank, inky darkness. It squirmed like writhing maggots, undulating in and out of the void-like block.

Where his eyes saw a cool blue that emitted a sense of warmth and comfort, Umbris saw a hate-filled chasm of... nothing.

It was the same feeling he'd gotten on the docks when coming into close proximity to the Lumenators' magic. What that meant, precisely, he was unsure.

Icy feet danced down Kullen's spine. He recoiled, instinctively retreating from the wonder.

"What is it?" Natisse asked.

"I don't know." Kullen looked to her. Upon averting his gaze, the malady plaguing his gut dissipated, her form solid and true. "Do you not feel it?"

Natisse scrunched her face in concentration, squeezing shut her eyes. After a moment, she shook her head. "Nothing."

Kullen grunted. So the queer effects didn't extend to all dragonblood magic, only, perhaps, that of the Shadow Realm. "There's something… off about the stone. Something… wrong. I don't know how to explain it, except it makes me feel sick."

Natisse raised an eyebrow. "And that's not something that happens often?"

"Never." Until recently, that was. "I have no idea why it's causing this reaction. Neither does Umbris. But one thing is certain: I can't use my magic anywhere near this stone. The results would be…" He shuddered at his recollections of the Shadow Wraiths—as he'd begun to think of them. Even moments ago when he and Natisse had slid together, he sensed them there, waiting, keeping their distance this time, but hungry as they'd been on the docks. "…unpleasant."

Something in the Shadow Realm had changed of late, and he would need to discover what. At first, he'd thought it was merely due to his weariness, but now he wasn't so sure.

"Then let's get bloody out of here," she said, gritting her teeth. "Though maybe you should take a second to bind that up."

Kullen followed the line of her eyes. A gash had opened along his side—courtesy of the gnashers, it appeared—but the pain hadn't even registered amidst all the other injuries he'd already received at the hands of Chuldok and Bareg's pet.

"What's a bit more blood?" he asked, trying to sound nonchalant. In truth, he barely felt it, and the trickle wasn't crippling. "It'll hold until we're safely away from here. After that, I'm spending the next week in a bathtub with all the food and drink I can handle, a full flight of the finest healing potions, and no Orken. That last bit especially."

"Sounds pretty damned good right about now." Natisse chuckled. "Maybe that pleasant fantasy will be enough to get us out of here. Though a weapon or six should help." She had lost her Orken dagger amid the battle—probably buried hilt deep within one of the beasts. But they seemed easy to come by. Even now, she bent and retrieved two more from the belt of the nearest dead Orken—the one whose throat had been splayed by Kullen's thrown stiletto.

Kullen followed suit, taking advantage of the slight reprieve to find truly useable weapons

To his delight, the Orken had stored a trio of longswords similar to those used by the Elite Scales. No doubt to train in opposition to their human counterparts against the eventuality the Emperor dispatched the unit upon them. Kullen belted one of the swords to his hip and carried the other in hand. He stowed a dagger on the opposite side, along with the remaining tools stolen from Chuldok. The hammer, he left behind, deciding against his recent inclinations toward misjudging the bulky armament. He was now weighed down with enough steel to at least have a fighting chance against the Orken.

Neither he nor Natisse needed encouragement to hurry. It took them less than a minute to arm up, then they were on the move toward one of the adjoining rooms. Kullen gave the stone obelisk a wide berth, eyeing it warily through his once-again human eyes. He couldn't begin to hypothesize its purpose or why it made him so uneasy, but he would find out. Someone would know—the Emperor, perhaps, or one of the Lumenators. Assidius, maybe. Turoc, certainly.

They reached the door closest to them, deciding one was no different from another since what lay beyond was as big a mystery to them as the rest of the Keep. Kullen pulled it open only to be met by five Orken. And there, Bareg stood at their head.

71
Natisse

Natisse froze mid-step, her eyes locked on the open door and the squad of Orken standing there. None wore armor or carried drawn weapons. The largest of the pack, a giant Orken with shoulders almost too large to fill the doorway, carried an enormous moon-shaped axe slung across his back, while the other Orkenwatch regulars had a collection of two-handed greatswords and spike-studded maces with heads as large as hers.

A goldband led them, the same Sniffer she'd seen departing the torture chamber where she'd found Kullen. But it was the second, smaller Sniffer beside the Orkenwatch commander that caught Natisse's attention.

He appeared to her eyes like any other Orken of his particular breed: a long, broad nose with wide nostrils, eyes set close together and sunken deep beneath his sloping brow, tusks jutting up from his lower jaw, teeth filed to sharp points. His weapons, too, were utterly unremarkable—a collection of human-sized daggers slung in two bandoliers across his chest.

Yet, unlike every Orken she'd encountered, this Sniffer wore a hat. And no ordinary hat. She knew this hat. It was the same horribly hideous, floppy, red, velvety hat Baruch had loved so much—all the same scuffs and stains. The dark bloodstains were new, though. Dalash's blood? One of the other Crimson Fang's? For there was no doubt in Natisse's mind: *this* Sniffer had been present for the Orkenwatch assault on the Burrow, likely even *led* it.

Righteous, hate-fueled indignation rose up within her. Her vision turned red and blurry, her face flushing hot. Every fiber of her being screamed at her to abandon caution and fly at the Sniffer, to rip Baruch's hat off his Ezrasil-damned head and hack him to pieces. Vengeance for Dalash, justice for her still-living comrades.

It would be folly to attack, but that didn't stop her from instinctively reaching within herself to call upon Golgoth's fire. The inferno raging in her belly sprang to life, heat surged in her veins, and she felt herself on the verge of exploding from the very core of her being.

And yet, no fire manifested. Try as she might, the rage would not produce flames. Her pulse throbbed in her ears and every shred of her body smoldered, yet it was no *magical* energy seething within her—just that old and familiar bundle of fear and hatred and anger all tied up with a nice bow of disgust.

All of this happened in the space between heartbeats, but it left Natisse feeling downright drained, hopeless. It took all her willpower just to remain standing in the face of her ire, trapped and made inert by her failure to access Golgoth's revenge. She wanted to unleash it—oh, how she wanted. But nothing she did would dissolve that barrier, and that feeling of helplessness shattered her very soul.

Neither Kullen nor the Orken appeared to notice the war raging within her. Kullen stood utterly still, drawn sword held low in a casual grip, his posture entirely on alert and his eyes locked on the Sniffer up front. For their part, the five Orken appeared far too surprised by the presence of the two humans to do more than provide a shocked stare.

Kullen broke the silence first. "It's over, Bareg. There's no more hiding what you've done, no more covering up your guilt. But I offer you this one chance: turn around and flee Dimvein, and maybe, *maybe,* the Emperor won't order the Orkenwatch to hunt you down and gut you like the traitor you are."

Whatever reaction he might've expected, it likely wasn't the mirthless laugh that rumbled from the goldband's lips.

"Funny, funny human." The Orken, Bareg, gestured to the Orken at his back. "You alone. With little fire-hair woman." He shot Natisse a contemptuous sneer. "No more questions. No more talk. Here, you die."

"I'd say the same to you," Kullen shot back in a voice of casual contempt, "but I'd much rather keep you alive long enough to drag your broken, beaten arse in front of the Emperor so you can identify every member of your little conspiracy."

Natisse was taken aback by Kullen's bravado. It took guts to remain so calm when unarmored and outnumbered. Then again, in the short time she'd known him, Kullen had never backed down from a fight, no matter the odds. Perhaps it was the fact he had Umbris at his command or he merely *was* so dauntless—whatever the case, Natisse found his strength and composure oddly reassuring.

With her resolve renewed, she asked, "What do you think? We let them surrender now, or we beat them into submission?"

A hint of a smile flickered across Kullen's face. "Don't get me wrong, after enjoying Chuldok's *hospitality* for the last few hours, I'd love nothing more than to crack skulls and shatter bones. But!" He held up a finger, shaking it in the Orkens' faces with mock severity. "But, I'm a decent fellow. Most of the time, at least. You four have one chance to prove you're loyal to the Emperor. In the name of Emperor Wymarc, arrest Ketsneer Bareg for treachery against the Karmian Empire and the people of Dimvein."

His words had no effect whatsoever. The huge Orken just glared at Kullen with a blank expression—Natisse couldn't be certain the giant one even spoke the Imperial tongue. The two

Orkenwatch regulars behind Bareg exchanged glances but made no move. The bastard Sniffer wearing Baruch's hat just sneered and muttered something in the Orken tongue.

Bareg's laughter echoed through the hall. "You not find allies among Orken. Orken loyal to Ketsneer." He thumped a fist on his chest. "Orken loyal to Orken!" He growled something in his own language, and the four Orken behind him echoed it in a loud, ringing shout.

"Glory and blood for Orken-kind, eh?" Kullen shook his head. "Haven't heard that one before." He snapped something at the Orken in their tongue. "But that one you've heard, yes?"

The word, whatever it meant, had an instantaneous effect. The huge Orken's face creased into a furious snarl and he reached for the enormous axe strapped to his back. Surprise showed on Bareg's face, but the other three Orken merely snarled back at Kullen and drew their weapons.

"You die!" Bareg grated in the Imperial language.

A tumultuous roar erupted, and the giant Orken in the back surged forward, stampeding past his comrades like a dragon rushing through a pottery shop. The two Orkenwatch regulars in the middle ranks were bowled over, and Bareg and the other Sniffer were pushed roughly aside to make way for the giant's rush.

Natisse's heart leaped into her throat as the giant made straight for Kullen, swinging his moon-shaped axe with all the force of his mighty muscles. Natisse saw the shearing, sweeping blow coming right for her—it would face little resistance cutting through Kullen and continuing on its path to take off her head. In desperation, she threw herself to the side and out of the way of the blurring steel.

A bellow echoed behind her, ringing with fury and pain. It took her brain a heartbeat to register the sound—Orken, not human. When she finally regained her feet and spun back around, she found the brute frozen motionless over Kullen. The giant

Orken stood hunched over, his body doubled nearly in half around the sword that Kullen, kneeling to evade the axe, had buried to the hilt in his foe's belly. A full foot of bloody steel protruded from the Orken's back and crimson gushed from the wound to sluice down Kullen's face and chest.

Kullen snarled something sharp and harsh in guttural Orken, then released his grip on his sword and twisted out from beneath his dying enemy. He climbed slowly to his feet and slid the second sword from its sheath at his belt.

"One down," he said, his voice still deadly and calm. "Who's next?"

Natisse was as stunned by his composure as the four Orken remaining. Bareg and the Sniffer hadn't been knocked over but had recovered enough to draw their weapons. The two Orkenwatch regulars were still picking themselves up from the ground—that was how quickly everything had transpired.

Bareg's eyes flicked past Kullen, seeming to see the dead Orken and gnashers behind them for the first time. "You kill Orken and *azukha*."

"*Mauhul* needed some friends to keep him company in whatever those overgrown rodents have for an afterlife." Kullen gave a little shrug. "As did Chuldok."

Bareg bared his tusks and drew the long, jagged-edged dagger he wore on his hip. "We serve your flesh as stew tonight."

"That's gross." Kullen pulled a disgusted face. "All right. Come on, then!" He beckoned with his free hand.

"The Sniffer's mine," Natisse snarled. She leveled her two daggers at the Orken in the hat. "He was there when they arrested and killed my friends."

If Kullen had anything to say on the matter, he never got the chance. Bareg's barked command sent the two Orkenwatch regulars into action.

The first charged sword tip first, aiming to skewer Natisse before a fight could even ensue. She batted the attack away, then fell back and uncoiled her whip. She gave it a snap, cracking the air. The Orken would find her no easy kill. He snorted and charged again, this time calculating a downward slice meant to shear her in two.

Natisse deftly spun away, then lashed out with her whip, low and hard. The cord tangled around the Orken's leading leg, and its tip drove deep into the back of his ankle. Her following pull didn't have the same effect as what defaced Chuldok, but the result was catastrophic.

The Orken's rear tendon shredded and the force of the action brought him down to the ground in a split. Blood poured out onto the stone. She had every intention of darting in and ending it with a swift stab of her short sword, but instead, found herself soaring backward after what felt like being hit by a runaway wagon.

She landed in a long skid that ended with a hard slam against the stone block in the middle of the chamber. Before she could compose herself, she heard a heavy *boom* but there was no time for further inspection. Her attacker was on her in an instant, slashing down wildly with his long greatsword. She rolled aside but not far enough. The blade raked down her back, taking a thin sliver of skin with it.

The unexpected shock froze her for an instant, allowing the Orken to deliver a second attack. Though she continued rolling, she braced for a killing blow. But it never came. A loud clatter of steel caused her to opened her eyes—which she hadn't realized she'd even closed. The Orken stood, arm raised with a thin dagger piercing his wrist.

Unable to waste any more precious time, she rose, slicing and slashing the whole way up. Three lacerations to the Orken's legs, and another two to his torso sent him stumbling backward. Back to the obelisk, she leaped, then used it as a springboard, thrusting her back leg outward. She flew through the air, sword poised, and thrust downward with both hands. It found its new home lodged between the Orken's eyes. But she didn't relinquish her grip. The weight of her fall dragged the blade with her, flaying the Orken's face down the middle, until it cut free at the chin.

The Orken remained standing for a second before folding in on himself and crashing to the ground in a puddle of blood.

Only then did she realize that there were no more Orken remaining. For a moment, she was furious that Kullen had killed the Sniffer—she'd wanted to be the one to put the blade in him, for Dalash. Yet there were two corpses too few.

"Where did—?" she started to ask, then caught sight of the closed door and realized what had made such a hard slam just moments ago.

"Bastard coward fled!" Kullen sneered. "Him and your Sniffer friend."

"Let's go after them, then!" Natisse demanded. The thought of Dalash's killer escaping was more than she could handle. She would watch that damned Sniffer die if it was the last thing she did. And if they'd gone to find reinforcements, it just might be.

"Good idea, why didn't I think of that?" Kullen snorted. "And you're welcome, by the way. Pretty sure that puts us back at even."

Natisse was too enraged to retort, already stalking toward the door. She gave it a pull, but it wouldn't budge.

"Binteth take it!" She tried again, with equal success.

Kullen lent a hand, but stopped after a half-hearted effort. "Shite-sucking cowards and traitors locked it!"

Natisse nearly lost herself in a fury of curses, but Kullen's next words left her cold.

"I know." He turned to her. "It's wood and iron. Nothing a bit of Dragonfire can't get through." He stepped back from the door and gestured to it with a grand flourish. "I leave it to you and your magic."

Ice filled her veins. She'd kept her secret long enough, and now the time had come for her to come clean.

"I…" The words died on her lips. How could she say it, at a time like this? What would he think of her? It would be no better than losing her sword before a desperate battle or forgetting to don leathers.

And yet, she had no choice. They had to find a way out, and at the moment, that way wasn't her.

"I can't." Shame overwhelmed her at the admission. "Golgoth is gone. I'm unable to access her magic."

72
KULLEN

Kullen would never admit it aloud, but he was exhausted. He'd slept only a handful of hours apiece the last few days—ever since the attack on the Refuge, he'd been too busy to sit still and rest—and the torture had sapped his strength. The pain only made things worse. Finally, having a chance to inspect the wounds on his chest, he was grateful to see they weren't as extensive as he'd originally thought. Strapped to that torture table, he'd been sure the gnasher had dug down to scrape bone with its sharp fangs. Truth was, he'd suffered worse.

Adding to the myriad injuries left by *Mauhul* were a fresh pair of gashes inflicted by Orken swords. He'd barely escaped the last clash with his head still attached.

He and Natisse had been lucky to encounter Bareg's little group unawares. Out on the streets of Dimvein, covered head to toe in banded mail armor, even those few Orkenwatch would've been nearly impossible to defeat in his current condition. Fortunately, Orken hide did little better at turning steel blades than human skin.

But their good fortune had all but run out. Bareg would doubtless even now be summoning reinforcements from the *countless* Orken within Tuskthorne Keep, likely arming and armoring up, too. In a matter of minutes, there would be a ferocious greeting party waiting to welcome Kullen and Natisse with drawn weapons and bared fangs.

But that wasn't all. The fatigue Kullen felt went far beyond just the physical. He could feel the Shadow Realm's cold seeping into his limbs, and his connection to Umbris fraying like a sawn rope. He hadn't yet called on the dragonblood power, yet the innate magic infused into his body through his bond with the Twilight Dragon was enough to activate whatever ill effects the mysterious obelisk was imposing on him. Just being near it was taking a toll. He didn't know how much longer he could ignore the ill effects. All he knew was he needed to get *away* from that stone before it got him killed or rendered him unconscious.

The situation was grim, the battle ahead bloody. And it turned out he'd be fighting it *alone?*

"What do you mean, *can't?*" His words came out sharp, his voice edged with enervation. "You've done it before. You know how to do it. You're telling me you've forgotten—"

"Of course not!" Natisse's eyes flashed. Anger replaced her uncertainty in a moment. "I know *how* to call on the magic. It's just..." She ground her teeth, blood rising to her cheeks. "Something's stopping me from calling on it. When I try to reach for it, it's like there's a wall there, blocking me from reaching it or it from reaching me."

Kullen stared at her, mouth agape. How was this a problem *again?* He was far from an expert when it came to the finer points of the magic as a concept—he only had his experience and those Jarius had shared with him to draw on—but hadn't he already spoken with Natisse about confronting her fears? That was how *he* had pushed past the barrier that blocked his access to Umbris's magic.

With effort, he fought to remain in control. He doubted that his anger would succor her. "Remember, we talked about this?" he said, trying to keep his voice calm, his tone carefully neutral. "The fear of fire would stop you from—"

"That's not it!" Natisse threw up her hands and stalked a few paces. "Don't you think I've already considered that? If this was just about what happened to me, the fear I felt about the fire itself, I'd have dealt with that already. But this…" She looked as if she wanted to punch something—either him or the black wood door, Kullen wasn't certain. "This isn't fear."

"It's always fear of *some* sort," Kullen said, shaking his head. "I can't tell you what it is. No one can. Only *you* can figure it out."

"And what about you?" Natisse demanded. "You dare to chide me over this when you yourself just flopped to the ground and blew our cover?"

She wasn't wrong. Perhaps her own inability to summon Golgoth's magic had something to do with whatever properties resided within the stone block? He drew in a deep breath, forced himself to think clearly. "You're right. However, I'm not going to lie, this is a rubbish time for this to happen, but I get it. We can deal with it another time. Once we're out of here. Didn't you say there was a third door?"

"Over there," she said, pointing, no lack of disappointment at not being able to follow Bareg and his Sniffer evident on her face.

"Let's give that a try, see if we can find another way out that doesn't require magic."

Natisse's face was tight, her expression strained, but she managed a little nod. "Sure." Even her voice sounded on edge.

Kullen studied her a long moment. It was clear whatever was happening with her was bothering her, but it fell to *her* to understand it. All he could do was give her the space to sort out it out in her head and let her come to terms with it on her own. Hopefully before it was too late for them to escape Tuskthorne Keep alive.

"Stay here," he told her, pointing to the door. "Watch my back. You hear anyone coming this way, you give a shout and I'll come running."

She opened her mouth to protest, but a thunderous reverberation stole the words from her tongue.

Kullen swore.

He followed the sound to the door they'd barred upon coming in. He'd almost forgotten about the Orken who had been dispatched to put down the rebellion and were now intent upon re-entering their chamber and continuing their strange work.

"We have to move," Kullen said. "Together. Now."

Kullen led the way, bloody sword held at the ready. The slams from the other side of the barred door continued.

"That door won't hold forever," Natisse said, running.

They reached the third door and threw it open. Despondency at the sight of what lay beyond settled in. Stacked wall to wall, buckets, bags full of material obviously used to construct the Orken art wall forced a new sense of dread. They were going to have to fight again.

The door burst into splinters behind them.

"Kullen!" Natisse shouted. "They're coming!"

Six Orken spilled through the door on the opposite end of the room. These carried no armor, but wasted no time collecting weaponry from the racks along the wall on their roaring charge. Four angled for Kullen, the remaining two making straight for Natisse.

A loud *twang pierced the air* and something dark hissed across the open chamber. An Orken flew backward as if punched by a giant invisible hand. When his body finally stopped rolling, Kullen caught sight of the black-fletched shaft protruding from his chest.

He had just time enough to cast a glance in Natisse's direction. She had snatched up a pair of crossbows from a mount on the wall and managed to load them—an impressive feat of strength, given they were Orken-sized weapons. Her second bolt took down one of the Orken coming for Kullen.

"Ready for round two?" Kullen asked.

"More like round four," Natisse responded.

He roared his defiance at the Orken, who answered with a growled war cry in their own tongue. Raising his sword, he charged at full speed, waving his free hand in the air like a madman. A cruel smile creased the lips of the nearest Orken.

Clearly, the brute was buying his act of half-naked, bleeding lunatic barreling head-on toward certain death.

The Orken's sword rose, and Kullen went low. He drove his sword sideways into a perfect thrust as he evaded the huge Orken, and the brute went down howling in agony and bleeding from a deep puncture wound just below his ribs. A fatal wound, Kullen knew without looking. Even Orken couldn't survive long when bleeding from a laceration to a major organ blood vessel.

The remaining two Orken weren't so easily fooled. Even as they saw Kullen's agile evasion and vicious attack on their comrade, their warrior-trained minds registered the true danger they faced and their pace slowed. They were ferocious, hungry for battle and bloodshed, but they were no fools to throw their lives away. Orken could be as cunning as they were ruthless—which made them a truly deadly foe to face.

Natisse loosed another two quarrels in the span it took him to cross the room, but both missed. Now, with him in close combat, she couldn't keep up the barrage without putting him in danger. He heard her moving in behind him, but shouted, "Stay back!"

"And let you have all the fun?" Natisse countered. "Fat chance."

A heavy mace split the air above Kullen's head as he ducked and followed through into a roll. The movement pained him deeply, but what else was new? Now, as he rose to a crouch, he found himself sandwiched between two warriors. Each fell into a fighting stance, waiting for the other to make a move.

"Come on!" Kullen taunted. "If you don't kill me, the smell of you will."

The Orken snarled and converged on him. Kullen rose and deflected the first attack, sending a greatsword directly at the mace-wielding Orken's throat. This caused the mace-wielder to halt his strike and dodge his own comrade's weapon. Kullen took advantage of the confusion to slash two long cuts across the swordsman's arms. They were hasty attacks, so neither cut very deep, but he would need time to enact his plan.

Natisse came in from behind, her whip finding its way around the mace's shaft. The thong pulled taut, but the Orken didn't give at all. Instead, he glared at her and smiled before jerking the weapon back and sending Natisse face first into the stone.

The sword-bearer drove in with a two-handed stab that caught Kullen just above the hip. Blood poured out like a fountain.

"Kullen!" Natisse shouted, rising from her fall.

Kullen groaned, pressing one hand futilely against the wound. Then, he growled, burying the pain, and kicked downward to hobble the Orken. Barefooted as he was, there was no leather or steel to add weight to the blow, so no satisfying *crack* awarded him. But it would be enough. With both enemies occupied for a moment, Kullen reached into his pants pocket and drew out a small orb—one of two little tricks he'd had on him just in case. In that moment, he was happy he'd not wasted them.

"Get back!" he shouted to Natisse through gritted teeth.

His arm flashed downward and sent the globe shattering against the floor. Smoke poured up from the spot, immediately concealing both him and the Orken. Now, Kullen had the advantage. His dragon-eyes activated and he could clearly see the two Orken struggling to hold their breath against the barrage. One sucked in accidentally and ended up doubled over in a coughing fit. With two swift flicks of his blades, the Orken were no more.

Kullen fell over, so spent he didn't care that he lay in a pool of Orken blood. He'd had enough. They wouldn't survive another encounter. Shekoth's pits, they might not survive the trip out unhindered.

He looked to Natisse. "Listen to me!" he snarled, his voice rising to a furious shout. "Right now, you are our *one* chance of getting out of here alive. We're not getting out that way"—he swept his sword toward the storage closet—"and there's no telling how many more Orken are going to come at us from behind. If we stand around here and wait, we're going to die, cut down by Orken or fed to the gnashers you said are on the other end of *that* tunnel!"

Natisse opened her mouth, but Kullen was far from done.

"My dragonblood magic is useless here. Without knowing what that stone will do, I can't risk summoning Umbris." He thrust a bloody finger at her. "Which means *you* are our only hope. We've got minutes until every Orken in Tuskthorne Keep knows we're here and comes howling for our heads. Whatever you have to do, whatever epiphany you need to have, do it right bloody *now*. Otherwise we're both going to die terribly!"

73
Natisse

Natisse's cheeks burned, shame twisting like a ball in her stomach. Much as she hated to admit it, Kullen was right. They couldn't remain in this chamber much longer—no telling how soon Bareg would return with more armed Orken to capture or kill them. Not to mention if anyone down the corridor heard the clash of battle.

Indeed, she'd barely survived the last skirmish. Even facing just *one* Orken alone after bringing down two with the crossbow, she had come dangerously close to death. Her hands, arms, and shoulders ached from the jarring impact of blocking the brute's heavy weapon. One of her stolen daggers was dented and bent, the other marked by chips along its now jagged edge. And that was just facing off against a single foe. Then, being tossed around like a child at the end of her whip… Their luck couldn't hold out much longer.

But what could she do? It wasn't fear of the flames, that much she knew. She was still hesitant to unleash Golgoth's Dragonfire—she'd seen the damage it could inflict, both on people and on their surroundings—but there was no doubt in her mind she needed it. Badly. Without the fire, Kullen was right, they would not survive.

The fear of certain death at the end of Orkenwatch blades far outweighed anything flames could do.

So what, then? Why could she not call on the fire burning within her? What stood between her and Golgoth?

She wished she could speak with the Queen of the Ember Dragons, to try and make sense of it, but the presence Natisse had come to feel so closely was distant, impossibly faint. The power in her veins had transformed from the controlled burn of a carefully-constructed fire to the mindless, rampaging ferocity of a wildfire. She could feel it slowly killing her, just as Kullen had warned.

"I'm trying!" she shot back, unleashing her anger in the hope that it would somehow cause the magic to manifest on its own, as it had in the past. "I've done everything I can think of, but it's just not working!"

Despite the frustration turning her words bitter and tightening every muscle, no fire sprang to her command. At least not on the outside. Internally, the sizzle of flames increased, forcing her to press a hand against the wall just to stay upright.

"Keep trying, then." Kullen's face was hard as he tried to stand. All traces of his formerly unflappable calm had fled, replaced by worry that darkened his eyes. "The only other choice is death, and you don't strike me as the sort who gives up and lies down to die."

Those words struck home deep within Natisse. Again, he was right. She had spent her entire adult life fighting—for Uncle Ronan's missions, to help the poor and destitute of Dimvein, and, most important of all, to protect her friends. The Crimson Fang had been her life for so long she couldn't remember a time she wasn't fighting. Even in her earliest memories of the day her family had been killed by Dragonfire, she'd been fighting. Fighting to survive against impossible odds.

Now, the tables had been turned. The odds were in her favor. She had been gifted a weapon of immense power—a weapon that might've saved her family, but which *would* save her friends once she found where they were being held captive. If only she could access Golgoth's magic, it would be the key to her salvation. So much power, just beyond her reach.

Then it struck her. *That's it!* The realization drove the breath from her lungs. *That's what is stopping me.*

Golgoth's power was immense, she knew it with every ounce of her. Yet, though her head wanted to wield the magic, her heart feared that it was too much. Too much fire, too much power for one person. Ezrasil's bones, it was the power of a bloody *dragon,* the Queen of the Ember Dragons herself. No human should wield so much power!

And *that* was why she couldn't control it: because she didn't believe anyone deserved it. Not the Magister who had tried to dominate Golgoth, not the Emperor, and certainly not *her.* That knowledge had caused her to resist the magic. And in resisting, she had set her soul at war with itself.

For in truth, the fire was now as much a part of her as the breath in her lungs and the blood in her veins. She knew that, felt it to the core. Her bond with Golgoth was far more than merely physical—it permeated every part of her, as if it always had been and would always be. Which, she supposed, it was. The bond only ended when *she* died. Golgoth was forever, a being of elemental purity that only existed in the Mortal Realm because of her connection to a human. As long as there was fire in the world, Golgoth would continue. Her magic would endure long beyond Natisse's death.

So why did Natisse fear it? Was she truly alarmed by fire? No, she *used* it every day, in countless ways. Certainly, there was plenty to worry about from fire left to run rampant—it could ravage everything in its path. Yet a fire constrained and controlled was as much a tool as Natisse's fingers, lashblade, or belt knife. And what had Natisse to fear from a tool? Just as a sword could neither be good nor evil, nor could the magic. Not on its own.

Only the one who *wielded* it mattered. Intention and purpose mattered. A sword raised in defense of the innocent still shed blood, but a sheathed blade hanging on the belt of a cruel man could inflict far more pain. What mattered most was how the tool was used.

Natisse knew without a shred of doubt why she used the magic. Not to gain power, but in her defense and the defense of those for whom she cared. To balance out the inequity in Dimvein and bring justice to those who could not see justice done for themselves. And what could be more noble than that? What could be more *good* than that?

In that moment, Natisse understood what truly hindered her. The magic was part of her, but unless she chose to control it, it would control her. Just as fire burned through everything in its path, so, too, would the magic. It would burn through her body and soul, as it had so many times already. Her pain, rage, and fear would give it life, but in doing so, would destroy her. Or, she could accept the inevitability of the power and *use* it, channel it, give it life in a way that would benefit those around her. Like a spark fanned into the fire that drove off the cold and brought light in the darkness, Natisse needed to be in command of the fire.

And when she wielded it, truly accepting the gift she'd been given, the magic would be her salvation.

Golgoth! She shouted through the mental bond, trying to reach the Ember Dragon across the planes of reality. *Golgoth, I accept your power. I accept its immensity and the responsibility inherent in such power. Never will I use it to cause harm to anyone upon which we don't mutually agree deserves it. We are friends. I accept your bond and trust you accept mine.*

Suddenly, Natisse felt as if something within her had shattered. Not a physical breaking of bones or tearing flesh, but it was no less real for its intangibility. Power rushed through her with staggering force, nearly sending her to her knees, but this time the fire didn't hurt, didn't harm, didn't consume. Instead, it swirled within her, infusing her with life and vitality, scouring all trace of exhaustion from her muscles and restoring her depleted reserves of strength.

Golgoth's satisfaction resonated deep within her mind. "*I*

accept your bond and trust you with my power. Together, as one, let us bring justice to those deserving."

Natisse opened her eyes—she hadn't realized they were closed—and as she did, the world around her seemed to shine with new light. Every torch in the chamber called to her, reached out fiery hands as if to embrace her. She reached back for them. Dropping her mortal weapons, she stretched out her arms, raised them high, and summoned the flickering lights to her as if they were part of her.

Come to me, she commanded them. How she didn't know, but it came to her instinctively, as if Golgoth's mind had melded with her own. *Come to me and lend me your aid.*

The torches were snuffed out in an instant, but the fires did not die. Instead, they hurtled toward her like globes of pure energy, enveloping her upturned palms and burning as brightly as they had when feeding on oil-soaked wood. Now, however, they fed on *her* power—on the power of her soul, connected to the Fire Realm through her bond with Golgoth. It was a mutual bond, each devouring the fragments of the other that gave them life.

A gasp from nearby brought Natisse's attention to where Kullen stood. The Black Talon's dark eyes were wide, his mouth agape, a look of rapt wonder on his handsome face.

Natisse smiled, her own delight mingling with Golgoth's.

"You were right," she said, her voice resonating with an impossible timber that could only have come from a dragon's throat. "Fear was holding me back. Fear of how much power there is, how much I can call on." She shook her head. "No longer."

Kullen appeared at a loss for words, but his eyes flicked to the door barring their path. Natisse turned toward it. Fueled by the inferno dancing around her, she felt as if she could break it down with a mere thought. It was nothing more than wood and metal, fuel to be consumed.

"You might want to step back," she said, her voice booming through the chamber. "I've never tried this before."

Kullen complied, giving her space as she advanced to place her burning palms against the door.

"Wait!" he said.

Natisse glanced over her shoulder.

"Remember what I told you about Jarius?" Kullen spoke quickly, urgently. "How he used a sword to channel and focus his power?" His gaze flicked to the fires burning on her hands, and he bent to scoop up one of the daggers she'd dropped, which he held out to her. "Maybe that'll work better than a blast of Dragonfire?" He gave her a wry grin. "Less likely to burn us both alive, too."

Natisse accepted the dagger and the advice. She had never tried anything like it before, but the way he said it, she somehow understood how to make it work. Gripping the hilt of the dagger in both hands, she placed its tip against the door at chest height and drew on the fire—both burning in her palms and swirling like a maelstrom within her belly.

COME TO ME.

And it did.

74

KULLEN

Kullen was nearly blown away—*literally*—by the power that burst out of Natisse in an explosive corona. A wave of blistering heat slammed into him, lifting him off his feet and hurling him backward with the force of a charging bull. He landed hard on his feet and felt a wincing sting from his fresh side wound. When he recovered, what he saw took his breath away.

Natisse still stood before the door, but where there had once been a barrier of solid wood and wrought metal, now only scorched and twisted wreckage remained. It looked as if the dagger glowing red-hot in her hands had carved the door into splinters, leaving only a sliver hanging off its hinges, black wood charred and blackened. Smoke rose from the pile of cinder on the ground and liquid metal dripped in great gobbets.

Natisse turned to look at him, almost shyly, her expression a curious mixture of elation, triumph, and surprise. "How's that?"

Despite his shock, Kullen couldn't help laughing. The great rolling belly laugh shook his entire body and, once again, left him sucking in a deep breath through his teeth. He clutched his side and said, "Yeah," Wiping away the tears of mirth. "Yeah, that works just fine."

Only then did Natisse lower the dagger, then dropped it altogether. Dragonfire had warped the already pitted, dented steel, and the blade cracked as it struck the floor, rendered brittle and fragile by the intense calefaction. Yet Natisse herself appeared no worse for the wear. Even her clothing—*his* clothing—remained untouched by the blast, barely rumpled.

"Ezrasil's bones!" she gasped, letting out a little breath and dropping her arms to her sides. "That's… that's a lot of power!"

Kullen couldn't argue that. "How do you feel?" he asked, stumbling over to her on aching legs. Though his new wound wasn't gushing blood as it had, him having wrapped it in one of the canvas strips he'd found unlit, the pain remained.

"Forget that," Natisse said, seemingly noticing the extent of his damage for the first time. "How do *you* feel?"

Kullen waved off the question. "Did you overexert yourself? Use too much power?"

"I…" Natisse frowned. "No, actually. I didn't." She held up her hands, flexing her fingers and testing her wrists and elbow joints. "I feel better than I have in a long time. I'm not fighting it anymore, so it feels… right."

Kullen nodded. "That's how it felt the first time I stepped into the Shadow Realm, too. Right." Even though nearly two decades had passed since that moment, he'd never forget the sensation. "Almost as if you were born to it. Or it was created for you."

"Something like that," Natisse said, nodding. Her brow wrinkled. "Is that how it is? Are we born to it? Like the Magisters who—"

"No." Kullen shook his head. "The way it was explained to me, there is nothing about blood or birth that dictates access to the magic. Only the dragon can decide. Only they can choose their bond. Some say they recognize their soul's counterpoint in another, while others believe that in the choosing, they *make* their bond compatible. Sort of like romance…" He gave her a sly smile. "Or so I hear."

Natisse returned the smile. Her eyes told the whole story, sparkling with a new life—new fire, as it was.

Both smiles quickly faded as the sound of war cries filled the air.

"Damn!" Kullen swore, gaze darting through the still smoldering doorway. "Pretty sure every Orken in Tuskthorne Keep heard or felt that. It'll be harder than ever to get out. Come on!"

"Will it?" Natisse flexed her fingers again, and when they straightened, tongues of orange tipped them. "Will it really?"

She grinned and, damn it, Kullen could help but join her. Inwardly, however, his gut clenched. There was no telling how many Orken awaited them ahead, or what obstacles would bar their path. Yet the sight of Natisse's success brought him a measure of comfort. At least he wouldn't be facing this battle alone.

He stared back at her, watching the joy etched onto her face. And her smile nearly melted his heart as easily as her magic had those iron supports. There they were in the middle of Shekoth in flames and Kullen had to fight to shove down feelings he hadn't experienced since Hadassa. Was it her enrapturing beauty, the confidence she almost always carried, most recent events notwithstanding—or the power she now yielded? He thought it a fair combination of all three and then some.

"You're something, you know that?" he asked, stepping back through the doorway.

"Something good?"

"Something," he repeated. "Now, unless we want to see what happens when the Black Talon gets caught snooping around Tuskthorne Keep, we need to move."

Someday, he would acknowledge what his heart was urging, but now wasn't the time for such things.

"Come on," he said again, starting up the corridor again. "Stay close behind me."

"You think I'm going to let you lead the way?" she asked, her words almost scornful. "After what you just witnessed?"

Kullen shrugged. "You're not the only one who can pick up a crossbow. Unless you want to be the one taking a crossbow bolt face-first…?"

Natisse stepped back, sweeping a grand gesture with her burning palm. "Maybe it *is* better you lead." She chuckled. "My face is far too pretty to be ruined."

"You won't hear me arguing that." Only after it came out did Kullen realize what he'd just said. Heat rushed to his cheeks, and he was glad his back was already turned so Natisse couldn't see it.

They traveled as quickly as their many wounds would allow. It had been a long time since Kullen had come so close to death so many times in a row.

To Kullen's relief, the disruption he felt in his soul lessened with distance from the monolith. Had the situation not been so dire, he would've spent more time studying the unfamiliar stone in the hopes of finding an answer. Something about that thing and the Lumenator magic shared a common bond, and Kullen needed to understand why. But the questions would have to be held until *after* they escaped and brought news to the Emperor of the Orkenwatch's treachery.

He still found it difficult to wrap his head around the idea that *all* of the goldbands were involved in the treasonous plot against the Empire. The Emperor was among the most perceptive, insightful people Kullen had ever known—how could he fail to see Turoc's culpability right under his own nose? Emperor Wymarc had invested the Tuskigo and the rest of his Orkenwatch commanders with immense authority, apparently without worry they would turn against him. Had the Imperial monarch grown so comfortable in his rule and the loyalty of the Orken that he'd been too blind to see the truth? That sat poorly with Kullen. If age had begun causing Emperor Wymarc to slip, to miss crucial details…

No. He cut off the thought before it could take root in his mind. *No, that's not it at all. Turoc and the goldbands were just adept at hiding it. They've fooled even Assidius all this time.*

The thought came as little comfort.

From up the tunnel ahead, he heard the sounds of clanking armor, clattering weapons, and shouted commands in the Orken tongue. He slowed, heart hammering in his chest. As he'd feared, Bareg had summoned reinforcements. No telling how many Orkenwatch now barred his path to freedom.

He tightened his grip on his sword and glanced over his shoulder at Natisse.

"I hear it," she said, her voice barely above a whisper. "Come what may, I'm ready." She raised her hands as if even now preparing to summon Dragonfire.

The confidence in her voice surprised Kullen—and oddly reassured him, too. A marked change had come over her in the last few minutes, ever since the magic had once more sprang to her command. Whatever had been blocking her connection to Golgoth was clearly gone, blown away by her willpower like smoke on the wind. Now, she exuded raw power in a way he'd never seen from her before. The fire burning in her eyes and the heat radiating off her in tangible waves would have instilled fear in him had he faced it across a battlefield. Not for the first time, he was glad to have her on his side for the moment.

They took the next length of the corridor with slow, calculated steps, unsure where their new threat would come from or when it would arrive. Reaching what at first appeared to be a dead end, they turned a corner and spotted two large doors opening into a vast chamber at least as large as the one they'd just escaped. Yet where the other had been a mostly empty, cleared expanse of open space, this was crammed with a variety of potential hiding places —or obstacles, depending on what the next few minutes held.

Platforms, crates, climbing chains, and maze-like rope structures filled the room. Kullen's eyebrows rose. The sight bore a strong resemblance to the training course Swordmaster Kyneth had run him through every day for two years. Such things— balance beams, hemp ladders for dexterity and speed—seemed terribly out of place here, for the Orken were anything but agile. Yet the heavy chains, double-thick ropes, and mammoth logs used in their design were easily twice the size of Swordmaster Kyneth's obstacles—built for Orken frames, no doubt.

He'd only had a glance before his attention was drawn to the titanic, armored figures clanking their way along the straw-covered ground marking the space between the stations. The Orken carried no shields, but they needed none. Their heavy banded steel armor would more than suffice to turn aside mundane weapons. A bristling wall of axes, swords, halberds, and spears had begun forming just within the training facility—if that truly was what he'd seen. Together, they would prove to be a difficult trammel to Kullen and Natisse's freedom.

But they hadn't yet fully formed. Orken were still lumbering across the chamber to join the formation. Bareg stood atop a raised platform, crossbow in hand, shouting orders in Orken to his men. Of the Sniffer who had been at his side before, Kullen saw no sign. Yet he didn't care. He had eyes only for the Ketsneer.

"On my signal," he told Natisse without looking back, "hit them with everything you've got. One blast powerful enough to knock them down. Then make a run for it. Understood?"

"What are you—" Natisse began.

Kullen didn't hear the rest of her question. Lifting his sword high, he raised his voice in a throaty roar and barreled down the corridor at full bore. There was no time for hesitation or uncertainty now, only action. The moment the Orken collected themselves and formed a proper wall, Kullen and Natisse would be trapped within a tunnel that might as well have been a grave. Kullen had no desire to kill any more Orken than necessary—some might still be loyal to the Emperor—which meant he had to take chances.

Every Orken head snapped in his direction, prepared to face whatever threat Bareg had told them would come calling. These bared their tusks, braced themselves, and hefted their weapons to strike him down the moment he drew within range. Those not yet formed up or facing elsewhere whirled, surprised but reacting with impressive speed to close ranks. By the time Kullen covered ten sprinting paces, two dozen Orken stood ready to kill him.

Kullen had no doubt he looked like an utter madman, staggering along from so many injuries and yet charging so many enemies alone. But he *wasn't* alone.

I need your strength, he told Umbris through their bond.

"*It is yours, Bloodsworn,*" came the rumbling response.

Immense power surged through him. Every cut, bruise, and laceration was filled with the vitality of Umbris's magic. It would not heal him, but for now, it masked his discomfort enough for him to do what needed to be done. Everything but him moved in veritable slow motion. His form flickered and began to morph. Still shrouded in the darkness of the corridor, he cloaked himself in shadows, and he could feel himself losing his grip on the Mortal Realm.

Just before his voice would no longer be heard, he roared, "Now!"

75
Natisse

Natisse had absolutely no idea what Kullen meant by "on my signal." Nor did she have any idea how he hoped to survive a head-on collision with a fully-formed line of heavily armed and armored Orken with a blast of Dragonfire coming at him from behind.

But she trusted him. The realization surprised her. She *trusted* him. Not just his skill at arms—though he'd proven himself a damned fine comrade to have at her side in combat. No, this went deeper. She didn't hesitate with him, didn't question what his ulterior motives might be. He'd simply come out and said everything straight to her face. No lies, no half-truths, no deceit—not that she'd recognized, at least.

So when he broke into a run hollering like a madman and charging the Orkenwatch, she trusted that he knew what he was doing.

Heat rose steadily like a furnace, brimming with devastation just under the surface. It felt ravenous as ever, yearning to be free, to expand, to devour everything in its path. Such was the nature of fire. It had a will of its own, yet it answered to her command.

Even as the Dragonfire sprang to her palms, she saw Kullen begin to flicker. The shadows seemed to close in around him, enveloping him like a cold embrace, and his physical form wavered and dissipated. Then she heard his shout.

"Now!"

The signal was unmistakable, and she heeded as he'd known she would. An explosion of raw force in the form of flames erupted from her outstretched hands. She had no need of the Orken short sword to channel it—somehow, she instinctively knew that a tight, concentrated beam of fire would cut through the Orken like a red-hot knife through a block of lard. If Kullen had wanted to kill, he wouldn't had specified "knock them down." No, she needed the magic to burst forth from her in an arc as broad and powerful as she could manage.

The blazing pillar tore through the spot where she'd last seen Kullen only a heartbeat earlier, barreling on its way toward the Orken. She had a single instant to hope Kullen had gotten free of the path before it plowed into the Orken line.

Body after body hit the ground, rolling and patting themselves in a vain attempt to put out the magic inferno. Maybe they wouldn't all die, but she'd damn sure leave her mark.

Natisse tried to call back the fire, to control it, but there was no stopping it now. It seemed to feed on the many torches and oil lamps, swirling around in a firestorm. It sucked all the air out of the room, burning it away and leaving the Orken to choke and wheeze. Their many training devices went up in great columns, spreading the maelstrom even further and wreaking more havoc. Dozens of smaller blazes sprang up in its wake, and they, too, began to grow and expand, feeding on everything around.

The sheer magnitude of the display stole Natisse's breath. She'd been right to be afraid of the power, she realized. In the wrong hands, it could have upturned cities, nations even. Out of control, it could turn all of Dimvein to ash—as it had all those years ago, when Golgoth rampaged through what was formerly known as the Imperial Commons before it became the Embers.

However, this was different. Natisse was in control. *She* commanded the fire. Feet planted, jaw set firmly, she summoned the searing, blindingly bright tongues of magic-given-life back under her submission, and it heeded her call. Like a whirlpool, it funneled back to her hands, continuing to destroy everything in its wake on the way.

When it fully dissipated, not a single Orken remained standing.

Vim and vigor billowed up as the fire absorbed back into her hands. It flowed in and filled her warmly like a fine wine. But the fire had grown, fed on the fuel of the wood and hay, amplified by the light of torches. And all that extra power now coursed through her, nourishing her body with power and vitality she could never have imagined.

Natisse charged in, unsure where Kullen was. But she couldn't wait for him. She needed to finish her part to end the threat and escape Tuskthorne Keep.

Two figures had escaped the blaze. One, she recognized as the goldband, Bareg, who'd tortured Kullen. He leaped from platform to platform, high above, escaping the torrent of fire. He moved with agility impressive even for his smaller-than-average Orken build. Powerful leg muscles catapulted him with what looked like ease. When one platform began to burn, he threw himself to another. Then, finally, he cast himself down and broke into an all-out sprint for the exit.

But it was the *second* figure that demanded Natisse's attention. The smaller, leaner Orken with the broad nostrils of a Sniffer had somehow escaped her fury and now rushed through the smoldering obstacles.

"Oh, no you don't!" Natisse felt the words bubble up from her lips, her hand snapping up of its own accord. The magic surged within her, given life by her anger, and barriers of pure flame leaped up from the ground in front of the fleeing Orken. The Sniffer yipped and fell back before becoming roast Orken. His head snapped side to side, seeking another path out. Natisse stretched out her other hand and one after another, streams of fire cut off his escape. He had no choice but to retreat—back towards *her.*

"You invaded my home!" she shouted, her voice amplified by Golgoth's power. "You hurt my friends, killed Dalash."

The Orken spun around, his beady black eyes narrowing to focus on her. A blast sent him stumbling toward Natisse, nearly knocked him off his feet. Somehow, he managed to remain upright, but the steaming hot wind blew Baruch's hideous-looking hat off his head, carrying it straight to Natisse.

She snatched it out of the air and held it reverently before her like the most exquisite of jewels, or a relic of some long-dead kingdom. "And you stole this. One of the few things I have left to remember them."

As she looked at the worthless Sniffer quivering before her, the heat fueled her rage. Yet the fury didn't touch her mind. She was calm, her thoughts focused, sharp. She knew what she had to do—what she'd wanted to do ever since she found the blood staining the Burrow, cradled Dalash's lifeless body.

However, outright murder like this…

Natisse made no effort to quench the flames that tore the training room asunder. Kullen had told her not to kill anyone, but Natisse had promised Golgoth she'd only use her magic to harm those who deserved it. By her estimation, not a single Orken following the commands of that bastard Bareg was uncounted amongst that lot. Besides, she hadn't blocked any path to escape. All they need do was rise and run. She wouldn't stop them.

She stalked forward, feeling Golgoth's power in her. Then she stopped.

In her time of greatest need, Golgoth had returned to her. Regardless of how she felt about the Sniffer, she couldn't take the chance at offending the Queen of Embers.

So she would do it without the magic.

She placed the hat carefully on her head, tilted it to the exact angle that Baruch had worn it so many times.

"You and me," she snarled at the Sniffer. "Only one of us is walking out of here alive."

The Sniffer bared his stubby tusks and growled something in Orken. Natisse didn't understand the words but had no need to. There was no doubt in her mind, the Orken relished the opportunity to kill her—she could see it shining in his globular black eyes, could see it written into every craggy line on his brutish face. And she welcomed it.

She stood waiting, arms at her side, eyes locked on her enemy. She had no weapons, but that wouldn't stop her from executing justice for Dalash's needless death.

The Sniffer moved impossibly swift, hands darting up to his bandoliers and snatching daggers free. He hurled the blades at her, first with his left hand, then his right. Natisse was already spinning away as the first dagger sliced toward her. It whistled past so close it tugged at the ornate vest Kullen had given her, tearing a ragged line in the cloth. The second hurled dagger missed by a wider margin, clattering on the ground behind her.

But Natisse had no time to slow. She reversed directions abruptly, wheeling backward to evade the Sniffer's next dagger. The Orken was growling, his arms a blur as he drew and threw one after another.

Natisse evaded the fourth dagger, and only then did she make her move. Her hand snapped up to the dragonblood vial at her neck and she called on Golgoth's power. Not to blast away her enemy—Golgoth wouldn't approve, she knew—but just to feel the fire coursing through her veins.

As the magic flooded her body, time slowed to a near standstill. She could see the dagger carving a deadly path toward her head, another behind it aimed at her chest. The two blades appeared to hang suspended in the air, and behind them, the Sniffer had already drawn another to throw.

Natisse felt Golgoth's power fueling her muscles. She moved, faster than she'd ever moved before, reaching up to snatch the dagger from the air. The instant her fingers closed around it, she spun away from the next weapon and, using her body to conceal her movement, hurled the Sniffer's weapon back at him.

He never saw it coming. His eyes, fixed on the empty space where she'd been standing a heartbeat earlier, had no chance to register the blur of steel splitting the air between them. The dagger buried to the hilt in his eye socket with such force it snapped his head back and sent him toppling to the ground. There he lie, nevermore to rise.

Natisse stifled a hiss of pain as the Sniffer's last dagger carved a furrow along the outside of her left arm. She'd known she couldn't fully evade it so had accepted the inevitable wound as Haston had taught her during the countless hours they'd spent training to hone her knife skills. None of the Crimson Fang had been able to match Haston's ability with a dagger—until now, and only because of Golgoth's magic.

Natisse marched toward the Sniffer and stood over the Orken's corpse, staring down silently. She had no words, but none were needed. Dalash's death had been made right. The Sniffer who'd killed him had received just punishment for his unnecessary cruelty. For that was precisely what it had been. Dalash was no fighter. He wouldn't have taken up weapons in defense of the Burrow. But still, the Orken had stabbed him, unarmed and defenseless. Though Golgoth wouldn't have approved of being involved, this dead Orken deserved what he got.

The fury within her abated, and with it, the searing in her veins dimmed and died. Suddenly, she was overcome by lassitude. She had drawn so much power, and it left her in need of rest. Any further *bloodsurge* would result in something dire, she knew.

She took in her handiwork, wishing the whole of the tower would just catch alight and burn away. Yet, in that moment, all she could do was wonder where in Shekoth's pits Kullen had gone.

76

KULLEN

Kullen embraced the shadows, releasing his mortal form and slipping into the Shadow Realm. They were there, waiting, the creatures, lurking in the darkness, closer now than before. Yet he knew he could outrun them a little longer. One last *bloodsurge*.

"Now!" Even as the shout left his lips, the world shifted to varying shades of gray. The shadows called to him, drawing him forward. He trickled through the razor-thin patch of darkness cast by the towering, heavily armored Orken, heading on a direct course toward a dark spot beneath the raised platform upon which Bareg stood.

Then Natisse's Dragonfire blazed to life behind him, and the blast of immensely powerful magic caught his immaterial form and sent it spinning away. He hadn't considered the effects a pillar of light would have on him even lost in the shadows. The fire seared the tether binding him to the Mortal Realm, so hot and bright it nearly severed the connection to his flesh. All of Kullen's iron willpower went into retaining his grip on reality. But control was no longer within his grasp. He was at the mercy of the dancing shadows, flittering and flickering like a candle in the wind. His thoughts became muddled and confused, disoriented as he was by the sudden burst of flames.

He felt as if he was being torn apart, cast in every direction all at once. Finally, as the stream of fire leveled out, he was able—if by accident—to find a patch of black where the light was obscured by something. What it was, Kullen didn't know, but he didn't care either. When he rematerialized, gasping for air in the burning room, he stood twenty paces away from his original target, and facing the wrong way.

The super-heated air scorched his lungs just as it did the present Orken, but he forced himself to focus on the task at hand. Staggering back from gale-force winds, searing hot and blindingly bright, he struggled to locate Bareg before he managed to escape again.

Natisse recalled her flames, giving Kullen a reprieve from the onslaught. Yet not *all* the fires had been snuffed out. A trail of charred and blackened wreckage marked the path of her magical Dragonfire, and in its wake, hundreds of smaller fires caught the many flammable devices strewn throughout the room: straw bales, wooden platforms, log beams, and more, all caught up in the inferno.

Smoke rose in thick, dark pillars, quickly growing choking and stinging his nose and throat. The heat, too, grew all but unbearable—Kullen almost reached for the icy chill of the Shadow Realm. Yet the sight of a dark, armored form racing through the smoke kept him firmly grounded in reality. Bareg had abandoned his perch-top efforts to escape the flames—abandoned his Orken, too—and now broke out toward the archway at the far end of the chamber.

Kullen sprang up the side of the nearest of the platforms that had not yet succumb to destruction. The climb was easy—the wooden supports offered plenty of handholds—and it took him a matter of seconds to scramble up. With the fires below, he had a clear view of the fleeing Ketsneer. Bareg tore across an uneven bridge, swaying beneath his weight. A means of training for balance? Like all Sniffers, he was far more agile and quick than their heftier counterparts. Still, he was jostled around like a wagon on a rocky road.

With a wordless roar of anger, Kullen took off after him. His course took him through not only plumes of obscuring smoke, but a flight of steps built unevenly to test the Orken's footing. On this, Kullen had no trouble maneuvering. Proving to be a little more difficult was the thirty-foot-deep chasm dotted with raised pillars, the flat tops of which acted as stepping stones from one side to another. How Bareg had cleared them so quickly, Kullen didn't know. But he ran toward the pit as fast as his injuries would allow and took the first leap.

He landed, his bare foot catching hold easily enough. However, the moment it touched, the next pillar descended a foot. Having no knowledge of this trick, Kullen had already found himself airborne and unable to redirect course. He had less than a second to make a decision between possibly missing the pillar and plummeting to his potential death or…

He slid into shadow once more, finding plenty of darkness within the chasm walls. This time, he not only heard the snarling Shadow Wraiths, but he caught his first true view of one. Human only in the most basic of descriptions, he was face-to-face with a creature of nightmares. Where a mouth should've been was a gaping maw, all jagged teeth and slithering tongue. Hollow, cold eyes glared at him, white and milky like one born without sight. Its skin was thin and fragile looking, having the appearance of parchment left out in the sun too long.

It lunged for him, hands ending in dagger-sharp fingers. Kullen had no experience fighting in the Shadow Realm. And while he'd never run from battle in the Mortal Realm, this was far beyond even his skill. He cast his gaze past the creature, searching for the edge of the pit. The Shadow Wraith hissed—but it wasn't a hiss. It was a whisper. Words, spoken in Imperial Common.

"Do not resssssissssst," it said with ear-raking sibilance. "Sssstay with usssss."

It reached for him once more and Kullen barely evaded its grasp. Like most things about the Shadow Realm, he didn't know what being touched by the thing would do to him. Perhaps that was all it would take for him to be sucked into Umbris's world forever. As he retargeted the edge of the pit, he spotted something in the distance—a wide pillar of pure energy streaming upward as far as he could make out.

He was drawn to it as if dying and being offered new life. All pretense of escaping fled from him, and all he could see was that glorious light. How far was it? How long would it take to get there? Thoughts in the back of his mind screamed that Natisse was still fighting for her life, that Bareg was escaping, that a Shadow Wraith was after him, and he could get himself stuck in this realm forever, but he didn't care.

He longed to be in that light, basking in it, drinking it in.

Then, a mighty roar cut through his thoughts. Deep *whomping* billows of wind blew him a dozen yards away, and then, Umbris descended like one of Ezrasil's winged warriors.

"*Kullen,*" he said. "*Go now!*"

The sound of the Twilight Dragon's words appeared to have an almost magical effect, dragging Kullen back from his confused state. His mind snapped back to the reality he faced, the Orken and Tuskthorne Keep, Natisse and Turoc's treachery against the crown.

His eyes found the edge on the far side of the pit and he willed himself there. With a thought, he rematerialized, fingertips clutching to the stone lip. Dizziness and fatigue blanketed him, but he had no time for such maladies. He pulled himself up, feeling the wound in his side tear deeper as he did so. Tossing one leg over, he rolled to his feet and continued his pursuit.

His gaze darted to his prey. Bareg had managed to stay a good twenty paces ahead of him. More familiar with the gauntlet than Kullen, he deftly avoided large spears falling from the ceiling at seemingly random intervals. As much as Kullen wished he could avoid the obstacle by magical means, there was no way he'd be stepping foot back in the Shadow Realm until he had a long talk with Umbris.

However, the more pressing problem was that in a hundred paces, Bareg would be through the archway and Kullen might lose him forever.

In desperation, Kullen did the only thing he could: he tore free one of the spears buried into the stone and hurled it at the fleeing Ketsneer. Like an arrow loosed from a hunter's bow, the oversized dart blurred through the air on its course toward the Sniffer's back. Yet even as it left Kullen's hand, he knew the throw had been off. His aim was true, but fatigue, the choking smoke and the gaping wound on his side had impacted the power of his cast. Instead of punching into the base of Bareg's spine, the spear flew between the Ketsneer's legs.

But Cliessa hadn't fully turned her back on him. The spear missed Bareg's flesh, but the long shaft snagged between his legs, tripping him up. He went down in a tangled heap, rolling arse over elbows. His head smacked hard against the stone wall and he didn't move.

Hope surged in Kullen's chest. He broke into a dash. Luckily, the trap had been sprung and no more spears fell. He zigged and zagged through the expanse as if running through a forest full of saplings and closed the distance between him and his quarry.

A sound like a half growl, half groan drifted up from the face-down Ketsneer. He stirred but barely moved. Bareg's large Orken frame reminded Kullen of an onyx shark cutting through the waters of Blackwater Bay, dark and glinting with steel, sharp but subtle movements. A small pool of blood gathered around his skull, and his right leg lay twisted at a terrible angle, transfixed by a long shard of wood snapped off from the spear.

A grim smile spread across Kullen's lips. The Ketsneer wasn't going anywhere in a hurry.

"It's over, Bareg!" Kullen called, approaching the downed Sniffer—close enough to see the pain etched into Bareg's brutish face but out of range of the Orken's claws and jagged-edged dagger he wore on his hip. "The only way you're walking out of here alive is in chains."

"Never!" Bareg glared up at Kullen, eyes blazing and tusks bared. "Orken not surrender. Orken not be prisoner. Years too many prisoner already. I live free. I die free!"

He lunged for Kullen with surprising speed, even for an Orken. His long, claw-like fingernails raked at Kullen's legs, the desperate attack of a cornered predator.

Kullen swung his sword low—an awkward blow but powerful enough to knock aside Bareg's hand. The Orken's armor kept Kullen's blade from biting into flesh, but the *clang* of metal on metal was accompanied by the audible *snap* of shattering bones. Bareg howled and pulled his arm back, hand dangling and fingers limp.

"Don't try it," Kullen said, a grim finality in his tone. "Much as I'd rather bring you before the Emperor alive, he'll accept my word and your head as proof enough of your treachery. But you have a chance to regain some of the honor you lost the moment you betrayed the Empire you swore to protect. Identify the rest of your traitors—and the one called Red Claw, the one calling the shots—and you can still redeem yourself."

"No honor is lost!" Bareg sneered, lip curling up, nostrils flaring wide. "My choice for Orken-kin. Always for Orken-kin. My choice for freedom from humans. In this, I have honor. Red Claw knows this."

Kullen saw the Ketsneer gathering himself for one final, desperate, futile attack. From the fanatical tone of Bareg's voice and the certainty in his eyes, there was no doubt in Kullen's mind that the Orken had resigned himself to his fate. He simply wanted to drag Kullen to the grave first.

He braced himself, and when Bareg lunged, propelling himself forward with the power of his arms, Kullen was ready. His sword drove down point first, and sharp steel punched into the crown of the Orken's head. The blade burst out of Bareg's mouth and buried a hand's width into the stone floor. The Ketsneer writhed, pinned in place like a grisly trophy, blood gushing down the steel of the blade. His struggles quickly grew faint, until with a horrible, gurgling gasp, he lie still.

Kullen stared grimly down at the dead Orken. Bareg had given him no choice. He'd fought to the bitter end, preferring a warrior's death to a traitor's execution. Kullen could almost admire that —*almost,* for the Orken had betrayed the oaths of his people and his service to Empire and Emperor both.

Emperor Wymarc would need a full report of today's happenings. The deaths of Ketsneer Bareg and Arbiter Chuldok were only the beginning. There were more yet still, traitors to the crown, and threats to the Empire. The Orken blood spilled today was far from the end.

77
NATISSE

Natisse rushed through the flames, grateful for Golgoth's power to shield her from the worst of the heat. The dragonblood magic did nothing to prevent the smoke from stinging her eyes or clogging her lungs, however. She coughed, choking on the acrid fumes, and fought to ignore the dizziness washing over her from lack of oxygen.

Her gut tightened as she caught sight of a dark figure looming within the smoke. They held a drawn sword raised high, point downward. In the haze, Natisse couldn't tell if they were Orken or human but braced herself for a battle. If it *was* an Orken barring her path, she would have to take them down without her *bloodsurge*. She was still unsure of her constraints, and the exhaustion plaguing her already felt damning. She raised the two daggers she'd removed from the nameless Sniffer's corpse.

The sword plunged downward, and the violent motion set the smoke around the figure swirling, clearing a gap. Natisse breathed a sigh of relief.

"Kullen!" she called.

She raced toward him, heart soaring, and reached him just as he pulled his sword clear of a fresh corpse—Bareg.

He spun toward her, blade coming halfway up as if to defend

from an attack. Yet when his eyes fixed on her, his face lit up like a watchtower. He appeared as relieved and elated as she felt, his shoulders straightening as if a great burden had been lifted.

"Not going to lie," he said, giving her a wry smile, "it's pretty impressive what you've done with the place." He gestured with his free hand to the immolated chamber. "Maybe I should have specified not to set the *entire* place on fire, though."

Natisse snorted. "Do they not teach you how to say 'thank you' in your fancy assassin school?" She pretended anger, an act as counterfeit as his chastisement. "Because I'm pretty sure that's the third time in the last hour I've saved your life—"

"*Yours*, too," he added.

"—and every time you've got some wise-arse remark," Natisse finished, as if he hadn't spoken. She waggled a finger in his face. "Clearly, something we'll have to work on. For next time."

His eyes brightened. "So you think there'll be a next time, then?"

Natisse hadn't given the words much thought, but now that she'd spoken them aloud, she found the idea less-than-repulsive.

"We'll see." She shrugged. "Kind of hard to consider anything beyond our immediate state of affairs. You know, my *immolation*."

Kullen surveyed their surroundings and inclined his head. "Fair point." His gaze finally took in Baruch's horrible hat. "Problem sorted?"

She nodded. "Sorted." The Sniffer's corpse would be reduced to ash—a fitting end for the whoreson.

"Good." Kullen gave her a tight smile. "Unfortunately, mine's not. Not completely, at least." He gestured to the dead Orken at his feet. "I wanted to bring him in alive to give answer for his actions. He had another proposal. But that means all I've got to go on is my word and what little I unearthed during my visit here."

"Will it be enough?" Natisse couldn't help asking the question. "If the goldbands were wrapped up with Magister Branthe—and whoever he was working for—"

"Who I can't identify, thanks to his stubborn insistence on dying here." Kullen dug a toe into Bareg's lifeless body, a look of frustration on his face. "But what I found in Turoc's chambers and everything I learned while they tortured me should suffice." He shook his head. "Ezrasil alone knows how the Emperor's going to handle this, but no two ways about it, things in Dimvein are about to get unpleasant."

Natisse had to agree with that. She'd never liked the Orkenwatch—they had always been the greatest threat to the Crimson Fang's missions, a foe they had trained relentlessly to avoid—but they had served a purpose in keeping the Emperor's peace in the city. What happened to Dimvein without them? Could the Imperial Scales maintain order alone, or would the city—particularly the poorer areas—descend into lawlessness?

If the latter, it made the Crimson Fang's existence all the more imperative. They didn't need to take on any more of Uncle Ronan's "missions." Perhaps they could help to protect the defenseless, to shield the poorest from those who would use the Orkenwatch's forced absence to stir up further dissent and seize command of the streets.

But for that, she needed her comrades at her side.

"Come on," she said, gesturing toward the archway. "We're not out of the shite yet."

Kullen grimaced. "True that." He followed her pointed finger. "I'll lead, you get ready to loose that Dragonfire should we encounter any trouble."

Natisse shook her head. "I can't."

Kullen's head snapped back around toward her. His expression hardened, and he looked as if he was about to lose his composure on her once more.

She held up a hand to stop him. "You're the one who warned me that *bloodsurging* has its limits. I feel I'm dangerously close to mine."

"Ahh." Kullen's face softened, and he gave her an understanding nod. His lip twitched once, his brow furrowing as if an idea had just occurred to him. "Think you could manage a spark or two?"

Natisse closed her eyes, listened for Golgoth's presence. It was there—albeit weak. Her veins no longer seared with fiery rage, no longer raw and burning. But still, she could feel the lingering fatigue threatening to claim her if she drew on too much more energy. "If there's no other choice…" She shrugged one shoulder.

"It'll be enough," Kullen said, a hard, predatory smile on his lips.

"You going to tell me what you're planning this time, or should I be expecting another vague *signal?*" Natisse asked, scowling.

Kullen laughed. "I've been told the surprise is half the fun!"

Natisse's brows knit.

"Fine, fine!" Kullen raised his hands, palms patting the air. From within one of the pockets of his cloak—which had survived the fire with only a bit of singeing around its lower hem—he drew out a small glass orb filled with some acidic green fluid. "The moment I throw this, you light it on fire. Easy as that."

Natisse had no idea what exactly was in the strange, spherical object but had spent enough time around Serrod's alchemy to know that the addition of fire would likely produce a violent reaction. "Good enough for me." She raised her right hand. "I'll have the spark ready."

A broad staircase rose just beyond the archway. Clearly, it was built for Orken feet, each one twice the size of any found in Dimvein. It switchbacked several times, enough that Natisse could surmise it led to the main level of the tower. And perhaps, their freedom.

With no attempt at stealth, Kullen burst through the door at the topmost level. There, not even ten paces away, the double iron doors stood open, and through them Natisse caught a glimpse of the night sky. Beyond the film of Thanagar's dome, the sky shone with bright stars and an even brighter moon. They were so close, yet between them stood yet another pack of Orken.

Lined up against the far wall, prisoners stood in chains.

Among them, the young lady Natisse had given Gulma's keys stood with a puffy black eye and blood trickling down from her ear.

"This complicates things," Kullen said. Already the Orken were responding to their intrusion. "As soon as you light those flames, fight your way to get those people to freedom. Yeah?"

"Quit wasting time," Natisse said, raising her hands and already feeling the tingle of Golgoth's magic at her fingertips.

"Yes, noble lady."

Kullen's arm flashed back, then forward, and the glass orb hurtled across the Keep's entry hall to shatter at the feet of the Orken on the opposite side of the prisoners. The instant the acidic green mixture made contact with the air, it evaporated into a brightly colored mist that enveloped the Orken. Even from where she stood, the stench burned Natisse's nostrils and brought bile floating to her throat. The Orken nearest the point of impact staggered back, retching and gasping for breath.

Golgoth, be with me once more, Natisse begged as she stretched her hands toward the rising mist.

A single spark answered the call, hurtling toward the cloud of noxious gas.

The cloud exploded into a controlled fireball. Unlike Natisse's magical flames, these didn't burn hot but sent everyone within their influence toppling to the ground. Much to Natisse's chagrin, that included a couple of the captives.

She darted for them, leaping over the long table barring her path.

"Go!" Natisse shouted. "Let's go!"

Behind her, she heard the charge of an Orken, turned to meet it and got a spray of blood in her face for the effort. One of Kullen's stilettos protruded from the beast's neck, severing his jugular and dropping him in an instant.

"Now!" Natisse cried.

The prisoners all moved at a harried pace, but the chains

binding their legs to one another made it a much slower and more painful task than they had time for.

She glanced over her shoulder as Kullen charged toward them, vaulting the downed Orken. He played the role of rear guard while Natisse guided them out. As the Orken within choked on the fumes and flames, Natisse, Kullen, and those of the escaped prisoners who remained, sucked in a lungful of fresh air.

Ahead of her, Kullen swore. No less than a dozen more Orken milled about the courtyard. The explosion had sent them to arms already, and Natisse feared they would have to fight their way free. She reached for the vial hanging around her neck, reaching out to Golgoth to summon her to the Mortal Realm. Not even an army of Orken could stand against the Queen of the Ember Dragons.

But before she could form the thought, the sound of beating wings tore the night and a powerful wind buffeted her. The night itself seemed to darken right in front of her, the stars dying like snuffed-out candles. Shadow coalesced a heartbeat later into a sleek, powerful form that shone as dark as the lightless sky, with only the faintest hint of deep violet to separate Umbris's bulk from the heavens.

Prisoners cried out in terror, but Natisse worked to ease their minds. "Don't be alarmed! He's with us. This is our freedom."

The Orken cowered before the great Twilight Dragon, and Umbris did his part drawing a large ring of flames around them.

"Got room for half a dozen, friend?" Kullen asked Umbris.

Natisse heard no reply but for the deep growl that shook the courtyard.

Some took coaxing, but the ring of fire and the angry Orken did much to persuade the escapees to climb aboard.

As they rose above Dimvein, Natisse looked back at the place that would be the source of many nightmares to come. She'd gone in there to find old friends, but she found something far greater: herself, and the power residing in her because of her new friend, Golgoth. She'd made peace with the abundance of power made available to her, and she would keep true to her promise to use it only for good.

And as their next assignment, she would use it to free the Crimson Fang—and with them at her side, they could return to the true mission for which they had been trained: protecting and caring for the people of Dimvein.

78

KULLEN

"I could've summoned Golgoth, too, you know," Natisse said in Kullen's ear. "I told you my connection is fine." Her voice held a trace of mild irritation.

"I know you did." Kullen had to shout to be heard over the wind. "But you said you were approaching the edge of your limits. Besides, Umbris draws far less attention flying over the city than the Queen of the Ember Dragons."

He took Natisse's grunt as acknowledgement. In truth, he hadn't given it much thought, merely acted out of instinct. He'd operated alone for so long that such things had become second nature to him. Yet Natisse was right. She had her own dragon, and as she'd proven after escaping Pantagoya, she could more than handle herself.

Thoughts of Pantagoya reminded him of the dragonblood vial they'd been sent to retrieve. He desperately wanted to ask her about it but decided now wasn't the time.

They'd already visited one of Kullen's safe houses in the Embers, set the prisoners free, and warned them that they'd be watched not by the Orkenwatch but by the Black Talon himself. If any of them stepped out of line, they'd find themselves returned to the Palace dungeons by his own hand. They hadn't stayed long—

just enough to relieve them of their bindings and watch them depart into the night.

Kullen had business with the Emperor.

"Just tell me where you want me to leave you," he said, albeit reluctantly. He felt oddly dismayed to part company with her. But he had his priority. He could always find her later. "That warehouse that hid the secret passage to your underground tunnels, or—"

"No!" Natisse's voice was sharp, edged with biting steel.

Only then did Kullen remember her account of what had happened to her people. The raid by the Orken, the deaths of her friends. He could understand her not wanting to return to her home with such a grim spectacle awaiting.

"I'm not leaving your side until you uphold your end of the bargain," she said.

Kullen raised an eyebrow. "You sure about that?" He twisted in his seat to look over his shoulder at her. "There's a chance that once the Emperor finds out who you are—and I *will* have to tell him when I explain why I think your friends should be freed—he'll order you thrown into the dungeon alongside them."

"That's a chance I'll just have to take." Natisse's jaw set in a stubborn cast, her face growing hard. "You gave me your word. I expect you to live up to it, just like I've lived up to mine."

Kullen fought to keep the dismay from showing on his face. It wasn't just that her insistence on accompanying him would throw a wrinkle into his plans to retrieve the dragonblood vial from wherever she'd stashed it. By her tone and the look on her face, it felt as if she was *only* at his side because of what he'd promised her. Was she merely using him to free her friends?

He wanted to deny it. He'd thought they had made immense strides of progress in the last few days. He'd grown to trust her—far more than he'd trusted anyone since Jarius and Hadassa—and her actions had led him to believe she felt the same. But her response put a dent in his certainty.

"I'll do everything in my power, as I promised," he told her. "I am nothing if not a man of my word."

Natisse's face softened a fraction. "I know you are."

Again, her response surprised him. Perhaps he *had* been right about her—about them. Though he'd only known her—truly known her—for a few days, he couldn't help feeling the way he did. No one had held his interest so completely in years... not since Hadassa, and he'd never allowed himself to fully entertain that particular notion. Yet, the beautiful, fiery-haired, and fiery-spirited woman riding behind him was the first person in a long time to enrapture him thusly. And deep inside, he'd accept either reasoning for her staying with him a few more hours, even if at the end, he'd be at the mercy of Emperor Wymarc when the monarch found out about the deal they'd struck. Truth be told, he *would* keep his promise to her, help her free her friends from the dungeon. He just had to hope the Emperor would understand.

"Before we do that, though," he said, sternness entering his tone, "I need to report to the Emperor what I learned in Tuskthorne Keep. He needs to know that the Orkenwatch are scheming against him. If not all of them, enough that they're a threat. That *has* to be my first priority here."

"I understand," Natisse said. The way she said it told Kullen she meant it. "You need me to back you up, I'm here."

Those were the words he hadn't even realized he'd longed to hear—she would reaffirm his story, she would have his back.

They climbed high, marking the Palace as their destination, and Umbris flew with haste to reach it. Within him, so many conflicting emotions and thoughts wrestled for dominance over his mind. The budding relationship with Natisse—something he hadn't even realized he desired. His whole life, he'd been alone. But when she was with him, he felt different. He felt as if they'd been together, fighting side by side for an eternity.

Clashing with those confusing emotions, the pit in his stomach sank deeper at the thought of what Emperor Wymarc was going to say. About her, about the Crimson Fang, about the rebellion.

Then, a sudden fear that Turoc had somehow already heard of the happenings at Tuskthorne Keep, and his dagger had already found its spot in the Emperor's back.

But no, Assidius would never allow such a thing. He may've been a conniving weasel, but he would protect the Emperor with his own life. If not his, that of the Elite Scales that were never far from his side.

Thanagar, fully expectant of Kullen's return and aware of the haste in which he'd desire to reach the Emperor, didn't even stop him. He did, however, scrutinize Natisse. Perhaps he sensed the new depth of her relationship with Golgoth, or feared the stranger entering the Palace to be so close to his bond. It didn't matter.

You will find him in his private study, Thanagar said within Kullen's mind. He wondered if Natisse heard it too, but her silence answered the question for him.

Though when he turned to her, the scowl on her face as she watched the White Dragon hover beside them spoke of something deep in her heart. He let the matter go, for now.

They landed in the Emperor's garden, quickly disembarking and sending Umbris back home. The air split before them, a colorless portal appearing and receiving the Twilight Dragon into the Shadow Realm.

Then, a memory returned to Kullen. That pillar of light he'd seen in the Shadow Realm. What had it been? He'd meant to ask Umbris, but things had gotten too hectic with the prisoners and their escape. Umbris had mentioned something akin to the great pillar of light in the Pantagorissa's tower. Had this anything to do with those words?

Tomorrow, when Kullen brought Umbris a big, juicy pork shoulder, they would share a conversation about that and much more.

True to Thanagar's word, Kullen and Natisse found the Emperor alone in his private study. He sat at his desk, drafting a letter with a quill pen. Assidius hovered at the Imperial monarch's elbow, a frown on his face.

Emperor Wymarc looked up before Kullen entered the room—no doubt warned by Thanagar.

"Kullen, what in Ezrasil's name happened to you?" His eyebrow arched as he took in the bloody scene. "And you... Natisse, was it?"

"Y-yes, Majesty," Natisse stammered. Kullen saw she'd been caught off guard by the Imperial monarch's recollection of her name.

"Assidius, fetch the Royal Physicker and spare not a moment!" the Emperor commanded as he rose from his seat. He crossed the room with a speed that belied his age and forced the two of them to sit upon his leather-covered sofa.

"I'm afraid I bear grim tidings," Kullen told him.

"Surely such things can wait until after you're attended to."

"I fear there's no time to waste, Your Grace," Kullen said, his face wrought with concern.

Emperor Wymarc stopped his fussing over them and turned an inquisitive eye. "Go on."

As Kullen recounted what he'd uncovered—the scrimshaw hidden in Turoc's chamber, Bareg and Chuldok's complicity in Magister Branthe's schemes—though he kept the details of Natisse's involvement in his escape intentionally vague, leaving out all mention of her dragonblood magic. Throughout, Emperor Wymarc's face steadily darkened, his expression growing more and more grim.

Kullen recounted Bareg's questions about Assidius.

Emperor Wymarc listened, his face ashen and nearly as pale as his hair. Kullen had not even finished before he'd said all the Emperor needed to hear. "I desperately wanted you to be wrong, Kullen."

"As did I, Majesty." Kullen's jaw clenched.

"Turoc has served me faithfully—or appeared to—since I first took the Imperial throne." Emperor Wymarc shook his head. "I still find it hard to believe, and yet—"

The door opened and the Seneschal returned with the Royal

Physicker in tow.

"Physicker Erasthes will work to patch you up."

Erasthes lowered his leather bag and began unpacking items of aid, but his eyes never left Kullen's and Natisse's many wounds, appraising them with grave features.

"Seneschal." Emperor Wymarc's tone was grave. "Kullen has uncovered evidence that Ketsneer Bareg and Arbiter Chuldok were wrapped up in Magister Branthe's conspiracy. There is some proof, too, that Tuskigo Turoc was complicit."

"I cannot believe it," Assidius said.

"Have you found anything that could refute such proof? Anything at all that would indicate Turoc is not complicit?" Desperation peppered the question. Kullen knew the Emperor would want nothing more than for there to be a simple misunderstanding. But Kullen was sure there would be no such proof.

"I have not, Divine Majesty." Assidius's sour expression gave the man the appearance of one who'd just sucked on a sour firecherry. "On the contrary, my visit to Tuskthorne Keep only adds credence to the Black Talon's belief in the Tuskigo's guilt."

Kullen's eyebrows shot up. "You were in the Keep?"

"I've only just returned," Assidius said.

Kullen surveyed the Seneschal with fresh eyes. Though the man always wore plain clothes, he did look far too rumpled for his usual primness.

"Following your last visit, on Imperial orders, I launched investigations of my own. One of my contacts informed me of an unauthorized raid conducted by the Orkenwatch on a seemingly ordinary warehouse in the One Hand District late last night."

Kullen felt Natisse stiffen beside him, the tension radiating off her with heat as intense as her dragon magic.

"Within the warehouse," Assidius went on, "they discovered a small army of Blood Clan pirates masquerading as Embers-folk. Among the items in their possession was an arsenal of weaponry, a fortune in Imperial coin, and letters of correspondence between the pirates and one 'Red Claw.'"

It was now Kullen's turn to stiffen. "Any luck figuring out who Red Claw is?"

"Not as of yet." Assidius's expression soured further. "However, upon questioning some transients in the area, we received word of Orken activity in and around the building prior to the raid. One actually identified both Tuskigo Turoc and his Ketsneer, placing them around the vicinity in the days leading up to the Orkenwatch assault."

"Coincidence?" Emperor Wymarc asked. "Or were they merely reconnoitering the locale in anticipation of the attack?"

"That's not their style," Natisse said through clenched teeth. Thankfully, she had the wherewithal to add, "Your Majesty."

The Emperor stared at her, seemingly unsure what to make of her declaration.

"Though she speaks out of turn," Kullen said, glaring at her, "she's not wrong, Your Grace. The Orkenwatch thrive on surprise and fear. They never struck me as the reconnaissance types."

"Indeed," the Emperor said.

Kullen winced as Erasthes pressed a cloth damp with some alchemical cleansing liquid against his exposed muscle and tissue.

"Nonetheless," Assidius's lip curled into a sneer. "I took that exact question to Ketsneer Bareg not two hours ago. The Keep was in chaos, as I told you, Majesty. Prisoners ran free. Blood flowed. He proved far from cooperative, saying he answered only to his Tuskigo and he had more important things to deal with."

"Brazen bloody bastard," Kullen said.

That had been right around the time Bareg had been called away from questioning Kullen. Certainly the personal appearance of *Zadruzak* himself would suffice to demand the Ketsneer's presence. Which meant he owed Assidius his life, in a way. That didn't sit well with him at all.

Neither Emperor Wymarc nor Assidius seemed to notice Kullen's reaction. Emperor Wymarc was pensive, his brow furrowed and eyes downcast, while Assidius's gaze remained fixed on his monarch.

"I've heard enough, and we've wasted enough time," the Emperor said, his voice stern and commanding. "Assidius, take a contingent of Scales and stop Tuskigo Turoc from departing the Palace. Relieve him of his weapons, on my order, and have him escorted here."

"Yes, Your Magnificence," Assidius hissed. He glided out of the room, feet lost beneath the train of his robes. With the snap of his fingers, four Elite Scales fell into formation behind him.

The Emperor paced the room, stroking his beard with concern. "This is outrageous," he whispered. Then, he returned to his desk and sat, face buried in his hands.

"This is going to sting," Erasthes said, lifting a threaded needle to Kullen's chest.

Kullen nodded as the Physicker began the process of stitching his most grievous of wounds.

Natisse placed a hand on his leg, and instantly, he no longer cared about the pain. He looked over to her, finding comfort in her presence.

Moments later, the door reopened and Turoc, gripped tightly by the soldiers, two on each side, barged through. Kullen had no delusions that as strong and well trained as the Elite Scales were, Turoc couldn't have thrown them aside with his thickly muscled arms if he so desired to.

"What is meaning of this?" the Orkenwatch commander demanded. "Why little men interrupt departure?" He stood ramrod straight, as if he'd just had a thornbush shoved somewhere unpleasant. He glowered at his captors, then at Assidius, and finally, his eyes fell upon Kullen. Only the Emperor himself was spared his visible ire. "And why insist on take weapons?"

"Because you have betrayed me!" Emperor Wymarc's voice thundered through the study. He exploded to his feet and slammed a palm onto the table. "After everything I've done for you and your people, after how I've treated you, this is how you repay me?"

Turoc's blocky face contorted in confusion. "Not know of

what you speak, I do, Sir." He took a step toward the Emperor and the soldiers moved with him, hands on their hilts and ready for an attack. "What is this betrayal?"

"You tell me, Turoc." The Emperor's voice dropped to barely above a whisper, but one ringing with terrible menace. "Tell me what you, Bareg, Chuldok, Magister Branthe, the Blood Clan, and all of my other enemies have planned."

Turoc's face turned to stone.

"That is an order, Turoc!" Emperor Wymarc barked, fists clenched in barely controlled rage. "Speak the truth, or suffer the consequences."

"I speak truth, Sir." Turoc's huge jaw muscles clamped tight, his lower tusks grinding audibly against his upper teeth. "Always, I do."

Kullen rose from the couch despite Erasthes's many protests. "Look at me!"

The entirety of the study's occupants turned to him. The last of which was Turoc, who merely angled his head.

"Your Ketsneer and his mutilation-happy Arbiter did this. Now they stand before whatever abomination you call God, answering for their crimes."

Turoc's face paled, jaw slacking at the revelation that his men were dead. His fist rose to his forehead in whatever religious gesture Kullen had seen Bareg and Chuldok perform.

"They had much to say about you when they presumed it would be my soul on the other end of this life. They let slip irrefutable proof that the goldbands had conspired with enemies of the crown to dismantle this Empire. 'Orken loyal to Orken' they said, proud, as those shite-suckers watched me squirm under a gnasher's teeth."

Assidius let out a small gasp, having not heard that portion.

"Your little Kingdom within that tower has been destroyed," Kullen continued. "Dozens, perhaps hundreds who stood behind Bareg's words lay in ruins." He pulled the scrimshaw from his pocket, holding it up for the room to see. "And I found this in your very quarters. Proof enough to make you complicit if their words of admission were not enough."

Turoc stood stock still, chin raised and mouth closed.

"You have *nothing* to say for yourself?" Emperor Wymarc demanded.

"Much to say, I do." Turoc straightened. "And much to consider. You dishonor me, Sir."

"You dishonor yourself," Emperor Wymarc said, slumping in his chair, expression cold. "It is settled then. The Orkenwatch is hereby dissolved, and every remaining Orken is confined to Tuskthorne Keep until such a time as a full investigation can be conducted."

The Elite Scales drew their weapons, expecting Turoc to attack, but he didn't even raise an arm.

"See it is done, Seneschal," Emperor Wymarc said, waving vaguely in Assidius' direction. "At once."

"Of course, Majesty." His curled beard rose along with his lips, a wicked grin splitting his face in a triumphant smile. Kullen knew Assidius hated the Orken as much as Kullen despised the Seneschal, but to show his pleasure at such a time bordered on disrespect for the Empire's loss. "Do I have your permission to call upon the Elite Scales, Imperial Scales, and, if necessary, General Tyranus's forces, as I see fit?"

Emperor Wymarc sighed heavily. "You do."

The thought of Dimvein being overrun by the full force of the Imperial Army brought dread to Kullen's heart. He looked to Natisse, whose face showed similar emotions. What had begun as an investigation into which of the goldbands had conspired with Magister Branthe and the others had now erupted into all-out war with an unknown number of enemies. How far did this treachery go? Were other nations involved?

Despite General Tyranus's numbers, Kullen feared they may not be enough to keep Dimvein from falling should the threat prove greater even than they thought.

"By your will, Divine Majesty." Assidius bowed low—*too* low—

and turned to Turoc. "Tuskigo Turoc, by order of the Emperor, I hereby place you under ar—"

At that moment, the door burst open and a pale-faced young man appeared. "Grandfather!" Prince Jaylen was far from recovered; indeed, he looked half-dead, as if he'd just run across the entire Empire.

Emperor Wymarc leaped to his feet. "Jaylen, you should be in bed re—"

"Grandfather!" Prince Jaylen cut off the Emperor with a shout. "There's no time for resting now. Not for any of us." He looked between Turoc, Assidius, Kullen, Natisse, the soldiers, and the monarch. "Finally free of that chair, I desired to take Tempest out for a flight, see if that would help me recover my strength, and that's when I spotted them!"

"Them?" Kullen asked.

"Them who?" Emperor Wymarc demanded at the same time.

"The Blood Clan!" Prince Jaylen nearly collapsed, so weak he was from fatigue. Erasthes caught him and helped him into the seat Kullen had previously occupied. But Jaylen shrugged the Physicker off of him and stood again. "They're coming, Grandfather! The Horde and the Clan, sailing together. On their way here right now. Based on their speed, their entire fleet will sail into Blackthorne Bay in two days!"

Emperor Wymarc looked to Kullen. A thick blanket of silence smothered the room until the Emperor finally said, "Get me General Tyranus." His face grew pale. "May Ezrasil have mercy on us, for war is coming to Dimvein."

The story will continue in ***SILVER SPINES.***

THANK YOU FOR READING RED CLAW

We hope you enjoyed it as much as we enjoyed bringing it to you. We just wanted to take a moment to encourage you to review the book. Follow this link: *Red Claw* to be directed to the book's Amazon product page to leave your review.

Every review helps further the author's reach and, ultimately, helps them continue writing fantastic books for us all to enjoy.

Want to discuss our books with other readers and even the authors? Join our Discord server today and be a part of the Aethon community.

Facebook | Instagram | Twitter | Website

You can also join our non-spam mailing list by visiting www.subscribepage.com/AethonReadersGroup and never miss out on future releases. You'll also receive three full books completely Free as our thanks to you.

Also in the series:

BLACK TALON

RED CLAW

SILVER SPINES

GOLDEN FLAMES

Did you love Black Talon? Get more books by the authors

In the West, there are worse things to fear than bandits and outlaws. Demons. Monsters. Witches. James Crowley's sacred duty as a Black Badge is to hunt them down and send them packing, banish them from the mortal realm for good. He didn't choose this life. No. He didn't choose life at all. Shot dead in a gunfight many years ago, now he's stuck in purgatory, serving the whims of the White Throne to avoid falling to hell. Not quite undead, though not alive either, the best he can hope for is to work off his penance and fade away. This time, the White Throne has sent him investigate a strange bank robbery in Lonely Hill. An outlaw with the ability to conjure ice has frozen and shattered open the bank vault and is now on a spree, robbing the region for all it's worth. In his quest to track down the ice-wielder and suss out which demon is behind granting a mortal such power, Crowley finds himself face-to-face with hellish beasts, shapeshifters, and, worse … temptation. But the truth behind the attacks is worse than he ever imagined … ***The Witcher* meets *The Dresden Files* in this weird Western series by the Audible number-one bestselling duo behind *Dead Acre*.**

GET COLD AS HELL NOW AND EXPERIENCE WHAT PUBLISHER'S WEEKLY CALLED PERFECT FOR FANS OF JIM BUTCHER AND MIKE CAREY.